PULITZER PRIZE
FEATURE STORIES

PULITZER PRIZE FEATURE STORIES

Edited by David Garlock

Iowa State University Press / Ames

DAVID GARLOCK is currently head of the magazine sequence in the Department of Journalism at the University of Texas. During his 30-year career as writer, publisher and journalism educator, Garlock has judged newspaper contests around the country and presented writing/editing seminars and workshops. He is also an independent magazine consultant who has directed an international magazine publishing firm and started a city magazine. In 1993-94, Garlock won the Teaching Excellence Award and gave the 1994 commencement address in the College of Communication at the University of Texas.

© 1998 Iowa State University Press, Ames, Iowa 50014

♾ Printed on acid-free paper in the United States of America

First edition, 1998

International Standard Book Number: 0-8138-2389-7

Library of Congress Cataloging-in-Publication Data

Pulitzer Prize feature stories / edited by David Garlock.—1st ed.
p.   cm.
ISBN 0-8138-2389-7
1. Feature stories—United States. 2. Pulitzer prizes. 3. Reporters and reporting—United States.   I. Garlock, David.
PN4726.P815   1998
070.4′4′0973—dc21   97–44251

The last digit is the print number: 9 8 7 6 5 4 3 2 1

CONTENTS

PREFACE

"YOU CAN WIN A PULITZER PRIZE for a feature story?"

To be honest, I've never actually heard anyone ask that question, but as many non-deadline writers will quickly agree, newsroom respect for feature writers varies greatly. And you can hardly blame the detractors. Much of what passes for feature writing is soft, puffy and less-than-scintillating. The genesis of this book was that very concern.

During eight years of teaching writing at the University of Texas, I have scoured the market for effective texts to use in feature writing classes—texts loaded with pertinent examples of what a feature story can be. The end result: *Pulitzer Prize Feature Stories*—a compilation of the best non-deadline and on-deadline feature stories over the past two decades. This is the first time all the winners have been published in one complete volume.

I don't use the "non-deadline" vs. "on-deadline" designation lightly. For years, I have taught college journalism students that a feature story begins exactly the same way as a hard-news piece, with extensive research and reporting. It can easily turn into explanatory or investigative journalism if the trail leads that way. A soft-focus Christmas feature on a free clinic treating needy patients only stays soft until you see the glint of a needle on the floor. Then the reporting focuses on how these clinics (and perhaps others) handle needles, syringes and medical waste products.

Early in my career, I learned that lesson firsthand while writing a deadline feature on how one of the world's largest military food distribution warehouses delivered nonperishable products to U.S. personnel around the world.

During a first tour of the cavernous facility, I noticed the dark, dingy look of the warehouse and how poorly some of the cases of food were marked. Silent alarms began to go off in my head. The finished "feature" exposed how the military was wasting millions of taxpayers' dollars by secretly burning food in the middle of the night. The result: a congressional investigation and a nightmare for the army.

Was that a feature? Damn right.

It often seems there is no end to the parade of books on effective writing—books usually featuring selected excerpts of award-winning stories to make a point. I have nothing against most of these books. In fact, I've used many as texts in writing classes at the University of Texas. However, I've long wished for an anthology of the best feature writing of the last two decades.

Thus, when Iowa State University Press asked me to edit this volume, I jumped at the chance.

In compiling this book, I've minimized the role of the editor and maximized the real stars—the Pulitzer Prize winners. I've added some of my own thoughts on each work, but in a concise manner. During interviews with the winners, I focused on their writing techniques and strategies that led to such masterful work. I *did* feel my writing colleagues would be interested in how each Pulitzer Prize winner learned of his or her prize. I assumed their stories would be interesting and meaningful and wasn't disappointed. Some of the tales are hilarious. All are intriguing.

Finally, I asked each author to review my final comments for accuracy, errors in fact and anything else they disagreed with. Most did just that. None found any serious disagreement.

What I ended up with was exactly what I sought—a book in which the outstanding writing of these Pulitzer super stars is left to shine on its own.

My friend Tom Fensch, former head of the magazine sequence at the University of Texas, and author of numerous books and anthologies on writing, warned me that compiling this volume wouldn't be easy. I sailed serenely through that warning. How hard could it be? You simply write the newspapers for permission, pay the small fees required to reprint the work, interview the writers and scan in their stories. Simple.

Receiving the permissions was indeed fairly easy and the authors, by and large, proved to be generous and forthcoming with their time.

Acquiring copies of the physical stories, however, turned out to be a whole different deal. Reprints from the earliest years are hard-to-impossible to come by. Pulitzer Prize-winning stories that ran in the early-to-middle 1980s usually can't be found on most news retrieval services and databases, including Lexis-Nexis. Papers such as *The Washington Post* and *The Wall Street Journal,* plus chains such as Knight-Ridder, spare no expense in reprinting their winning pieces. However, through the years, the reprints often collect dust—and finally seem to totally disappear.

A precious few authors, such as Jacqui Banaszynski, Sheryl James and Peter Rinearson still have access to the original reprints. Peter sent a couple reprint copies of his mind-boggling "Making It Fly"— at 29,000 words, the size of a small daily paper. Nan Robertson was also kind enough to send one of her treasured (and rare) original copies of *The New York Times Magazine* containing the stunning "Toxic Shock." Several other Pulitzer winners were equally helpful.

Far too often, however, no high-quality copies remain of some of the finest journalism of the last two decades. Worse, many of the stories in this book have been reprinted along the way in a shortened fashion (even by some of the winning newspapers), frequently without informing the reader.

To acquire many of the stories, I was finally reduced to pulling them off film in dusty libraries or requesting the film from distant libraries. A top-of-the-line scanner helped convert the stories to manuscript form but the scanner had trouble reading much of the copy that appears from the bowels of a Flintstone-era basic microfilm reader.

I attempted to leave the stories as pristine as possible, including putting in the original sidebars, for example, when I could find them. For readability, however, I standardized subheads, ellipses, indenting, etc., where possible. Yet, much of the material was reprints of the original work, and editorial decisions had been made that changed the layout and heads from the original (and later epilogues were often added to the reprints), so the challenge was obvious.

Feature writing is a comparatively recent Pulitzer Prize category, having been added on April 7, 1978, according to Seymour Topping, administrator of the Pulitzer Prize Board at the graduate school of journalism at Columbia University. The Board's 1978 minutes give no hint as to why the decision was made. Topping points out: "Obviously, a subcommittee must have made the proposal which was then accepted by the Board."

It would have been interesting to be a fly on the wall to hear the discussion about what would be required to win a Pulitzer in the features category. For example, notice how the feature rules were written more specifically than those for beat, investigative or spot reporting:

> For a distinguished example of feature writing giving prime consideration to *high literary quality* and *originality.*

Perhaps the Pulitzer Board was trying to send feature writers a message right from the beginning.

Regardless, the first winner could hardly have been a more appropriate choice to set the right "literary" tone: Jon Franklin, the 1979 winner for the riveting "Mrs. Kelly's Monster." (Franklin would come up with another first in 1985, winning the initial Pulitzer Prize awarded for explanatory journalism.)

Franklin says he was attempting to work "Chekov's story-form theories into journalism ... a good story that would have a beginning, middle and end ... highly paced ... sort of what Bolero was to Ravel." Or, perhaps, what features should be to literature.

Franklin has his own theories on why features were annointed by the Pulitzer Board on that spring day in 1978. In the 1970s and '80s, he noticed many other writers producing feature stories using the same nonfiction/short-story form. Franklin feels the Pulitzer category was a logical recognition of this new genre.

The works represented in this anthology are indeed sterling examples of literature, written by true storytellers who let the drama and action play out, understand the role of conflict and resolution in a narrative, and don't hesitate to channel their passion and rage into the narrative when appropriate.

Yet, all of these writers are also ace reporters. The inestimable Rick Bragg of *The New York Times* seems to take quiet glee in showing up at an important event to write a news feature and, as in the case of one of his 1996 Pulitzer Prize-winning features, "A Killer's Only Confidant: The Man Who Caught Susan Smith," becoming the only reporter to snare the big interview.

Teresa Carpenter's 1981 masterpiece, "Death of a Playmate," another feature written in the midst of worldwide controversy, could easily have won a Pulitzer in investigative or in any of several categories. The same holds true for several of the stories reprinted here. Much of Bragg's work, the Pulitzer efforts of Isabel Wilkerson (1994) and David Zucchino (1989) were written directly on deadline.

But the beauty of this anthology is the wide spectrum of the work. The poetic writings of Alice Steinbach in "A Boy of Unusual Vision" and Howell Raines' touching and lyrical "Grady's Gift" are real literature. Massive explanatory efforts are also part of the collection, such as Saul Pett's "The Federal Bureaucracy," John Camp's "Life on the Land," Jacqui Banaszynski's "AIDS in the Heartland" and Peter Rinearson's "Making It Fly."

A staple of many features, tragedy, is well-represented with "The Stalking of Kristin," George Lardner Jr.'s heartbreaking account of his daughter's senseless murder, "Adam & Megan" by Dave Curtin, "A Gift Abandoned" by Sheryl James and Lisa Pollak's "The

Umpire's Sons." And a couple of magnificent profiles are included: "Zepp's Last Stand" by Madeleine Blais and Ron Suskind's inspiring two-parter: "Against All Odds" and "Class Struggle."

Steve Twomey's "How Super Are Our Supercarriers?" adventure tosses the reader right on the flight deck of the carrier America as a F-14A Tomcat fighter jet screams down onto a postage-stamp size carrier flight deck. The jet is quickly hooked and so are the frazzled readers. Twomey doesn't give us shore leave until we know everything about these floating fortresses.

And finally, perhaps surprisingly to some, only two true first-person accounts have won the feature Pulitzer Prize: Raines' "Grady's Gift" and Nan Robertson's "Toxic Shock," a gripping, harrowing and thoroughly frightening masterpiece about her near-death experience with the deadly condition.

The Pulitzer Prize-winning stories in this anthology are powerful reminders of what's *right* in American journalism. Although each won a Pulitzer in the feature writing category, many were originally entered in other categories before being moved to features. The quality of the research, reporting and writing of these unique features is stunning. No two are written exactly the same way. But they all hold to one constant: strong emotions and content—powerful, touching, frightening, harrowing journalism.

Like most works of this nature, the final product involves many people who offered their help, advice and assistance with this project.

The roughness of some of the copy and the adventure of scanning so many thousands of words required the help of an additional copy editor. Fortunately, I worked with such a person every day in the Journalism Department at the University of Texas. Tania Hannan proofed every word in this book, made sure the spelling and context were correct, caught the sentences/paragraphs the scanner/computer would unexpectedly delete and was quick to tell me when my own words were less-than-graceful. I owe her a large debt for her inestimable work in this book.

The scanning also required some technical help and my wife, Susan Garlock, an engineer in real life, took on the thankless and time-consuming task of setting up the scanner and getting it to work on our IBM computer. She was also there to fix things and figure out an amazing number of idiosyncrasies that seemed to pop up in the scanning process. At times, the scanner would seem to take on a life of its own and Sue was always there to end that new life. Her help, support and encouragement with this book was priceless.

Thanks are also due to many others for their help, advice and assistance, including:

University of Texas professors Ron Anderson, Susan Dillon, Maxwell McCombs and Rusty Todd.

Professor Griff Singer, associate chair, Department of Journalism, University of Texas.

Dr. Tom Fensch, former head of the magazine sequence at the University of Texas. Tom's "best of" writing anthologies inspired this work in the first place. In addition, his book, *The Hardest Parts,* remains one of the premier texts for teaching young feature writers.

Richard Oppel, widely respected editor of the *Austin American-Statesman* and Edward Jay Friedlander of the University of South Florida, co-author of *Feature Writing for Newspapers and Magazines.*

Murry Greenwald for originally teaching me what quality journalism can accomplish.

Judi Brown, Jane Zaring and Gretchen Van Houten of Iowa State University Press were wonderfully patient about some of the pitfalls in the preparation of this book—and a joy to work with.

Claudia Weissberg of the Columbia University Graduate School of Journalism.

Special heartfelt thanks go out to James A. Michener for taking the time to read some of the work in this anthology and offering his positive comments—which meant more than he could ever know.

PULITZER PRIZE
FEATURE STORIES

1979

JON FRANKLIN

IF THE PULITZER BOARD adds a new category in the near future, keep an eye on Jon Franklin. In 1979, he won the first Pulitzer Prize awarded for feature writing, for "Mrs. Kelly's Monster," a two-part series on the intricacies of brain surgery. Then, in an unprecedented Pulitzer achievement, Franklin followed that up in 1985 by winning the first Pulitzer given for explanatory journalism.

Franklin is convinced many feature writers miss the point in their writing, often failing to look behind the story to find the compelling dramatic complication. In *Writing for Story,* Franklin says, "A story consists of a sequence of actions that occur when a sympathetic character encounters a complicating situation that he confronts and solves."

Notice that Franklin doesn't differentiate between short story, script, sonnet, novel ... or feature story. The key words for him are "complicating situation." He uses an award-winning story he wrote in 1983, "The Ballad of Old Man Peters," to explain.

Peters had received a certificate of appreciation from a local church for his efforts in serving as a translator for foreign travelers who were down on their luck. A national newspaper reporter had gotten wind of the award and interviewed Peters, writing a long piece on the award and what a superior translator the man was.

Happening upon the story long after the trail was cold, Franklin was fascinated by how a black sharecropper's son could have learned six languages in the first place. After some patient interviewing and prodding, Franklin discovered a man who was so afraid of his ignorance, he drove himself to become a figure of truly heroic proportions (conflict/resolution). The certificate was long-forgotten.

Influenced by writers such as Truman Capote (especially *In*

Cold Blood), Ernest Hemingway, Jack London and John Steinbeck, Franklin admits he ended up on a newspaper to pay the bills while hoping it would lead to a literary career, preferably in fiction. In the 1970s and 1980s, Franklin noticed writers seemed to be producing feature stories using the nonfiction short-story form.

The Pulitzer Board seemed to agree, voting on April 7, 1978, to add a new category (No. 12) for feature writing, with prime consideration being given to "high literary quality and originality." In choosing "Mrs. Kelly's Monster" for the inaugural Pulitzer for feature writing, the Board followed their new rules to the letter.

Interestingly, *The Baltimore Evening Sun* didn't seem as quick to recognize the value of "Mrs. Kelly's Monster," running the relatively short feature over two days (December 12-13, 1978) and burying the story on the bottom of page C1 both days, without any front page promotion.

Franklin recalls the editors deciding to run the story over two days, yet at the same time being concerned the readers wouldn't follow the story through the second part. He says he was asked to figure out a way to tell the readers—in advance—what was going to happen the second day.

An unhappy Franklin agreed to do an italicized precede. "If you can write stuff people will read, you can write stuff they won't. I broke rhythms, used marginal syntax, etc. It had all the info, so the editors were happy. The irony is that it may have been the most skillful grafs I ever wrote, and I wrote them so that people wouldn't read them!"

Franklin says his plan worked. The precede was written so badly, callers flooded the switchboard trying to find out how the story ended.

Here are the two precedes:

Day One

The organ of the mind defied scientists and philosophers for centuries, but in this decade it began, slowly, to yield. Now the drama of science turns inward to the elusive chemical and physical processes of intelligence and personality. There is hope that the grim disorders of the brain may soon be preventable, treatable, even curable, and in the coming months The Evening Sun *will print tales from this most intimate of frontiers.*

The following story, the first of two parts, focuses on the tragic drama of Dr. Thomas Ducker, Edna Kelly and Mrs. Kelly's monster. Mrs. Kelly's ultimate death illustrates that neuroscience is young and that its promise is a highly qualified one. In 1978, the gray tunnels of the brain are finally accessible, but they remain frightening and dangerous places to be.

Day Two
In this decade the drama of science turns inward to the elusive chemical and physical processes of intelligence and personality. In the coming months the Evening Sun *will focus on the scientists and doctors who work on the gray frontier as well as on the patients, who are drawn there by desperation. The following story concludes a two-part report on the tragedy of Mrs. Edna Kelly.*

Mrs. Kelly's Monster

The Baltimore Evening Sun

December 12, 1978

FRIGHTENING JOURNEY THROUGH TUNNELS OF THE BRAIN

IN THE COLD HOURS of a winter morning, Dr. Thomas Barbee Ducker, University Hospital's senior brain surgeon, rises before dawn. His wife serves him waffles but no coffee. Coffee makes his hands shake.

Downtown, on the 12th floor of the hospital, Edna Kelly's husband tells her goodbye.

For 57 years Mrs. Kelly shared her skull with the monster. No more. Today she is frightened but determined.

It is 6:30 a.m.

"I'm not afraid to die," she said as this day approached. "I've lost part of my eyesight. I've gone through all the hemorrhages. A couple of years ago I lost my sense of smell, my taste, I started having seizures. I smell a strange odor and then I start strangling. It started affecting my legs and I'm partially paralyzed.

"Three years ago a doctor told me all I had to look forward to was blindness, paralysis and a remote chance of death. Now I have aneurisms; this monster is causing that. I'm scared to death ... but there isn't a day that goes by that I'm not in pain and I'm tired of it. I can't bear the pain. I wouldn't want to live like this much longer." As Dr. Ducker leaves for work, Mrs. Ducker hands him a paper bag containing a peanut butter sandwich, a banana and two Fig Newtons. Downtown, in Mrs. Kelly's brain, a sedative takes effect. Mrs. Kelly was born with a tangled knot of abnormal blood vessels in the back of her brain. The malformation began small, but in time the vessels ballooned inside the confines of the skull, crowding the healthy brain tissue.

Finally, in 1942, the malformation announced its presence when one of the abnormal arteries, stretched beyond capacity, burst. Mrs. Kelly grabbed her head and collapsed.

After that, the agony never stopped.

Mrs. Kelly, at the time of her first intracranial bleed, was carrying her second child. Despite the pain, she raised her children and cared for her husband. The malformation continued to grow.

She began calling it "the monster."

Now, at 7:15 a.m. in Operating Room 11, a technician checks the brain surgery microscope and the circulating nurse lays out bandages and instruments. Mrs. Kelly lies still on a stainless steel table.

A small sensor has been threaded through her veins and now hangs in the antechamber of her heart. Dr. Jane Matjasko, the anesthesiologist, connects the sensor to a 7-foot-high bank of electronic instruments. Waveforms begin to move rhythmically across a cathode ray tube.

With each heartbeat a loudspeaker produces an audible popping sound. The steady pop, pop, pop, pop isn't loud, but it dominates the operating room.

Dr. Ducker enters the operating room and pauses before the X-ray films that hang on a lighted panel. He carried those brain images to Europe, Canada and Florida in search of advice, and he knows them by heart. Still, he studies them again, eyes focused on the two fragile aneurisms that swell above major arteries. Either may burst on contact.

The one directly behind Mrs. Kelly's eyes is the most dangerous, but also the easiest to reach. That's first.

The surgeon-in-training who will assist Dr. Ducker places Mrs. Kelly's head in a clamp and shaves her hair. Dr. Ducker checks his work. "We can't have a millimeter slip," he says, assuring himself that the three pins of the vise are locked firmly against the skull.

Mrs. Kelly, except for a 6-inch crescent of scalp, is draped with green sheets. A rubber-gloved palm goes out, and Doris Schwabland, the scrub nurse, lays a scalpel into it. Hemostats snap over the arteries of the scalp. Blood splatters onto Dr. Ducker's sterile paper booties.

The heartbeat goes pop, pop, pop, 70 pops a minute, steady.

It is 8:25 a.m.

Today Dr. Ducker intends to remove the two aneurisms, which comprise the most immediate threat to Mrs. Kelly's life. Later, he will move directly on the monster.

It is a risky operation, destined to take him to the hazardous frontiers of neurosurgery. Several experts told him he shouldn't do it at all, that he should let Mrs. Kelly die. But the consensus was he had no choice. The choice was Mrs. Kelly's.

"There's one chance of three that we'll end up with a hell of a mess or a dead patient," Dr. Ducker says.

"I reviewed it in my own heart and with other people, and I thought about the patient. You weigh what happens if you do it against what happens if you don't do it. I convinced myself that it should be done."

And Mrs. Kelly said yes.

Now, the decision made, Dr. Ducker pulls back Mrs. Kelly's scalp to reveal the dull ivory of living bone.

The chatter of the half-inch drill fills the room, drowning the rhythmic pop-pop-pop of the heart monitor. It is 9 o'clock when Dr. Ducker hands the 2-by-4-inch triangle of skull to the scrub nurse.

The tough, rubbery covering of the brain is cut free, revealing the soft gray convolutions of the forebrain.

"There it is," says the circulating nurse in a hushed voice. "That's what keeps you working."

It is 9:20.

Eventually, Dr. Ducker steps back, holding his gloved hands high to avoid contamination. While others move the microscope into place over the glistening brain, the neurosurgeon communes once more with the X-ray films.

The heart beats strong, 70 beats a minute, 70 beats a minute, 70 beats a minute.

"We're gonna have a hard time today," the surgeon says, to the X-rays.

Dr. Ducker presses his face against the microscope. His hand goes out for an electrified, tweezer-like instrument. The assistant moves in close, taking his position above the secondary eyepieces.

Dr. Ducker's view is shared by a video camera. Across the room, a color television crackles, displaying a highly magnified landscape of the brain. The polished tips of the tweezers move into view.

It is Dr. Ducker's intention to place tiny, spring-loaded alligator clips across the base of each aneurism. But first he must navigate a tortured path from his incision, above Mrs. Kelly's right eye, to the deeply buried Circle of Willis.

The journey will be immense. Under magnification, the landscape of the mind expands to the size of a room. Dr. Ducker's tiny, blunt instrument travels in millimeter leaps.

His strategy is to push between the forebrain, where conscious thought occurs, and the thumb-like forward projection of the brain, called the temporal lobe, that extends beneath the temples.

Carefully, Dr. Ducker pulls these two structures apart to form a deep channel. The journey begins at the bottom of this crevasse.

The time is 9:36 a.m.

The gray convolutions of the brain, wet with secretions, sparkle beneath the powerful operating theater spotlights. The microscope landscape heaves and subsides in rhythm to the pop, pop, pop of the heart monitor.

Gently, gently, the blunt probe teases apart the tiny convolutions of gray matter, spreading a tiny tunnel, millimeter by gentle millimeter into the glistening gray.

Dr. Ducker's progress is impeded by scar tissue. Each time Mrs. Kelly's monster flooded her brain with blood, scars formed, welding the structures together. To make his tunnel, Dr. Ducker must tease them apart again.

As the neurosurgeon works, he refers to Mrs. Kelly's monster as "the AVM," or arterial-veinous malformation.

Normally, he says, arteries force high-pressure blood into muscle or organ tissue. After the living cells suck out the oxygen and nourishment, the blood drains into low-pressure veins, which carry it back to the heart and lungs.

But in the back of Mrs. Kelly's brain, one set of arteries pumps directly into veins, bypassing the tissue. Over the years the unnatural junction, not designed for such a rapid flow of blood, has swollen and leaked. Hence the scar tissue.

Some scar welds are too tight, and the damaged tissue too weak, to endure the touch of metal. A tiny feeder artery breaks under the pressure of the steel probe. The television screen turns red.

Quickly, Dr. Ducker catches the ragged end of the bleeder between the pincers and there is a crackling bzzzzzzzt as the electricity burns it shut. Suction clears the field of blood and again the scene is gray. The tweezers push on.

"We're having trouble just getting in," Dr. Ducker tells the operating room team.

Again a crimson flood wells up. Again Dr. Ducker burns the severed bleeder closed and suctions out the red. Far down the tiny tunnel, the white trunk of the optic nerve can be seen.

It is 9:54.

Slowly, using the optic nerve as a guidepost, Dr. Ducker probes deeper and deeper into the gray.

The heart monitor continues to pop, pop, pop with reassuring regularity, 70 beats a minute, 70 beats a minute. The neurosurgeon guides the tweezers directly to the pulsing carotid artery, one of the three main blood channels into the brain. The carotid twists and dances to the electronic pop, pop, popping of the monitor.

Gently, ever gently, nudging aside the scarred brain tissue, Dr. Ducker moves along the carotid toward the Circle of Willis, near the floor of the skull.

This loop of vessels is the staging area from which blood is distributed throughout the brain. Three major arteries feed it from below, one in the rear and the two carotids in the front.

The first aneurism lies ahead, still buried in gray matter, where the carotid meets the circle. The second aneurism is deeper yet in the brain, where the hindmost artery rises along the spine and joins the circle.

Eyes pressed against the microscope, Dr. Ducker makes his tedious way along the carotid.

"She's so scarred I can't identify anything," he complains through the mask.

It is 10:01 a.m. The heart monitor pop, pop, pops with reassuring regularity.

The probing tweezers are gentle, firm, deliberate, probing, probing, probing, slower than the hands of the clock. Repeatedly, vessels bleed and Dr. Ducker cauterizes them. The blood loss is mounting, and now the anesthesiologist hangs a transfusion bag above Mrs. Kelly's shrouded form.

Ten minutes pass. Twenty. Blood flows, the tweezers buzz, the suction hose hisses. The tunnel is small, almost filled by the shank of the instrument.

The aneurism finally appears at the end of the tunnel, throbbing, visibly thin, a lumpy, overstretched bag, the color of rich cream, swelling out from the once-strong arterial wall, a tire about to blow out, a balloon ready to burst, a time-bomb the size of a pea.

The aneurism isn't the monster itself, only the work of the monster which, growing malevolently, has disrupted the pressures and weakened arterial walls throughout the brain. But the monster itself, the X-rays say, lies far away.

The probe nudges the aneurism, hesitantly, gently.

"Sometimes you touch one," a nurse says. "And blooey, the wolf's at the door."

Patiently, Dr. Ducker separates the aneurism from the surrounding brain tissue. The tension is electric.

No surgeon would dare go after the monster itself until the swelling time-bomb is diffused.

Now.

A nurse hands Dr. Ducker a long, delicate pair of pliers. A tiny, stainless steel clip, its jaws open wide, is positioned on the pliers' end. Presently, the magnified clip moves into the field of view, light glinting from its polished surface.

It is 10:40.

For 11 minutes Dr. Ducker repeatedly attempts to work the clip over the neck of the balloon, but the device is too small. He calls for one with longer jaws.

That clip moves into the microscopic tunnel. With infinite slowness, Dr. Ducker maneuvers it over the neck of the aneurism.

Then, in an instant, the jaws close and the balloon collapses.

"That's clipped," Dr. Ducker calls out. Smile wrinkles appear above his mask. The heart monitor goes pop, pop, pop, steady.

It is 10:58.

Dr. Ducker now begins following the Circle of Willis back into the brain, toward the second, and more difficult, aneurism that swells at the very rear of the circle, tight against the most sensitive and primitive structure in the head. The brainstem. The brainstem controls vital processes, including breathing and heartbeat.

The going becomes steadily more difficult and bloody. Millimeter, millimeter, treacherous millimeter the tweezers burrow a tunnel through Mrs. Kelly's mind. Blood flows, the tweezers buzz, the suction slurps. Push and probe. More blood. Then the tweezers lay quiet.

"I don't recognize anything," the surgeon says. He pushes further and finds a landmark.

Then, exhausted, Dr. Ducker disengages himself, backs away, sits down on a stool and stares straight ahead for a long moment. The brainstem is close, close.

"This is a frightening place to be," whispers the doctor.

In the background the heart monitor goes pop, pop, pop, pop, 70 beats a minute, steady. The smell of ozone and burnt flesh hangs thick in the air.

It is 11:05 a.m.

December 13, 1978

IT WAS TRIPLE JEOPARDY—SURGEON VS. THE MONSTER

IT IS 11:05 A.M., the Day of the Monster.

Dr. Thomas Barbee Ducker peers into the neurosurgery microscope, navigating the tunnels of Mrs. Edna Kelly's mind.

A bank of electronic equipment stands above the still patient. Monitor lights flash, oscilloscope waveforms build and break, dials jump and a loudspeaker announces each heartbeat, pop, pop, pop, 70 pops a minute, steady.

The sound, though subdued, dominates the room.

Since 8:25 a.m., when an incision was opened in the patient's scalp above the right eye, University Hospital's chief neurosurgeon has managed to find and clip off one of two deadly aneurisms.

Now as he searches for the second aneurism he momentarily loses his way in the glistening gray tissue. For 57 years the monster has dwelled in Mrs. Kelly's skull, periodically releasing drops of blood and torrents of agony, and in the process it altered the landscape of the brain.

Dr. Ducker stops and ponders, makes a decision and pushes ahead, carefully, carefully, millimeter by treacherous millimeter.

The operating room door opens, and Dr. Michael Salcman, the assistant chief neurosurgeon, enters. He confers briefly with Dr. Ducker and then stands in front of the television monitor.

Thoughtfully, he watches the small tweezer instrument, made huge by the microscope, probe along a throbbing, cream-colored blood vessel.

An aneurism on an artery is like the bump on a tire that is about to blow out, Dr. Salcman says. The weakened wall of the artery balloons outward under the relentless pressure of the heartbeat and, eventually, it bursts. That's death.

He says the aneurisms appeared because of the monster, a large malformation of arteries and veins in the back of the brain. Eventually Dr. Ducker hopes to remove or block off that malformation, but today the objectives are limited to clipping the two aneurisms.

Then, those hair-trigger killers out of the picture, he can plan a frontal assault on the monster itself.

But that will be another day. This day the objectives are the aneurisms, one in front and one in back. The front one is finished. One down, one to go.

The second, however, is the toughest. It pulses dangerously deep, hard against the brain's most sensitive element, the brainstem. That ancient nub of circuitry, the reptilian brain, controls basic functions like breathing and heartbeat.

"I call it the 'pilot light,' " says Dr. Salcman, "because if it goes out ... that's it."

Dr. Ducker has a different phrase. It is "a frightening place to be."

Now, as the tweezer probe opens new tunnels toward the second aneurism, the screen of the television monitor fills with blood.

Dr. Ducker responds quickly, snatching the broken end of the tiny artery with the tweezers. There is an electrical bzzzzzzt as he burns the bleeder closed. Progress stops while the red liquid is suctioned out.

"It's nothing to worry about," he says. "It's not much, but when you're looking at one square centimeter, two ounces is a damn lake."

The lake drained, Dr. Ducker presses on, following the artery toward the brainstem. Gently, gently, gently, gently he pushes aside the gray coils. For a moment the optic nerve appears in the background, then vanishes.

The going is even slower. Dr. Ducker is reaching all the way into the center of the brain and his instruments are the length of chopsticks. The danger mounts because, here, many of the vessels feed the pilot light.

The heartbeat goes pop, pop, pop, 70 beats a minute.

Dr. Ducker is lost again in the maze of scars that have obscured the landmarks and welded the structures together.

Dr. Salcman joins his boss at the microscope, peering through the assistant's eyepieces. They debate the options in low tones and technical terms. A decision is made and again the polished tweezers probe along the vessel.

The scar tissues that impede the surgeon's progress offer testimony to the many times over Mrs. Kelly's lifespan that the monster has leaked blood into the brain, a reminder of the constant migraines that have tortured her constantly since 1942, of the pain she'd now rather die than further endure.

Back on course, Dr. Ducker pushes his tunnel ever deeper, gentle, gentle, gentle as the touch of sterile cotton. Finally the gray matter parts.

The neurosurgeon freezes.

Dead ahead the field is crossed by many huge, distended, ropelike veins.

The neurosurgeon stares intently at the veins, surprised, chagrined, betrayed by the X-rays.

The monster.

The monster, by microscopic standards, lies far away, above and back, in the rear of the head. Dr. Ducker was to face the monster itself on another day, not now. Not here.

But clearly these tangled veins, absent on the X-ray films but very real in Mrs. Kelly's brain, are tentacles of the monster.

Gingerly, the tweezers attempt to push around them.

Pop, pop, pop .. pop ... pop .... pop ..... pop ...

"It's slowing," warns the anesthesiologist, alarmed.

The tweezers pull away like fingers touching fire.

.... pop ... pop .. pop . pop, pop, pop.

"It's coming back," says the anesthesiologist.

The vessels control blood flow to the brainstem, the pilot light.

Dr. Ducker tries to go around them a different way.

Pop, pop, pop . pop .. pop ...

And withdraws.

Dr. Salcman stands before the television monitor, arms crossed, frowning. "She can't take much of that," the anesthesiologist says. "The heart will go into arrhythmia and that'll lead to a ... call it a heart attack."

Dr. Ducker tries a still different route, probing clear of the area and returning at a different angle. Eventually, at the end of a long, throbbing tunnel of brain tissue, the sought-after aneurism appears.

Pop, pop, pop . pop .. pop .. pop ...

The instruments retract.

"Damn," says the chief neurosurgeon. "I can only work here for a few minutes without the bottom falling out."

The clock says 12:29.

Already, the tissue swells visibly from the repeated attempts to burrow past the tentacles.

Again the tweezers move forward in a different approach and the aneurism reappears. Dr. Ducker tries to reach it by inserting the aneurism clip through a long narrow tunnel. But the pliers that hold the clip obscure the view.

Pop, pop .. pop ... pop .... pop .....

The pliers retract.

"We're on it and we know where we are," complains the neurosurgeon, frustration adding a metallic edge to his voice. "But we're going to have an awful time getting a clip in there. We're so close, but ... "

A resident who has been assisting Dr. Ducker collapses on a stool. He stares straight ahead, eyes unfocused, glazed.

"Michael, scrub," Dr. Ducker says to Dr. Salcman. "See what you can do. I'm too cramped."

While the circulating nurse massages Dr. Ducker's shoulder, Dr. Salcman attempts to reach the aneurism with the clip.

Pop, pop, pop . pop .. pop ... pop ...

The clip withdraws.

"That should be the aneurism right there," says Dr. Ducker, taking the place at the microscope again. "Why the hell can't we get to it? We've tried, 10 times."

At 12:53, another approach.

Pop, pop, pop . pop .. pop ... pop ...

Again.

It is 1:06.

And again, and again, and again.

Pop ... pop ... pop, pop, pop ... pop ... pop-pop-pop ...

The anesthesiologist looks up sharply at the dials. A nurse catches her breath and holds it.

"Damn, damn, damn."

Dr. Ducker backs away from the microscope, his gloved hands held before him. For a full minute, he's silent.

"There's an old dictum in medicine," he finally says. "If you can't help, don't do any harm. Let nature take its course. We may have already hurt her. We've slowed down her heart. Too many times." The words carry defeat, exhaustion, anger.

Dr. Ducker, stands again before the X-rays. His eyes focus on the rear aneurism, the second one, the one that thwarted him. He examines the film for signs, unseen before, of the monster's descending tentacles. He finds no such indications.

Pop, pop, pop, goes the monitor, steady now, 70 beats a minute.

"Mother nature," a resident surgeon growls, "is a mother."

The retreat begins. Under Dr. Salcman's command, the team prepares to wire the chunk of skull back into place and close the incision.

It ends quickly, without ceremony. Dr. Ducker's gloves snap sharply as a nurse pulls them off.

It is 1:30.

Dr. Ducker walks, alone, down the hall, brown paper bag in his hand. In the lounge he sits on the edge of a hard orange couch and unwraps the peanut butter sandwich. His eyes focus on the opposite wall.

Back in the operating room the anesthesiologist shines a light into each of Mrs. Kelly's eyes. The right pupil, the one under the incision, is dilated and does not respond to the probing beam. It is a grim omen.

If Mrs. Kelly recovers, says Dr. Ducker, he'll go ahead and try to deal with the monster itself. He'll try to block the arteries to it, maybe even take it out. That would be a tough operation, he says, without enthusiasm.

"And that's providing she's in good shape after this."

If she survives. If. If.

"I'm not afraid to die," Mrs. Kelly had said. "I'm scared to death ... but ... I can't bear the pain. I wouldn't want to live like this much longer."

Her brain was too scarred. The operation, tolerable in a younger person, was too much. Already, where the monster's tentacles hang before the brainstem, the tissue swells, pinching off the source of oxygen.

Mrs. Kelly is dying.

The clock in the lounge, near where Dr. Ducker sits, says 1:40.

"It's hard even to tell what to do. We've been thinking about it for six weeks. But, you know, there are certain things ... that's just as far as you can go. I just don't know ... "

He lays down the sandwich, the banana and the Fig Newtons on the table before him, neatly, the way the scrub nurse laid out instruments.

"It was triple jeopardy," he says, finally, staring at his peanut butter sandwich the same way he stared at the X-rays. "It was triple jeopardy."

It is 1:43 and it's over.

Dr. Ducker bites, grimly, into the sandwich.

The monster won.

ANALYSIS

JON FRANKLIN definitely *didn't* fly by the seat of his pants in writing "Mrs. Kelly's Monster." "Mrs. Kelly was actually the fifth in a series of stories that I was doing ... to try out Chekhov's story-form theories in journalism," he explains. "I was looking for a good story that would have a beginning, middle and end." Franklin admits his story is "highly paced ... sort of what *Bolero* was to Ravel."

Franklin also carefully outlined his feature in the short story format he prefers:

Complication/Ducker gambles
　1. Ducker enters brain
　2. Ducker clips aneurysm
　3. Monster ambushes Ducker
Resolution/Ducker accepts defeat

Franklin leaves little to chance. He even chooses each noun and verb with unusual care—switching tense from present to past when necessary for literary flow. A student of the short story, Franklin devises his feature stories with care: A snappy lead is followed by an immediate complication. The body of the story leads to an appropriate resolution—satisfactory or not.

In "Mrs. Kelly's Monster" the subject of the story dies, a most unsatisfactory ending. Or was it? Franklin solved that problem by making Dr. Thomas Ducker, the surgeon who operated on Mrs. Kelly's brain, the focal point of the story.

Franklin begins with an effective descriptive lead showing Ducker awakening before dawn and eating only waffles because, "coffee makes his hands shake." The author admits that even the first verb in the story, "rises," wasn't chosen by accident. Franklin is a stickler for active verbs. And subtly noting the importance of a brain surgeon's hands not shaking in the first paragraph was an important early tip for readers of what was to come.

Shifting between the doctor routinely preparing for his day of work and the patient waiting in the hospital, Franklin creates both human interest and tension. As a frightened but resolute Edna Kelly waits in her hospital bed, Ducker's wife hands her husband a paper bag containing lunch: a peanut butter sandwich, a banana and exactly two Fig Newtons. Ducker could be a plumber or a carpenter heading off to a day's work. The sharp reader will note food is prominently mentioned at the beginning and the end of the piece.

By the third paragraph, Franklin brings the complication into focus: Mrs. Kelly may die during the operation, a risk she willingly accepts.

Finally, notice how skillfully the author foreshadows coming events by dropping hints into the narrative or changing words as Mrs. Kelly's condition deteriorates. An example: Mrs. Kelly is *covered* early in the piece. Later, she is *shrouded*. A small change but one with ominous overtones.

Throughout this story, Franklin seems to be sitting right beside the doctor, peering into his own high-powered microscope. He actually had unusual access, having spent several years doing a book on the trauma unit at Johns Hopkins.

Two examples serve to show how well Franklin marries keen observational powers with solid reporting and near-lyrical writing:

The gray convolutions of the brain, wet with secretions, sparkle beneath the powerful operating theater spotlights. The microscopic landscape heaves and subsides in rhythm to the pop, pop, pop of the heart monitor.

The going becomes steadily more difficult and bloody. Millimeter, millimeter, treacherous millimeter the tweezers burrow a tunnel through Mrs. Kelly's mind. Blood flows, the tweezers buzz, the suction slurps. Push and probe. More blood. Then the tweezers lay quiet.

In writing this story, Franklin uses two literary devices to create pace and tension—the use of time and the steady beating of Kelly's heart.

He uses the time element almost as a benchmark in the story. Beginning at 6:30 a.m., when Mrs. Kelly is preparing for surgery, and ending at 1:43 p.m., when she dies. Franklin mentions the exact time during the story at least 14 times.

Even more effectively, Franklin frequently inserts into his text the *pop, pop, pop, pop ... pop ... pop* of Kelly's heartbeat being broadcast from a loudspeaker in the operating room. Sometimes, to create more tension, Franklin adds:

70 beats a minute, 70 beats a minute, 70 beats a minute.

These tactics are mesmerizing to the reader. And as the operation nears the crucial life or death part, Franklin also ratchets up the tension for the reader by writing short, choppy sentences and increasing the use of *pop . pop ... pop .. pop*. Even the number of dots between each pop change as the danger increases.

At the end of the story, the reader is nearly as drained as Dr. Ducker. Even though the ending is sad and Ducker's valiant efforts unsuccessful, we have experienced a thrilling literary ride and learned a great deal about the complexities of brain surgery. Franklin isn't really keen on sad endings. By eliminating references to Mrs. Kelly in the last few paragraphs, and focusing on Ducker, the reader ends with a heroic vision of the doctor—who will live to save more lives. Subtle but telling. Just like Jon Franklin.

JON FRANKLIN is currently a professor in the creative writing program at the University of Oregon. He holds a bachelor's degree in journalism from the University of Maryland and has published several books, including *Writing for Story,* a fascinating "cookbook" on the preparation of dramatic nonfiction.

1980

MADELEINE BLAIS

MADELEINE BLAIS says she has always been interested in "the stories of people who are usually on the outskirts or walking a curious edge."

Edward Zepp, a well-known figure in South Florida newsrooms in the 1970s, seemed an interesting choice for such a story, she recalls. "As a frail, garrulous old man [Zepp] fit the usual category." Blais admits she knew little about World War I and this seemed a chance to further her education. She wrote the story for the paper's *Tropic Magazine*.

Unlike many feature writers who view editors with a wary eye, Blais credits her editors with much of the story's success. "My editor Lary Bloom suggested I meet with Zepp. Lary had this way of rolling his eyes and looking vague, the signal he thought he was onto something."

Blais says another editor, Doug Balz, helped her to see the value of the use of travel in the story—Zepp's journey back to the past as the train raced to his final destiny, for example.

Blais learned about her Pulitzer Prize as it came over the wire in the newsroom. "At the time I was worried I was not worthy, or old enough [32] for such an honor," she says. Quickly recovering from that thought, Blais knew what to do next: "We had a spontaneous gathering at my house on Miami Beach that night and people brought everything from KFC to a $100 bottle of champagne, which in a way captured what I have always loved about journalists—the urge to celebrate!"

Has winning the Pulitzer changed her career? "Not fundamentally. You're only as good as your next story, whether you've won a Pulitzer, or a good posture or a biggest tomato prize."

Zepp's Last Stand

The Miami Herald

November 11, 1979

ALL HIS LIFE Edward Zepp has wanted nothing so much as to go to the next world with a clear conscience. So on Sept. 11 the old man, carrying a borrowed briefcase filled with papers, boarded an Amtrak train in Deerfield Beach and headed north on the Silver Meteor to our nation's capital. As the porter showed him to his roomette, Ed Zepp kept saying, "I'm 83 years old. Eighty-three."

At 9 a.m. the next day, Zepp was to appear at the Pentagon for a hearing before the Board for Correction of Military Records. This was, he said, "the supreme effort, the final fight" in the private battle of Private Zepp, Company D, 323rd Machine Gun Battalion, veteran of World War I, discharged on Nov. 9, 1919—with dishonor.

Something happens to people after a certain age, and the distinctions of youth disappear. The wrinkles conquer, like an army. In his old age, Zepp is bald. He wears fragile glasses. The shoulders are rounded. His pace is stooped and slow. It is hard, in a way, to remove 60 years and picture him tall, lanky, a rebel.

The old man, wearing a carefully chosen business suit which he hoped would be appropriately subdued for the Pentagon, sat in the chair of his roomette, as the train pulled out of Deerfield Beach. With a certain palsied eagerness he foraged his briefcase. Before the train reached full speed, he arranged on his lap the relics from his days at war. There were his dog tags and draft card, even his Department of War Risk life insurance policy. There was a letter written to his mother in 1919 in France, explaining why he was in the stockade. His fingers, curled with arthritis and in pain, attacked several documents. He unfurled the pages of a copy of the original court-martial proceedings which found him in violation of the 64th Article of War: failure to obey the command of a superior officer. There was also a copy of the rule book for Fort Leavenworth, where Zepp had been sentenced to 10 years at hard labor.

When Ed Zepp was drafted in 1917, he told his draft board he had conscientious objections to fighting overseas. The draft board told him his objections did not count; at the time only Quakers and

Mennonites were routinely granted C.O. (conscientious objector) status. "As a Lutheran, I didn't cut any ice," he said. Zepp was one of 20,873 men between the ages of 21 and 31 who were classified as C.O.'s but inducted nonetheless. Of those, only 3,999 made formal claims once they were in camp. Zepp's claim occurred on June 10, 1918, at Fort Merritt, N.J., the day before his battalion was scheduled for shipment overseas. Earlier, Zepp had tried to explain his position to a commanding officer, who told him he had a "damn fool belief." On June 10, Zepp was ordered to pack his barracks bag. When he refused, a sergeant—"Sgt. Hitchcock, a real hard-boiled guy, a Regular Army man"—held a gun to his head: "Pack that bag or I'll shoot."

"Shoot," Zepp said, "you son of a bitch."

Conscientious objection has always been a difficult issue for the military, but perhaps less difficult in 1917 than in recent times. Men who refused to fight were called "slackers" and "cowards." By the time the United States entered the war, the public had been subjected to a steady onslaught of "blatant propaganda," according to Dr. Raymond O'Connor, professor of American history at the University of Miami.

The government found ways to erode the spirit of isolationism felt by many Americans and replace it with a feeling of jubilant hostility against the Germans. It was patriotic to despise the Kaiser. It was patriotic to sing: *Over There, Oh, I Hate To Get Up In The Morning* and *Long Way to Tipperary.* A new recruiting poster pointed out that "Uncle Sam Wants You." The war's most important hero was Sgt. York, a conscientious objector who was later decorated for capturing Germans. They made a movie of Sgt. Alvin York's heroics.

They made an example of Pvt. Edward Zepp, a kid from Cleveland.

Zepp was formally released from the Army 60 years and two days ago.

But Zepp has never released the Army.

At his upcoming hearing at the Pentagon, Zepp was after a subtle distinction, two words really, "honorable discharge," meaningless to anybody but himself. It would be a victory that couldn't even be shared with the most important person in his life, his wife Christine, who died in 1977.

In 1952, Zepp appeared before the same military board. At that time the Army agreed that he was a sincere C.O. His discharge was upgraded to a "general discharge with honor." He became entitled to the same benefits as any other veteran, but he has never taken any money: "I have lived without their benefits all my life." The board refused to hear his case again; only a bureaucratic snafu and the intercession of Rep. Daniel Mica (D., Palm Beach) paved the way to the hearing scheduled for Sept. 12.

For 41 years, Zepp worked as the money raiser for The Community Chest, now called The United Way, in Cleveland. He learned how to get things done, to get things from people.

For years, he has sought his due from the Pentagon. His persistence was not only heroic, but also a touch ornery. Here is a man who refused to fight in World War I but who takes a blackjack with him to ward off potential punks every time he leaves his Margate condominium at night. He talks about how there are just wars, and maybe we should have gone all out in Vietnam, "just like we did in Hiroshima, killing the whole city" and in the next breath he talks about the problems that occur when "the Church starts waving a Flag."

It is impossible to tell how much of his fight is hobby and how much the passion of a man who says he cannot die—he literally cannot leave this earth—until his honor is fully restored.

To some, his refusal to fight meant cowardice; to Zepp, it represented heroism. It is an ethical no-man's-land. War leaves no room for subtle distinctions.

For his day in court, Ed Zepp was not taking any chances. His health is failing; he is at the age of illness and eulogy. He has an understandable preoccupation with his own debilities (proximal atrial fibrillations, coronary heart disease, pernicious anemia). Many of his references, especially his war stories, are to people now gone. At $270 for a round-trip train ticket, the plane would have been cheaper, but Zepp thought flying would be too risky; it might bring on a seizure, a blackout, or something worse.

On the train the old man talked obsessively about what happened during the war. He told his story over and over and over—clack, clack, clack, like the train on the rails. Except for this constant talk, there was nothing about him that revealed his mission. As he hesitantly walked the narrow, shaking corridors, making his way from car to car, he did not have the air of a man headed for the crucial confrontation of his life. He looked like a nicely dressed elderly man who might be taking the train out of a preference for gravity or perhaps in sentimental memory of the glory days of railroading.

"This was the war to end war," Zepp said on the way to the dining car. "The war to make the world safe for democracy. *Democracy.* They gave me a kangaroo court-martial."

All his life, Zepp has believed he was denied the very freedoms he had been recruited to defend. He has nursed his grievances like an old war injury, which, on one level, is exactly what they are. "They murdered me, you know. They tried to, in a way."

His refusal to fight turned him into a fighter. "I was cursed," he said. "It made a killer out of me, almost."

He said he was seeking only one thing: "My honor. My good name. I don't see how a great nation can stigmatize as dishonorable a person who was following the dictates of his conscience. When I die, I want it said of me, 'Well done, thou good and faithful servant.'"

Ed Zepp turned to the young waiter, in his starched white mess coat, who had been patiently waiting for him to order lunch. He ordered a turkey sandwich: "I can't eat much. My doctor says I should eat lightly. I take enzyme pills to help me digest."

September 1979, Sebring, Fla.: Ed Zepp's light lunch has just been placed before him. September 1917, Cleveland, Ohio: Ed Zepp's appeals to the draft board have been rejected twice.

During any long trip, there is a distortion of landscape and time; the old man's talk echoed the feeling of suspension that comes with being on the road. The closer he got to the Pentagon, the closer he got to 1917.

Before he was drafted at the age of 21, Zepp had already earned a business degree and worked as a clerk at Johns Manville. At the time, his native Cleveland was heavily industrialized, with much social and political unrest. Socialist Eugene Debs was a frequent visitor; Zepp says the man was "fire." He remembers listening to his speeches and once joined a Debs march, clear across town, to a large hall on the west side. Debs preached workers' rights and counseled against war. So did Zepp's pastor, who was censured by the Lutheran Church for his outspoken views against the war. "War," says Ed Zepp, "was an ocean away."

Zepp's parents were Polish immigrants, Michael and Louise Czepieus. His father was a blacksmith, "not the kind who made shoes for horses, but rather he made all the ironwork pertaining to a wagon." There were five children, and all of them were sent to business school and ended up, says Zepp, "in the office world."

"I was a top-notch office man all my life," he says. In any family there is talk about somebody's lost promise, failed opportunity, and in the Zepp family, there was talk, principally among his sisters, about how, with his meticulous mind, he would have been a great lawyer, but for the war, but for what happened over there.

The waiter removed the empty plates from Zepp's table, and the next group of hungry passengers was seated.

Three p.m., Waldo, Fla., in the club car. Ed Zepp is nursing a soda, and on the table in front of him, like a deck of marked cards, are the original court-martial proceedings.

Eighty miles an hour.

The train was moving almost as fast as Edward Zepp is old, and he seemed impressed by that. "It is," he said, "a wonderful way to see the countryside." The world passed by in a blur.

Despite his ailments, there is something energetic and alert about Zepp; for two months before the hearing, he swam every day for half an hour to build stamina. Sipping his soda, he wondered whether he had chosen the correct clothes. His suit was brown and orange. He had a color-coordinated, clip-on tie and a beige shirt. "I have another suit that my wife, Christine, picked out for me, but it has all the colors of the rainbow, and I didn't want to show up at the Pentagon looking like a sport in front of all those monkeys. Oops. I'd better be careful. They probably wouldn't like it if I called them monkeys, would they?"

This trip was partly in memory of Christine, Zepp's third wife, whom he married in 1962, shortly before he retired to Florida. His first marriage was brief; during the second marriage he had two children, a son who died in his early 30s ("He served in Korea and he was a teacher.") and a daughter, now 46 years old, a psychiatric social worker who lives near Boston.

"Christine would want me to do this. She was a fighter, she was a real person. She was the only one I really cared about. And what happened? She died. All the guys in my condominium thought I would be the first to go, but she passed away on May 1, 1977, two days before my 81st birthday. Do you know what she said to me before she died? 'I want to be buried with my wedding ring on.' I met other women at the square dances at the senior center. One of them said, 'Ed, let's go to the Bahamas for a week. Get your mind off this. It's too much pressure.' But I couldn't go away. Christine and I are married, even in death."

When Ed Zepp speaks of his third wife, his face sometimes gets an odd look; there is a dream-like minute or so. The voice catches, the blue eyes become rheumy, his words come out in a higher pitch. Just as it seems as if he will break down and sob, composure returns. The same thing often happens when he speaks of what happened during the war.

"Anyone who reads this court-martial," said Zepp, "will acquaint himself with all the vital points of my case: how the draft board refused to listen; how the Army loused it up in Camp Sherman when they failed to inform me of General Order Number 28; how, at Fort Merritt, Sgt. Hitchcock held the gun to my head and forced me to pack, and then they Shanghaied me out of the country on the SS Carmania, and in France they gave me a kangaroo court-martial."

General Order Number 28, issued by the War Department on March 23, 1918, was an effort by the government in mid-war to expand the definition of those who qualified for C.O. status. Men who had already been drafted, but had sought C.O. status, were supposed to be informed by a "tactful and considerate" officer of their right to choose noncombatant service.

"General Order Number 28 was never read or posted during the time I was at boot camp at Camp Sherman in Chillicothe, Ohio," Zepp maintains. "This was how it was done—gospel truth: 250 of us were lined up in retreat. Lt. Paul Herbert, went through the ranks, asking each man, 'Any objections to fighting the Germans?' Well, I thought they were looking for pro-German sympathizers. I wasn't a pro-German sympathizer. My parents were Polish. I did not speak up.

"Then at Fort Merritt, Sgt. Hitchcock, he was a hard-boiled sergeant, put the gun on me. He never told the court-martial about that. He approached me in a belligerent manner; there was no kindly and courteous officer informing me of my rights as specified in General Order Number 28.

"They shipped me overseas against my will, and for two months in France I still didn't know what action would be taken against me for defying Sgt. Hitchcock and Capt. Faxon. They kept me busy with regular military work. I helped erect a machine gun range, I had rifle practice, I learned how to break a person's arm in close combat.

"During that time, Lt. Herbert propositioned me with a nice soft easy job. He came to me and said, Zepp, how about calling the whole thing off. I'll get you a nice soft easy job in the quartermaster." Zepp repeated Herbert's words in the buttery tone of voice he always uses when he repeats Herbert's words. "He tried to make a deal. But I had no confidence. I smelled a rat. And to prove to you beyond a shadow of a doubt it was not a sincere offer, find one word in the court-martial proceedings that he offered me a job. He was trying to make a deal. It was a trap."

"And then they Shanghaied me out of the country and gave me a kangaroo court-martial. I wasn't even allowed to face my accusers." During Zepp's court-martial many of the basic facts which are part of his litany are mentioned. The sergeant who held a gun to his head testified, but no mention was made of that action. Capt. C.W. Faxon said he believed Zepp had "sincere religious objections." Sgt. Steve Kozman admitted to giving the defendant "a few kicks in the behind" on the way to the SS Carmania.

In his testimony, Zepp told about how, the same evening he refused to pack his barracks bag, "Lt. Paul Herbert came up to me and spoke in a general way about my views and called them pro-German. He also asked me if I had a mother and I said 'Yes', and he asked me if I had a sister and I said 'Yes', and he said, 'Would you disgrace them by having your picture in the paper?'"

Zepp argued that in light of General Order Number 28 the Army had no right to ship him overseas without first offering noncombatant service. The heart of Zepp's case, as he spoke it before that tribunal long ago, showed his instinct for fine, if quixotic distinctions:

"I did not willfully disobey two lawful orders, but I was compelled to willfully disobey two alleged lawful orders."

Savannah, Ga. 7 p.m. The train had crossed state lines, and Zepp had just entered the dining car for an evening meal of fish and vegetables. His conversation once again crossed the borders of geography and time.

Even at dinner, it was impossible for him to abandon his topic.

"Let me tell you about what happened after the court-martial. They put me in a dungeon; there were rats running over me, the floor was wet, it was just a place to throw potatoes, except they'd all rot. It was later condemned as unfit for human habitation by the psychiatrists who interviewed me. That was a perfect opportunity to act crazy and get out of the whole thing. But I stuck by my conscience. I was not a coward. It's easier to take a chance with a bullet than stand up on your own two feet and defy."

He talked about how the Army discovered he had "office skills" and he spent much of his time as a clerk—"sergeant's work, or at least corporal's."

He said he was transferred to Army bases all over France during the year 1919; the best time was under Capt. John Evans: "I had my own desk, and Captain Evans put a box of chocolates on it, which he shouldn't have, because it turned me into a 250-pounder. I had the liberty of the city, and Capt. Evans gave me an unsolicited recommendation." Zepp quoted it by heart: "Private Zepp has worked for me since Jan. 3, 1919. During this time he has been my personal clerk, and anyone desiring a stenographer will find him trustworthy and with no mean ability."

In August of 1919, as part of his clerical duties, Zepp was "making out service records for boys to return home to the United States, and finally the time came for me to make one out for myself."

In September he arrived in Fort Leavenworth where once again he served as a clerk: "They made me secretary to the chaplain, and I taught the boys how to operate a typewriter.

"Finally on Nov. 9, 1919, they released me. I still don't know why I didn't serve the complete sentence. I never asked for their mercy. I think it must have been my mother, she must have gone to our pastor, and he intervened."

Zepp paused, and his look became distant. There was that catch in his voice; he cried without tears.

Dinner was over.

Ten p.m. Florence, S.C. After nursing one beer in the club car, Zepp decided it was time to get some sleep. As he prepared to leave for his roomette, he said, "They tried to make Martin Luther recant, but he wouldn't. Remember: 'If they put you to shame or call you faithless, it is better that God call you faithful and honorable than that the world call you faithful and honorable.' Those are Luther's own words. 1526."

It was hard to sleep on the train; it rocked at high speeds and it made a number of jerking stops and churning starts in the middle of the night in small towns in North Carolina.

Ed Zepp asked the porter to wake him an hour before the 6 a.m. arrival in Washington, but his sleep was light and he awoke on his own at 4. He shaved, dressed, and then sat in the roomette, briefcase beside him. The train pulled in on time, before sunrise.

Wandering the almost-empty station, Zepp had a tall dignity, eyeglasses adding to his air of alertness. He sat by himself on a bench, waiting for his lawyer who was due at 7. Zepp's lawyer was a young fellow who had read about his client in *Liberty Magazine*. Thirty-four years old, John St. Landau works at the Center for Conscientious Objection in Philadelphia. Landau called the old man in Florida and volunteered his services. They made plans to meet at Union Station, and Zepp told the lawyer, "Don't worry. You'll recognize me. I'll be the decrepit old man creeping down the platform."

Landau, himself a C.O. during the Vietnam War, arrived at the appointed hour. The two men found an empty coffee shop where they huddled at a table for about an hour. Zepp told his lawyer he had not brought his blackjack to Washington, and the lawyer said, smiling, "I take it you are no longer a C.O."

At 8:30 they left to take the Metro, Washington's eerily modern subway system with computerized "farecards," to the Pentagon.

Zepp was easily the oldest person on the commuter-filled subway. He did not try to speak above the roar. His was a vigil of silence. When the doors sliced open at the "Pentagon" stop, the hour of judgment was upon him.

"The gates of hell," he said, "shall not prevail."

It would be hard to surmise, given the enthusiasm of his recital, that Zepp was in Washington on not much more than a wing and a prayer. In April, the Pentagon had mistakenly promised him a hearing; it was a bureaucratic bungle. On May 9, he was told there had been an error; there was no new evidence in his case; therefore there should be no new hearing. On May 31, Rep. Mica wrote to the review board requesting a new hearing on the strength of his office. It was granted for Sept. 12, but Zepp had been forewarned in a letter from the Pentagon that just because he was getting his hearing, he should not conclude from this concession that "the department" admits "any error or injustice now ... in your records."

Just before Zepp was ushered into the small hearing room at 11, he gave himself a pep talk: "I am going to be real nice. Getting even doesn't do anything, punching someone around. I want to do things the Christian way. And I'll use the oil can. When I was at the Community Chest, I called all the women 'darlings' and I would polka with them at the parties. I used the oil can profusely."

Zepp departed for the hearing room.

The fate of the World War I veteran, defended by a Vietnam era lawyer, was to be decided by a panel of five—four veterans of World War Two, one veteran of the Korean War. The chairman was Charles Woodside, who also served on the panel that heard the appeal of the widow of Pvt. Eddie Slovik, the first deserter since the Civil War to be executed. Less than a week before Zepp's hearing, newspapers carried a story about how Slovik's widow, denied a pension by the Army, had finally died, penniless, in a nursing home.

Landau stated Zepp's case, saying that the defendant accepted the findings of the 1952 hearing, the findings which concluded Zepp had in fact been sincere: "The reason we're here is that we believe the general discharge ought to be upgraded to an honorable discharge. ... What we see as the critical issue is the quality of [Mr. Zepp's] service."

The first witness was Martin Sovik, a member of the staff of the Office for Governmental Affairs of the Lutheran Church Council.

Like Landau, Sovik, had also been a C.O. during Vietnam.

He confirmed that in 1969 the Lutheran Church of America supported individual members of the church, following their consciences, to oppose participation in war. One member of the panel asked Sovik how you can determine whether a person is in fact a C.O.

"That decision is made within a person's mind—obviously you can't know whether a person is a C.O. anymore than whether he is a Yankees' fan or an Orioles' fan except by his own affirmation."

Next, the old man took his turn. The panel urged him to remain seated during the testimony. The old man marshalled the highlights of his military experience: *Shanghaied, nice soft easy job, tactful and courteous officer, hard-boiled sergeant, gun at my head, face my accusers, unfit for human habitation, unsolicited recommendation.* The words tumbled out, a litany.

Every now and then Zepp's composure cracked, stalling the proceedings. "I'm sure it's hard to recall," said Woodside.

"It's not that," said the defendant. "I'm just living it. This was indelibly impressed, it is vivid on my mind, like something that happened yesterday."

At 1:00 a luncheon recess was called. Woodside promised that he would continue to listen with sympathy when the hearing resumed.

"Govern yourself by the facts," said Zepp. "Then we'll both be happy."

As they were leaving the hearing room, Zepp turned to Landau and Sovik and apologized for breaking down. "You're doing all right, you're doing just fine," said Sovik.

"I can't help it. Every now and then my voice breaks," said Zepp. "It touches me."

Sovik, putting his hand on the old man's arm, said: "It touches us all."

The afternoon was more of the same: *Lt. Herbert was not making me a sincere offer, German sympathizer, disgrace your sisters, sincere religious objections.*

Finally the executive secretary of the Corrections Board, Ray Williams, the man most familiar with Zepp's case, asked the defendant:

"Mr. Zepp, since you received your general discharge under honorable conditions back in 1952 as a result of a recommendation of this board, have you ever applied to the V.A. for any benefits?"

Zepp: "No I haven't."

Williams: "You understand you are entitled to all the benefits of an honorably discharged soldier."

Zepp: "That's right. The one thing that bothers me is my conscience, my allegiance to the Almighty. I have to see this thing through. ... I don't think that a person who follows the dictates of his conscience and is a true Christian should be stigmatized as a dishonorable person. And I think he shouldn't even get a second-rate discharge."

Williams: " ... In all good conscience you can say that your discharge is under honorable conditions."

Zepp: "I personally feel it would behoove the United States of America, who believes in freedom of conscience, religion or the Bill of Rights, that a person who follows, truthfully follows, the dictates of his conscience, and you are obligated to follow that because you've got a relationship with God, and I don't think that we should stigmatize anybody like that as being a dishonorable person.

"And the reason I'm here at my advanced age—83, arthritis and all that—my inner self, my conscience, says, 'Now here. You go to the board and make one last effort.'" Zepp paused. He hunched forward and made ready to sling one final arrow: "In view of the fact, Mr. Williams, that there's not much difference, then why not make it honorable? There isn't much difference. Let's make it honorable and we'll all be happy."

Zepp's lawyer closed with this plea:

"The military has come a long way since 1918 in their dealing with these individuals who have religious scruples about continued military service. ... I would contend that it's in part because of individuals like Mr. Zepp who were willing to put their principles on the line many years ago ... that it took individuals like that to finally work out a good system of dealing with conscientious objection. And that's what the military has now after many, many years. That, in its own right, is a very important service to the military."

The panel closed the proceedings. A decision was promised sometime within the next month.

Back at Union Station, waiting for the return trip: gone now the derelict emptiness of the early morning hours. In the evening the station was smart with purpose: well-dressed men and women, toting briefcases and newspapers, in long lines waiting for trains. The old man sat on a chair and reviewed the day. He smiled and his eyes were bright.

"I feel very confident. I sensed victory. I put all my cards on the table and I called a spade a spade. Did you see how I went up afterwards and I shook all their hands, just like they were my friends? I even shook the hands of Williams, my enemy, and I leaned over and I said to him, 'I love you, darling.' I acted as if I expected victory and I did not accept defeat. I used the oil can profusely."

He paused. Zepp looked up, seeming to study the ceiling. He cupped his chin with his left hand. The old man was silent. A college girl across from him watched him in his reverie, and she smiled a young smile.

Finally, the old man spoke. He seemed shaken. His voice was soft, filled with fear, the earlier confidence gone. The thought had come, like a traitor, jabbing him in the heart:

"What next?"

"I'll be lonesome without this. Here's my problem. Now that I don't have anything to battle for, what will I do? There's nothing I know of on the horizon to compete with that."

He paused. His face brightened. "Well, I can go swimming. And I can keep square dancing. Something happens to me when I square dance; it's the—what do they call it?—the adrenalin. I am a top form dancer. Maybe I can go back to being the treasurer of the Broward Community Senior Center. I did that before my wife became sick, but I quit to take care of her. I always was a fine office man. Maybe I'll become active in the Hope Lutheran Church. In other words, keep moving. Keep moving. That's the secret.

"All I know is that I could not face my departure from this earth if I failed to put up this fight."

At 7:20, there came the boom of an announcement over the loud-speaker; the voice was anonymous and businesslike:

"The Silver Meteor, bound for Miami, Florida, scheduled to depart at 7:40, is ready for boarding. All passengers may now board the Silver Meteor, which stops in Alexandria ... Richmond ... Petersburg ... Fayetteville ... Florence ... Charleston ... Savannah ... Jacksonville ... Waldo ... Ocala ... Wildwood ... Winter Haven ... Sebring ... West Palm Beach ... Deerfield Beach ... Fort Lauderdale ... Hollywood ... Miami."

Edward Zepp boarded the train, located his roomette and departed for home. Within minutes of leaving the station, exhausted by the day's excitement, he fell asleep.

On Tuesday, Oct. 2, 1979, the Pentagon issued the following statement:

"Having considered the additional findings, conclusions and recommendations of the Army Board for Correction of Military Records and under the provisions of 10 U.S.C. 1552, the action of the Secretary of the Army on 4 December 1952 is hereby amended insofar as the character of discharge is concerned, and it is directed: (1) That all Department of the Army records of Edward Zepp be corrected to show that he was separated from the Army of the United States on a Certificate of Honorable Discharge on November 1919. (2) That the Department of the Army issue to Edward Zepp a Certificate of Honorable Discharge from the Army of the United States dated 9 November 1919 in lieu of the General Discharge Certificate of the same date now held by him."

"In other words," said Edward Zepp, "I was right all along."

A week later, a copy of the Pentagon's decision arrived at Zepp's Margate condominium. He discovered the decision was not unanimous. One member, James Hise, had voted against him.

"I'm so mad I could kick the hell out of him. A guy like that shouldn't be sitting on the Board. I am going to write to the Pentagon and tell them he should be thrown off the panel. It would be better to have just a head up there loaded with concrete or sawdust than this guy Hise, who doesn't know the first thing about justice. If he can't judge better than that, he should be kicked off. He's a menace to justice in this world.

"I'd like to go up there and bust his head wide open."

ANALYSIS

MADELEINE BLAIS says she only set out to "tell a good story and stretch myself in storytelling" when she began with Edward Zepp. She credits the power of the story for its success, rather than her writing. That's a nice humble thought, but Blais' storytelling skills are the obvious reason a profile of a bitter old man with a shop-worn story won a Pulitzer Prize.

Blais says she was "conscious of using metaphor to make the material even more coherent. Many of the images are borrowed from the military, from the world of prayer or the spirit—and also related to the aging process. This was a conscious decision on my part."

From a literary point of view, there were several ways for

Madeleine Blais to document Zepp's lifetime efforts to obtain an honorable discharge: She could have used a straight narrative or even utilized the train ride to send him back to 1917 and document a chronology forward to the moment he faced the review board.

She finally chose a harder path, focusing on Zepp's fateful train ride on the Silver Meteor to Washington, effectively using the journey to take Zepp back and forth—contrasting his distant refusal to obey a direct order with his lifelong battle to upgrade his general discharge with honor to a full honorable discharge.

Blais uses time well in this story, using specific dates and times to make a musty six decades spring to life:

September 1979, Sebring, Fla.: Ed Zepp's light lunch has just been placed before him. September 1917, Cleveland, Ohio: Ed Zepp's appeals to the draft board have been rejected twice.

The closer he got to the Pentagon, the closer he got to 1917.

The train was moving almost as fast as Edward Zepp is old.

Zepp may well have been a true Lutheran Conscientious Objector, but Blais works some much-needed humor into this thoughtful story by including some of the old man's fiery rhetoric. In fact, the quotes serve as a delightful counterweight to the 83-year-old gentlemen's single-minded quest:

"Shoot ... you son of a bitch."
[To the sergeant who pulled a gun and threatened to shoot Zepp if he didn't pack his bag as ordered.]

"Maybe we should have gone all out in Vietnam ... just like we did in Hiroshima, killing the whole city."

"I'm so mad I could kick the hell out of him ... I'd like to go up there and bust his head wide open." [The one person who didn't vote to upgrade his discharge.]

By using the "bust his head wide open" quote as her final sentence, Blais has finished with a powerful thrust and let the reader decide how this remark plays against Zepp's mission to finally have his conscientious objector status acknowledged by the Pentagon.

Blais' story resonates with skilled reporting and astute observations; as a result, in the end, the reader perhaps knows Edward Zepp better than he does himself.

MADELEINE BLAIS is currently a professor of journalism at the University of Massachusetts. She holds a master's degree in journalism from Columbia University, was a 1986 Nieman Fellow at Harvard University and has written two books.

1981

TERESA CARPENTER

"Death of a Playmate," one of a package of stories dealing with high-profile deaths, is an edgy story about the sensational death of Dorothy Stratten, *Playboy* magazine's Playmate of the Year. The story is notable for its gritty, candid, true-crime feel.

Author Teresa Carpenter, not *The Village Voice,* holds all rights to the story, extremely unusual for a story of this magnitude. Carpenter wrote this stunning piece in the midst of a worldwide media frenzy over Stratten's death. To make her job harder, the two main principals, Stratten and her husband, Paul Snider, were dead. Plus, her lover, Peter Bogdanovich, and Hugh Hefner weren't talking.

Carpenter has the reputation of a reporter who tackles the tough stories, whether the key people will talk to her or not. She seems to relish throwing a net around those surrounding the main character, reeling them in, thus developing the story from the outside in.

In "Death of a Playmate," Carpenter talked to everyone who would deal with her, and once she acquired the coroner's report, among other leads, doors began to open and the key people started talking.

Top reporters routinely use law-enforcement methods in piecing together crime stories, sometimes helping and sometimes hindering the police. In "Death of a Playmate," Teresa Carpenter takes this detective skill to a high art.

Notice how this story compares to "The Stalking of Kristin," George Lardner's 1993 Pulitzer Prize story about the brutal killing of his daughter. Both Carpenter and Lardner had to recreate the circumstances leading up to especially vicious killings without being able to talk to those most involved in what happened. Yet, both authors, working with different motivations and goals, created journalistic magic—and the readers of *The Washington Post* and *The Village Voice* were the ultimate beneficiaries.

NOTE: "Death of a Playmate" replaced "Jimmy's World" as the Pulitzer winner when *The Washington Post* had to return the Pulitzer after reporter Janet Cook admitted "Jimmy" was a composite of several children.

Death of a Playmate

The Village Voice

November 5, 1980

IT IS SHORTLY PAST FOUR in the afternoon and Hugh Hefner glides wordlessly into the library of his Playboy Mansion West. He is wearing pajamas and looking somber in green silk. The incongruous spectacle of a sybarite in mourning. To date, his public profession of grief has been contained in a press release: "The death of Dorothy Stratten comes as a shock to us all. ... As Playboy's Playmate of the Year with a film and television career of increasing importance, her professional future was a bright one. But equally sad to us is the fact that her loss takes from us all a very special member of the Playboy family."

That's all. A dispassionate eulogy from which one might conclude that Miss Stratten died in her sleep of pneumonia. One, certainly, which masked the turmoil her death created within the Organization. During the morning hours after Stratten was found nude in a West Los Angeles apartment, her face blasted away by 12-gauge buckshot, editors scrambled to pull her photos from the upcoming October issue. It could not be done. The issues were already run. So they pulled her ethereal blond image from the cover of the 1981 Playmate Calendar and promptly scrapped a Christmas promotion featuring her posed in the buff with Hefner. Other playmates, of course, have expired violently. Wilhelmina Rietveld took a massive overdose of barbiturates in 1973. Claudia Jennings, known as "Queen of the B-Movies," was crushed to death last fall in her Volkswagen convertible. Both caused grief and chagrin to the self-serious "family" of playmates whose aura does not admit the possibility of shaving nicks and bladder infections, let alone death.

But the loss of Dorothy Stratten sent Hefner and his family into seclusion, at least from the press. For one thing, Playboy has been earnestly trying to avoid any bad national publicity that might threaten its application for a casino license in Atlantic City. But beyond that, Dorothy Stratten was a corporate treasure. She was not just any playmate but the "Eighties' first Playmate of the Year" who, as Playboy trumpeted in June, was on her way to becoming "one of the few emerging film goddesses of the new decade."

She gave rise to extravagant comparisons with Marilyn Monroe, although unlike Monroe, she was no cripple. She was delighted with her success and wanted more of it. Far from being brutalized by Hollywood, she was coddled by it. Her screen roles were all minor ones. A fleeting walk-on as a bunny in *Americathon*. A small running part as a roller nymph in *Skatetown U.S.A.* She played the most perfect woman in the universe in an episode of *Buck Rogers in the 25th Century* and the most perfect robot in the galaxy in a B spoof called *Galaxina*. She was surely more successful in a shorter period of time than any other playmate in the history of the empire. "Playboy has not really had a star," says Stratten's erstwhile agent David Wilder. "They thought she was going to be the biggest thing they ever had."

No wonder Hefner grieves.

"The major reason that I'm ... that we're both sittin' here," says Hefner, "that I wanted to talk about it, is because there is still a great tendency ... for this thing to fall into the classic cliché of 'smalltown girl comes to Playboy, comes to Hollywood, life in the fast lane,' and that somehow was related to her death. And that is not what really happened. A very sick guy saw his meal ticket and his connection to power, whatever, slipping away. And it was that that made him kill her."

The "very sick guy" is Paul Snider, Dorothy Stratten's husband, the man who became her mentor. He is the one who plucked her from a Dairy Queen in Vancouver, British Columbia, and pushed her into the path of Playboy during the Great Playmate Hunt in 1978. Later, as she moved out of his class, he became a millstone, and Stratten's prickliest problem was not coping with celebrity but discarding a husband she had outgrown. When Paul Snider balked at being discarded, he became her nemesis. And on August 14 of this year he apparently took her life and his own with a 12-gauge shotgun.

The Pimp

It is not so difficult to see why Snider became an embarrassment. Since the murder he has been excoriated by Hefner and others as a cheap hustler, but such moral indignation always rings a little false in Hollywood. Snider's main sin was that he lacked scope.

Snider grew up in Vancouver's East End, a tough area of the city steeped in machismo. His parents split up when he was a boy and he had to fend for himself from the time he quit school in the seventh grade. Embarrassed by being skinny, he took up body building in his late teens and within a year had fleshed out his upper torso. His dark hair and mustache were groomed impeccably and women on the nightclub circuit found him attractive. The two things it seemed he could never get enough of were women and money. For a time he was the successful promoter of automobile and 'cycle shows at the Pacific National Exhibition. But legitimate enterprises didn't bring him enough to support his expensive tastes and he took to procuring. He wore mink, drove a black Corvette, and flaunted a bejeweled Star of David around his neck. About town he was known as the Jewish Pimp.

Among the heavy gang types in Vancouver, the Rounder Crowd, Paul Snider was regarded with scorn. A punk who always seemed to be missing the big score. "He never touched [the drug trade]," said one Rounder who knew him then. "Nobody trusted him that much and he was scared to death of drugs. He finally lost a lot of money to loan sharks and the Rounder Crowd hung him by his ankles from the 30th floor of a hotel. He had to leave town."

Snider split for Los Angeles where he acquired a gold limousine and worked his girls on the fringes of Beverly Hills. He was enamored of Hollywood's dated appeal and styled his girls to conform with a 1950s notion of glamour. At various times he toyed with the idea of becoming a star, or perhaps even a director or a producer. He tried to pry his way into powerful circles, but without much success. At length he gave up pimping because the girls weren't bringing him enough income—one had stolen some items and had in fact cost him money—and when he returned to Vancouver some time in 1977 Snider resolved to keep straight. For one thing, he was terrified of going to jail. He would kill himself, he once told a girl, before he would go to jail.

But Paul Snider never lost the appraising eye of a pimp. One night early in 1978 he and a friend dropped in an East Vancouver Dairy Queen and there he first took notice of Dorothy Ruth Hoogstraten filling orders behind the counter. She was very tall with the sweet natural looks of a girl, but she moved like a mature woman. Snider turned to his friend and observed, "That girl could make me a lot of money." He got Dorothy's number from another waitress and called her at home. She was 18.

Later when she recalled their meeting Dorothy would feign amused exasperation at Paul's overtures. He was brash, lacking altogether in finesse. But he appealed to her, probably because he was older by nine years and streetwise. He offered to take charge of her and that was nice. Her father, a Dutch immigrant, had left the family when she was very young. Dorothy had floated along like a particle in a solution. There had never been enough money to buy nice things. And now Paul bought her clothes. He gave her a topaz ring set in diamonds. She could escape to his place, a posh apartment with skylights, plants, and deep burgundy furniture. He would buy wine and cook dinner. Afterwards he'd fix hot toddies and play the guitar for her. In public he was an obnoxious braggart; in private he could be a vulnerable, cuddly Jewish boy.

Paul Snider knew the gaping vanity of a young girl. Before he came along Dorothy had had only one boyfriend. She had thought of herself as "plain with big hands." At 16, her breasts swelled into glorious lobes, but she never really knew what to do about them. She was a shy, comely, undistinguished teenager who wrote sophomoric poetry and had no aspirations other than landing a secretarial job. When Paul told her she was beautiful, she unfolded in the glow of his compliments and was infected by his ambitions for her.

Snider probably never worked Dorothy as a prostitute. He recognized that she was, as one observer put it, "class merchandise" that could be groomed to better advantage. He had tried to promote other girls as playmates, notably a stripper in 1974, but without success. He had often secured recycled playmates or bunnies to work his auto shows and had seen some get burnt out on sex and cocaine, languishing because of poor management. Snider dealt gingerly with Dorothy's inexperience and broke her in gradually. After escorting her to her graduation dance he bought her a ruffled white gown for the occasion—he took her to a German photographer named Uwe Meyer for her first professional portrait. She looked like a flirtatious virgin.

About a month later, Snider called Meyer again, this time to do a nude shooting at Snider's apartment. Meyer arrived with a hairdresser to find Dorothy a little nervous. She clung, as she later recalled, to a scarf or a blouse as a towline to modesty, but she fell quickly into playful postures. She was perfectly pliant.

"She was eager to please," recalls Meyer. "I hesitated to rearrange her breasts thinking it might upset her, but she said, 'Do whatever you like.'"

Meyer hoped to get the $1,000 finder's fee that Playboy routinely pays photographers who discover playmates along the byways and backwaters of the continent. But Snider, covering all bets, took Dorothy to another photographer named Ken Honey who had an established track-record with Playboy. Honey had at first declined to shoot Dorothy because she was underage and needed a parent's signature on a release. Dorothy, who was reluctant to tell anyone at home about the nude posing, finally broke the news to her mother and persuaded her to sign. Honey sent his set of shots to Los Angeles and was sent a finder's fee. In August 1978, Dorothy flew to Los Angeles for test shots. It was the first time she had ever been on a plane.

Even to the most cynical sensibilities, there is something miraculous about the way Hollywood took to Dorothy Hoogstraten. In a city overpopulated with beautiful women—most of them soured and disillusioned by 25—Dorothy caught some current fortune and floated steadily upward through the spheres of that indifferent paradise. Her test shots were superb, placing her among the 16 top contenders for the 25th Anniversary Playmate. And although she lost out to Candy Loving, she was named Playmate of the Month for August 1979. As soon as he learned of her selection, Paul Snider, by Hefner's account at least, flew to Los Angeles and proposed. They did not marry right away but set up housekeeping in a modest apartment in West Los Angeles. It was part of Snider's grand plan that Dorothy should support them both. She was, however, an alien and had no green card. Later, when it appeared her fortunes were on the rise during the fall of 1979, Hefner would personally intervene to secure her a temporary work permit. In the meantime, she was given a job as bunny at the Century City Playboy Club. The Organization took care of her. It recognized a good thing. While other playmates required cosmetic surgery on breasts or scars, Stratten was nearly perfect. There was a patch of adolescent acne on her forehead and a round birthmark on her left hip, but nothing serious. Her most troublesome flaw was a tendency to get plump, but that was controlled through passionate exercise. The only initial change Playboy deemed necessary was trimming her shoulder-length blond hair. And the cumbersome "Hoogstraten" became "Stratten."

Playboy photographers had been so impressed by the way Dorothy photographed that a company executive called agent David Wilder of Barr-Wilder Associates. Wilder, who handled the film careers of other playmates, agreed to meet Dorothy for coffee.

"A quality like Dorothy Stratten's comes by once in a lifetime," says Wilder with the solemn exaggeration that comes naturally after a tragedy. "She was exactly what this town likes, a beautiful girl who could act."

More to the point she had at least one trait to meet any need. When Lorimar Productions wanted a "playmate type" for a bit role in *Americathon,* Wilder sent Dorothy. When Columbia wanted a beauty who could skate for *Skatetown* Wilder sent Dorothy, who could skate like an ace. A happy skill in Hollywood. When the producers of *Buck Rogers* and later *Galaxina* asked simply for a woman who was so beautiful that no one could deny it, Wilder sent Dorothy. And once Dorothy got in the door, it seemed that no one could resist her.

During the spring of 1979, Dorothy was busy modeling or filming. One photographer recalls, "She was green, but took instruction well." From time to time, however, she would have difficulty composing herself on the set. She asked a doctor for a prescription of Valium. It was the adjustments, she explained, and the growing hassles with Paul.

Since coming to L.A., Snider had been into some deals of his own, most of them legal but sleazy. He had promoted exotic male dancers at a local disco, a wet underwear contest near Santa Monica, and wet T-shirt contests in the San Fernando Valley. But his chief hopes rested with Dorothy. He reminded her constantly that the two of them had what he called "a lifetime bargain" and he pressed her to marry him. Dorothy was torn by indecision. Friends tried to dissuade her from marrying, saying it could hold back her career, but she replied, "He cares for me so much. He's always there when I need him. I can't ever imagine myself being with any other man but Paul."

They were married in Las Vegas on June 1, 1979, and the following month Dorothy returned to Canada for a promotional tour of the provinces. Paul did not go with her because Playboy wanted the marriage kept secret. In Vancouver, Dorothy was greeted like a minor celebrity. The local press, a little caustic but mainly cowed, questioned her obliquely about exploitation. "I see the pictures as nudes, like nude paintings," she said. "They are not made for people to fantasize about." Her family and Paul's family visited her hotel, highly pleased with her success. Her first film was about to be released. The August issue was already on the stands featuring her as a pouting nymph who wrote poetry. (A few plodding iambs were even reprinted.)

And she was going to *star* in a new Canadian film by North American Pictures called *Autumn Born.*

Since the murder, not much has been made of this film, probably because it contained unpleasant overtones of bondage. Dorothy played the lead, a 17-year-old rich orphan who is kidnapped and abused by her uncle. Dorothy was excited about the role, although she conceded to a Canadian reporter, "a lot [of it] is watching this girl get beat up."

A Goddess for the '80s

While Dorothy was being pummeled on the set of *Autumn Born,* Snider busied himself apartment hunting. They were due for a rent raise and were looking to share a place with a doctor friend, a young internist who patronized the Century City Playboy Club. Paul found a two-story Spanish style stucco house near the Santa Monica Freeway in West L.A. There was a living room upstairs as well as a bedroom which the doctor claimed. Paul and Dorothy moved into the second bedroom downstairs at the back of the house. Since the doctor spent many nights with his girlfriend, the Sniders had the house much to themselves.

Paul had a growing obsession with Dorothy's destiny. It was, of course, his own. He furnished the house with her photographs, and got plates reading "Star-80" for his new Mercedes. He talked about her as the next Playmate of the Year, the next Marilyn Monroe. When he had had a couple of glasses of wine, he would croon, "We're on a rocket ship to the moon." When they hit it big, he said, they would move to Bel-Air Estates where the big producers live.

Dorothy was made uncomfortable by his grandiosity. He was putting her, she confided to friends, in a position where she could not fail without failing them both. But she did not complain to him. They had, after all, a lifetime bargain, and he had brought her a long way.

As her manager he provided the kind of cautionary coaching that starlets rarely receive. He would not let her smoke. He monitored her drinking, which was moderate at any rate. He would have allowed her a little marijuana and cocaine under his supervision, but she showed no interest in drugs, save Valium. Mainly he warned her to be wary of the men she met at the Mansion, men who would promise her things, then use her up. Snider taught her how to finesse a come-on. How to turn a guy down without putting him off. Most important, he discussed with her who she might actually have to sleep with. Hefner, of course, was at the top of the list.

Did Hefner sleep with Dorothy Stratten? Mansion gossips who have provided graphic narratives of Hefner's encounters with other playmates cannot similarly document a tryst with Dorothy. According to the bizarre code of the Life—sexual society at the Mansion—fucking Hefner is a strictly voluntary thing. It never hurts a career, but Hefner, with so much sex at his disposal, would consider it unseemly to apply pressure.

Of Stratten, Hefner says, "There was a friendship between us. It wasn't romantic. ... This was not a very loose lady."

Hefner likes to think of himself as a "father figure" to Stratten who, when she decided to marry, came to tell him about it personally. "She knew I had serious reservations about [Snider]," says Hefner. "I had sufficient reservations ... that I had him checked out in terms of a possible police record in Canada. ... We didn't get anything. ... I used the word—and I realized the [risk] I was taking—I said to her that he had a 'pimp-like quality' about him."

Like most playmate husbands, Snider was held at arm's length by the Playboy family. He was only rarely invited to the Mansion, which bothered him, as he would have liked more of an opportunity to cultivate Hefner. And Stratten, who was at the Mansion more frequently to party and roller skate, was never actively into the Life. Indeed, she spoke disdainfully of the "whores" who serviced Hefner's stellar guests. Yet she moved into the circle of Hefner's distinguished favorites when it became apparent that she might have a real future in film.

Playboy, contrary to the perception of aspiring starlets, is not a natural conduit to stardom. Most playmates who go into movies peak with walk-ons and fade away. Those whom Hefner has tried most earnestly to promote in recent years have been abysmal flops. Barbi Benton disintegrated into a jiggling loon and, according to Playboy sources, Hefner's one time favorite Sondra Theodore went wooden once the camera started to roll.

"Dorothy was important," says one Playboy employee, "because Hefner is regarded by Hollywood as an interloper. They'll come to his parties and play his games. But they won't give him respect. One of the ways he can gain legitimacy is to be a star maker."

There is something poignant about Hefner, master of an empire built on inanimate nudes, but unable to coax those lustrous forms to life on film. His chief preoccupation nowadays is managing the playmates. Yet with all of those beautiful women at his disposal, he has not one Marion Davies to call his own. Dorothy exposed that yearning, that ego weakness, as surely as she revealed the most pathetic side of her husband's nature—his itch for the big score. Hefner simply had more class.

Dorothy's possibilities were made manifest to him during *The Playboy Roller Disco and Pajama Party* taped at the Mansion late in October 1978. Dorothy had a running part and was tremendously appealing.

"Some people have that quality," says Hefner. "I mean ... there is something that comes from inside. ... The camera comes so close that it almost looks beneath the surface and ... that magic is there somehow in the eyes. ... That magic she had. That was a curious combination of sensual appeal and vulnerability."

After the special was aired on television in November, Dorothy's career accelerated rapidly. There was a rush of appearances that left the accumulating impression of stardom. Around the first of December her *Fantasy Island* episode appeared. Later that month, *Buck Rogers in the 25th Century*. But the big news of the season was that Hefner had chosen Dorothy Playmate of the Year for 1980. Although her selection was not announced to the public until April, she began photo sessions with Playboy photographer Mario Casilli before the year was out.

Her look was altered markedly from that of the sultry minx in the August issue. As Playmate of the Year her image was more defined. No more pouting, soft-focus shots. Stratten was given a burnished high glamour. Her hair fell in the crimped undulating waves of a '50s starlet. Her translucent body was posed against scarlet velour reminiscent of the Monroe classic. One shot of Stratten displaying some of her $200,000 in gifts—a brass bed and a lavender Lore negligee—clearly evoked the platinum ideal of Jean Harlow. Dorothy's apotheosis reached, it seemed, for extremes of innocence and eroticism. In one shot she was draped in black lace and nestled into a couch, buttocks raised in an impish invitation to sodomy. Yet the cover displayed her clad in a chaste little peasant gown, seated in a meadow, head tilted angelically to one side. The dichotomy was an affirmation of her supposed sexual range. She was styled, apparently, as the Compleat Goddess for the '80s.

By January 1980—the dawning of her designated decade—Dorothy Stratten was attended by a thickening phalanx of photographers, promoters, duennas, coaches, and managers. Snider, sensing uneasily that she might be moving beyond his reach, became more demanding. He wanted absolute control over her financial affairs and the movie offers she accepted. She argued that he was being unreasonable; that she had an agent and a business manager whose job it was to advise her in those matters. Snider then pressed her to take the $200,000 from Playboy and buy a house. It would be a good investment, he said. He spent a lot of time looking at homes that might suit her, but she always found fault with them. She did not want to commit herself. She suspected, perhaps rightly, that he only wanted to attach another lien on her life.

This domestic squabbling was suspended temporarily in January when it appeared that Dorothy was poised for her big break, a featured role in a comedy called *They All Laughed* starring Audrey Hepburn and Ben Gazzara. It was to be directed by Peter Bogdanovich, whom Dorothy had first met at the roller disco bash in October. According to David Wilder, he and Bogdanovich were partying at the Mansion in January when the director first considered Stratten for the part.

"Jesus Christ," the 41-year-old Bogdanovich is supposed to have said. "She's perfect for the girl. ... I don't want her for tits and ass. I want someone who can act."

Wilder says he took Dorothy to Bogdanovich's house in Bel-Air Estates to read for the role. She went back two or three more times and the director decided she was exactly what he wanted.

Filming was scheduled to begin in late March in New York City. Paul wanted to come along but Dorothy said no. He would get in the way and, at any rate, the set was closed to outsiders. Determined that she should depart Hollywood as a queen, he borrowed their housemate's Rolls Royce and drove her to the airport. He put her on the plane in brash good spirits, then went home to sulk at being left behind.

They All Laughed

The affair between Dorothy Stratten and Peter Bogdanovich was conducted in amazing secrecy. In that regard it bore little resemblance to the director's affair with Cybill Shepherd, an escapade which advertised his puerile preference for ingenues. Bogdanovich, doubtless, did not fancy the publicity that might result from a liaison with a 20-year-old woman married to a hustler. A couple of days before the murder-suicide, he spoke of this to his close friend Hugh Hefner.

"It was the first time I'd seen him in a number of months because he'd been in New York," says Hefner. "He was very very up. Very excited about her and the film. ... I don't think that he was playing with this at all. I think it was important to him. I'm talking about the relationship. ... He was concerned at that point because of what had happened to him and [Cybill]. He was concerned about the publicity related to the relationship because of that. He felt in retrospect, as a matter of fact, that he ... that they had kind of caused some of it. And it played havoc with both of their careers for a while."

Stratten, as usual, did not advertise the fact that she was married. When she arrived in New York, she checked quietly into the Wyndham Hotel. The crew knew very little about her except that she showed up on time and seemed very earnest about her small role. She was cordial but kept her distance, spending her time off-camera in a director's chair reading. One day it would be Dickens' *Great Expectations;* the next day a book on dieting. With the help of make-up and hair consultants her looks were rendered chaste and ethereal to defuse her playmate image. "She was a darling little girl," says makeup artist Fern Buckner. "Very beautiful, of course. Whatever you did to her was all right."

Dorothy had headaches. She was eating very little to keep her weight down and working 12-hour days because Bogdanovich was pushing the project along at a rapid pace. While most of the crew found him a selfish, mean-spirited megalomaniac, the cast by and large found him charming. He was particularly solicitous of Dorothy Stratten. And just as quietly as she had checked into the Wyndham, she moved into his suite at the Plaza. Word spread around the set that Bogdanovich and Stratten were involved but, because they were discreet, they avoided unpleasant gossip. "They weren't hanging all over one another," says one crew member. "It wasn't until the last few weeks when everyone relaxed a bit that they would show up together holding hands." One day Bogdanovich walked over to a couch where Dorothy sat chewing gum. "You shouldn't chew gum," he admonished. "It has sugar in it." She playfully removed the wad from her mouth and deposited it in his palm.

Bogdanovich is less than eager to discuss the affair. His secretary says he will not give interviews until *They All Laughed* is released in April. The director needs a hit badly and who can tell how Stratten's death might affect box office. *Laughed* is, unfortunately, a comedy over which her posthumous performance might throw a pall. Although the plot is being guarded as closely as a national security secret, it goes something like this:

Ben Gazzara is a private detective hired by a wealthy, older man who suspects his spouse, Audrey Hepburn, has a lover. In following her, Gazzara falls in love with her. Meanwhile, Gazzara's sidekick, John Ritter, is hired by another wealthy older man to follow his young bride, Dorothy Stratten. Ritter watches Stratten from afar— through a window as she argues with her husband, as she roller skates at the Roxy. After a few perfunctory conversations, he asks her to marry him. Hepburn and Gazzara make a brief abortive stab at mature love. And Gazzara reverts to dating and mating with teeny-boppers.

Within this intricate web of shallow relationships Dorothy, by all accounts, emerges as a shimmering seraph, a vision of perfection clad perennially in white. In one scene she is found sitting in the Algonquin Hotel bathed in a diaphanous light. "It was one of those scenes that could make a career," recalls a member of the crew. "People in the screening room rustled when they saw her. She didn't have many lines. She just looked so good." Bogdanovich was so enthusiastic about her that he called Hefner on the West Coast to say he was expanding Dorothy's role—not many more lines, but more exposure.

Paul Snider, meanwhile, was calling the East Coast where he detected a chill in Dorothy's voice. She would be too tired to talk. He would say, "I love you," and she wouldn't answer back. Finally, she began to have her calls screened. Late in April, during a shooting break, she flew to Los Angeles for a flurry of appearances which included the Playmate of the Year Luncheon and an appearance on *The Johnny Carson Show.* Shortly thereafter, Dorothy left for a grand tour of Canada. She agreed, however, to meet Paul in Vancouver during the second week of May. Her mother was remarrying and she planned to attend the wedding.

That proposed rendezvous worried Dorothy's Playboy traveling companion, Liz Norris. Paul was becoming irascible. He called Dorothy in Toronto and flew into a rage when she suggested that he allow her more freedom. Norris offered to provide her charge with a bodyguard once they arrived in Vancouver, but Dorothy declined. She met Paul and over her objections he checked them into the same hotel. Later, each gave essentially the same account of that encounter. She asked him to loosen his grip. "Let the bird fly," she said. They argued violently, then both sank back into tears. According to Snider, they reconciled and made love. Dorothy never acknowledged that. She later told a friend, however, that she had offered to leave

Hollywood and go back to live with him in Vancouver, but he didn't want that. In the end she cut her trip short to get back to the shooting.

Snider, by now, realized that his empire was illusory. As her husband he technically had claim to half of her assets, but many of her assets were going into a corporation called Dorothy Stratten Enterprises. He was not one of the officers. When she spoke of financial settlements, she sounded like she was reading a strange script. She was being advised, he suspected, by Bogdanovich's lawyers. (Dorothy's attorney, Wayne Alexander, reportedly represents Bogdanovich too, but Alexander cannot be reached for comment.) Late in June, Snider received a letter declaring that he and Dorothy were separated physically and financially. She closed out their joint bank accounts and began advancing him money through her business manager.

Buffeted by forces beyond his control, Snider tried to cut his losses. He could have maintained himself as a promoter or as the manager of a health club. He was an expert craftsman and turned out exercise benches which he sold for $200 a piece. On at least one occasion he had subverted those skills to more dubious ends by building a wooden bondage rack for his private pleasure. But Snider didn't want to be a nobody. His rocket ship had come too close to the moon to leave him content with hang-gliding.

He tried, a little pathetically, to groom another Dorothy Stratten, a 17-year-old check-out girl from Riverside who modeled on the side. He had discovered her at an auto show. Patty was of the same statuesque Stratten ilk, and Snider taught her to walk like Dorothy, to dress like Dorothy, and to wear her hair like Dorothy. Eventually she moved into the house that he and Dorothy shared. But she was not another Stratten, and when Snider tried to promote her as a playmate, Playboy wanted nothing to do with him.

Paul's last hope for a big score was a project begun a month or so before he and Dorothy were married. He had worked out a deal with a couple of photographer friends, Bill and Susan Lachasse, to photograph Dorothy on skates wearing a French-cut skating outfit. From that they would print a poster that they hoped would sell a million copies and net $300,000. After Dorothy's appearance on the Carson show, Snider thought the timing was right. But Dorothy had changed her mind. The Lachasses flew to New York the day after she finished shooting to persuade her to reconsider. They were told by the production office that Dorothy could be found at Bogdanovich's suite at the Plaza.

"It was three or four in the afternoon," says Lachasse. "There had been a cast party the night before. Dorothy answered the door in pajamas and said, 'Oh my God! What are you doing here?' She shut the door and when she came out again she explained 'I can't invite you in. There are people here.' She looked at the photos in the hallway and we could tell by her eyes that she liked them. She took them inside, then came out and said, 'Look how my tits are hanging down.' Somebody in there was telling her what to do. She said, 'Look, I'm confused, have you shown these to Paul?' I said, 'Dorothy, you're divorcing Paul.' And she said, 'I don't know, I just don't know.'"

When Lachasse called the Plaza suite the following week a woman replied, "We don't know Dorothy Stratten. Stop harassing us."

"Paul felt axed as in every other area," says Lachasse. "That was his last bit of income."

They All Cried

During the anxious spring and early summer, Snider suspected, but could not prove, that Dorothy was having an affair. So as the filming of *They All Laughed* drew to a close in mid-July, he did what, in the comic world of Peter Bogdanovich, many jealous husbands do. He hired a private eye, a 26-year-old freelance detective named Marc Goldstein. The elfish Goldstein, who later claimed to be a friend of both Dorothy and Paul, in fact knew neither of them well. He was retained upon the recommendation of an unidentified third party. He will not say what exactly his mission was, but a Canadian lawyer named Ted Ewachniuk who represented both Paul and Dorothy in Vancouver claims that Snider was seeking to document the affair with Bogdanovich in order to sue him for "enticement to breach management contract"—an agreement Snider believed inherent within their marriage contract. That suit was to be filed in British Columbia, thought to be a suitable venue since both Snider and Stratten were still Canadians and, it could be argued, had only gone to Los Angeles for business.

Goldstein began showing up regularly at Snider's apartment. Snider produced poems and love letters from Bogdanovich that he had found among Dorothy's things. He instructed Goldstein to do an asset search on Dorothy and to determine whether or not Bogdanovich was plying her with cocaine.

Even as he squared off for a legal fight, Snider was increasingly despairing. He knew, underneath it all, that he did not have the power or resources to fight Bogdanovich. "Maybe this thing is too big for me," he confided to a friend, and he talked about going back to

Vancouver. But the prospect of returning in defeat was too humiliating. He felt Dorothy was now so completely sequestered by attorneys that he would never see her again. Late in July his old machismo gave way to grief. He called Bill Lachasse one night crying because he could not touch Dorothy or even get near her. About the same time, his roommate the doctor returned home one night to find him despondent in the living room. "This is really hard," Paul said, and broke into tears. He wrote fragments of notes to Dorothy that were never sent. One written in red felt-tip marker and later found stuffed into one of his drawers was a rambling plaint on how he couldn't get it together without her. With Ewachniuk's help, he drafted a letter to Bogdanovich telling him to quit influencing Dorothy and that he [Snider] would "forgive" him. But Ewachniuk does not know if the letter was ever posted.

Dorothy, Paul knew, had gone for a holiday in London with Bogdanovich and would be returning to Los Angeles soon. He tortured himself with the scenario of the successful director and his queen showing up at Hefner's Midsummer Night's Dream Party on August 1. He couldn't bear it and blamed Hefner for fostering the affair. He called the Mansion trying to get an invitation to the party and was told he would be welcome only if he came with Dorothy.

But Dorothy did not show up at the party. She was keeping a low profile. She had moved ostensibly into a modest little apartment in Beverly Hills, the address that appeared on her death certificate. The apartment, however, was occupied by an actress who was Bogdanovich's personal assistant. Dorothy had actually moved into Bogdanovich's home in Bel-Air Estates. Where the big producers live.

Several days after her return to Los Angeles, she left for a playmate promotion in Dallas and Houston. There she appeared radiant, apparently reveling in her own success. She had been approached about playing Marilyn Monroe in Larry Schiller's made-for-TV movie, but she had been too busy with the Bogdanovich film. She had been discussed as a candidate for *Charlie's Angels* although Wilder thought she could do better. She was scheduled to meet with independent producer Martin Krofft who was considering her for his new film, *The Last Desperado*. It all seemed wonderful to her. But Stratten was not so cynical that she could enjoy her good fortune without pangs of regret. She cried in private. Until the end she retained a lingering tenderness for Paul Snider and felt bound to see him taken care of after the divorce. From Houston she gave him a call and agreed to meet him on Friday, August 8, for lunch.

After hearing from her, Snider was as giddy as a con whose sentence has been commuted, for he believed somehow that everything would be all right between them again. The night before their appointed meeting he went out for sandwiches with friends and was his blustering, confident old self. It would be different, he said. He would let her know that he had changed. "I've really got to vacuum the rug," he crowed. "The queen is coming back."

The lunch date, however, was a disaster. The two of them ended up back in the apartment squared off sullenly on the couch. Dorothy confessed at last that she was in love with Bogdanovich and wanted to proceed with some kind of financial settlement. Before leaving she went through her closet and took the clothes she wanted. The rest, she said, he should give to Patty.

Having his hopes raised so high and then dashed again gave Snider a perverse energy. Those who saw him during the five days prior to the murder caught only glimpses of odd behavior. In retrospect they appear to form a pattern of intent. He was preoccupied with guns. Much earlier in the year Snider had borrowed a revolver from a friend named Chip, the consort of one of Dorothy's sister playmates. Paul never felt easy, he said, without a gun, a holdover from his days on the East End. But Paul had to give the revolver back that Friday afternoon because Chip was leaving town. He looked around for another gun. On Sunday he held a barbecue at his place for a few friends and invited Goldstein. During the afternoon he pulled Goldstein aside and asked the detective to buy a machine gun for him. He needed it, he said, for "home protection." Goldstein talked him out of it.

In the classifieds, Snider found someone in the San Fernando Valley who wanted to sell a 12-gauge Mossberg pump shotgun. He circled the ad and called the owner. On Monday he drove into the Valley to pick up the gun but got lost in the dark. The owner obligingly brought it to a construction site where he showed Snider how to load and fire it.

Dorothy, meanwhile, had promised to call Paul on Sunday but did not ring until Monday, an omission that piqued him. They agreed to meet on Thursday at 11:30 a.m. to discuss a financial settlement. She had been instructed by her advisers to offer him a specified sum. During previous conversations, Paul thought he had heard Dorothy say, "I'll always take care of you," but he could not remember the exact words. Goldstein thought it might be a good idea to wire Snider's body for sound so that they could get a taped account if

Dorothy repeated her promise to provide for him. They could not come up with the proper equipment, however, and abandoned the plan.

On Wednesday, the day he picked up the gun, Snider seemed in an excellent mood. He told his roommate that Dorothy would be coming over and that she had agreed to look at a new house that he thought might be a good investment for her. He left the impression that they were on amiable terms. That evening he dropped by Bill Lachasse's studio to look at promotional shots of Patty. There, too, he was relaxed and jovial. In an offhanded way, he told Lachasse that he had bought a gun for protection. He also talked of strange and unrelated things that did not seem menacing in the context of his good spirits. He talked of Claudia Jennings, who had died with a movie in progress. Some playmates get killed, he observed. Some actresses are killed before their films come out. And when that happens, it causes a lot of chaos.

Bogdanovich had somehow discovered that Dorothy was being trailed by a private eye. He was furious, but Dorothy was apparently not alarmed. She was convinced that she and Paul were on the verge of working out an amicable agreement and she went to meet him as planned. According to the West Los Angeles police, she parked and locked her 1967 Mercury around 11:45 a.m., but the county coroner reports that she arrived later, followed by Goldstein who clocked her into the house at 12:30 p.m. Shortly thereafter, Goldstein called Snider to find out how things were going. Snider replied, in code, that everything was fine. Periodically throughout the afternoon, Goldstein rang Snider with no response. No one entered the house until five when Patty and another of Paul's little girlfriends returned home, noticed Dorothy's car and saw the doors to Snider's room closed. Since they heard no sounds, they assumed he wanted privacy. The two girls left to go skating and returned at 7 p.m. By then the doctor had arrived home and noticed the closed door. He also heard the unanswered ringing on Snider's downstairs phone. Shortly before midnight Goldstein called Patty and asked her to knock at Paul's door. She demurred, so he asked to speak to the doctor. The latter agreed to check but even as he walked downstairs he felt some foreboding. The endless ringing had put him on edge and his German shepherd had been pacing and whining in the yard behind Paul's bedroom. The doctor knocked and when there was no response, he pushed the door open. The scene burnt his senses and he yanked the door shut.

It is impolitic to suggest that Paul Snider loved Dorothy Stratten. Around Hollywood, at least, he is currently limned as brutal and utterly insensitive. If he loved her, it was in the selfish way of one who cannot separate a lover's best interests from one's own. And if he did what he is claimed to have done, he was, as Hugh Hefner would put it, "a very sick guy."

Even now, however, no one can say with certainty that Paul Snider committed either murder or suicide. One of his old confederates claims he bought the gun to "scare" Bogdanovich. The coroner was sufficiently equivocal to deem his death a "questionable suicide/possible homicide." One Los Angeles psychic reportedly attributes the deaths to an unemployed actor involved with Snider in a drug deal. Goldstein, who holds to a theory that both were murdered, is badgering the police for results of fingerprintings and paraffin tests, but the police consider Goldstein a meddler and have rebuffed his requests. The West LAPD, which has not yet closed the case, says it cannot determine if it was Snider who fired the shotgun because his hands were coated with too much blood and tissue for tests to be conclusive.

And yet Snider appears to have been following a script of his own choosing. One which would thwart the designs of Playboy and Hollywood. Perhaps he had only meant to frighten Dorothy, to demonstrate to Bogdanovich that he could hold her in thrall at gunpoint. Perhaps he just got carried away with the scene. No one knows exactly how events unfolded after Dorothy entered the house that afternoon. She had apparently spent some time upstairs because her purse was found lying open in the middle of the living room floor. In it was a note in Paul's handwriting explaining his financial distress. He had no green card, it said, and he required support. Dorothy's offer, however, fell far short of support. It was a flat settlement of only $7500 which, she claimed, represented half of her total assets after taxes. "Not enough," said one friend, "to put a nice little sports car in his garage." Perhaps she had brought the first installment to mollify Paul's inevitable disappointment; police found $1100 in cash among her belongings, another $400 among his. One can only guess at the motives of those two doomed players who, at some point in the afternoon, apparently left the front room and went downstairs.

It is curious that, given the power of the blasts, the little bedroom was not soaked in blood. There was only spattering on the walls, curtains, and television. Perhaps because the room lacked a charnel aspect, the bodies themselves appeared all the more grim. They were nude. Dorothy lay crouched across the bottom corner of a low bed. Both knees were on the carpet and her right shoulder was drooping. Her blond hair hung naturally, oddly unaffected by the violence to her countenance. The shell had entered above her left eye leaving the bones of that seraphic face shattered and displaced in a welter of pulp. Her body, mocking the soft languid poses of her pictorials, was in full rigor.

No one, least of all Hugh Hefner, could have foreseen such a desecration. It was unthinkable that an icon of eroticism presumed by millions of credulous readers to be impervious to the pangs of mortality could be reduced by a pull of the trigger to a corpse, mortally stiff, mortally livid and crawling with small black ants. For Hefner, in fact, that grotesque alteration must have been particularly bewildering. Within the limits of his understanding, he had done everything right. He had played it clean with Stratten, handling her paternally, providing her with gifts and opportunities and, of course, the affection of the Playboy family. Despite his best efforts, however, she was destroyed. The irony that Hefner does not perceive or at least fails to acknowledge is that Stratten was destroyed not by random particulars, but by a germ breeding within the ethic. One of the tacit tenets of the Playboy philosophy—that women can be possessed—had found a fervent adherent in Paul Snider. He had bought the dream without qualification, and he thought of himself as perhaps one of Playboy's most honest apostles. He acted out dark fantasies never intended to be realized. Instead of fondling himself in private, instead of wreaking abstract violence upon a centerfold, he ravaged a playmate in the flesh.

Dorothy had, apparently, been sodomized, though whether this occurred before or after her death is not clear. After the blast, her body was moved and there were what appeared to be bloody handprints on her buttocks and left leg. Near her head was Paul's handmade bondage rack set for rear-entry intercourse. Loops of tape, used and unused, were lying about and strands of long blond hair were discovered clutched in Snider's right hand. He was found face-down lying parallel to the foot of the bed. The muzzle of the Mossberg burnt his right cheek as the shell tore upward through his brain. The blast, instead of driving him backwards, whipped him forward over the length of the gun. He had always said he would rather die than go to jail.

Goldstein arrived before the police and called the Mansion. Hefner, thinking the call a prank, would not come to the phone at first. When he did he asked for the badge number of the officer at the scene. Satisfied that this was no bad joke, Hefner, told his guests in the game house. There were wails of sorrow and disbelief. He then called Bogdanovich. "There was no conversation," Hefner says. "I was afraid that he had gone into shock or something. [When he didn't respond] I called the house under another number. A male friend was there to make sure he was [all right]. He was overcome."

Bogdanovich arranged for Stratten's cremation five days later. Her ashes were placed in an urn and buried in a casket so that he could visit them. Later he would issue his own statement:

DOROTHY STRATTEN WAS AS GIFTED AND INTELLIGENT AN ACTRESS AS SHE WAS BEAUTIFUL, AND SHE WAS VERY BEAUTIFUL INDEED—IN EVERY WAY IMAGINABLE—MOST PARTICULARLY IN HER HEART. SHE AND I FELL IN LOVE DURING OUR PICTURE AND HAD PLANNED TO BE MARRIED AS SOON AS HER DIVORCE WAS FINAL. THE LOSS TO HER MOTHER AND FATHER, HER SISTER AND BROTHER, TO MY CHILDREN, TO HER FRIENDS AND TO ME IS LARGER THAN WE CAN CALCULATE. BUT THERE IS NO LIFE DOROTHY'S TOUCHED THAT HAS NOT BEEN CHANGED FOR THE BETTER THROUGH KNOWING HER, HOWEVER BRIEFLY. DOROTHY LOOKED AT THE WORLD WITH LOVE, AND BELIEVED THAT ALL PEOPLE WERE GOOD DOWN DEEP. SHE WAS MISTAKEN, BUT IT IS AMONG THE MOST GENEROUS AND NOBLE ERRORS WE CAN MAKE.

PETER BOGDANOVICH

Bogdanovich took the family Hoogstraten in tow. They were stunned, but not apparently embittered by Dorothy's death. "They knew who cared for her," Hefner says. Mother, fathers—both natural and stepfather—sister, and brother flew to Los Angeles for the service and burial at Westwood Memorial Park, the same cemetery, devotees of irony point out, where Marilyn Monroe is buried. Hefner, and Bogdanovich were there and after the service the family repaired to Bogdanovich's house for rest and refreshments. It was all quiet and discreet. Dorothy's mother says that she will not talk to the press until the movie comes out. Not until April when Stratten's glimmering ghost will appear on movie screens across the country, bathed in white light and roller skating through a maze of hilarious infidelities.

Playboy, whose corporate cool was shaken by her untimely death, has regained its composure. The December issue features Stratten as one of the "Sex Stars of 1980." At the end of 12 pages of the biggest draws in show business—Bo Derek, Brooke Shields, etc.—she appears topless, one breast draped with a gossamer scarf. A caption laments her death which "cut short what seasoned starwatchers predicted was sure to be an outstanding film career."

Hype, of course, often passes for prophecy. Whether or not Dorothy Stratten would have fulfilled her extravagant promise can't be known. Her legacy will not be examined critically because it is really of no consequence. In the end Dorothy Stratten was less memorable for herself than for the yearnings she evoked: in Snider a lust for the score; in Hefner a longing for a star; in Bogdanovich a desire for the eternal ingenue. She was catalyst for a cycle of ambitions which revealed its players less wicked, perhaps, than pathetic.

As for Paul Snider, his body was returned to Vancouver in permanent exile from Hollywood. It was all too big for him. In that Elysium of dreams and deals, he had reached the limits of his class. His sin, his unforgivable sin, was being small-time.

ANALYSIS

TERESA CARPENTER had much to ponder as she began her story on the gruesome and sordid murder of Dorothy Stratten. Crime stories are tricky enough, but when they involve covering brutal murder/suicides—especially before the police have sorted it all out—reporters have to tread even more gingerly.

Carpenter finally decided to focus on Stratten's life and career by taking a detailed look at how Stratten interacted with three of the main men in her life—Hugh Hefner, Paul Snider and Peter Bogdanovich—and the roles each played in her life.

Making the entire story all the more difficult, Bogdanovich never did speak directly with Carpenter, choosing to reply instead by written statement. Stratten's family also decided not to comment until the movie opened. This meant Carpenter had to write a moment-by-moment account of the life and death of Dorothy Stratten by talking to only one of the four key players in the story: Hefner. She seemed to have an impossible task in writing a feature/profile. And yet, when she was done, a Pulitzer followed. Significant lessons can be learned from this story.

Carpenter opens her 1980 story interviewing Playboy founder Hugh Hefner. Carpenter sets the mood for the entire story by devilishly noting that Hefner was somberly attired in green silk pajamas:

The incongruous spectacle of a sybarite in mourning.

She uses a long, descriptive summary lead that begins and ends with Hefner, not unlike Stratten's Playboy/movie career.

As the only key player she could initially interview, Carpenter often makes Hefner the central compass point for the tragedy— a knowing, if jaded, father-figure. Carpenter sprinkles Hefner's quotes throughout the story while seemingly interviewing everyone who knew anything about Stratten's burgeoning career.

The use of the chronology method of writing is extremely effective and probably the only way Carpenter could have done the story under the circumstances.

Sharp readers will also notice, perhaps due to the lack of key sources, Carpenter hasn't written a quote-driven piece. She uses quotes where necessary, but her amazing reporting and sense of detail carry the action as the reader is left feeling the author was continually present at all the key points in Stratten's rise and fall.

Having to write so carefully, Carpenter was still able to demonstrate conclusively what may have driven Snider to end Stratten's life: Snider knew he lacked Hefner's class, was gradually being frozen out of the Playboy Mansion and felt he was losing his beautiful "rocket to the moon." Perhaps more devastatingly, Carpenter shows how Snider could see he was losing his wife to the sophisticated Bogdanovich. And by documenting Snider's purchase of a shotgun, coupled with his precarious mental state, Carpenter leaves the reader with a highly-plausible murder scenario.

In her remarkable conclusion, Carpenter manages to weave Hefner and Bogdanovich back into the end of the story, pointing out the irony of how the shooting affected all the men closest to Stratten. To prevent her story from spilling over into an exploitative vein, Carpenter is careful not to dispense blame or create an undue cause and effect. But her conclusion takes the gloves off and challenges the entire Playboy mentality:

Snider ... had bought the [Playboy] philosophy—that women can be possessed ... He acted out dark fantasies never intended to be realized ... he thought of himself as perhaps one of Playboy's most honest apostles.

Carpenter's overall excellent reporting ratchets up a notch near the end, carefully and meticulously laying out the death scene. Her description of Stratten in death is equal parts gruesome and coolly poetic:

Dorothy lay crouched across the bottom corner of a low bed. Both knees were on the carpet ... Her blond hair hung naturally, oddly unaffected by the violence. ... The shell had entered above her left eye leaving the bones of that seraphic face shattered and displaced in a welter of pulp. Her body, mocking the soft languid poses of her pictorials, was in full rigor.

Although some may disagree with Carpenter's strong broadsides against the entire Playboy culture and Hefner ("a sybarite in mourning") in general, this is a strong advocacy story, one not for the squeamish. Carpenter gives no quarter—not to Snider, not to Bogdanovich, not to Hefner. And some of Carpenter's death-scene descriptions hardly portray Dorothy Stratten as a fresh-scrubbed prom queen.

Carpenter didn't have to take the gloves off in this story. She simply never put them on.

TERESA CARPENTER received a bachelor's degree in English from Graceland College in Iowa and a master's degree in journalism from the University of Missouri. She is the author of *Without a Doubt, Mob Girl and Missing Beauty.*

1982

SAUL PETT

BY 1982, THE LATE SAUL PETT had begun to feel like the bridesmaid. He was 64 years old and tired of hearing it was only a "matter of time" before he would finally win a Pulitzer. "I have been nominated for a Pulitzer more often even than Stassen ran for president," Pett wrote in the *AP Log*.

He noted at least six times when he could have won and cited a common question he heard at editors' conventions and press club bars: "Saul, I'm trying to remember, when did you get your first Pulitzer?

"Now I can tell them: at 3:12 p.m. EST, April 12, 1982."

AP newsfeatures editor Jack Cappon, who had originally come up with the idea for a story on the U.S. bureaucracy, also remembers the day well. The two men walked into a long-overdue party in the AP newsroom that day shortly after 3 p.m. According to Pett, "There were people standing and waving and throwing kisses ... they were waiting with champagne uncorked, with beautiful warm smiles, with arms outstretched ... a feeling that I could feel and touch and remember. They were as joyful as I was."

Cappon is more succinct. "The climax to a great career."

Pett had won the 1982 Pulitzer Prize for the following monumental feature story.

The Federal Bureaucracy

Associated Press

June 14, 1981

EDITOR'S NOTE—"The government of the United States is so big you can't say where it begins and where it ends. It is owned by everybody and run by nobody." It has frustrated presidents and defied definition. It is now the subject of great debate. Herewith is a rare and fascinating look at the processes, sometimes ennobling, sometimes maddening, by which the government came to be what it is.

WE BEGIN WITH THE SENTIMENTS of two Americans two centuries apart but joined in a symmetry of indignation.

One said this: "He has erected a multitude of new offices and sent hither swarms of officers to harass our people and eat out their substance."

The other said this: "The government is driving me nuts. The forms are so complicated I have to call my accountant at $35 an hour or my lawyer at $125 an hour just to get a translation."

The latter opinion belongs to Roger Gregory, a carpenter and small contractor of Sandy Springs, Md., a man of otherwise genial disposition.

The first statement was made by Thomas Jefferson of Monticello, Va., in the Declaration of Independence, in the bill of particulars against the king of England that launched the American Revolution.

It is one of the ironies of history that a nation born out of a deep revulsion for large, overbearing government is now itself complaining, from sea to shining sea, about large, overbearing government.

Somewhere between Thomas Jefferson and Roger Gregory, something went awry in the American growth hormone. And now in our 40th presidency, Ronald Reagan is trying to saddle and tame a brontosaurus of unimaginable size, appetite, ubiquity and complexity.

In designing a government, James Madison said, "The great difficulty is this: you must first enable the government to control the governed and, in the next place, oblige it to govern itself." Has it?

One is often told that in a democracy the people get the government they deserve. In the process, do they also get more government than they want? Does anybody recall voting for the regulations which resulted in three years of litigation between the city of Los Angeles and the U.S. Department of Labor over whether the city was guilty of discrimination against the handicapped by refusing to hire an assistant tree-trimmer with emotional problems?

The government of the United States is so big you can't say where it begins and where it ends. It is so shapeless you can't diagram it with boxes because, after you put the president here and Congress there and the judiciary in a third place, where in the hell do you put the Ad Hoc Committee for the Implementation of PL89-306? Or the Interdepartmental Screw Thread Committee? Or the Interglacial Panel on the Present?

The government of the United States is so unstructured it is owned by everybody and owned by nobody and run by nobody. Presidents run only a part of it. Presidents can't even find and sort out the separate parts.

Jimmy Carter tried. On the crest of promises to streamline and make sense out of the federal bureaucracy, he began by looking for the blueprint. He appointed a panel and the panel looked everywhere, in the drawers, in the closets, in the safe, but they couldn't find it.

"We were unable," the panel concluded, "to obtain a single document containing a complete and current listing of government units which are part of the federal government. We could find no established criteria to determine whether an organizational unit should be included or excluded in such a list."

President Carter never did find out what he was president of. As a candidate, he had flayed the "horrible, bloated bureaucracy." As president, he managed to reduce one or two minor horrors but added to the bloat.

Other presidents have found the bureaucracy an immovable yeast. Franklin Roosevelt ran into so much resistance from the old departments, he created a flock of new agencies around them to get action. Harry Truman complained the president can issue an order and "nothing happens." He tried to reorganize the bureaucracy with the help of Herbert Hoover but not much changed. John Kennedy said it was like dealing with a foreign power.

Since 1802, the population of the United States has multiplied 55 times while the population of government has grown 500 times. Since 1802, and most especially in the last 50 years, the government has been transformed, far beyond the ken of men who started it, in size, power and function. The capital of capitalism now subsidizes rich and poor, capital and labor.

The number of civilian personnel (2.8 million) and military personnel (2.1 million) employed by the federal government has remained fairly constant in recent years. But federal programs have brought vast increases in state and municipal personnel.

Growing, Growing ... Groan

Thus, government in the United States on all levels now employs 18 million people. One out of six working Americans is on the public payroll. Government on all levels now costs more than $832 billion a year. Clearly, it is the nation's largest single business and the least businesslike.

None violates Polonius' advice to Laertes more severely than Uncle Sam. He is both a borrower and a lender. He borrows in cosmic amounts and lends on a celestial scale. He lends at less interest than he borrows. And every year, billions slip through his fingers and disappear into the sinkholes of waste, mismanagement and fraud.

But governments are rarely designed for efficiency, especially democratic governments, and most especially this one. This one has grown spectacularly as people demanded more and more of it and as politicians and bureaucrats saw or stimulated those demands. This government was designed for accommodation and consensus. It began on the docks of Boston, not the other side of town, at the Harvard business school.

Poor old Uncle. He does many essential things that only governments can do. He is capable of great change, a necessity for governments that would survive. He has held the place together 205 years in more freedom and comfort than history ever knew. But he is a creature of diverse forces. He gets it on all sides and is perceived in many ways.

A big, bumbling, generous, naive, inquisitive, acquisitive, intrusive, meddlesome giant with a heart of gold and holes in his pockets, an incredible hulk, a "10-ton marshmallow" lumbering along an uncertain road of good intentions somewhere between capitalism and socialism, an implausible giant who fights wars, sends men to the moon, explores the ends of the universe, feeds the hungry, heals the sick, helps the helpless, a thumping complex of guilt trying mightily to make up for past sins to the satisfaction of nobody, a split personality who most of his life thought God helps those who help themselves and only recently concluded God needed help, a malleable, vulnerable colossus pulled every which way by everybody who wants a piece of him, which is everybody.

In one lifetime, the cost of all government in the United States has become the biggest single item in our family budgets, more than housing, food or health care. Before World War II, the average man worked a month a year to pay for it; now it takes four months. Now it consumes a third of our Gross National Product. In 1929, it took a tenth.

Our federal income tax began in 1913 but it didn't begin to bite until Pearl Harbor. At that, we have been spared the irony that befell Mother England. Her income tax began as a "temporary war measure" in 1799, to fight Napoleon.

It is in the nature of government measures to achieve immortality. Few die. Governments expand in war and contract slightly in peace. They never go back to their previous size. Peacetime emergencies also have a way of becoming permanent. The Rural Electrification Program was set up in 1935 to bring electricity to American farms. Today more than 99 percent of farms are electrified but the REA goes on, 740 people spending $29 million a year.

When we were kids, the word trillion seemed a made-up word like zillion. Now it's for real. Last year, the federal government owed $914.3 billion. Next year it will owe $1.06 trillion. It is owed $176 billion in direct loans. It has also guaranteed loans for $253 billion. If Chrysler and the others default, the government debt would rise to nearly $1.5 trillion.

Like the man said, it all mounts up.

If you would begin to visualize the physical presence of the government, you must brace yourself for more statistics. The government of the United States now owns 413,042 buildings in the 50 states and abroad, excluding military installations abroad. That cost nearly $107 billion. It also leases 227,594,942 square feet of space at an annual rental near $870 million. It owns 775,895,133 acres of land, one-third the land mass of the United States. Uncle is big in real estate.

The government of the United States is so big it takes more than 5,000 people and $210 million a year just to check part of its books. The government is the nation's largest user of energy. A check by a House committee found the government was saving less energy than much of the nation and the Department of Energy, itself, had an "abysmal" record of conservation. The government uses enough energy to heat 11 million homes. It owns 449,591 vehicles. It leases others.

Among others, the government finds it needs the services of 67,235 clerk-typists, 65,281 secretaries, 28,069 air traffic controllers, 27,504 computer specialists, 13,501 internal revenue agents, 5,771 economists, 5,479 voucher examiners, 3,208 psychologists, 16,467 general attorneys, 38 undertakers, 519 nonmilitary chaplains, 1,757 microbiologists, 658 landscape architects, 3,300 librarians, 62 greenskeepers, 16 glassblowers, 8,092 carpenters, 66 saw sharpeners, 4 bicycle repairers, 6 tree fellers, 5 swineherds, and 15 horse wranglers.

... And the Government Taketh Away

"The government is driving me nuts," says Ruby Beha of "Ruby's Truck Stop" on U.S. 50 near Guysville, Ohio. "And the more you make, the more they take."

She complains of high taxes and government forms which require half her waking life, she says, to fill out. She couldn't agree more with Alexis DeToqueville, the 19th century French observer of governments, who said, "The nature of despotic power in democratic ages is not to be fierce and cruel but minute and meddling."

Unlike King George, King Sam sends hither swarms of officers with bundles of money and oodles of regulations. In his great urge to protect everybody from everything, from disaster and discrimination, from pestilence and pollution, he sends money with strings attached.

In this, he is damned if he does, and damned if he doesn't. If he sends money without regulation, he risks monumental larceny. If he sends it with regulations, he risks an outraged citizen.

He has an outraged citizenry. More than the size of bureaucracy, Americans who complain about government complain they are up to their esophagus in indecipherable forms, choking red tape, maddening detail and over-zealous bureaucrats.

In Janesville, Wis., an inspector from the U.S. Department of Agriculture cites a small meat packing plant for allowing the grass to grow too high outside the plant. What, one cries to the heavens, does that have to do with the meat inside?

"I guess," says Dan Wiedman, the man in charge of sanitation at the plant, "he feels that if the outside isn't neat, the inside isn't sanitized."

In New York, the president of Columbia University says that among the sums he must raise is $1 million a year for government paper work.

In Sheldon, Iowa (population 4,500), the mayor has to fill out 27 feet of government forms, in quadruplicate every year, most of them concerning minority employment. Sheldon has no minorities.

In Cambridge, Mass., the president of Harvard says that the federal government, with the strings it attaches to federal funds, tries to decide "who may teach, what may be taught, how it should be taught, and who may be admitted to study."

In Hanover, Wis., (population 200), three men operate a small junkyard called Hanover Auto Salvage. One man is the owner but all three work 60 hours a week and all three draw equal amounts of income from the business every week. The Department of Labor says the two non-owners should be paid overtime. They did not ask for the overtime. Why, they ask, should they be paid more than the owner for the same work?

In Baltimore, Md., Stefan Graham, director of the zoo, is told by the U.S. Department of Agriculture he must do something about the high bacteria count in a pool occupied exclusively by three polar bears.

The bears have been there a long time. They have lived longer than your average polar bear. They are in good health. The man from Agriculture agrees but regulations are regulations. How, asks the zoo keeper, do you get bears to change their personal habits to keep the bacteria count down? Dunno, says Agriculture, but comply or get rid of the polar bears.

In New York, Mayor Ed Koch is told that unless he installs elevators for the handicapped in subway stations, he risks losing federal funds for mass transit. The elevators system would be so expensive, says Koch, it would mean that each subway ride by each handicapped person would cost the city $50. It would be cheaper to transport them by limousine or cab.

In North Carolina and other places in the South where blacks can now attend white colleges, the Department of Education threatens to withhold federal funds unless black colleges are made more attractive to whites.

In Washington, D.C., Sen. Daniel Patrick Moynihan (D.-N.Y.) complains that for the better part of a year his staff had to negotiate with the Senate Ethics Committee over whether the senator had used the letter "I" more times than the franking privilege rules allow.

"Personally phrased references ... shall not appear more than five times on a page," according to Section 3210(a)(5)(c) of the rules. "The essence of the argument," says the senator, "was whether the term we, as in 'we New Yorkers,' implied the term I."

In Janesville, Wis., a small banker complains that since they ask the same questions every year, why can't federal and state bank examiners share the answer and eliminate one of the inspections?

In New York, a long investment prospectus from Merrill Lynch Pierce Fenner and Smith includes this cautious paragraph:

"Section 13. Masculine Pronouns. Masculine pronouns, whenever used herein, shall be deemed to include the feminine, and the use of the masculine pronoun shall not be deemed to imply any preference for it or any subordination, disqualification or exclusion of the feminine."

God forbid anybody should think that the mighty Wall Street firm was so male chauvinist, so illegally macho, they wouldn't accept money from female investors.

The men (there were no sex discrimination laws then) who wrote the Constitution of the United States were deliberately imprecise. They left room for growth and change. Their descendants often are compulsively detailed.

Somebody in Washington gets an idea. Wouldn't it be nice, especially since there is a lobby of the handicapped, if street curbs had ramps for people in wheelchairs at intersections? Simple? No.

The word goes forth from Washington across the land, whenever federal funds are involved in road construction, that ramps be installed at intersections, each to be a specific width, length, pitch and non-slip material.

The first thing that happens is that in a heavy rain the water running along the gutter is diverted by the ramps and deposits its debris, not in sewers, but out in the street. The second thing that happens is that in the winter, snow plows rip up the protruding grades. The third thing that happens is that blind people relying on canes complain that the ramps confuse their perception of where the curb ends and the street begins.

Government by the Rules ...

Washington's passion for detailed regulation has its ironic inconsistencies. For example, the government asks fewer questions of a man buying a Saturday night special than it does of a man importing a salami from Italy. And the man who buys a gun is allowed to leave with his purchase before his answers are verified.

Washington was far more cautious when the city of Des Moines planned to build a viaduct over a railroad in 1971. The estimated cost then was $1.3 million and the feds would put up half in matching funds. But it took five years for the city to persuade Washington that its regulations about environment and noise would be satisfied. By then the viaduct cost $4.1 million. It would have been faster and cheaper if the city had built the viaduct itself, footing the entire bill.

The federal government is easily ridiculed for its bureaucratic excesses, its stifling regulations, its intrusive Big Brotherism. But against that, one needs to recall it was the federal government, not the states or private industry or private charity or the free marketplace, that sustained the country in the Great Depression and saved it from revolution. It was the federal government that ended slavery in the South and had to come back 100 years later with "swarms of officers" to make that liberation real.

It is the federal government that insists management pay labor overtime for overtime work, that cushions the shock of dismissal and prevents child labor. It is the federal government that keeps the poor and the aged out of county poor farms and back attics. It is the federal government that keeps Wall Street honest, makes bank deposits safer, makes the air and the water cleaner, reduces deaths in the mine shafts of Pennsylvania, keeps horrors like thalidomide from disfiguring our babies, makes American airways the safest among the world's busiest, and keeps chaos out of our airwaves by controlling shares to the small Citizen Band owner and the big television networks.

It is the federal government and its loans which keep many small and large business men in business, many farmers on the family farm, many students in college. It is the federal government which injected new life into many downtown areas of the dying cities, with money for new hotels, parking garages, civic centers and open plazas. It is the federal government that gave Detroit its Renaissance Center and Baltimore a revitalized harbor.

"I have no apologies for the federal government being interested in people, in nutrition, education, health and transportation," Hubert Humphrey once said. "Who's going to take care of the environment and establish standards? You? Me? Who's going to work out our transportation problems? The B & O railroad?"

Others ask, who would do all this with better planning and greater efficiency? Chrysler? Lockheed? The New York Central Railroad?

Elmer Staats, as head of the General Accounting Office, spent 15 years ferreting out waste, fraud and sloppy management in Washington. He found plenty. He is not naive about the bureaucracy. He says:

"Americans have come to expect more and more from government while trusting it less. Many of the same individuals who bemoan the growth of government are the first to seek its help when their own interests are involved.

"They decry the government bureaucrats but are unwilling to accept positions in government because the salaries are too low or the ethical requirements too high. They speak out at every opportunity against the encroachment of government but fail to speak up when asked to volunteer for community endeavors. They most often assert demands or speak of rights rather than duty, obligation or responsibility. They see nothing inconsistent with pleading for tax reduction yet expecting public services to remain the same.

"The once prized characteristic of American society of hard work and self-reliance too often has given way to the view that 'someone else should do it' or someone else should pay the bill, that someone else being government."

The men who created our government were suspicious of government. They feared any restrictions of individual liberty. They were more interested in preventing the accumulation of power than in promoting its efficient use. Thus, they gave us a government of checks and balances and separation of powers in a design that built in tension, competition, even mutual suspicion between branches of government. It was not a blueprint for a smoothly coordinated team.

James Madison, the "father of the Constitution," said that under that document the states would be more powerful than the central government and the federal taxing powers would not be "resorted to except for supplemental purposes of revenue." He said federal powers were "few and defined" while state powers were "numerous and indefinite." Federal powers would be "exercised principally on external objects ... war, peace, negotiation and foreign commerce." State powers would extend "to all the objects which ... concern the lives, liberties and properties of the people."

When Mr. Jefferson was in the White House in 1802, the entire federal establishment in Washington numbered 291 officials; the entire executive branch, 132 people. Congress consisted of 32 senators and 106 representatives, all of whom had to get along with a total staff of 13 among them. (Congress has 3,500 today.) The Supreme Court had six justices, one clerk among them.

In the Beginning ...

The business of the national government then was defense, minting money, conducting foreign relations, collecting revenue, maintaining lighthouses for navigation and running the postal service, which in those days belonged to the Treasury Department and—would you believe?—turned a profit.

Almost all the things that governments do that affect the lives and fortunes of its citizens were done by the state and local governments, and that wasn't much. Then and for decades after, the national government got along on customs and excise taxes.

The chief proponents of a strong central government then were business leaders and they wanted it only strong enough to protect commerce, provide a nationwide free home market and a sound currency and banking system.

The public attitude toward the poor reflected the young country's sense of rugged individualism, reliance on family and a strong work ethic. The poor were thought to be poor because of personal failure.

From the Revolution to the Great Depression a century and a half later, help for the needy came mostly from family, charity, and local government. Local public relief bore a stigma.

The federal government grew slowly in its first 150 years. On the expanding frontier, it was involved in territorial jurisdiction and land grants for public education, roads, flood control, drainage, canals and railroads. Until 1893, federal money largely went to pensions, public buildings and river and harbor improvements. There were short term federal deficits because of the Civil War, the recession of 1890 and World War I, but nothing like what would come later.

The first federal regulation of the private sector came in 1863 with the creation of the Office of the Comptroller of the Currency as part of the national banking system. In the next 40 years, only two regulatory agencies were added—the Interstate Commerce Commission and the Animal and Plant Health Inspection Service.

Generally, the federal government remained aloof from most domestic affairs. Generally, it was a quiet time and presidents were not overworked. Grover Cleveland could take afternoons off, riding in his Victoria drawn by a matched pair while the citizenry tipped their hats and said, "Good afternoon, Mr. President."

If it were possible to chart the American dream, you would have a steadily climbing line from 1776 to 1860, a sharp drop for the Civil War and then again a rising line with minor dips, rising, rising, rising to a pinnacle in 1929. We were prosperous. We were buoyant. We were supremely confident.

Then the wheels fell off.

Suddenly, 12 million Americans, one out of four of the country's breadwinners, were looking for jobs that didn't exist. More than 5,000 banks failed and 86,000 businesses went out of business and, in 1932 alone, 273,000 families were evicted from their homes.

In the spreading hunger and deepening humiliation, middle-class neighbors knocked on back doors for handouts. Some people ate weeds and some people fought over leftovers in the alleys behind restaurants and rioting farmers dumped cans of milk rather than sell for two cents a quart and in many places people talked of revolution from the left or the right and across the land nobody seemed to be able to do anything about anything. With all the property foreclosures, with tax revenues way down, the state and city governments were virtually helpless to help, private charities dried up, and the whole blessed country seemed at a dead stop.

Only the federal government had the resources to help and under Franklin Roosevelt it did. This was the watershed, the great turn in history in which laissez-faire died and the basic philosophy of American government was profoundly altered.

Federal Emergency Relief. Social Security. Unemployment compensation. The Civilian Conservation Corps. The National Labor Relations Act. The Securities and Exchange Commission. The Agricultural Adjustment Administration. The Tennessee Valley Authority. The Work Progress Administration.

The cartoons showed men leaning on shovels but it was WPA, or a form of it, that built 10 percent of the new roads, 35 percent of the new hospitals, 70 percent of the new schools. Denver was given a new water supply system; Brownsville, Texas, a port; Key West, the roads and bridges that connect it to the Florida mainland.

WPA built the Lincoln Tunnel between New York and New Jersey, the Camarillo Mental Hospital in California, the canals of San Antonio, the Fort Knox gold depository in Kentucky, Dealey Plaza in Dallas and Boulder Dam on the Colorado River.

Franklin Roosevelt made the economic welfare of Americans a federal commitment. In his turn, Lyndon Johnson took the ball and ran with it—ran away with it, some say.

The '60s were a time of high employment and great economic growth. Every American, it was thought, could be assured a job, a minimum standard of living, adequate diet, decent housing and sufficient health care.

Everything looked possible if you threw enough money and expertise at it—the moon, Vietnam, the policing of the world in our image, the end of poverty, racial injustice, decay of the cities and the sliding quality of life. Thus, we got:

More aid to the poor. More foreign aid. Supreme Court decisions to ensure the rights of minorities and the accused. Food stamps. Medicare. Affirmative action. Job training. Child care. School lunches. Housing and rent subsidies. Corporate subsidies. Educational aid. Urban renewal. Consumer programs. Wars on poverty and cancer and pollution. Projects to combat heart disease, reduce mental illness, raise reading scores, reduce juvenile delinquency.

All of it part of what seemed like an unquestioning national momentum to take the risk and inequity out of life, in ghettos and board rooms, in factories and farms, in schools and homes. And people voted for the candidates who made government bigger, Republican as well as Democratic, and before long Washington was into everything from the number of Hispanic teachers in Waukegan to the number of prongs in the electric plugs of a bakery in West Warwick, R.I.

The cost of domestic social programs rose from 17 to 25 percent of the Gross National Product between 1964 and 1974. Defense outlays grew, too, but as a slice of the federal budget domestic programs became twice as large as defense.

Much was attempted, much was accomplished, much ended up a mess. Where failure resulted, it usually was attributed, in retrospect, to an excessive confidence in what government could do. The war on poverty fed and housed the poor but largely failed to make them self-sufficient. Subsidized housing provided better housing but no less crime in the disrupted neighborhoods. Federal efforts to improve student learning fell far short of their spectacular promises.

Ed Koch was a congressman who voted with the flood tide of federal largesse, a fact he now regrets as the mayor of New York swamped in federal regulations.

"The bills I voted for came to the floor in a form that compelled approval. After all, who can vote against clean air and water or better access and education for the handicapped?

"As I look back, it is hard to believe that I could have been taken in by the simplicity of what Congress was doing and by the flimsy empirical support—often no more than a carefully orchestrated hearing record or a single consultant's report offered to persuade members that the proposed solution could work throughout the country."

Washington Weeds

While the rapid growth of the federal government began in the '30s, it is since 1960 that its restrictive effects have deepened profoundly on individuals, business and lesser governments. Between 1961 and 1973, Washington sprouted 141 new agencies, more than a third of the current total, and none disappeared.

Twenty years ago, federal money going to the state and local governments was slightly more than $7 billion. Now there are nearly 500 programs that cost $88 billion. Then, there were few regulations tied to the money. Now there are 1,260 sets of rules. Then, federal aid went almost entirely to the 50 states. Now it also goes directly to 65,000 cities, towns and wide bends in the road.

A commission appointed by Congress last year concluded that the constitutional system of shared and separate powers among federal, state and local governments is "in trouble."

"The federal government's influence," the commission said, "has become more pervasive, more intrusive, more unmanageable, more ineffective, more costly and, above all, more unaccountable. The intergovernmental system today is a bewildered and bewildering maze of complex, overlapping and, often, conflicting relationships."

Gov. Bruce Babbit of Arizona, a Democrat, aimed his shaft directly at Congress:

"It is hard to see why a national Congress, responsible for governing a continental nation, should be involved in formulating programs for rat control, humanities grants for town hall debates on capital punishment, educating displaced homemakers, training for use of the metric system, jellyfish control, bike paths and police disability grants.

"It is long past time for Congress to ... ask with the shades of Jefferson and Madison, 'Is this a truly national concern?' Congress ought to be worrying about arms control and defense instead of the potholes in the streets. We just might have both an increased chance of survival and better streets."

Almost since he yawned, stretched and left the cave to get organized, man has made bureaucracy part of his history.

Julius Caesar levied a 1 percent general sales tax. He also levied an inheritance tax, which contained history's first and most picturesque tax loophole. Close relatives of the deceased were exempt.

It is because of bureaucracy that we think of Bethlehem at Christmas, not a suburb.

"And it came to pass in those days that there went out a decree from Caesar Augustus that all the world should be taxed. ... And all went to be taxed, everyone into his own city. And Joseph went up to Bethlehem ... to be taxed with Mary, his espoused wife, being great with child."

Long before Ronald Reagan, there was a Roman historian, Tacitus, who viewed bureaucracy with gloom and doom. "The closer a society is to ruin," he said, "the more laws there are."

If true, we are not alone. In recent years, in most places of the world, small government has grown large and large government has grown larger. The rising tide of paternalism from national capitals has been nearly universal.

Sweden, where someone calculated a new law or ordinance was passed every eight hours of the last decade, now spends more than half of its national income on government. Other countries which spend relatively more on government than we do include the United

Kingdom, France, Belgium, Canada, West Germany, Austria, Holland, Denmark, Norway and Italy. Among the major powers, only Japan spends less than we do; it has virtually no military establishment and meets welfare needs through the private business sector.

We are not alone in our irritation.

In Italy, it took Giuseppe Grottadauria two-and-a-half years to get his residence papers switched from Messina to Rome, without which he couldn't vote, buy a car or register his son's birth.

In Italy, it can take four hours in a line at the post office to pay a phone bill. It can take years to get a phone installed and months to register in a university, by which time the new student is taking final exams.

In Sweden, the government intruded on a national pastime. It decreed that people picking and selling wild berries must be registered for income tax. The result was that for two years Sweden had to import berries while thousands of tons rotted in the forests.

In Nanking, China, the requisitioning of 1.3 acres of land took three months and the signatures of 144 officials in 17 different organizations on 46 documents.

In Japan, Mihoko Yokota returned from eight years in the United States and applied for a driver's license. She was asked for proof of residence. She tried to register her new address in Kamakura but was told she needed a form from her last address in Japan. She asked her mother in Hiroshima to send the form by special delivery but when she went to the Kamakura post office to register her new address in order to receive the mail she was told she needed proof of residence which she could not get from the Kamakura city office until her mother in Hiroshima sent the form which could not be delivered until the post office had the form from the Kamakura city hall which finally meant that the form from Mihoko's mother had to be hand-carried by a friend travelling between the two cities. And if you're wondering what yamemasho means, it is the closest the Japanese come to saying, to hell with it.

Students of sanity know there are two ways to react to the Catch 22 situations, the claustrophobic red tape, the sins, excesses and sheer idiocy of big government. One way is to react with indignation; the other, with humor. A carefully calibrated combination of both comes highly recommended for dealing with the following:

The Pentagon's XMI tank program, costing $13 billion, produces a tank which can't run in any but dust-free conditions like those in the lab.

The National Aeronautics and Space Administration asks Congress for $1.1 billion for a new telescope. Turns out NASA made a small bookkeeping error. It will cost $2.2 billion.

The Department of Health, Education and Welfare (now the Department of Health and Human Services) estimates that in fiscal 1979 it blew $2 million in overpayments or payments to ineligibles in three major welfare programs. Ideally, it says, it hopes to reduce this slippage to 4 percent. That's still $1.1 billion.

Various federal agencies do nothing about $2.5 to $3 billion owed the government by contractors and grantees for questionable book-keeping. One tiny part of HEW blew $1.5 million by letting the statute of limitations expire before trying to recover improper charges.

The government has 12,000 computers. The General Accounting Office spot-checks the payroll computer at the Department of Housing and Urban Development. It feeds the computer fictitious names. Turns out the infernal machine would have paid Donald Duck.

By one estimate, the government spends $9 billion a year on out-side consultants. Two-third of the contracts are reportedly let without competing bids. Many of the consultants are former officials of the agency seeking the consultation. Many of the resulting studies end up in drawers and are never used.

One consultant is paid $440 for working Sept. 31, 1978. (Thirty days hath September.) The Environmental Protection Agency pays $360,000 for a study which shows, among other things, that the average speed of trucks in Manhattan is 68 mph. (!)

The new Department of Education pays $1,500 a week for six weeks to a consultant (a former Education official) to design an office layout for its top executives. The Energy Department consults out-siders to explain an act of Congress (the Civil Service Reform Act). Another department hires a consultant to find out how many consultants it has.

A bureaucrat in the Bureau of Labor Statistics makes one mistake in computing used car prices nationally, which pushes up the Consumer Price Index by two-tenths of 1 percent, which increases benefits for millions of people getting regular checks based on the Index.

The General Accounting Office estimates that in the past five years it saved taxpayers nearly $21 billion that otherwise would have gone down the drain because of waste, bad management and uncollected bills. Since the GAO makes only special checks at the behest of Congress, that figure has to be regarded as the tip of an iceberg colored red.

Private-wise ...

Horrendous as that is, there are those who suspect that private industry is in no position to look down its corporate nose at government.

Clark Clifford, the Washington attorney who has dealt with both for years, says he has also seen "scandalous waste" in the private sector. Paul O'Neill, a former high official of the Office of Management and Budget and now a senior vice president of International Paper Co., adds, "The steel and auto industry made huge mistakes. If you put the Washington press corps on the back of industry you'd find equal stupidity."

With a couple of differences. Private industry has a better line: profit. A widget that saves money is highly prized and rewarded.

Government has no bottom line and money becomes an abstraction, as if it belonged to nobody. In government, if your department spends less this year, you're apt to get less from Congress next year. A bureaucrat who finds he can get by with fewer people may find his own grade and salary reduced.

Also, private industry generally can still fire people. The government of the United States generally can't. Once in, federal employees are tough to get out, like headless nails.

An agency fired an employee for beating his supervisor with a baseball bat. The Federal Employees Appeals Authority ordered the culprit reinstated in the same job under the same supervisor with eight months back pay. Reason: the employee was given insufficient notice of dismissal.

It took a Commerce Department manager 21 months and mounds of paper work to fire a secretary who consistently failed to show up for work for reasons of health which proved phony. The manager had to devote so much time to the case his own work suffered and he received a reprimand.

In New York, a postal worker was fired for shooting another man in the stomach during a difference of opinion. The attacker went to jail but appealed his dismissal. He won reinstatement and $5,000 in back pay on the grounds that the papers were filled out wrongly. So they filled them out rightly and this time the firing stuck but the postal gunslinger kept the $5,000.

Nearly all federal employees are protected by Civil Service or other rigid umbrellas. They are also represented by 78 labor unions and associations. Civil Service was begun in 1883 to replace the old spoils system by which all federal workers could be fired every four years. Merit replaced politics as a condition of employment.

But in 1919, a congressman was complaining on the floor of the House about all the "clinkers" in government who couldn't be purged: "They are in all departments, killing time, writing answers to letters that do not need an answer, stupidly pretending to do work that live employees must do over again."

Fifty-nine years later, President Carter complained to Congress: "It is easier to promote and transfer incompetent employees than to get rid of them. It may take as long as three years to fire someone for just cause. ... You cannot run a farm that way, you cannot run a factory that way, and you certainly cannot run a government that way."

Added to the Civil Service complications were the difficulties created by equal opportunity legislation. An administrator would have to think hard about firing a member of a minority for incompetence. If the incompetent countered with a discrimination suit, the administrator would have to hire his own lawyers to defend himself. If the decision went against him, he could lose pay or position.

In 1978, out of 2.8 million people on his payroll, Uncle Sam managed to fire 119 for inefficiency. Later that year, Carter got some civil service reform out of Congress and in the next go-round 214 employees were sacked for the same reason. Not exactly a spectacular leap forward. There remained a huge permanent core entrenched in concrete and beyond the reach of presidents to touch.

Low-level federal workers are said to be paid somewhat more than their counterparts in the private sector. Many higher levels are paid much less than they could earn on the outside.

Federal pensions are generally better than private ones and in recent years, along with cost of living increases, 99 percent of federal employees were given annual merit raises. Were there really that many that good?

In the Carter administration, Carol Foreman headed food inspection and consumer services in the Agriculture Department. "I have a staff of 10,000," she once said. "A few are very dedicated, a few are very talented, and then there are the others."

Bureaucratic Boons

The goof-offs and foul-ups in government obviously get more attention than the people doing their job. Few Americans were aware of the calibre of Foreign Service officers until the hostages came back from Iran. Few are aware of the young lawyers who pass up golden offers from big firms to work in legal aid for the poor. The doctors in public health get no attention every day they prevent epidemics until they fail. The men and women who leave fat corporate jobs to work much harder for much less in government get no space in the papers until one of their number is caught with his hand in the till.

Most students of government agree that the trouble with government is not the bureaucrats, good, bad or indifferent, but the chaotic system that incubates and nourishes them.

What we have is a big, implausible, ramshackle house, distorted by random additions, by corridors that go nowhere and rooms that don't connect, a house loosely expanded through the years for numberless children, most of them unexpected. There was no family planning. There was no architect.

"Congress has the power but not the incentive for coordinated control of the bureaucracy while the president has the incentive but not the power," said Morris P. Fiorina, a political scientist, speaking generically.

Congress can create, change or kill an agency through its funding power. Presidents can only hope to mobilize public opinion. Presidents seek re-election and a place in history. Members of Congress seek re-election but, each being one of 535, cannot count on immortality. Congressmen get re-elected, not for the broad strokes of history, but for the post offices or sewage systems or dams they bring their constituents.

And back there, everybody is for saving money in general but not in particular. The taxpayer in Colorado may not shed a tear over cuts in urban renewal funds for New York, but don't touch his water projects. And vice versa, the taxpayer in New York. And the rural congressman, who couldn't care less about a Model Cities program, votes for Model Cities in a trade for a vote for farm subsidies from the urban congressman. "A billion here, a billion there," said Everett Dirksen. "Pretty soon, you're talking about real money."

Even the pure in heart can't escape the swelling effect of politics. Two powerful Republican senators (Jesse Helms and Robert Dole) had candidates for the job of assistant agriculture secretary for governmental and public affairs. The Reagan administration solved the dilemma by splitting the job between the two choices but not the salary. Each will be paid $52,750 a year.

There is, we are told, a constituency for every dollar in the federal budget. Everyone seems to have a compelling reason and consistency is not always the rule of the day.

The American Medical Association, which once opposed Medicare as socialized medicine, now opposes cuts in Medicare on which many doctors depend heavily for their income.

In 1978, the snow was so heavy that cities in Michigan asked for federal money to help with the snow removal. In 1979, the snow was so light that ski areas in Michigan asked for federal aid. Rain or shine, Uncle Sam often finds himself in a no-win situation.

If he insists on taking more time to examine the eligibility of people asking for welfare, does he risk causing some of them to starve or freeze? If he doesn't guarantee a loan for Chrysler, will he be responsible for throwing thousands of auto workers out on the street? If he sends a mother to jail for food stamp fraud, won't he have to feed her children in a foster home at greater cost? If he cuts subsidies for the merchant marine and airlines, will he have enough ships and planes in the next war?

Presidents come, presidents go, but in Washington there remains a permanent bureaucracy with its own ideas, momentum, inner resources, cozy ties with key members of Congress and ingenious ploys for survival. Nothing evokes the fancy footwork of a bureaucrat so much as a presidential attempt to cut his budget.

Ask Amtrak to cut the fat out of its operation and it comes back with a dandy plan to eliminate railroad routes going through the home districts of powerful committee chairmen in Congress who would never tolerate it. Ask Interior to save money and it proposes to close the national parks earlier or shut down the elevators in the Washington Monument, neither of which the public would take lying down.

Generals are very good at this, although lately they haven't had to be. Ask a general in the Pentagon to cut and he goes dutifully before an appropriations committee, with whose chairman he is secretly wired, and he says, loyally, yes, he can oblige the president. But on further questioning, his expression grows more pained until finally, in all candor, he lets it be known in hushed tones, that the proposed reduction would leave the entire East Coast of the United States defenseless.

Recurring Red-Tapeworm

Deeply embedded in the inner workings of the permanent government, like the wheels and timing mechanism of a bank vault, there are "iron triangles" of power and expertise which continue to hum, quietly and smoothly, regardless of the passing sounds of elections.

At the three corners, there are the bureaucrats running a given program, the key congressmen favoring it and the special interest groups benefiting from it. They are welded together for mutual self-interest and survival. They can defy presidents.

Bryce Harlow, who has been around Washington almost as long as the Monument, who worked on the Hill and served in high places in the Eisenhower and Nixon administrations, likens the triangles to complexes of bees.

"They form like bees around a flower, and they stroke it and milk it and make it give forth its honey. They are in all departments of the government and they don't much care who is president or who is the Cabinet member in charge. To a large extent, America is governed by these complexes.

"Let's begin with an administrative undersecretary in the Agriculture Department. We'll call him Jack Brown ..."

Jack knows everybody. He knows the key people in his department who are dependent on him. He knows John Doe and Horace Smith in the Office of Management and Budget. They have been working together for years on agricultural budgets. They socialize together.

Jack Brown also knows Bill Gordon, a veteran member of the professional staff of the House subcommittee on farm appropriations. Jack and John and Horace and Bill and their wives go to the same conventions together, to meetings of the cotton council, the soybean council, the Grange, the Farm Bureau.

"Everybody knows everybody and they all get on well together." Harlow concludes, "and they are all milking the same flower."

More and more professional bureaucrats are people who were trained in specialized sciences and technologies and seek to apply their expertise in government. They have counterparts on the staffs of Congress and in state and local governments. They form a network of experts on which presidents, Congress, governors and mayors rely. They speak their own language. They sometimes agree more with each other than with the people they work for.

It used to be, says Sen. Daniel Moynihan, who was an assistant secretary of labor under Kennedy, that "when the Labor Department needed a policy, it sent out for one, you might say, from the AFL-CIO." Now it gets policy from in-house experts.

Samuel Beer, a professor of government at Harvard, maintains that most of the Great Society programs began with the professionals in government, not with the public demanding them.

"In the field of health, housing, urban renewal, highways, welfare, education and poverty, it was in very many cases people in government service, acting on the basis of specialized and technical knowledge who conceived the new programs, initially urged them on the attention of the president and Congress, and, indeed, went on to lobby them through to enactment."

Whether the programs begat the constituents or the constituents begat the programs, whichever came first, the chicken or the egg, we now have a lot of chickens in Washington. And they all know how to lobby. They all know how to bring pressure for and against.

It used to be, someone said, that politics was about a few things; now it's about everything. It used to be that the major power blocs which shaped government were business, labor and agriculture. Now power is fragmented into a thousand insistent voices, which have to be heard and reconciled.

They are highly organized for the annual fight over the federal pie and fight frequently for their slice with the help of interested bureaucrats. They have become so effective as to cause some students of government to fear that power in this country has shifted from the people and their elected representatives to organized interest groups and bureaucrats.

E Pluribus Unum is in trouble. If ever we were one out of many, we are now many out of one. John Gardner, founder of Common Cause, calls the centrifugal forces of special interest groups a "war of the parts against the whole."

The parts multiply like the denizens of a rabbit warren on New Year's Eve. Everybody, it seems, wants something or opposes something and, in the melee, bureaucracy grows larger and more shapeless and threatens to become, in itself, a government of too many people, by too many people, for too many people.

ANALYSIS

ALTHOUGH SAUL PETT would spend six months researching and writing an amazing 8,500 words on the scope and influence of the federal bureaucracy, the story had humble beginnings.

Jack Cappon, Pett's editor and now AP general news editor, recalls "reading how the White House was vainly trying to reduce staffing and it just struck an idea." Cappon decided to assign a story that focused on the specific scope and enormity of government—not the usual piece on waste and mismanagement.

Cappon, who still marvels at Pett's ability to write with "detached humor" says Pett nailed the concept on the second draft and ultimately produced a text that required very little editing. "I was the only editor involved ... I'm sure Saul felt that was more than enough."

The fact that Saul Pett was able to create an informative and whimsical story about a subject as boring and self-important as the federal government is a story in itself. Instead of writing with a sarcastic literary chip on his shoulder, as could easily have been expected, even understood, Pett documented the absurdities in the government and tried to laugh along with the system. It allowed him to write the story through a literary looking glass, laughing with the bloated government's foibles. In doing so, he greatly illuminated the problems and kept the readers along for the full ride.

One 100 word-plus sentence/paragraph Pett wrote early in the story stands out like a beacon on how he planned to "humanize" the story and discuss the idiosyncrasies of the government of the United States with loving affection:

A big, bumbling, generous, naive, inquisitive, acquisitive, intrusive, meddlesome giant with a heart of gold and holes in his pockets, an incredible hulk, a "10-ton marshmallow" lumbering along an uncertain road of good intentions somewhere between capitalism and socialism, an implausible giant who fights wars, sends men to the moon, explores the ends of the universe, feeds the hungry, heals the sick, helps the helpless, a thumping complex of guilt trying mightily to make up for past sins to the satisfaction of nobody, a split personality who most of his life thought God helps those who help themselves and only recently concluded God needed help, a malleable, vulnerable colossus pulled every which way by everybody who wants a piece of him, which is everybody.

Faced with the prospect of violating a cardinal rule of writing features—producing a story overflowing with numbers, Pett decided to attack the problem head on. He neither shirked the subject of figures nor over-stuffed the story with them. Instead, he consistently found clever ways to bring them to life:

Before World War II the average man worked a month to pay for it [the cost of government]; now it takes four months.

Now it consumes a third of our Gross National Product. In 1929, it took a tenth.

[The government] owns 774,895,133 acres of land, one-third the land mass of the United States. Uncle is big in real estate.

The government uses enough energy to heat 11 million homes. It owns 449,591 vehicles. It leases others.

Pett also used some specific examples of government intrusion to propel his narrative forward with devastating effectiveness:

•A USDA meat inspector who cites a small meat-packing plant for allowing the grass to grow too high outside the plant.

•A small city mayor who has to fill out 27 feet of government forms yearly in quadruplicate, mostly concerning minority employment, although the town has no minorities.

•A zoo director who is told by the USDA to do something about the high bacteria count in a pool occupied exclusively by three polar bears who have already lived longer than most polar bears and are in good health. The inspector can't think of a way to reduce the bacteria either, but warns the zoo they will have to get rid of the bears if they can't succeed.

Finally, the massive story is tied together by a compelling lead mentioning Thomas Jefferson and the Declaration of Independence and a clever ending playing on the same subject:

[the] bureaucracy ... threatens to become ... a government of too many people, by too many people, for too many people.

Pett's career masterpiece was a muscular effort, creating an informative and entertaining story out of a subject seemingly without charm or humor. His Pulitzer might have been too long in coming for Saul, but for the rest of us, his final effort was worth the wait.

THE LATE SAUL PETT was a graduate of the University of Missouri School of Journalism, published two books and conducted in-depth interviews with many U.S. presidents.

1983

NAN ROBERTSON

AS SOON AS SHE BEGAN to recover from the deadly toxic shock syndrome that nearly took her life, veteran reporter Nan Robertson was motivated to turn her horror into a story.

And although 15 years have passed since she was raced to a hospital, Robertson still carries the outrage and passion inside—emotions that fueled a magnificent story detailing a mystery disease that doctors barely understood.

"I wrote it because I wanted to save lives," Robertson stresses. "Doctors were misdiagnosing toxic shock over and over again as scarlet fever, a very serious case of influenza or as food poisoning."

Although most experienced feature writers (often with strong encouragement from their editors) go to great lengths to avoid writing in the first-person, no matter how personal the story (for example: "The Stalking of Kristin," 1993 Pulitzer), Nan Robertson literally had no choice.

Yet, her harrowing, profound narrative of surviving TSS is an instructive lesson in how to report the most deadly life experience in a frank and educational way. Along the way, she gave her readers a medical lesson and a first-rate reading experience.

Although Robertson's story understandably offers little in the way of humor, she can now laugh over how the piece first started. "Arthur [Gelb] called me when I was in intensive care at St. Anthony's Hospital in Rockford, Ill., with tubes coming out of every orifice. The phone rings and the nurse puts it up to my ear. Artie Gelb is shouting, 'Nan, what a great story! Unlimited wordage! You'll get the cover of the magazine!'

"I lay there listening to this maniac saying these things after I had barely come through. I said, 'Oh, fuck off, Artie. I'm living this thing. I don't want to write about it.'"

A couple of months later, she called Gelb and told him she

would "write the definitive piece on toxic shock syndrome," which she did.

Robertson is nothing if not thorough. She clearly remembers the anxiety she experienced awaiting the announcement of the Pulitzer. Two high-placed contacts had called her in April of 1983, telling her she had won the prize. The second call, coming just five days before the official announcement, only increased her anxiety. To relieve the stress, Robertson says she spent that weekend with her best friend at an inn in East Hampton, Long Island.

"Then being really neurotic," she recalls, "I thought, the Columbia University campus will be bombed over the weekend, destroying all evidence that I won!"

The explosion never came and Robertson went to lunch with a *Times* editor at Sardi's on April 18, 1983, the day of the announcement, arriving back at the office just before 3 p.m.

Here's how she remembers the magic moment:

It was announced over the intercom in the city room, at which point the building fell down. Everybody ran to my desk and there was an enormous amount of hugging, kissing and cheering. The publisher, Punch Sulzberger, ran down from the 14th floor. It was an absolute mob scene for several hours.

Robertson remembers Gelb telling her he had never seen a more emotional Pulitzer celebration at *The Times*. "First of all, Nan, we were afraid you wouldn't live when the news came you were gravely ill with toxic shock and then after they had saved your life at this hospital in Rockford, we thought you'd be maimed irretrievably," he said. Gelb pointed out that Robertson had lived, had not been maimed irretrievably and had written a masterful story that saved a lot of lives. "And then," he said, "to top everything, you win the Pulitzer. Everybody just felt this was justice redeemed."

Robertson says she was also overjoyed to receive a letter several days later from the chairman of the Pulitzer jury for features that year, calling "Toxic Shock" "a stunning achievement, one that students of our craft will be reading for several years to come ... as fine and heroic a piece of newspapering as I expect to see."

Fifteen years later, those words still ring true.

Toxic Shock

The New York Times

September 19, 1982

I WENT DANCING the night before in a black velvet Paris gown on one of those evenings that was the glamour of New York epitomized. I was blissfully asleep at 3 A.M.

Twenty-four hours later, I lay dying, my fingers and legs darkening with gangrene. I was in shock, had no pulse and my blood pressure was lethally low. The doctors in the Rockford, Ill., emergency room where I had been taken did not know what was wrong with me. They thought at first that I might have consumed some poison that had formed in my food. My sister and brother-in-law, whom I had been visiting, could see them through the open emergency-room door: "They were scurrying around and telephoning, calling for help, because they knew they had something they couldn't handle, that they weren't familiar with," was the instinctive reaction of my brother-in-law, Warren Paetz.

I was awake and aware, although confused and disoriented. The pain in my muscles was excruciating. I could hear the people bent over me, blinding lights behind them, asking me how old I was, when I had stopped menstruating, and, over and over, what I had eaten for Thanksgiving dinner the previous afternoon, Thursday, Nov. 26, 1981, and what I had had the day before.

The identical, delicious restaurant meal my mother, Eve, and I had consumed on Thursday centered on roast turkey with the classic Middle Western bread stuffing seasoned with sage that I had loved since childhood. I had eaten slowly, prudently, because I had had only three hours' sleep the night before, catching an early plane to Chicago to connect with a bus to Rockford, a city of 140,000 in north-central Illinois where all my family lives. Immediately after finishing my Thanksgiving dinner, I threw it up. It was 4 P.M. at the Clock Tower Inn in Rockford. I thought excitement and fatigue had made me ill. Neither I nor my mother, a gutsy 90-year-old, was overly concerned.

That was how it began: almost discreetly. I felt drained; my legs were slightly numb. The manager, apologizing all the way, drove us back to my sister's house in the hotel van. I was put to bed in the downstairs den.

I awoke, trancelike, in the middle of the night to find myself crawling and crashing up the stairs to the bathroom. The vomiting and diarrhea were cataclysmic. My only thought was to get to the bathtub to clean myself. I sat transfixed in my filthy nightgown in the empty tub, too weak to turn on the water. Warren and my sister, Jane, awakened by the noise of my passage, carried me back downstairs, with exclamations of horror and disgust at the mess I had created. Warren, an engineer who is strong on detail, remembers it as five minutes before 3 A.M.

As I lay in the darkened den, I could hear their voices, wrangling. Jane said it must be the 24-hour-flu: "Let's wait until morning and see how she is." Warren said: "No, I can't find a pulse. It's serious. I'm calling an ambulance. Nan, do you want to go to the hospital now?" "Yes," I said. His choice, of course, was Rockford Memorial—the status Protestant hospital in Rockford where my family's doctors practiced.

The ambulance came within a few minutes in the wake of a sheriff's car and a fire truck. People in uniforms spoke gently, gave me oxygen. Lying in the ambulance, I could feel it surging forward, then beginning to turn right, toward Rockford Memorial, 15 minutes across town. I heard an emergency technician, 18-year-old Anita Powell, cry out: "Left! Left! Go to St. Anthony! She has no pulse! Rockford Memorial is 15 minutes away—she'll be D.O.A. [dead on arrival] if we go there! St. Anthony is three minutes from here—she'll have a chance."

"Do what she says," my sister told the driver. We turned left to St. Anthony Hospital, and my life may have been saved for the second time that night, following Warren's decision to call the ambulance.

In the early hours of Friday, Nov. 27, the baffled young medical staff on holiday emergency-room duty telephoned several physicians. One of them was Dr. Thomas E. Root, an infectious-diseases consultant for the Rockford community. He arrived at 7:30 A.M.

Dr. Root was informed about the vomiting, the diarrhea, the plummeting blood pressure. By then, a faint rash was also beginning to stipple my body. I did not develop the last of the disease's five classic acute symptoms—a fever of more than 102 degrees—until later. But Dr. Root is a brilliant diagnostician. And, incredibly, he and his colleagues had treated two similar cases within the previous year. "I think she has toxic shock syndrome," Dr. Root said to his colleagues. "Let's get going."

Most doctors have never seen, or have failed to recognize, a single case of this rare malady. Yet the St. Anthony doctors had treated two before me. The first, an 18-year-old who was hospitalized for six months in 1981, was left with total amnesia regarding the first weeks of her illness, but no other apparent damage. The second, a 17-year-old boy, who had a mild case, was out of the hospital within a week with no lasting damage.

"The most striking thing about you was your terribly ill appearance," Dr. Root recalled later. "Your whole legs and arms were blue—not just the fingers and toes. But the central part of your body, the trunk and your face, were more an ashen color. You were in profound shock. Your blood was not being pumped to your extremities. There was just almost no circulation at all. Your eyes were red, another important clue. But you were 55 years old, and you had not worn tampons since the onset of your menopause 11 years before." Nevertheless, Dr. Root made the diagnostic leap to toxic shock syndrome.

This is the story of how, almost miraculously and with brilliant care, I survived and prevailed over that grisly and still mysterious disease. Almost every major organ of my body, including my heart, lungs and liver, was deeply poisoned. I narrowly escaped brain damage and kidney collapse. The enzyme released into my bloodstream that reflected muscle destruction showed almost inconceivable damage—an abnormally high reading would have been anything over 100 units; I showed 21,000 units. At first, the Rockford doctors thought they would have to amputate my right leg and the toes of my left foot. Because of the treatment, my legs were saved. But the dry gangrene on eight fingers persisted.

The end joints of my fingers were amputated. In all, three operations were performed. The first, at St. Anthony on Jan. 14, 1982, was delayed in a successful effort to save more of each digit. The other operations, involving corrective surgery, took place at the University Hospital in New York at the end of April and again in May. The Illinois doctors theorized that gangrene had not affected my thumbs because the blood vessels in them were larger and nearer to a major artery.

This is also the story of how—with luck and expertise—this life threatening disease can be avoided or detected, monitored, treated and destroyed before it reaches the acute stage. Yet few physicians know how to test for it or what to do about it once the strain of a common bacterium, *Staphylococcus aureus,* releases its toxins. Toxic shock syndrome strikes healthy people like a tidal wave, without warning. Only two weeks before in New York, my internist of 25 years had said, after my annual physical checkup, which included a gynecological examination: "If you didn't smoke, Nan, you'd be perfect." Later, other doctors told me that smoking constricts blood vessels, further impeding circulation and thereby worsening gangrene when it occurs.

But, "Nobody should die of toxic shock syndrome," says Don Berreth, a spokesman for the United States Public Health Service's Centers for Disease Control in Atlanta, "provided one gets prompt treatment and appropriate supportive care." This view is shared by Dr. Kathryn N. Shands, the physician who until last June headed the Federal toxic shock syndrome task force at the C.D.C. and who has studied every case reported to it from January 1980 to last June.

Toxic shock is rooted in the public mind—and in the minds of many doctors as well—as a tampon-related disease. It is true that of menstruating cases, about two-thirds occur in women under the age of 25, almost all of whom are using tampons when the disease strikes. They are at very high risk.

But about 15 percent of all cases are nonmenstruating women, such as myself, men and children. In this group, there has been no recorded case of a recurrence of toxic shock.

Dr. Shands, warns, however, that a tristate study—conducted by the Wisconsin, Minnesota and Iowa departments of health—showed that menstruating women who have had toxic shock syndrome and who have not been treated with an antistaphylococcal antibiotic and who continue to wear tampons have possibly as high as a 70 percent chance—horrifyingly high—of getting toxic shock again. Some people have had their second episode six months later; others as soon as one month later." The shockingly high rate of recurrence among menstruating women indicates that most doctors may misdiagnose toxic shock the first time around, or that sufferers may not seek medical aid if the case is relatively mild.

The disease was first given its present name in 1978 by Dr. James K. Todd, an associate professor of pediatrics at the University of Colorado and director of infectious diseases at Denver Children's Hospital. Writing in the British medical publication *Lancet,* Dr. Todd described seven cases of the devastating malady he called toxic shock syndrome and suggested that staphylococcus bacteria may be the cause. His patients were seven children from 8 to 17 years old: three were boys and four were girls of menstrual age. One boy died with "irreversible shock" on the fourth day after being hospitalized. One girl, aged 15, suffered amputation of the end joints on two toes.

By June 1980, the national Centers for Disease Control had linked toxic shock with tampon use. The findings were based on a study it had conducted after surveys of victims of the disease by the Wisconsin state health department had suggested a correlation. Publicity about the disease ballooned, spreading alarm across the nation, particularly among the estimated 52 million American women who wear tampons.

Also that June, the C.D.C. toxic shock task force invited the major tampon manufacturers to Atlanta to brief them on the results of the studies. Shortly thereafter, the Federal Food and Drug Administration (F.D.A.) issued a ruling requesting tampon manufacturers to include warnings about their products.

As part of its surveillance, the C.D.C. began to take cultures of women patients at family-planning clinics for *Staphylococcus aureus*—a procedure as simple as obtaining a Pap smear to test for cervical cancer. It was found that 10 percent of the menstruating patients carried the bacterium in their vaginas, a statistic that still holds. "But it is not necessarily the particular strain that causes toxic shock syndrome," Dr. Shands pointed out in a recent telephone interview. Only "about 1 percent of all menstruating women," she said, "carry the poison-producing strain of the bacterium in their vaginas during their menstrual periods." Infectious-disease experts say that approximately 2 percent of the general population carry the poison-producing strain of Staphylococcus aureus in the mucous membranes of their noses.

In September 1980, the C.D.C. reported that of 50 toxic shock victims contacted who had become ill during the previous two months, 71 percent had used superabsorbent Rely tampons. Of the control group of 150 healthy women, 26 percent used Rely. From January through August of 1980, 299 cases had been reported. The death rate was 25 persons, or 8.4 percent.

Late in September 1980, after the C.D.C. toxic shock task force had met with F.D.A. officials in Washington about the matter, Procter & Gamble announced it would withdraw its Rely tampons from the market. (Other superabsorbent tampons, however, are still being marketed.) The company is now facing about 400 lawsuits from the surviving victims, or the next of kin of those who died. The plaintiffs have won every one of the half-dozen or so cases that have come to trial, and last month Procter & Gamble settled out of court with a woman whose original trial was the first against the company.

In October 1980, Procter & Gamble blitzed the country with advertisements encouraging women to stop using the superabsorbent Rely tampon. Then, both publicity and the number of reported cases among menstruating women fell precipitously in virtually all states.

One of the few exceptions is Minnesota, where the health department has vigorously ridden herd on doctors and hospitals to count and report all toxic shock cases. There, the incidence has remained at about nine cases a year for every 100,000 menstruating women. The severity of the disease can range from mild to fatal: The death rate in cases *reported* in 1981 was 3.3 percent overall, but the actual count is almost certainly higher, according to experts on the disease.

A National Academy of Sciences advisory panel also warned last June that toxic shock syndrome had not disappeared. Indeed, the academy's experts concluded, the disease is probably under-reported by physicians who don't recognize the symptoms in victims or don't report the cases they do identify to state authorities. State health agencies, however, are still giving notice of about 30 to 50 cases a month to the Centers for Disease Control in Atlanta.

Between 1970 and April 30, 1982, the Centers for Disease Control received word of 1,660 toxic shock cases, including 88 deaths. Although only 492 cases were reported in 1981, down from a high of 867 in 1980, the Institute of Medicine of the National Academy of Sciences estimated that the true number is about 10 times greater, or at least 4,500 a year. That estimate is based on figures from Minnesota.

Last month, the *Journal of the American Medical Association* carried an article by three doctors from the Yale University School of Medicine that said a review of five toxic shock studies found flaws that could lead to biased conclusions against tampons. However, an editorial in the same issue of the journal, while agreeing that there were deficiencies in the studies (the largest of which found tampon users were up to 18 times more likely than nonusers to develop the disease), said that "only substantial new research evidence evoking alternative explanations for the existing observations would be sufficient to negate the association between TSS in menstruating women and tampon use."

In the cases of non-menstruating victims, *Staphylococcus aureus* can enter the body through a post-surgical wound or boil; is found inside women who have recently given birth; or anywhere on the skin. According to Dr. Root, there is no evidence that it can be sexually transmitted. In my case, among many theories, a tiny sore on the vaginal wall "may have favored the staphylococcus getting there from somewhere on your skin and then growing," according to Dr. Root. The staph was also found in my colon and urinary tract.

I was one of the dangerously ill cases. For at least four days after toxic shock struck me, the Rockford doctors did not believe I would live. Dr. Edward Sharp, a leading surgeon at St. Anthony, who would later perform the first amputation of the ends of my fingers, alternately bullied and coaxed me to fight on, and was "amazed" that I survived. "If ever anybody had a good reason to die, you did," he said later. "Your age alone! If you had been a 15- or 20-year-old, it wouldn't be so unusual. Of course, this just means you're as tough as nails."

It also means the treatment was swift and superlative, once Dr. Root decided I had the syndrome. Afterwards, Dr. Root recalled: "There are two aspects to the therapy. One is the right antibiotic to treat the staphylococcus germ. Almost all staph is resistant to penicillin now." So he prescribed beta-lactamase-resistant antibiotics to inhibit and wipe out *Staphylococcus aureus* and to prevent recurrences. Last June, the National Academy of Sciences' advisory panel on toxic shock emphasized, however, that, in the disease as it usually appears in menstruation, "evidence is not available to indicate that such treatment ameliorates symptoms or shortens the course of the acute illness."

The two-pronged attack on the disease in my case began, as it would in all others, with "vigorous therapy for the cardiovascular collapse, the shock." And what that involves, Dr. Root said, "is massive amounts of intravenous fluid. Your body has to have a certain amount of fluid within the blood vessels, the heart, to be able to pump effectively."

The amount of fluid that flowed from wide-open bottles and flushed through me in the first 24 hours "would stagger the imagination of many physicians," Dr. Root declared. "You got approximately 24 liters, or quarts, of fluids. I think it was because of the 24 liters, 10 of which replaced fluid lost from vomiting and diarrhea before coming to the hospital, that your kidneys managed to make it through without being terribly damaged. You gained, with those fluids, about 40 pounds in the first day. Your body blew up."

At one point, a nurse emerged from the intensive-care cubicle where I lay and blurted out to my sister and brother-in-law: "Your sister has become a conduit."

"But if we hadn't kept that adequate volume of fluid in your blood, then the kidneys would have gone and we would have lost the whole ball game because everything would have collapsed," Dr. Root explained. "The single most important thing in your therapy, in my opinion, was the incredible volume of fluid we put into you, keeping some measure of circulation going. And then, as the effects of the poison weakened, that circulation eventually picked up and was enough to restore you back to normal."

I was left, however, with eight partially dead and gangrenous fingers; bilateral foot-drop, a form of paralysis in both feet caused by lack of blood flow resulting in damaged nerves, which can leave the patient with a permanent limp, and severely poison-damaged muscles all over my body.

"Shock basically means that your legs and arms were getting no circulating blood anymore, that the amount of blood in your body was so depleted because, first of all, you'd lost volumes and volumes of fluid from your diarrhea and vomiting," Dr. Root told me. "Secondly, with toxic shock, the whole body is damaged, so that the blood vessels, instead of holding the fluid that's circulating through them, leak it, and the blood doesn't flow well; it gets too thick. Your body is made so that at all costs it preserves the blood flow into the brain and the kidneys and the heart. When you lose blood pressure, those organs get the blood flow and the legs and arms don't."

About 12 hours into my hospitalization I slipped into a moderate coma, from which I did not emerge for two days. My brother-in-law went to the Rockford retirement home where my mother lives to tell her I might not make it. Forever gallant, she never showed me her grief and dread during the two months I was hospitalized in St. Anthony. Her tears were secret tears. The day before I was transferred to the Institute of Rehabilitation Medicine in New York, my mother confessed, "I have cried more in the last eight weeks than I have in all my 90 years."

In the first hours, a catheter was inserted into my heart so that the doctors could judge how much fluid to give me. Another tube ran from my trachea to a respirator to enable me to breathe.

Within the week, in a profound gift of friendship, Pat Novak, a close friend since college days and a doctor's daughter, came out to Illinois from New Jersey to stay by my side until the worst was over. She kept a daily diary which she later sent to me. These were her first impressions:

"I drove into St. Anthony Hospital and donned the gloves, mask, hat and apron required for the isolation unit. There, lost in a huge white bed, was a small face swathed in tape, with tubes from each nostril. Nan's sister, Jane, was there talking loudly, getting limited response from the brown eyes that opened occasionally as the head nodded, indicating a positive or negative response. A gurgling and hissing came from the respirator pumping oxygen directly into her lungs through the thick plastic tube in her nose.

"After asking permission of the nurses, I reached over to touch Nan. I stroked her tightly stockinged legs. Her eyes were wet with tears of welcome and gratitude. I saw the hands, fingers ending in charred and blackened tips, lifeless and distorted. Her arms were webbed in maroon rashes from her armpits to her wrists, sores and lesions and Band Aids, wounds of the battle of the past few days."

Shirley Katzander, another dear old friend who had already become my "information central" back East, arrived from New York for a visit. "Your hands were a mummy's hands," she told me long afterward. "The fingers were black and shriveled, with small, perfect black nails. I almost fainted when I saw them. Thank God you were asleep when I walked in and could not see my face."

It was clear by then that the ends of my fingers would have to be amputated. Both thumbs had been spared from gangrene, which meant that I could possibly retain 40 percent of my hand function, using my thumbs and palms only. The day the surgeon told me he would have to amputate, I was filled with horror. I was certain I would never be able to write again. I was still on the respirator, and speechless. My friend and executive editor at *The New York Times*, Abe Rosenthal, telephoned. Pat Novak broke the news. Abe began to cry. When he had composed himself, he said something that carried me through many of the hardest days: "For Chrissake, tell Nan we don't love her for her typewriter; tell her we love her for her mind."

Then I was swept with rage, rage that fate had once again struck me down, after 10 dark, troubled years following the traumatic death of my husband, Stan Levey, at the age of 56. Through my long struggle and the help of others, I had finally emerged the previous summer onto what Winston Churchill had called the "broad, sunlit uplands" of life.

But now, as soon as they took me off the respirator, I began to heap my anger onto my family, the doctors and the nurses. I reviled everyone who entered the room. I became impetuous, demanding, argumentative, impossible. One day, when my sister materialized at the foot of the bed, I looked at her with hatred. "Go home," I said, icily.

For at least 10 days I was possessed by fury, at everyone. One morning, I awoke and felt for the first time cleansed and filled with hope. "You have everything to live for," I told myself. That morning in late December 1981, my recovery truly began. It has been a long road back.

Among my Illinois doctors, I shall always cherish Dr. Root, the first to diagnose me correctly, and with whom I later had many instructive and comforting talks, and Dr. Sharp, the surgeon who took a risk and decided to wait before operating on my fingers, putting me as soon as possible into physical therapy. I had dry gangrene, akin to frostbite gangrene, not the wet burn gangrene that gets infected and spreads and so must be removed immediately. Day after day until mid-January 1982, as I winced with pain, Dr. Sharp would rip away bits of the hard black sheaths around my fingers to find, triumphantly, healthy pink flesh beneath. Then the physical therapists would pull and bend the joints of my fingers to bring them back to life and flexibility. "We saved an inch of your fingers," he said later—which meant I retained a whole middle joint on each of the eight affected digits.

Waiting to be operated on was agonizing. I longed for it to be over. Finally they had saved all the tissue they could. Dr. Sharp operated on Jan. 14, 1982, more than six weeks after the onset of toxic shock. I awoke from the anesthesia to find my hands suspended from bedside poles, swathed in bandages like boxing gloves. The healthy thumbs stuck out.

Two days later, Dr. Sharp unwound the bandages. I was afraid. Then I forced myself to look at what my hands had become. I felt a surge of relief and surprise. I rotated the hands, front and back, and told the doctors with a smile: "I can live with this." My truncated fingers did not repel me. Nor did they shock my family and friends. "This is the worst they will ever look," Dr. Sharp said.

Meantime, the doctors and therapists were fighting to save me from footdrop paralysis. I began to stand and walk in orthopedic shoes, with steel braces up to my knees. I exercised my legs and arms and hands obsessively, in bed and out. Under the sheets, I wore cross-shaped board splints attached to what I called "bunny boots" on my feet. I loathed them because they prevented me from turning on my side to sleep. I kept removing them. "If you don't wear them," Dr. Sharp finally warned me, "you will be a cripple for life." I wore them, after first making an enormous fuss, and was soon walking short distances—without braces, unaided and with only a slight limp when I was tired.

As yet another index of how catastrophic the sweep of toxic shock syndrome can be, I was treated by 14 doctors during the eight weeks at St. Anthony. They ranged from cardiologists and lung specialists to a podiatrist who cut thick crusts from my toes and the soles of my feet. The cost of the eight weeks' hospitalization in Rockford was $35,000, not counting the doctors' fees. Ahead lay additional tens of thousands of dollars in New York, in hospital stays, additional surgery and daily out-patient therapy on my hands, which will continue for months to come.

On Jan. 26, 1982, my brother-in-law and sister put me on a plane, homeward-bound to New York. For weeks, I had wanted to return to the city that was the center of my life and my career, and by then, thanks to my Illinois doctors, I was well enough to make the trip. I had had the good fortune to be accepted by the Institute of Rehabilitation Medicine, of New York University Medical Center, on East 34th Street, commonly known as the Rusk Institute, after its founder, Dr. Howard A. Rusk, the great father of rehabilitation for the disabled. I went there by ambulance directly from the airport.

It is a place with miracles in every room, with people in wheel-chairs crowding the halls like the pilgrims at Lourdes. During 17 days there as an inpatient, the beneficiary of some of the most sophisticated physical and occupational therapy available anywhere, I progressed by quantum leaps. It seems incredible to me, considering the vast need, that there are only a half-dozen civilian rehabilitation centers associated with university hospitals around the United States, outside the Veterans Administration network.

I was so rare, as the first and only case of toxic shock seen at the hospital despite its worldwide reputation, that the doctors and nurses looked at me as if I were a piece of the Ark. "They will not believe your medical records from St. Anthony," Dr. Sharp had predicted, and he was right. Dr. Root had also delivered himself of a statement the day before my discharge from the Rockford hospital. "You now know more about toxic shock syndrome," said this expert, "than the majority of physicians in the United States."

For instance, the terrifyingly high rate of recurrence in menstruating victims—70 percent—indicates that most doctors may misdiagnose toxic shock the first time around, or that the sufferers may not get to a doctor if the case is relatively mild. My gynecologist in New York, Dr. Howard Berk, who has seen several hospitalized toxic shock cases some time after acute onset, said he advises his patients "to call me immediately and urgently if they have sudden high fever, vomiting or diarrhea during their menstrual period—it could point to toxic shock syndrome." Although it is most unlikely that I will ever get the disease again, because I have not menstruated for more than 11 years, Dr. Berk is monitoring me carefully. He now examines me every three months; takes cultures of my nasal mucosa and vagina for Staphylococcus aureus, and immediately after my discharge from Rusk began a program of local estrogen therapy to strengthen the vaginal walls, thus preventing irritation.

Publicity and the performance of the tampon manufacturers in warning users about toxic shock have been spotty since Procter & Gamble took superabsorbent Rely off the market in late 1980. A new

F.D.A. ruling issued last June 22—and effective in December—requires a warning on the outside of tampon boxes and a longer explanation of the association between toxic shock and tampons on the leaflet inside the package.

Right now, the major manufacturers of superabsorbent tampons have warning notices on the boxes or on their inside instruction leaflets, or both.

This year, International Playtex Inc., which manufactures Playtex superabsorbent tampons, has been running a television commercial that begins: "Brenda Vaccaro for Playtex tampons. If I was a mother of a teenager, I'd tell her to buy Playtex tampons ..." —thus aiming at the age group that is at the highest risk of getting toxic shock syndrome.

When Walter W. Bregman, president of Playtex, U.S., was asked to comment on that television advertisement, he said: "The objective of the current Brenda Vaccaro commercial is to appeal and communicate to a variety of women, both in terms of age—in other words, those both older and younger than Brenda—and those with and without children. It is not intended to reach only teenagers, and, in fact, Burke day-after recall research indicates this commercial most effectively communicates to women 25 to 34 years of age."

Government research has shown that a blood-filled tampon can provide a place for the growth of *Staphylococcus aureus*. "What we think probably happens is that the staph either grow better in the presence of menstrual fluid and a tampon, or they produce toxin better in the presence of menstrual fluid and a tampon," said Dr. Shands of the C.D.C. toxic shock task force. The bacterium was not found on unused tampons, but could be grown on them. One study showed that the "supers" absorb more fluid, making the vaginal walls dryer and more subject to irritation. Dr. Shands pointed out that the risk of using superabsorbent tampons is greater than the risk of using less absorbent tampons. At least one case of toxic shock in women using sea sponges had also been recorded.

Testing for *Staphylococcus aureus* might be a good idea in my case, but not in many others, according to Dr. Kathryn Shands. "You could pick up *Staph. aureus* from someone else at any time," she said, by touching them or from particles of a sneeze. In addition, you could pick it up and carry it in your nose, and you'd certainly never know it, and transfer it to your vagina at any time. So suppose you went to your gynecologist today and said, 'Please do a culture for *Staph. aureus,* and he did and said, 'It's negative. There's no *Staph. aureus.*'

There's nothing to prevent your picking up *Staph. aureus* on Saturday."

She went on: "So in order to have some reasonably high degree of certainty that you will not develop toxic shock syndrome with this menstrual period, you would have to go in the day before your menstrual period and every day during your period and have *Staph. aureus* cultures done. And you would have to do it for every menstrual period every month. Pretty expensive for you and pretty much a waste of time. And if you multiply it by the millions of menstruating women in the United States, it becomes a ridiculous exercise: the entire health budget could be used up doing just that."

Asked if there is any way a young woman can eliminate the risk of coming down with toxic shock syndrome, Dr. Shands replied: "She could not use tampons." She hastened to add: "What we've tried to do is put the whole thing into perspective. You are more likely to be killed in a car accident than you are to get toxic shock syndrome. Not *die* from toxic shock syndrome, but *get* toxic shock syndrome. And yet people make the choice every day to drive cars. And if you want to take protective measures, you are far likelier to *die* from lung cancer from smoking cigarettes than you are to *get* toxic shock syndrome when using tampons."

From a doctor's point of view, such a perspective is no doubt reasonable. From my point of view, as I continue the torturous process of regaining the use of my hands and right leg, such statistics seem irrelevant.

The day after I was admitted to Rusk, Dr. Krisjan T. Ragnarsson, my chief physician there, did the first evaluation of me based on my Rockford medical records and his own hospital's neurological, muscle and mental tests. My first question of the day was: "Will I ever take notes again?" Dr. Ragnarsson nodded and said, "Yes." "Will I ever type again?" I persisted. His rosy face darkened. Then he smiled. "Oh, well, all you newspaper people are hunt-and-peck typists with two fingers, anyway," he responded. I said, "Dr. Ragnarsson, I have been a touch typist, using all 10 digits, since I was 18 years old." He looked somber again. I did not pursue my queries.

For a long time, pain was my daily companion. The worst is now over, but Dr. Ragnarsson believes it could be one or two more years, or never, before normal sensation returns to my finger tips and my right foot. The recovery time depends on how far up the toxic shock struck my limbs, since the nerve endings regenerate at the rate of about an inch in a month.

I have been an outpatient at Rusk five afternoons a week since my discharge last Feb. 12.

On Feb. 13, back in my own apartment and alone after 10 and a half weeks of being hospitalized, I totally panicked for the first time. Because of the long Lincoln-Washington holiday weekend, I was not immediately able to arrange for a nurse's aide to help me readjust. I could not turn a single knob on any door, or any faucet, or the stereo, or the television set. I could not wash myself, dress or undress myself, pull a zipper, button a button, tie shoelaces. Punching the telephone numbers with one thumb, I called Nancy Sureck, perhaps the most maternal of all my friends, awakening her and her husband, David. "Help," I said. Nancy was at my side within the hour, taking charge. The next week I hired a wonderful nurse's aide for the mornings; afternoons I was at Rusk; evenings, a half-dozen close women friends took turns coming in to fix dinner and pop me into bed. Harriet Van Horne, another earth mother, always arrived, like Little Red Riding Hood, with a basket of exquisite home-cooked goodies.

It was months before I could open a taxi door on my way to and from the outpatient hand clinic at Rusk. The cabdrivers of New York, with one exception, invariably sprang to my rescue with a gallantry that amazed, amused and touched me. I had decided to try a frontal, self-confident approach to all strangers in this tough city. I would hail a cab, hold up my hands and say with a smile, "I have a bum hand— could you open the door for me?" Without an instant's hesitation, the drivers would leap around to the back door and open it with a flourish. As we approached our destination, I would hand them my wallet, tote bag or purse and they would hold up each bill and coin like a rosary or miraculous medal or baby to be blessed. "This is a dollar bill," they would say. "This is a quarter," and then return the rest of the money to its place. One driver said, "Even my wife won't trust me with her wallet," and another muttered, "Anyone takes advantage of you should be shot."

Once, in bitter cold that turned my fingers purple because I could not bear yet to wear gloves or mittens, or stick my fingers into my pockets, I could not find an unoccupied taxi. An off-duty cabbie finally stopped in the rush-hour crush for my young, beautiful occupational therapist Gail Geronemus, while she explained why he should take me. As we reached one end of my block, we saw a fire engine blocking the other end. A policeman approached the taxi. "Back up," he commanded. "Hey, hey, this lady's come straight from surgery!" cried the driver, lying with that brilliant New York penchant for instant invention. "We've got to get her through to Number 44!" "Back up," the stone-faced cop repeated. The two men exchanged a stream of obscenities. When I had recovered from my laughter, I told the cabbie that I could make it to my apartment in the middle of the block. As usual, he hopped around to open the back door. I got to my lobby, and burst into tears of fatigue and relief.

The one and only stinker cabbie was an elderly man who refused to roll down his window or open the back door for me. I finally asked a woman on the street corner to help; she complied with alacrity and without asking why. "You roll down the window, you get a gun to your head," the driver said. When I had settled inside, he snarled, "You got only one bum hand, why didn't you open the door with the other?" I shrieked back: "Because all the fingers on both my hands have been amputated!" He almost dissolved into a heap of ashes. "I'm sorry, lady," he said, while a surge of gratifying catharsis rolled through me. I reflected later that I had finally expressed my deepest, pent-up resentments for the first time since my rages in St. Anthony.

Every day of my recovery had brought its frustrations and disasters—and triumphs. On March 25 at the Rusk Institute's hand clinic, Gail, my occupational therapist, said, seemingly casually: "Why don't you try out our electric typewriter?" I was stunned with the enormity of her suggestion. I had thought it would be months before I would be able to attempt such a thing. I went to the typewriter. With incredible slowness and apprehension, I pecked out, "Now is the time ..." As the letters appeared on the paper, I began to sob. Gail and Ellen Ring, my physical therapist, rushed to my side. "Are you in pain?" they chorused. "These are tears of joy," I said.

Almost six weeks after I had begun outpatient therapy at Rusk, Gail wrote this evaluation of me: "Patient tends to protect her hypersensitive stumps by using her palms and thumbs instead of her fingers. She self-splints her hands [holds wrists, hands and fingers rigidly upright] by using her palms and thumbs instead of her fingers to complete various tasks." The tasks I could not properly perform then included picking up coins and unscrewing jar lids.

But, day by day, my occupational and physical therapists were bringing my hands back to life and function. Traumatized by toxic shock, gangrene and then surgery, my finger tips—the most sensitive part of the body, I had been told—had stiffened straight out, the opposite of a stroke victim's fingers that often curl into claws. As an outpatient, I began to wear custom-made "splints," which consisted of castlike wrist braces, leather nooses for each finger and rubber bands that passively pulled my fingers down into fists so that I could grasp objects. These splints perform much like braces on a child's teeth, without active effort on the wearer's part.

There were endless, excruciatingly boring but vital exercises at home. At the clinic, I pawed through coffee cans heaped with raw rice, kidney beans, macaroni and gravel to toughen my finger ends: this invariably set my teeth on edge. I hated the touch of metal of any kind, such as the nails I had to pick up and put in the holes. But there is no way to win at physical therapy without working through pain to healing. "There are the survivors, and there are those who would rather take 50 pills and just slip under," a nurse at Rusk told me. "All human beings divide into those two groups. I have even seen babies who do not want to live—who literally pined away and died."

By early May, I was able to open taxi doors with two hands, and the door knob crisis was over. I was buttoning my blouses and dresses in a trice with a button hook, and awkwardly cutting the top off my breakfast soft-boiled egg with a knife encased in a tube of foam that provides a wider gripping surface. By mid-June, I could punch a push-button telephone with my index finger. (I am still having trouble cutting meat.) By late July, my therapists were "thrilled" with my progress in hand strength, dexterity and range of motion.

Just as important, Dr. Barry M. Zide, a skilled young plastic surgeon at University Hospital, with which Rusk is associated, liberated me from much of my pain in two operations on my fingers last April 29 and May 26. One of my doctors at Rusk had run into Dr. Zide, a kind of Alan Alda in "M*A*S*H"—witty, irreverent and all heart as well as talent—in the hospital corridor just after failing, as had two other doctors, to remove the Illinois surgical stitches from my fingertips without causing me agony. "No problem," said Dr. Zide. "I'll throw a nerve block in her wrists." The next day, painlessly, he took the sutures out, and I fell in love with yet another doctor.

He then told me to brace myself for more surgery. With a sinking heart, I heard him say: "I can see by the way your nails are coming in that you are set up for chronic infection as soon as the nails grow back. In addition, the unpadded skin at the fingertips will never withstand the constant trauma of daily living. The bone below this thin skin is surely going to become exposed and infected."

First on the left hand in April and then on the right in May, Dr. Zide amputated up to half an inch of some fingers, removing the nailbeds and infected bone. The thicker, more resilient skin on the palm side of my fingers was then draped over the newly shaped bone. Within a week, I was making tremendous progress in the use of my hands and becoming increasingly independent in every facet of my daily life.

My story is almost over except for one crucial detail: My deepest fear did not materialize.

I have typed the thousands of words of this article, slowly and with difficulty, once again, able to practice my craft as a reporter. I have written it—at last—with my own hands.

ANALYSIS

WRITERS FREQUENTLY COMPLAIN they have trouble with certain types of stories, but Nan Robertson's problems had nothing to do with writer's block or lack of time. Robertson wrote "Toxic Shock" after recovering from losing the end joints of all eight of her fingers.

"When I was typing the piece on the computer, it was extremely painful," she concedes. "It was about a month after my last series of amputations that I began to type the piece. It was so painful and the stumps were so swollen and sore, I could only type about 250-500 words a day. And I would go home with my finger ends just screaming."

On the positive side, Robertson points out it was effective therapy for toughening the stubs of her amputated finger ends and less excruciating than her usual regimen of pawing through coffee cans filled with rice, macaroni or gravel.

Like many writers, Robertson feels a need to devise a compelling lead before she proceeds further. She has long won prizes within *The Times* for her leads and says, "Unless I get the lead right, the story doesn't seem to hang right."

For "Toxic Shock," she "wanted to do a cinematic lead, something that absolutely knocks the reader in the eye—a visual thing. I wanted to show the reader how fast [toxic shock] comes and how devastating it is."

On a secondary note, she wanted to develop a contrast between going dancing "at a ball at the Plaza Hotel with a man I had just fallen in love with" and being near death 24 hours later.

"The lead was the easiest thing," she admits:

I went dancing the night before in a black velvet Paris gown, on one of those evenings that was the glamour of New York epitomized. I was blissfully asleep at 3 A.M.

Twenty-four hours later, I lay dying, my fingers and legs darkening with gangrene.

Robertson also spent some care with the ending:

I have typed the thousands of words of this article, slowly and with difficulty, once again able to practice my craft as a reporter. I have written it—at last—with my own hands.

(In fact, for the cover of *The New York Times Magazine*, Robertson's lead and ending were stitched together in large type around a photo of her amputated finger ends typing on a keyboard.)

After the lead, Robertson uses some amazingly descriptive language to move the story forward, including:

I awoke, trancelike, in the middle of the night to find myself crawling and crashing up the stairs to the bathroom. The vomiting and diarrhea were cataclysmic.

Later, in a taut ambulance ride to the hospital, Robertson recreates the exact dialogue as emergency medical technicians increase the tension of the moment:

"She has no pulse! ... She'll be D.O.A. if we go there [Rockford Memorial]!"

Robertson initially sticks with the first-person voice until she discusses toxic shock syndrome in detail. At that point she skillfully slows down the story by presenting a complex and comprehensive explanation of TSS in the third person. Back in the intensive care unit, as doctors initially doubt she will live, Robertson returns to first person as the text immediately pulls the reader forward again.

Recognizing that switching voices would slow the story down, Robertson says: "It was a risk I had to take. I realize these transitions are very difficult but it had to be made because there was no way I could give the medical information in first person."

As such, Robertson's story differs from the other compelling medical story in this book ("Mrs. Kelly's Monster") because she felt the need to work in vital TSS information outweighed the literary convenience of a seamless narrative.

Robertson says she also interviewed all the doctors, nurses, physical therapists and ambulance attendants she dealt with as one tactic to recreate the exact dialogue and quotes that make this story so riveting.

"I'll tell you something [else] that doctors and psychiatrists know," she continues. "If you are going through a trauma, everything is burned in your memory. I was still conscious, so I could hear the ambulance driver shout to the driver and hear my sister saying 'do what she says' ... before I began to lose consciousness."

Robertson says she "also sprung my medical records from the moment I was admitted to the emergency room at St. Anthony's Hospital on Thanksgiving night in 1981." She hired a young doctor to translate the medical jargon into plain English—and help with other medical questions.

Robertson skillfully uses her ordeal to present readers with the far-reaching implications of the disease, often using her TSS as a jumping-off point to discuss how tampon manufacturers are dealing with TSS, who is vulnerable to the disease, reoccurrence possibilities, etc. Robertson continually fills her article with such minute and major details.

Robertson makes no attempt to protect her vulnerabilities or spare herself unnecessary embarrassment in this story, offering intense personal details about her illness, her body, even how badly she treats her family and friends at some points. Some of the paragraphs about her personal battle and suffering are hard to read, yet crucial to the narrative, such as this quote from her doctor:

"You got approximately 24 liters, or quarts, of fluid. I think it was because of that 24 liters, 10 of which replaced fluid lost from vomiting and diarrhea before coming to the hospital, that your kidneys managed to make it through without being terribly damaged. You gained, with those fluids, about 40 pounds in the first day. Your body blew up."

Or this telling sentence:

As I winced with pain, Dr. Sharp would rip away bits of the hard black sheaths around my fingers to find, triumphantly, healthy pink flesh beneath.

Although interviewing people even while still in her hospital bed and unable to take written notes, Robertson still called on her ability to inspire trust to snare great quotes. Robertson says empathy is one of the most valuable tools of a feature reporter. "Your interviewing technique rises out of your own personality," she believes.

Robertson says she especially admires the interviewing skills and hard work of Rick Bragg, also of *The New York Times* (1996 Pulitzer).

Finally, Robertson's text is further enhanced by little anecdotes she interjects that bring her experience home to the reader on a very personal and realistic level. A classic example of this is the courtesy shown by many otherwise cynical New York cabdrivers when they realized Robertson's finger ends had been amputated and she couldn't open the taxi doors by herself.

It's unlikely that many readers, including the most sophisticated, will experience a better first-person story than this one—a fact the 1983 Pulitzer Prize judges validated.

NAN ROBERTSON has been the Eugene Roberts Visiting Professor of Journalism at the University of Maryland since 1994. She is the author of two books: *Getting Better: Inside Alcoholics Anonymous* (William Morrow) and *The Girls in The Balcony: Women, Men, and The New York Times* (Random House). Robertson is a graduate of the Medill School of Journalism at Northwestern University.

1984

PETER RINEARSON

WHEN PETER RINEARSON, still on the sunny side of age 30, took over the aerospace beat at *The Seattle Times* in 1982, he had a couple of strikes against him as far as local giant Boeing was concerned. First, his predecessor "had covered Boeing on a very familiar basis for longer than I had been alive," Rinearson recalls. "Boeing has a reputation for being cautious with the press and the company's public relations representatives were especially cautious with me.

"It probably didn't help that I'd covered the state legislature previously and had a reputation among Boeing lobbyists as a skeptic of some of the company's legislative initiatives," he believes.

Starting such a major beat without sources, Rinearson says he needed a way to get inside the company. As luck would have it, Boeing was about to put two jetliners into commercial service. "I'd read Tracy Kidder's *Soul of a New Machine,* which was the story of the creation of a computer, and John Newhouse's *A Sporty Game,* which described the excitement of the commercial jetliner business."

Rinearson decided to propose a "Kidder-style" treatment on the birth of a jetliner to his editors. "I pitched the idea to Boeing and my editors as a six-week project and there was a fair amount of enthusiasm for it," he recalls.

When word of his Pulitzer came in April of 1994, Rinearson was writing a book and on leave of absence from the paper. "I'd completely forgotten about it," he remembers. "I got a phone call from one of the assistant city editors. He opened the conversation by saying, 'I need a quote.'" Momentarily puzzled, Rinearson tried to remember what he could have left out of a story.

"I asked him what kind of quote he needed and he told me

I'd won the Pulitzer Prize for Feature Writing and the quotation he needed was my reaction.

"This was a bizarre moment," according to Rinearson. "My work had been a finalist in National Reporting but the judges moved it to the Feature Writing category to give it the prize. What a lottery! I'd won in a category I didn't even enter."

Actually, Rinearson says his greatest pride came a few months later when an editor handed him a short AP story that said the Pulitzer Board had created the Explanatory Journalism category, citing "Making It Fly" as a justification for the new category.

Rinearson says he was prepared (by friends) for less-than-enthusiastic reactions in the newsroom if he won the Pulitzer. He feels two pieces of advice from one such friend helped him deal with the award. "First, if you win a Pulitzer, get out of the newsroom as fast as you can for as long as you can. Second, treat the prize as nothing more than a tool to achieve more with your career. A major prize should be viewed as part of the means rather than an end in and of itself."

Rinearson did both, extending his leave and assuming a very low profile in the newsroom when he returned. Within a couple of years he left *The Seattle Times* to write books and start a software company.

But the following story, breathtaking in its scope and detail, is a masterpiece in any Pulitzer category—National, Explanatory or Feature.

Making It Fly
The Seattle Times

June 19–26, 1983

DURING A 2½-MILE DRIVE *skirting the edge of Miami's international airport, Frank Borman and Tex Boullioun agreed to an enormous gamble.*

Borman, president of Eastern Airlines, and Boullioun, then presi-

dent of Boeing's commercial airplane division, knew the gravity of the decision they were making. But it wasn't apparent from their casual, confident manner during the four-minute automobile ride on a sun-drenched August day in 1978.

Boeing and Eastern had talked for much of 1977 and 1978 about a new airplane, one on which both Borman and Boullioun would risk the futures of their companies.

They had some ideas. The airplane would be a much-updated derivative of the popular single-aisle Boeing 727, with two engines instead of three. It would have about 160 seats. Eastern and British Airways together would launch the airplane, giving Boeing the sales orders and cash to begin production.

Then, on that August morning in Miami, Borman surprised Boullioun and other Boeing executives who had gathered at Eastern's headquarters at the edge of the airport. Borman asked to see data on a hypothetical plane about 15 seats bigger than they'd talked about earlier.

Boeing officials, though not eager to increase the size of the plane, obliged and laid out the material for Borman, who was noncommittal. Boullioun had to leave early, and Borman said he'd see him to the airport terminal.

Once together in the back of the car, Borman told Boullioun he liked the bigger airplane design and was willing to gamble on it.

"All at once Borman had a flash that a 175-passenger airplane was what Eastern wanted," Boullioun recalled. "He said, 'If you'd build that, we'll go.' "

Boullioun replied: "You've got it."

And so, with a handshake—just as the car jiggled over some railroad tracks—the Boeing 757 was born.

"It was a recognition of months and months of negotiation," Borman recalled recently. "Finally we had an accommodation. We knew we were going to be able to do it. They laid out just the airplane we wanted."

Launching a commercial airplane project sobers an airline because it must hazard millions of dollars on a plane that won't fly for years.

But an airline's risks pale next to those of an airplane manufacturer, which may spend $1.5 billion or more on a new design. Not many new aircraft are launched, because a sales flop literally can drive a manufacturer out of the commercial airplane business, as Lockheed proved with its L-1011 jetliner.

"It's the world's biggest poker game. The risks are fantastic," said

Ken Holtby, a Boeing vice president. "We bet the company over and over again in terms of our net worth."

Today the 757 is in service with both Eastern Airlines and British Airways and is proving Boeing's claims that it would be the world's most fuel-efficient airplane.

But bringing together the elements to make a new idea fly is an immensely detailed process. In the case of the 757, it began well before Borman and Boullioun shook hands, and still isn't finished.

"Sometimes I sit back in amazement and look up at an airplane flying overhead," said Malcolm Stamper, president of the parent Boeing Co. "It's flying people at these tremendous speeds over long distances. And, you think, it was just a bunch of parts, pieces of paper on the ground.

"I think when you build an airplane for the first time it's an excitement, because it didn't exist. Take the 757. Somebody said, "We'll cut out this piece of sheet metal and we'll bend it this way. And we'll go get this wire and we'll string it this way. And this pipe and bend it.

"And they put all these things together and they're inanimate. Nothing's moving. Then they fill it up with fuel, light it up, and it takes off and flies! It becomes alive all of a sudden."

PART I: THE BIG GAMBLE

BOEING loses millions of dollars on every new 757 it sells.

But someday—if fate cooperates, if the wager pays off, if enough of the twin-engined jetliners are sold—the 757 will become hugely profitable. Or at least that's Boeing's hope.

It's all part of what Sanford McDonnell, chairman of McDonnell Douglas, has called a "sporting business that rivals Las Vegas."

More than one airplane manufacturer has been driven from the jetliner field by the commercial failure of a jetliner which was a technological success. Lockheed bowed out of the business two years ago after losing $2.5 billion on its L-1011, a popular wide-body jetliner similar to the DC-10.

In fact, of all the jetliners ever made in Europe or the United States, only two, the Boeing 707 and 727, are said certainly to have made a profit. The DC-9 and 747 may yet become profitable. The DC-8, the DC-10, the L-1011, even the 737 ... all these airplanes, and more, have lost money for their manufacturers.

So when Boeing elects to risk $1.5 billion or more to build a new airplane, it does so warily and with great forethought.

The 1978 decision to build the 757 was not reached easily or quickly. It involved sophisticated forecasts of international politics and economics and the advancing state of technology.

But the world airline industry is volatile, and unexpected developments can destroy the best-laid plans. An airplane concept that is promising one year may be pointless the next, ruined by the changing needs of the industry. There's a saying in the airplane-manufacturing industry: "Long-range forecasting is the day after tomorrow."

Still, Boeing predicts both the 757 and its companion, the 767, will be moneymakers. Design and manufacturing costs have been contained and the long-term market for the planes is large, company officials say.

Boeing's confidence is not universally shared. The 767 is competing directly with a similar airplane, the Airbus A-310, and the slightly smaller 757 is judged by many to be too similar to the 767 in passenger capacity.

What's more, the market for airplanes is small. Only about 300 airlines in the world buy jetliners, and some place only modest orders.

The 757 is praised by its customers and suppliers and undoubtedly is a technological marvel, but critics contend that Boeing misread the crystal ball and built the wrong airplane—a fine airplane, but the *wrong* fine airplane.

Carl Munson, Boeing's vice president for strategic planning, said the company built the 757 and 767 because it couldn't afford to sit still while the world changed.

"You either are continually modernizing your product line or you're going backwards," he said. "You have to spend and improve just to stay in the same place from a marketing perspective."

The company, which has built two-thirds of the jetliners in the Western world, updates existing airplanes as much as possible before launching new ones, Munson said. But that only works for so long.

When the time comes to launch a brand-new airplane, as Boeing did in 1978 with both the 757 and 767, the company must gaze into the future and take huge a gamble—take what Boeing Chairman T.A. Wilson has called "a hell of a risk decision."

TEN YEARS AGO, Boeing was searching for a new project.

Hopes had centered on a supersonic transport, but Congress cut off federal funds for the SST in March 1971. Boeing, racked by depression in the airline industry and early troubles with its 747 program, was forced to reduce Puget Sound employment from 101,000 in 1968 to 38,000 at the beginning of 1972.

What was next?

The company was strongly attracted to the concept of a joint venture with overseas aerospace interests.

E.H. "Tex" Boullioun, then president of the Boeing Commercial Airplane Co., began negotiating with potential overseas partners who might share some of the responsibilities the Seattle company traditionally had assumed on a new-airplane project. Such an arrangement would reduce Boeing's risks and costs.

It was an attractive idea because it could lend to a new airplane an international flavor which could help sales overseas, and would skirt anti-trust laws which prohibit too much collaboration between U.S. firms.

At the same time, it would not reduce Boeing's percentage of work on a new airplane because the company already subcontracts about 50 percent of its manufacturing, mostly to other U.S. firms.

"It was my belief," Boullioun said, "that it was in the best interests of the United States to combine with the European nations in the technology of airplanes, as long as we always put out 50 percent of an airplane, both in weight and in dollars."

Boeing wasn't the only company thinking about internationalism. Britain's Rolls-Royce was making engines for Lockheed L-1011s, and the inherently international Airbus Industrie first flew its 240-passenger A–300 late in 1972.

That same year, Boeing struck a 50-50 deal with Aeritalia, Italy's government-owned aircraft manufacturer, to build a quiet, short-haul airplane. It was dubbed the 7X7.

Italian engineers were dispatched to Seattle to receive instruction. Italy paid Boeing, which was strapped for cash.

But Boeing lost interest and unilaterally withdrew from the partnership, leaving behind a badly upset Italy.

"As we were developing this quiet airplane, we came into the 1973 period and the Yom Kippur War and fuel prices went from 9 cents a gallon to 35 and 36 cents a gallon real quick," said John Swihart, who played a role in Boeing's airplane-development plans throughout the 1970s.

"As soon as that happened, there was a great change in emphasis, because you needed fuel efficiency more than you needed the quiet-noise aspect."

Boeing's focus shifted to new designs stressing fuel efficiency, but the name 7X7 stuck.

It wasn't any single airplane or idea. The concept kept changing. Sometimes it had four engines, sometimes three, sometimes two. Sometimes it was a short-haul plane, sometimes medium-haul.

Sometimes the engines were mounted on top of the wings, sometimes below.

Wilson was quoted in mid-1973 on why "X" was in the name: "The design boys wanted a specific number. I said no: A number would imply we know what the hell we're going to build and we don't. So the 7X7 is whatever we're going to do next."

Gradually, the 7X7 designs focused on wide-body configurations with two passenger aisles, but it wasn't even determined whether the airplane would have two engines or three.

Nothing was unusual about Boeing trying to intrigue airlines with numerous and ever-changing concepts. For every new airplane model Boeing builds, literally hundreds of designs never escape the drawing boards. The company has fleets of planes that never flew, and fine balsa models of discarded designs adorn the offices of many Boeing executives.

Boeing and its competitors even try to "sell" designs they know they wouldn't build. "You're trying to show the customer that, by golly, you've still got good ideas," a Boeing sales executive explained.

EVEN WHILE the 7X7 design was being offered around in various twin-aisle guises, Boeing began to talk in 1974 about a second new airplane. It would have a single aisle and less capacity than the 7X7.

All-new designs are extremely costly, however, so the second airplane Boeing had in mind would be a substantially modified 727.

It was to be called the 727-300 and would feature a stretched body, refined wings, moderately improved engines and new landing gear. "It was all of the technology that we could put in, in a cost-effective manner," said Duane Jackson, a lead designer on the project.

Boeing had United Airlines in mind as the first, or "launch" customer, for the 727-300, and United was interested. Braniff said it could use the plane by 1977, too.

But customer interest, though essential to creation of a new airplane, is not enough to ensure it will be built. Showing a design, even negotiating a possible deal, is a far cry from agreeing to take the gamble.

In the case of the 727-300, however, Boeing was ready to go. And it seemed, at least to Boeing, that United was ready to buy 50 of the planes for about $600 million.

Boeing announced that the program was officially going ahead with United as the first customer. But then the press release was abruptly withdrawn, because on Aug. 28, 1975, United announced it was not buying the 727-300.

Edward Carlson, United's chairman, praised the plane and blamed economic conditions and the lack of "reasonable (tax) incentives" for halting the purchase.

But Edward Beamish, the airline's senior vice president for corporate planning, today recalls that United really was "not all that close" to launching the 727-300. "We decided it wasn't a good investment" because it didn't offer enough of an improvement in fuel efficiency, he said.

"It was a matter of disappointment," remembers Jackson, the Boeing designer.

Jackson and a small group of designers spent the remainder of 1975 trying to breathe life back into the 727-300 by finding design changes that might cut the cost of the airplane enough to attract United.

But every time the designers eliminated some costly innovation, they also reduced the airplane's value to the airline. "We spent four or five months understanding that there wasn't another alternative that would satisfy," Jackson said.

The 727-300 was dead, another plane that never flew.

Nevertheless, Boeing remained committed to the idea of two new airplanes, a double-aisle 7X7 and a single-aisle 727-like airplane.

In January 1976, the 7N7 was born from the ashes of the 727-300. It was to retain many key body sections and concepts of the 727, but would have broad innovations, too.

Eventually, after 339 rejected designs, the 7N7 would evolve into the 757 of today.

The 7N7 was destined to become the twin-aisle 767.

SINGLE-AISLE and double-aisle airplanes each have virtues, and Boeing wanted to build a new one of each type.

A wide body has a spacious feeling and the second aisle allows easier passenger movement, especially when food carts are blocking one aisle. A wide body also can carry an appreciable amount of cargo.

A single-aisle airplane has a narrower body which slices through the atmosphere more easily and hence is substantially more fuel-efficient to fly. But it carries much less cargo than a wide-body, and passengers may feel cramped on long flights.

Boeing saw the 7X7 with two aisles and the 7N7 with one aisle. The 7X7 was to be a derivative of the single-aisle 727, though much more updated than the 727-300 idea United had rejected.

Although the 7N7 would retain many of the 727's body sections, thus saving vast sums on tooling and production experience, it also would employ advanced technology where it really counted—especially in the engines and wing.

One reason Boeing wanted to build two new airplanes at once was to hedge its bets.

If it had known exactly what kind of airplane would be needed in the 1980s, a single plane would have been enough. "Frankly," Boeing vice president Ken Holtby once explained, "our ability to forecast is so lousy that the only way you can survive is to cover all your bets."

Munson, Boeing's strategic planner, said launching both the 757 and 767 amounted to using a shotgun to hit a target. A rifle wouldn't do because Boeing had to fire the shot years in advance, and didn't know where the bulls-eye would be.

The company began moving forward on the 757 on two fronts, domestic and foreign.

Within the U.S., it looked to Eastern Airlines as a possible launch customer for the narrow-body airplane. Outside the country its attention focused on Great Britain and its multiple attractions in the form of three government-owned industries.

One of them, British Airways, wanted a 757-like airplane for its many short-haul routes in Europe. It was a large international airline and an attractive launch customer, and if Boeing could get both it and Eastern to buy the 757 in substantial numbers, the company could put the airplane into production.

Another industry, Rolls-Royce, was a jet-engine manufacturer that was hungry for a strong connection with a U.S. airplane manufacturer. Boeing was its first choice, for Rolls saw in Boeing's planes a large and enduring market for its engines—which sell for about $3 million each and require periodic replacement.

The third industry, which then was a group of companies but now is a single entity known as British Aerospace, was a potential risk-sharing partner in the manufacture of the 757. It was especially attractive because it had the capability to design and produce a high-technology wing.

Producing state-of-the-art wings is such a challenge that neither France nor West Germany was eager to take on the challenge of making wings for the A-310 (the earlier A-300 Airbus uses a British-made wing, as does the Concorde supersonic transport).

Boeing makes all its own wings. But in the case of the 757 it was willing, even eager, to break tradition. The wing was an expensive challenge, and Boeing would have been happy to let the British take it on.

Bringing British Aerospace's substantial resources onto the Boeing team also probably would deny them to the Airbus A-310, a threat to Boeing's other new program, the 767. Airbus needed Britain to make its wings.

BOEING'S British plan was simple: It wanted a launch order for 757s from British Airways, and it offered the government of Prime Minister James Callaghan a market for Rolls-Royce engines and a partnership of sorts with Boeing on the 757 airframe.

The arrangement suited Rolls-Royce and British Airways.

Sir Kenneth Keith, chairman of Rolls-Royce, visited Seattle and said Rolls would go forward with Boeing if two major airlines would become launch customers for the plane with Rolls-Royce engines. The engine deal was "clinched" at a Seattle meeting between Sir Kenneth and Boullioun, said John Hodson, a Rolls-Royce vice president.

The British government, which must approve airplane purchases by British Airways, was keenly interested in selling Rolls-Royce engines.

"If there was any political pressure, it was that an association with Rolls-Royce was necessary to make the purchase," said Roy Watts, deputy chairman of British Airways. "I don't think you'll find it written down anywhere. But if we'd tried to buy the 757 with Pratt & Whitney engines, we would have had a hell of a fight."

But the Boeing plan didn't sit well with British Aerospace.

Boeing's scheme called for a joint venture with British Aerospace to create the 757 airframe, but the Seattle company didn't believe a billion-dollar enterprise could succeed without a definite leader.

As one Boeing executive put it: "Everybody's equal, but somebody's more equal than the others. Throughout those discussions we felt we'd have a partner, but one partner was going to be in charge, and that was us."

British Aerospace felt it deserved an equal partnership—if not with Boeing, then with Airbus or McDonnell Douglas. Lockheed was talking to the British, too, although rather nebulously.

All but Boeing were talking full partnerships—but Boeing was the world's most successful planemaker, and Rolls-Royce and British Airways were pushing for the Boeing connection.

Michael Goldsmith, a top British Aerospace official who negotiated with Boeing, said the Seattle company had been talking partnerships initially, but eventually offered only a subcontracting role. "Boeing offered us to build so many wings at a very snappy price" while Airbus was talking with British Aerospace about a partnership in what eventually would be a whole family of airplanes, Goldsmith said.

For its part, Boeing's enthusiasm for the deal began to dim when it saw British estimates of the cost to build the wing. British Aerospace's figures were far higher than Boeing's estimates.

"One thing we would never do is go to a higher cost," a Boeing official said. "They, either from their cost-estimating techniques or their own efficiency, couldn't approach what we felt the wing ought to cost."

"They'd added a safety factor in their bid," Boullioun added. "I think it was 30 percent banged right on top of it. I told the ministers over there in the industry that 'You're a lot better than you think you are. You ought to step up and have some courage and do it.' "

Goldsmith said British Aerospace could have gambled by shaving its price if it was to be a partner in the 757 project. But as a subcontractor, it had no incentive to offer more than a cautious price—a price where it was almost certain to make a profit, he said.

Boeing continued talks with the British, but also began looking for a possible U.S. manufacturer to take on the 757 wing.

In late June 1978, Prime Minister Callaghan came to the United States and met separately with Wilson and Boullioun of Boeing, Eastern Airlines President Frank Borman, and McDonnell Douglas President Sanford McDonnell.

He sought and received assurances that the Rolls-Royce engine would be used by Eastern Airlines on the 757 and Boeing's top leaders thought their meeting had gone well.

Then, in July, Callaghan met with President Valery Giscard d'Estaing of France and Chancellor Helmut Schmidt of West Germany.

By early August, reports were circulating that Britain would split its allegiance, linking British Aerospace with manufacture of the Airbus A-310 and Rolls-Royce and British Airways with the Boeing 757.

That led Boeing to decide to build the 757 wing itself, without any risk-sharing partners at all. It would mean spending more and risking more than the company liked—especially since it had just commenced the 767 program.

In a series of announcements on Aug. 31, 1978, Boeing, Rolls-Royce, British Airways and Eastern Airlines revealed that the 757 was going forward, with a total of 40 orders worth more than $1 billion.

The British government announced "approval of two major decisions critical to the future of Britain's aerospace industry"—approval for Rolls-Royce to produce the engines for the 757, and the addition of British Aerospace at a risk-sharing, 20 percent partner in the Airbus A-310 program.

There was a catch, however. The governments of France and West Germany both had to give approval for British Aerospace participation in Airbus, and both governments were upset that British Airways was going to purchase the Boeing 757 instead of the Airbus A-310.

Still, approval finally was granted—but only after Britain suggested that British Airways might someday also buy the A-310, if it could be adapted for Rolls-Royce engines. France and Britain didn't have a good alternate source of wings, anyway.

Callaghan has since told an interviewer he was pleased by the results of his negotiations, which allowed each of the three British companies to follow its own inclinations. "Rolls-Royce was the national asset we had to preserve, which meant establishing it in the U.S. market was the central consideration," he said.

Those political decisions had profound implications for the world of commercial aviation.

For Boeing, the decisions meant the company would have to assume almost all the risk of two new airplane programs simultaneously, while linking the 757 to a British engine for its first years of commercial service.

For McDonnell Douglas, and to a lesser extent for Lockheed, the decisions represented another lost opportunity and a sign of declining influence.

For Airbus, the decisions meant new strength and a new and valuable partner, Britain.

Today Boeing seems confident about the outcome of its competition with Airbus, and Boullioun suggests Britain erred tactically by choosing to help build A-310s instead of 757s.

"We'll build literally two or three times more 757s than they'll ever build 310s, because I think the 767 is going to hurt the 310," Boullioun said.

But Airbus seems confident, too. "The way we see it," Goldsmith said, "the A-310 series of aircraft have a very good chance."

WHEN THE 7N7 program started in 1976, Boeing designer Jackson called up Boeing's corporate headquarters and established a new model number. It was 761—the in-house number for the 7N7.

The first new 7N7 design studied was numbered 761-1. The next was 761-2. And so on.

"We started hundreds of models within that series," Jackson said. "For example, if we study a short-body concept, we'll call that a 761 dash whatever the next number is."

Boeing thought, and for a time hoped, that the 757 would be a 164-passenger design, which was number 761-262. British Airways and Eastern Airlines were attracted to a larger size because it would reduce per seat operating costs. When Eastern's Frank Borman requested a larger version of the plane, British Airways and Boeing agreed.

By late summer of 1978, the larger 757 had become model 761-280. It looked a good deal like a lengthened 727, with a high T-tail, but had two big engines under the wings instead of three small engines on the rear of the fuselage.

The details of the 761-280 weren't all worked out, so Boeing, Rolls-Royce, Eastern Airlines and British Airways had only an idea of what was being sold and bought when their leaders shook hands on the deal in August 1978. It wouldn't be until March 1979, after details were nailed down, that contracts would be signed.

Even without contracts, Boeing and Rolls-Royce began spending millions of dollars on a program to produce the 761-280 in less than four years.

Hodson explained Rolls-Royce's willingness to proceed on faith: "When two people like Boullioun and Kenneth Keith have shaken hands, it's only up to the lesser mortals to dot the I's and cross the T's. It's going to happen."

But the task was bigger than imagined in 1978, for the 757 refused to sit still.

Model 761-280 kept evolving. The high T-tail eventually was dropped, the nose was flattened and widened, the electronic gear and cockpit were updated radically—and much of this happened late enough in the process that some Eastern Airlines engineers were nervous about Boeing's ability to pull it off in time.

With the changes came ever-higher model numbers. The 757 in production today is model 761-340.

As for 761-280, the airplane which led to handshake agreements back in 1978, it's just another plane that never flew.

The Quest for Simplicity

No ONE really understands the Boeing 757. No single person knows how to design or build it. No one human, or even a modest group of humans, could fully fashion its complexities.

But anyone could fly a 757—even a nonpilot, under ideal conditions.

Advancing technology, be it in an airplane, a telephone system or a computer program, often seeks simplicity through complexity. It's not a new idea.

In fact, 44 years ago the French aviator and philosopher Antoine de Saint-Exupery blessed technology for making airplanes that pilots could fly as if by second nature. Looking back at earlier flying machines, he wrote:

"There was a time when a flyer sat at the center of a complicated works. ... The indicators that oscillated on the instrument panel warned us of a thousand dangers. But in the machine of today we forget the motors are whirring. The motor, finally, has come to fulfill its function, which is to whirr as a heart beats—and we give no thought to the beating of our heart."

Saint-Exupery disappeared during a flight over the Mediterranean in 1944. But his "ultimate principle of simplicity" is evident in the aircraft of today.

"We consistently have found that the best (cockpit) displays are the ones which are kept simple in appearance and function," said H.G. Stoll, senior project engineer for the flight deck used in the Boeing 757 and 767. "The crew procedures are simple and the workload is the lowest of any commercial airplane."

NEVERTHELESS, a new-generation jetliner is "about the most complex piece of mechanical equipment that man's ever made," said John Swihart, a Boeing engineer who rose to become vice president of domestic sales.

The computers and displays in the 757-767 cockpit exceed the sophistication of those used in the Space Shuttle, Swihart said.

"My expertise is only in airplanes and some nuclear stuff, and I can tell you that no nuclear reactor is anything as complicated as a commercial airplane, by quite a little bit," he said.

Phil Condit, former director of engineering on Boeing's 757 program, estimated it would take the combined knowledge of 50 to 100 hand-picked engineers to know what is necessary to design a 757 or a similar airplane. Perhaps even that is an underestimate, because many engineers might rely on assistants for important detail information, he said.

Bill Robison directs manufacture of the 757 and is well-acquainted with the immense task of bringing a plane together. He estimates it would take 50 of the supervisors who work for him, pooling their knowledge and experience, to know how to manufacture a new jetliner like the 757.

If those figures seem high, consider that at one point more than 10,000 Boeing employees were assigned to the 757 program and a similar number of non-Boeing workers were employed through subcontractors. At its peak, the program employed about 1,500 engineers and a like number of engineering-support personnel.

Modern jetliners incorporate a wide range of technologies. The 757 and 767, for instance, use superlight composite materials created by advanced and sometimes secret processes, a new aerodynamic wing design that resulted from more than 36,000 hours of wind-tunnel testing and sophisticated new electronic systems.

An airplane has been described as a large number of spare parts flying in close formation. In the case of the 757, there are about 3 million parts, held together by about 415,000 fasteners, many of them expensive titanium rivets. There are about 95,000 separate part types.

The plane's 130 on-board microprocessors control everything from cabin pressure to flight path. Many are substantial computers which communicate among themselves, using a "party line" arrangement.

The plane's electrical and electronic systems, including the microprocessors, are interconnected by 37,857 individual wires totaling 65.9 miles in length and weighing a total of 2,646 pounds.

The 757 also carries a host of intricate mechanical contraptions. Its two British-made Rolls-Royce jet engines each deliver 37,400 pounds of take-off thrust, and represent an enormous investment of time, money and technology.

"Nobody will develop an engine these days for under $1 billion," said John Hodson, a vice president of Rolls-Royce. It could take a team of 300 engineers five years to refine engine technology and new developments into a new engine, and the engineering force might rise to 2,000 at the peak of development, he said.

"You've got enormous energies involved in an engine," Hodson said. To dissipate the heat, the turbine blades must have tiny cooling air passages running through them—and yet the blades must remain strong.

To meet such design and production challenges, high technology tooling and testing equipment is necessary. "The facilities that you need cost millions and millions of dollars," Hodson said.

Since air flows through a jet engine at high velocities, internal parts must be designed with aerodynamic and vibrational characteristics in mind. Layer upon layer of blades must resonate at appropriate frequencies. The wrong vibration frequency at cruise speed could create a fatigue failure within minutes and "the blade would just fall off," Hodson said.

AS WITH THE entire airplane, sophistication has yielded simplicity of operation in the engines. They require little attention from the 757's two pilots. Computers monitor engine operation, and although the pilots watch a few engine indicators on cockpit video screens, they can mostly ignore the engines unless a problem develops.

The "ultimate principle of simplicity" extends to the maintenance of the 757, too.

On-board electronic systems are in modules, and built-in computers tell maintenance workers which modules, or boxes, should be replaced to get a plane flying again almost immediately. Boxes removed from the planes are taken to repair shops where more new technology is used to diagnose and repair problems.

So, the 757 is an amalgamation of hardware that can be repaired quickly by maintenance personnel who may not really understand what they are repairing, and flown by pilots who may have little grasp of the technology they command.

Consider, for instance, the plane's inertial-reference unit, a device made by Honeywell that uses a trio of lasers to perform navigational feats which in older planes were performed, less precisely, by a gyroscope.

The IRU, as it is called, keeps track of the 757's vertical and horizontal accelerations and decelerations and by adding and subtracting is able to deduce the altitude and location of the plane. The IRU is so sensitive that it detects the effects of wind and displays wind speed and direction on a cockpit video screen.

A 757 pilot will know how the IRU helps him fly the plane. He will know there are three IRUs cross-checking each other, and that if all agree precisely regarding the 757's location, he can use them to land the airplane automatically in fog.

But will he really understand how an IRU works?

John Armstrong, 757 chief test pilot, explained the IRU this way:

"There are no moving parts. It's a triangular-shaped device and they have a laser beam and they measure the bending of the beam itself. You set in your position before you start moving. Then, as you move around, it keeps track of the position you're at. It can tell where you are any place on the globe."

Armstrong paused, and then captured the essence of both the IRU and the 757 in a phrase: "It's sort of complicated."

PART 2: MAKING THE DECISION

AN AIRLINER hurtling down a runway reaches "decision speed"— the point at which it's too late to abort the takeoff.

Industrial projects often have decision speeds, too. As a huge venture accelerates, as millions of dollars are invested and manpower and machinery are committed, there comes a point when it would be disastrous to try to turn back.

Boeing's multi-billion-dollar 757 project was moving slowly on its runway when Eastern Airlines and British Airways announced in August 1978 that they would be launch customers for the new single-aisle jetliner. But the runway was long, and enormous managerial, engineering and manufacturing challenges lay ahead before it could fly:

• Timetables had to be created, thousands of employees hired, dozens of subcontractors selected and hundreds of millions of dollars of new tooling designed and built.

• The airplane's 95,000 part types had to be designed and either manufactured or acquired from what ultimately would be 1,300 outside suppliers and 37 major subcontractors in the U.S. and seven foreign countries. Intricately shaped pieces produced by different manufacturers, possibly thousands of miles apart, sometimes had to fit within a tolerance of less than two one-thousandths of an inch.

• Working from blueprints and other documents, Boeing manufacturing engineers had to create hundreds of thousands of pages of directions, literally instruction books for the assembly of a new airliner.

• Additional airplanes had to be sold beyond the combined order of 40 placed by British Airways and Eastern Airlines. Unless a sufficient number of airplanes is sold in the first few years of a program, interest costs and other expenses make it almost impossible for the program ever to make money—no matter how many planes are sold in the long run.

Beyond these and other known challenges, for which effort and expense could reasonably be planned, there were unknown variables of known types. These "known unknowns" included such questions as: "How much would the design evolve during the course of the project? What would these changes cost?"

Finally, there were what Boeing president Malcolm Stamper calls the "unk-unks." These "unknown unknowns" are the booby traps of any new airplane project. They can be terribly expensive, and an airplane manufacturer must be financially prepared for them.

In the case of the 757, the Rolls-Royce engines provided a modest example of an unk-unk. The 757 was on the verge of certification when icing conditions unexpectedly caused engine damage. Rolls-Royce and Boeing put people on round-the-clock schedules to find a solution quickly. The solution was found, but the expense was great and the delay significant.

Adding to the uncertainty and challenge in the early days of the 757 project was the presence of the 767 program, which had a few months' head start and commanded first call on Boeing's resources.

"There were a lot of rumors that Boeing was never going to build this airplane," said Benjamin Gay, who oversaw construction of the 757 for Eastern Airlines. "We had a contract. I saw metal being cut. But you still heard rumors that Boeing was not going to build the airplane."

FOR A LONG TIME, the 757 didn't have many orders—and by some measures, it still doesn't. The modest number of orders fed rumors of cancellation, as did nagging concerns that Boeing had blundered into making the airplane too large—at 178 seats, too close in size to the 210-seat 767.

"Some people felt the 757 wasn't the right size for the market, this sort of thing. That the 150-passenger plane was the one," Gay said.

John Lampl, an American who worked in British Airway's London public-relations office in 1979, recalls, "There was all this talk because the 767 was also being built. Could Boeing really build and introduce two airplanes at the same time? People were really wondering.

"It seemed to be that Boeing was putting more and more emphasis on the 767. And the 757 was sort of getting shoved aside."

Adding to the anxiety, especially later in the program, was the way the airplane kept changing. Never had a Boeing aircraft gone through so many metamorphoses.

"At one point we were concerned that they were trying to do a little too much, biting off a lot late in the program, or later in the program," Gay said. "I think we were kind of amazed at how many changes were going into this thing during 1980 and 1981."

The 757 grew and shrunk and grew again before the airlines said they would buy it. Then, before the contracts were signed, the tail of the airplane was changed radically. Soon after the contracts were signed, Boeing changed the airplane's nose and began altering its electronics in a way which affected the fundamental character of the aircraft.

The transformation effectively linked the 757 technologically with the new 767 rather than with the tried-and-true 727, the Boeing airplane the 757 was intended to replace. The changes were improvements, but they raised eyebrows.

"There was just this talk," Lampl said, "the fact that this late in what was seemingly the production stage there was the redesigning of a major portion of the airplane. If they're doing this so late in the game, is this airplane really going to come off the assembly line in 1983 or whatever?"

Eastern Airlines president Frank Borman said Boeing was willing to make all the improvements in the 757's design without increasing the cost of the contract. Today's 757 is "enormously" better than the one Eastern ordered, he said.

Boeing had a short timetable for making the 757 project fly, but "fortunately we all pulled together and we were able to make those schedules," said Bill Robison, director of manufacturing for the 757. "But there was a risk. There was more compression in the schedule of the 757 than any other airplane the Boeing Co. has ever tried to make."

Boeing imported a lot of engineers and paid a lot of overtime to get the 757 into commercial service with Eastern Airlines by the end of 1982. A typical Boeing new-airplane schedule, which isn't generous in timing, would have called for deliveries in late summer of 1983.

HOW DID BOEING KNOW, back in 1978, that it could get the 757 designed, built, and certified by December 1982?

"I'll give it to you the other way around," Robison said. "How did we know we couldn't?"

Was it really that much of a challenge? Was the timing really that close?

"Yeah, it was that close," Robison said.

If the schedule had called for completion two months earlier, in October instead of December, could Boeing have done it?

"No, we couldn't have done it. It would have been impossible."

E.H. "Tex" Boullioun disagrees.

Boullioun, as president of Boeing's commercial-airplane division, negotiated the 757 contracts with Eastern Airlines and British Airways. He also was the one who decided the airplane could be produced and certified for commercial flight by December 1982.

Boullioun chuckled over Robison's statement that the airplane couldn't have been produced two months earlier. "I know they won't agree, but I think they could have (done it)," he said. "I've seen those guys do things they didn't have any idea they could do."

Boullioun said he even would have committed the company to produce the airplane by September or October of 1982 if that's what the customers had wanted. Boeing's engineering and manufacturing arms would have found a way to do it, he said.

"They always like that little extra in there," Boullioun said. "It's like the grasshopper in the rut. He's hopping along in the rut, but he gets the hell out of there when a wheel comes by."

Boullioun said those charged with producing the airplane "squawked" when he told them he wanted the plane by December 1982 rather than the summer of 1983. "But then they had to come back and show why they couldn't do it," he said. "They couldn't show that positively."

Robison remembers telling Boullioun back in August of 1978 that more time was necessary. "He said, 'Oh, Robbie, you're better than that. You don't know how good you are. You just go put that (schedule) back to December because that's what I'm going to sell airplanes at.'"

So the airplane was scheduled for unveiling (called "rollout") in January 1982, with first flight a month later and certification by the Federal Aviation Administration in December 1982.

The schedule was timed about six months behind the other new Boeing jet, the 767, which was to be certified in July of 1982.

The 767 had received formal "go-ahead" by the Boeing board of directors in July 1978, when United Airlines ordered 30 of the twin-aisle airplanes. By contrast, the first 757 orders were announced in August 1978, but the company didn't formally commit to the program until the following March.

Boeing executives say the delay did not indicate a lack of resolve about the program. They explained that the size of the 757 had been increased in August 1978 to suit Frank Borman, president of Eastern

Airlines. Boeing needed time to refine the general design and clarify particulars before contracts were signed.

Still, a high Boeing official said "there was much soul-searching as the management struggled with the go-ahead decisions on these airplanes. ... There was concern inside and outside Boeing that the company had bitten off more than it could chew."

Boeing kept careful tabs on its financial exposure in the 757 project. Every month, company management received a report on what it had invested in the 757 project—and how much it could lose if the project were aborted.

THE STAKES for Boeing went up after the contracts were signed, but the company's point of no return—its "decision speed"—may not have been reached until Oct. 11, 1979.

That was the day Boeing signed more than $1 billion in contracts for the 757's fuselage sections with four major subcontractors—a record for civil aviation, and an expensive commitment to the future of the 757 program.

Even after the major subcontracts were let, Boeing kept track of what it would cost to cancel the program at any time. Every subcontractor provided Boeing with a frequently updated "termination dollar curve," said Jack Edwards, director of material on the 757 program.

"If we have to cancel, we knew right at the moment the maximum amount that we would have to pay," he said.

Top executives of companies that worked closely with Boeing—Eastern Airlines, British Airways and Rolls-Royce—say they had no doubts the 757 program would go ahead.

"I don't think there ever was a point where it was remotely close to being canceled," said John Hodson, a vice president of Rolls-Royce, which made the engines for the Eastern Airlines and British Airways 757s. "I have had my finger on Boeing's pulse pretty closely for the last 3½ years, and it never even missed a beat."

One Boeing engineer says the company could not afford not to go ahead with the 757. The plane was needed to reduce the possibility that airlines might re-engine their huge 727 fleets instead of buying new aircraft.

Also, there was the threat of McDonnell Douglas.

In 1978, McDonnell Douglas competed for the British Airways order that Boeing ultimately won with the 757. McDonnell's 180-seat design was called the Advanced Transport Medium Range (ATMR). Later, as voices in the industry began to wonder aloud whether a 150-

seat airplane might sell better than the 757's 178-seat design,
McDonnell transformed the ATMR into a 150-seater.

But it never sold or launched the airplane—and still hasn't. Elaine
Bendel, a McDonnell spokeswoman, said the 150-seater is called the
D3300 now and may yet be launched.

Paul Johnstone, until recently Eastern's senior vice president for
operations, thinks McDonnell was one of three main sources of
rumors that the 757 program might be killed.

McDonnell, he says, "was trying to rush a 150-seater, the ATMR
or whatever it was they were calling it."

Another source "was probably from Airbus Industrie, who wanted Boeing the hell out of the market. And the third source, amazingly enough, may well have been from some of the 767 people over
there (at Boeing) who all of a sudden saw an airplane (the 757) that
was better then theirs," he said.

"The 767 has become, I think, the stepchild—and stepchildren
don't like it. They had the 757 guys in that role, second-class citizens,
I think that helped the 757 immeasurably, because I think all the guys
got their dander up and said, 'By God, we're not going to be second-
class citizens. We'll kick their butts.' "

WAS THERE SUCH competition within Boeing itself?

Boeing 757 engineers praise the 767 and 767 engineers praise the
757. But, at a party in January celebrating the certification of the 757,
a huge cheer went up when a snide comment about the 767 was made
over the public-address system.

It's the kind of thing Boeing tries to deny, but there is a friendly
rivalry between the two programs.

"The 767 got the best of everything," said a rank-and-file engineer
on the 757 program, emphasizing the final word of the sentence.
"They got the money. They got the appropriations. They got the management. Corporate gave them whatever they wanted. And we got
what was left over."

The 757 was to be a derivative of the 727, making it a comparatively low-cost program. The 767, which got an earlier start, was to
be the all-new showpiece. It was to be, in the words of the 757 engineer, "Boeing's baby."

It seemed to some of these working on the 757 that their achievements were shrouded in obscurity and they were relegated to "me-
too" status: Boeing had this great airplane it was building, the 767. It
was the first new Boeing since the 747 in the mid-1960s. It would be

ultra-modern. It would be fuel-efficient. It would be a great seller. And, oh yes, Boeing was also making this other airplane, the 757.

"We weren't denied anything," said the 757 engineer. "But we certainly did have to try a little harder."

Eastern's Johnstone says that "in a lot of ways, they picked what Boeing thought was the second team to work on the 757. I think those guys are just as happy as clams. They're rapidly becoming the first team."

Although it downplays the existence of rivalry between programs, Boeing frequently uses internal competition to stimulate innovation within a single program.

"That process is extremely important," said Phil Condit, who directed 757 engineering for several years.

For example, sometimes the company creates an A team and a B team to compete on potential designs. The approach often sparks new ideas.

"When people start doing something some way, they sort of get locked in with their thinking. They don't start exploring," said Joe Sutter, the Boeing vice president who oversees new-product design. One way to break up reliance on old ideas, he said, is to "pop in a new team and get a sort of challenge going forth and back."

Sometimes the B team successfully challenges the established thinking of the A team, Sutter said. An example was the 737, a relatively small jetliner which was planned with two engines mounted on the rear of the fuselage until a B team proved that putting them under the wings would allow six extra passenger seats at the same operating costs.

"Boeing has always used sort of a system of checking the doers," Sutter said.

Another check: While all the engineers on the 757 project report to the 757 organization for direction, some of them report administratively to a separate engineering organization. The separate reporting arrangement is meant to insulate them from potential reprisals if they question the decisions of others.

This arrangement, with some people reporting in two different directions, is used widely throughout Boeing, not just in engineering.

But the reporting arrangements, and everything else that shows up on the organization chart, are only a superficial reflection of the way Boeing workers really relate to each other, Condit said. "There are all sorts of formal relationships, and then millions of informal relations."

If those relationships were somehow dissolved, a fanciful idea, it would add years to the time necessary to create a new jetliner, Condit said. "It would be a monumental task to put it all back together again."

THE SCHEDULE for creating the 757 took shape in the fall of 1978 on huge sheets of paper covering one wall of Bill Robison's office.

Long horizontal lines were drawn across the sheets, and on these lines Robison and a few others charted the gestation period of the airplane. Industrial engineers picked hypothetical go-ahead and completion dates for intermediate landmarks.

"We spent a considerable amount of effort pre-planning," Robison said. "Nothing was left to chance."

The paper on Robison's wall evolved gradually into the 757's "master phasing plan"—a comprehensive set of deadlines for key achievements in finance, engineering, customer introduction, hardware development, engines, procurement, facilities, manufacturing, flight test and deliveries.

The deadlines all were interrelated. For example, once a deadline for completion of 90 percent of the airplane's engineering had been established, a corresponding deadline for finishing a mockup of the airplane could be set. Knowing when the mockup must be finished made it possible to set a date to begin mockup fabrication. All of it was based on Boeing's past experience in creating new airplanes.

When Robison and his colleagues laid out those first schedules, they were like a team of cooks planning a mammoth feast of 95,000 ingredients—except they still didn't know exactly what parts would be needed, or where they would come from, or how they would be put together.

As Robison pondered the schedules, he kept in mind an industrial management technique used by Boeing—the idea that parts should arrive when needed, and virtually no sooner. The Japanese, who use the technique widely, call it "just in time" scheduling and inventory control.

Storing parts in warehouses is expensive. So is the interest cost on capital tied up in inventory. The just-in-time approach reduces both of these costs, and provides quality control because faulty parts and assemblies are discovered almost immediately, when Boeing attempts to use them.

The approach is central to Boeing's method of operation. It does not want major assemblies from subcontractors to arrive more than five days before needed.

"If you're buying something that's costing you over $100,000 apiece and you have to keep it sitting here for six months, why, that's pretty expensive," said Edwards, the 757 director of materiel.

Added Jack Traynor, a procurement manager: "Not only is it expensive to bring it in early, but if you have it here for any length of time you might have changes that have to be incorporated in it. So the closer you work to the line, the more up-to-date the configuration is and the less work we have to do here in our assembly line."

On the other hand, there are real problems when something arrives late, creating a parts shortage.

"Let's say the example is a shortage way up in the wing somewhere," Boullioun said. "Holy crimeny, you can't put it together! You do put it together, and you've got to take it apart. And then everything piles up. And so it's a real mess."

BY LATE DECEMBER 1978, Robison had finished his master-phasing chart. It told management how long it would take to build the 757. With the basic timing established, Boeing entered a "cost-definition phase."

Normally, Boeing completes cost estimates before formally committing to a new program. But in the case of the 757, both initial customers were eager to get the program under way and there was a threat that orders could be lost to competing airplanes.

So Boeing took a gamble. It made a rough estimate in its costs and signed contracts on the basis of that estimate.

Officially, Boeing won't reveal the cost of creating the 757, but Wall Street analysts put it at $1.5 billion to $2.5 billion. One high-level Boeing executive put the figure at $3 billion for the 757 and 767 combined. Another said the combination cost $4 billion, plus $2 billion in tooling costs.

Boeing contends it saved no money by building the two airplanes simultaneously, even though they shared a large percentage of identical parts. Any savings achieved by commonality of parts apparently was lost to the higher cost associated with the rushed development of the 757, one executive said.

Overtime expenses soared. More than 1,000 employees worked overtime during the last Christmas holidays, when the first two airplanes were delivered to Eastern Airlines.

"What we did to compress the 757 schedule was to put this thing on a six- and seven-day week," Robison said.

Now, ironically, it appears the hurry may not have been necessary. Other "unk-unks" intruded: Airline deregulation, world-wide recession and the air-traffic controllers' strike cut sharply into passenger traffic and airline revenues.

As a result, an industry which was making hundreds of millions of dollars profit annually in the 1970s now is losing similar amounts. Braniff Airlines and Laker Airways have gone out of business and other major carriers may follow. New orders for expensive jets have all but disappeared.

Today, the 757's first customers, Eastern Airlines and British Airways, are in weak financial shape. British Airways has reduced its 757 order by two airplanes and Eastern is working on schemes to pay for its new planes. Eastern may delay acceptance of its 757s due in 1984 and 1985.

If they could have known what the future would hold, the airlines probably would have welcomed a stretched-out delivery schedule.

But back when the decisions were made, it made sense to turn out the fuel-efficient 757 as quickly as possible. So Boeing's management accelerated the project down the runway until the 757 was reality.

PART 3: DESIGNING THE 757

BOEING'S NEWEST JETLINER, silvery metal with the blue numerals 757 emblazoned on its tail, turned heads like a celebrity as it taxied into Montreal's Dorval International Airport last September.

It came to rest at an Eastern Airlines gate where top Boeing officials were waiting to give the airline's president, Frank Borman, his first ride in the airplane he had helped launch with a $900 million order four years earlier.

A gate agent stepped up to the 757's door, popped out a butterfly-shaped handle and turned it clockwise. Grasping the door firmly, while the top brass of Boeing and Eastern looked on, she pushed and pulled.

The 323-pound door moved only a few inches. It wouldn't budge beyond that. Try as she might, she couldn't get it open.

"See?" said Paul Johnstone, then Eastern's senior vice president for operations.

Johnstone chuckled later and explained that he had purposely cnosen a small woman to open the heavy door—or try to—so Boeing executives could see first-hand that something was wrong. "I mousetrapped 'em," he said.

Although the 757 passenger door met elaborate engineering criteria and reliability tests, in Eastern's view the airplane at Dorval International was a flawed product.

The airline was to take delivery of the first airplane in December, just three months away, and it wanted a door every gate agent, regardless of his or her weight or strength, could open.

The 757 door took about 70 pounds of strength to open, twice as much as a 727 door. There were several reasons, including that it weighed more because the 757 sits higher off the ground and the door must contain a longer escape slide for emergency evacuation.

Boeing hadn't ignored the question of how much strength was necessary to open the door, said Jim Johnson, 757 director of engineering. On the contrary, engineers had calculated everything from the door's weight to the viscosity of its oil to the effects of friction on the door's bearings and rollers.

D.P. Tingwall, chief product engineer for engineering computing, said door loads were examined by computer and the design of cam parts was modified on the basis of the computer's findings.

And yet an error was made.

"We didn't give proper consideration to a small-framed woman with light weight," Boeing's Johnson said. A small person didn't have enough leverage to move the door, he said.

Boeing first encountered the door problem last July 8, when Nancy Ballard, a 115-pound Eastern gate agent at Seattle-Tacoma Airport, had enormous difficulty opening a 757 door in a test at Boeing Field.

"This young girl damn near got herself a hernia trying to open the damn door," said Johnstone, now retired from Eastern. In fact, Ballard came away from the test with a muscle bruise the size of a baseball on one arm, where she had repeatedly leaned for leverage while trying to push the door open.

"I was able to open the door, but believe me, it was a strain," she said.

It took a dozen engineers eight 56-hour weeks to solve the problem by designing a dual-spring mechanism, but the solution hadn't yet been installed when Johnstone sprang his mousetrap in Montreal.

THE DOOR PROBLEM wasn't the only thing discovered relatively late in the development of the 757 that required re-engineering.

In the fall of 1981, an anesthetized 4-pound chicken was loaded in a pneumatic gun and fired at 360 knots head-on into a stationary 757 cab.

The expectation was that the chicken would deflect off the cabin's sloping metal roof. Instead, it pierced the airplane's skin.

"It looked like you had thrown a shotput through it," said Ed Pottenger, a Boeing engineer.

This shocking result, and the realization that it might be repeated if the 757 hit a bird in flight, led to some urgent redesigning of the cabin roof of both the 757 and 767. The challenge was great because several 767s already were flying and had to be cut apart.

The changes were particularly painful because beefing up the cab added 70 pounds to the weight of each airplane, and saving weight is an aeronautical engineering objective pursued with almost religious intensity.

"There are people in the Boeing Co. who kill their grandmothers for five pounds. I'm dead serious," said Leroy Keith, the Federal Aviation Administration official who oversees certification of jetliners and other transport aircraft.

Overcoming those obstacles was only a small part of the engineering that went into the door and cabin of the 757—and the door and cabin represented but a fraction of the 65,000 "engineering events" involved in creating the airplane's detailed design.

At its peak, 1,500 engineers and a like number of assistants were involved in the 757 project. Although it was building two new airplanes simultaneously, Boeing didn't want to swell its engineering ranks temporarily, so it imported engineers from subcontractors around the country.

Often using computers (which helped design 47 percent of the airplane's parts), the engineers tackled large questions such as what shape the tail should be and how far back the wings should be swept, and such seemingly small questions as whether a piece of hardware should be hollow and how many inches wide a restroom should be.

Along the way, the engineers helped contribute to a dramatic change in the nature of the airplane. The 757 Boeing started to build is far different from the 757 it actually built, largely because of improvements in the airplane's cockpit and electronics.

The 757 has 95,000 different part types and a total of 3 million separate parts. Engineers selected or designed each one. Other engineers decided when material would be needed to make the parts and when the parts themselves would be needed.

Phil Condit, who held the top two engineering posts on the 757 project before being named its vice president and general manager in January, said he didn't make important engineering choices so much as designate times when they must be made by rank-and-file engineers.

"I couldn't absorb enough data to possibly make these kinds of decisions," he said.

Although the engineering details of the 757 far exceed the grasp of any single human mind, the problems involved in the design of the passenger door and cockpit offer some insight into the complexities of conceiving and creating a new airplane.

A BOEING 757 passenger door doesn't attract attention, which is just fine with its creators. "A door looks simple," Condit said. "That's the way you want it to look. You don't want the passenger worrying about whether it's going to work."

In fact, the simple-looking passenger door contains about 500 parts, held together by 5,900 rivets. Its mechanical systems were designed by a battalion of engineers and fashioned by custom-made tools that cost millions of dollars.

The curving 4-inch-thick door must contain highly reliable mechanisms, including a system to control the speed at which it rotates on elaborate hinges, and a system that enables the door to power itself open and deploy an escape slide in an emergency.

The slide is stored in the door, but whenever the door is closed and "armed" the slide automatically attaches to the sill of the doorway. In an emergency, the slide is pulled out of the door as the door opens. The slide inflates automatically.

The slide must reach the ground in an emergency even if the airplane is resting nose-up and tail-down, or is listing to one side with a broken landing gear. And the slide must inflate rapidly and reliably even in 25-knot winds.

The complexities of the 757 passenger door are all the more remarkable because of the utter simplicity of the door's basic concept. The door is, in essence, a plug not unlike a bathtub stopper or a bottle cork.

But unlike a cork in a bottle, which is wedged in from the outside, the 757 door is wedged from the inside. The pressurized cabin air helps hold the door in place.

With the first turn of the door handle, internal mechanisms unlatch the door and reduce its height and wedge shape by folding in "gates" at the top and bottom. The door swings into the cabin briefly, unplugging the doorway, then slides back through the opening at a 25-degree angle and swings wide to fold against the outside of the airplane.

But to think of the door only as a piece of hardware is to overlook what is perhaps its most telling characteristic: compromise. The door, like the whole airplane, is as much a collection of engineering trade-offs as it is a collection of parts.

"To the last detail, everything we do is a compromise," Johnson said. Boeing engineers refer to these compromises as "trades," and there are lots of them in a door.

For example, the door must be wide enough to provide passengers comfortable entry, yet not so wide it robs seating space. Its window must give adequate vision of what is outside, and yet not use up too much of the space needed for its mechanical innards.

The door must be strong enough to hold out an alien environment of sub-zero temperatures, low air pressures and speeds approaching the sound barrier. And yet, like the rest of the airplane, it must be as light as possible to maximize fuel efficiency.

"I can't overstress the complexity of this set of trades that are continually going on," Condit said. "How much off am I? What happens if I put a little more wing area on? How does that balance?"

Engineers have different concepts of what is important. "You get a hydraulics guy, and he thinks the airplane ought to have 80 million miles of hydraulic lines in it," said John Armstrong, chief test pilot of the 757 program. "And the propulsion guy thinks that the airplane's just a vehicle to carry his engines around."

"Weight is the all-important driving force behind almost everything," said Keith, the FAA official. "You can build something that is totally safe, fire-resistant and fail-safe, but it would be made out of titanium and it would be heavy and it would be prohibitively costly. So you've got a series of trades.

" ... It's just one series of compromises. In performance, handling qualities, systems, reliability, comfort, economy, structure, fabrication."

That all the trades are made and an airplane is created and tested in just four or five years is remarkable, Keith said. "You've got a magnificent flying machine out of the deal in a relatively short time period. It just never ceases to amaze me."

EARLY IN 1978, a cockpit designer named Tom White made a pie-in-the-sky suggestion—a suggestion that, if accepted, would fundamentally change the future of Boeing's new family of jetliners.

The 757 program was a year away from its eventual launch and the proposed configuration of the airplane kept changing. "Semi-fluid," one designer called it.

But Boeing was certain of one thing: although much of the 757 would be new, including its engines, wings and interior design, to save development costs it would use updated versions of the 727 cockpit, tail and body cross-section. In short, it would be a 727 derivative.

In a one-page memo dated March 23, 1978, White asked why the company shouldn't forget about making the 757 a derivative. Instead, he proposed putting the all-new Boeing 767 wide-body nose and state-of-the-art digital electronics on the narrow-body 757. It would be a challenge, since there was almost four feet of difference in the diameters of the two airplanes, but he thought it was possible.

White was suggesting more than just a nose job for the 757. It would be a complete personality change. It would make the 757 a sister to the 767, which was a 1980s airplane, rather than a half-sister to the 727, a 1960s airplane. But it also would cost Boeing a fortune in additional development costs and add substantial weight to the airplane.

White argued the updating would make the 757 attractive to airlines for years and might result in the FAA eventually approving a common pilot rating for both airplanes. This would cut operating costs for airlines flying both the 757 and 767.

The idea of creating a common cockpit for the 757 and 767 wasn't new to White's boss, Del Fadden. It had come up every few months. But never before had a designer developed the idea so imaginatively or made it seem within the realm of possibility. Fadden encouraged White.

But the suggestion went nowhere. It just wasn't what Boeing had in mind.

Over the summer of 1978, the 767 program was launched with United Airlines as its first customer. The 757 program was announced in late August, although it wouldn't get the official go-ahead from Boeing until the following March.

During that summer it dawned on Boeing management that the 757 was looking less and less like a 727 derivative. There was talk about using a non-727 tail for improved aerodynamics, and the latest cockpit design called for an advanced safety-and-maintenance monitoring system that could reduce the flight crew from three to two. Without a formal policy decision having been made, the 757 was evolving away from the 727.

In October, Ken Holtby, a Boeing vice president who had run the 747 division for four years, took charge of coordinating development of the 757 and 767. Management felt the two programs sometimes were plowing the same ground.

"One of the things that became immediately obvious was that many of the decisions that had been made on one program or another really should have been applied across the board," Holtby said. "We found a lot of differences between the airplanes that really couldn't be justified."

Holtby told the product-development organization to study ways to increase the commonality of the two airplanes. Much of the job fell to Doug Miller, a chief designer.

One of the first things Miller did was call Tom White. Together they went to Boeing's Everett plant to look at a mockup of the 767 cab, which used a new design Boeing had been developing for years. They set out to prove the cab could be used on the narrower 757.

Soon there were a lot of people working on the common-cockpit idea, and excitement grew. Pete Morton, senior project engineer on the 757, became a powerful advocate. H.G. Stoll, Morton's counterpart on the 767, remembers a phone call in which Morton spelled out the common cockpit idea.

"At first I thought it looked like it was way out as far as an idea," Stoll said. "After all, (if) somebody says you're going to take the front end of a Cadillac and put it on your Datsun, your first reaction is that it's not a good idea."

Morton and Miller approached Condit, who, as chief engineer, was impressed with the idea of common parts between the airplanes, but thought a common FAA pilot rating was "pretty elusive, a pretty high-risk thing to be going after."

Eventually, the idea worked its way up the corporate-ladder to Holtby, the vice president who had urged greater commonality between the airplanes.

"I had to be persuaded," Holtby recalls. "There are a lot of factors that go into that kind of a decision, including our capability. Quite a few of the guys were recommending against it because they didn't feel we had the resources to do it. So there was quite a bit of debate."

Boeing decided to take the gamble.

Today, both airplanes have identical cockpits, developed jointly by 757 and 767 engineers. ... Boeing perceives the evolution of the cockpit as a triumph. ... White still seeks new design ideas. ... Condit, who is only 41, has risen from engineering to become vice president and general manager of the 757 division.

And hanging on Condit's office wall, framed and signed, is one of White's original renderings of how he thought the 767 cab could be fitted to the 757.

INSIDE AND OUT, the cab is the most expensive part of a jetliner's fuselage to engineer and manufacture.

The cab's exterior is of irregular shape. None of the metal is flat, even the contours are not uniform. Inside the cab, an impressive number of electronic and mechanical devices must be sandwiched into a small area.

Morton estimates 120 to 150 engineers were involved in creating the cab and cockpit on the 757 and 767, including those who designed the exterior, crafted the interior and figured out how to fit in all the instrumentation.

Cab design is based on the position of a pilot's eyes, hands and feet. The 757 and 767 cockpits are designed for people from 5-foot-2 to 6-foot-3. The shorter height was included in the design in the expectation that women pilots will become numerous during the useful life of the airplanes.

Boeing selected earth tones of brown and beige for the interiors because a NASA study found those colors reduce anxiety in high stress environments. Sheepskin-covered seats were installed.

Boeing ran tests on how computer screens should offer information, seeking answers to such questions as whether pilots might be distracted if screens automatically changed displays. (Answer: Yes. So Boeing designed systems so that nonessential screens would update displays only when requested to do so, or in emergencies.)

Boeing engineers also used computers in wind-tunnel studies to simulate the airplanes' handling characteristics long before they ever flew. Test pilots expressed their preferences, and engineers changed computer software and the airplanes' control surfaces until they found configurations that gave both airplanes desirable flying qualities.

The goal, which Boeing says it achieved, was to build two airplanes that seemed similar to pilots, even though they are quite different.

"Cockpits are the place in the airplane that have the most compromises that I know of," Morton said. "Everything comes together there.

"For example, if I want a good view of a panel, I don't want a big control column there," he said. "But the guy that's responsible for the control column would like a good meaty one that a guy can wrap his hands around and really pull. And he doesn't care if it blocks my instruments.

"And then I want a nice compact cockpit. I don't care if there's a quarter of an inch behind a panel. But the guy who has to go buy the equipment wants 18 inches behind there. And there's another guy with the responsibility to cool it. He puts ducts in the back of that thing ... "

The 757's front window, or "No. 1 windshield" as it is called, demonstrates the compromises that can be involved in a single jetliner component.

A big window gives a pilot good outside vision, but leaves less room for instrumentation. Glass contributes nothing to the strength of the cabin, so big windows mean big posts, which block vision. Structural engineers would just as soon have portholes as picture windows.

Glass must be strong enough to withstand the impact of a large bird at high speed. But thick glass doesn't transmit light as well as thin glass.

Glass is a poor insulator, so large windows can chill a cab at night and let in excess sunlight by day. Big windows can mean glare problems, too.

The aerodynamics of the cabin are crucial, both for fuel efficiency and to keep noise levels low. Curved windshields help aerodynamically, but can create optical distortions, including double-light reflections.

The No. 1 windows, which are made in England, are the same for both the 757 and 767. There are two of them, one on the right side and one on the left. They are flat. The side windows, known as Nos. 2 and 3, are curved and differ between the two airplanes because their fuselages have different shapes.

The narrower 757 has smaller Nos. 2 and 3 windows and they are closer to the pilot's shoulders. But Boeing shaped and positioned them so that they give essentially the same field of view as the larger and more distant side windows on the 767.

The reason? Again, to make the airplanes feel alike to pilots.

In some places, engineers could not resolve differences between the two airplanes, but the variances aren't major. For example, the No. 2 windshield opens in both planes to allow an escape route for pilots, but the mechanisms differ due to fuselage shapes.

AFTER ITS STOP in Montreal last September, the 757 flew on to England with a load of Eastern and Boeing officials.

On the way, a duck hit one of the cockpit's No. 2 windows, not an unusual incident.

"It's usually not a big deal," said Less Berven, an FAA pilot who was co-piloting the flight. "All it did was just to make him into jelly and he slid down the side of the window."

The window didn't break—but then Boeing knew it wouldn't because the window had gone through a series of "chicken tests."

Boeing is a little touchy about the subject of chicken tests, and points out they are required by the FAA. Here's what happens:

A live 4-pound chicken is anesthetized and placed in a flimsy plastic bag to reduce aerodynamic drag. The bagged bird is put in a compressed-air gun.

The bird is fired at the jetliner window at 380 knots and the window must withstand the impact. It is said to be a very messy test.

The inch-thick glass, which includes two layers of plastic, needn't come out unscathed. But it must not puncture. The test is repeated under various circumstances—the window is cooled by liquid nitrogen, or the chicken is fired into the center of the window or at its edge.

"We give Boeing an option," Berven joked. "They can either use a 4-pound chicken at 200 miles an hour or a 200-pound chicken at 4 miles an hour."

The British government requires that the metal above the windows also must pass the chicken test. This was the test the 757 failed. It had not been conducted on the 767, which has no British customers.

The 757 failure meant both airplanes had to be modified, since the metal overheads are structurally identical. Sixteen 767 cabs already had been completed, and had to be cut apart so reinforcing metal could be installed.

Mort Ehrlich, an Eastern Airlines senior vice president, said he watched Airbus Industrie conduct chicken tests in Toulouse, France.

"A few of us who were there uttered the classic remark about how hard it is to be a chicken in Toulouse," he said. "I guess the same is true in Seattle."

PART 4: PULLING IT TOGETHER

IT TAKES MONTHS to manufacture the myriad parts and details of a Boeing 757 but, in only a single work shift, workers and machines merge the pieces into the image of an airliner.

It's called the "come-together," and that's just what the airplane does in a matter of hours inside a cavernous hangar at Boeing's Renton plant.

From nose to tail, the 757 takes shape in a series of operations as big as hoisting tons of metal by crane and as small as the painstaking alignment of body sections to tolerances measured in thousandths of an inch.

Yet the come-together, impressive as it is, is just a fragment of the puzzle of assembling a 757. One could spend days touring facilities involved in making the 757 and still come away with only a general idea of the process.

"All you've got to do is bring people in here and show them this place," said Bill Robison, director of manufacturing for the 757. "I don't know what they expect. I don't know what they think we do.

"Or sometimes I really don't know how to display it to them ... the vastness of that factory ... the gee-whiz numbers you can quote to them, like 60,000 assemblies. It's hard for people to comprehend."

The hangar in which the come-together and final assembly take place is known as the 4-81 Building. It adjoins the 4-80 Building, where 737s are assembled. The two actually form a single structure, the largest at the Renton complex.

Like the Kingdome, it is an edifice which seems bigger inside than out. It swallows men and machines, making the snap of a rivet gun or the hum of an electric ceiling crane sound remote. Viewed from a lofty perch inside the hangar, workers almost vanish in the vastness of the enclosed space.

The scope of the Boeing operation is all the more overwhelming when compared to the manufacturing facilities of Boeing's rival, the European consortium Airbus Industrie. Though impressive in its own right, the Airbus operation is dwarfed by Boeing's.

After the come-together, Boeing 757s, their metal skins covered with yellow-green protective coating, are assembled on a line with six stations. At each station certain tasks are done to the interior and exterior: wiring the cockpit, installing the galleys, hanging the engines ...

When an airplane has migrated the length of the hangar, past all six stations, it is moved outside and the five planes behind it each move up to the next station. This leaves an open spot at the first station, where the next 757 will start to come together.

The first time a 757's wings take to the air they are suspended by cable from two cranes crawling just beneath the ceiling of the 4-81 Building. That is the beginning of the come-together, and laborers pause to gaze aloft at the sight: two wings mated to either side of a short, hollow section of fuselage.

Crane operators slowly bring the suspended wing assembly into place over an array of steel scaffolds, beams, braces and ramps at the first station. These imposing contraptions, rising from the hangar floor, are known at Boeing as "tools."

Tools range from scaffolding to hand-held devices, from mammoth computer-driven riveting machines to steel frames in which airplane subassemblies are created. Many tools are one-of-a-kind, and they must meet exacting standards because many parts of the airplane must fit together with precision.

Increasingly, tools are replacing skilled laborers.

"We've poured well over $2 billion into high-productivity machinery in the plant in the last four or five years," said John Swihart, a Boeing vice president, referring to Boeing's whole commercial-airplane operation.

"If you throw in the development cost of the two new airplanes on top of that, we've poured about $6 billion into making us the most productive airplane manufacturing company in the world. We've got machines today that are 40 percent more productive than what we used four years ago. We're building more pounds of airplanes today than we were at our best point, with half the people."

The tooling onto which the wing assembly is lowered contains hydraulic jacks to level the fuselage, plus a maze of walkways and work areas.

The next section to be lowered into place during the come-together is the aft section of fuselage, which extends from just behind the wings to the back end of the airplane. Neither the vertical tail nor horizontal tail (the small set of wings at the back of a jetliner) are attached to the tubular section at this point.

Finally, huge doors open to let a tractor pull the forward fuselage section into the hangar. One crane hooks onto the front of the nose section and another hooks to the rear. The hollow shell is hoisted and set in alignment with the two wing sections.

Suddenly an airplane has taken shape, although the individual sections still are more than a foot apart. Over the next several hours, workers will inch them together, measuring and leveling with surveying tools.

But even after the come-together is complete, the 757 is still weeks away from screaming down a nearby runway for its first flight.

THE COME-TOGETHER and much of the assembly of the 757 is done at the Renton complex, but the manufacture of the airplane is spread around the U.S. and the world.

The nose, for instance, is made at Boeing's Wichita plant, the tail by Vought in Texas, the engines by Rolls-Royce in Derby, England.

In fact, only 48 percent of the first 757 to roll off the production line was made "in-plant" at Renton. Sixteen percent was made at other Boeing locations and 36 percent by non-Boeing companies in the U.S. and abroad.

These figures change. Until last year, Rockwell was a major subcontractor on the 757, making much of the airplane's fuselage. Now Boeing is doing the work at Renton.

Jim Madewell, who was general manager of the Rockwell project, said the company had initial problems applying the ultra-thin skin on the 757 fuselage sections without introducing subtle wrinkles.

The problem was resolved with experience, but soon Boeing needed more work in its Renton plant and Rockwell needed to use its capacity for the B-1 bomber project, so the companies agreed to cancel their contract, Madewell said.

Before recession hit the airline industry a couple of years ago, Boeing was so busy it didn't have capacity either to engineer or manufacture the 757 without outside help.

Major subcontractors were selected partly for their willingness to loan aerospace engineers to Boeing. Nearly 1,000 engineers relocated temporarily in the Seattle area, remaining on the payrolls of the subcontractors but working at Boeing's direction on the 757 and 767 programs.

"We simply told them that without the engineers, there would be no contract awards," Frank Gregory, Boeing's director of personnel, said in mid-1979. "The engineer shortage is so severe that it was a do-or-die situation."

The arrangement often suited the subcontractors. A Northern Ireland company, Short Bros., dispatched engineers to Seattle for a year to design inboard flaps for the 757, which the firm later manufactured. "I think our engineers came back better engineers," said Jim McKerrow, Short Bros.' new business manager. "There was an educational value."

Jack Edwards, who headed procurement for the 757 project, estimated that as many as 400 Boeing employees were involved in finding suppliers and subcontractors and striking deals.

"The contractors are very complicated," Edwards said. "We're talking billions of dollars."

Early on, Boeing decided which parts of the airplane would be made in-house and which parts would be acquired elsewhere. Procurement teams assembled lists of potential suppliers for each part or section of the 757. To be considered, a supplier had to demonstrate it could comply with Boeing contractual terms in areas such as price, production rate and quality.

"We look at their financial situation to see that they can handle this kind of thing, because on most programs we ask them, in effect, to share costs—to defer non-recurring charges until we start delivering airplanes," Edwards said.

Altogether, 37 major subcontractors were signed up for the 757 project, plus hundreds of major suppliers.

Once contracts were let, Boeing could not afford to assume the subcontractors would meet their obligations. Late arrival of a part or assembly would delay construction of the airplane, so Boeing representatives visited subcontractors frequently to observe work progress.

Subcontractors also submitted documentation of progress each week for Boeing to review. "If we see where we're running into any problem items, we can immediately react," Edwards said.

"You're always running into somebody who's going bankrupt," said E.V. Fenn, who was general manager of the 757 program for most of its formative years. "Or somebody's having problems."

Problems are commonplace because of the complexity of the manufacturing process and the evolving nature of the airplane's design. The design literally changes up until the day the airplane is delivered, though most major changes occur relatively early in development.

Boeing tries to anticipate potential changes and negotiates contracts accordingly. The idea is to keep cost increases to a minimum—and assure that parts are delivered on time.

SOMETIMES CONTRACTS and foresight aren't enough to produce the parts Boeing needs to build an airplane. When that happens, the company turns to the world's largest machine shop for help.

It is the Boeing Fabrication Division, with headquarters in Auburn and a sizeable operation near Boeing Field. It receives little outside recognition, but supports dozens of Boeing programs—from hydrofoils to helicopters, from spaceships to jetliners.

The division turns out 1.25 million machined parts a month. Just to shave some of these metal parts to proper shape may require as many as 12 different cutting heads on a million-dollar machine.

"Auburn," as the Fabrication Division is known, "supplies the lifeline items for the assembly line, the things that are totally critical to keeping the airplanes on schedule," said Fenn, who managed the division at one time. Manufacture of wing spars, skins and other critical items can be kept close to home this way, he said.

The Fabrication Division also is the manufacturing equivalent of a military rapid-deployment force. When a subcontractor is late or there's a rush change order, Boeing can put a great deal of manufacturing power to work quickly.

"Auburn's got a quick-reaction capacity, so the line never falters," Fenn said.

"Auburn" more closely resembles a stereotypical factory than most Boeing manufacturing operations. Huge rooms, some smelling of oil, house millions of dollars worth of machinery.

Another contrast between the machine shops of Auburn and other Boeing divisions is that many Auburn workers have no idea what they're making. The shapes they create often seem almost abstract.

"We never worry about what it is," said one man working on a metal part. "As long as I have something to do, that's what I worry about."

Jay Hess tends a precision boring mill at the Auburn division. The machine was automated last fall. "I did it for 18 years by hand," Hess said. "It was harder work, but it becomes a part of you. I've been doing it by pushbutton for two months, and it's a big adjustment."

As Hess spoke, workers started a 15-minute break. A ping-pong table appeared in a flash and four men played a spirited game until the break was over. Then the table vanished and work resumed.

In addition to making critical parts for aircraft, the Fabrication Division makes the tools that make the airplanes.

For instance, the 757's doors are assembled in Renton on frames made by the Fabrication Division. Each door is made on a different series of frames.

Altogether, 36 frames are used to manufacture 757 doors and the cost of making each frame averages $750,000, according to Lloyd Susee, 757 door-shop supervisor.

The expense is due to the precision required. Control points along the lines of the frame must be accurate to tolerances of .0025 of an inch, so that doors—which must mate with the airplane—will enjoy similar tolerances.

"Everything," Susee said with emphasis, "has got to fit."

THE WING SKINS of the 757 begin as large sheets of inch-thick aluminum at Auburn.

They are stacked flat and on edge along with the larger wings of 747s and 767s and the smaller wings of 727s and 737s, all inside a "skin and spar mill" which is almost a quarter-mile long.

The aluminum sheets are carved and contoured at Auburn to thicknesses of as little as 8 one-hundredths of an inch. The work is automated, with one man watching over a sprawling machine that works its way down the wing.

"All you've got to do is put the right cutter in and make sure nothing goes wrong," an operator said.

A close look at an aluminum wing skin reveals its thickness is not uniform. Surplus weight is an enemy of efficient flight, so the metal is shaved surprisingly thin in many places to eliminate each unnecessary ounce.

Thinner skins, fewer fasteners and use of composite materials such as graphite are factors in reducing the wing weight, part of an intense and successful campaign by Boeing to keep the 757's weight as low as possible.

"It doesn't make it any weaker," said Bill Arthalony, supervisor on the 757 wing line in Renton, referring to the thin skin of the wing. "The wing when it's airborne doesn't weigh anything."

The key to a strong wing is strong fasteners, said Ken Storkel, a factory manager in Renton.

The aluminum skins are subjected to bombardment by millions of tiny balls like buckshot. This "shot peening" releases stress, strengthens the metal and imparts a texture.

The skins next are dipped into tanks of nitric acid for cleaning, then tested for cracks with a dye penetrant.

The 63-foot-long skins and the wing's "stringers" are moved from Auburn to Renton. Two stringers, running from the body of the airplane to the wingtip, connect three side-by-side skins into a single large surface called a panel assembly. There is one panel assembly for the top of the wing and another for the bottom.

The skins are attached to the stringers by mammoth computer-controlled machines known as Drivematics. The skins are held on edge while the machine moves methodically from one end to the other, pausing every few moments to automatically drill, ream and countersink a hole, install a rivet and microshave its head to present a smooth skin.

"It's a tremendous labor saver," Storkel said. "It does cut jobs, but we call it a productivity improvement. That's the only way you can compete."

Meanwhile, spars for the front and rear of each wing are fashioned from aluminum on a balcony in one of Boeing's many buildings in Renton. Each spar has a graphite skin.

The panel assemblies and spars are brought together and wrapped around wing ribs on a series of enormous jigs. Titanium rivets are used to hold everything together. Some of the rivets are cooled to 40 degrees below zero before insertion, yielding a tight fit as they warm to normal temperatures and expand.

Finally, the wings are removed to the floor of the factory, where flaps and slats and other assemblies are added.

The wings are tested for fuel tightness, too, since thousands of pounds of jet fuel will be stored in them. There is no bladder or lining; the fuel is directly in contact with the inside of the aluminum wing.

"What we're building is a fuel cell," Arthalony said.

"It just happens it is also a wing," added Storkel.

HUMAN INGENUITY found a lot of ways to save weight in the 757. And that saved money.

Boeing estimates the weight reductions will save more than $100 million on the production costs of the first 300 757s.

From engineering to manufacturing, Boeing employees pondered ways to trim an ounce or a pound. Dick Burnham, an engineering assistant, came up with numerous ideas—little thoughts that added up.

For example, it occurred to Burnham that carpet padding wasn't needed under that portion of the carpeting extending up the side wall of the airplane. The padding was removed.

The walls, partitions and ceilings of the 757 are made of composite materials. The ceiling panels are a crushed honeycomb product, strong and yet so light that the panels for the entire 525-square-foot ceiling weigh only 180 pounds—and almost half of that is for the hardware that holds the panels up.

Seats in the 757 are manufactured in sets of three—and a set weighs a total of only 55 pounds. New seats, soon to be released, will weigh only 47 pounds a set.

Computers are beginning to reshape the role of the American worker, and the signs of change are unmistakable at Boeing. Computers increasingly are challenging human ingenuity for supremacy in areas such as saving weight.

Even the colors on the 757's tail are getting a computer assist.

"Five years ago we were putting a sign painter out there and we'd hope the customer would like the results," said Robison, the director of manufacturing. Each plane was slightly different because it was painted by hand, but "today we're giving them a computer-generated stencil, and every one of them is identical."

The same is true of carpets for airplane interiors. Garth Cooper, lead operator of manufacturing-engineering computer graphics, says it once took 120 days to design and finish a template that could be used to cut carpeting. Now a computer does it in only 10 days.

"Up until now we've had to cut these templates by hand," Cooper said, but now a computer-driven machine also does that. The next step is to have the machines cut the carpet, too.

D.P. Tingwall, chief project engineer for engineering computering, said Boeing is trying to assess how to make a "quantum step forward in the use of these (computer) tools, based on what we've learned and what we know we can do with them."

Machines can do some kinds of work with a speed and consistency that humans can't match. One example is the 757's hydraulic tubing, bent to shape by machines which turn out identical results every time.

These changes portend a shift in the labor force toward white-collar workers.

"Now one of two workers at Renton are blue-collar," Robison said. "In 20 years, based on our increases in productivity, that might be one in 20."

Productivity: One Key to Success

BOEING'S manufacturing success is built on ever-improving productivity, the art and science of doing more and more with less and less.

The object is to save the company as much money as possible and keep its costs competitive by automation and getting more work out of people per hour.

"Running the business is a simple thing," said Malcolm Stamper, Boeing's president. "You just try to be as productive as possible."

The airplane industry is highly competitive, with manufacturers clawing at each other with low-ball offers to airlines. Boeing management believes the company's future depends on keeping up its manufacturing efficiency.

"If you don't build as efficiently as you can, you can't compete in the world," Stamper said. "You either have to work faster or use more mechanical advantages."

Despite a reputation among some of its employees as an easy place to be lazy, Boeing is renowned for its productivity. One recent chronicler of the aircraft industry, John Newhouse, refers to "Boeing's astonishing productivity" which gives it the "ability to assemble airliners faster than any competitor in the world."

Although robotics are being used increasingly at Boeing, skilled and experienced employees remain the key to productivity. Every airplane is assembled a little more efficiently than the one before, and Boeing depends on employees to move toward lower manufacturing costs.

There is speculation that Seattle's relative geographic isolation has been a major factor in Boeing's success. Unlike southern California, aerospace workers here cannot easily move to competing aerospace firms, and employees tend to stick with Boeing—unless they get laid off.

The company is constantly adjusting the size of its workforce and layoffs are viewed as an unpleasant consequence of remaining productive. But layoffs also can damage productivity, because the company loses experienced workers.

"Every time we have to lay off somebody, we're sending a good guy out the door. No question about it," said Joe Sutter, a Boeing vice president.

"We don't like to do that, for two reasons. Some of them are going down to other areas where they can get work. They take all that Boeing training away with them. But we just hate to have to do that to them, too."

Stamper said it pains him when Boeing lays off thousands of workers. "I was hungry as a kid, because my old man worked in an auto plant in Detroit. When he got laid off I didn't eat."

The move toward automation concerns union leaders, but they say it's inevitable.

"How can you resist it?" asked Robert Bradford, executive director of the Seattle Professional Engineering Employees Association (SPEEA). "It's like the flood. My concern is we have to manage it."

"I don't think there's any way of thinking union representation can oppose new technology," said Tom Baker, president of the local Aeromechanics Union. "That's unrealistic. New technology is on the way, but the union needs to get the employer to look at it in a responsible way."

Bradford and Baker, who between them represent the engineers and technicians who design the 757 and the mechanics who assemble it, say Boeing is not forthright enough about its intentions regarding automation and other issues. The company may not want to tip its hand for competitive reasons, but Boeing employees have a legitimate need to know what the future may hold, they say.

"There are going to be different jobs and fewer of them, and more competition for them," Bradford said. He and Baker believe employees must be trained for the increasingly automated future.

Boeing has a responsibility to work with the unions to keep technology an ally of its employees, not an enemy, the union leaders suggested.

"Technology is what's creating the productivity. We're working smarter," Bradford said. A calculator is said to allow an engineer to work with 20 times the efficiency of a slide rule, and it may be that computers are creating similar gains over calculators, he said.

Boeing attempts to promote productivity with a variety of programs. For instance, it pays an employee up to $10,000 for a cost-saving suggestion. In 1982, 22,000 employees submitted 51,000 suggestions and the company paid $4.3 million in awards.

One employee, Tom King, has averaged $1,000 a month in extra take-home pay by making cost-saving suggestions on the 757 program—more than 180 separate suggestions since the beginning of 1982.

"Employee involvement is a key to the process of change," said John Black, productivity manager for the 757 program. "Responsive change maintains our competitive edge to improve productivity. And improved productivity means greater profit, more jobs and a higher standard of living."

Black said the first thing he did when he took charge of productivity planning on the 757 program in 1979 was examine what he calls "the Boeing culture."

"We spent quite a while looking at what the Japanese are doing, what the west Europeans are doing. And their culture. And recognizing that we're not going to bring the Japanese culture over here and we're not going to bring the west European culture here. We have our own culture within the Boeing Co."

An important element of Boeing's culture, Black said, is cooperation between management and the workforce on issues of productivity. It's a non-adversarial relationship, he said.

Bradford and Baker agreed this is largely true, but cautioned that Boeing needs better communication with unions and should plan more openly. "I think we may begin butting heads over automation," Bradford said.

The Boeing workforce is changing as society changes, Black said. The methods by which employees can be motivated are changing as traditional values and institutions change.

"Twenty years ago, the average education of the blue-collar

hourly employee in the (Boeing) factory was eighth-grade. Today it's a year of college," Black said.

The percentage of minority and female workers is growing. The average employee age is 41 and growing older as layoffs reduce the ranks of younger workers.

"We have to understand that we're going to have to do things differently," Black said.

One innovation imported from Japan and used in the 757 program is the "quality circle," in which small groups of employees meet with management to discuss possible improvements and cost savings for the company and ways to improve morale among workers. A productivity technique used with increasing frequency, it was first adopted in this country by Lockheed, a Boeing competitor.

Pride in the company and its airplanes must be maintained, said Black, who is enthusiastically proud of both. He even wrote a country-Western song, "757 Fly," which he calls "a statement of Boeing culture."

The company had the song recorded in Los Angeles. It goes like this:

"757 fly, where angels fear to go. The Boeing people build them best, best is all we know ... Well this airplane company seems to have a hold on me. We'll be building Boeings until the end of time ..."

PART 5: WILL IT REALLY FLY?

"WE ALMOST LOST ONE."

That was the urgent communique from one top federal aviation official to another last Nov. 16 after a particularly dramatic 2-hour, 17-minute flight by a Boeing 757.

LeRoy Keith, who heads the Federal Aviation Administration's certification program for jetliners, was at FAA headquarters in Washington, D.C., when the phone call came.

Darrell Pederson, a Keith lieutenant, was on the line from Seattle. He was supervising Boeing's efforts to prove the 757 airworthy, and his call attracted attention because it interrupted an important meeting.

Keith recalls Pederson's message. "He said, 'Well, ... we had ... we almost lost one.' He was quite frank about it."

During a certification flight, a 757 had ingested ice in its huge Rolls-Royce engines, setting off cockpit alerts and creating a roar that one person on board said sounded disturbingly like a car without a muffler.

Keith said Pederson sounded shaken on the telephone. "He said it had an icing encounter and went back to Boeing Field drifting down on minimum-power setting, and got back and found the fan blades were damaged on both engines."

Later there would be differences of opinion about just how serious the problem had been, and whether the airplane really had been in any peril.

The crew intentionally had been seeking ice build-up on the airplane's wings to prove its performance under such conditions and had lingered in circumstances which any commercial pilot would have avoided. It was not a situation likely to be encountered by an airplane carrying passengers, because commercial pilots don't go looking for trouble.

The objective of flight testing is to uncover potential problems, even those that are extremely unlikely. Boeing and FAA officials agree that every new airplane design has unforeseen snags that need to be discovered and corrected, and it's not fair to judge an aircraft until this process is complete.

Despite these caveats, no one took the icing incident lightly.

"It sounded really serious," Keith said. "And in fact, it was."

A Boeing flight engineer with significant responsibility for the program described the Nov. 16 flight this way: "They were descending into terrain and didn't have power to climb. It's very dangerous. You can lose a plane that way. We don't fly with parachutes because we expect to land in the middle of a runway every time."

The engine problem, coming so late in the 757's development, posed logistical difficulties for Boeing, Rolls-Royce and the 757's first customer, Eastern Airlines. The airline wanted its first plane within a month, but the FAA wasn't about to certify it until there was conclusive proof that the problem had been solved.

For their part, neither Boeing nor Rolls wanted an airplane operating with any safety question lingering.

John Winch, who directs Boeing's flight-test and certification programs, said the company went to unprecedented lengths to ensure both the 757 and 767 were thoroughly tested.

The FAA's certification procedures for the Boeing 757 and 767 are said to be the most comprehensive in history. After suffering the sting of criticism over difficulties experienced by the McDonnell Douglas DC-10 long after it was certified for flight, federal officials intensified their efforts to be certain the 757 and 767 certification programs were beyond reproach.

"I think the real reason we're being tougher is because these are a lot more complex airplanes than we had eight years ago, or 10 years ago with the 747," Keith said.

The 757 and 767 have two-man crews and equipment for low-visibility landings, both of which required additional certification efforts, said Brian Wygle, Boeing vice president of flight operations.

The 757 carries more than 100 computers, and federal inspectors sought proof that both the airplane's hardware and the intricacies of the computer software were fail-safe.

Certification is a painstaking process—and an expensive one. "You spend $1.5 million to $2 million per airplane just to put the (certification instrumentation) parts in," a Boeing engineer said. It has been estimated that flying jetliners that are equipped for flight testing and certification costs more than $50,000 an hour.

The task of certifying two airplanes simultaneously added to the challenge. At the peak of the certification effort, 17 aircraft (including models other than 757s and 767s) were involved in flight testing, said James Lincoln, manager of the data section of Boeing flight-test engineering.

The whole program, another official said, "cost hundreds of millions of dollars."

Flight testing has a splashy reputation, a lingering image of the do-or-die pilot tempting fate to prove his machine. But a Boeing flight-test engineer said "we don't do much of that 'white knuckles and silk scarves' stuff any more."

Still, in their more dramatic moments, flight tests aren't for the faint of heart.

Testing and certifying an airplane involves pushing it into what Phil Condit, general manager of the 757 program, calls "far corners"—performance situations one hopes an airplane will never have to encounter in actual service.

Far corners can be terrifying to the uninitiated.

A 757 cruises with maximum fuel efficiency at 80 percent of the speed of sound, or mach .8. Its maximum intended speed is mach .86. But Boeing pressed the airplane to mach .92 in flight testing. A far corner.

Such flights, said Rick Lentz, 757 flight-test aero-analysis lead engineer, "can be frightening, because the plane responds with buffeting. The tail assembly is groaning and wings are flapping—and until you've been through this a few times, you're not sure it will hold together."

The fear is personal, not corporate, Lentz added. Anxiety is normal for a person who hasn't been through it before, although Boeing is confident the airplane will perform as intended, he said.

The vibrations of some manuevers, Lentz said, "will literally rattle your teeth."

Not every dramatic test takes place in the air. Boeing routinely destroys one airplane of each model to see what it takes, to see if it's really as tough as the engineers say it is.

The 757 test happened last July 16. Enormous pressures were applied to a 757 airframe inside a hangar. The wings were bent upwards ... first two feet ... then five ... eight ... 10 ... At 11 feet, 6 inches of deflection, both wings snapped.

"It's like loading a bridge," Condit said. "You just keep loading it until the thing finally goes 'kaboom!' That's exactly the sound it makes. I felt it in my knees. I don't know if that was the excitement or the boom."

The results were pleasing, because the airplane proved 12 percent stronger than engineering estimates, and because, in a tribute to Boeing engineering and quality control, both wings failed at the same place and at almost the same moment—just 14 thousandths of a second apart.

IMAGINE WHAT must go through the mind of a test pilot about to take off in a jetliner which never has flown before.

Wind-tunnel tests say the aircraft will fly. Engineers say the design will soar like a dream. Mechanics and inspectors have looked over the huge machine.

But will it really fly?

John Armstrong, chief test pilot for the Boeing 757 program, said he felt little anxiety about taking off for the first time ever in a 757 on Feb. 19 of last year.

"Excitement" is what he remembers of the moments before hurtling into the air from Renton Municipal Airport.

Armstrong and Boeing called it a "perfect first flight" upon landing, although later they admitted that a design problem, later corrected, prompted them to temporarily shut down one of the 757's two engines during the flight.

Armstrong, piloting the "No. 1" 757, had general good fortune throughout the 11-month flight-test program—a program which involved five different airplanes, each conducting separate tests specified years in advance.

Like the rest of the 757 project, the requirements of a 1,254-hour flight-test program were scheduled with precision back in late 1978 and 1979, before Boeing irrevocably committed itself to the financial and other risks of a new-airplane program.

A chart created at the end of 1978 shows Armstrong's 757 was to fly 375 hours of tests, between February and December 1982 when certification was to be complete. The timetable was met.

The inside of Armstrong's 757 would be almost unrecognizable to a frequent flyer on regular commercial-airline flights.

There are few seats. Water barrels, like metal beer kegs in appearance, are positioned where seats might otherwise be. By filling the barrels in differing configurations, Boeing engineers can simulate the effects of different passenger loads.

There are racks of computerized equipment attached to thousands of wires which snake through the airplane. The wires carry signals from sensors all over the plane, and computers record the data and help make sense out of it.

Four thousand channels of information were stored simultaneously by the on-board flight-test computers on the 757. A decade ago, the 747 flight-test computer equipment filled a jumbo jet from stem to stern and succeeded in recording only 800 channels, while the 757 accomplished a much larger task with room to spare inside a shorter, much narrower airplane. That's a result of a decade of computer evolution.

Several engineers and technicians are on board during test flights, monitoring the gear and the airplane's performance. The atmosphere is business-like, competent, yet markedly relaxed. A flight attendant from a commercial airline might wince at the freedom of movement inside a test-flight airplane, even during takeoffs or landings.

WHEN LOCAL TELEVISION viewers see news stories on the 757 or 767, they are sometimes treated to rather unusual footage of a Boeing airplane touching its tail to the runway during takeoff. It's an interesting sight—and not always explained by the newscaster, who may be reporting Boeing sales figures or some other issue unrelated to flight tests.

The tail dragging is known as "Vmu" testing, and it was one of the missions of 757 No. 1. It took place last June in southern California, at Edwards Air Force Base, the same place the Space Shuttles have landed.

Twenty-eight times the 757 dragged its tail down the Edwards runway. Each was a test of the characteristics of the 757 at minimum-speed takeoffs (Vmu stands for Velocity-minimum unstick, with "unstick" signifying the wheels departing the runway).

The object was to determine the lowest speed of safe takeoff under various conditions so that a schedule could be established to guide pilots in selecting appropriate take-off speeds.

Avoiding damage to the airplane during the tail scraping involved careful work by the pilots and the temporary addition of an oak skid to the bottom side of the rear of the airplane.

Pilots lifted the nose of the airplane off the ground rapidly, lowering the tail in what is called "rotation." When they sensed the tail was about to touch the ground, they would slow the rate of rotation.

"It's a hard test to fly, to be precise about it," said Les Berven, the FAA pilot who flew the Vmu tests with Armstrong. "You have to rotate just fast enough to make sure you've gotten the tail on the ground before lift-off, but not so fast that you hit it."

The judgment, Berven said, is "seat of the pants."

Though Armstrong's 757 was put through its paces relatively uneventfully, the opposite was true of 757 No. 3, flown by a fellow test pilot, Kenny Higgins.

Problems began the first time the airplane was flown: the landing gear would not retract fully.

The flight continued, with the wheels hanging out of the airplane at a strange angle, but it was cut short at 39 minutes. The basic airworthiness of the airplane was established, however.

Five days later, a more difficult problem developed.

Higgins was bringing in No. 3 for a landing at Boeing Field after a flight of more than three hours when he had trouble with the airplane's flap system. A transmission part froze, forcing the airplane to land about 20 knots too fast.

To Boeing's total surprise, all four tires on the right-hand side caught fire when the brakes locked up. The wheels were ground flat. On the left-hand side, two tires and wheels were flattened.

Fire trucks moved in and put out the flames. Boeing workers jacked the airplane up and changed wheels and tires, then taxied the airplane off the runway and into a hangar.

Flight-test problems are instructive, and Boeing set out to learn from the bad landing. In this instance, finding the cause of the difficulties was challenging— "a real witch hunt," in the words of Jim Johnson, director of engineering on the 757 project.

The snag was in computer programming.

In the end, it was proved that the flap problem was unrelated to the locking of the wheels, which was a failure of the plane's anti-skid system. A freakish set of electrical impulses confused four of five computers controlling the anti-skid system, Condit said.

It took several weeks before the bugs were all worked out, although temporary repairs were made within two days.

"It took us about a day and a half to isolate the problem," Johnson said. "Very quickly, through what we call cuts and jumpers, where we go into a circuit board and make a cut and put in a new wire ... we were flying."

The same fixes were made in all the 757s—and in all the 767s, where the same potential problem existed.

But Higgins' troubles with No. 3 weren't over. He had yet to fly the Nov. 16 "ice flight."

Ice on a jetliner can be deadly, as was demonstrated by the crash of an Air Florida 737 into the Potomac River near Washington, D.C.'s, National Airport on Jan. 13, 1982. The problem is most threatening when the ice is irregularly shaped, because it can dramatically change the shape of the airplane's airfoil, destroying much of its lift.

For most of its 2 hours and 17 minutes, the Nov. 16 flight was uneventful. The pilots were intentionally building up two inches of ice on the 757's wings, then shedding it with anti-ice systems.

But the unexpected struck rudely toward the end of the flight when chunks of ice broke off the center hubs of the two Rolls Royce engines and damaged the fan blades.

Rather than heating the engine's "spinner cone"—the hub in the center of the outer fan blades—Rolls had elected to use a flexible tip it believed would flex to keep ice from building up.

The Nov. 16 flight proved dramatically that the flexible tip wouldn't always work.

Immediately upon ingestion of the ice, both engines began to rumble and cockpit instruments showed high levels of engine vibration. The vibration could be felt throughout the airplane, including the cockpit.

Higgins and Dick Paul, the FAA pilot on board, cut back the engine power, alternately idling one engine, then the other. They aborted the tests, retracted the flaps and raised the landing gear.

The left-side engine was vibrating particularly badly on the return to Boeing Field, and the pilots agreed to land with the engine idling rather than possibly push it too far by running it hard.

Finding ice hadn't been easy for Boeing. There had been a weeks-long search for the appropriate test conditions. Then, suddenly, there was an abundance of ice—and an unexpected problem.

Engineers in the back of the airplane, monitoring banks of instruments and watching the ice on the wings, were pleased with the amount of ice they finally had found.

But in the cockpit, where the engine performance was alarming the pilots, there was no elation. Upon landing, Higgins told the FAA: "I was not happy."

ROLLS AND BOEING solved the problem by substituting a heated spinner core for the flexible tip. It was a rush job, with round-the-clock shifts in the Rolls-Royce's plant at Derby, England, producing the spinner on a few day's notice.

The airplane was certified and rushed into service by Eastern Airlines, which took delivery of its first two 757s at the end of December.

But the FAA made the certificate valid for only six months. The airplane was perfectly safe, the FAA said, but it wanted a seat in the cockpit repositioned so that FAA personnel who occasionally ride along on commercial flights could have a better view of pilot activities.

Boeing and the FAA dug in over the issue, and it looked for a time as if the matter would end up in court. But in late May, the FAA granted a permanent certificate after Boeing agreed to move the 757 seat just 7½ inches.

Hundreds of Boeing flight-test employees gathered at Longacres on Jan. 22 to celebrate the certification of the 757. The FAA came in for more than a little ribbing, including a skit in which an outlandish chair with a chicken attached to it was displayed and proclaimed to be, by a supposed FAA representative, a "damn good seat."

But the flight-test crews gave themselves a bad time, too. The test pilots and their airplanes were roasted in good humor.

When it was Higgins' turn, a top Boeing engineer named Pete Morton explained the astronomical odds against all the problems Higgins had encountered with 757 No. 3. He gave Higgins a T-shirt with the slogan "Extremely Improbable."

Higgins, having weathered a stormy certification filled with unlikely events, replied: "Extremely improbable to me means that it happened yesterday."

PART 6: AN ACT OF FAITH

SELLING JETLINERS is a bit like peddling religion. Buying one requires an act of faith.

The salesman demands part of the payment up front, but the airline has to wait—sometimes for years—for the payoff. Meanwhile, there may be doubts: Will the airplane be ready on time? Will it do what the manufacturer says? And will the maker be there, indefinitely, continuing to tend to the buyer's needs?

"You sell on the basis of the relationship of the top people and engineers of the two companies," the manufacturer and the airline, said E.H. "Tex" Boullioun, who's had a hand in selling hundreds of Boeing jetliners.

"The company that's buying—the airline—is putting up a third of their money, or part of their money, for something that's not going to be delivered for two to four years," Boullioun said.

"And so they have to have faith in the people (making the airplane). ... They're going to buy on the integrity of the people they're talking to, and their past performance," he said.

The airline's risk is greater if the plane has never flown. When British Airways and Eastern Airlines became the customers that launched the Boeing 757 project almost five years ago, they paid millions for an airplane that was nothing more than drafting paper, images on a computer screen and wind-tunnel models.

Although Boeing assigns salesmen to each of the world's airlines, "there's no such thing as a single guy selling an airplane anymore," said John Swihart, Boeing's vice president for domestic sales.

"We all sell," said Carl Munson, Boeing's vice president for strategic planning. "Anybody at Boeing management is prepared to jump on an airplane and go try to sell an airplane any time."

Boullioun and other top Boeing executives travel the world talking to airline chiefs. Sometimes, though not frequently, they will load a new jetliner with executives, engineers and maintenance personnel and fly it to an air show or on a tour of world airlines. The idea is to stir up interest.

Until a few years ago, Boeing also spent millions of dollars on payoffs to foreign airline officials who were in a position to influence purchasing decisions. After a federal crackdown on such practices and payment of stiff fines by Boeing for these illegal "sales commissions," the company says the practice has been ended.

Typically, selling begins years before contracts with airlines are signed. Boeing courts the customer with technical arguments, financial schemes and the less quantifiable lures of product prestige, confidence in Boeing's competence and the kinship formed by long personal associations.

Even after the airplane is delivered, the selling continues. Boeing is widely regarded as a foremost practitioner of the art of product support, and its reputation for taking care of its customers is a crucial sales tool. "We want to help them make money," said Jim Blue, who headed Boeing product support for several years.

Boullioun tells a story which illustrates both the importance of establishing a personal relationship with airline executives and helping the customer after the sale.

Boullioun, who for years was president of the Boeing Commercial Airplane Co., said Delta Airlines was exclusively a Douglas customer until it purchased five 747s in about 1970.

He recalls that not long after Delta took the 747s, its president, David Garrett, told him the jumbo jets were too large for his airline to operate profitably. He showed Boullioun why.

The Boeing executive said he was impressed by Garrett's argument and offered to try to get the 747s off Delta's hands. "I was able to put together a deal where Flying Tiger would take those airplanes. It was not a sale for Boeing," Boullioun said.

Soon thereafter, Delta ordered the first of 116 Boeing 727s. Then it ordered $1.5 billion worth of Boeing 767s. And on Nov. 12, 1980, it placed a record-breaking order for 60 Boeing 757s valued at $3 billion.

The 757 order was crucial to Boeing because it gave the new airplane commercial credibility. Until the Delta sale, there had been no large orders since those placed by Eastern Airlines and British Airways two years earlier.

Last December, Delta ordered 33 short-range 737s, and Robert Oppenlander, the airline's senior vice president for finance, said Boeing would be front-runner for a 150-seat airplane Delta wants to buy.

When Boullioun relieved Garrett of his unwanted 747s a decade ago, there was nothing in it for Boeing directly.

"But in my mind, a relationship was established there," Boullioun said. "So he's willing to gamble his resources. And by God, Boeing will come through."

A PARADOX of selling airplanes is that the market is tiny but the amounts of money involved are huge.

Boeing estimates that between now and 1995 there is a market for $167 billion worth of new jetliners, but in the non-Communist world there are only about 300 potential customers. That makes every customer vitally important.

"Twenty of those airlines will need 50 percent of the world's production. So you try to be as responsive as possible," Munson said. "It's not like in the consumer business. You don't have people walk in off the street to buy like you do with automobiles."

Another anomaly is that airlines typically don't know what they want because the industry is so volatile that planning sometimes seems futile. Boeing employs about 300 people to analyze airline needs and finances, but choosing airplanes for the future is largely guesswork.

Swihart said Boeing's analysts sometimes gather more information on the airlines than the airlines have themselves. "They know the airline completely," he said. "In fact, for many of the smaller airlines, again, they depend on us."

Boeing analysts use information on airports, airline schedules and financial data to put together sales proposals for a particular airplane. "We'll develop scheduling plans: where an airline ought to fly, what time of day ... show them how the airplane fits," Swihart said.

A Boeing salesman carries ideas back and forth between the manufacturer and the airline. He lobbies the airline to buy, but he also may lobby Boeing to build what "his" airline wants or needs. "We do an awful lot of in-house marketing," said Hal Crawford, until recently Boeing's salesman to Eastern Airlines.

When it becomes clear that an airline is seriously considering a particular Boeing offering, the salesman becomes an orchestrator. He calls on Boeing engineers, analysts, maintenance supervisors, top executives—anyone whose sales efforts he thinks could help clinch the order.

"As a salesman at Boeing," Crawford said, "I can draw on anyone in the corporation, including the chairman of the board."

Swihart said, "We've got financial experts who can round up 20 banks, and maybe we test the water with the banks and see what kind of credibility these (airline) people have. And so we'll put together a banking consortium to finance the airplane for them."

In the later stages of negotiations, an airline will ask Boeing and its competitors to submit formal proposals, including prices. That's when the bargaining really begins in earnest, and that's when complicated deals are struck.

Price negotiations are tricky because neither Boeing nor an enginemaker wants one airline to know that they might have given someone else a better deal. One way around this is to charge a fairly standard "sticker price" for an airplane (in the case of the 757, about $40 million in 1983 dollars), then sweeten it with bargains in other areas, such as reduced maintenance costs, or credit for future purchases of spare parts, or attractive financing arrangements.

These sweeteners, which accomplish the same thing as price reductions, are known as "incentives," "inducements" or "concessions."

One incentive used occasionally is an offer by Boeing (or a competitor) to buy an airline's unneeded planes while selling them new ones. Another is to order to sell, at a favorable price, the data needed by an airline to operate its own computerized flight simulator.

Yet another is financing. Boeing likes to downplay its role as a participant in financing schemes, but it is forced to compete with Airbus Industrie of Europe and McDonnell Douglas—both of which have used attractive financial packages to help clinch sales.

Engine-makers battle with incentives, too. General Electric, Pratt & Whitney and Rolls-Royce compete vigorously and may offer such things as a free engine-maintenance shop in return for a large order of engines on a new airplane.

"I don't mind telling you what form Rolls-Royce puts concessions in," said John Hodson, a Rolls vice president. "They will either give or sell at a very low price the initial tooling needed to set up an overhaul shop. ... We provide engineers to help them in the introductory period. We provide those either free or for a very nominal sum. ... We will put a lease engine at their disposal so that they only have to buy the minimum number of spare engines until they've got their overhaul facility working."

When Delta was considering engines for the 757 in 1980, it looked both at Pratt & Whitney and Rolls-Royce. Eastern Airlines and British Airways were using a Rolls-Royce engine, but both Pratt and Rolls said they could do much better with a new design—and both engine-makers desperately wanted the Delta order.

Delta's Oppenlander recalls the price-performance guarantee and incentive battle between the two engine-makers: "It was a beautiful competition. It was ideal from the buyer's standpoint."

Pratt won the competition, partly by guaranteeing its engine would outperform any Rolls engine by about 8 percent. This was a guarantee made on the basis of engineering estimates, since neither company's engine will be ready for service until 1984.

There is a theory at Rolls-Royce, postulated by many executives including the director or marketing, Alan Smith, that Pratt gambled that it would drive Rolls out of the 757 market if it won the huge Delta order.

The theory, which Smith calls "a bit more than a rumor," is that Pratt guaranteed 8 percent better performance than any Rolls engine because it thought there would be no new Rolls engine.

Under such a guarantee, Pratt might pay Delta cash to the extent its engine is not 8 percent better than a Rolls engine.

But Rolls didn't drop out of the competition, and now Rolls executives gleefully expect Pratt will have to pay a fortune to Delta to meet its guarantee.

"Delta doesn't talk much," Smith said. "How much Delta will benefit, and Pratt will bleed, we'll never know."

Richard Coar, president of Pratt & Whitney, concedes the 8 percent guarantee figure is "about right." But he said the guarantee is based on his engine's superior technology, which he said is at least 8 percent better in fuel economy.

Coar predicted Rolls-Royce will drop its new engine in less than 18 months, after the performance of Pratt's engine is demonstrated. "They'll have to drop the engine to cut their losses," he said.

And if Rolls-Royce doesn't drop out?

"If they want to go bankrupt a second time," Coar said, "they are welcome to."

BOEING HAS RECEIVED ORDERS for only nine new 757s in the past two years, though not for lack of trying.

A combination of factors may be to blame. The airline industry is in recession, United and some other airlines don't want a plane the size of the 757, and some airlines may be waiting to evaluate new engines which will be available in a few years.

Whatever the reason, Boeing's salesmen are getting turned down a lot these days. So it seems especially ironic that Boeing rejected its first chance to sell the 757, six years ago.

The date was Tuesday, April 12, 1977. The time 8:30 a.m. The place, Miami.

Eastern Airlines president Frank Borman was ready for a new, fuel-efficient airplane, and he had one question for Boeing chairman T.A. Wilson: "Are you ready to produce?"

The 757 was only an idea under development, called the 7N7, and its design was far from settled. Other customers weren't ready to order, and "we kind of knew we didn't have the right airplane yet," Swihart said.

Boeing and Eastern officials met all morning at Eastern headquarters, with Wilson winding up a Boeing presentation just before noon. The gist was that Boeing wanted Eastern's business, but not yet. The answer to Borman's request was no.

EASTERN didn't wait long to react. If it couldn't buy from Boeing, it would buy elsewhere. That afternoon it voted to accept an offer from Airbus Industrie for the lease of four new A-300s—thus opening North America to Airbus for the first time.

Airbus, anxious to get established in the crucial North American market with its 240-seat airplane, offered incentives described by those familiar with them as "incredible."

The Europeans let Eastern use the first four airplanes free for six months, then leased the planes at reduced rates—rates which pretended the 240-seat airplanes had only 180 seats, the size of airplane Eastern wanted.

A year later, on April 6, 1978, Eastern agreed to buy 23 A-300s. Swihart estimates Airbus lost $10 million on each airplane it sold Eastern. "It's an absolute give-away subsidy, no question about it," he said.

Airbus can afford to sell below cost because it enjoys the backing of several European governments and apparently considers such sales worthwhile to establish credibility. "The Eastern deal gave us credentials in the rest of the world," an Airbus official said recently.

Boeing didn't give up on Eastern after the Airbus purchases. Boeing's engineers produced volumes outlining the evolving design of the proposed new Boeing airplane, which Crawford delivered to Eastern during frequent trips to Miami. His goal was to learn every aspect of every problem of the company, so he could explain how a 757 would solve those problems.

"I've worked the flight line," he said. "I've been out at night watching airplanes. I've talked to their ground crews. I've talked to their guys in the hangar.

"I've talked to their field engineers. I've talked to their performance engineers, their power-plant engineers. I've talked to their service managers, their stewardesses, their cabin attendants, their finance guy, their financial-analysis guys—you cover them all.

"And then finally, hopefully, and as does happen, you end up with the executive decision-makers," Crawford said.

Finally all the pieces came together.

On Aug. 31, 1978, after months of selling, the results were announced in a story on the front page of *The Seattle Times*. The story began:

"British Airways and Eastern Airlines announced plans today to order more than $1 billion worth of Boeing 757s."

Super Simulator Helps Train Pilots Quickly in
Boeing's New Airliner

CARL YOUNG, an Eastern Airlines pilot with a gentle southern drawl, spoke evenly when a red indicator light came on in a Boeing 757 cockpit during takeoff.

"We've got a fire here, Virgil," he said.

Virgil Tedder, his co-pilot, consulted a checklist and made a couple of adjustments. A display in the center of the control console said **"L ENGINE FIRE"**—a fire in the left engine of the two-engine airplane.

Outside the cabin windows, it was dark. Inside, panel lights and futuristic video screens glowed subtly. The cockpit was tilted back, nose up, in the early moments after takeoff. There was a hiss of air rushing over the 757's smooth nose, but the mood inside was quiet. Both men were intent.

"Fire went out," Tedder reported seconds later.

The airplane, powered by the remaining engine, made a wide circle to return to Boeing Field. Suddenly, one of the two video screens whose purpose is to alert pilots to problems went blank—another failure. But essential information from the screen transferred automatically to a companion display.

Young edged the airplane down toward the runway. Tedder pushed down a large lever, and landing gear could be heard rumbling into place. The cabin bumped on touchdown, but no more than usual.

The pilots shut down the flight deck and stepped out of the cockpit—not into a passenger cabin or an airport, but into a large, bright, mostly empty room. On the other side of plate-glass windows were computers.

"You can't tell me I haven't been flying," Young said.

But he hadn't.

Carl Young and Virgil Tedder had only been pretending, and the perils of their flight had only been drills, not actual emergencies. The two veteran pilots had been playing an electronic game so realistic and enthralling it would make a video-arcade junkie weep with envy.

The game is a multi-million dollar full-flight simulator at the Boeing Customer Training Center, less than a mile from Boeing Field. In this machine and others somewhat like it, airline pilots receive training in new airplanes before they ever take control of a real one.

Viewed from the outside, the simulator is a metal box on legs, like some stilt-legged mechanical creature one might see in a Star Wars movie.

The device is pure Star Wars on the inside, too. The array of controls is identical to those of the "Century 21" flight deck Boeing has incorporated in both the 757 and 767. Video displays offer sophisticated data in soft colors. Flight and maintenance instruments are linked to a computer which simulates flight circumstances—and emergencies—with an accuracy that pilots say is remarkable.

Looking through the cockpit "windows," a pilot sees realistic computer-generated color video images. When a pilot "takes off" in the simulator he sees an identifiable airport and its surroundings. The simulation of Boeing Field, for instance, may show a fuel truck on the runway and Mount Rainier in the distance.

The simulator, built in England by Rediffision Simulation Ltd., also imitates the noise and motion of flight. Six hydraulic systems under the simulator raise and tilt the cockpit to mimic a real airplane. The only thing that's missing is the feeling of acceleration, that feeling of being pushed into one's seat upon takeoff—and most people don't miss that until its absence is pointed out to them.

During the simulated flight by Young and Tedder, a Boeing instructor, Dant Bourn, observed the pilots. He played the role of air-traffic controller and threw them curves, like the engine fire and display-screen failure, by manipulating a special computer console.

In the computer room nearby, operators tended machines that can conjure up images of Moses Lake at noon and Bombay, India, at midnight, with equal ease.

Before a pilot graduates to a full-flight simulator, he receives several weeks of instruction using small computerized learning stations and other aids. After sessions in the simulator, the pilot has to fly a real 757 for only one hour, for the benefit of a Federal Aviation Administration inspector, in order to receive federal approval to fly the airplane in commercial service.

"Flying the airplane is rather anticlimactic after flying the simulator," Young said. "Simulators are getting so realistic. We are in fact approaching the point where pilots will be certified in this plane on a simulator only," he predicted.

Not many pilots have the opportunity to receive their training directly from Boeing. Most airlines send a selected number who return to the airline to train others. In the case of Eastern, the first airline to fly the 757, only eight of 4,400 pilots received 757 training in Seattle.

Large airlines often have their own simulators, though not necessarily the full-motion and vision simulators used by Boeing. The airlines' Boeing-trained pilots use the simulators to pass along the specialized skills necessary to fly a new airplane.

In the Boeing Customer Training Center one can find pilots from almost anywhere in the world. It's not unheard of to find Taiwanese and Chinese pilots bumping into each other and getting along. English is only one of many languages heard here, although all of Boeing's instruction is in English.

But training pilots, though important and expensive, is far from the only thing an airline does to ready itself for a new type of Boeing jetliner. There are plenty of other preparations to make.

SUSAN BORMAN liked what she saw.

The colors were right, the textures were right, the uniforms were right.

It was her first trip ever in a Boeing 757, the airplane her husband, Frank Borman, Eastern president, had helped launch with an order. The couple was aboard a Boeing flight from Montreal to London last September.

Mrs. Borman had visited Renton more than two years earlier to examine mockups of the 757 interior and express preferences about what passengers should find when they stepped inside the airplane. The interior design was a particular concern of hers.

Eastern's 757s use earth tones and striped seat-upholstery patterns that change subtly as one walks the length of the airplane. Eastern's interior design is more subdued than most airlines'.

"This is not a flying circus," Mrs. Borman said.

During the September flight, while her husband got a firsthand opportunity to assess the 757's performance ("This is an incredible airplane"), Susan Borman inspected the decor and explained the quasi-military uniforms Eastern flight attendants wear.

"This is our first uniform after the cutsey-pie," she said. "We're excited about the look. I think people like a structured environment. It gives a sense of security, and this is a business where people want security."

A lot goes into the interior design of an airplane. Substantial areas of Boeing's Renton plant are devoted to making elements of the 757 interior. Extensive use is made of expensive composite materials, which save weight.

The airlines are responsible for much of the interior design, working with Boeing and an interior-design firm, Walter Dorwin Teague Associates. The airlines also purchase seats from any of several manufacturers other than Boeing.

Choosing the paint design generally is easier because airlines typically have a color scheme already in use on other airplanes. (One trend in exterior design—a trend employed by Eastern—is to keep large portions of the airplane polished metal rather than painted. This lends a flashy appearance, but that's a small consideration next to the weight savings realized by using less paint.)

Eastern made a last-minute change in the 757's paint scheme. Boeing's 757s carried the numerals 7-5-7 on their tails in mammoth size, and last November Eastern decided to keep the same-sized numerals on its 757s, too.

That decision was made in Panama City on Nov. 8, when a 757 in Boeing paint landed to refuel on its way back to Miami from Buenos Aires. The Eastern Airlines board of directors and some Boeing officials got off the airplane, and someone asked why Eastern didn't keep the numbers.

Russ Ray, an Eastern board member who doubles as vice president of marketing, took to the idea immediately, seeing its promotional value. "I don't know of another commercial airplane flying around that has its model designation on the tail," he said.

The decision was made then and there to keep the numerals on for the first couple of years, during the period that Eastern is the only U.S. airline flying the new jetliner. The first time the 757s need repainting, Eastern plans to take the super-sized numerals off.

BECAUSE EASTERN intended to begin commercial service with the 757 at the first of the year, the November decision to change the paint meant some fast shuffling of promotional material. Photos of the airplane used in advertising should have the numerals, Eastern decided.

One service Boeing provides every customer is a "photo flight" for each paint scheme on a given Boeing model. The customer's airplane is flown around Washington state for an hour or two while another jetliner flies alongside with photographers on board.

Half the seats are removed from the photographers' airplane to give them freedom of movement. They holler their preferences to a coordinator on a radio who asks the pilots of the two planes to fly a little closer together, or a little farther apart, or to move ahead or drop back to give the photographers the perspective they want.

When Eastern decided to change the paint on its tail, it meant a new photo flight would be necessary. But by the time the paint actually was changed, it was December and the weather was uncooperative. The airplanes could fly above the clouds, but that would allow no variety for backdrops in the photos.

More than once Boeing's photographers got on an airplane and waited on the ground while a 757 scouted the state looking for a break in the weather: No luck.

"I need those pictures bad," Jim Ashlock, Eastern's director of public relations, said on Dec. 13. He wanted to assemble promotional material on the 757 for the press.

Finally, there was a break in the weather on a day when a 757 destined for Eastern was available. The photos were taken in a tandem flight over western Washington and shipped to Ashlock in Miami.

Just two weeks later the 757 entered commercial service for the first time—flown by Eastern pilots trained on simulators in Seattle, its interior decorated in earth tones and its tail wearing a huge 757.

PART 7: THE DELIVERY

IT HARDLY LOOKED LIKE an airplane about to enter commercial service.

Some passenger seats were missing. A rack jammed with electronic equipment was strapped to the floor in the first-class section. Technicians and engineers swarmed over the airplane, inside and out.

Seats were pushed forward on their tracks, with carpets rolled back and mechanics climbing in and out of floor recesses. Six technicians were crammed into a cockpit meant for two pilots.

A team of mechanics worked on a recurring problem with the right-wing forward flaps. A heavy-set man looked up at the tail, eyeing the airplane's rudder alignment. A pair of workers used an array of photo-electric cells to aim the airplane's landing lights.

It was Friday, Dec. 17, 1982, and Boeing was late delivering its first 757 to Eastern Airlines. Not contractually late, because the manufacturer had given itself a cushion of extra time. Such buffers, both in projected dates of completion and projected airplane performance, let Boeing almost always point to "better than anticipated" results.

Nevertheless, it already was two weeks past the date Eastern had been told it would receive the first of its silver-and-blue 757 twinjets.

The airline, which had launched the 757 project, was getting impatient. It had announced plans to begin 757 service Jan. 1 and had purchased television advertising to herald the new jetliner during the Rose Bowl and other New Year's Day football games. Even more important, millions of dollars in safe-harbor-leasing tax benefits to Eastern were riding on getting delivery before the end of 1982.

On that overcast day a week before Christmas, while technicians scurried and chiefs paced impatiently, Boeing had yet even to acquire Federal Aviation Administration certification which would allow the 757 to be operated commercially.

An engine-icing problem on a test flight a month earlier had sidetracked certification. The engine had been modified, but was yet to be proved in icing conditions.

Deadlines and timetables were being revised continuously. The target had been certification by Nov. 23, but the days and numbers kept changing. Hundreds of Boeing employees were destined to keep working on the program during the traditional long Boeing holiday recess. There was even talk of working Christmas Day.

Things were, in short, a mess.

"Every time you set a number, it slips. I don't even want to set another one," lamented Bill Robison, director of manufacturing on the 757 project.

Robison was standing with Paul Johnstone, then senior vice president of operations for Eastern, since retired. Johnstone is an amiable man, but he was growing perturbed by the delays in delivery of the jetliner.

Johnstone was head of a delegation that had come to Seattle from Eastern's Miami headquarters to look over the new Boeing jet before accepting it. Every Boeing airplane is subjected to such inspections when it is delivered to an airline. Just as a careful car buyer scrutinizes a new automobile carefully before driving it off the lot, an airline examines a $30 million airplane before flying it home.

EASTERN'S inspection of the 757 program really had begun in 1979, when the airline sent an ex-Boeing engineer, Ben Gay, back to Seattle to be Eastern's on-site representative. Gay had an impossible job keeping track of an enormous program, but he was assisted by Boeing employees whose sole jobs are to help represent the interests of airlines.

Gay's mission was to make sure the airplane would meet Eastern's needs—that every light bulb could be replaced easily, that the cockpit would please Eastern's pilots, that the carpets were the right colors.

"You can't see it all," Gay said. "I can go out quite a bit, but I can't cover all of it. Too much for one man."

But one man is enough when Boeing's high level of quality control is considered, Gay said. "If we had doubts about Boeing's ability to build a decent airplane, not only design-wise but quality and workmanship-wise, we'd have people up here. But they've proven to us in the past that they can build a good airplane with good workmanship, and if it isn't right they fix it."

Gay's activities were reaching a high pitch in the closing days of December as the first 757s were being readied.

The particular airplane under inspection on Dec. 17 was No. NA007, the newest of the new 757s. It had flown for the first time only two days earlier.

On that shakedown flight, 39 problems had been detected—not big problems, but typical little first-flight problems: an annoying sound of hissing air around a seat in row 20, an electrical-access panel that fell off the first time the airplane ever landed.

Now Johnstone, Gay and other Eastern personnel waited for a planned 1 p.m. demonstration flight of the airplane which, in just two weeks, was supposed to carry the first paying Eastern Airlines 757 customers.

Hours ticked by. Mid-day came and went and still the airplane sat outside Plant 2 at Boeing Field. Technical problems kept cropping up. Even the modest 1 p.m. timetable could not be met.

Johnstone recognized the possibility Eastern might not get its first two 757s certified and in service by the end of the month. Every minute seemed precious. "We're down to moving hours out of the schedule, not days or weeks," he said.

Many of Johnstone's thoughts that Friday afternoon were 900 miles south at Edwards Air Force Base near Los Angeles, where another 757 was facing obstacles of a more substantial nature.

It was Boeing 757 No. 3, a flight-test airplane flown by pilot Kenny Higgins. The pilot and his crew were almost desperately trying to build up ice on the airplane's engines to prove that the icing problem had been remedied.

On a routine flight test Nov. 16, both Rolls-Royce engines on 757 No. 3 had been damaged when ice built up on their spinner cones, hubs for the forward set of fan blades. The ice had broken off in chunks large enough to bend blades and cause dangerous engine vibration.

After a sometimes-heated debate with Boeing over the cause of the problem, Rolls responded by installing heated spinner cones to prevent ice build-up, and it was presumed the problem was solved. But presumption alone would not win an FAA airworthiness certificate. The "fix" had to be proven.

Boeing and Rolls worked out a strategy in which they would take FAA personnel on a flight through the same sort of supercooled weather conditions that caused the engine damage on Nov. 16. The jetliner would use one engine with a heated spinner and one without—as a control—for the test. The idea was to damage the unmodified engine as before, while demonstrating the safety of the engine with the heated spinner.

But proof was elusive. Day after day, 757 No. 3 flew across the western United States seeking appropriate weather conditions, and day after day it had no luck.

"We had a week of totally dry weather in this half of the whole United States," said John Hodson, a Rolls-Royce vice president.

Finally, Boeing asked the Air Force to help it make ice. At Edwards, a KC-135 tanker was loaded with water. The tanker, a derivative of the Boeing 707, normally is used to refuel another airplane in flight with an arm-like boom. This time, however, the tanker dispensed water into the freezing air.

The 757 flew about 70 feet behind and the water had turned to ice by the time it hit the airplane and its engines. It was a last-ditch attempt to create icing conditions, prove the engine modification, win certification and get the first two airplanes to Eastern by the end of the year.

Johnstone knew the test was under way as he paced around the 757 on Boeing Field, but he didn't know how it was going to turn out.

He would have been relieved to know that, in fact, over the next few days the test would succeed, certification would be granted, and Eastern would receive its first two 757s before the end of the year.

DECEMBER'S ILL WINDS weren't the first turbulence the 757 program weathered during its five-year flight.

By 1981 the health of the airline industry was fading, and Boeing faced the prospect of canceled orders for the new airliner. Some airlines, such as American, eventually withdrew plans to buy the new and expensive 757. They couldn't afford it.

Eastern president Frank Borman went before Congress in 1981 and 1982 to plead for tax breaks so that his company's "launch" order for the 757 could proceed.

"The performance of the (airline) industry in 1980 and 1981 jeopardized not only Eastern's participation in that (757) program, but the entire Boeing program," Borman told the Senate Finance Committee on March 18, 1982.

Borman told the senators he had been in Seattle in July 1981 attempting to cancel or delay a third of Eastern's order for 757s. Then Congress passed safe-harbor leasing, which improved the situation.

"We went back and did our numbers and found that with the provisions of safe-harbor leasing we could indeed continue the $909 million capital (757) order," Borman testified. "And we went to Boeing and said, 'With the new tax law, it's go,' and Boeing is in fact producing our airplanes. And they are coming down the assembly line, ready or not."

Safe-harbor leasing was an ingenious, controversial mechanism which allowed unprofitable companies to sell unusable tax breaks to profitable companies. Fortune magazine called it "an obscure form of tax-avoidance boogie-woogie." Here's how it worked:

With or without safe-harbor leasing, a company acquiring capital assets (in this case, airplanes) is entitled to tax breaks such as depreciation. But tax breaks are little good to an unprofitable company which pays no tax anyway. In fact, they can even hurt a money-losing airline.

That's because a profitable airline might get a $10 million tax break on a $30 million Boeing jetliner, making its true cost only $20 million, while an unprofitable airline would have to pay the full $30 million for the same airplane.

Under safe-harbor leasing, an unprofitable company could sell its tax breaks to a profitable company for cash. In the hypothetical case of the $30 million jetliner, ABC Airline could sell its $10 million tax break to XYZ Oil Co. for, say, $8 million.

The $8 million in cash for ABC Airline would reduce the true out-of-pocket expense for a $30 million jetliner to $22 million. XYZ Oil, meanwhile, would get a $10 million tax reduction for the $8 million it paid—a quick $2 million profit.

Technically, ABC would temporarily sell the jetliner to XYZ, then lease it back. It is a complicated shuffle of paperwork in which nothing really is exchanged except tax breaks and cash. Both the profitable and unprofitable company are sheltered from taxes in a "safe harbor."

No one loses—except the federal treasury, which, in this hypothetical example, would be out the $8 million.

Safe-harbor leasing was pushed through Congress in 1981 by Borman and others, who argued that unprofitable companies like Eastern were suffering and could not afford to buy needed equipment, such as Boeing 757s.

By early 1982, however, it was clear that Uncle Sam was being taken to the cleaners.

Alan Greenspan, a conservative economist, labeled safe-harbor leasing "food stamps for American business." Profitable companies were gobbling up available tax credits from unprofitable companies, and some big profitable companies—including General Electric—used the loophole to pay no taxes at all for 1981.

In February 1982 the mood in Congress was turning against safe-harbor leasing. Senate Finance Committee Chairman Robert Dole called for repeal of the tax loophole.

Borman and leaders of other unprofitable companies returned to Congress. Borman's argument was compelling: Eastern had proceeded with the 757 order only on the promise of safe-harbor leasing, and revoking that promise would be unjust and disastrous.

Congress chose a middle course, eliminating much of safe-harbor leasing but allowing a timed phase-out for several key and depressed industries, including airlines.

The 757 seemed safe again, although as Eastern's financial picture continued to deteriorate there were other doubts whether it would be able to complete the purchase of 757s.

By Dec. 17, when Johnstone was examining the first of the new jetliners, financial packages involving safe-harbor leasing had been assembled. Once the jetliner was ready, Eastern would have money available for transfer to Boeing, Johnstone said.

The actual purchase of a completed Boeing jetliner is conducted in a variety of ways.

Typically about a third of the price has been prepaid to Boeing during the course of manufacture. But increasingly, as airlines have fallen on hard times (or developed shrewdness in such dealings), Boeing itself has provided financing for part of the purchase price and the whole deal has grown more complicated.

In the case of the sale to Eastern, final funds were to be transferred by wire, with telephone conference calls between several cities confirming the movement of funds from one New York bank account to another. The moment the money changed accounts, the airplane changed hands.

For competitive reasons, Boeing and the airlines tend to obscure the details of such financial transactions. But Eastern's 1982 annual report provides some details.

For instance, the report reveals that the British government provided roughly $10 million financing per 757 "at an attractive interest rate" because of the purchase by the airline of Rolls-Royce engines. More to the point, the report said Eastern made $12.8 million on the sale of the tax benefits associated with the first two 757s.

The report says Eastern will raise another estimated $130 million through the sale of the tax benefits associated with 13 additional 757s and four Airbus A-300s due for delivery this year.

"We would have had to cancel the (757) program had we not had safe-harbor leasing," Borman said in an interview last month. "There's no question. It's fact."

EASTERN AIRLINES is looking to the 757 as part of the solution to its financial woes. The 757 is the world's most efficient jetliner, on a per-seat basis, and the airline hopes that its position as the only U.S. operator of the airplane for two years will give it some competitive advantage on costs.

"Frank Borman sees it as a vehicle to thwack his competition with," said Alan Smith, a Rolls-Royce official.

Boeing has faced lean years recently, too, and also is looking to the 757 to help restore the strong profitability of the past. Announced total orders for the 757 actually have fallen rather than risen during the past two years, but Boeing claims the airplane eventually will be the world's all-time best-seller.

This is a point of speculation and dispute. While Boeing contends the 757 is about the right size to capture a large share of future sales, other aviation-industry forces—notably Europe's Airbus Industrie—believe the still-to-be-built 150-seat airplane will be far more attractive than the 185-seat 757.

The Airbus view, shared by many others, is that the 757 is a technological success but is likely to be a financial failure—the same bittersweet combination that characterizes the European Condorde SST.

"The 757 would sell beautifully if it had 150 seats," said Reinhardt Abraham, chief technical executive of Lufthansa German Airlines. "My personal opinion always was that the 757 was too close to the 767 and A-310, and it is meeting its own (Boeing) competition. Only huge airlines will be able to fly both the 757 and 767."

But M.J. Lapensky, president of Northwest Airlines, offered a sharply contrasting view. "I don't know what's magic about 150 seats," he said, adding that the 757 is sized perfectly at 185 seats to fill the gap in capacity between the 140-seat 727s and 290-seat DC-10s.

However, Lapensky added that Northwest won't order any 757s until it becomes apparent which of three available engines (two made by Rolls-Royce, one by Pratt & Whitney) offers the best economy.

Wolfgang Demisch, an aerospace analyst for the Wall Street firm of First Boston, takes a middle view.

Demisch suggests that the 757 will be a money-losing burden for Boeing in the short run because the company will sell relatively few in each of the first few years of production.

But he believes that the long run will show Boeing has sized the airplane correctly—that the 185-seat airplane will prove more valuable than the 150-seat airplane, because the shortage of air-traffic controllers and growing congestion in air space will force airlines to fly fewer flights with larger-capacity airplanes.

And although it is costing Boeing a bundle to build an airplane which isn't yet selling well, it could have cost Boeing much more not to build the 757, Demisch contends.

Airbus elected to build its second jetliner, the A-310, at the same 210-passenger size as the 767—a size where there is a known strong market and where appropriate new-technology engines already were under development.

In Demisch's view, Airbus probably would have sized its airplane smaller, at about 160 seats, if the 757 hadn't already been under development to fill that need.

"I think in essence that the 757 has ... rattled Airbus sufficiently by its presence that they didn't launch a competitive entry," Demisch said.

"There was a time when Airbus was feeling pretty buoyant a couple of years back, and if there hadn't been a 757 at that point there would have been a large, gaping hole between 140 seats for the 727 and 210 seats for the 767," he said. The temptation to build an airplane in the middle "would, I think, have been irresistible."

"As it is, that opportunity was preempted, and as it stands now I think Airbus is probably regretting that they didn't go ahead and do it anyhow," Demisch said. "Basically, I think it means Boeing is going to be gaining market share, courtesy of the 757, which protected them at the short-to-medium-haul length."

Successful jetliner models seem to stay in production about 20 years. When a jetliner is retired it generally is because its technology is outmoded, not because it is physically worn out.

By incorporating state-of-the-art technology in the 757, Boeing attempted to create an airplane that would be flying well into next century. In fact, the 757 and 767 share a cockpit design which Boeing calls, ambitiously, the "Century 21 flight deck."

The cockpit can be updated readily by replacing computer software (programs), eliminating the need for challenging or impossible hardware changes. This simplicity and flexibility should add to the longevity of the 757.

But a Boeing airplane design is not static. As long as the 757 is in production it likely will be refined. Derivative versions of the airplane are under study, so one day soon men and women may be creating 757 freighters, or stretched or shortened passenger models.

IN RENTON and around the world, people continue laboring to make the 757—and make it a success.

The range of human endeavor on any given day is impressive.

On Wednesday, April 20, 1983, a day picked at random, Barry Buckworth was running a 90-foot-long milling machine at the Hawker de Havilland plant in Bankstown, Australia.

The machine, first of its kind in Australia, was automatically shaping three 757 wing-shear ribs simultaneously. The ribs were destined for the 40th Boeing 757, and Buckworth's job was to monitor a video screen and blow away metal shavings with an air hose.

That same day, in Burbank, Calif., Ken Tuttle was running a similar milling machine, although he was sweeping away the metal shavings rather than blowing them off. Tuttle is an employee at Menasco, another Boeing subcontractor, and his milling machine was simultaneously shaping the outer housings of the left-hand main landing gears of six 757s.

In Derby, England, 20-year-old Martin Spooner squirted lubricating oil onto carbon-hardened steel he was milling for Rolls-Royce. Working in oil-laden air, Spooner was creating tooling for the manufacturer of the 757 engines.

In Minneapolis, Richard Butler, a group leader at a Honeywell factory, was looking after a high-technology machine which used ultrasound energy to drill and mill dense glass. The glass would become the heart of a laser-gyro inertial navigation system used on the 757.

At the Boeing plant in Wichita, Kan., Sharon Baily drilled holes and mounted parts of ribs in the nose section of 757 No. 33, while Jessie Bishop Jr. cut out wheel-well door panels of graphite, using a concentrated spray of water at 50,000 pounds of cutting pressure per square inch.

At Boeing's Vertol Division in Philadelphia, which mostly makes helicopters, Larry Troutman supervised assembly of the fixed leading-edge structure of the right wing for 757 No. 37. The structure is a 2,100-pound device, 64 feet long and containing 700 parts.

On that day, Art Flock of Delta Airlines was in Everett pondering how his airline wanted its 60 757s painted. And near Boeing Field in Seattle, Rob Wood, chief pilot of Britain's Monarch Airlines, was giving a test to two of his pilots in a 757 full-flight simulator.

At Renton Municipal Airport, Eastern's Ben Gay told Boeing to send 757 No. 6, destined for his airline, back into the paint hangar for more polishing.

"My main effort since those early deliveries has been to look for early in-service problems," Gay said. "There's a lot of little things. But overall, you'd give the airplane an excellent grade."

Nearby, top officials of Rolls-Royce and Pratt & Whitney laid out for Boeing executives the first glimpse of the "I-2500," a collaborative engine proposed to power a 150-seat airplane Boeing and other manufacturers are considering building.

And on that day, April 20, Tom White finished two sketches of a proposed control box that airline personnel could use to load the 757's cargo hold automatically. Late in the day, he and his coworkers began a new project, a theoretical redesign of airplane passenger cabins in which convention is tossed aside and new ideas are given free reign.

In the Renton plant, Ken Baesler climbed from the inside of a 757 wing which he had been checking for leaks with a mixture of pressurized air and ammonia. In another building, Paul Duxbury was helping assemble the wings, driving titanium fasteners with a rivet gun.

In the final-assembly hangar at Renton, Bill English installed a wing part, tightening a ¾-inch nut to 100 foot-pounds of pressure. A Boeing inspector, J.J. Johnson, witnessed the operation and then stamped a seal on the nut to signal his approval. The pressure on the nut cannot be altered without breaking his personalized seal.

On the underside of the same 757, Dennis Kitchen spent an hour installing a nose landing gear, pushing the 3,000-pound installation dolly away like Superman when he was finished (the dolly was riding on a cushion of air).

And inside yet another 757 that day, Tanjer Gillard filled a Dixie cup with shiny white acrylic enamel and began to paint the heads of screws in a doorjamb. A finishing touch.

All these men and women, and thousands more, were contributing to the 757 program, an industrial venture of massive proportions— whether measured by the yardstick of economics, technology, politics, utility, or even romance.

All these men and women, and tens of thousands more, were helping to make it fly.

7?7: What Will Boeing Gamble on Next?

WHAT'S NEXT after the 757?
　　Like a card shark pondering the next play, Boeing's gaze is shifting back and forth between its hand and the faces of its opponents.

The ante is a billion dollars or more. But the stakes are even higher.

In Boeing's hand are several cards. Perhaps those figuring most prominently are plans for 150-seat jetliners of a modern, fuel-efficient design. Consensus seems to be that the next major project will be in this class.

Airline leaders are calling for such an airplane, although many acknowledge they couldn't afford to buy one even if it were available. The airline business is in recession, and airlines are notorious for second-guessing their purchase decisions.

"Boeing may have a problem in the fact that there's a terrible amount of uncertainty across the whole spectrum of airline customers as to what the hell they really want," said M.J. Lapensky, president of Northwest Airlines. "I guess if I were making airplanes I'd really love it if people knew what they wanted, in a very clear fashion."

One voice calling consistently for a 150-seat airplane has been that of David C. Garrett Jr., president of Delta, the major U.S. airline that is, perhaps, in the best shape financially.

"The development of a short-range, advanced-technology airplane is imperative if we are to fly into the 21st century prepared to remain a viable enterprise, provide the level of transportation convenient and necessary to the public, and operate effectively within the framework of the free-enterprise system created by airline deregulation," Garrett said in a recent speech.

The problem with an all-new airplane of this size is that it would be terribly expensive to produce, said Joseph Sutter, executive vice president of the Boeing Commercial Airplane Co.

Airlines may want the plane, "but they want it at a helluva low price," he said.

Boeing and the airlines may find that derivative versions of existing airplane models are more economical than all-new airplanes, when the high capital costs of new airplanes are taken into account, Sutter said.

Airbus Industrie, a consortium of plane-makers backed by European governments, already has announced its 150-seater, called the A-320. But the announcement was made at the Paris Air Show two years ago, and though the announcement has been periodically and dramatically renewed, the engineering and construction program still hasn't been launched.

Airbus hasn't been able to line up sufficient orders from airlines to commit to the program.

Meanwhile, Airbus, Boeing and McDonnell Douglas all are courting Japan's industrial capacity and money as a potential partner on a 150-seat airliner project.

Boeing is said to be a frontrunner, though skeptics wonder whether Boeing wouldn't just be providing Japan with the technology it needs to become a threatening new manufacturing competitor.

Boeing's major choices for the 150-seat market are a longer stretched version of the 737, called the 737-400 or 737-500, and an all-new 150-seat airplane called, for now, the 7—7.

The 7—7, which presumably could be named the 777, probably would retain the "Century 21 flight deck" used on the 757 and 767. Common instrumentation and layout potentially could yield common pilot training and certification, making all three Boeing models that much more attractive to airlines through increased flexibility and lower training costs.

A new 737 would retain a cockpit largely consistent with existing 737 cockpits, providing commonality advantages of a different kind.

Sutter said Boeing could produce a 737-400 or 737-500 before Airbus could build the A-320. Sutter said Boeing would wait until after the A-320 is launched before starting work on the 7—7, and use the extra time to advance the technology of the new Boeing airplane. It might even use some sort of turbo-prop engine, he said.

Meanwhile, Boeing recently introduced a larger version of its 747 jumbo, is readying a larger 737 and is prepared to build a stretched version of the 767, increasing capacity from about 210 seats to about 250.

This larger 767 is being eyed by airline executives. It would be a highly attractive replacement for DC-10s and L-1011 wide-bodies if and when two-engine jetliners are approved for transoceanic flights.

Other airplanes, such as a new four-engine airplane to take the role once filled by the 707, may be in the company's cards, too.

But if Boeing has firm ideas about its plans, it isn't sharing them.

"Anything is possible," said Carl Munson, vice president for strategic planning. "I refuse to be categorical in the long term about anything being either inevitable or impossible, because I don't believe anybody can look into a crystal ball and be categorical.

"The industry's changing dramatically right now."

ANALYSIS

PETER RINEARSON says the original idea to write "Making It Fly" came from a newsroom colleague, Ross Anderson, who would later win his own Pulitzer: "During a conversation one day at my desk, he threw out the idea that I write the story of the 767, which Boeing was just beginning to deliver to United Airlines. I rushed to the photo lab to bounce the idea off my closest friend in the newsroom, a photographer named Chris Johns, now with *National Geographic* ... [and] one of the best journalists I've known. ... The first words out of his mouth were 'You can call it Making It Fly.'

"I set out hoping to understand Boeing better, and to share that understanding with Seattle readers, who really didn't have much of a clue what the company did—other than build airplanes, of course. I think I achieved both of those goals. It was more work and more rewarding than I had imagined."

The story soon took on a life of its own. The six-week project turned into months of seven-day work weeks and 18-hour days. "I even worked on it on Christmas Day," he admits. "I was totally consumed—there was so much to do!" A subtle irony: Rinearson had adopted Boeing's own impossible schedule for his story.

As his editors began to get restless, Rinearson continued to provide the paper with daily beat coverage of Boeing, pointing out his series was allowing him unmatched access to top Boeing sources. Rinearson received a much-needed boost when his editors decided to hold the story to help launch a new joint Sunday edition of *The Seattle Times* and *Post-Intelligencer,* pending court approval of a Joint Operating Agreement. Rinearson kept writing and when the approval came—five months later—his story had grown to a mini-novel size 29,000 words.

"To the paper's credit," Rinearson is quick to point out, "they let me stick with it and they played it up big. The editors gave me a dozen or so blank pages, spread out over a week, to run the 29,000-word account. They gave me the extended service of a first-rate photographer, Alan Berner. The paper's graphic department, arguably the best in the country, did a superb job, too."

The irony of "Making It Fly" being used as a justification for creating the Pulitzer Explanatory Journalism category certainly isn't lost on Rinearson. As "Making It Fly" is a textbook example of explanatory journalism, his puzzlement over winning in features rather than national reporting is easy to understand. "Had I entered in the features category, who knows whether I would have even made it through the preliminary screening," he astutely points out.

"Making It Fly" compares in some ways with David Zucchino's "Being Black in South Africa." Both are several-part entries written in no-nonsense prose. Both tell a tremendous story and are highly educational, although Zucchino's series is more of a traditional feature.

Like Zucchino, notice how Rinearson writes straight-to-the-point leads for each of his sections:

Boeing loses millions of dollars on every new 757 it sells.

We almost lost one.

Selling jetliners is a bit like peddling religion.

Buying one requires an act of faith.

It hardly looked like an airplane about to enter commercial service.

Even more impressive is how Rinearson structured his series by mortaring on layers and layers of detail. His complete mastery of the Boeing manufacturing process at the end of this series is a far cry from his earlier concerns about lacking sources and trust from the giant aircraft manufacturer.

And as it lacks the one (or several) central reoccurring characters to "humanize" the narrative, such as those found in "AIDS in the Heartland," "Life on the Land" and "Mrs. Kelly's Monster," Peter Rinearson's masterpiece is all the more impressive as a work of newspapering.

Even if it really isn't a feature story!

PETER RINEARSON is currently president of two companies, Alki Software Corp., which is helping newspapers to publish interactive content on the Web, and Raster Ranch Ltd. He has written four books about Microsoft Word and co-authored Bill Gates' book, *The Road Ahead.* He plans to finish a comprehensive "Boeing book" in the future.

1985

ALICE STEINBACH

ALICE STEINBACH HAS the observational powers of a journalist, the ear of a musician and the pen of a poet.

And as an experienced feature writer, she is always on the prowl for her next story. "One of the joys and horrors of daily journalism," Steinbach calls the never-ending search for new story ideas. Stopped at a red light in Baltimore one day in 1984, her eyes focused on a young girl walking down Charles Street. A dozen years later, Steinbach still remembers the scene vividly.

"Out of the corner of my eye, I saw this young girl, 14 or 15 years old and cute, dressed in the latest fashion." As Steinbach thought back to her own high school days, she "saw this white cane flash out and I was startled because I suddenly realized she was blind.

"That told me there was something wrong with how I felt about blind people. I found myself wondering: Why should I be so shocked to learn that a cute, with-it girl was blind?"

Steinbach decided some "revisionist thinking" was called for. She decided to acquire it by finding and writing a story about a blind teen-age girl.

But a problem developed: She couldn't find a blind teen-age girl like the one she had seen on Charles Street. In fact, she couldn't find a girl like that at all.

One name, however, started to come up consistently in her phone calls—Calvin Stanley, a boy who was one of the first totally blind children to be main-streamed in public school from the beginning.

It turned out Steinbach had found the person she was looking for, although he initially seemed to be the wrong age, gender and not at all typical of his age group. But he ultimately turned out to be a boy who would lead to the Pulitzer Prize.

As you read "A Boy of Unusual Vision," notice how the language of the poet infiltrates this story at every level. Consider the difficulty of writing a highly-visual, colorful narrative about a young boy who sees none of this.

Alice Steinbach took a month of her life to craft a literary masterpiece that stands the test of time. It seems fitting that "A Boy of Unusual Vision" was written by a woman whose vision so colorfully takes in the world.

A Boy of Unusual Vision

The Baltimore Sun

May 27, 1984

FIRST THE EYES: They are large and blue, a light, opaque blue, the color of a robin's egg. And if, on a sunny spring day, you look straight into these eyes—eyes that cannot look back at you—the sharp, April light turns them pale, like the thin blue of a high, cloudless sky.

Ten-year-old Calvin Stanley, the owner of these eyes and a boy who has been blind since birth, likes this description and asks to hear it twice. He listens as only he can listen, then: "Orange used to be my favorite color but now it's blue," he announces. Pause. The eyes flutter between the short, thick lashes, "I know there's light blue and there's dark blue, but what does sky-blue look like?" he wants to know. And if you watch his face as he listens to your description, you get a sense of a picture being clicked firmly into place behind the pale eyes.

He is a boy who has a lot of pictures stored in his head, retrievable images which have been fashioned for him by the people who love him—by family and friends and teachers who have painstakingly and patiently gone about creating a special world for Calvin's inner eye to inhabit.

Picture of a rainbow: "It's a lot of beautiful colors, one next to the other. Shaped like a bow. In the sky. Right across."

Picture of lightning, which frightens Calvin: "My mother says lightning looks like a Christmas tree—the way it blinks on and off across the sky," he says, offering a comforting description that would make a poet proud.

"Child," his mother once told him, "one day I won't be here and I won't be around to pick you up when you fall—nobody will be around all the time to pick you up—so you have to try to be something on your own. You have to learn how to deal with this. And to do that, you have to learn how to think."

There was never a moment when Ethel Stanley said to herself, "My son is blind and this is how I'm going to handle it."

Calvin's mother:

"When Calvin was little, he was so inquisitive. He wanted to see everything, he wanted to touch everything. I had to show him every little thing there is. A spoon, a fork. I let him play with them. The pots, the pans. *Everything.* I showed him the sharp edges of the table. 'You cannot touch this; it will hurt you.' And I showed him what would hurt. He still bumped into it anyway, but he knew what he wasn't supposed to do and what he could do. And he knew that nothing in his room—*nothing*—could hurt him.

"And when he started walking and we went out together—I guess he was about 2—I never said anything to him about what to do. When we got to the curbs. Calvin knew that when I stopped, he should step down and when I stopped again, he should step up. I never said anything, that's just the way we did it. And it became a pattern."

Calvin remembers when he began to realize that something about him was "different": "I just figured it out myself. I think I was about 4. I would pick things up and I couldn't see them. Other people would say they could see things and I couldn't."

And his mother remembers the day her son asked her why he was blind and other people weren't.

"He must have been about 4 or 5. I explained to him what happened, that he was born that way and that it was nobody's fault and he didn't have to blame himself. He asked, 'Why me?' And I said 'I don't know why, Calvin. Maybe there's a special plan for you in your life and there's a reason for this. But this is the way you're going to be and you can deal with it."

Then she sat her son down and told him this: "You're *seeing,* Calvin. You're just using your hands instead of your eyes. But you're seeing. And, remember, there is *nothing* you can't do."

It's spring vacation and Calvin is out in the alley behind his house riding his bike, a serious looking, black and silver two-wheeler. "Stay behind me," he shouts to his friend Kellie Bass, who's furiously pedaling her bike down the one-block stretch of alley where Calvin is allowed to bicycle.

Now: Try to imagine riding a bike without being able to see where you're going. Without even knowing what an "alley" looks like. Try to imagine how you navigate a space that has no visual boundaries, that exists only in your head. And then try to imagine what Calvin is feeling as he pedals his bike in that space, whooping for joy as the air rushes past him on either side.

And although Calvin can't see the signs of spring sprouting all around him in the neighboring backyards—the porch furniture and barbecue equipment being brought out of storage, the grass growing emerald green from the April rain, the forsythia exploding yellow over the fences—still, there are signs of another sort which guide him along his route:

Past the German shepherd who always barks at him, telling Calvin that he's three houses away from his home; then past the purple hyacinths, five gardens away, throwing out their fragrance (later it will be the scent of the lilacs which guide him); past the large diagonal crack which lifts the front wheel of his bike up and then down, telling him he's reached his boundary and should turn back—past all these familiar signs Calvin rides his bike on a warm spring day.

Ethel Stanley: "At 6, one of his cousins got a new bike and Calvin said 'I want to learn how to ride a two-wheeler bike.' So we got him one. His father let him help put it together. You know, whatever Calvin gets he's going to go all over it with those hands and he knows every part of that bike and what it's called. He learned to ride it the first day, but I couldn't watch. His father stayed outside with him."

Calvin: "I just got mad. I got tired of riding a little bike. At first I used to zig-zag, go all over. My cousin would hold on to the bike and then let me go. I fell a lot in the beginning. But a lot of people fall when they first start."

There's a baseball game about to start in Calvin's backyard and Mrs. Stanley is pitching to her son. Nine-year-old Kellie, on first base, has taken off her fake fur coat so she can get a little more steam into her game and the other team member, Monet Clark, 6, is catching. It is also Monet's job to alert Calvin, who's at bat, when to swing. "Hit it, Calvin," she yells. "Swing!"

He does and the sound of the ball making solid contact with the bat sends Calvin running off to first base, his hands groping in front of his body. His mother walks over to stand next to him at first base and unconsciously her hands go to his head, stroking his hair in a soft, protective movement.

"Remember," the mother had said to her son six years earlier, "there's *nothing* you can't do."

Calvin's father, 37-year-old Calvin Stanley, Jr., a Baltimore city policeman, has taught his son how to ride a bike and how to shift gears in the family's Volkswagen and how to put toys together. They go to the movies together and they tell each other they're handsome.

The father: "You know, there's nothing much I've missed with him. Because he does everything. Except see. He goes swimming out in the pool in the back yard. Some of the other kids are afraid of the water but he jumps right in, puts his head under. If it were me I wouldn't be as brave as he is. I probably wouldn't go anywhere. If it were me I'd probably stay in this house most of the time. But he's always ready to go, always on the telephone, ready to do something.

"But he gets sad, too. You can just look at him sometimes and tell he's real sad."

The son: "You know what makes me sad? *Charlotte's Web*. It's my favorite story. I listen to the record at night. I like Charlotte, the spider. The way she talks. And, you know, she really loved Wilbur, the pig. He was her best friend." Calvin's voice is full of warmth and wonder as he talks about E.B. White's tale of the spider who befriended a pig and later sacrificed herself for him.

"It's a story about friendship. It's telling us how good friends are supposed to be. Like Charlotte and Wilbur," he says, turning away from you suddenly to wipe his eyes. "And when Charlotte dies, it makes me real sad. I always feel like I've lost a friend. That's why I try not to listen to that part. I just move the needle forward."

Something else makes Calvin sad: "I'd like to see what my mother looks like," he says, looking up quickly and swallowing hard. "What does she look like? People tell me she's pretty."

The mother: "One day Calvin wanted me to tell him how I looked. He was about 6. They were doing something in school for Mother's Day and the kids were drawing pictures of their mothers. He wanted to know what I looked like and that upset me because I didn't know how to tell him. I thought, 'How am I going to explain this to him so he will really know what I look like?' So I tried to explain to him about facial features, noses and I just used touch. I took his hand and I tried to explain about skin, let him touch his, and then mine.

"And I think that was the moment when Calvin really *knew* he was blind, because he said, 'I won't ever be able to see your face ... or Daddy's face,'" she says softly, covering her eyes with her hands, but not in time to stop the tears. "That's the only time I've ever let it bother me that much."

But Mrs. Stanley knew what to tell her only child: "I said, 'Calvin, you *can* see my face. You can see it with your hand and by listening to my voice and you can tell more about me that way than somebody who can use his eyes.'"

Provident Hospital, November 15, 1973: That's where Calvin Stanley III was born, and his father remembers it this way: "I saw him in the hospital before my wife did, and I knew immediately that something was wrong with his eyes. But I didn't know what."

The mother remembers it this way: "When I woke up after the cae-sarean, I had a temperature and couldn't see Calvin except through the window of the nursery. The next day a doctor came around to see me and said that he had cataracts and asked me if I had a pediatri-cian. From what I knew, cataracts could be removed so I thought 'Well, he'll be fine.' I wasn't too worried. Then when his pediatrician came and examined him he told me he thought it was congenital glau-coma."

Only once did Mrs. Stanley give in to despair. "When they knew for certain it was glaucoma and told me that the cure rate was very poor because they so seldom have infants born with glaucoma, I felt awful. I blamed myself. I knew I must have done something wrong when I was pregnant. Then I blamed my husband," she says, looking up from her hands which are folded in her lap, "but I never told him that." Pause. "And he probably blamed me."

No, says her husband. "I never really blamed her. I blamed myself. I felt it was a payback. That if you do something wrong to somebody else in some way you get paid back for it. I figured maybe I did some-thing wrong, but I couldn't figure out what I did that was that bad and why Calvin had to pay for it."

Mrs. Stanley remembers that the doctors explained to them that the glaucoma was not because of anything either of them had done before or during the pregnancy and "that 'congenital' simply means 'at birth.'"

They took Calvin to a New York surgeon who specialized in con-genital glaucoma. There were seven operations and the doctors held out some hope for some vision, but by age 3 there was no improve-ment and the Stanleys were told that everything that could be done for Calvin had been done.

"You know, in the back of my mind, I think I always knew he would never see," Mrs. Stanley says, "and that I had to reach out to him in different ways. The toys I bought him were always toys that made a noise, had sound, something that Calvin could enjoy. But it didn't dawn on me until after he was in school that I had been doing that—buying him toys that would stimulate him."

Thirty-three-year-old Ethel Stanley, a handsome, strong-looking woman with a radiant smile, is the oldest of seven children and grew up looking after her younger brothers and sisters while her mother worked. "She was a wonderful mother," Mrs. Stanley recalls. "Yes, she had to work, but when she was there, she was with you every minute and those minutes were worth a whole day. She always had time to listen to you."

Somewhere—perhaps from her own childhood experiences—Mrs. Stanley, who has not worked since Calvin was born, acquired the ability to nurture and teach and poured her mothering love into Calvin. And it shows. He moves in the sighted world with trust and faith and the unshakable confidence of a child whose mother has always been there for him. "If you don't understand something, ask," she tells Calvin again and again, in her open, forthright way. "Just ask."

When it was time to explain to Calvin the sexual differences between boys and girls, this is what Mrs. Stanley said: "When he was about 7 I told him that when you're conceived you have both sexes. It's not decided right away whether you're going to be a boy or a girl. And he couldn't believe it. He said, 'Golly, suppose somebody gets stuck?' I thought, 'Please, just let me get this out of the way first.'"

"And I tried to explain to him what a woman's sexual organs look like. I tried to trace it on the table with his fingers. I said, well you know what yours look like, don't you? And I told him what they're called, the medical names. 'Don't use names if you don't know what they mean. Ask. Ask.'"

"When he was little he wanted to be Stevie Wonder," says Calvin's father, laughing. "He started playing the piano and he got pretty good at it. Now he wants to be a computer programmer and design programs for the blind."

Calvin's neatly ordered bedroom is outfitted with all the comforts you would find in the room of many 10-year-old, middle-class boys: a television set (black and white, he tells you), an Atari game with a box of cartridges (his favorite is "Phoenix"), a braille Monopoly set, records, tapes and programmed talking robots. "I watch wrestling on TV every Saturday," he says. "I wrestle with my friends. It's fun."

He moves around his room confidently and easily. "I know this house like a book." Still, some things are hard for him to remember since, in his case, much of what he remembers has to be imagined visually first. Like the size and color of his room. "I think it's kind of big," he says of the small room. "And it's green," he says of the deep rose-colored walls.

And while Calvin doesn't need to turn the light on in his room he does like to have some kind of sound going constantly. *Loud* sound.

"It's 3 o'clock," he says, as the theme music from a TV show blares out into his room.

"Turn that TV down," says his mother, evenly. "You're not *deaf,* you know."

From the beginning, Ethel and Calvin Stanley were determined their blind son would go to public school. "We were living in Baltimore county when it was time for Calvin to start school and they told me I would have to pay a tuition for him to go to public school, and that really upset me," Mrs. Stanley says. "I had words with some of the big honchos out there. I knew they had programs in schools for children with vision problems and I thought public education should be free.

"We decided we would move to Baltimore city if we had to, and I got hold of a woman in the mayor's office. And that woman was the one who opened all the doors for us. She was getting ready to retire but she said she wasn't going to retire until she got this straight for Calvin. I don't know how she did it. But she did."

Now in the fourth grade, Calvin has been attending the Cross Country Elementary School since kindergarten. He is one of six blind students in Baltimore city who are fully mainstreamed which, in this context, means they attend public school with sighted students in a regular classroom. Four of these students are at Cross Country Elementary School. If Calvin stays in public school through the 12th grade, he will be the first blind student to be completely educated within the regular public school system.

Two p.m., Vivian Jackson's class, Room 207.

What Calvin can't see: He can't see the small, pretty girl sitting opposite him, the one who is wearing little rows of red, yellow and blue barrettes shaped like airplanes in her braided hair. He can't see the line of small, green plants growing in yellow pots all along the sunny window sill. And he can't see Mrs. Jackson in her rose-pink suit and pink enameled earrings shaped like little swans.

("Were they really shaped like little swans?" he will ask later.)

But Calvin can feel the warm spring breeze—invisible to *everyone's* eyes, not just his—blowing in through the window and he can hear the tapping of a young oak tree's branches against the window. He can hear Mrs. Jackson's pleasant, musical voice and, later, if you ask him what she looks like, he will say, "She's nice."

But best of all, Calvin can read and spell and do fractions and follow the classroom work in his specially prepared braille books. He is
smart and he can do everything the rest of his class can do. Except
see.

"What's the next word, Calvin?" Mrs. Jackson asks.

"Eleven," he says, reading from his braille textbook.

"Now tell us how to spell it—without looking back at the book!"
she says quickly, causing Calvin's fingers to fly away from the forbidden word.

"E-l-e-v-e-n," he spells out easily.

It all seems so simple, the ease with which Calvin follows along,
the manner in which his blindness has been accommodated. But it's
deceptively simple. The amount of work that has gone into getting
Calvin to this point—the number of teachers, vision specialists and
mobility instructors, and the array of special equipment is staggering.

Patience and empathy from his teachers have played a large role,
too.

For instance, there's Dorothy Lloyd, the specialist who is teaching
Calvin the slow and very difficult method of using an Optacon, a
device which allows a blind person to read a printed page by touch
by converting printed letters into a tactile representation.

And there's Charleye Dyer, who's teaching Calvin things like
"mobility" and "independent travel skills," which includes such tasks
as using a cane and getting on and off buses. Of course, what Miss
Dyer is really teaching Calvin is freedom; the ability to move about
independently and without fear in the larger world.

There's also Lois Sivits who, among other things, teaches Calvin
braille and is his favorite teacher. And, to add to a list which is endless, there's the music teacher who comes in 30 minutes early each
Tuesday to give him a piano lesson, and his home room teacher, Mrs.
Jackson, who is as finely tuned to Calvin's cues as a player in a musical duet would be to her partner.

An important part of Calvin's school experience has been his contact with sighted children.

"When he first started school," his mother recalls, "some of the
kids would tease him about his eyes. 'Oh, they're so big and you can't
see.' But I just told him, 'Not any time in your life will everybody
around you like you—whether you can see or not. They're just
children and they don't know they're being cruel. And I'm sure it's
not the last time someone will be cruel to you. But it's all up to you

because you have to go to school and you'll have to deal with it.'"

Calvin's teachers say he's well liked, and watching him on the playground and in class you get the impression that the only thing that singles him out from the other kids is that someone in his class is always there to take his hand if he needs help.

"I'd say he's really well accepted," says his mobility teacher, Miss Dyer, "and that he's got a couple of very special friends."

Eight-year-old Brian Butler is one of these special friends. "My *best* friend," says Calvin proudly, introducing you to a studious-looking boy whose eyes are alert and serious behind his glasses. The two boys are not in the same class, but they ride home together on the bus every day.

Here's Brian explaining why he likes Calvin so much: "He's funny and he makes me laugh. And I like him because he always makes me feel better when I don't feel good." And, he says, his friendship with Calvin is no different from any other good friendship. Except for one thing: "If Calvin's going to bump into a wall or something, I tell him, 'Look out,'" says Brian, sounding as though it were the most natural thing in the world to do when walking with a friend.

"Charlotte would have done it for Wilbur," is the way Calvin sizes up Brian's help, evoking once more that story about "how friendship ought to be."

A certain moment:

Calvin is working one-on-one with Lois Sivits, a teacher who is responsible for the braille skills which the four blind children at Cross Country must have in order to do all the work necessary in their regular classes. He is very relaxed with Miss Sivits, who is gentle, patient, smart and, like Calvin, blind. Unlike Calvin, she was not able to go to public school but was sent away at age 6, after many operations on her eyes, to a residential school—the Western Pennsylvania School for the Blind.

And although it was 48 years ago that Lois Sivits was sent away from her family to attend the school for the blind, she remembers— as though it were 48 minutes ago—how that blind 6-year-old girl felt about the experience: "Oh, I was so *very* homesick. I had a very hard time being separated from my family. It took me three years before I began getting used to it. But I knew I had to stay there. I would have given anything to be able to stay at home and go to a public school like Calvin," says the small, kind-looking woman with very still hands.

Now, the moment: Calvin is standing in front of the window, the light pouring in from behind him. He is listening to a talking clock which tells him, "It's 11:52 a.m." Miss Sivits stands about 3 feet away from him, also in front of the window holding a huge braille dictionary in her hands, fingers flying across the page as she silently reads from it. And for a few moments, there they are as if frozen in a tableau, the two of them standing in darkness against the light, each lost for a moment in a private world that is composed only of sound and touch.

There was another moment, years ago, when Calvin's mother and father knew that the operation had not helped, that their son was probably never going to see. "Well," said the father, trying to comfort the mother, "we'll do what we have to do and Calvin will be fine."
He is. And so are they.

ANALYSIS

Fairly short and lyrical, Alice Steinbach's story is different from many of the feature stories in this anthology. Crafted into a series of highly-visual scenes, Steinbach creates a wonderfully readable profile of a little blind boy, and how he relates to those around him.

In fact, it could be argued that the story is more about how those around Calvin Stanley, such as his mother, *relate to him.*

Some editors might have asked Steinbach to add a few grafs to this piece—talking directly to the doctors, how other school systems handle blind students, etc. But extra research here would break the flow and only take away from the dulcet tune Steinbach is playing for us.

Another reason this piece works so well is that Steinbach doesn't take features like "A Boy of Unusual Vision" lightly. Before agreeing to even write the story, she met with Calvin and his parents and warned them of all the negatives that could come from a story about a boy such as Calvin. "I'm interested in stories, not articles," she stresses. "I didn't want to compromise this boy in any way."

Steinbach didn't *even agree* to write the story until she was certain all the literary elements were in place, including:

A strong plot: Hard-working parents nurture and support Calvin's being mainstreamed through school.

A strong main character, capable of telling the story: Calvin's mom.

Once underway, Steinbach doesn't use an outline and writes almost by feel, or perhaps, by sound: "I can hear dissonance when I write," she explains. "I hear what I'm writing. I don't read it."

Steinbach says this ability allows her to know when a word is wrong or if a sentence is too short or too long. "I can't explain it. It's just there," she says.

Although stressing strongly that she doesn't consider herself a poet, Steinbach says, "I wanted to make [Calvin] a little bit like poetry ... there were moments that were so striking—like when I was in Calvin's room one night:"

Much of what he remembers has to be imagined visually first. Like the size and color of his room. "I think it's kind of big," he says of the small room. "And it's green," he says of the deep rose-colored walls.

Steinbach's lead is also novel and creative. This may be the only Pulitzer Prize-winning story to begin with a three-word sentence fragment followed by a colon. The opening sets the stage for the remainder of the article:

First, the eyes: They are large and blue, a light, opaque blue, the color of a robin's egg.

Not surprisingly, Steinbach likes to have her lead nearly perfect before she ventures much further into the story. "It tells me where I'm going," she explains.

Steinbach uses her colons to set off quotes with great effect throughout her story. It's an interesting technique. She's trying to give the story a cadence, a rhythm—much as Jon Franklin used exact times and a *pop ... pop ... pop* in "Mrs. Kelly's Monster."

"I think of writing as being musical," Steinbach says. "Punctuation is the rhythm and the words are the melody. I think of a semicolon like a semi stop in music and a colon is a full stop.

The author follows her visual and colorful lead throughout the story. Even though Calvin can't see, he has favorite colors.

As such, Steinbach dots her prose with a vivid use of color: opaque blue, emerald green, exploding yellow, purple hyacinths, rose-colored, rose-pink.

In the best feature stories, the action flows from quotes heavily laced with flavor and detail. The writer often assuming the position of tour guide, trying to "stay out of the way," letting the sights carry the day. Alice Steinbach has done that masterfully in this story. The quotes are so strong, plentiful and filled with splendid details. Steinbach saw it all, and noted it all. She spent quite a bit of time at the Stanley household and it shows. Her observational powers and keen sense of detail are the major reason this story works well as a heroic tale.

Steinbach works hard on her paragraphs. The results are some mini-classics. One paragraph in the story seems to sum up her ability to observe even the smallest details and present them in a compelling and interesting fashion:

Two p.m., Vivian Jackson's class, Room 207.

What Calvin can't see: He can't see the small, pretty girl sitting opposite him, the one who is wearing little rows of red, yellow and blue barrettes shaped like airplanes in her braided hair. He can't see the line of small, green plants growing in yellow pots all along the sunny window sill. And he can't see Mrs. Jackson in her rose-pink suit and pink enameled earrings shaped like little swans.

("Were they really shaped like little swans?" he will ask later.)

Again, note the cadence of repetition of the phrase, *"he can't see"* in this paragraph. Steinbach repeats it three times (and introduces the quote with a fourth *"can't see"*).

"I spend a lot of time thinking about creative paragraphing," Steinbach admits. "You can do a lot with flow and stopping people and starting them; speeding things up and slowing them down. I think paragraphing is a very overlooked tool in feature writing."

In several instances, Steinbach acquires memorable quotes and uses them with maximum sensitivity and skill to paint an unforgettable portrait of this special boy:

Something else makes Calvin sad: "I'd like to see what my mother looks like," he says, looking up quickly and swallow-

ing hard. "What does she look like? People tell me she's pretty."

Although she feels organization is her biggest challenge, the way Steinbach structured this article is effective. After writing the compelling and slightly jarring lead, she quickly transitions to Calvin's mother explaining how his blindness came to be, followed rapidly by a cut to Calvin riding his bike at break-neck speed in the alley behind his house.

A quote about Calvin's bike prowess would have been interesting, but Steinbach's on-the-spot reporting of the ride in the alley significantly brought the adventure to life. As Steinbach proves in this story, witnessing such an adventure has it all over a quote:

Now: Try to imagine riding a bike without being able to see where you're going. Without even knowing what an "alley" looks like. Try to imagine how you navigate a space that has no visual boundaries, that exists only in your head. And then try to imagine what Calvin is feeling as he pedals his bike in that space, whooping for joy as the air rushes past him on either side.

In the bike paragraph, Steinbach has again used repetition to set the pace (*try to imagine*). She seems to be making the bike a metaphor for Calvin's ability to conquer any hurdle, and his family's unwavering encouragement and support.

Amazingly, Steinbach says the bike narrative required almost no additional writing. "I wrote it all down in my notebook virtually the way it appeared [in print]."

Steinbach's use of transitions in this story is excellent. Notice how, after the bike scene, she backtracks to Calvin's birth (a point at which many writers would have taken the safe path and finished the story by returning Calvin chronologically to the present). Instead, Steinbach veers yet again—to how his mom raised and nurtured him, before jumping to Calvin's performance in school. (One side note: Steinbach says she probably would have mentioned that the Stanley's were African-American if the story hadn't used photos.)

In theory, this story shouldn't flow as well as it does, moving in so many different directions. Steinbach says the story took a month to produce—three weeks of spending significant time with the family and one week to write.

Near the end of the story, Steinbach shows Calvin working one-on-one with his braille teacher, who is also blind. It's a wonderful touch, again focusing on how Calvin relates to others. Bringing out the teacher's regret about not having been allowed to attend a public school like Calvin was an interesting angle. The whole scenario Steinbach creates is poignant and telling, a deft lead-in to the final close.

ALICE STEINBACH is currently a reporter and feature writer for *The Baltimore Sun*. She has studied at the University of London and recently released her first book: *The Miss Dennis School of Writing and Other Lessons from a Woman's Life*.

1986

JOHN CAMP

LONG BEFORE HE BECAME a best-selling novelist, writing his acclaimed "Prey" series under the name John Sandford, John Camp won a Pulitzer Prize for his five-part series on the plight of American farmers.

Six years after being named a Pulitzer Prize finalist for a feature story on American Indian culture, Camp would win the Pulitzer by chronicling the lives of a Minnesota farm family over the course of a year—from spring planting through harvest.

Although the paper had always devoted extensive coverage to farms, by late 1984 the *St. Paul Pioneer Press* had concluded that the next year presented the region with the worst farm outlook since the Great Depression. "It was a very serious crisis," Camp recalls today. "A large percentage of farms went down during the middle 1980s, for a combination of reasons."

Before deciding to focus on the Benson family, the *Pioneer Press* had "discussed the possibilities of [using] four or five different families, that either people in the office knew about or people in the Department of Agriculture knew about," Camp explains. "As it turned out, the photographer, Joe Rossi, knew the Bensons from when he was working as a newspaper reporter in Worthington, Minn.

"When we went down there, everything sort of fit—the farm had been in the family for quite a while and was being passed now to David."

Camp gives ample credit to his editors for the success of the series, pointing out the *Pioneer Press* had a compressed management, without many levels, making it easy to pitch ideas. "The executive editor at the time, Deborah Howell, was very approachable and it was only a matter of saying, 'we have to do something about this.' And she was the type of person who actually listened.

"So it was given a very high priority at the top, which always makes it easier to get through," Camp noted the head of the photo department handled the actual layout and the managing editor did the editing—and later visited the farm.

The Pulitzer also helped bring Camp some other benefits. "I didn't like being a columnist," he says bluntly. "I didn't have enough opinions to be a columnist. ... Shortly after I finished the last piece of "Life on the Land," I dumped the column and went back to writing."

Camp started to get some indications he might win a Pulitzer after the series won the American Society of Newspaper Editors (ASNE) feature award. "An editor from some paper said I was going to win the Pulitzer because (ASNE) was kind of a precursor." Someone else told him that he might win because he had been a finalist before and didn't win.

"I started to get stressed out, because I really wanted to win," he admits. "I was talking to a friend, Bill Gardner, the day before the awards were announced [and] apparently the Knight-Ridder people had found out who their winners were. Deborah came by and said, 'Are you going to be around tomorrow? I need to talk to you about some stuff. ...'

"Gardner looked at me and said, 'You won. She knows.'

"She never really did tell me but I think she told other people in the newsroom because when the Pulitzers started coming across the wire a large crowd of people was there."

After winning, Camp's thoughts turned to his father. "My dad was always a big newspaper reader, and still is. He used to talk about *The Cedar Rapids Gazette* and how it had a Pulitzer. It was kind of neat when I called him up and told him now I had one."

Camp also notes with amusement another first relating to the Pulitzer Prizes. In 1968, while in the Army in Korea, Camp edited a tiny post newspaper. "My officer-in-charge was the intelligence officer, Bill Keeler, and he wanted to be a newspaperman after he got out. He eventually ended up at *Newsday* and when I won the Pulitzer he was all excited and called me up to congratulate me.

"And Keeler won last year [for national reporting]. We're the only two-man newspaper shop in Korea to win Pulitzers!"

Life on the Land:
An American Farm Family

St. Paul Pioneer Press

May–December 1985

MAY 12, 1985

DAVID BENSON sits on the seat of the manure wagon, behind the twin black draft horses, reins in his hands, and he says this:

"Machinery can be intoxicating. You sit there on top of a huge tractor, rolling across those fields, and you feel like God. It's an amazing feeling, and a real one, and I think some people get so they don't feel complete without it.

"That's one of the reasons they keep buying bigger and bigger tractors, these enormous four-wheel drives tearing up and down the fields. Tearing up and down. They are incredibly expensive machines, they'll run you $16 an hour in fuel alone, and you can do in one day what used to take you three or four—but then the question arises, are you doing anything useful on the three or four you saved? You buy this gigantic machine with its incredible capability, and all of a sudden, you're done.

"And you start thinking, 'My God, if I bought another 600 acres I could do that, too.' So you buy it, and then you find if you only had a bigger machine, you could buy even more. At the end of it, you're doing 2,000 acres on this fantastic Star Wars machinery and you're so far in debt that if anything goes wrong—and I mean if they stop eating soy sauce in Ireland—you lose the whole works, including the place you started with.

"And it's not the same as losing in the city. These people are going around asking, Jeez, what did I do wrong? They said this was the American way, you try to get bigger and take a few risks, but nobody ever told me that if I lose they were going to take away everything, my whole way of life and my children's way of life and our whole culture and the whole neighborhood and just stomp us right into the ground.

"My God, you know, people are bulldozing farmsteads so they can plant corn where the houses used to be because there's nobody to live in these houses any more. That's happening."

David Benson. He has horses, but he's not a back-to-the-land dabbler, not an amateur, not a dilettante—he has a couple of tractors, and a barn full of machinery. But he finds a use for horses. He likes them.

And unlike a lot of farmers in Minnesota, he's making it. Making it small, but he's making it.

Go down to Worthington. Get off Interstate 90, off the state highway, off the blacktopped county road, and finally go down the gravel track and into the farm lane, listening to the power lines sing and the cottonwoods moan in the everlasting wind, watching a red-orange pickup a mile away as it crawls like a ladybug along a parallel road between freshly plowed fields, leaving behind a rising plume of gravel dust, crawling toward the silos and rooftops that mark the Iowa line. ...

A Mailbox on a Post

The landscape is not quite flat—it's a landscape of tilted planes, fields tipped this way or that, almost all showing the fertile loam of recent plowing. The black fields dominate the countryside, interrupted here and there by woodlots, by pasturage where lambs play in the fading sunlight, by red-brick or purple-steel silos, Grant Wood barns and Sears-Roebuck sheds, and by the farmhouses.

There's a turn-of-the-century farmhouse here. Gray with white trim, it could be any one of a thousand prairie homes. There's a single rural mailbox on a post across the road from the end of the driveway. It says Benson on the side, but the paint has been scoured by the wind and the name is almost illegible.

There is a tire swing hung from a cottonwood with a yellow rope, and a kid named Anton kicking a black-and-white soccer ball in the driveway.

The walk to the porch is guarded by lilacs and lilies of the valley and a patch of violets. A tortoise-shell cat named Yin lounges on the porch, watchfully making way for visitors; a familial tiger-striper named Yang watches from the side yard. Just before the porch is a strip of iron set in a concrete block: a boot scraper, and well-used.

The door swings open and Sally-Anne Benson is there, navy sweatshirt, blue jeans, tan work boots.

"Hi," she says, "Come in. David is still in the field, with the oats."

From behind her come the kitchen smells of fresh bread and noodles and sauce, and blonde Heather is turning to go up the stairs to her bedroom.

"We're going over to Grandpa's to do the chores," Sally-Anne says to Heather.

These are some of the Bensons. The Bensons in this house are

David, 38, and Sally-Anne, 35, husband and wife, and their children, Heather, 11, and Anton, 8. Sally-Anne is small with thin wrists and curly brown hair, blue-gray eyes, a quick smile, and a tendency to bubble when she's had a few glasses of white wine. She answers to the nickname "Sag" or "Sag-oh" which is an acronym of her maiden name, Sally-Anne Greeley. David has a red walrus mustache and the beginning of crows-feet at the corners of his eyes, smile lines at his mouth, and a storyteller's laugh. The children are blonde, blonder than seems real, or even possible.

Rhythm of Work Blissful

The Bensons in the white house up the road and around the corner on the blacktop are Gus and Bertha Benson, David's parents.

Gus, 82, is mostly retired, though on this day he's been fanning oats—cleaning the oats to be used as seed—for the planting. He has white hair combed straight back, a white stubble on his pink face, and powerful, heavy hands. Bertha is 75. Her hair is a steel brown-gray, she wears plastic glasses, and after 56 years of farming, she still can't watch when chickens are butchered. She can pick them, the hens who make the fatal mistake of not laying, but she can't watch them topped with a corn knife.

David and Sally-Anne do the bulk of the heavy farm work now. Gus particularly likes to work with the beef cattle, and Bertha keeps house and recently has taken up weaving and rugmaking, and cans and freezes produce during the summer; last year she got in 100 quarts of applesauce. Heather and Anton have their chores. Together they live on 160 acres of the best land God ever made.

And they work it hard. They have the crops, the cattle, a growing flock of sheep, chickens, geese, and a boxful of tiny turkeys on the back porch.

The day started with David getting up at 6:15 a.m. and apologizing for it. "Boy, I got up earlier, but I just couldn't ... Oh, boy, I just laid back down and the next thing I knew it was after 6 ... "

He's planting oats, and has been hard at it for the previous two days, sitting up on top of the John Deere, first disking, then chisel-plowing a small patch of compacted ground, then hooking up a grain drill to seed the oats.

"You sit up there, going back and forth, when you're disking, and your mind goes on automatic pilot," he said. "You can think of any-thing, and sooner or later, you do. It's a liberating experience, really. You put in maybe 400 hours a year on a tractor, and you spend a good part of it just ... thinking. It's even better when you're working with the horses, because everything moves fairly slowly and you don't have the tractor engine, so it's quiet. There's a rhythm to it. It's almost ... blissful, is that the word?"

The Land Comes First

At noon, Sally-Anne brings out lunch, cheese sandwiches and fresh milk from Bluma, the milk cow, and homemade bread and a chunk of cake. David climbs stiffly off the tractor and drops down into the roadside ditch and leans back into last year's tall brown grass, out of the eternal prairie wind.

"It's just going so well, going so well," he says, looking across the barbed-wire fence toward the field. "Just need to get it in, this is beautiful weather, but I wish the wind would lay off."

He looks up at the faultless blue sky. "And we could use some rain, use some rain. Sure. We sure could."

He lies in the ditch eating, his face covered with dust, alternately eating and explaining: "We'll grow beans and corn and oats and alfalfa for hay, and the alfalfa puts nitrogen back in the soil; of course, we won't grow all those at once, we'll rotate through. You've got to be strict about it, you can't decide just to knock off a little extra here and there, or you'll kill it, the land."

He's almost apologetic about the chisel plow. "Normally we don't need it, but last year we brought in some heavy earth-moving equipment to build that terrace down there, and it compacted the ground enough that disking won't do it."

He needed the terrace to correct a drainage problem. "If you don't build water structures, you're going to wash ditches, and that's another way you can kill it," he says.

Kill the land. The nightmare. The land must be cared for, the Bensons say. But the land is in trouble right now. Neither David nor Sally-Anne Benson would be considered solemn, but David will sit in his dining room chair after supper, leaning his elbows on the strawberry-patch oilcloth that covers the table, and talk like this:

"The strength of the Midwest culture was that it had people who were developing an interest in the land, and in developing a community that had some continuity to it. Without that, we have an ethereal culture that just isn't satisfying to most people, and can't be— people who don't really know what they want.

"We are living in the middle of one of the largest areas of fertile land on the planet. Normally you'd think that people would go to a place like that. Would want to live there, to form a good rooted culture, where you could form your own ties to the land and to the neighborhood and even to those people you just see driving by, but whose whole lives you know and they know yours. ... "

The connections between the people, the land, the crops, the food, the neighborhood, the community—they're impossible to put a hand on, but they are real. Much of its connecting web can be explained in stories of times past, of incidents that somehow hallow a particular patch of ground or even make it a place of humor, or sadness, or dread.

Gus and Bertha sit at their dining room table, at what their children call the home place, and remember it.

"Spring is always the moving time for farmers," says Bertha. "We bought this place in 1938, and we moved here in the spring of 1939, from Stanton, Nebraska. That's where Gus was born, in Stanton, and two of our children—the other two were born here. Gladys and Shirley and Marilyn and David, 17 years apart, the four of them, and we enjoyed every one. ...

"When we moved here, we couldn't tell what color the house was, it was so bad, but we were more concerned about the land. When we bought it, the land cost $95 an acre, and we were trembling and afraid, because we thought if we did something wrong, we could lose it and lose everything we saved."

They had been married in Nebraska in 1929, and spent the next 10 years as renters, building up a working capital of $3,000. It all went into the new place in Minnesota.

"We moved up here because it was dry in Nebraska for so many years, you couldn't farm. We came up here on a trip and we thought it was so beautiful in Minnesota, so beautiful," Bertha says.

Unfreezing the Car
And it was cold, and windy, and the life was rough. They laugh about it now, Bertha and Gus, but at the time ...

"When Marilyn was born, it was so cold I had to start a fire with corn cobs in a pan, and put it under the engine to get it warmed up so we could start it," Gus recalls. "She was ready for the hospital, 4 in the morning, and I can still remember the cold ... "

"And remember when we got electricity ... "

"Oh, yes, when we got the electricity," says Bertha. "That was in, when, 1948?"

"1948, that's when it was."

"I remember," says Bertha, a glow in her face, "we got an electrician from Dundee to do the house, all the way from Dundee because all the other electricians were busy. The whole neighborhood went on at the same time. We were one of the last, because we were so close to the Iowa border, we were like in a corner. But I remember how the lights came on, and we sat with all the lights all evening, sat with the lights on us. ...

"The electricity is the best thing for farm wives. Before that we took soft water from the cistern, and regular hard water from the well in a pail. I think I could go back to that way of living, except that I want my hot water. Hot water is the most wonderful thing!"

"Oh, we had a wedding here, too," says Gus.

"One of Shirley's girls, Christina," says Bertha. "They had their wedding in the yard, and dancing in the corn crib, and a hay ride in the afternoon."

"They decorated the corn crib," says Gus. "They cleaned it out and decorated it and danced in there."

"We never thought David would come back," Gus says suddenly. "We thought we'd be the last. We thought he would be an engineer. He was living in San Francisco, and one day he called and said, 'Don't sell the farm, we might come back.'"

David and Sally-Anne have their memories too, some of their courtship in Sally-Anne's hometown of Lexington, Mass., and some of San Francisco, where they spent some time when they were in their early 20s, and many, now, of their 14 years on the farm.

Memories Grow Fast

Of walking the beans. Of haying time. Of rebuilding the aging machinery. Of David on the John Deere, dragging a plow, Sally-Anne on the David Brown 990 with the disk, the wind whistling across them both, the sun beating down. ...

Sally-Anne, laughing: "You remember at a party putting those chickens asleep?"

David: "Nothing like it. Hypnotizing chickens. We had one asleep for three or four minutes I think, just stretched stone cold out on the ground ... a rooster.

"By the way," he says to Sally-Anne, "do you see we've got another transvestite rooster coming along?"

"Oh, I saw that, he's getting big, too, he's almost as aggressive as the top one ... "

"Well, not that bad ... "

David explains: "We decided to get rid of all our roosters. We ate them, every one, or thought so. Then all of a sudden, here comes this chicken out of the flock. I mean, we thought all along he was a hen, but he starts getting bigger and growing some wattles and pretty soon he's crowing all over the place. He was hiding in there, pretending to be a hen. Now we've got another one coming out of the closet, he's getting bigger. ...

"I remember when we were kids, we used to chase the chickens down—chickens have got pretty good speed over the short haul, and have pretty good moves. Anyway, you'd get a rock and just chuck it at them, and every once in a while you'd lay it right alongside their heads, just throwing it at them on the run.

"And then you'd be hiding out behind the corncrib, because it'd drop over and you were sure it was dead. But it never was. It'd always get up and walk around like nothing happened. I'm not sure you can hurt chickens, to tell you the truth.

"No kid should grow up without chickens; chickens have got to be good for you. ... "

Some Memories Difficult

Some of the memories are funny, like the chickens. Some are not.

Sally-Anne: "One time we had this horse, named Belle, and that year there was an unusual mold that grew on the corn stalk, and Belle ate some of it. It turns out that it destroys your muscle control. She couldn't control the way she moved ... like polio in people. Anyway, we had the vet out, and he said that's what it was.

"There was nothing we could do, and David had to shoot her.

David got the gun and brought her out of the barn, and kept backing away from her so he could get a clean shot and she kept going to him, kept trying to walk up to him, because she trusted him and she didn't know what was wrong with her. ... "

Sally-Anne shivers as she tells the story. "I didn't want to watch. It was just awful, but finally he got back and shot her. The vet said there was nothing wrong with the meat, so David and a friend skinned her and butchered her ... it was still pretty bad, but then, after a while, another friend came over and said 'Ah, Taco Bell, huh?' And that made it better, somehow. God, it was awful."

A farm of 160 acres can't really support six people, and the Bensons know it. They talk about buying more land, of going into debt, the very experience they saw drag down so many of their neighbors.

In the meantime, Sally-Anne teaches at the Worthington Montessori school in the mornings, and David does casual work as a mechanic. Sally brags that he can fix most things, especially Volvos. "If you live anyplace around Worthington and own a Volvo, you probably know him," she said.

The life suits them. More land would be nice, but the spectre of debt is overpowering. The Bensons, for now, have no debt—they don't even need spring operating loans. Between grain sales, auto mechanics, and Sally-Anne's job, they are self-supporting and self-financed. They're proud of their ability to survive, but there is no sense of victory when they see a neighbor fail.

Instead, there is a sense of loss. It's their community evaporating, the Bensons' along with everyone else's.

"I don't know," says Dave. "Maybe what we need is some kind of creative financing like they do for home mortgages. Some kind of rent-share program where younger farmers can have a chance, can move into these homesteads and take them over and work them like they should be.

"And if they fail anyway? Well, at least we tried. If we don't try, we're going to kill it, the land."

Strong stuff, deeply felt; but it's hard to stay solemn for too long at the Bensons.

"When are you coming back?" they ask the visitors at the table. "Three or four weeks? Gee, that'd be just about right time for haying."

Sure would like to see you for haying, yes indeed, they say. Bring a hat. Bring gloves. Bring beer. Love to have you.

JUNE 30, 1985

Making Hay

A scorching sun, south wind, the sweet smell of fresh-cut alfalfa mixed with gravel dust thrown up by passing cars and the scent of diesel fuel; down on the farm, south of Worthington, staring dry-mouth and aching through the shimmering heat waves toward the gleaming white grain elevators of the town—the town with its beckoning bar, the cold beers, and the air conditioning—that stands a mile farther south on the Iowa line.

Wherever farm people get together, the farm crisis dominates serious talk. But talk is not the real material of the spring and early summer on a farm. Talk may dominate a prairie winter, when the planting loans are in doubt. With the crops in the ground, the spring and summer are for work.

"Man can't save himself," said the hard-sweating Calvinist who stopped at the Benson farm to throw hay. "Work can't be redemptive in itself, but it's an honor. It's not given to everyone to have the honor of good work."

Hay is the first crop in the barn. The initial cutting comes around the first week of June.

"Hay is the crop where you get your heart broken most often," David Benson said as he stood on the edge of the farmyard, nibbling at the bottom of his reddish-blond mustache and squinting over an alfalfa field south and east of the house. Benson's face was caked with dust, with heavier lines in the crow's feet around his eyes.

"After you cut it, you need at least two or three days of good hot weather to dry it out, and the drier you can get it on the ground, the better off you are. This time of year, though, you get these evening thunderstorms. You get a good day to swath, get it down, and then watch the clouds building up and the rain coming in. It can break your heart."

While a day or two of rain won't completely ruin fresh-cut hay, sometimes the rains last longer than that. Benson recalled a time a few years ago when he and his family were eager to take a vacation trip, but had to get the hay in first.

"We cut it early because we wanted to get away. We even baled it a little green. So we got out of here just as everybody else was swathing.

"When we left, everybody had hay down and drying. When we came back, like a couple of weeks later, it was still out there in the fields. A rainy spell hit, and they couldn't get it in. A lot of people lost the whole first crop—it was worthless by the time the rain stopped. It was laying out there looking like sludge."

Swathing Time

This year Benson began swathing early in the first week of June, chugging remorselessly through the alfalfa field while purple martins darted around the swather, gobbling the insects set into flight by the passing machine.

A 20-mile-an-hour wind and a blistering sun dried the fresh-cut alfalfa as efficiently as if it had been shoveled into an oven; and the aroma of the cooking hay spread softly across the landscape.

With the swathing done, the Bensons watched the sky anxiously, the puffy white clouds popping up in the west, born of the afternoon's rising humidity. Nothing came of them; the days stayed dry.

"This is good hay. This might be the best hay we've ever had on the first cutting. Usually the first cutting is kind of tall and steamy and coarse, but this is very good hay," Benson said as he turned piles of hay with his foot during an exploratory trip through the main field.

The swathing is hot and tiring, but the baling is the real back-breaker. The baler is pulled by a David Brown 990 tractor, with

Benson's wife Sally-Anne in the driver's seat. The hay rack—hay wagon—is towed behind the baler. The baler scoops off the long rows and carries the hay into a chute where it is packed by a hydraulic ram and tied into bales by a device too crazy to describe. As the ram packs more and more hay into the chute, newly tied bales are expelled from the rear of the baler, to be grabbed and stacked on the rack.

"You've got to stack the bales just this way," Benson told a helper, laying out a pattern along the back of the rack. "If you do it right, you can stack them six high and everything will stay on the rack."

He is sweating profusely now, swinging a hay hook in one hand, grabbing the baling twines with the other, stacking the bales into a head-high wall as they pop out of the machine every 30 seconds or so. The hay is abrasive, and nicks the forearms and lightly-clothed chests with dozens of tiny pin-prick cuts; sweat gets into the cuts and a characteristic hay rash develops.

"It's a good thing we moved that hay around in the barn this morning," Benson said as he piled the bales. "That's just the kind of warm-up you need when you're our age. When you're 16 and in good shape, it seems like you can throw all day. You get older, you need something you can start slow with."

There are six Bensons on the farm now. Gus, 82, and Bertha, 75, own it and are semi-retired; their son David, 38, and his wife, Sally-Anne, 35, are both management and principal labor; David's and Sally-Anne's two children, Heather, 11, and Anton, 8, do the chores.

As in most farm families, everybody works.

With the school in recess for the summer, the two children are expected to do several hours' work each morning, and one or two more in the late afternoon.

They are still children; their work isn't heavy, but is considered necessary both for its intrinsic instructional value as well as product.

The children's morning jobs may vary, anything from house or field work to such special jobs as sanding and lacquering a firewood box to trapping gophers in the oat field.

Everybody Works

"David said he would give us a dollar each," Anton said confidently as he and his sister picked their way through the oats toward a stick that marked the gopher trap. "After we trap all these, we're going to go see if the neighbors need help with theirs."

The problem with pocket gophers is that they leave behind mounds of dirt, six or eight inches high, up to two feet in diameter, as they tunnel. Besides destroying small amounts of the crop, the mounds harden in the sunlight and can damage farm machinery at the harvest.

A gopher tends to work in one direction, leaving behind a series of increasingly fresher mounds. By following the trail of mounds, the trapper will soon arrive at the freshest. He looks for an indentation on the side of the mound, which is the dirt-blocked mouth of the newest tunnel.

Carefully digging out the tunnel with his hand, the trapper may set any of several kinds of traps in the tunnel itself, with a holding chain leading to the outside, where it is firmly staked into the ground.

The open hole is then covered with a piece of wood, a shingle, or newspapers, the edges carefully sealed with dirt to prevent any light leakage. If it's all done right, the gopher will walk right into the trap.

"We got one," Anton said breathlessly as he dug around the hole with a spade. It was their first.

"Pull it out, pull it out," urged Heather. "Is it dead?"

"No, no, it's not dead," said Anton, "it's moving."

The fuzzy, dirt-brown, nearly blind gopher squirmed feebly in the trap. "We've got to kill it."

Nobody wanted to kill it. The children's eyes eventually fell on a friend who said, finally, "OK. Give me the shovel." The gopher died with a quick thrust of the shovel's edge against the back of its neck.

"Poor thing," said Heather.

"Let's show Dad," said Anton. The gopher was placed on the lid of an oil can and taken home for the reward.

"Poor thing," Heather said again, on the way back to the farm house.

The children's evenings are less dramatic, carrying water and feed to the animals, collecting eggs from the chicken house.

The worst of their spring jobs, hands down, is walking the corn, and later, walking the beans. They start in mid- to late June, and carry into July. It's a job for the entire family and any friends and relatives who want to volunteer. It's a tough one.

A Tough Row

"Walking (the corn) isn't done much any more," said Sally-Anne.

"You can get rid of most of the weeds with chemical herbicides, but we don't want to get into that. We used some when we first came back, when the thistles had just about taken over, but when we got them down (to a tolerable level), we just started walking them."

The principal piece of farm machinery involved in walking the corn—and the beans, of course—is a sharp hoe. The idea is to walk along a row of knee-high corn and root out the waterweed and the creeping jenny and the nightshade and especially the Canadian thistle.

The posture is head-down; on a sunny day, the derivation of the term "redneck" becomes painfully clear. As row fades into row, with hits on the water bottle at the end of each round, an ache grows just below the shoulder blade and in the back just above the pelvis. And the thistle seems to grow thicker as the hours wear on, and the hands become tender and ripe with burning scarlet sore spots.

"You can sacrifice a corn plant to get a thistle," Sally-Anne said. "But try not to do it too often."

"Oops," said one of the walkers.

"A fine obituary for a corn plant," said another. "Oops."

"The thistles are growing right up against the corn. I can't believe it."

"Pull that creeping jenny. If you let it go, it can climb right up a corn plant and choke it."

"Tell us about that Rodney Dangerfield movie you saw on Home Box Office. ... "

"How many rounds do we have left?"

"You know, walking the beans isn't all that bad," Sally-Anne said late one afternoon, as she sat at her dining room table drinking tea. "At this time of year, David's in the field so much that I hardly get to see him, and then he's so tired and dirty he just wants to wash up, eat, and go to bed ... when you're walking the beans, you can go along together, and talk about things."

She smiled and the lines around her eyes crinkled. "The only problem is that you usually run out of talking before you run out of beans."

Anton twits his father: "Why don't we get one of those big tractors and a tank and just spray them down with Lasso (herbicide)," he asks, fully aware of his father's antagonism for solutions built on lethal chemistry and brute horsepower.

Walking the corn, and the beans, has the status of a Midwestern myth; the Bensons possess a record by Iowa/Minnesota folksinger Greg Brown, a man whose reputation is swelling through the cornbelt countryside, mostly because of songs like "Walking the Beans."

It's a mile-long row, that's a lot of room to grow,

"I think he's walked beans," said Sally-Anne.

His shoulders straining under the dark-blue cowboy shirt, the Rev. Ronald Lammers swung fresh bales off the battered hay rack and threw them onto a ladder-like elevator, which carried them up to the loft in Gus Benson's barn; a good quarter-hour's work for a man of Calvinist convictions, and a pleasure to see the undoubted sinners higher in the barn sweating to keep up with him.

Midmorning, the sun glowing evilly through a haze of humidity. The farm buildings farther south shimmer above the fields of corn, oats, and alfalfa, patches of broken color against the haze.

A short round of haying has already been completed this morning, Lammers driving into the farmyard as the tractor and hay rack rolled in from the other direction, just in time to be recruited to throw bales. As a Christian Reformed minister, Lammers presides over a white clapboard church at Bigelow, a church whose shrinking congregation reflects the emptying of the great Minnesota prairie farmlands.

"When I started, eight years ago, there were 22 families (in the congregation), and now we're down to 14. The way it's supposed to work, you have a turnover. The older people die as the younger people marry and have children. Now the younger people marry and move away. They just vanish from the landscape," Lammers said later, when the hay was safely in the barn.

With the sun and the heat and the heavy lifting, the breaks are frequent: the workers need the time to put water back in their bodies.

And it's cool at the picnic table under the trees in Gus Benson's back yard. Bertha Benson's garden is doing fine, just there beside the picnic table, lettuce and beets and tomatoes growing cheerfully in the good black dirt. Most of them look cheerful, anyway, aside from one or two that were trampled the night before when a horse got loose and paid the garden an impromptu visit. Evidence of the visit remains in a soil-enriching pile at one corner of the vegetable plot.

Lammers is a soft-spoken, serious, graying man. At 41, he is a thesis away from a master's degree in the Old Testament from the respected Calvin Theological Seminary in Grand Rapids, Mich. He pushed his black plastic glasses back up his nose with an index finger and said quietly that our national farm debate doesn't seem to consider the morality of the new situation.

"One thing that's never talked about is justice. We have all these arguments between the left and the right about who's got the better idea to get the economic pumps working, but nobody talks about justice. The final worth of a nation isn't determined by how much money its people make, but whether they are just. People who dedicate themselves to injustice," said the Calvinist, "will inevitably perish. Those who strive for justice will endure."

Good Neighbors

Their mutual interest in the farm issue is part of the cement in the relationship between the Calvinist minister and the Bensons. None of the Bensons belong to Lammers' congregation—Bertha takes the children to Indian Lake Baptist Church, and David describes himself and Sally-Anne as "sort of Quaking Unitarians. I have an interest in the Quakers and we've met with the Unitarians."

The minister and the farmers met in the most prosaic of ways. A car owned by a church deacon broke down in Lammers' yard, and the deacon called David Benson to fix it.

"I found out what a good mechanic I had in my own backyard, so to speak, and we started trading labor. I'd do some work on the farm and he'd work on my car, and that's how we got to be friends. We talk about everything; we talk about what's happening with the farms. It's something that worries us both."

"I'd seen him around for years, but never said anything to him. Then once we said a few things, we found out what an interesting guy he was, and we never stopped talking," said David.

Their approach to politics and life seems radically different, although they share a deep sincerity.

David Benson talks of a relative, human morality, a complex mix of manners and tradition and economic pressures. Ronald Lammers approaches the problem through the revealed word of God.

Benson is profoundly concerned with the disappearance of the small farm and the rise of giant agri-business enterprises, issues so complex he sometimes finds it difficult to express the dangers of the phenomenon and the urgency of a resolution. Lammers uses David Benson's language in a general discussion of the topic, but has no trouble finding fluent expression of the troubles.

Because, he said, it has all been discussed before, and with the greatest of eloquence.

"Woe unto them that join house to house, that lay field to field, till there be no place, that they may be placed alone in the midst of the earth," said Lammers. "That's Isaiah 5. He was talking about the Near East, but he was talking about this place, too. We're changing from a farm culture to a plantation culture, and the people working them will soon be peons. That's injustice. And squeezing people off ancestral lands, that's not only injustice, that's the stuff from which revolutions are made."

As Lammers ponders the problem of the farm, the younger Bensons disappear around the big red barn, headed for the corn field with hoes over their shoulders.

Value of Work

"There are parts of the world where five acres will support a family. What does it mean when you live out here, in the richest earth God ever made, and 1,000 acres might not support a family, no matter how hard they work?" Lammers asked. "Work has always been an honor; work is an honor. But what does it mean when people can't work hard enough to live? When they just can't do it? You know, in (biblical) Israel, the people failed to husband the land. That was what Isaiah was talking about. Eventually the whole land was blown away with the wind. If we don't listen to Isaiah, it could happen here."

Work may not be enough. But the Bensons work:

Sally-Anne Benson chopping Canadian thistles in the hot sun, her face glowing fiery red with heat, despite the woven straw hat; David Benson rolling the cultivator down the endless rows of new beans, five hours with barely a stop, the hot wind blowing the dust and grit into his eyes and ears and teeth; Heather Benson, laying out the table, putting together a quick dinner because her parents are late in from the field, and she knows they'll be tired almost to sickness; Anton Benson, pulling a full round of evening chores while his parents work on in the long lingering twilight of the summer solstice.

Working on the Benson farm, just off Nobles County Road 4, nine miles south of Worthington, a mile north of the Iowa line, out on the prairie in Minnesota.

AUGUST 25, 1985

When Bertha Benson stands with her hands in the soapy water of the kitchen sink and looks out through the east window, she can see down across the salad garden and sweet corn patch, across the steel-colored pond and the deep-green alfalfa and cornfields to the next farm home, where her son David and his family live.

There's a tree belt around David's house, old cottonwoods mostly, and an aging orange-brick silo behind it. Early in the morning, after her husband Gus has gone out to the barn and Bertha is cleaning up the breakfast dishes, she can see the sun climbing over the cottonwoods around David's house.

"In January when the days get longer, I say to Gus when he comes back in, 'Oh, you should see the sun over David's house; already it's over the trees. Spring is coming.'

"You know, in the bottom of winter, the sun is so far down, it seems to stay down forever. Then it jumps. One day it's down, and the next day you can see it's higher. Spring is coming."

In the summer—right now, in August—the sun is slipping down the sky again, hiding behind the trees and the orange-brick silo as the season slides inexorably into autumn. Bertha Benson, gray-haired, bespectacled, measures it all through the east window over the kitchen sink.

There are six people and two houses on the Benson farm, nine miles out of Worthington on the prairie in southwestern Minnesota. There are Gus and Bertha, the elders, in the main house; their son, David, and his wife, Sally-Anne, in a second house; and David's and Sally-Anne's children, Heather and Anton.

Three generations, split evenly between male and female; two houses, and many windows.

Bertha's kitchen window discloses private places—the garden, the pond, the fields. The front room window is sharply different. It faces west, looking over public places, the driveway, at the shop where David runs his Volvo repair service.

"You know what I saw from this window ... really, I didn't see it, that was the scary thing," Bertha said with her soft Scandinavian vowels, fingertips poised thoughtfully on her cheek.

"It was when David and Sally had just come back to farm.

"There was a big storm. A famous storm, so many people were killed. The telephone was out—we used to say that you could tell when a storm was coming, because the phone would go out—and David was over here for chores. Sally was at their house, with Heather, who was just born.

"The snow was so thick you couldn't see anything. David wanted to walk back to his house because we couldn't call on the phone. He didn't want to leave Sally there alone with the baby. So he walked back, and I ran to my window to see him go.

"I couldn't see him. There was nothing out there. Only snow. We couldn't get out of the house after that. We didn't know for two days that he had made it home. ... "

This is summer, a good distance yet from the first lashing winter winds. The David outside the west window is another one: the summer David, laughing and talking and pounding on an orange '73 Volvo while a friend lies on the ground and strips a large black number on the side.

"Ninety-nine," said Bertha. "Is that a lucky number?" She peered out the west window and shook her head. "I wish they wouldn't do it; I hope nobody gets hurt. I won't go. If I went, I would sit with my hands over my eyes."

She is talking about an automobile race that night.

This is a good week at the Benson farm. The field work is light—the second cutting of hay is already in, though the family will spend a few hours pulling weeds from the soybean fields. The work that must be done is ... fun: freezing corn, canning peaches and tomatoes, squeezing cider from early apples, making applesauce.

Rebuilding the car.

The car is a rusted-out, stripped-down Volvo. The engine isn't too bad, and the transmission works after a fashion, though it has no reverse gear.

"When you throw it in reverse, it's like the shifter fell in a hole," David said.

But it's a machine granted beauty by circumstance. The Nobles County Fair has announced an Enduro Race, 250 laps on a quarter-mile black-dirt track, where speeds approach and sometimes exceed 45 mph. This is the car for it, this broken-down orange Volvo, now dubbed the *General Ole* (pronounced Oh-Lee) with the Swedish flag on the roof.

The flag is for Volvo and Benson and Rolf Carlson, a Worthington psychotherapist who kicked in $50 to have the tires put on new rims. He gets credit in black paint, on the front fender: Tires by Rolf, Ph.D. David takes credit on the back fender: Benson Volvo. Bob Yeske, an auto body man from the town of Bigelow, provides race-crew experience and mechanical backup.

The driver is a Hollander, the bearded Bigelow building contractor Marvin DeVries, who in his younger days drove sprint cars on the local racing circuit. Marv is supposed to get "Marvelous Marvin" in script letters under the driver's side window. As it works out, there's never time to do the painting, and Marv settles for the ride and lets the credit go. ...

That's the week: freezing, canning, the Enduro Race, with a brief timeout for Heather's 12th birthday.

If the spring and first weeks of summer are times for the fields—for the plowing, planting, cultivating, walking the beans and corn, haymaking—the late high summer is the time for the kitchen.

Vegetables are ripening in the gardens, the trees are heavy with big, blushing, tart apples, the groceries advertise unbeatable deals on long-season produce from Georgia and California. It's time for the pressure cookers, for the freezer bags, for the Ball and Kerr jars whose lids go dink when they seal. ...

The corn is one thing.

It starts with David and Sally-Anne down in the sweet corn patch behind Gus and Bertha's place, where the tassels are so laden with pollen that walking through the patch is like breathing water. The day is hot, and loud country-western music blares from a battered radio hidden in the middle of the patch at the end of a 150-foot extension cord.

"We've done tests," David said, tongue in cheek, "Country-western keeps the 'coons out of the corn patch better than anything else.' "

"Even better than Duran Duran?"

"Yeah, even better," he said solemnly. He turned and looked down the patch where his wife was thrashing through the corn. Everybody calls Sally-Anne "Sago"—Sag-oh—an acronym of her maiden name, Sally-Anne Greeley.

"I think Sago is going crazy," David said. He raised his voice. "Jeez, Sago, I think we've got enough. ... Sago, stop. ... " He dropped his voice again. "When she gets the bit in her teeth, it's hard to stop her. We could be doing this until midnight if we don't get her out of here."

The ears of sweetcorn are fat, but the kernels are the pale, pearly yellow-white that almost sing of sugar; nothing with the telltale fullness or the dark-dried silk escaped Sago's grocery sacks.

"Look at it all, we've got to get it before it goes bad," she said with chin-out determination, snatching an ear off another stalk. A line of sweat glistened on her upper lip and her cheeks were dappled with pollen.

"Sago, we've got enough, we've got too much, oh boy," David pleaded. "Sago ... "

After a while: "OK. I'm done."

The corn is shucked on the picnic table behind the house, the pile of clean corn growing quickly, the shuckers—Bertha, David, Sago, and the kids—calling attention to special prizes. "Oh, look at this one—oh, that's a good one. Let's keep that one out. ... "

Sago and Bertha moved inside before the shucking was done and got the kettles ready. Gus used a whetstone to put a fine edge on a set of paring knives. When the last of the corn was clean, David carried it inside and Sago began feeding it into the kettles of boiling water.

"Five minutes," said Bertha. "If you go longer, I think you get a taste of the cob."

The work was done assembly-line fashion. Sago blanched the corn, David and Gus cut it from the steaming cobs, and Bertha packed it into one-pint freezer bags. The corn sometimes popped off in individual kernels, sometimes in slabs the size of a middle and ring finger held together. Most of the slabs are packed; others are passed around for instant consumption.

"Twenty-five pints," Bertha announced when they finished, a smile like a quarter-moon lighting up the bottom of her face. "Big pints. Sometimes three cups in a sack. That's good."

That's just the corn. Not all of it, but some of it. And there's more: tomatoes, peaches, beans; it's produced all week in the steamy kitchen, Bertha Benson, director.

With the canning done, and the crew gone on to other things, Bertha sat in her front room and talked about the canning and the work of her life and pronounced herself satisfied.

"I enjoy the housework—I especially enjoy the baking. Sometimes I'd get so carried away with the baking that I'd forget to do the other things. ...

"It was not just work in the house that women used to do. We had chickens, and I took care of the chickens and sold the eggs. We used to have hundreds of chickens, 400 one time. The worst was carrying water from the windmill to the chicken house. The girls (her three daughters) used to say they have long arms from carrying water.

"Separating milk was my job, and the older girls would help. I was happy when that ended, but you know, you give up things, too ... the milk truck would come and take the milk and drop off some butter, and one time one of the younger girls asked me where butter comes from. ...

"Sometimes I would help in the fields, but only in a pinch. That was Gus' job, he did the field work, and he took care of the tractor, the machinery. I did the housework, and took care of the children, though Gus is handy around the house and makes good oatmeal. ... "

Sally-Anne Greeley Benson also loves the farm life, though she grew up in New England as the daughter of an official of the Massachusetts Institute of Technology.

"Bertha made it a lot easier. She wasn't born on a farm, either. Farming isn't something you just do. You have to know an awful lot and she taught me an awful lot," she said.

She is not, however, satisfied to divide the life she shares with

David Benson into housework and fieldwork, women's work and men's work.

"When David grew up, he was expected to help his father with the farm work. He had older sisters to help his mother with the housework. So, he didn't do housework. He didn't know how to do housework." She smiled: "He's a lot better now than when we first came here."

Sago sat at her table behind a cup of hot cider she had just "nuked" in the microwave. She had made the cider herself, the day before.

"There's a lot of housework that just plain isn't fun. It's drudgery. Most field work is at least a little bit fun.

"You're outside, you're working hard, you might feel like it's killing you, but you can feel like it's really important. Housework doesn't always feel like that," she said.

Sago works in the fields more than Bertha ever did. She routinely does disking and chisel, and runs the haybaler. She says matter-of-factly that she can drive anything from motorcycles and cars to trucks and tractors.

Her dislike for some types of housework—which she does anyway—is not a matter of unhappiness.

"It has to be done," she said. "You can look at David when he comes in and his face is all white and exhausted and he just about falls in bed, and you go ahead and do it (housework). It's really all a matter of adjustments, back and forth. One of the really good things about David is that he adjusts. That's really good."

Bertha's work has impressed Sago with the routine of the seasons, as she sees them through the kitchen window. Sago has no window in her kitchen. She remembers listening. ...

"I remember I was pregnant with Heather. It was the first part of August. David had cut across the fields on a moped to do some chores, and I heard this voice. It was, 'Sago, Sago,' really low, and quiet—and then I realized it was David, and I knew, I knew, we had some serious business. He'd hit a fence post that was lying down in tall grass and went over and broke his collar bone. He could barely walk back, and he could barely get his breath to call me, and I went running out. ... I can remember that, 'Sago, Sago.'"

Race day started clear and cool. Sago and the kids picked apples at a friend's home—they have no apple trees of their own—while David worked on the Volvo—painting, bracing, figuring tactics.

At noon, the family broke off work for Heather's birthday party.

Heather smiled shyly as the family gathered around the dining room table, clasped hands, sang a grace song and "Happy Birthday."

Heather opened her gifts—she seemed particularly pleased by a calendar featuring American Impressionist paintings. Then it was back to work, David on the Volvo, Sago with the apples.

The Bensons are in possession of an ancient hand-powered apple press. The press is a machine—two machines, actually—of almost sublime simplicity and efficiency. The first part grinds whole apples to a juicy pulp, and the second, a screw press, squeezes the apple juice from the pulp.

The press produces a torrent of cinnamon cider, which Sago caught in an ice cream bucket and transferred to plastic milk jugs. Halfway through the cider run she got cups from the house and took a long draught of cider. She swallowed, caught her breath, her cheeks sucked in. "Wooo, that is ... tart. That is good."

In the distance, from up near the other house, there was a burst of noise, a popcorn sound, like old thunder or a distant light machine-gun fire.

"That's the car; they're running it," she said.

The county fair. Pole barns and cattle judging, the smell of manure and new-mown grass, gasoline fumes and oil smoke, sandy hot dogs and a thousand gallon jugs of air-aging mustard.

Long rows of clouds rolling in on the grounds as The Car is backed off the transporter. The car is ugly. The doors are chained shut, there is only one seat inside if you don't count the one strapped vertically onto the driver's door as padding, and there is no glass at all. No headlights, tail lights, or windows. In place of the windshield is a wire screen, which supposedly will stop the bigger mud clods thrown off the track.

"What do you think the average value of these cars is?" David was asked, as the Benson crew looked over the competition.

He shrugged. "About $150," he said.

"The thing about an Enduro Race," explained the driver, Marvelous Marvin De Vries, "is keeping the car alive. If you can make it through the first hour, you should make it all the way. But in those first few laps, you can go out like this." He snapped his fingers.

The track was a muddy quarter-mile oval with a low bank at the turns. The floodlit infield swarmed with drivers and pit crew, dressed in cowboy shirts and cowboy hats and cowboy boots or running shoes, and billed hats and striped bib overalls and heavy-soled boots, or some combination of those. The exceptions are a half-dozen drivers like Marvin, who wear white drivers' jumpsuits with red piping.

The pre-race ceremonies are quick: a crew meeting, the raising of the colors by a veterans' group color guard—the flag has 48 stars, but it's a perfectly good flag—and the cars begin rolling onto the track.

Nothing is new. Nothing is clean. The auto bodies look like hammered brass ashtrays. Fifty-eight cars start the race. Three finish. The 55 cars that die do so in a variety of colorful ways—some blow engines, some catch fire, some shred tires, some lose drive shafts, some are wrecked, some disappear over the low bank and never return. One is abandoned in midtrack, and the remaining cars drive around it for 150 laps or so.

The General Ole lasts about 20 minutes.

"He's running on a flat," David shouts. "The left front is gone." Sago is tense, standing on a stack of tires, turning, turning, as the Volvo goes around.

Under track rules, repairs can be done only if the race is stopped to clear the track. There is no guarantee it will happen—you could only wait and hope. The Bensons turn and turn, and finally the tire comes apart and tangles the axle so badly the rim begins to drag. It's the end. Marv sadly bounces the General Ole onto the infield, and a moment later, as he walks away, another car smashes into it, crushing the right front fender and ripping open the radiator.

Later, with the track quiet, the pit crew pushed the mortally wounded Volvo back on the transporter and passed around the Bud Lites.

"You know what," said Marvelous Marv. "We've got to do this again."

"Hey, it was a good time, wasn't it?" asked David.

And Sago is laughing.

During the race, while Marv was running on the rim, Heather and Anton sat in the grandstand with friends. As her younger and more demonstrative brother did everything but handstands, Heather sat tensely quiet, watching intently.

Of all the Bensons, she is the quietest. From the infield, her shy smile flashed out across the track once or twice, alive under her blue Volvo cap. When the crisis came, she stood to watch. That was all.

What about Heather? She would like to live on a farm, she said, like her mother and grandmother. But there are other things, too. She doesn't know.

Earlier on race day, she would briefly put on an inexpensive pair of pearl earrings she had gotten as a gift.

"Oh, Heather, you look so grown up," said Sago, pushing out her bottom lip. And Heather did look grown up, just for an instant.

At the birthday table, the family had linked hands for the grace song:

"The silver rain, the shining sun, the fields where scarlet poppies run," the three women sang, a complex of alto voices from three generations, "and all the ripples of the wheat are in the bread that we do eat. ...

"So, when we sit to every meal, with thankful hearts we always feel, that we're eating rain and sun, and fields where scarlet poppies run."

Heather has a west-facing window in her bedroom, with a view over the checkerboard prairie toward the horizon with its glorious prairie sunsets. It's a good place, she said, to sit and look out at things.

OCTOBER 20, 1985

It was Monday noon, the 14th of October, Columbus Day—a day of high clouds, cool winds and fractured sunshine.

Blackbirds gathered on roadside power lines, flocking for the arduous trip south. Skunks traffic-flattened on the road wore their long, opulent winter fur. And on the rich prairie farmland around Worthington, Minn., it was a day of waiting.

David Benson, 38, drove an aging Volvo northwest along a tar road toward the KRSW radio tower. The road ran through an ocean of soybeans and corn, over flat prairie creeks, past small herds of black-and-white Holsteins grazing their still-green pastures.

Benson did a running commentary on the grain fields—on their cleanliness, soil types, productivity. He pointed out patches of weeds whose seeds had been planted in otherwise clean fields by flowing water. He was intent in his judgments: Benson operates a small farm near Bigelow, nine miles south of Worthington. He grows beans and corn as cash crops, and hay for 39 head of beef cattle, six work horses, a pony, 14 sheep, and an aging milk cow named Bluma.

On this day, almost nothing was moving in the fields—in his fields, or any other. The beans were dark brown and full, the corn a light, bright tan, with heavy ears hanging down from the stalks. Here and there, on the edges of the cornfields, brilliant yellow kernels flashed from split-open husks.

"Everything is, ohhh, man, everything is beautiful, and that's what could break your heart," Benson said. Crowsfeet deepened at the corners of his eyes as he peered at the sun-dappled landscape. "You look out there, and you could cry. You can feel the mood of the whole county: it's getting lower every day. Lower and darker. If we get some snow, ohhh, man, that would do it. That would kill us."

This year's harvest in southwestern Minnesota could be substantial if the farmers could get at the crops. So far, they hadn't been able to. Fall work was more than a month behind.

"For all practical purposes, the harvest hasn't started," said Gene Lutteke, manager of the grain elevator at Bigelow.

Harvest a Month Late

"A few years back, I did a spot of work for a man who was having a little trouble with cancer," said another man, who came out of a country Standard station to pump gas. "I remember we were all done, cleaned up, and I put the last of the machinery away on the 17th of October. This year, he hasn't even been out in the field yet."

The problem is water. Too much water. The soybeans have never had a chance to dry out, and the very process of picking them would destroy them. They are so soft they can be eaten like fresh peas.

The corn is tougher, closer to picking, but still too wet.

"I can pick a bit of it, maybe, in the next couple of days, if we don't get any more rain," Benson said. "I can pick it and grind it and feed it right away. I just can't crib it. But the corn isn't worth much this year anyway, and a snowstorm or two won't wipe it out. It's the beans that could break your heart."

The night before, Benson stood on the edge of a 60-acre soybean field, and counted his metaphorical chickens.

"We'll get, ohh, gosh, at least 30 bushels to the acre, and maybe a little more. They look great, don't they? Even if the price stays right where it is, that's $150 an acre; that's almost $9,000 sitting right there. If we get a snowstorm or a sleet storm, it'll pull them right down and we won't get a thing. And it's getting so late in the year, we could get snow. We could get some sleet. Boy, it would break your heart."

In one short spell of drier weather, Benson managed to cut some hay, but the rains returned before he could bale it. With much more rain, it would be gone. Sludge, he calls it.

"I love that last cutting of hay because all the swallows turn out, diving around the tractor. They eat all the bugs they can find before they head south," Benson said. "It's like working in a field full of big butterflies. It's absolutely delightful. This year I was out there by myself—the swallows'd all gone south before I had a chance to do the final cutting. I really missed seeing them."

The weather has been the main topic in the Worthington area since the second week of August.

Farm Work Only Part of It

"I've never seen anything like this fall. In all my years, nothing like this," said Gus Benson, 83, David's father. "It seems like it rained every day—it didn't, but it never got dry, that's for sure."

And this Columbus Day was yet another day when no field work could be done. It was clear enough, and a fine drying wind was blowing. But it had rained again only two days before, further saturating the soggy countryside.

The condition of the fields was no excuse for idleness, however. Like more and more small-farm families, the Benson family puts together an annual income with a pastiche of part-time jobs and farming.

One of Benson's part-time jobs involves work as a repairman for local radio stations, climbing the towers that soar hundreds of feet over the patchwork prairie.

It's a job that his wife, Sally-Anne, doesn't like, won't talk about, and doesn't want to hear about. When David gets a climbing job, her normally cheerful face turns grim, and it hangs in the background of her mind until he's back on the ground.

Both reactions—David's willingness to climb, and Sally-Anne's unhappiness with the work—run in the family. David's father, Gus, never had much fear of heights, either. When Gus was young, he did a good deal of farm windmill repair, and his wife, David's mother, Bertha, didn't want to hear about that, either.

"There's our tower over there," David said, pointing through the Volvo's mud-spattered windshield.

The tower is on a low hill near Chandler, surrounded by cornfields. From a distance, it looks like a short piece of red-and-white thread dangling from the clouds.

"We have to fix a beacon," Benson explained. "Some kids climbed up there one night and broke it. It's going to cost somebody, oh, better than $1,000 for a new light and the work. The insurance company, I guess."

Paid Sightseeing Trip

He really isn't afraid of the open height?

"Not really. You're working on the inside of the tower," he said, with his tongue in cheek. "If you fell, it wouldn't be the height that killed you. It'd be hitting all those support bars on the way down.

You'd kill yourself falling 15 feet in there, so 700 feet won't make any difference."

The work is at the 280-foot level.

"Those kids had to be nuts to climb up there at night," a friend said standing at the base of the tower and peering straight up the slender steel structure. A prairie wind rustled through the surrounding corn field and hummed across the tower's support cables. "You're a little weird yourself, David."

"It makes a change," he said. "And it's beautiful up there—boy, you can see for miles. You can see over to Blue Mound, over to the ridge where South Dakota starts. You can see down to Worthington."

Benson works with rudimentary equipment: blocks taken from barn hoists, a kid's pack full of tools worn backward on the chest. He wears an insulated jumpsuit as protection against the wind, and replaces his farmer-standard billed cap with a woolen watch cap.

"It can get cold," he said, just before he started up the tower. It took 20 minutes to climb the 280 feet to the broken light, and four hours to complete the repairs. Benson gets $25 an hour for the job.

"It's a handy kind of work to do, if you're a farmer and don't mind working up high," he said when he got down. "You can earn a quick $100 cash money for three or four hours work. It comes in handy."

As soon as he was back on the ground, he called Sally-Anne to let her know.

Jobs Here and There Help

To an outsider, grain farm work appears to be sporadic. There's plowing, planting, cultivating, and harvesting, each in a separate compartment of weeks. It looks different to a farmer. To a farmer, there's never enough time for the work to get done.

"It's hard to make a living with straight farming, especially with prices like they are now," Benson said. "But if you're going to farm, you can't have a regular job, even part-time, because you need such big blocks of time off. So you get a lot of little jobs."

To keep the Benson farm going, Sally-Anne teaches half-days at a Worthington Montessori school, and David fixes cars in the farm shop, climbs radio towers, and trades work on various kinds of agricultural and construction equipment—he has a strong local reputation as a diesel mechanic and specialist in Volvos and Volkswagen Rabbits.

They also keep costs down by producing and preparing most of their own food. And David, of course, keeps the family cars running.

"There's always something to do. Sometimes I think, you know, after the kids are grown, Sago and I ought to take a long sabbatical somewhere," Benson said late on a rainy Saturday night in the farm's shop.

Sago's old car was on its last legs, so David had driven to the Twin Cities where he located a diesel Volkswagen Rabbit with a good body and interior, and a blown engine. He happened to have another Rabbit with a cracked block, that he'd bought for parts, and now he was making one machine from the two.

The Money's Not All Gravy

"In our best year, I guess we pulled in, gross, about $26,000, including Sago's money. But then, when you're running a farm, you have expenses, just like you do in any business. So the $26,000 wasn't all for groceries. We get away a little cheaper than most guys because we can substitute labor where most of them use chemicals—cheap labor is one of the advantages of an extended family. And I think our equipment is sized better for the farm than most people's. ...

"But you get very tired when you get into the Cities and you hear people say, 'Aw, the good farmers are making it,' or 'It's the farmer's own fault,' and you know how hard you work, and how hard your neighbors work, and you aren't making anything. ...

"I'm not going to say that some farmers didn't get greedy when things were looking good and got in over their heads buying land. But that's not all of it. Look at soybean prices. That one field we were in. If I get those beans off, and sell them right now, we'll get maybe $9,000 or a little less. If I could sell them for the average price we got last year, they'd go for $12,500. Same crop. Same expenses, or even a little higher—and we get 25 or 30 percent less, off a price that wasn't that good to begin with. It gets real tough."

Benson's case is stated on a half-page of blue-and-white charts in the Worthington *Daily Globe*'s Saturday Farm Report.

The charts include bar graphs, which are particularly interesting for one striking aspect—the graphs for current corn and soybean prices don't have any bars on them. That's because the prices have fallen below the bottom level of the graph.

Instead of rescaling the graphs, the newspaper, to call attention to the problems of farmers, simply prints the current price of the crops where the bars should be. On Friday, Oct. 11, corn stood at $2.15 a bushel at Worthington; last year's average was $2.90. Soybeans stood at $4.67, Worthington bid. Last year's average was $6.90. That's down 30 percent.

As Benson works under a trouble light to fit the replacement head on the newer Rabbit, he talks both economics and social history: the problems of making a living while preserving the land, the false assumptions of economy-of-scale theories, the uses of labor as a replacement for foreign oil, the philosophical reasons for maintaining national agricultural population.

A House Full of Books

Although it embarrasses him when friends call him a Prairie Intellectual, that's precisely what he is. Sago, too. In the north bedroom of the old farmhouse, where they live with their children, Heather and Anton, there are 1,000 books or more. There are an even dozen works by Lewis Mumford, a half-dozen by Thorstein Veblen. There are books by Ayn Rand and Alan Watts, Barry Goldwater and Hunter S. Thompson, Upton Sinclair and Tom Wolfe.

They have "The Golden Bough" by Sir James George Frazer and "The Journey to Ixtlan" by Carlos Casteneda; "The Female Eunuch" by Germaine Greer and "The Courage to Be" by Paul Tillich. There are works by Nietzsche and Balzac and Chekhov and Whitman and Emerson and Kafka and Tolstoy and St. Thomas Aquinas, all in paperback glory. They also own a tattered copy of "The Exorcist" by William Peter Blatty, and Benson said, "My God, don't write that down," when the book was mentioned.

On a rainy Saturday night, with auto grease covering his hands, a battered green-and-white billed hat perched on his reddish hair, the drizzle graying out background noise, he mixed those writers in casual conversation as he fit together the rebuilt car. And he talked about Charles Dickens' "Great Expectations."

Repairs Go on Back Burner

A road company of the Guthrie Theater of Minneapolis was to present a dramatized version of the Dickens novel Sunday night at the Memorial Auditorium in Worthington. He wants to go ... but he'd like to work on the car, too.

"I have to admit I like Sunday nights in the shop," he said. "It's quiet. You can think about things. It's nice to see an engine go together—I really like that. I don't know. You think Sago would let me out of the Dickens thing?"

No. Sago won't. The following night, the whole family, except Gus, is scrubbed and seated in the balcony. David entered a mild protest—"Listen, Sag, I could get that car going for you." But she shook her head and he went along.

Afterward he said, "I'm glad I went, though I kind of wanted to work on the car." Kidded again about his Prairie Intellectual status (how he might have lost it if he hadn't attended the Guthrie produc tion), he asked: "I wonder how much of being a Prairie Intellectual means doing what your wife tells you?"

Many Hang on Hopefully

And that, for the most part, has been the late summer and fall on the Benson farm. Rain, odd jobs, a growing tension over the harvest delays.

"People are in bad shape," Benson said. "The countryside is being depopulated. Too many people just can't make a living anymore. There are too many people who are supporting their farming habit by working other jobs, and they're saying to themselves, 'If we just quit farming, we'd have more money.'

"Now, if on top of it all we have a real crop disaster, if we get a snowstorm that beats down the beans before we can get them out—that'll finish a lot more people. There must be thousands of people sitting on a razor's edge, and that would be the end of them."

The growing nervousness about the harvest is allayed a bit by visits from family and friends: over the weekend, one of David's older sisters, Marilyn Beckstrom, a minister with the United Church of Christ, came down to Gus Benson's house for a visit. She brought a friend, Bob Shoemake, a Methodist minister, and Shoemake's parents, Earl and Vivian Shoemake, of Paducah, Ky. Earl Shoemake is a Baptist minister.

Bob Shoemake, a longtime friend, came equipped with a pair of barber shears and scissors. He promised David a free haircut and a professional shave in return for an oil change. After dinner, accompanied by a good deal of hilarity, he kept his promise in Gus Benson's kitchen.

"Another advantage of an extended family," Benson said around a hot towel.

And later: "Your family keeps you going; everybody moans and groans, but nobody says they want to do anything different."

Even later one night, he stood in the side yard of his house with his 9-year-old son, Anton, and picked out the Big Dipper, the Little Dipper, the North Star, the Pleiades, and other constellations in a sky that looked like black velvet touched by sugar.

"Look at the Milky Way," he said, his face turned up, his finger tracing the grains of stars across the sky. "You can't see anything like this in the city; you just can't do it. It looks like you could fall right into it."

What's the weather?

Things turn quickly on the farm.

Benson climbed the radio tower last Monday, and the fields were soggy. But the day was dry, and so was Tuesday. So Tuesday, he sneaked out, picked the end rows of the corn fields, taking in a single wagonload of corn. It was still wet, but fine for grinding. And he turned over the hay he'd cut before the last rain ... and Tuesday night he and Sago baled it, Sago on the tractor and David throwing the bales on the hay rack.

Wednesday was dry again. Humid, but no rain. Thursday was the same. Friday, two days ago, he picked the end rows of the bean fields.

"We got the field open, but the beans are still wet," Sago said by phone late Friday. "If the weather holds, we might get in Sunday. We hate to work Sunday, but if the weather holds. ... "

If the weather holds, the Bensons are out there this minute, bringing in the big cash crop. It'll be a good one.

If the weather holds.

DECEMBER 8, 1985

The November landscape was brown and black and tan, spotted with stark clusters of leafless trees, dark evergreen windbreaks, and here and there a glint of silver from a frozen pond. It was a rough, grainy Middle Ages landscape painted in bleak northern earth colors by Pieter Bruegel the Elder, and revealed by John Deere.

But a winter storm was prowling down to the south, over Iowa somewhere, and the fast-talking television weathermen said the border country was in for it. Anyone who must go on the road should carry blankets and a source of heat. If the car goes into a ditch, stay with it.

Along the Minnesota-Iowa border, farmers pushed their tractors and looked to the south. The sky was an edgeless slab of mean gray cloud that obliterated any hint of the sun. The prairie wind, whipping in from the northeast, cut your face like splinters of broken glass.

Time was trickling away. Snowflakes in the air, one here, one there, like ghosts of summer fireflies. Every time you looked up, there were more of them. At mid-morning, the grain elevator at Bigelow, Minn., three miles to the south, had been sharp on the horizon. By mid-afternoon, it was hidden by the falling snow.

On the west side of an unmarked gravel road, a combine was broken down with no more than a dozen rows of corn still standing in the field. The John Deere service man crouched at the front of the machine, his back hunched against the wind, trying to wring a last mile out of the 1985 harvest.

On the east side of the road, David Benson pulled his corn picker out of the field and stopped. It wasn't riding right. It had a tired sag. He had been having trouble with cornstalks wrapping into the picking gears, but this was something else. He climbed down from the tractor to look.

"Oh man, look at that," he said to a friend. "It just gave out." He pointed at a main support strut in the picker's frame. The quarter-inch-thick steel strut was twisted and folded like a piece of fabric. Benson's picker is old; he bought it for $92 at a spring auction.

"It's going to take time, take too much time," he said, looking south. "The corn is good. I bet we're getting 90 to 100 bushels an acre. Boy, I'd like to get it out."

The cure for the corn picker was simple but time-consuming. Tow it carefully back to the farm shop, straighten the folded strut with a winch and reinforce it by welding in a couple of pieces of angle iron.

But with winter coming in, other tasks were pressing—the barn to close up, two wagons of corn to unload, animals to move. Night comes early. By 6 p.m., it's too dark to work.

Across the road, the neighbor was working again, snow squalls whipping around his ungainly green combine. The prairie was flat enough, and the neighbor's corn was tall enough, that a man on the road couldn't see beyond it. There was only the wall of corn, and the sky. But as the combine chopped the last rows, the countryside beyond it became visible, as though the machine were pushing back a theater curtain.

Farm Year, Poker Are Alike

A farm year knits together personalities and opportunities, market prices and snowstorms, machines and philosophical tendencies that produce different quantities and qualities of oats and corn and soybeans and alfalfa.

It's an accumulation of quick conversations behind hot waiting tractors, of grunts and warm drinking water exchanged on 100-degree days on hay racks, of equipment breakdowns and apple picking, of kitchen smells and dim, cool milkings in the bottom of the barn, of country music blaring from the corn patch to repel the raccoons, of nights so dark and so far from city lights that the Milky Way looks like Manhattan.

A farm year is like a poker game. A poker game is not simply a matter of who won and lost—knowing the game is knowing how the cards were played, the tension, the bluffs, the hard decisions, the bets.

A year on the farm is a playing of cards, each card an individual, yet each related, each card a memory and simultaneously a new day, cards that are played out in hands that are always familiar and always subtly different.

David Benson is a large man with blue eyes that turn down at the outside edges. He has a walrus mustache and an unruly mop of blondish hair, smile lines in his cheeks, and crow's-feet at his eyes.

He has what friends teasingly call an act. With intellectuals, he talks like an intellectual; with other friends, he's full of yups and ain'ts and gol-lies.

It's not an act. His two sides are simply that.

He reads Lewis Mumford and Alan Watts and has a reputation as a fine diesel mechanic and welder. He drives 90 miles on Sundays to a Unitarian church in Sioux City, Iowa, to hear discussions of moral philosophy, and on Sunday nights he rebuilds Volvos and Volkswagens. He reads each night before sleeping, serious works on ecology and feminism, political theory and economics, and he is building a new house.

He climbs hundreds of feet up radio towers to earn extra money by replacing burned-out or damaged beacon lights, and he gives public radio a break on his price for high-tower work because he values public radio.

'Can't Afford a Mistake'
Sometimes, sitting around a dinner table, he talks like this:

"The future of farming is in the hands of the older farmers. The financial system we have right now makes it almost impossible for new farmers to get started. The financing terms are so bad that a new farmer, once he buys his land and equipment, can't afford to make a single mistake, ever. If he does, it's all gone. Everybody makes mistakes. Everybody.

"You don't even have to make a mistake. You can do everything the extension people tell you to do, you can do everything the government wants you to do, then we get a new president and he changes something, and everything is up for grabs. Somebody changes the rules, and what used to be a good practice is now a mistake, and you're out of business."

Talk at the kitchen table. Talk and food, food and talk. The two are inextricably tied together. For the Benson families, as with many farm families, the kitchen table is at the center of life.

There are two houses at the Benson farm. One shelters David, 38, and Sally-Anne, 36, and their children, Heather, 12, and Anton, 9. It is about a mile, by road, from the main farmstead, where David's parents, Gus, 83, and Bertha, 76, live. The farm is nine miles south of Worthington and just north of the Iowa line.

The kitchen tables are important in both homes. This is where the plans are made, the reverses are assessed, the stories are told. This is where the talk is.

And the talk, in this bitter year of 1985, often has to do with the agricultural crisis.

"Older farmers, the ones who want to get out and retire, have it in their power to provide more favorable terms for new people coming in," Benson said. "Maybe they could farm shares, maybe just taking a little less money."

Older Farmer's 'Only Hope'

"You know a bank isn't going to do that—a bank is set up to make as much money as possible. That's what it's for. But an older farmer, who has taken a good living out of the land over the years and wants to retire, maybe he'd be willing to take a little less for moral or philosophical reasons. It might be the only hope we have. We may be at the point we have to depend on altruism to save us, because nothing else works."

The present system of farming frightens all the Bensons, the older Gus and Bertha as well as the younger David and Sally-Anne.

"If you are pushed to the financial wall, you'll take extreme measures to save yourself," David Benson said. "Forget good farm practice—water structures, conservation, and all that. You'll have to get the most possible profit every year just to pay off the debt load.

Short-term View Wrong

"That means you'll soak the place in pesticides, which may be a terrible decision in the long run. You'll soak the soil with fertilizer instead of trying to build it up naturally, which may be a terrible thing in the long run. You'll plow it the fastest way that takes the least amount of fuel—you'll cut every possible corner. And in the long run, you'll destroy the land.

"That's what the system encourages right now. It encourages the absolute shortest possible view of every problem we have. It's an awful thing, and you can already see the result. The countryside is being depopulated. People who can't make it are being forced out. They're losing everything—their farms, their neighborhoods, their way of life, their whole culture."

Why should older farmers take less than a farm is worth?

"There are a couple of good answers," Benson said. "You owe something to the land. It has made you a place to live and work all your lives, so you ought to see that it gets into the right hands—somebody who will take care of it.

"And sometimes, taking less will get you more. Look at all of these old farmers who sold out six years ago for $1,400 an acre and 14 percent interest on contracts-for-deed. Nobody can make those payments. So the guy they sold it to, he just quits. He gives the place back.

"Now the old farmer, who used to be retired, gets back a farm that's worth $750 an acre, if anybody is buying, and it's not in nearly as good shape as it was six years ago. So he never really got that big price, did he? He would have been better off selling it on more reasonable terms, something the guy would have a chance to pay off, than take what looked like all that big money."

The farm, Benson said, is the basic ecological unit on the planet, and should be used to hold the planet together. As the family passes around lamb stew and cranberry bars, he warms to the topic:

"Christianity once came out of work and the land, but it's gotten more theoretical, and I think that's unfortunate. The churches represent the moral leadership of the culture, and I think the effort to save the land, that impulse, might best come from the pulpit. Social sciences? Maybe. But I don't think so. I don't think you can trust social science the way you can trust the instinct to religion. ..."

The kitchen table is not just a place for philosophy. It's also a place for good stories and good memories that once were bad and now have the warm familiarity of a worn flannel nightshirt.

Sally-Anne seems always conscious of her children, hugging them, talking to them, touching their heads. Her stories are less of farming and economics than of family.

Sally-Anne Tells a Family Story
"Oh, God, one time, Anton swallowed some popcorn the wrong way, it went down into his lungs, and he had trouble breathing," she said. "He just seemed like he couldn't breathe, or he'd just kind of doze off, like he wasn't all there. ... "

Her hands dance in the air as she tells the story, and the legs of her chair scrape the floor as she becomes more agitated.

"We rushed him into the hospital, and when we got there, he was all right again ... and then he started fading out again," she said. "Finally the doctor told us we ought to take him to Children's Hospital in St. Paul. We put him in the car and headed up the highway, 80 miles an hour. ... "

"A cop stopped us, a highway patrolman," David interrupted, "and I stopped and jumped out of the car. ... "

Sally-Anne pushed back in, excited by the story. "And the patrolman took one look at David's face and he said, 'You've got trouble, don't you,' and David told him, and he said, 'Go on up the highway, don't worry about the speed limit but keep it under control.'

"So we took off again, and all the way up, nobody bothered us— the patrolman had called ahead and cleared us. And Anton kept fading out, and we'd say, 'C'mon, Anton, c'mon Anton,' and we got up to the hospital and rushed him inside and the doctor took him. ...

"They took him back to examine him, and came out and said it was popcorn and they could get it out. David and I, we just went out to the car and sat there and cried. We just cried. What a day that was. God, I'll never forget that, Anton fading out, and sitting there in the car. ... "

The children, both blond and round-faced and blue-eyed, chip in their own stories of snowstorms past, of skating on the farm pond, of doing evening chores, and of social trauma on the school bus.

Bertha talks about her youth in Finland, the memories of war, of bombs and bullets. Gus talks of warming the crankcase of the Ford with a hubcap full of burning corncobs so he could get Bertha to the hospital for the birth of their middle daughter. Bertha tells of the night they got electricity, of her hands bathed in electric lamplight. Gus brags of picking 150 bushels of corn a day, by hand. David tells of riding a motorcycle to San Francisco, where he lived through the final years of the '60s, right there on Haight. Sally-Anne laughs about a hair-raising hitchhiking trip through Canada, just before she and David settled down with farming.

'You Know What You're Eating'

The kitchen table also is the place for food.

"One of the best things about living on the farm is that you know what you're eating," Sally said. "Our kids are going to be healthy."

The Bensons raise all their own meat—beef and lamb and chicken. They milk an aging cow, Bluma, and maintain a chicken house for the eggs. They raise most of their own vegetables, eating fresh in season, and frozen and canned through the winter. They pick apples for sauces and cider. On any given day, the kitchens of Bertha and Sally-Anne are redolent with the odors of fresh bread or pies, meat stews, and vegetables.

"Grandpa (Gus Benson) always figured food was fuel, and he wanted plenty of it," Sally-Anne said. "David grew up that way, too, and it's a necessary thing—sometimes, when it's cold, and you have to work outside, it seems like you can't eat enough to keep yourself going."

Kitchen operations are passed deliberately and carefully down the generations. Heather goes to Bertha's kitchen to learn about apple pies. Together, they build a pie from scratch, an extended process that involves discussion of all the reasons for each different action and ingredient.

"What about nutmeg?"

"Just a little. Here. Just shake it on, just a touch. ... But plenty of butter. The more butter the better it is. So never skimp on butter. ... "

"And you roll this?"

"You pinch it, here. That seals it up, and it makes it look nice. ..."

The farm year began in late spring. The entire world seemed composed of different shades and tints of green. The air was soft and humid and still. The only breeze was artificial, born of the motion of the hayrack, and, at that, not enough to ruffle the hair on a forearm. In the shade of the windbreak, it was almost cool. As the tractor moved out the front gate past the mailbox, crunching over the gravel shoulder, sunlight fell on the bare necks and lightly clothed shoulders, and heat prickled on the skin.

"You gotta make hay while the sun shines," Sally-Anne Benson said cheerfully, swinging her legs off the rack as her husband, David, towed it out to the west field with the David Brown tractor.

Sally-Anne Benson's nickname is Sago, an acronym of her maiden name, Sally-Anne Greeley, with the "o" tagged on for reasons of euphony. She is a small woman, 5 feet tall, 105 pounds, and pretty. She is a teacher (mornings only) at a Worthington Montessori school, the mother of Heather and Anton Benson, a good cook, an enthusiastic dancer, a maker and drinker of apple cider, a milker of cows and a doer of any number of other things, including a frequent driver of tractors. She drives at hay-making.

"You have to keep the moisture down, so you wait late enough in the morning to get the dew off," she said. "You mostly won't get out much before 10 or 11. A hot day with the sun shining and a good wind will really dry the hay out."

First Cutting of Hay a Good One

In the field, David and Sally-Anne traded places, David hopping on the rack while she drove the tractor over windrows of hot yellow hay.

If haying was a card, it would be the queen of diamonds—a sweetness with a definite edge to it. Hay is the first crop of the year, the first payback.

And the first cutting of hay on the Benson farm was a good one. It was baled and stacked while the sun shined and the daily temperature climbed over 100 degrees.

The drying alfalfa smells like ginger and something else, a sweet, fat odor riding the silky summer breezes with gravel dust and gasoline fumes, riding into the elbow-out side windows of dusty old automobiles.

Baling means long, lingering hours of twilight as the solstice approaches. Old, weathered gray wood in the hay rack. Warm water from glass jars, and never enough of it. Hay cuts on forearms. Twine grooves in the pads of fingers. Sweat-soaked leather gloves. T-shirts sticking to the back and chest. Dry lips. The sun carving at the eyes. Arms leaden and aching with fire.

Baling is noise. A baler is a strange, violent piece of machinery. Trailed behind a tractor, it picks up pre-cut and dried windrows of hay—alfalfa, mostly—smashes and pounds them into a bale, ties the bale with twine, and ejects the bale from an upward-slanting chute that just touches the front edge of the hayrack.

Hayrack is the open wagon pulled behind the baler. You stand at the front edge of the rack, knees bent to absorb the shock of the bumpy ride, hands protected by leather gloves which are sweat-soaked in minutes, and when the bale comes up, you reach out with the stronger arm, snag the twine with your fingers, lift and grunt, balance the bale on your out-thrust hip, take three or four quick steps to the back of the rack, and push the bale onto the stack.

And go back for another.

"Like this. Stack it like this. That'll tie it together," David Benson shouted as the first bales pushed over the lip of the rack.

There is a pattern to stacking, as Benson demonstrated. The first bale is set all the way to the back, with its long side parallel to the side of the rack. The rest of the bales are placed with their long sides parallel to the back of the rack. The pattern is reversed on the next level, so the bales always cross each other from one level to the next.

"We're going to be stacking these up over our heads, so you want to tie them together like that—so the whole pile doesn't fall off on the road back to the barn. It gives you just that little bit of stability," Benson said.

The work was hard and unremitting. The stackers took turns grabbing, swinging and stacking, the baler hammering all the while, Sago half-turned in her tractor seat as it rolled up and down the field.

When the rack was full, it was towed back to the barn. The bales were swung off the rack and onto an elevator, a piece of machinery that looks like a cross between a conveyor belt and an escalator. It's even noisier than the baler.

"You guys unload the rack, and we'll go up to the top and stack," Benson said. The men on the bottom began pulling bales off the rack and dropping them onto the elevator. Up in the loft, the bales popped off much the same way they had popped out of the baler. Benson and a friend hooked and grunted and lifted, as they had on the rack, and carried the bales as far back and high in the barn as possible.

Heat of the Barn Weighs in the Lungs
The barn, in its own way, is as bad as the field. Balers are exposed to the fierce, slicing sunlight, but in the barn the heat is close, dense and heavy, sitting in the lungs like soup.

"When I was 16, a friend and I hired out all over to bale," Benson said. "We could throw bales all day. Boy, were we in shape. Baling will do that for you. It takes a little longer after 35."

"You ought to start a spa for yuppies," Benson was told. "The Benson Hay Plan—$150 a day, good meals, guaranteed to whip the body into shape in only 14 days."

"You'd have to be able to stand yuppies, for 14 days."

"A major drawback."

"Not more than 30 bales left, now."

"You said that 30 bales ago."

"Yeah, but I was lying then."

Early summer.

"Remember," David Benson asked, "going out there with the hoes and chopping the weeds out?"

The Bensons have hoes. A lot of hoes, kept sharp with a grinder, one for every member of the family, for cousins and sisters and out-of-town visitors.

A hoe, for the Bensons, is a philosophical statement.

"The soil has been here since the glaciers left, and you could grow just about anything on it," Benson said. "Since we've started farming it, we haven't done it any good. We send a lot of it right down to the Gulf of Mexico every year, pour all kinds of chemicals on it. Who knows what we'll wind up doing to it?

"There's an alternative to all that. If you're willing to take a little less, you can get along without all the fertilizers and the Lasso and Bigfoot (herbicides). It means you've got to do handwork, but that's OK, too—you build up a relationship with the land by working on it. You put so much work into a piece of land, and you start getting protective. That's got to be good for it, in the long run."

Hoeing is one of the bad jobs of the farm year. It's not particularly hard work, like haying, nor does it take much skill, as plowing does. It's hard in a different way. It demands attention, but lacks drama. The work is constant, but there is little sense of progress.

The principal villain in the soybean field is the Canadian thistle, a tall, tough, bristly plant that crowds beans and chokes combines. It grows in shapeless patches that pay little attention to the order of bean rows.

The individual thistles seem to grow best near the stems of corn or beans. The thistles have to be hooked out with the hoe, rather than simply attacked with brute force.

Hoeing the Beanfield Is 'the Worst'

"This has got to be the worst," Sally-Anne Benson said, halfway through a round of hoeing in the bean field. A thistle patch trailed across the rows in front of her. She was sweating hard, her face brown and unhappy in the hot summer sun. Two friends were working with her, and they both stopped.

"I thought you said it wasn't that bad," said one, leaning on his hoe.

"I keep forgetting," she said.

The Bensons have relatives and friends in the Twin Cities who come down with their families to help. "It's a family get-together, and it's a good chance for David and I to talk," Sally-Anne said one night at the kitchen table.

"Most of the time, he's on the tractor and I'm doing something else, or I'm on the tractor and he's doing something else, or I'm at the house and he's in the field, or I'm at school and he's in the shop. This is one thing we do together, at least."

But not on this day. The relatives had not come down yet. David was cultivating the corn with the tractor, and the bean field stood there, demanding attention, its thistles spreading and sprouting with great glee.

"This," Sally-Anne said, "is the worst."

At the end of each round of hoeing (a round is one trip up and down the length of the field), Sally-Anne drank water from the gallon glass jugs left at the ends of the rows. Her face glowed with heat and dehydration.

"Maybe you're too small to do this," a friend told her.

"Why?"

"Your body's surface area is a lot bigger compared to your weight than with larger people. Maybe you dehydrate a lot more than we do."

"I don't know. It sure is hot."

"How many more rows?"

"Just down to three—you can see the end.

Four more rounds, maybe."

"Two hours?"

"I don't think I can do it two more hours."

"How about this? See, you set up a Benson Academy of Performing Arts and you apply for a grant from the arts council, and then you hire a bunch of starving artists from the cities, and give them hoes and tell them that this is a performance of life and death and they are out here to kill. Maybe we could tape it and run it on public TV."

"How about this? We get some Hare Krishnas and tell them the thistles are the manifestation of evil, and they could dance through the fields with their hoes, Hare-Hare, Rama-Rama. ... "

And passers-by, had there been any, would have seen two large dust-covered men and a small, tired woman doing an impromptu Hare Krishna dance with hoes, in a blazing sun in the Benson soybean field, not far from the Iowa line, in southwestern Minnesota.

Autumn

If a playing card were chosen to represent the 1985 soybean harvest, it would be what? The ace of hearts? A warm card, a card of the highest level. Soybeans are the cash crop, the money crop, the crop that will decide how the year goes. Even a small crop is a pleasure to harvest.

David Benson, the worry lines etched around his eyes, stood at the edge of his field, plucked a few pods, shelled out the small, yellow soybeans, and popped them into his mouth.

"Soft. They're so soft, they're mushy," he said. "Run these beans through a combine and you'd lose them, you'd just mash them up."

The trouble began in early August.

"Rain came just about the second week of August—right after I bought that Deutz (tractor)," he said. "I remember we only used it once, and after that, it was always too wet to get in the fields. The rain was OK at first. We already had the oats out, and the second cutting of hay, and the corn needed a touch of wet weather. But it never stopped. It just kept going. Here it is the middle of October, and we're usually finishing up everything, just about now. We haven't been able to get in the fields. We haven't even touched the beans."

At the house, Gus Benson, from his easy chair next to the kitchen table, said, "I've never seen anything like it in 83 years. It's never been this wet and this late."

"It's getting cold," David said. "If we get snow, it'll drag the beans right onto the ground. You can't combine that way. We'd lose the crop. That's $9,000 in beans in that one field down there, and it'd be gone just like *pfffft*.

"It happened one time to us—not snow, but hail. I remember, we ran up and stood in the doorway and watched the hail come down and take the beans right out. Took them right out. I tried to get in and combine, but there wasn't any point in it. We'd get a few beans, but it cost us more in fuel than we were getting out. Of course, nothing's ever a total loss—I plowed those beans under, and next year that soil was terrific. Beans make good manure; it's the kind of manure you wish you could afford to put on the land, build it up."

Weather Turns Dry
Two weeks later, everything changed. The rains broke and the weather turned dry.

By Monday, Oct. 28, the harvest was on. It was a Monday of the full moon. Not the harvest moon of September, but the hunter's moon.

To a man traveling down Highway 60, the major diagonal roadway from Mankato to the southwest corner of Minnesota, the hunter's moon was like a lamp flying along the edge of the road, illuminating the landscape.

On other trips, on other days, the landscape had been still. The windbreaks around the farmhouses, as seen in the moonlight, had looked like vast ships in a dark ocean anchorage, their blue mercury-vapor yardlights serving as warning lights at the peak of unseen main-masts.

And all of the small towns had gone to sleep early. Lake Crystal, Madelia, St. James, Butterfield, Mountain Lake, Bingham Lake, Windom, Heron Lake, Brewster—all strung out on Highway 60 like rosary beads, and all asleep by 11 p.m.

Farmers' Hours
But different farmers' hours were kept beneath this hunter's moon. The landscape was alive with combines that crawled and clawed their way through endless miles of rust-brown soybeans.

Grain trucks roared down sideroads and onto the highway, the elevators were lit and working hard, and locomotives maneuvered grain cars onto elevator sidings.

The towns were awake. The Dairy Queens and groceries were

open. Clusters of dusty, tired men in work shirts and pinstriped bib overalls gathered around the back of pickup trucks, their smiles flashing in the electric light. The harvest. A month late, but coming in.

A Time for Fields

Benson got his beans out in a week of hard work, sitting on top of the combine, churning through dark, clean fields. Not a time for talking. Just a time for the fields.

A bean combine, like most working farm equipment, makes no concession to beauty. It's an ungainly thing, like a giant green stinkbug, groaning and lurching through the fields, pulling dried bean plants in the front, spewing shredded leaves and stems from the back. The pale yellow beans go into an interior tank, to be dumped later in high-side wagons.

Some farmers take the beans straight into the local cooperative elevator. On the Benson farm, the wagons are towed to the main farmyard and dumped into storage bins.

"You can't really know what it feels like unless you've done it. Gosh, it just feels so good to get them out," Benson said. "Remember going out there with the hoes and chopping the weeds out? This is the payoff. These beans are clean. Look at those beans."

Later comes a colder judgment.

"The beans, I'd say, were mediocre," he said. "I mean, they're all right, but we got maybe 30 bushels an acre, average. We've gotten used to more than that—35, 40 bushels an acre—but that wet weather back in August maybe kept the pods from forming like they usually do. Maybe—I don't know."

Though the crop was only fair, the feeling remains warm.

"I'm glad we got them off," he said. "Gosh, it makes you feel good."

Closing down the year. Snow whips through Gus Benson's farmyard, and wagons of corn wait to be unloaded.

"We've got to close the big door," David Benson said. "That's always a job."

The "big door" is the huge, drop-down door to the barn's hayloft. Eight feet wide and perhaps 10 feet tall, it hangs upside down beneath its open doorway all through the summer.

To lift it into place, ropes are run from the back of the door to a series of pulleys inside the roof of the barn, then down to the ground floor. A single thumb-thick tow rope emerges from a ground-level door directly beneath the big door. That end of the rope is tied to a pickup truck bumper, and the pickup hauls the door up.

On the first attempt, a side rope broke and the door fell back.

"Gol-darned rope has probably been here since 1938," Benson muttered. Working bare-handed to untie the broken rope, and retie the new one, was a slow, clumsy task. When he was done, Benson climbed back into the pickup and put it in gear.

"Easy, easy, easy ... get the hooks, get the hooks. ... "

As the door swung up, the light in the barn died and the outside sounds were muffled. The change was anything but subtle, the loft changing from airy balcony to comfortable cave with the creaking swing of the great door. The metallic sound of the catch-hooks confirmed the closing.

Corn Is Last Crop In

The closing of the barn is one acknowledgment of winter's approach. The final acknowledgment—the final concession—comes with the corn harvest.

"When the last of the corn is in, that's it," Benson said. "There's all kinds of other stuff you keep doing, but that's it, really. After that, it's getting ready for winter, and waiting for spring."

As the storm came in, Benson towed the broken corn picker back to the shop and left it. There were other tasks to be done—two loads of waiting corn to be unloaded, the house to be converted to its winter configuration.

The high-sided grain wagons were towed under a rack that looked much like a child's swing set without the swings. A winch, run by a tractor's power takeoff, was hooked to the front corners of the wagon. When the winch cable was tightened, the front of the wagon lifted from the ground, and the corn slid through small doors at the back.

Beneath the back of the wagon was the lowest step of the corn elevator, which boosted the corn to the top of the crib, where it was dropped inside. The process was simple, efficient, and noisy.

"The corn is hardly worth growing, if you were going to try to sell it," Benson said as he watched the elevator carry the neat yellow ears into the crib. "We feed most of it, so we're OK. Even if we don't sell the beef, we can always eat it."

As the snowstorm intensified—the television weathermen now were calling it a blizzard—the Bensons began talking about the conversion of their home.

When David and Sally-Anne married, and then later moved back to his parents' farm, they bought an aging house. Although they worked to make it livable, it never had good insulation or modern heating systems.

The House Needs Winterizing

The Bensons heat with wood, kerosene, and sometimes oil; wood is the mainstay. In the spring, the big Ashley woodstove is moved out of the front room to storage. In the fall, it regains its dark, glowering prominence in front of the couch.

"It's always nice to have visitors at a time like this," Benson said cheerfully. "We can use the help moving the stove."

The conversion was quick but heavy. The big old upright piano was pushed and carried from one wall to the next while Sally-Anne ran around with a broom, chanting, "wait, wait just a minute."

When she was satisfied with the new arrangement of furniture, the Ashley was mounted carefully on cinderblocks and the chimney pipe was fitted carefully on top of it.

Sally-Anne further winterized the house by taping large pieces of transparent plastic over drafty windows. All of the Bensons worked together to shovel snow around the house's foundation to prevent wind from getting beneath the house.

"The hardest part of living here is the winter," Sally-Anne said. "The wind never stops, and when it's 10 below, or 20 below, you feel like it's cutting your face open. It can go on like that for days. You don't go outside except when you absolutely have to. You feel like you're living in a cave."

As the Bensons rearranged the living room for winter, the storm intensified.

"Can you see Bigelow? The lights?" Sally asked at 9 p.m.

No. There was nothing out there but the suffocating white mill of the storm.

Near dawn, the storm began to weaken. By mid-morning, Bigelow was visible again. Drifts blocked the road outside the house, but David, expecting them, had left a car in a non-drifting area of the road during the night. The Bensons were still mobile.

The next two days were cold. On the third day, the weather turned milder, and Benson thought about the corn again.

"Maybe I could use the bigger tractor and pull the picker through there," he said. He decided to try. Repairs on the picker took two hours, and he pulled it down to the cornfield and through the snow. It worked.

"I figure two hard days and it'll be done," he said with evident pleasure, ice bristling from his mustache, as he towed the first full wagon back to crib. "You see us go through there? She pulled right through." He patted the tractor.

It didn't work quite that way. He spent the rest of the week struggling with the increasingly crusty snow and breakdowns with the picker.

"It's the ice going through it," he said. "It puts a heck of a strain on all the machinery."

But he did finish.

For the work he had done, for all the planting, cultivating, hoeing, the waiting for the rain to stop, the tension of the late fall—for all that, he finished without fanfare, although you almost expected there to be some.

There was not. He pulled the picker over the last rows of corn, through the snow, and drove home.

On a cold, snowy November day, I climbed the soft steps of baled hay to a place near the peak of the Bensons' big red barn, and made some final notes.

A barn is a place of mysteries. A place of birth and death and endless sweat. A place of hatches up and down, of unexpected turnings and gates and barriers, a place where you can build a castle or a fort or a nest in the bales of hay.

In seven months of reporting on the Benson family and their farm, I had been in and out of the barn 20 or 30 or 40 times. So, on the last day, as I left for the barn, Sally-Anne asked, half teasing, "Going to think?"

I was. When I stepped inside the barn, I found Gus Benson's big hound, Moses, curled up on a bale of hay a few feet from Bluma, the aging milk cow. I stepped over Moses and climbed the steps made by the bales until I reached the peak. Six half-grown barn cats—four tigers and two calicos, the survivors of the summer litters—climbed right along with me, curious about the intrusion.

A barn is basically a large wooden envelope designed to keep the worst of the weather off whatever is stored inside—hay, animals, miscellaneous equipment, and tools. It is not designed to be as weatherproof as a house. Up near the top of the barn, light and snow were filtering in through cracks around the big door, a hole in a windowpane and other places.

The cats stepped carefully around the snow and sat down to watch. And I sat down to think about the year, the faces and names, the things we did, the way the farm looked and felt.

To tell the story of a farm family, over a growing year, is difficult if you are determined to do it honestly. As you accumulate information, you find too many bits that will not fit into a smooth story—the low cards in the deck, in a way.

But an accumulation of low cards can make a powerful hand—you'd bet the house on four deuces in draw poker. So what do you do with the small bits, the pieces that characterize the land, the people, the work?

In the months of interviewing and writing, I never told how the Bensons fight occasionally, as any sane couple does, and how, when they have a difference of opinion, they call each other "honey" in every other sentence.

Nor did I say much about the killing of animals—the butchering of chickens, the transportation of sheep to the locker, David's comment that the beef cattle "represent a lot of corn and work," or his suggestion that he can maintain a personal relationship with his animals at the same time he quite happily sends them to slaughter.

I never wrote much about Sally-Anne's hunger for seafood or about Heather playing beginner's Bach on the old upright $25 piano.

I never wrote anything about the stock tank used as a swimming pool, about the tire swing in the backyard, about the sweat-inflamed forearm cuts left by haying, about how the handles of the hoes are worn concave by years of use, about how drivers wave to each other when passing on country roads under the assumption they're acquaintances or wouldn't be there.

I never wrote about the peculiar cast of the sun on the prairie at dawn. I never wrote about Gus Benson's hands, which all by themselves look like 50 years of farming—or how the Bensons link hands, big and small, rough and smooth, to say grace before meals.

In a year with the Bensons, I've been writing about the face cards. I could have done as well with the deuces and treys.

ANALYSIS

CAMP FEELS HIS "semi-rural" Iowa background helped him hit it off with the Benson family in preparing "Life on the Land." "I grew up in an area where we were always in the countryside," Camp says. "I sort of spoke the language."

Although Camp doesn't favor quote leads, he used a long,

free-form quote from David Benson on the harshness of being a farmer to open the series. "That was such a great sequence," he marvels. "We were just getting to know each other."

It also served as a telling summary lead of the farm crisis.

Notice how Camp follows the quote with a wonderfully descriptive paragraph, highlighted by the following 80-word sentence:

Get off Interstate 90, off the state highway, off the black-topped county road, and finally go down the gravel track and into the farm land, listening to the power lines sing and the cottonwoods moan in the everlasting wind, watching a red-orange pickup a mile away as it crawls like a ladybug along a parallel road between freshly plowed fields, leaving behind a rising plume of gravel dust, crawling toward the silos and the rooftops that mark the Iowa line.

Camp also does an effective job in the May 12 opening section of visually setting the stage for the rest of the series: describing the farm and its history, introducing the characters and, finally, explaining why the Bensons stay on the farm.

Camp credits taking art courses for a sense of imagery and his ability to write visually. "I tell people to think about Haiku," he says. "Because when you are opening a feature story you want a lot of things very close to the top that appeal to the senses—all of the senses. If you can get taste and smell in there, particularly, it evokes things in people immediately ... pulls them in."

The following sentence/paragraph is a classic example of Camp's visual talents and ability to write with imagery. Notice how he effectively uses (and does not use) punctuation, primarily semi-colons and commas:

Sally-Anne Benson chopping Canadian thistles in the hot sun, her face glowing fiery red with heat, despite the woven straw hat; David Benson rolling the cultivator down the endless rows of new beans, five hours with barely a stop, the hot wind blowing the dust and grit into his eyes and ears and teeth; Heather Benson, laying out the table, putting together a quick dinner because her parents are late in from the field, and she knows they'll be tired almost to sickness; Anton Benson, pulling

a full round of evening chores while his parents work on in the
long lingering twilight of the summer solstice.

Camp admits to taking some ribbing for writing sentences that
top 80 words. "People used to say, 'can't you make it a hundred?'"

Camp feels the ability to produce different sentence lengths is
an important component of effective writing. "I also try to vary
the form, style and length of my sentences [and] try to write relatively short paragraphs because I'm aware of the effect of
white space in newspapers."

Short paragraphs perhaps, but paragraphs chock full of rich-
ness and detail, yet often unconventional enough to catch a
reader off guard—and transport them to a place where their
senses rule:

The drying alfalfa smells like ginger and something else, a
sweet, fat odor riding the silky summer breezes with gravel dust
and gasoline fumes, riding into the elbow-out side windows of
dusty old automobiles.

Camp feels the observational powers that allow this type of
writing are teachable. "A great exercise for people trying to
write visually is to go sit in a place like a bar and describe in the
smallest detail the inside of the bar. People are astonished at the
immediacy and the strength of their writing when they do that."

In "Life on the Land," Camp also knew when to listen as
well as observe. "There's a scene during the automobile race
where there's a 48-star flag. But I'm not the one who saw the
flag. The photographer said, 'Did you notice the flag is 48
stars?' I looked up and sure enough it was. There was a lot of
back-and-forth (like that) between myself and the photographer—who had a great eye for this. I thought he should have won
the Pulitzer for photography."

Effective interviewing skills are equally important, Camp
says, as is finding articulate people to interview in the first
place. "David is now a county commissioner," Camp says. "He
is very articulate and so is she—and so were the children for
their ages."

Camp admits to periodically asking uninformed questions
that may lead to a reaction and generate quotes. "[I'll] keep

coming back to something over and over again, asking the same question in a variety of ways, hoping they will have thought [more] about it." His premise? if you ask questions that are pushy, interesting or provocative enough, over an ample period of time, people will begin to think about their answers and ultimately provide well-thought-out responses.

And, perhaps thinking back to David Benson's free-form quotes that open the initial story, Camp offers: "Sometimes, when you are interviewing people, it's best to keep your mouth shut. There just seems to be a hump you have to get over."

Camp says writing this series didn't take long but the reporting required "more or less just living there. It was about a four-hour drive down to their farm and a lot of times the photographer and I would go down separately."

The long, monotonous drive gave him plenty of time to sort his thoughts and mentally prepare his story on the way home, allowing him to immediately begin writing after returning to the paper. He estimates the 23 trips he made to the farm accounted for 8,500 miles.

Although he wrote the series in an on-the-spot, day-by-day chronology, Camp says he decided not to write the series in the first person to preserve objectivity and keep a little needed distance. "I would not stay overnight at their house," he stresses. "I always stayed at a Holiday Inn because I didn't want to get [too] close."

But he skillfully slips himself and the photographer into the story in the last few paragraphs, telling the farmers they will return just in time for the hay harvest.

Camp brings himself in again at the very conclusion of the story, referring to himself as "I" for the first time, climbing the steps of the barn to "make some final notes."

He points out the final section was the only time he went first person, and only because "I was trying with this series to write as well as I could, and when I got to the end, I tried to write around the first-person part and it just didn't make it. Finally, it came down to the point where I had to step out from behind the third-person objectivity and just say what I thought ... it was much clearer that way."

And by inserting himself into the end of the 20,000 word series, Camp provides his readers some insights and observations that would have been lost otherwise.

Notice how Camp uses the mini-epilogue to tell how many of the "low cards in the deck" didn't fit smoothly into his narrative, "cards" he wants to report about anyway—such as how the Bensons fight like every other married couple, slaughter and eat their animals and make do without many of the luxuries they crave.

His ending is an inspired, thoughtful and subtle conclusion:

In a year with the Bensons, I've been writing about the face cards. I could have done as well with the deuces and treys.

Camp also set the ending up, of course, by skillfully inserting card analogies into the narrative several times, including:

A farm year is like a poker game. A poker game is not simply a matter of who won and lost—knowing the game is knowing how the cards were played, the tension, the bluffs, the hard decisions, the bets.

A year on the farm is the playing of cards ...

If haying was a card, it would be the queen of diamonds ... Hay is the first crop of the year, the first payback.

If a playing card were chosen to represent the 1985 soybean harvest, it would be what? The ace of hearts? A warm card, a card of the highest level. ... Soybeans are the cash crop, the money crop ...

What Camp may be missing, of course, is that he gave the readers both the face cards AND the small cards in this terrific series. The Pulitzer Board responded by dealing him the final ace.

JOHN CAMP is currently one of the most successful novelists in the world, having produced many best-selling thrillers, including *Rules of Prey, Shadow Prey, Eyes of Prey, Silent Prey, Winter Prey, Night Prey, Mind Prey* and *Sudden Prey,* under the pseudonym John Sandford. He holds both a bachelor's degree in American studies and a master's degree in journalism from the University of Iowa.

1987

STEVE TWOMEY

THE NIGHT BEFORE the 1987 Pulitzers were to be announced, Steve Twomey was certain he had lost. "I felt, that's it, my brush with glory has come and gone," he recalls.

Twomey should have been optimistic. He had already won a prestigious American Society of Newspaper Editors award for the Supercarriers story and was fully aware the story was a Pulitzer finalist. Plus, *The Philadelphia Inquirer* had a distinguished history of winning Pulitzers. But Twomey knew the editor, Gene Roberts, usually notified the winners the night before the announcement—to ensure they would be at work the next day. Twomey hadn't received that call.

The clincher came when his wife, an assistant city editor for the *San Jose Mercury News,* called from the West Coast to see if he had heard anything. Aware the *Inquirer* arranged for the spouses to be present for the announcement, Twomey now knew for sure he had lost.

Knowing he didn't have to be in tip-top shape the next day, Twomey concedes he, "had a lot of wine that night." However, for an accomplished reporter with such highly-tuned instincts, Twomey now realizes he missed two key pieces of information.

Just back from France, where he was the paper's Paris correspondent, Twomey was temporarily renting the third floor of a house from another *Inquirer* reporter. If Roberts called Twomey that night, the secret could spread quickly throughout the newsroom—before the "surprise" announcement the next day.

Also, Twomey's wife had indeed called him from the West Coast, but not from her home. She called from San Francisco International Airport, where she was about to board the red-eye for Philadelphia.

"I got up the next morning, quite hungover and went to work, thoroughly depressed," Twomey recalls vividly. A little after noon, the editorial page editor asked him to come up to the sixth floor to check a fact in an editorial. Walking into the room, Twomey faced a broadly-smiling Gene Roberts, who said: "Congratulations, you've won the Pulitzer Prize!"

How Super Are Our Supercarriers?

The Philadelphia Inquirer

October 5, 1986

AIR BOSS LOOKED AFT. Through the haze of a June morning off Sicily, an F-14A Tomcat fighter was already banking in low over *America*'s wake, a couple of miles out and coming home to the Bird Farm. Air Boss looked down. Damn. Still no place to put the thing.

On the flight deck below, opposite Air Boss's perch in the control tower, an A-7E Corsair II bomber sat astride the No. 4 steam catapult amidships. By now, the A-7 should have been flying with the rest of the day's second mission. Nobody would be landing while it straddled *America*'s only available runway.

"What's taking 'em so long down there?" Air Boss growled. He had left his leather armchair in his glass booth in *America*'s superstructure. He was standing up for a better look, which he always does when the flight deck crunch is on.

The ship's 79,724 tons suddenly shuddered. Steam billowed from No. 4. The A-7 had vanished, rudely flung out over the Mediterranean by the "cat stroke," like a rock from a slingshot. Finally.

"Launch complete, sir!" said Mini Boss, his assistant.

"Clear decks!" Air Boss boomed into the radio to his launch crews. It would be close, maybe too close. "Secure the waist cat! Prepare to recover aircraft! Hubba, Hubba!"

The F-14 was closing at 150 miles per hour. A mile out now. On the deck, crews were frantically stowing launch gear. They had to seal the long slit down which the catapult arm—the "shuttle"—races as it yanks a plane along the deck and flips it heavenward. They had to shut hatches and make them flush with the deck. *America* had to become seamless for its bird.

"Commmme on, commmme on," said Air Boss. His eyes flitted from the looming F-14 to his crews working below. The plane's variable wings were swept wide for landing, 64 feet tip to tip. Its wheels were down, its twin tail jets were spewing heat waves. It was a pterodactyl about to prey on the carrier.

"We're not going to make it!" said Air Boss.

"We'll make it!" said Mini Boss.

Unless they made it, the F-14 would have to be waved off, sent around for another approach. In peacetime, that is not fatal. It costs fuel—266 gallons a minute for an F-14, $1,100 an hour—but no more. In war, a carrier's ability to cycle its jets in seconds—to launch them, land them, rearm them, refuel them, launch them again—could mean victory or defeat. America is not at war now. But *America* trains as if it is.

"We're not going to make it!" Air Boss said again.

"We'll make it!" said Mini.

Catapult crews had almost finished. The F-14 was just off the stern and plunging, a long hook dangling from its belly that would, it was hoped, catch one of four cables laid across the rear flight deck to stop the plane cold. It was time to decide: Wave it off or land it. The last of the crew was scampering out of the landing area.

"They made it!" said Mini.

Over the stern, down, down.

Bam.

Fifty-six thousand pounds of F-14 slammed home. Simultaneously, the pilot pushed to full throttle. Heat blasted down the aft flight deck. If the hook missed all the cables, the pilot would simply keep going, over the now-dormant site of the No. 4 catapult, flying off and coming around again. But he was no "bolter." He snagged a wire for a clean trap. Time from the last launch to the first landing: 45 seconds.

Air Boss grinned.

Mini Boss grinned.

Hubba, hubba.

IT IS HARD NOT TO LOVE the dance of the carrier deck—the skill, beauty and sheer guts of men launching and landing warplanes on a 1,000-foot slab on the sea.

Seventy-five times on an average day, up to 400 times during crises such as Libya, *America*'s crew members dodge sucking jet intakes and whirring props to hitch aircraft to the catapults and send them flying. That many times, they help them home and snare them and park them. They can launch planes a minute apart. They can launch and land at the same time. They can do it in the dark or in the rain. Their average age is 19½.

Engines whine, then race—and a plane disappears from the deck in 2.5 seconds. Its exhaust heat bathes launch crews. The air reeks of jet fuel. Steam seeps from the catapult track. The next plane is already moving forward to take the "cat stroke," and there's another behind it. Noise overwhelms the deck. All the while, the carrier slices through the blue.

"There's no way to describe it," said an A-7 pilot aboard *America*. "There's no way to see it in a movie. You've got to come out here and smell it and see it. It's too dynamic. The whole thing's like a ballet."

In all, the United States' carriers number 14; no other nation has more than four. They are the largest engines of war; no one else's are half as big. They bear the names of battles won, *Coral Sea, Midway* and *Saratoga;* of leaders gone, *Eisenhower, Forrestal, Kennedy, Nimitz* and *Vinson,* and of Revolutionary War vessels, *Constellation, Enterprise, Independence* and *Ranger.* One evokes the place where man first flew, *Kitty Hawk.* And one is called *America.*

With their pride of escorts, the 14 carriers and 878 carrier-based fighters and bombers are the most tangible sign of U.S. power that most people around the world ever see. They are the heart of the nation's maritime defense, its glamour boys. They are the costliest items in the military budget, the price of one carrier and its escorts equaling the bill for 250 MX ballistic missiles.

Yet, for all their impressiveness and for all the importance the Pentagon attaches to the vessels, many congressmen and defense analysts argue that the supercarriers' day is history. The critics fear they are now unnecessary, too expensive, and, worse, easy marks. Some of the doubters are even Navy men: Stansfield Turner, a retired admiral and the former director of the Central Intelligence Agency; Elmo Zumwalt, the retired Chief of Naval Operations, and Eugene J. Carroll Jr., a retired admiral who once commanded *Nimitz.*

"Like the battleship the carrier replaced, its magnificence cannot nullify basic changes in the nature of war at sea," Sen. Gary Hart, the Colorado Democrat, writes in a new book on U.S. defense, *America Can Win.* "The day of the large aircraft carrier ... has passed."

Today, all surface ships are highly vulnerable to two things—missiles and submarines. A British frigate was sunk in the 1982 Falklands War by a single Exocet missile fired from an Argentine jet it never saw. The Soviet Union has 304 attack submarines, enough to dispatch 21 to hunt each U.S. aircraft carrier. By opting for 14 big carriers—a 15th, the 91,487-ton *Theodore Roosevelt,* will join the fleet soon—the United States could lose, perhaps fatally, a very large portion of naval power in a very short time from a very few Soviet missiles and torpedo hits.

In short, it might have the wrong navy for the late 20th century. "When you concentrate your total offensive capability into 15 platforms, the targeting system of the adversary becomes very focused," said Carroll, the ex-carrier captain, who is now deputy director of the Center for Defense Information, a private Washington research group.

No one doubts that the United States ought to have carriers. They have uses. The answer to vulnerability, critics say, is to have more of them, to spread the risk. The big ones, however, cost big bucks. *Roosevelt* and two other new, huge, nuclear-powered carriers authorized by Congress, the *Abraham Lincoln* and the *George Washington,* will cost $3.5 billion apiece. Without planes. Add those and add the cruisers and frigates that must escort any carrier—the Navy concedes they need protection—and it costs $17 billion to put a carrier group to sea. That is 10 times the 1986 Philadelphia city budget. The cost of the three carrier groups combined would be enough to pay for all city services—police, fire, sanitation, everything—for 30 years without any resident paying any taxes.

That is money that cannot be spent on other military items. And most of that money goes for "the purpose of protecting this goddamn carrier," said Robert Komer, who was an undersecretary of Defense for policy during the Carter administration. Even most of the carrier's planes are there to protect it.

Instead, many critics say, it's time to think small. Overhauling the big carriers at the Philadelphia Naval Shipyard—*Independence* is there now, under the Service Life Extension Program—is merely fixing up the past. The nation should have smaller, cheaper carriers. They can do the job. And the nation could then afford more carriers, and more would cut the impact of losing any given one if war comes.

Of course, to speak of cutting losses in any war seems surreal. Only the Soviet Union could really challenge the U.S. Navy. But any sea battle with the Soviets would trigger nuclear war, many analysts say. In that case, it wouldn't much matter if the United States had 15 supercarriers or 30 medium ones. The game would be over. Still, the Pentagon plans for old-fashioned conflict. Its theory is that because nuclear war is final, no nation would start one. But the Soviets might be willing to start a regular war, so it's vital to have good conventional armed forces. In that context, debating what kind of navy to have does make sense.

And the U.S. Navy has no doubt that it wants big carriers. It would even like seven or eight more, up to 22 or 23. In fact, the Reagan administration, under Navy Secretary John. F. Lehman Jr., has made big carriers the key to a strategy that would take them right into the teeth of Soviet defenses in wartime. That is how much confidence it has in carriers' ability to survive today. Critics, said Adm. Henry H. Mauz, commander of *America*'s battle group, "are well-meaning people, I'm sure. But they're wrong."

Lehman even said in testimony before Congress last fall that to build small is communistic, to build big is American. "Should carriers be bigger or smaller? There is no absolute answer to that question," he said. " ... [But] our tremendous edge in technology is a permanent edge built into the nature of our culture and economic system, compared to the Soviets. It is to that advantage we must always build, not to go to cheaper, smaller, less capable ships in large numbers. That is an area in which a totalitarian, centralized, planned economy excels."

Big is beautiful.

AMERICA'S CREW SOMETIMES gets lost. There are so many decks and passageways that sailors don't know where they are. "I get fouled-up all the time," said an officer who was consulting a deck plan on a bulkhead.

Crew members can ask someone for help, though it'll often be a stranger. With 4,950 men—there is not one woman—who work different hours on different decks, most don't know each other, even after spending six months at sea on the same ship. Usually they learn about a fellow crew member by reading about him in the ship's daily newspaper or seeing him on one of two television stations that beam live news and old movies and TV shows. (The most popular fare is a raunchy movie about a riot in a women's prison, one aired repeatedly and so bad that the crew says it's great.)

Many days, there is no sensation of being at sea. Unless they stand on the flight deck or work in the "island"—the starboard-side command structure that rises above the flight deck—crew members can't see the ocean. There are no portholes. And *America* is so massive, it is often unaffected by the water's roll. Being belowdecks can feel like being in a building.

When it left Norfolk, Va., on March 10, for a Mediterranean patrol, *America* took $9 million in cash because at sea it becomes its own economy. The crew gets paid. The crew buys things at the ship's stores. The proceeds are then used to pay the crew. Eighteen thousand meals are fixed a day, 280,000 gallons of sea water are distilled. The Navy loves to boast that there is a barber shop, a bakery, a photo lab, a post office, a printing plant, a tailor, and a public relations staff. In other words, much of the crew has nothing to do with weapons or war. They are service-sector Navy.

The bigness does have an objective, of course: to fly a lot of planes and carry fuel and bombs for them. A U.S. carrier has 80 to 90 planes, more than all four Soviet mini-carriers combined. *America* has eight types of planes, more types than either the three British or two French carriers can hold.

Besides 24 F-14s and 34 A-6 and A-7 bombers, *America* has four planes to refuel its planes in the air, four to detect enemy planes, four to jam enemy electronic equipment, 10 to hunt for submarines, and six helicopters to find downed pilots and to hunt for submarines. All told, there are 86 aircraft, which together can deliver 480,00 pounds of bombs, as much as 10 World War II-era aircraft carriers. When they're not flying, the planes can be stored and repaired on the hangar deck, which runs almost from bow to stern below the flight deck.

The aircraft fly off a deck that is 1,047.5 feet long, not the biggest in the Navy, an honor that belongs to *Enterprise* at about 1,100 feet. But if stood on end, *America*'s flight deck would be almost twice as high as William Penn's hat on City Hall. It is 252 feet wide. All told, the deck covers 4.6 acres, an expanse coated with black, coarse, non-skid paint. The crew has plenty of straightaway to jog in the hot sun when the planes aren't flying. Five lengths is a mile.

The flight deck is so big, *America* can launch four planes almost at once, two from bow catapults and two from catapults amidships, on an extension of the flight deck that angles left. The angle enables the ship to launch and land simultaneously in some cases. While a plane is launched forward, another lands on the angle. If it misses all the arresting cables, it keeps going left, thereby avoiding the bow cata-pults.

Despite its weight, *America,* which is 22 years old, can glide through the water at 30 knots. The power is not nuclear but conventional boilers that drive four 22-foot-high propellers. In fuel for the ship and planes, in crew pay and in food and supplies, each hour of patrol costs taxpayers $22,917. That is $550,000 a day. That is $99 million for the normal six-month cruise—not counting the bills that its escorts run up.

Overall, *America* exudes seductive and expensive power, a sense magnified by the stateroom of Capt. Richard C. Allen. There, in the bowels of a ship designed for war, is an elegant living room with cof-fee table, sofa and wing chairs. The carpeting is bulkhead-to-bulk-head. The dining table can seat at least 10. Several lamps lend a soft light to the room.

Its occupant is a serious man who was born 46 years ago in

Wisconsin and flew carrier jets until his eyes went bad. He wears wire-rims now; they give his soft and narrow face the look of a teacher. Allen, who has commanded *America* since July 1985, seemed perplexed by a suggestion that his ship might be at risk or should be anything but the size it is.

Two carriers half as big, for example, would mean two of everything, Allen said—two engine rooms, two sets of catapults, two bridges. Thus, two small carriers would be more than the cost of one big one. But neither would be as stable in rough seas, hampering flight operations, and neither would have so many planes able to do so many things. Even with the advances in missile and submarine warfare, he would much rather command a carrier now than during World War II. Besides, because *America* is big, it can take many bomb hits. And it is much harder to find than an airfield ashore.

"It's mobile, it's moving, it's never in the same place," the captain said. "Like right now. You're on it. Do you know exactly where we are? I'll share with you: We're southwest of Sicily. Tonight, we'll go north of Malta. This morning, we were east of Sardinia. The carrier moves. As a result, the targeting problem against a carrier is very complex. ...

"It's extremely remote a carrier would ever be totally put out of—I mean, *sunk*. I think it's just something beyond imagination as I see it, by any threat that we see today or in the near future. This is a very capable piece of machinery."

LIBYA. THEY WERE ACTUALLY going to hit Libya. Night had fallen. It was April 14, 1986. Allen looked down from the bridge at a dimly lighted flight deck jammed with aircraft, bombs and bullets bound for Benghazi. It was no drill. "I don't believe we're really doing this," he thought. "It's just unbelievable."

The crew had manned battle stations in record time. "All you have to do is tell somebody, 'We're going to go kill something,' and the level of interest goes up logarithmically. I mean, people become—they're *motivated*."

Thirty-eight planes from *America* would go. Somewhere in the darkness of the Mediterranean, the scene was being repeated on the *Coral Sea*. One by one, planes roared away. The most beautiful were the F-14s because, in order to get extra lift, they always flipped on their afterburners just before the "cat stroke," sending twin cones of flame 20 feet down the flight deck and lighting up the dark sea.

He was proud, Allen said, "to watch the complexity of the carrier pull together and to watch the thing take shape, until *boom,* there you are at night, and the cats start firing, and things happen just as they were planned."

And in the early hours of April 15, as the planes began coming back, crew members belowdecks watched the closed-circuit television shot of the flight deck to see whether the bombers had bombs under their wings. They didn't. And all 38 planes returned. The crew cheered wildly. (Fearing terrorist reprisals against the crew's families in the United States because of the carrier's role in the raid, the Navy requested that no crew member's name be used in this article, except Allen's, and it told crew members not to discuss Libya.)

"I just never thought the national decision would be to engage," Allen said. "I'm extremely proud of the President for having had the guts to do what he did."

Whatever its merit or morality, the U.S. raid on Libya to counter terrorism showed what carriers do best. They can sail to remote places and deal with Third World crises. They can, as the Navy puts it, "project power." Virtually every day of 1985, four U.S. carriers were somewhere at sea on patrol. Not the same four, of course, but a rotation that enables crews to avoid prolonged periods away from home. No other nation can deliver so much airpower wherever it wants. It is this ability to pop up anywhere swiftly that even critics of big carriers say makes carriers worth having.

It was carrier planes that forced down the civilian jet bearing the four hijackers of the cruise ship *Achille Lauro*. Carriers stood off Grenada and Lebanon during land operations in 1983. It is carriers that would be called on to reopen the Strait of Hormuz should Iran ever carry out its threat to cut oil lanes in its war with Iraq. Often, the mere arrival of the carrier is enough; none of its jets has to fire a shot.

"The carrier is an enormous politico-military capability," said Rear Adm. Jeremy J. Black, assistant chief of the Royal Navy Staff. "It is evident power. As you approach the thing, it emanates power. And wherever it will be, it will be a symbol of *American* power. That in itself is so significant."

"The aircraft carrier," said Norman Polmar, a noted U.S. defense analyst, "has demonstrated that it can move to the troubled area. It can remain offshore, in international waters, for days or weeks or months. ... You're going to see many more low-level conflicts and confrontations, and aircraft will be necessary for us to observe, deter and, if necessary, fight."

Used this way, carriers are not at much risk. Grenada or Libya do not have the military skill to mount a serious threat. Or so the Navy thinks. Carriers stood off North Vietnam for years, launching air strikes but never taking one in return. The Navy has plans for big carriers, however, that would put them at risk.

Imagine: On May 30, 1987, Soviet tanks and infantry swarm across central Europe. For the moment, the conflict is conventional. The European Allies are barely holding on, and they need troops from the United States. Convoys are pieced together, civilian 747s commandeered. And carriers flood the Atlantic to baby these sea and air fleets across to Europe. They are to sink submarines and shoot planes. They are to sweep Soviet surface ships out of the sea lanes linking Old World and New.

That has been part of U.S. strategy for years. Navy Secretary Lehman has added a twist, however. After carriers make the oceans safe for passage, he wants to send them on aggressive forays close to the Soviet Union to finish off the Soviet navy and then bomb land targets. Carriers would sail near the Kola Peninsula, off the Soviet Union's far north coast. They would sweep into the Baltic Sea. They would cruise off the Soviet's Pacific coast. By crushing the Soviets on their flanks with carrier power, Lehman argues, the United States would take pressure off the war in central Europe.

This "forward strategy" fuels a push by Lehman for a 600-ship Navy. The number of warships had slipped to 479 after Vietnam, and the Carter administration had decided not to build carriers to succeed the aging *Coral Sea* and *Midway*, which were both due to be retired. It thought big ships were too vulnerable and expensive. The number of carriers was set at 12.

But Lehman sought—and got—congressional approval during the first Reagan term for three giant nuclear-powered carriers and all their escorts, which together will consume 41 percent of Navy construction costs from now to the year 2000—$60 billion. Two of the carriers will replace *Midway* and *Coral Sea*, and the third will represent a net gain. So, the number of big carriers will actually rise to 15.

Lehman says the fleet expansion centered on big carriers is crucial to the "forward strategy." The United States must get the enemy in his lair, and only big carriers can do it. But it's not the same enemy as it used to be.

"CAPTAIN SAID TO TELL YOU we got a Udaloy coming in."

Churning on an opposite course in the twilight, the sleek visitor whipped past on *America*'s port side, swerved across its wake and pulled up off the starboard side about 1,000 yards away. Its speed and course now matched the carrier's. From the flight deck, a few crew members gave a look, but they had seen one before.

The Udaloy is a new class of Soviet destroyer. Each has 64 surface-to-air missiles, eight torpedo tubes, eight antisubmarine missiles and two helicopters. The ships steam at 32 knots. *America's* crew calls them "tattletales."

Soviet destroyers and frigates routinely weave in and out among U.S. battle groups. The high seas belong to no one; the Soviets have every right to sail wherever they want. The encounters are always courteous. Both sides follow the rules of the road. What the Soviets are doing is taking notes. They watch the pattern of flight operations and the types of exercises. They see how the task force moves. They watch how different planes perform.

"The Soviets? Oh yeah, they'll come right off the quarter, 1,000 yards, 500 yards, follow us around, back and forth," Allen said the next day as the Udaloy hovered. "Whatever we do, they do. If we turn, they turn. ... They take pictures. They pick up garbage. They do weird things. Usually they just follow you around."

Such open-ocean presence reflects the new Soviet Navy. Russia had never been a sea power, under the czars or under communism. Just 20 years ago, Soviet ships spent a fleet total of 5,700 days at sea, according to U.S. estimates. Last year, they spent 57,000. The Soviets now have the world's largest navy, with 283 major surface ships and 381 submarines, split between 77 ballistic missile-launching submarines (for delivering nuclear warheads to the United States) and 304 attack submarines (for sinking ships, such as U.S. ballistic missile-firing submarines or the carriers). That is 664 warships, compared to the 541 the United States has at the moment. That is three times the total of U.S. attack submarines, the kind needed to find Soviet attack submarines before they find U.S. carriers.

Assigned to the Soviet navy are 1,625 aircraft, mainly operating from land. Their job, too, is to sink U.S. ships. Most formidable, perhaps, is the new Backfire bomber, which can fly at 1,100 knots for 3,400 miles without refueling, bearing big air-to-surface missiles. At the end of 1985, there were 120 Backfires, with more being added each year.

Some Soviet planes are even at sea. Four modest aircraft carriers have been built, and each has 113 planes and 19 helicopters. Like British "jump jets," the planes take off and land by moving vertically. Last year, the Soviet Union launched an American-size carrier of at least 65,000 tons and designed for 60 planes and helicopters. It will not be operational for several years, however, because the Soviets must first master the dance of launching and landing so many aircraft.

Though the Soviet navy is large, there is disagreement about how

much of a threat it is, at least away from its coastal waters. In a study
last year, the Center for Defense Information said that 145 of the
Soviets' surface ships were too small, less than 2,000 tons, to venture
into the open sea for long. It said the Soviets have a limited ability to
resupply ships at sea, which *America* does very well. (It has to: A battle group gulps 10,000 barrels of fuel a day.) Nor do the Soviets have
as many anchorages in other countries as the United States has. And
while the Soviets now have carriers, no one argues that the vessels are
any match for U.S. carriers.

Nonetheless, Lehman and other Navy officials tout the Soviets as
a huge, aggressive force, plying waters they never did before with
power they never had before. They point to the Gulf of Mexico,
where major Soviet naval forces sailed twice last year. "In many areas
of the world, the Hammer and Sickle now overshadows the Stars and
Stripes," the unabashedly pro-Navy magazine *Sea Power* intoned last
fall.

Much of this gloom-and-doom, of course, is to justify the need for
600 very expensive ships: The Pentagon must face a worthy foe. And
even the Center for Defense Information, in its study, said the Soviets
would be very tough adversaries close to home if Lehman's "forward
strategy" were ever tried. And farther out to sea, Soviet attack submarines and Backfire bombers could, indeed, threaten convoys and
their carrier escorts.

Yet even while highlighting Soviet power, the Navy says, in effect,
no problem. It's got a system.

MUCH OF THE TIME, *America* seems alone in the Mediterranean,
free of Soviet tattletales and steaming toward an empty horizon. Not
even fishermen chug by. But the Small Boys are never far away.

There are 10 sprinkled in a circle around *America*, two cruisers,
four destroyers and four frigates, sometimes moving in close, some
times sailing out of sight. One or two U.S. attack submarines are
often there as well, but because they are underwater, it's hard to be
sure; Allen said only that they are not there all the time.

America never leaves home without the Small Boys, whose crews
say that they are the true sailors and that the carrier is just the Bird
Farm. Battle groups are the key to what the Navy calls defense-in-
depth. The idea is to keep the $3.5 billion airfield at the center from
being sunk.

The first sentry is not a ship, however. It is a plane, one that does
not carry any weapons and cannot fly fast. The E-2C Hawkeye looks
like a small AWACs plane, the Air Force's Airborne Warning and

Control aircraft, that seems to have a giant mushroom on its back. The mushroom has radar.

Often the first plane to leave the carrier during launches, the E-2's job is to park in the sky and see what else is up there. Its radar can scan 100,000 feet up and in an arc 250 miles around *America*. If it identified enemy planes, the E-2 would call in what deck crews call the Super Hot Fighter Pilots, only they use a more descriptive word than *super*.

The men who fly the $38.7 million F-14 fighters are just about as smug and smooth as *Top Gun* portrays them. *America*'s pilots haven't seen the movie because they have been at sea. But they've seen the Kenny Loggins video clip, featuring shots of twisting, blasting F-14s. It was flown out to the ship. They love it.

"Yeah, that's us," said a 28-year-old pilot from Drexel Hill. "We're *cool*. We're *fighter pilots*."

Most are in their late 20s or early 30s. Handsomeness seems to be a job requirement. Catapulting off a carrier, which subjects them to a jolt seven or eight times the force of gravity, "is a lifetime E-ticket at Disneyland," said the Drexel Hill pilot.

"To be sitting in that machine and to know that 300 feet later you'll be going 200 miles per hour and the whole thing takes 2½ seconds—well, the level of concentration in sports or whatever has never reached *that* adrenaline high," said a 42-year-old pilot from Philadelphia, who has done it 1,250 times.

Their job is to hunt down enemy planes and destroy them before they can launch missiles at *America*. Or, as Adm. Mauz, the battle-group commander, put it, "We want to shoot the archer rather than the arrow."

F-14s, which can fly at more than twice the speed of sound, have Phoenix missiles with a range of 120 miles, as well as shorter-range Sidewinder and Sparrow missiles. The F-14s would be helped by four EA-6B Prowlers from the carrier, planes whose task is to scramble the radar of attacking enemy planes and baffle their missile guidance systems. Needless to say, the fighter pilots don't think anyone will get past them. What a silly suggestion; without the carrier, they would get wet.

"This is home," said the air wing commander, 40, who is in charge of all the pilots of all the various types of planes. "This is where dinner is. This is where the stereo is."

If attacking planes did skirt the F-14s and fire missiles, the next line would take over, the Small Boys. They would rely on Aegis, a defensive system just entering service aboard a new line of cruisers and destroyers; *America*'s battle group has one of the new ships, the cruiser *Ticonderoga*. The Aegis is designed to find and track dozens of hostile missiles at once—the exact number is classified—and launch shipboard missiles to destroy them. It can coordinate not only the cruiser's reply missiles, but also those of all the ships in the battle group, automatically. An attack would be swatted out of the skies. In theory.

If that fails, and missiles are still boring in, *America* has a modern Gatling gun called Phalanx. Mounted at three points on the edge of the flight deck, the computer-directed gun has six barrels that together fire 3,000 rounds a minute. That is supposed to shred any missiles. Judging by a test one day on *America*, the gun's noise alone might destroy them.

Soviet submarines would be found by *America*'s 10 S-3A Viking planes. Their electronics can look down through the water and spot a submarine. The plane then drops a depth charge or torpedo. The battle group also scours with sonar and can fire an array of weapons at submarines.

Actually, Navy officials hate to talk about all this defense. They say outsiders spend too much time worrying about how vulnerable carriers are. The ships are for offense, first. "It's sort of like your house," said the air wing commander. "You take steps to protect it, but you don't go around protecting it all the time. I'm not worried every day my stereo's going to be stolen. I'd rather go bomb something."

IT CAME OUT OF THE WEST just after launch, skimming 10 feet above the South Atlantic at 680 miles per hour. On the bridge of *Sheffield*, a British frigate, Lts. Peter Walpole and Brian Leyshon had seen a puff of smoke on the horizon but didn't know what it meant and hadn't seen the Argentine Super Etendard fighter. One mile out, they both recognized what was coming their way.

"My God," they said simultaneously, "it's a missile."

Four seconds later, the Exocet hit starboard amidships, above the water line, and veered down into the engine room, where its 363 pounds of high explosive detonated. In an instant, *Sheffield* lost electrical power and communications. Fires broke out. The edge of the hole in the ship's side glowed red from the blazes, but there was no water pressure to put them out. As flames crept toward the magazine, where ammunition is stored, the crew abandoned *Sheffield*.

A new, $50 million ship had been destroyed—and 20 of its crew killed—by a single, small computer-guided missile costing one one-hundredth as much.

What happened that Tuesday, May 4, 1982, during the Falklands War was the most stunning example in history of the power of the anti-ship missile. These weapons can strike from much greater distances than naval guns and, unlike shells, can be guided to their targets. Photos of *Sheffield*, listing and burning, depict the critics' nightmare of what will happen to carriers.

There is little chance, certainly, that one, two or even three Exocets could sink a U.S. carrier. It is just too big. And the Navy accurately says that the British had less ability to detect, track and destroy enemy planes than a U.S. battle group has. Britain's two Falkland carriers had no planes like Hawkeyes to spot the Super Etendards. They had far fewer fighters to attack them. No British ship had Aegis. Polmar, the military analyst, says a U.S. carrier force would have destroyed the Argentine air force "in two days."

But there are missiles that could threaten a carrier—cruise missiles. They are flying torpedoes with large warheads, launched up to 350 miles from their targets and often moving at supersonic speed. Backfire bombers can carry them. About 30 Soviet surface ships can carry them. And so do 62 Soviet submarines, including the new Oscar class. Each Oscar has 24 cruise missiles. Two are at sea now, with another joining the fleet every two years.

"We do not have an adequate defense for cruise missiles," said Adm. Carroll of the Center for Defense Information. "It's been the *bete noire* of naval strategy for some time now. We've made progress. We've got Phalanx and such. But I'll guarantee you that if you take those carriers in range of Soviet land-based aircraft and cruise missiles, there will be enough cruise missiles coming through the defense to hit the ships. I don't know how many will get through, but say it's one out of five. And if one out of five hits our ships? It's all over."

Aegis is supposed to deal with cruise missiles, but its performance has not been flawless. Initially, it knocked down only four of 15 attacking missiles in tests. Later, that rose to 10 of 11, but doubts remain. Moreover, a missile doesn't have to sink a carrier to render it useless. Each carrier has four very weak points—its catapults. Without them, planes don't fly. The Navy thinks it is highly unlikely that any enemy will get so lucky as to put all four out of action at once. But then, naval history is replete with lucky moments.

A carrier's greatest foe, however, is not in the air. It is the enemy it never sees. Gary Hart calls them the kings of the sea. And the Soviets have more of them than anyone. In March 1984, a Soviet nuclear-powered attack submarine rose up under *Kitty Hawk* in the Sea of Japan, bumping it and damaging both ships. It was an accident, not an attack. But the battle group had not detected the sub, even though at least five Small Boys were around *Kitty Hawk*.

Because it was peacetime, it was possible the escorts weren't "ping-ing" with sonar to find subs. The incident, however, illustrates how stealthy subs can be. They are a threat not only from their cruise missiles, but from their torpedoes. While the Navy believes its detection skills are good, they are not perfect. "We don't always know where they are," said Capt. Allen, "so we don't know whether we're being followed or not all the time."

Oddly, Allen has never been on a submarine at sea, despite being in the Navy for 27 years. Critics say that would be an excellent way for carrier captains to learn how their underwater adversaries work and think.

Given the air and sea threats to carriers, Lehman's "forward strat-egy" could end in the destruction of the heart of the Navy. It would be going right where the defenses are thickest. Stripped of even a few of its carriers, the Navy might then be unable to do its more impor-tant job, protecting the sea lanes. That, in turn, would jeopardize a war in central Europe.

"If we sail into battle against the Soviets depending on just 15 ships, we will, like the Spanish Armada, sail in expectation of a mir-acle," Hart writes in *America Can Win*. "Perhaps we will get one, although the precedent is not encouraging. Perhaps the opponent, despite numerous submarines and aircraft, will prove incompetent. But our survival, as a navy and a nation, would depend ... on massive incompetence, not on our strength."

Even if the strategy worked and the carriers sank huge portions of the Soviet navy, the cornered Soviets might shift first to tactical and then strategic nuclear weapons to stave off surrender. In that case, the carriers' size wouldn't matter.

ASTERN OF *AMERICA*, they formed a necklace of lights in the night sky, 15 planes strung out in a row. They had lined up to take their turns coming home. It was 11:30 p.m.

On a catwalk hanging over the side of the flight deck, four land-ing-signals officers stood peering into the dark. LSOs can tell, just by looking at wing lights, if a returning pilot is on the right glide path, dropping 100 feet for each quarter mile to the ship.

"You're high, high," an LSO said softly into his radio to the first inbound plane. It was too dark to see what kind it was.

No task in all of aviation is more difficult than landing on a carri-er at night. While modern jets can all but fly themselves and the carrier has runway lights, pilots have none of the usual reference points, such as the lights of a city. The sky is black, the water is black. They cannot tell where one stops and the other starts. All they can see is a short line of light. They cannot even see the ship, let alone the deck. No matter what instruments can say and computers can do, that is frightening.

The first plane drew nearer. It crossed the stern. Sparks shot from the flight deck as the arresting hook hit first, searching for one of the four cables. It found one, yanking an A-7 to a halt in 350 feet, one-tenth of the distance a plane needs on land. The lights of the next plane grew larger.

"Foul deck! Foul deck!" said two LSOs.

Until the A-7 could be unhooked and moved aside, until the arresting cables were back in position, until deck crews had moved, the LSOs would keep telling the next pilot his runway was blocked. If necessary, they would wave him off. On this night, they would not have to; the crews were perfect.

Sparks flew, engines roared. In 16 minutes, all the planes were down. The ship grew quiet for the night, sailing on.

"Sometimes," said an LSO, "I can't believe what we do out here."

ANALYSIS

STEVE TWOMEY calls "How Super Are Our Supercarriers?" "the most fun I've ever had doing a story." The end result was a joy for *The Philadelphia Inquirer*'s magazine readers as well. Twomey mixes intricate facts, solid reporting and compelling quotes to discuss whether the U.S. Navy's largest aircraft carriers are the hope of the future—or dinosaurs from the past.

More than anything else, his use of striking details makes this story memorable. He continually plugs pertinent and memorable facts into the text, giving readers a sense of the enormity of these supercarriers. Some examples:

America *carries 4,950 men (but no women); it takes $9 million in cash out to sea; 18,000 meals are fixed daily; 86 different aircraft on board can deliver 480,000 pounds of bombs; the flight deck is a 1,000-foot floating slab.*

His lead is a tense description of the difficult landing by an
F-14 on the carrier. Twomey's use of actual dialogue and Navy
"flavor" heightens the experience for the reader. Notice how
much information he dispenses in just a few sentences:

*The F-14 was closing at 150 miles per hour. A mile out now.
... The plane's variable wings were swept wide for landing, 64
feet tip to tip. ... It was a pterodactyl about to prey on the carrier. ... Unless they made it, the F-14 would have to be waved
off. ... It costs fuel—266 gallons a minute for an F-14, $1,100
an hour. ... (finally) Fifty-six thousand pounds of F-14 slammed
home. Simultaneously, the pilot pushed to full throttle.*

Twomey finishes his thrilling lead and then skillfully slows
down, discussing the pros and cons of aircraft carriers. He
moves back and forth in this story—from carrier "action" to
details about weaponry, the role of carriers and their perceived
vulnerability in the modern navy—without letting the story lag.

Twomey has a talent for bringing potentially mind-numbing
figures to life by comparing them to things people can relate to:

*It costs $17 billion to put a carrier group to sea ... 10 times
the 1986 Philadelphia city budget; the cost of the three carrier
groups combined would be enough to pay for all the city services ... for 30 years.*

Such comparisons are especially valuable in a story loaded
with figures. Twomey's story is a classic example of how astute
reporting and writing can weave overwhelming facts, figures
and details into a captivating story.

Yet, surprisingly, Twomey had a great deal of difficulty initially getting started with this story. "I was based in Paris and I
remember gazing out over Paris for days, uncertain how you
could marry the theoretical debate over the value of aircraft carriers with the day to day action I had observed by being there,"
he explains.

"There didn't seem to be any connection between watching
an F-14 land and whether we ought to have aircraft carriers."

Finally, knowing he wanted to write the story in the "chapter" format he prefers and remembering how a small Soviet ship
had bird-dogged the huge carrier, Twomey decided to begin
each chapter with a specific scene and then flesh it out greatly.

Notice how he begins a chapter by pointing out how the *America*'s crew often gets lost on the ship—and then begins to describe the size of the carrier in great detail. He uses this tactic throughout.

The chapter approach is important to Twomey. "Each chapter was plotted out in advance as to what I wanted to accomplish," he stresses. "I actually outlined the piece. The opening line of each chapter is utterly independent of the closing line of the preceding one."

Twomey says he learned the chapter approach from an *Inquirer* magazine editor who once told him an apparently seamless 150-inch story was "too long for a reader to go underwater without coming up for air."

"She told me you have to write them in chapters."

Outside of deliberately striving for jarring transitions in this article, Twomey doesn't spend much time analyzing his literary techniques. An instinctive writer, Twomey says he puts things in his story if they "just feel right or sound right to me."

Hubba, hubba!

STEVE TWOMEY currently writes a twice-weekly metro column for *The Washington Post*. He holds a bachelor's degree in journalism from Northwestern University.

1988

JACQUI BANASZYNSKI

NOT ONLY WAS IT IMPRESSIVE for a paper the size of the *St. Paul Pioneer Press* to win two Pulitzer Prizes for features in a three-year period (the paper had been a finalist five times the previous nine years), but the Midwestern daily won for a pair of superlative features—on the plight of Midwest farmers and AIDS.

At the helm for both Pulitzers, highly-regarded Executive Editor Deborah Howell was effusive in her praise of Jacqui Banaszynski's 1987 three-part series on the death of AIDS victim Dick Hanson: "Many stories have been done on AIDS victims, but we have seen none that have approached the sensitivity, scope and impact of 'AIDS in the Heartland,'" she told the Pulitzer Board.

The paper had decided "to look for a provocative and poignant and telling diagnosis-to-death story," Banaszynski recalls. She says it was important to find a gay man because "I wanted to be able to write not just about a disease, but about THIS disease and all that went with it ... the prejudice, the fear, the distancing, the judging, the self-doubt, the legal and financial and moral consequences, the lifestyle and the love.

"But I also wanted someone who was quintessentially Minnesotan. A neighbor ... someone who, if they weren't gay, would be immediately accepted as 'one of ours.'"

Photographer Jean Pieri found Dick Hanson, a farmer and prominent political activist, who agreed to suffer the invasion of privacy that would inevitably result from such a story. Banaszynski says she was reluctant at first to accept Hanson because of his high public profile.

But Banaszynski is also pragmatic—and competitive. She was aware that Hanson was the first openly gay member of the Democratic National Committee. "And given our competitive posture with the *Minneapolis Star-Tribune*, I wasn't about to let [this story] get away," she says.

"Finally, one day, [Pieri] showed up at my desk and plopped a batch of photos in front of me and essentially dared me not to see the story," Banaszynski says. "There was magic in those photos."

Banaszynski and Pieri had worked together before, covering the famine in the Sudan three years earlier. That story made Banaszynski a Pulitzer Prize finalist in international reporting for her resulting "Trail of Tears" story. "[Pieri] sees with her soul," Banaszynski remarks. (Anyone who reads "AIDS in the Heartland" will quickly recognize the same trait in Jacqui Banaszynski.)

Banaszynski says she originally approached this story as little more than a regular profile but changed her mind during an off-the-record dinner with Pieri, Hanson and his companion, Bert Henningson. The two men started to talk intimately about their lives, fears and families. "It was after a long day of interviews, when my notebook was closed and Jean's cameras were in their case," Banaszynski remembers. She started to realize the couple were a real love story and (along with Pieri) began to return to the farm on weekends. Banaszynski later said her notebook "slowly began to fill with sprinklings of journalistic gold."

After the paper agreed to the diagnosis-to-death story, Banaszynski says she had to ask the men for the same permission and explain what a disruption it would make in their lives. "The toughest thing I've ever done in my career may have been to ride that elevator up to their weekday apartment [in a senior citizen high rise] and ask their permission to watch them die," she remembers.

Although the 17,000-plus word series was set for three parts, she admits "we planned very little." Banaszynski didn't know how long Hanson would live or how fast he would deteriorate. And although she prefers to see stories develop in her mind—and on the page—it wasn't possible in this case. "I confess to a severe feeling of uncertainty. To put it bluntly, I was lost."

Banaszynski credits the "gutsiness" of Deborah Howell and the trust of her assignment editor, Jack Rhodes, for letting her "roam without a map or a deadline." She also sought direction by discussing the story in the newsroom and with friends and editors.

Banaszynski says she finally decided to write the series in four parts: a "set up" beginning introducing the men and their

situation; a piece about their families and communities; an intimate look at their relationship and, by extension, gay love; and,
finally, the death story.

Only when Hanson's health began to fail did the urgency of
the story come front and center. "As became true throughout
'AIDS in the Heartland,' the story eventually forced the issue,"
Banaszynski feels.

Still lacking her lead for the entire story, Banaszynski recalls
seeing Hanson in the hospital. "I visited him and asked Bert to
bring a photo album with him. ... Photo albums are hard to
look at without thinking of the moments that come alive in each
picture," she explains. "That night, sitting in the hospital with
a storm raging, paging through that faded album, became the
lead." She feels the albums also forced the two men to look at
Hanson's deterioration and talk more powerfully about the
past, the future and his fears.

Still mulling over how best to handle the italic lead-ins,
Banaszynski retreated to the far edges of the newsroom, "struggling with what must have been my 50th attempt at a set up,
when I hear [fellow Pulitzer Prize-winner] John Camp grump
behind me. I look up, startled and defensive and angry, just in
time to hear Camp say, '[expletive deleted], I hope that's not
your lead. That's [expletive deleted]. You can do better than
that.'

"I raged. I yelled at him. I went into the ladies' room and
cried. I probably complained to the editor. I threw my hardcopy
around the room ... all because I knew he was right."

This would become yet another bit of magic for Banaszynski
in writing "AIDS in the Heartland," and force her to face an
important truth: "I had to let go of Dick and Bert, worrying
how they would see the story and squarely switch my allegiance
to my audience."

The next morning she sat down at her keyboard, a day
before deadline, and wrote:

Death is no stranger to the heartland.

"From then on," she says, "those italic scenesetters became
my own little road maps, voices of truth that led the way for me
as a writer and, I hoped, the readers, to get through the stories."

She admits the scenesetters helped summarize and establish
the voice of each story and often took longer to write than the

rest of the stories. They set her back on firm ground. "Ultimately, they were what gave the package coherence of voice and vision."

In April of 1988, six months after Hanson died (and six weeks before Henningson would die), Banaszynski was finishing final page proofs and writing cutlines for a Bert Henningson epilogue piece when she learned she had won the Pulitzer. A few weeks later, after an assignment in Greenland, Banaszynski took a phone call from Henningson's mother, Ailys Henningson. Bert had died, she said, would Jacqui be willing to come to a memorial service in tiny Ortonville, Minn., and carry his ashes there from Minneapolis?

Banaszynski recalls her editor, Jack Rhodes, sending her out for a walk and a cry before starting on the obituary. "Two days later, I drove to Ortonville with Bert's ashes, sat with the family at the service, then ... sitting at his desk in the bedroom where he lived in the last months of his life ... wrote my last story of Dick and Bert—about all the dignitaries and old farm friends who attended the memorial.

"The next day I flew to New York and received the Pulitzer."

AIDS in the Heartland

St. Paul Pioneer Press

June 21, July 12, August 9, 1987

CHAPTER I

June 21, 1987

Death is no stranger to the heartland. It is as natural as the seasons, as inevitable as farm machinery breaking down and farmers' bodies giving out after too many years of too much work.

But when death comes in the guise of AIDS, it is a disturbingly unfamiliar visitor, one better known in the gay districts and drug houses of the big cities, one that shows no respect for the usual order of life in the country.

The visitor has come to rural Glenwood, Minn.

Dick Hanson, a well-known liberal political activist who homesteads his family's century-old farm south of Glenwood, was diagnosed last summer with acquired immune deficiency syndrome. His partner of five years, Bert Henningson, carries the AIDS virus.

In the year that Hanson has been living—and dying—with AIDS, he has hosted some cruel companions: blinding headaches and failing vision, relentless nausea and deep fatigue, falling blood counts and worrisome coughs and sleepless, sweat-soaked nights.

He has watched as his strong body, toughened by 37 years on the farm, shrinks and stoops like that of an old man. He has weathered the family shame and community fear, the prejudice and whispered condemnations. He has read the reality in his partner's eyes, heard the death sentence from the doctors and seen the hopelessness confirmed by the statistics.

But the statistics tell only half the story—the half about dying.

Statistics fail to tell much about the people they represent. About people like Hanson—a farmer who has nourished life in the fields, a peace activist who has marched for a safer planet, an idealist and gay activist who has campaigned for social justice, and now an AIDS patient who refuses to abandon his own future, however long it lasts.

The statistics say nothing of the joys of a carefully tended vegetable garden and new kittens under the shed, of tender teasing and magic hugs. Of flowers that bloom brighter and birds that sing sweeter and simple pleasures grown profound against the backdrop of a terminal illness. Of the powerful bond between two people who pledged for better or worse and meant it.

"Who is to judge the value of life, whether it's one day or one week or one year?" Hanson said. "I find the quality of life a lot more important than the length of life."

Much has been written about the death that comes with AIDS, but little has been said about the living. Hanson and Henningson want to change that. They have opened their homes and their hearts to tell the whole story—beginning to end.

This is the first chapter.

The tiny snapshot is fuzzy and stained with ink. Two men in white T-shirts and corduroys stand at the edge of a barnyard, their muscled arms around each other's shoulders, a puzzled bull watching them from a field. The picture is overexposed, but the effect is pleasing, as if that summer day in 1982 was washed with a bit too much sun.

A summer later, the same men—one bearded and one not, one tall and one short—pose on the farmhouse porch in a mock American Gothic. Their pitchforks are mean looking and caked with manure. But their attempted severity fails; dimples betray their humor.

They are pictured together often through the years, draped with ribbons and buttons at political rallies, playing with their golden retriever, Nels, and, most frequently, working in their lavish vegetable garden.

The pictures drop off abruptly after 1985. One of the few shows the taller man, picking petunias from his mother's grave. He is startlingly thin by now; as a friend said, "like Gandhi after a long fast." His sun-bleached hair has turned dark, his bronze skin pallid. His body seems slack, as if it's caving in on itself.

The stark evidence of Dick Hanson's deterioration mars the otherwise rich memories captured in the photo album. But Hanson said only this:

"When you lose your body, you become so much closer to your spirit. It gives you more emphasis of what the spirit is, that we are more important than withering skin and bone."

Hanson sat with his partner, Bert Henningson, in the small room at Minneapolis' Red Door Clinic on April 8, 1986, waiting for the results of Hanson's AIDS screening test.

He wouldn't think about how tired he had been lately. He had spent his life hefting hay bales with ease, but now was having trouble hauling potato sacks at the Glenwood factory where he worked part time. He had lost 10 pounds, had chronic diarrhea and slept all afternoon. The dishes stayed dirty in the sink, the dinner uncooked, until Henningson got home from teaching at the University of Minnesota-Morris.

It must be the stress. His parents had been forced off the farm and now he and his brothers faced foreclosure. Two favorite uncles were ill. He and Henningson were bickering a lot, about the housework and farm chores and Hanson's dark mood.

He had put off having the AIDS test for months, and Henningson hadn't pushed too hard. Neither was eager to know.

Now, as the nurse entered the room with his test results, Hanson convinced himself the news would be good. It had been four years since he had indulged in casual weekend sex at the gay bathhouse in Minneapolis, since he and Henningson committed to each other. Sex outside their relationship had been limited and "safe," with no exchange of semen or blood. He had taken care of himself, eating homegrown food and working outdoors, and his farmer's body always had responded with energy and strength. Until now.

"I put my positive thinking mind on and thought I'd be negative," Hanson said. "Until I saw that red circle."

The reality hit him like a physical punch. As he slumped forward in shock, Henningson—typically pragmatic—asked the nurse to prepare another needle. He, too, must be tested.

Then Henningson gathered Hanson in his arms and said, "I will never leave you, Dick."

Hanson is one of 210 Minnesotans and 36,000 Americans who have been diagnosed with AIDS since the disease was identified in 1981. More than half of those patients already have died, and doctors say it is only a matter of time for the rest. The statistics show that 80 to 90 percent of AIDS sufferers die within two years of diagnosis; the average time of survival is 14 months after the first bout of pneumocystis—a form of pneumonia that brought Hanson to the brink of death last August and again in December.

"For a long time, I was just one of those statistics," Hanson said. "I was a very depressing person to be around. I wanted to get away from me."

He lost 20 more pounds in the two weeks after receiving his test results. One of his uncles died and, on the morning of the funeral, Hanson's mother died unexpectedly. Genevieve Hanson was 75 years old, a gentle but sturdy woman who was especially close to Dick, the third of her six children. He handled the arrangements, picking gospel hymns for the service and naming eight of her women friends as honorary pallbearers—a first in the history of their tiny country church.

But Hanson never made it to his mother's funeral. The day she was buried, he collapsed of exhaustion and fever. That night, Henningson drove him to Glenwood for the first of three hospitalizations—42 days worth—in 1986.

"Dick was real morbid last summer," Henningson said. "He led people to believe it was curtains, and was being very vague and dramatic. We all said to be hopeful, but it was as if something had gripped his psyche and was pulling him steadily downward week after week."

Hanson had given up, but Henningson refused to. He worked frantically to rekindle that spark of hope—and life. He read Hanson news articles about promising new AIDS drugs and stories of terminal cancer patients defying the odds. He brought home tapes about the power of positive thinking and fed Hanson healthy food. He talked to him steadily of politics and all the work that remained to be done.

He forced himself, and sometimes Hanson, to work in the garden, making it bigger than ever. They planted 58 varieties of vegetables in an organic, high-yield plot and christened it the Hope Garden.

But Hanson returned to the hospital in August, dangerously ill with the dreaded pneumonia. His weight had dropped to 112 from his usual 160. He looked and walked like an old-man version of himself.

"I had an out-of-body type experience there, and even thought I had died for a time," he said. "It was completely quiet and very calm and I thought, 'This is really nice.' I expected some contact with the next world. Then I had this conversation with God that it wasn't my time yet, and he sent me back."

Hanson was home in time to harvest the garden, and to freeze and can its bounty. He had regained some of his former spunk, and was taking an interest again in the world around him.

"I'd be sitting next to him on the couch, holding his hand, and once in a while he'd get that little smile on his face and nod like there was something to hold on to," Henningson said. "And a small beam of life would emerge."

A month later, Hanson's spirits received another boost when he was honored at a massive fund-raising dinner. Its sponsors included DFL notables—among them Gov. Rudy Perpich, Lt. Gov. Marlene Johnson, St. Paul Mayor George Latimer, Minneapolis Mayor Don Fraser and Congressmen Bruce Vento and Martin Sabo—and radical political activists Hanson had worked with over the years, farmers who had stood with him to fight farm foreclosures and the West Central power line, women who remembered his support during the early years of the women's movement, members of the gay and lesbian community and other AIDS sufferers.

What started as a farewell party, a eulogy of sorts, turned into a celebration of Hanson's life. Folk singer Larry Long played songs on an Indian medicine man's healing flute. Friends gathered in a faith circle to will their strength to Hanson. Dozens of people lined up to embrace Hanson and Henningson. For most, it was the first time they had touched an AIDS patient.

"People are coming through on this thing and people are decent," Hanson said. "We find people in all walks of life who are with us in this struggle. ... It's that kind of thing that makes it all worth it."

So when the pneumonia came back in December, this time with more force, Hanson was ready to fight.

"The doctor didn't give him any odds," Henningson said. Hanson was put on a respirator, funeral arrangements were discussed, estranged relatives were called to his bedside.

"He wrote me a note," Henningson said. " 'When can I get out of here?' He and I had never lied to each other, and I wasn't about to start. I said, 'You might be getting out of here in two or three days, but it might be God you're going to see. But there is a slim chance, so if you'll just fight ...' "

People from Hanson's AIDS support group stayed at the hospital round the clock, in shifts, talking to him and holding his hand as he drifted in and out of a coma. Friends brought Christmas to the stark hospital room: cards papered the walls and a giant photograph of Hanson's Christmas tree, the one left back at the farmhouse, was hung.

The rest was up to Hanson.

"I put myself in God's healing cocoon of love and had my miracle," he said. "I call it my Christmas miracle."

He was released from intensive care on Christmas Eve day and since has devoted his life to carrying a seldom-heard message of hope to other AIDS patients, to give them—and himself—a reason to live as science races to find a cure.

"I'd like to think that God has a special purpose for my life," he said. His smile under the thinning beard is sheepish; faith is personal, and easily misunderstood.

"I don't want to come across like Oral Roberts, but ... I believe that God can grant miracles. He has in the past and does now and will in the future. And maybe I can be one of those miracles, the one who proves the experts wrong."

Hanson has spent his life on the front line of underdog causes— always liberal, often revolutionary and sometimes unpopular.

"Somewhere along the line Dick was exposed to social issues and taught that we can make a difference," said Mary Stackpool, a neighbor and fellow political activist. "That's what Dick has been all about—showing that one person can make a difference."

Hanson put it in terms less grand: "You kind of have to be an eternal optimist to be a farmer. There's something that grows more each year than what you put into the farm. ... I've always been involved in trying to change things for the better."

He was born into the national prosperity of 1950 and grew up through the social turmoil of the 1960s. A fifth-grade teacher sparked his enthusiasm in John F. Kennedy's presidential campaign. He was 13 when his father joined the radical National Farmers Organization, took the family to picket at the Land O' Lakes plant in nearby

Alexandria and participated in a notorious milk-dumping action.

He later led rural campaigns for Eugene McCarthy, George McGovern, Mark Dayton, and his current hero, Jesse Jackson. He led protests against the Vietnam War and was a conscientious objector. He organized rival factions to try to stop construction of the high-voltage power line that snakes through western Minnesota.

He was an early member of the farm activist group Groundswell, fighting to stop a neighbor's foreclosure one day, his own family's the next. The 473-acre Hanson farm has been whittled to 40 by bankruptcy; Hanson and Henningson are struggling to salvage the farmhouse and some surrounding wetlands.

He has been arrested five times, staged a fast to draw attention to the power line protest and stood at the podium of the 1980 DFL district convention to announce—for the first time publicly—that he was gay. That same year, he was elected one of the first openly gay members of the Democratic National Committee and, in 1984, made an unsuccessful bid for the party's nomination for Congress from the Second District. In 1983, he and Henningson were photographed in their fields for a 1983 *Newsweek* magazine story about gays responding to the AIDS crisis; neither knew at the time they carried the virus.

"He just throws himself into a cause and will spare nothing," Stackpool said. "He will expose himself totally to bring out the desired good."

Now the cause is AIDS. The struggle is more personal, the threat more direct. But for Hanson, it has become yet another opportunity to make a difference.

"He's handling this just as he would anything else—with strength and lots of courage and hope," said Amy Lee, another longtime friend and fellow activist. "And with that pioneering spirit. If there's anything he can do, any way he can help other victims, any time he can speak—he'll go for it."

Hanson has become one of the state's most visible AIDS patients. He and Henningson are frequently interviewed for news stories, were the subject of a recent four-part series on KCMT-TV in Alexandria and speak at AIDS education seminars in churches and schools throughout the state. Last month, Hanson addressed the state Senate's special informational meeting on AIDS.

"I want to take the mask off the statistics and say we are human beings and we have feelings," he said. "I want to say there is life after AIDS."

Rather than retreat to the anonymity of the big city, as many AIDS sufferers do, Hanson has maintained a high political profile in Pope

County. He is chairman of the DFL Party in Senate District 15. He and Henningson continue to do business with area merchants and worship weekly at the country church of Hanson's childhood, Barsness Lutheran.

"I've always been a very public person and I've had no regrets," Hanson said. "One thing my dad always emphasized was the principle that honesty was the most important thing in life."

Hanson and Henningson use their story to personalize the AIDS epidemic and to debunk some of the stereotypes and myths about AIDS and its victims. They are farmers who have milked cows, slopped hogs and baled hay like everyone else. Their politics and sexual orientation may disturb some. But their voices and values are more familiar, and perhaps better understood, than those of some of their urban counterparts.

"It makes people aware that it can happen here," said Sharon Larson, director of nursing at Glacial Ridge Hospital in Glenwood.

That honesty has carried a price. A conservative Baptist minister from Glenwood criticized their lifestyle at a community forum and again in a column in the *Pope County Tribune*. Some of Hanson's relatives were upset by the Alexandria television show and demanded he keep his troubling news to himself. There have been rumblings in his church from people concerned about taking communion with him, and a minor disturbance erupted in a Glenwood school when his niece was teased about him.

But his connections also carry clout.

"It brings it a little closer home to the guys in the Capitol who control the purse strings," a fellow AIDS patient said.

When they speak, Hanson and Henningson touch on a variety of topics: the need for national health insurance to guarantee equitable care, the cruelty of policies that force AIDS patients into poverty before they are eligible for medical assistance, the need for flex-time jobs so AIDS sufferers can continue to be productive, the imperative of safe sex.

They also stress the personal aspects of the disease: the need for patients to be touched rather than shunned, the importance of support from family and friends and, most dear to Hanson, the healing powers of hope.

"I know there are some who die because they give up," he said. "They have no hope, no reason to fight. Everything they're faced with is so desperate and dismal. ... I believe the biggest obstacle for us who have AIDS or an AIDS-related complex is fighting the fear and anxiety we have over the whole thing. Every positive thing, every bit of hope is something to hold on to."

Next month, Hanson and Henningson will celebrate five years together, perhaps with a gathering of friends and an exchange of rings. They exchanged vows privately that first summer while sitting in their car under the prairie night.

"We asked the blessing of the spirit above," Hanson said. "It was a pretty final thing."

At first blush, they seem an unlikely couple.

"Bert the scholar and Dick the activist ... In some ways they're just worlds apart," Stackpool said. "But politics brought them together, and now they take delight in those differences and in their special traits. They've figured out things many married couples never come close to figuring out."

Henningson is bookish and intense, a Ph.D. in international trade, a professor and essayist. He is a doer and organizer. He charts the monthly household budget on his Apple computer, itemizing everything from mortgage payments to medicine to cat food. He sets a hearty dinner table, which is cleared and washed as soon as the last bit of food is gone. He buries himself in his work during the week, becomes reclusive when he retreats to the farm on weekends and has worked hard over the years to control an explosive temper.

Hanson is more social, an easygoing, non-stop talker with a starburst of interests. He spent 12 years detouring through social activism before finally earning a bachelor's degree in political science at the university's Morris campus. He has a political junkie's memory for names, dates and events, thrills in company and is quick to offer refreshments, having inherited his mother's belief in friendship through food.

But they also have much in common.

Henningson, 40, grew up on a farm near Graceville, in neighboring Big Stone County. His life paralleled Hanson's in many respects: the radical farm movement, anti-war protests, involvement in liberal political campaigns.

Both suppressed their homosexuality until they were almost 30. Hanson kept so active with politics and the farm that he didn't have time for a social life. After acknowledging his homosexuality, his sexual life involved weekend excursions to the Twin Cities for anonymous encounters at the gay bathhouse.

"I had to taste all the fruit in the orchard," he said. "I had some real special relationships, but if they suggested it just be us I felt trapped, like they were closing in on me."

Henningson threw himself into graduate school, tried marriage and took on a demanding career in Washington, D.C., as an aide to former U.S. Rep. Richard Nolan. He divorced and returned to Minnesota, where he enrolled in a human sexuality program at the University of Minnesota. He had three homosexual involvements before meeting Hanson at a political convention.

"There were some major forces working in the universe that were compelling us together," Henningson said. "I don't know that we even had much to say about it. I've always believed in serendipity, but I also feel you have to give serendipity a little help. So I didn't sit back and wait for Dick to call—I called him."

Any doubts Hanson had about their relationship were squelched by his mother. She visited the farmhouse one Sunday morning with freshly baked caramel rolls, which she served Hanson and Henningson in bed. Henningson was accepted as part of the family, moved to the farm and eventually assumed financial responsibility for the family's farm operations.

"It was so good to work together, to sweat together, to farrow those sows and help the sows have those little piglets," Henningson said. "We literally worked dawn to dusk."

That hard but somewhat idyllic life has been altered drastically by AIDS. Hanson does what he can, when he can, perhaps baking cookies or doing the laundry. But the burden of earning an income, running the house and caring for Hanson has fallen heavily on Henningson's shoulders.

Hanson's medical bills—totalling more than $50,000 so far—are covered by welfare. Henningson's temporary job at the state Department of Agriculture, where he writes farm policy proposals, pays their personal bills, helps pay their apartment rent in the Twin Cities so Hanson can be near medical care during the week and allows them to keep the farmhouse.

"Dick's optimism is fine," Henningson said. "But you have to help optimism along now and then with a little spade work. I ended up doing all of the work with no help. What could have happened is that I could have grown resentful and blamed the victim.

"But I tried to put myself in his shoes—having pneumonia twice— and with all my anger and short temper, could I live with that? Could I even get through that? I'd probably have the strength to go to a field and dig a hole and when the time came crawl in and bury myself. But I don't know if I'd have the strength to do what he did."

So, their commitment to each other remains absolute, perhaps strengthened by facing a crisis together.

"When you know that somebody's going to stand by you, and when they prove that they will, when they go through what Bert's gone through this past year in putting up with me ... you just know it's very, very special what you have," Hanson said.

Each week, Hanson checks in at the AIDS clinic at Hennepin County Medical Center. He and Henningson make the three-hour drive to Minneapolis every Monday and spend their week in the Twin Cities. Henningson has work through June at the Agriculture Department. Hanson's full-time job is AIDS.

He has his blood tested to determine his white blood cell count—his body's natural defense system. It often is below 1,000; a healthy person's count would be closer to 5,000.

He has a physical exam, chats with two or three doctors, gives encouragement to fellow patients and collects hugs from the nursing staff. He is a favorite with the social workers, who tease him about his lack of interest in the women who flock to his examination room each week for a visit.

He does weekly inhalation therapy, breathing an antibiotic into his lungs to ward off the dreaded pneumonia. Then he buses to St. Paul for a long, healing massage from one of several local massage therapists who donate time to AIDS patients.

Thursday mornings find him at the University of Minnesota Hospital and Clinic for eye treatments. Doctors inject medicine directly into his eyeball to thwart a virus that is attacking his vision. Sometimes the needle punctures a blood vessel, leaving Hanson with bright red patches in his eyes.

On Thursday nights, he and Henningson attend an AIDS support group meeting, where as many as 30 patients, relatives and friends gather to share comfort and information.

For eight months, Hanson has taken AZT, or azidothymidine, an experimental drug believed to prolong life for AIDS sufferers. He takes other drugs to counter the nausea caused by AZT's high toxicity, and he is watched closely for bone marrow suppression. He uses various underground treatments, all with his doctor's knowledge. He rubs solvent on his skin to try to stimulate a response from his immune system, and spreads a home-brewed cholesterol agent on his toast, hoping it will help render the virus inert.

He watches his diet to prevent diarrhea and takes various prescription drugs for depression and anxiety.

His spare time, what there is of it, is devoured by long waits for the bus or slow walks to his various appointments. He naps often to keep his energy level up and spends evenings watching the Twins on TV. Reading has become painful for him, straining his eyes and making him dizzy.

"It comes back and back and back many times," he said. "Is this my total life? Has the illness become such an all-encompassing thing that my life will never be judged by anything but this brand of AIDS?"

Weekends are spent on the farm, where Hanson often can be found kneeling in his flower beds. The impatiens, moss roses and sweet Williams are planted especially thick this summer; Hanson was eager to see their cheerful pinks and reds cover the crumbling stone foundation of the old farmhouse. He insists on having fresh flowers in the house every day, even dandelions and thistles. Once, after pranksters broke the peony bushes in the church cemetery, Hanson gathered up the broken blossoms and took them home, placing them around the house in shallow bowls of water.

Or he can be found singing in the empty silo, practicing hymns for Sunday's church service. His voice is sweet and natural, with a good range. It is inherited, he says, from his mother, who sang to him when he was in the womb and tuned in opera on the radio in the farm kitchen when he was a youngster. He has sung for his brothers' weddings but is better, he says, at funerals.

On hot summer nights, he and Henningson sleep in twin beds in a screened porch upstairs. The room is kept cool by towering shade trees and constant breezes blowing off the marsh that winds in front of the house. From there, the men note the comings and goings of their neighbors: egrets and blue herons, Canada geese that feed on what Henningson calls Green Scum Pond, a doe and her buff-colored fawn. There is an owl in the nearby woods, a peregrine falcon nesting in the farmhouse eaves and an unseen loon that sings to them at dusk.

If the weekend is slow, the weather is mild and his energy is high, Hanson can be found in a dinghy somewhere on Lake Minnewaska, the sparkling centerpiece of Pope County. He's a skilled fisherman, and remembers weekends when he would haul home a catch of 200 pan fish for one of his mother's famous fries.

"I find that going out in the garden is a good way to get away from things, or going fishing, or just visiting with people and talking," he said. "I don't want my whole life to be branded by AIDS."

Hanson awakes in the Minneapolis apartment on a recent morning to the sound of his mother's voice.

"It wasn't part of any dream," he said. "Just her voice, crystal clear, calling."

He has been running a fever for several days and suffering headaches. His white blood cell count has dropped precipitously. His chatter, usually cheerful, is tinged with fear.

"I got pretty emotional about it," he said. "But Bert held me and said, 'Don't be afraid. Don't fight it.' And I remember a year ago when I was so sick, and she was reaching to me, and I was so scared I was almost pushing her away. And Bert said not to fight it, to let her comfort me even if she's reaching to me on a level we don't understand. ...

"There are days I think I'm just going to get out of this, put this whole thing behind me and get a job and go on with my life again. Then I have a rough day like this and I have to look at things much more realistically."

Hanson seldom talks of death. When his health is stable, there seems little point. He has beaten the odds before and will, he says, again.

"Intermittently, there has been some denial," said his physician, Dr. Margaret Simpson, director of the sexually transmitted disease clinic at Hennepin County Medical Center. "That's not too surprising. When you're feeling good, it's easy to think this isn't true.

"But he's deteriorating again, and it's worrisome. I don't make predictions, but I think now in terms of weeks and months rather than months and years."

Hanson senses that urgency. But he remains a fighter. His attitude, he says, is not one of delusion but of defiance.

"I think I'll know when the time is right and it's coming," he said. "Should it be, I'm ready to meet my maker. But I'm not ready to give up and say there's nothing that will turn around so I can live."

A week later, Hanson is in the hospital. The headaches are worse, and doctors do a painful spinal tap to determine if the AIDS virus has entered his brain. His white blood cell count is dangerously low, but a transfusion is too risky.

It is the first hospitalization in six months, and only an overnight stay for tests, but it evokes painful memories of the past and fears for the future.

Henningson telephones Hanson's sister.

"I told Mary it may be only three or four months and we have to respond to him accordingly," he said. "Not treat him as someone who's going to die, but accord him the time and attention you want. We can't just say, 'See you next week.' It's not a matter of dealing with certitude anymore, but a great deal of uncertainty about where it's going to lead."

Hanson is quiet this evening and seems distracted. The Twins game plays silently on the hospital room TV, but relief pitcher Jeff Reardon is losing and Hanson pays only passing interest. He gets up once during the evening to vomit and occasionally presses his hand to his temple. But he never mentions the nausea, the throbbing headache or the pain from the spinal tap.

Henningson sits next to him on the bed and thumbs through their photo album, recalling lighter times.

Suddenly, Hanson waves his hand vaguely, at the room, at his life. "I'll miss all this," he confided. "I'll just miss all these wonderful people."

Then he and Henningson discuss—gently—the logistics of his death. Should he be placed in a nursing home if he becomes invalid? Should life-sustaining measures be used if he falls into a coma again? Should he donate his body to research?

The morbid conversation is held in matter-of-fact tones and seems to soothe Hanson. It is Henningson's way of pulling out the emotions, the soft rage and futility that Hanson otherwise would keep tucked inside.

"Talking about things like that helps you understand your mortality, that it may not be much longer," Henningson said. "And that helps relieve your fears. Dick's fears are not so much for himself as for me. Will I live out here all by myself? Will I find someone else? I say don't worry about that, it's out of your control."

But Henningson, too, is shaken. He sits at the window next to Hanson's hospital bed, and holds his hand. Finally, he abandons the diversionary talk and cries. He is worried about losing the farm, about the political hassles involved in getting housing assistance, about getting a job after his contract with the state expires, about not having enough time left with Hanson.

And he can't help but worry about the AIDS virus in his body and his own health prospects. Although he guards his health carefully and is optimistic about medical progress on the AIDS front, he fears that the stress of caring for Hanson is taking its toll. He watches Hanson, and wonders if he is watching his own future.

Then he comforts himself with a wish.

"I want to be cremated and have my ashes thrown in Big Stone Lake. And from there I would flow to the Minnesota River, down to the Mississippi River, all the way to the Gulf. And I'll hit the Gulf Stream and travel the world.

"And I told Dick if he'd like to be cremated, they could put him in Lake Minnewaska, and he would flow to the Chippewa River and then into the Minnesota and the Mississippi and to the Gulf and around the world. And at some point we would merge and we'd be together forever."

He stops, perhaps embarrassed.

"You can't control what happens to people after they're dead," he said. "But even if it doesn't happen, it's a lovely, consoling thought."

CHAPTER II

July 12, 1987

Dick Hanson used to talk about being the first to survive AIDS; now he talks about surviving another week.

After a year-long battle with acquired immune deficiency syndrome, the Glenwood, Minn., farmer's health is deteriorating rapidly.

"We talk about holding on," said Bert Henningson, Hanson's partner of five years, who also carries the AIDS virus. "But we have to recognize what may be reality and prepare ourselves for it."

The funeral arrangements are checked and rechecked. Visits from family and friends take on more urgency. Precious moments alone, just Hanson and Henningson, are guarded and savored. Where once Hanson threw himself into radical political activism, he now hoards his dwindling strength.

Hanson has taken his battle with AIDS to the public, exposing his own dreams and despairs so that others will feel less alone. He wants others to learn from his loss. But the spotlight on Hanson is harsh, and sometimes catches unwilling players in its glare—relatives who would rather bear their grief in private, others who are angered and embarrassed by their connection with him and some who want no part of him at all.

"This whole illness is a test of humanity, of how we treat our fellow human beings," Hanson said. "If we do the leper thing, and put people away, that's one judgment. But if we do everything we can to give comfort and hope and try to find a cure, that's another judgment."

Chapter Two of Hanson's story is about that test of humanity.

Growing up, the men were like twins. Dick Hanson is barely a year younger than his brother Grant. They shared farm chores; Dick was a patient milker and had a gentle way with the animals, while Grant was a tinkerer who kept the machinery tuned and responsive.

They double-dated in high school, although the socializing never seemed to hold much interest for Dick. They even looked alike, with the same sandy hair that turned lighter in the sun.

"He looks different now, of course," Grant Hanson said.

At 38, Grant Hanson is sturdy from years of physical labor. His hair and beard are bleached from the summer, and his face carries a warm, healthy tan.

But Dick Hanson, 37, is wasting away from AIDS. His frail body is a sallow white, his skin seems translucent, his hair and beard have thinned and turned dark. He bears little resemblance to the ruddy, full-faced man who stands side-by-side with Grant and other relatives in family photographs.

And appearance isn't all that has changed because of AIDS.

Although Grant Hanson remains close to his brother and checks regularly on his condition, AIDS has created an unwelcome barrier between them.

"There's a paranoia about AIDS," Grant Hanson said. "Some people are certain the AIDS virus will live on a doorknob for days on end or you'll catch AIDS from mosquitoes. My wife is very fearful of the disease."

As a result of that fear, Grant Hanson's five children, ages 2 to 12, haven't been allowed to spend time with their Uncle Dick since he became seriously ill last fall. The family has visited the farm only once in recent months; the children stayed in the car while Dick Hanson chatted with them through an open window.

Dick Hanson seldom speaks of such rifts. He prefers to focus on the many kindnesses shown him by family and friends, and to dismiss any unpleasantries, blaming them on misinformation rather than maliciousness.

But he mentioned it recently at an AIDS education seminar in nearby Starbuck, when someone in the audience quoted a Christian radio doctor who said AIDS could be spread by casual contact.

"Because of things like that, I have five nieces and nephews who I can't see, who used to love to come out to the farm and enjoy being with Bert and me and doing things with us," Hanson said. "For a year now they haven't been allowed to do that. And it's one of the things I have missed most in the last year—getting to know these young people—and it has hurt me deeply. I can only hope it will change."

Hanson has become one of Minnesota's most visible AIDS patients, trying to educate others about the disease. That visibility has carried a price.

Some of his relatives have been hassled by gossip, letter-writers have accused him of flaunting his homosexuality, and a few family members are furious with him for holding the Hanson name up to public scrutiny.

But, on the whole, Glenwood and Minnesota are passing Hanson's test of humanity.

"You have to deal with so many different aspects of life when you're dealing with this, you're bound to run into some resistance or ignorance," Hanson said. "There are simple-minded people, and I don't bother to waste my time with them. But by and large, people are caring and giving and compassionate if given a chance."

Hanson says he expected no less, although he and Henningson knew they risked rejection by making their situation public. They have been featured in news stories and have spoken at AIDS education forums across the state and at the Minnesota Legislature.

"Our friends told us we were crazy, that we'd be lynched and branded by the hysterics," Hanson said. "But we had to balance that off with what we see as our part of it, what I like to think is the truth."

The slurs that come to him third-hand are more than offset by the favors he receives directly.

He and Henningson recently received a $50 check from strangers—two closeted gay men from Minneapolis who heard about them and wanted to help. Other strangers have sent smaller amounts—$5 or $10—or invaluable words of encouragement. A friend from the Glenwood area called Henningson last week to offer her savings if they needed it.

Neighbors sometimes mow the lawn, and others stop by to leave food in the freezer. Pearl Brosvick, Hanson's neighbor and godmother, brings rhubarb pie on the weekends and homemade doughnuts like those Hanson's mother made.

Brosvick, a childless 73-year-old widow, also sent Hanson a note last winter thanking him for escorting her to communion at Chippewa Falls Lutheran Church. Area residents had just received the news that Hanson had AIDS.

"I don't know that much about AIDS," she said. "And I don't really approve of homosexuality. I don't know if they're born this way and they can't function any other way.

"But we all do things we shouldn't and we can't judge each other."

Several local ministers have risked the wrath of their congregations by supporting Hanson. The Rev. Wayne Mensing of Immanuel and Indherred Lutheran churches in Starbuck urged people at an AIDS seminar to "take a stand and see these people as children of God and be with them in community." And the Rev. Marlin Johnson of Trinity Lutheran Church in Cyrus thanked Hanson and Henningson for sharing their story.

"Whether you agree or disagree or approve or disapprove is irrelevant," Johnson said. "This is such a big problem, you can't go running away off into the boondocks as if it didn't exist. If God can work good out of evil, then we are being blessed by these two fellows because they are so willing to be vocal about it."

Hanson cherishes such comments, little signs that people are listening and learning.

"I am so proud of this rural community," he said. "I think in the big cities it's very easy to get lost in the shuffle and impersonal aspect of the thing. But in the rural area, if you've given to the community all your life as I have, there's a level of decency. If a farmer gets sick or his barn burns down, the neighbors get together and bring food. There's a time to come together, even if you don't like the person, no matter what the differences.

"Not a lot of people understand or agree with my lifestyle, but they understand that sense of coming together and that sense of community. That, for me, makes life worth living."

Allen Hanson, 69, drives out to the farmhouse on a recent night to visit his son. They talk of the usual things—the family, the failing farm economy, their mutual dream of someday seeing Jesse Jackson in the White House.

But as he prepares to leave, Allen Hanson tells a strange story, about an age gone by when his own father was dying of inoperable cancer, and about a faith healer who came to town and called upon God, and how doctors later saved his father. And about a time when Allen Hanson himself was sick, stricken with gallstones, and the faith healer again called upon God, and the stones passed and he finally was freed of pain.

Allen Hanson stops his story and looks at his son, lying still as death on the couch.

"I just know if I could find someone like that," he said, "they could help the doctors and take away this illness of yours."

Dick Hanson stands up then, mustering a strength he hasn't felt for days, and clasps his father's hand in both of his. They stay that way for a long, awkward moment—two proud Norwegian farmers who seldom shared a handshake in all the years they shared a life.

Before letting go of his hand, Dick Hanson tells his father how good it is to see him, and how much he appreciates his concern.

It was the first time Allen Hanson had spoken with his son, even obliquely, about AIDS.

"We never discussed it," the elder Hanson said. "I can't explain why. ... I don't believe in this crying and everything. You got to take the good with the bad in life."

He sits this evening in the living room of a modest rambler near downtown Glenwood, where he moved after losing much of the family's century-old farm to foreclosure and selling the rest to his sons in an attempt to salvage the homestead.

He lives there with two of his five sons, Leland and Tom, and with Leland's wife and teenage daughter. Allen Hanson's only daughter, Mary Hanson-Jenniges, has walked over from her nearby apartment, and son Grant stops by on his bicycle. Allen Hanson's oldest son, John, lives with his family in Brooten, some 25 miles away.

It is an uncomfortable evening for Allen Hanson. He seems pleased by the company, but troubled by the conversation. He says he is confused about the strange and frightening disease that has attacked Dick, his third child, and that has fractured his family.

Allen Hanson says he never thought much about his son being gay, that it didn't really matter. Nor does he mind that Dick Hanson has taken his homosexuality and his fight with AIDS public. None of the townsfolk have said anything to him about it and, if they do, he's used to controversy.

As one of the first farmers in the area to try contour plowing, he was ridiculed by traditionalists who "probably thought I'd been drinking." As an early leader of the radical National Farmers Organization, he alienated neighbors who belonged to the conservative Farm Bureau.

But this issue is different, beyond Allen Hanson's understanding or control. "I'm sitting here thinking of what the heck I done wrong," he said. "The last year I lost everything I got ... the farm, my wife, everything."

He doesn't mention Dick directly in the litany of loss. But he spreads the family photo albums on his lap, pointing out the prouder times, the times that made more sense. Rather than talk about the son who is gay and dying of AIDS, he talks about the son who was, like him, a promising farmer and avid fisherman.

"Those pictures in there, years ago, he was built real good," he said. "He was strong. He could handle those bales like a good, healthy person, and he had good arms on him.

"And I can't help but think of the fun Dickie and I had fishing on this lake. We caught some fish there, I tell you ... Dickie and I haven't fished together for a couple years now."

He talks of the time Jesse Jackson visited Glenwood and drank some of his wife's good coffee, and the time he rode with the WCCO-TV helicopter to cover a story in the area. He brings out his daughter's wedding picture and many of the awards he won as a young farmer—anything to keep the conversation on safe, pleasant terrain.

But the anguish that has torn his family apart is not to be mended by nostalgia. Allen Hanson's memories are lost beneath the squabbling voices of his children—voices of grief, anger and resentment.

"You can't understand what this is doing to us as a family," Tom Hanson said. "It split us, big time."

The children—Dick Hanson's four brothers and one sister—share their stories reluctantly.

Each has been touched by AIDS in varying degrees and ways, depending on their ties to their brother. Their positions polarized after Hanson's story was aired on Alexandria television in April and, more recently, was covered by Twin Cities newspapers and TV stations. Between Hanson's avid crusade for AIDS education and the fishbowl existence of small-town living, they are robbed of the luxury of private emotions.

So they talk, some out of compassion for other families visited by AIDS, some out of a simple desire to support their brother, some out of a need to distance themselves from him, some out of anger at him for bringing his suffering—and its accompanying stigma—home.

Dick Hanson is painfully aware of the family's turmoil, but if he has criticisms or conflicts, he keeps them to himself.

"But I can't shelter people from reality," he said. "Even the people you love the most, sometimes you have to hurt them. I have to do what I think is right."

Tom Hanson, 28, is the youngest of Dick Hanson's brothers, a big, brusque man who family members say is prone to outbursts of rage. He lives in his father's house in town, having sold his dairy herd as part of a government buy-out. He still grows crops on 190 acres of the family's farmstead.

"Dickie helped me get the farm, the one thing I've always wanted," he said. "It's just like a twist in my stomach. It hurts because he helped me so much. But just because somebody does something good ... Every day something happens and I get madder and madder and madder."

Tom Hanson is angry at Dick Hanson for making news of such a shameful disease, at his sister, Mary, for siding with Dick, at his brother Grant because "he's not man enough" to say that homosex-

uality is wrong, at a local minister for refusing to denounce homosexuality from the pulpit, at the media for exploiting his family.

"I feel Dickie is helping the public by talking about this," he said.
"But he could have done it without bringing his name into it or his
picture or the town. This is not fair what he's doing to the family... .
It's not easy being single trying to go through this, having girls come
up and say, 'His brother's gay and he has AIDS. Is he gay, too?'

"At least I'm polite enough to call them 'gays.' And I still respected Dickie as my brother for years after I found out he was that way.
I've always been nice to Dickie. When he came out of the hospital, he
said he'd like to go ice fishing. So I moved the icehouse closer to shore
and drilled some holes for him and I tried to be nice. And in return,
the favor I get back is he comes on TV without consulting all the family, with no consideration what it'd be like in a small town. He never
stopped to think of the innocent people who would be suffering for
his glory."

He is cut short by his sister. The two haven't spoken for weeks,
their relationship strained by her steadfast loyalty to Dick.

"Can I ask you one question?" Mary Hanson-Jenniges is near
tears, her voice low and controlled. "Have you thought about what
life will be like without Dick? What will you complain about when
he's gone?"

She is 32, has a degree in psychology from St. Cloud State
University and works as a social service director at a Glenwood nursing home. She lived at Dick Hanson's farm for a time before she was
married, and later she and her husband were frequent visitors with
their lively daughter, now 2.

The baby no longer goes to the farm for fear she'll pass some childhood illness on to her uncle. Hanson-Jenniges often cooks for her
brother, making meals from their mother's recipes—glorified rice and
custard and other bland foods that Hanson can digest.

"As a result of my supporting Dick I've been shunned by some of
the family," she said. "I probably would have felt more comfortable
if he had not been public, because I'm more a private person. I can't
say I don't worry about what people think, because I do. But I'm
proud that Dick is my brother and has the courage to stand up and
do what he does.

"In the family, I was the first to know. I went through a mourning
period when he told me. I cried and cried and cried. I figured that was
the worst thing that could ever happen to me. Then three weeks later
my mom died.

"And for a while, there were probably a couple of months where

I hadn't adjusted to Mom's death, I almost felt angry at Dick for having AIDS. I just lost Mom and now the next most important person in the world may leave me, too. I think Grant is hurting inside just like I am right now. You start grieving before somebody's gone."

Grant Hanson is a quiet man who observes the rest of the family's emotion without comment, refusing to be drawn into the fray. "At this point in time, everybody's got their mind pretty well set," he said. "Being mad doesn't change anything."

Grant, a mechanic and a veteran of the U.S. Navy Seabees, is routinely tested for AIDS twice a year when he gives blood and reads everything he can about the disease. AIDS is his concern, he says, not people's sexual preferences.

"If there's truly a body chemistry so that there's a sexual desire in Dick for another man equal to mine for a woman, then I can understand that," he said.

Grant Hanson is careful not to say too much; he wants to protect his own family's privacy as much as possible. But he acknowledges that his affection for Dick Hanson is at odds with his wife's fear of AIDS, and their five children are caught in the middle.

"My desire would be that between what they hear at home and what they hear from the hygiene types at school, they'll make wise choices," he said. "It reaches a point where you let go of them on the bicycle, and it reaches a point where you can't control everything they do. You just hope they'll carry on what you've tried to teach them.

"And you pray for the people with AIDS. They say there is no cure, that the likelihood of a cure in this century is next to nil, so you just pray for time."

Leland Hanson, the fourth son, is 35 and unemployed. His wife works as a medical secretary and they are active in a Lutheran church in Sunberg. He says he is a recovering alcoholic; if he can overcome his desire for alcohol, he believes his brother can overcome his desire for homosexual relations.

"You look at where the gays were marching in the streets, and right in the Bible it says you'll die and your blood will be upon you," he said. "And AIDS is now in the blood. God will take that for just so long. He's still in control and now they're dying and there's not a damn thing we can do about it.

"If I was given a 95 percent chance of dying, and I'm dying from a sin that I committed, and God gave me another chance to live, I'd be hollering at the top of my lungs that this is wrong. But that's not what he did. God didn't give him a second chance so he could splatter his name across the paper.

"I went down to my church and the first two people I met said, 'Is Dick Hanson your brother?' And I walked away. Enough is enough."

John Hanson, 43, is the oldest and, he says, "the mediator between the whole bunch." Because he lives in another town, he is less entangled in family politics. He is a part-time farmer who buys hay and straw from area farmers and hauls it to dairy operations and to the race track in Shakopee. He sees Dick Hanson every few weeks when he brings his two teenage sons to the farm to do chores.

"I feel sorry for him. He seems to be a fairly good person. He's always been real nice to my family.

"But I wish they just wouldn't have so much publicity. We got kids in school and there's always some who pick on them, and this is an excuse. Down in the Cities, there's this gay business going on and they don't think too much of it. But up here in the small communities, it becomes a big deal.

"There are a few who ask, 'Are you related to that guy up in Glenwood?' My sons tell them we're not related."

There is talk. In a town like Glenwood, population 2,500, there is bound to be.

Much of the talk is rumor and unfounded, based on fears about AIDS and how it is spread.

Like the time Mary Hanson-Jenniges was chatting with a nursing home official from a neighboring county. He mentioned there was an AIDS patient in Pope County who died last winter. He was speaking of Dick Hanson.

Or the time Hanson-Jenniges was asked by a colleague if, because of her brother, she had been tested for AIDS. Flabbergasted, she didn't answer. But when a second person asked her the same question, she was ready.

"No, I haven't," she said. "I don't have sex with my brother or share needles with him."

But it is mostly just talk.

"Dick's problem hasn't been a big community issue," said John Stone, owner and editor of the local weekly newspaper, the *Pope County Tribune*. There has been no coverage of Hanson's illness or his public speeches in the *Tribune*.

"Dick has not been a real active member of this community for many, many years, and a lot of people have no idea who he is," Stone said. "I'm not sure people understand a person like him, who puts issues ahead of his own personal life. He's a crusader of sorts."

"The community interest is zip," agreed Gary Wenschlag, principal of Glenwood High School. "Most people feel he's just one of those weird people and they're not going to deal with it. It's like any other issue ... a few get right in the middle of it and the rest stay home and mow their lawns and go on about their lives."

Wenschlag spoke to a group of junior high school students about AIDS in April after Hanson's niece, a seventh-grader, left school for half a day when she was teased about him.

"Kids were teasing her that she had AIDS and that her uncle was a sexual pervert and things like that," he said. "The focus was more on the sexuality of it than on AIDS.

"So I told them to think of it from their perspective—maybe you have an uncle, or brother or someone who isn't exactly the person you might want them to be. And I tried to clarify the issue. She has an uncle who's gay; that's a fact. And he has AIDS; that's a fact. And when you go into the ninth grade, he'll be dead. That sounds pretty brutal, but that's the way it is and we need to confront that."

Hanson's presence has forced other townspeople to confront AIDS, too. He has been admitted without question at Glenwood's Glacial Ridge Hospital, although the medical staff wore gowns, gloves and masks when treating him—something that seldom occurs in Twin Cities hospitals except when doctors or nurses are drawing blood.

"People may have been a little skittish at first, but no one refused to treat him," said Sharon Larson, the hospital's director of nursing.

Hanson's family dentist cleared his calendar of patients to accommodate Hanson's need for dental work one day last year—and to avoid any panic among other clients. He continues to check on Hanson's health, and has offered to work Saturdays, if necessary, to treat Hanson. But he asked that his name not be published because he fears he will lose business if townspeople know he is treating an AIDS patient.

Local health officials capitalized on the curiosity surrounding Hanson by organizing AIDS education seminars in Glenwood and neighboring Starbuck that drew, combined, about 250 people. Hanson and Henningson were invited to tell their stories.

At the Glenwood seminar, a Baptist minister raised biblical objections to homosexuality, but was quieted by a Catholic priest who turned the conversation back to the topic—AIDS.

Some members of Barsness Lutheran Church, the tiny country church Hanson has attended since birth, were concerned about sharing communion wine with him. With Hanson's consent, the Rev. Carl Listug provided Hanson with a disposable plastic cup. Since then, Hanson has been welcomed warmly at the church, and has been asked to sing a solo when he is feeling well enough.

"Here is someone who was baptized in the church and grew up in the church and was confirmed in the church," Listug said. "We're not going to turn our backs on him now and have nothing to do with him because he's a homosexual and has AIDS. There's a history there."

Pastor Listug has been the minister of Barsness Lutheran Church for 18 years and has come to know the Hanson family well—burying, baptizing and marrying many of them. His parsonage is just down the gravel road from Dick Hanson's farm. Hanson used to teach Sunday school at the church, and Listug was a kind listener when Hanson struggled with his decision to be a conscientious objector to the Vietnam War.

So when Hanson was first hospitalized with AIDS last year, Listug paid a requisite visit.

"When I left the hospital, I realized I hadn't shaken his hand," he said. Listug's reluctance to touch Hanson forced him to face his own fears about AIDS.

"And I worked through that, and the way I came out of it was I'm not going to let that fear prevent me from ministering to Dick."

The next time Listug was called to Hanson's bedside, he made a point of taking the dying man's hand.

Since then, the minister has attended church-sponsored seminars about AIDS and homosexuality, trying to learn as much as he can so he can guide his congregation in their response to AIDS and its victims. He has preached about AIDS from the pulpit, encouraging compassion and acceptance.

"To me, this is a ministry issue and it doesn't mean that I approve of his whole lifestyle," Listug said. "The focus is on ministering to Dick, who has AIDS."

For those in the congregation who might be discomfited by Hanson's homosexuality and by the publicity he is receiving, the pastor offers some biblical wisdom, specifically, from the Book of Matthew.

"Matthew 7 said 'Judge not that you will not be judged,'" he said. "And in Matthew 9 and 10, Jesus was eating with sinners. He takes the risk of reaching out to people, even though the Pharisees are worried about their image.

"So if someone demanded that Dick not receive communion or not be allowed in church, I would say, 'Do you want me to abandon him? We're all sinners; the rest of us need grace, too.'"

Listug's approach is at odds with the Rev. Merrill Olson, pastor of the First Baptist Church in Glenwood.

"According to the Bible, homosexuality is wrong, an abomination unto the Lord," Olson said. "So a person who is homosexual and has AIDS has to realize the spiritual consequences of it, meaning they have to repent of it.

"So many churches and pastors override that whole issue. They say, 'We'll love them no matter what they've done.' But if we say we love them and accept them in spite of what they're doing, that's totally wrong."

Olson says Hanson would be welcome to worship in his church, but would not be allowed to receive communion until he repented of the sin of homosexuality.

Olson has purchased space in the *Pope County Tribune* to make his point, and spoke out against Hanson's homosexuality at the AIDS seminar in Glenwood. He objects to the promotion of condoms and safe sex in the war against AIDS, saying it is "treating the sin" rather than stopping it.

"As long as behavior doesn't change, we'll have AIDS and premarital sex and homosexuality and all kinds of debauchery and every immoral thing you can think of," Olson said.

Listug is aware of Olson's comments, and those of his other critics, and of the moral dilemma posed by AIDS.

But he again turns to Matthew, this time paraphrased on his favorite poster. It shows a starving child in dirty, tattered clothing, and carries the caption: "I was hungry and you debated the morality of my appearance."

"We can get into an academic thing of debating the morality of the issue instead of seeing the human being before us," Listug said.

The lush vegetable garden is overgrown and untended. Weeds poke through the thick straw mulch. The spinach and lettuce long ago flowered and turned bitter, before Henningson had a chance to harvest them. The other crops are ripening quickly under the humid summer sun—fat cabbages, gleaming white cauliflower and crisp broccoli, juicy peas and sweet strawberries. The raspberries are almost done for the season, and the tomatoes will redden soon.

"I found with the garden I don't have time to process it this year," Henningson said. "So I'm giving it away, all of it. Alice and John were here last Sunday and filled up their buckets with raspberries and I gave some cauliflower and broccoli to Mary."

He sits on the crumbled concrete stoop of the old farmhouse, looking at the garden that has been his pride and joy for the five years he has lived here with Hanson. Last summer, after Hanson fell ill, they named it the Hope Garden and look to it as a symbol of Hanson's stubborn will to survive.

"I find I just love to look at it," Henningson said. "I'll have to tell Dick there's a scarlet gladiolus on the way. He got those for his birthday. Two people gave him bags of gladioli bulbs and two people gave him begonias."

Hanson is asleep inside, on the couch in the front room. It is cool there, and blessedly quiet after the noise and smells of the Twin Cities, where Henningson works during the week while Hanson undergoes medical treatment.

It is Hanson's first visit to the farm in almost a month. He was hospitalized at Hennepin County Medical Center three times in June, for 13 days.

The garden has become a luxury for him, as have visits from friends and his beloved Minnesota Twins games. Watching the TV makes him dizzy. And he's been so exhausted he chose not to attend an annual Fourth of July party at the nearby lake home of Alice Tripp, a longtime friend and fellow political activist.

Dozens of friends would be there—compatriots who stood with him to try to block construction of the West Central power line, who campaigned with him for liberal Democratic candidates and who were arrested with him in farm foreclosure protests.

The party would have had special meaning this year: It marked the fifth anniversary of the night Hanson and Henningson exchanged private vows of commitment to each other, asking God to be their witness.

But Hanson and Henningson stayed home. "It would just be too hard to pull away from people and say goodbye," Hanson said. His melancholy is softened some by two red roses, given him that morning by Henningson to celebrate their years together. Hanson places them nearby so they catch his eye whenever he awakes from his frequent naps.

It is little things that tax him now. He suffered severe and unexplained headaches in early June. Doctors tried a host of pain-relieving medicines, but they only caused nausea and a dangerous loss of weight. They finally settled on methadone treatments and the headaches are less painful, but Hanson still cannot digest solid food.

Two weeks ago, an abscessed tooth had to be removed. The Novocain didn't take effect, but oral surgeons cut through the jawbone and pulled the tooth anyway, fearing that Hanson's weakened immune system would not be able to fight the infection by itself. Henningson left the building rather than listen to Hanson's screams. Hanson merely said: "It was the most unpleasant thing I've dealt with in a year-and-a-half with AIDS."

But Dick Hanson remains a fighter, struggling to maintain his weight—which has again dropped below 120—on a diet of Jell-O, Carnation Instant Breakfast and a chocolate-flavored protein drink. He still cherishes the quiet and fresh air of the farm, and watches the news each night with the avid interest of a lifelong political junkie. And he counts his small victories, like making it upstairs by himself to shower, or spending a few minutes on the stoop looking at the garden.

"I'm really thankful I've had the last six months," Hanson said. "The doctors gave up on me six months ago and I was in a very low physical condition. So I'm really thankful for all the things I've been able to do, all the speaking engagements, and talking at the Capitol. Maybe this is the purpose, maybe I was given this extra time in December so I could inspire the Legislature and the public through the media.

"The last couple of days in the hospital, and then here at home, I seem to have sensed spirits in the room, like people around me. The presence has been so real when I open my eyes up I expect to see them, and possibly I ... see the vague framework of someone.

"It seems they were there to comfort me and seems real natural with the environment. Mom was one of them, I know. The others I don't recognize. But I never knew my grandmothers. They died before I was born. So there are people in the family tree who would be concerned who I don't know.

"It's been scary in the past when I've felt the spirits. But this time it was a good feeling. Except maybe it means the time is closer for me to leave this world, and that always brings sad tears, to think of missing my friends and Bert and my family. But I guess it's kind of nice to know there is some kind of warning or signal, too, so if there's something I want to say or do before I leave ... like telling Bert how much I love him.

"Bert and I had a talk last night. He kind of prodded me like he does when he knows I need to talk. We talked about the time left, and he probed my wishes for a service, if it would be soon. He wanted to know if I had any changes in my mind for the plans we had talked about earlier."

He turns to Henningson then, trying to remember. "By the way, what did I say?"

"You left it up to me," Henningson answered.

Hanson shakes his head. "I left it up to you," he said. "Typical me ... when there are tough choices to make, leave it up to Bert."

Then, Hanson laughs, a surprisingly deep and healthy laugh.

THE FINAL CHAPTER

August 9, 1987

Dick Hanson died Saturday, July 25 at 5:30 a.m. Farmers' time, when the night holds tight to a last few moments of quiet before surrendering to the bustle of the day.

Back home in rural Glenwood, Minn., folks were finishing morning barn chores before heading out to the fields for the early wheat harvest. Members of the Pope County DFL Party were setting up giant barbecue grills in Barsness Park, preparing for the Waterama celebration at Lake Minnewaska.

In the 37 years Hanson lived on his family's farm south of Glenwood, he had seldom missed the harvest or the lakeside celebration. As the longtime chairman of the county DFL, it always had been his job to ran the hotdog booth.

But today he was in a hospital bed in downtown Minneapolis. The blinds of the orange-walled room were drawn against the rising sun. He had suffered a seizure the morning before. Doctors said it probably left him unaware of his surroundings, beyond pain and—finally—beyond struggling.

Yet those closest to him swore he could hear them, and knew what was happening, and knew it was time.

"Three times during the course of the night he brought his hands together and his lips would move, and you knew he was praying. I can't help but think he was shutting himself down," said Roy Schmidt, a Minnesota AIDS Project official and longtime friend who stayed with Hanson that last night.

Hanson died holding the hands of the two people most dear to him—his sister, Mary Hanson-Jenniges, and his partner of five years, Bert Henningson.

"Amazing Grace" was playing softly on a tape machine in the corner of the room. It was Hanson's favorite hymn, the one he had sung over his mother's grave barely a year ago.

This is the final chapter of Hanson's story. After having lived a year longer than he was expected to, he grew weary of fighting for his life and was willing—if not eager—for it to end. After his death, he

*was cremated. Mourners came to his childhood church for a memor-
ial service that was vintage Hanson—traditionally religious but politically radical and, inevitably, controversial.*

*Henningson is left behind on the farm with a legacy of love—and
death. For now he, too, is sick, suffering early symptoms of acquired
immune deficiency syndrome. No sooner will he finish grieving for
Hanson than he must begin grieving for himself.*

Dick Hanson spent the last weekend of his life at the farm where
he grew up. It is there he began his goodbyes.

Grant Hanson came to the farmhouse for the first time in months.
Of Hanson's four brothers, he was closest to Dick in age, tempera-
ment, and affection.

Grant was alone. His wife never had gotten over her overwhelming fear of AIDS and had forbidden Grant any close contact with
Dick, worried he would carry the virus home to their five children.

"I think Grant wanted very much to touch me and hug me,"
Hanson said. "But he said he couldn't lie about it to Joyce and she'd
just be so upset if she thought he got too close. So he just sat across
the room from me.

"But we had a very deep talk. He said if there was any of the four
brothers he could have farmed with, it was me. I guess I've always
known that, but it was nice to hear him say that. And it was just
something special that he came out and came into the house for the
first time."

Allen Hanson made two visits to the farm that weekend to see his
son. They never spoke directly of death.

"Dad has been coming out every Friday night on his own and has
sat for a long time and has not wanted to leave," Hanson said. "But
this last time seemed like a special time for him. He doesn't want to
talk about me dying. I guess I haven't found the right words to talk
to him about the situation. I was just hoping somehow he could see I
was at peace.

"My sister Mary came out with him on Sunday. It was hard for her
to see me use the cane and have trouble walking. I guess I stumbled a
few times, and when I went outside Bert had to hold my hand. She
just had to leave the room and go outside and cry. It was just too hard
for her. Bert talked to her and said he has watched me every day, and
he said I'm the same person. The inner person of me is still there, and
the outer body is something you just have to see past. It's like people
growing old together, you just have to accept it.

"So Bert stayed outside with Dad for a while and Mary came back in and sat on the couch and we just had a real deep conversation. I just said, 'Do you know that I'm at peace? I could go the next hour or the next day and be ready.' I think by the time she left she really believed me.

"I just felt like I was saying my goodbyes to each and every one of them. So even though I may never make it back, I felt I had a chance to be with them in a very special way."

Hanson was alienated from his three other brothers in early spring, when an Alexandria television station did a series of stories about him. The brothers were angered and embarrassed by Hanson's decision to tell his story publicly, and accused him of bringing shame on the family.

But Leland Hanson, a conservative Christian who is younger than Hanson by a year, telephoned after hearing his brother had been admitted to the hospital. Hanson's oldest brother, John, had stopped at the farm a few weeks earlier for a short visit. Hanson never heard from Tom, his youngest brother and longtime fishing companion.

Hanson entered the hospital two days later after a vicious bout of vomiting. He predicted it was his last hospitalization, and he seemed almost anxious to die. His characteristic cheerfulness was gone. He still talked occasionally of gaining weight and living several more months, but now the phrases of hope rang hollow, as if they were expected but not meant.

"The time is close," he said to friend Roy Schmidt, who pretended not to hear.

"He's pretty much given up," said his physician, Dr. Margaret Simpson. "Dick has always been an eternal optimist, and somehow he always bounced back before. But in the last two months, there's been a major turnaround. ... Most people just get tired of feeling this bad. They say, 'I don't want to die, but I don't want to live like this.'"

Yet a core of spunk remained. The sugar-water dripping into his veins perked him up, "giving me the opportunity to just gab away a few more days," he said.

A stream of visitors crowded to his bedside. He had to strain to see them through his blurred vision, or depend on his partner, Bert Henningson, to identify them. He comforted them as they cried, clutching their hands and reminding them each of some special moment or gesture that had enriched his life.

He insisted on sitting up as often as he could during the day, and tried to shake himself out of his morphine doze whenever he had visitors. Henningson teased that Hanson was just testing people "to see how interesting a conversationalist they are."

Hanson brightened most at the talk of politics. He scowled at the news that conservative Cardinal John O'Connor of New York was named to the president's AIDS task force. He smiled in satisfaction when a political crony from Glenwood reported she had been granted a long-sought audience with a state legislator after dropping Hanson's name.

A sympathy call from Gov. Rudy Perpich was cause for quiet pride—and prompt action.

"He praised me for being willing to be public, and for challenging people to be responsive in a public way to what we've done," Hanson said. "And he asked if there was anything he could do to help."

The next day, with Henningson's help, Hanson fired off a two-page letter to Perpich suggesting changes in state law to force nursing homes to accept terminal AIDS patients.

Hanson also remained a keen critic of the news media, constantly analyzing whether they were doing an adequate job to increase the public understanding of AIDS. He pumped Henningson for information about federal funding for AIDS research, laws guaranteeing compassionate treatment of patients or medical advances that might help the next generation of sufferers.

And he kept a healthy hold on his ego. He was fascinated to see himself in a follow-up story on the Alexandria television station, to witness the shocking change in his looks over the last two years.

He died just before *People* magazine ran a cover story about AIDS in America, and before *Newsweek* ran its dramatic photo package called "The Face of AIDS," a haunting panoply of 302 men, women and children who have died of AIDS in the past year.

Hanson would have been pleased to know his picture was included.

In the end, Hanson starved to death.

Since he became ill in late 1985, the AIDS virus had waged an insidious attack throughout his body. His skin broke out in herpes rashes. A related virus ate at his optical nerves, methodically destroying his eyesight. He frequently ran fevers as high as 104 degrees, and more frequently lay huddled under heavy blankets as icy rivulets of sweat soaked through to the mattress. Sometimes he had diarrhea, while other times he would go two or three weeks between bowel movements. His weight plummeted from 160 to 112.

He fought back with blood transfusions, eye injections, inhalation therapy, toxic drugs and home-brewed organic compounds, but his greatest medicines seemed to be faith and a stubborn will to survive. He defied the odds last August, and again in December, when he was expected to die from pneumocystis pneumonia, the most common killer of AIDS patients.

While he regained some of his lost weight and strength from the experimental drug AZT, he also was boosted by the fresh bounty of his garden and by home-baked treats from his country neighbors.

He used the time he had left to crusade, traveling the state, preaching a gospel of hope and acceptance for AIDS sufferers. For several months, he felt so good he vowed to be the first to survive the fatal virus. After a life of championing underdog causes, it would be his greatest triumph.

Then the nausea returned two months ago, leaving him unable to digest solid foods and launching a precipitous weight loss. As his 5-foot-10 frame shrunk and shriveled, his feet and hands and head seemed to grow enormous.

He walked with a cane, when he walked at all, shuffling to negotiate through doorways and around furniture. He fell once when he was alone, landing on his back on the bedboard, and was unable to move for almost an hour.

He had grown suddenly old. He trembled with the sheer effort of sitting up and with a constant chill that was impervious to the muggy summer heat. His face at times looked ancient, the forehead protruding atop the fleshless skull, the eyes bulging over pronounced cheekbones.

Yet the same face could look disarmingly young. The worry lines that once creased his forehead were gone and the soft laugh lines were pulled smooth as his skin stretched tautly over his skull.

The heavy gold-framed glasses no longer fit his face, edging each day nearer the tip of his nose, constantly threatening to slip off. His brown eyes were often cloudy and distant, like a child's lost in a world of fantasy.

The uncontrolled vomiting started a week before he died. He had nibbled on a neighbor's moist zucchini bread, declaring it so tasty he abandoned his precautionary avoidance of solid foods. When the retching began that night, nothing would stay down, not even medicine.

Three days later, he was rushed to the hospital, dangerously dehydrated. He weighed 107 pounds, his skin as dry as parchment and cold to the touch.

He refused a feeding tube and requested a Do Not Resuscitate order. He tried to decline all medicines, even painkillers, so death would come more quickly. Simpson insisted only on keeping him comfortable, sympathizing with his desire to die.

"She felt it was a terrific period of time I'd had, and that I had done a lot since December," Hanson said two days before he died. "She said I shouldn't feel guilty about not wanting to do every little thing possible to extend my life."

He lived on crushed ice those last four days. His sister, Mary Hanson-Jenniges, or Henningson stayed with him round-the-clock to spoonfeed him, wash his beard and change his soiled hospital gowns.

As he neared the end, he struggled against an increasingly dense fog brought on by the morphine he was given every eight hours.

"It's about all we can give him," Simpson said.

Hanson suffered a seizure on his third day in the hospital, while Henningson was giving him his morning shower.

It was part of the hospital ritual—a shower and a shampoo every other day if Hanson was up to it, a bed bath if he was not. It was the only physical intimacy the two men had left.

In the shower, Henningson chattered at Hanson about mundane things. He said he had stayed up late the night before, after leaving the hospital, to watch the magnificent thunderstorms that brought 100-year-rains to the city, thunderstorms that Hanson missed because he was fuzzy with morphine and because hospital policy required that the shades be drawn in case of shattering glass.

And Henningson updated Hanson about the latest political news—another ritual. As Hanson's eyesight failed and his headaches worsened, he relied on Henningson for his daily fix of news from Washington, D.C., or St. Paul or the Metrodome.

Henningson was telling him about the Iran-contra hearings, about Secretary of State George Shultz's startling testimony, when the seizure began.

"I was just saying, 'I'll tell you all about it when we get you back in bed,'" Henningson said later that morning. "And suddenly he started pushing out at me, very rigid and quite strong. I had to get a nurse to help me.

"And now there's no more recognition or response. He may be able to hear us, but there's no way to know. But if he is beyond hearing us, he's in effect been released. Now it's just a matter of the body going along. There will be no more pain, no suffering. Oh, I hope so."

The doctor said Hanson's organs were still strong, his farmer's heart and lungs pumping in defiance of the coma-like trance. He could live as long as two weeks like that, his eyes open but unblinking, his knees drawn up, legs twitching and arms tugging toward his chest, trying to curl up like a baby, his head cocked oddly to one side.

But others sensed it wasn't so.

Henningson ushered out the last of the day's many visitors, and drove to his South Minneapolis apartment for much-needed sleep. He awoke about 3 a.m. and cried and prayed and waited.

Hanson-Jenniges refused to return home to Glenwood that day and didn't bother with sleep that night. She sat at her brother's bedside, wearing the same clothes she had been in for three days, and watched his sunken chest move shallowly up and down. She prayed through the night for his death.

Alice Tripp, Hanson's old friend and political compatriot from Sedan, had driven to Minneapolis with Hanson-Jenniges. Tripp was asleep in the guest room of her daughter's house in suburban Minneapolis when something woke her about 4 a.m. She lay awake until daylight, thinking of the young man who had stood with her on countless picket lines and motivated her to run for governor in 1978, quietly convincing her and dozens of other women in rural Minnesota they could make a difference.

Jane Ireland, a chaplain from Hennepin County Medical Center, also awoke at 4 a.m. She was going to telephone Hanson's hospital room but, for some reason, didn't. Her concentration on him was so intense that later, when the phone did ring, she didn't hear it.

And back in Glenwood, Pearl Brosvick had trouble sleeping. She spent a restless night alone in the large farmhouse, where she had nursed her invalid husband for more than 20 years before he died, and where her godson, Dick Hanson, had whiled away rainy afternoons playing with other farm youngsters—the only children Brosvick ever had.

Sometime during the darkest hours of the morning, Hanson's breathing grew labored. His sister asked the nurse to give him a slow measure of oxygen through the mask—enough to smooth his breathing but not enough to keep him alive. She put some soothing music in the tape machine, just in case Hanson could hear, and called Henningson.

Henningson took his time returning to the hospital. He showered and finished his prayers and savored the quiet time, sensing it was about to end.

He reached Hanson's beside at 5:20 a.m. Ten minutes later, Hanson died.

"I think he waited for me," Henningson said.

Henningson's voice echoed in the vast basement vault of the Minnesota Cremation Society in South Minneapolis. He sat alone with Hanson's shrouded body, waiting for the cremation to begin.

Hanson always had been the stronger singer, his clear voice and natural pitch carrying the melody of folk songs while Henningson followed with a self-conscious harmony.

But this morning there was no one to hear Henningson as he sang Hanson's favorite hymns, "Amazing Grace" and "Swing Low, Sweet Chariot." And "Joe Hill," the ballad of the martyred union organizer.

"I've been singing him 'Joe Hill' for the last several weeks because in the song it says, 'I never died, said he,'" Henningson later told the six people—brought together only by a common friendship with Hanson—who waited for him in the hushed, formal parlor upstairs.

Henningson had been uneasy about the cremation. He faced criticism from some of Hanson's relatives who preferred a traditional burial. Others had wanted the body embalmed for a viewing.

But Henningson was determined to honor Hanson's wishes to be autopsied for study by AIDS researchers and then to be cremated.

"The ancient Greeks and the Indians, they all have the tradition of the funeral pyre where residual spirits are released," Henningson said.

"We had a philosophical difficulty with burial, doing that to the earth, and Dick was an environmentalist who cared for the earth. ... And I didn't want to put Dick in the earth with the AIDS virus in him. They can drain the blood in embalming, but the virus is still in the tissues. Burning is a purifying thing and it kills the virus."

Henningson had not known what to expect at the cremation. After months of being a no-nonsense caretaker for Hanson, Henningson suddenly felt shaken and unsure. The despair that gripped him in the wake of Hanson's death took him by surprise. His hands were icy when he entered the vault, and he said his voice trembled as he began to sing.

"Then I felt calmer and I put my head down," he said. "Then my head was pulled up, and I felt my mouth fall open and I felt warmer than I had been in days. And I knew the spirit had come into me and he was free and he was with me.

"They say the spirit stays around awhile so we can learn not to be apart. But I thought, 'I'm going to have to share you.' Then I just laughed out loud, because that's the way it always was, I always had to share my time with Dick. And there are lots of people now who will want part of his spirit."

It was already dark when Henningson arrived at the farm the next evening. He was tired and still had much to do. He had to prepare for Saturday's memorial service—last-minute visits with the minister and the florist, and a thorough cleaning to rid the house of countless medicine bottles, stained sheets, sweat-soaked bed cushions and other vestiges of terminal illness.

But those things would have to wait. Henningson went straight upstairs to the screened porch that overlooks the marshes in front of the farmhouse. He found the old pink candle, set it on the small table by the middle window and lit it, placing Hanson's Bible and the urn of ashes next to it. Henningson lay on one of the metal-frame cots, watched the candle's flame and remembered.

"We rehabbed the porch in the summer of '84 so we could use it," he said later. "The screens had been torn out by kids or whatever, so we screened it up and Dick's mother went to her auctions and got cots and a table for 50 cents or something ridiculous.

"It was dry that summer, not humid. The strawberries were especially good and I found a recipe for an old-fashioned, biscuit-type of shortcake. We would use the porch in the evenings. We'd spend all day with the hogs, then go up there and have our biscuits and strawberries and cream. There were good memories up there.

"That was an election year, and Dick was running for Congress. And often what I'd do, when Dick was out on the campaign trail, I'd light the pink candle and wait for him to come home. It was a nice signal for him to see as he drove in."

On this night, Henningson again lit the candle. But his sentimental vigil was brief, cut short by practicality. He fought sleep a while longer, but felt himself sinking into the thin mattress.

The last few months of caring for Hanson had extracted an ironic price. Stress had activated the AIDS virus, which had lain dormant in Henningson's body for so long but now was attacking his strength with a vengeful speed.

He blew out the candle, took two sleeping pills to ward off anxiety and set his alarm for 3 a.m., when he was scheduled to take his next dose of life-prolonging AZT.

The mourners came a week after the death, driving down the dusty prairie road to tiny Barsness Lutheran Church. As they entered the stuffy lobby of the white-washed sanctuary, they passed a table loaded with the treasures of Hanson's life—a "great bazaar," as Henningson called it.

They saw his degree from the University of Minnesota-Morris.

Photos of his biggest fish and proudest garden and of his family at his only sister's wedding. His formal campaign portrait from his run for Congress in 1984. His fishing license and the black rod and reel he used to take hundred of walleyes out of Lake Minnewaska.

His well-thumbed Bible was there, next to a rusty planting trowel and a jar of decorative corn from one of his harvests. His grubby powerline protest T-shirt was neatly folded and covered with shards of green glass and metal—the broken transformers and sawed-off bolts from the transmission towers downed during those protests.

There were a few buttons from his various political alliances, although Hanson had donated most of the collection to a DFL fundraiser. And a tattered red bandana he wore around his arm during farm foreclosure demonstrations—a symbol of his willingness to be arrested.

The display was crowned by a splendid bouquet of gladiolas—flowers that Hanson had grown in the garden next to the farmhouse.

Friends fingered the trinkets and remembered, their laughter torn with tears.

"We have lost a rare friend, a man of courage and vision who raised so many of our hopes," said Anne Kanten, assistant commissioner of the Minnesota Agriculture Department, who gave the eulogy at Hanson's request. "His tenacity frustrated us, and his courage absolutely scared us to death. The greatest tribute we can pay him is to continue the struggle. We have to march and lead and change the systems that need changing. That is the legacy Dick Hanson left us."

But Hanson's legacy, like his life, was burdened by disapproval and controversy. Some relatives and neighbors bristled at his public homosexuality and were disturbed to find reminders of it at the memorial service.

In the middle of the table in the church lobby lay a yellowed copy of *Equal Times,* a Minneapolis-based gay newspaper that carried a front page story about Hanson's fight with AIDS. Pinned to the paper was a small button, black with a pink triangle—the sign used to identify homosexuals in Nazi Germany and now a universal symbol of pride for gays and lesbians.

Conservative church members took exception to those items, not wanting it to look as if they condoned homosexuality. Others resented the presence of outsiders—a reporter and photographer who were chronicling Hanson's death, and a caravan of mourners from the Minneapolis gay community. And some still feared contact with the AIDS virus.

"People at the church said there was too much gay stuff involved in the service," Henningson said. "But that was a very significant part of Dick's life, that and his struggle in the last year. How can we deny that?"

The greatest resistance came from within the Hanson family, a large family—five siblings, three spouses and numerous nieces and nephews—that shrunk when asked to stand together at his death. A shaky and confused Allen Hanson greeted the mourners at the service, flanked only by his daughter, Mary, and son, Grant. Two of the three pews reserved for the Hanson family remained largely empty.

Leland Hanson came to the church with his wife and teenage daughter, but left abruptly before the service began. He declined to comment, but family members said he was angered at the presence of a photographer.

Tom Hanson waited until all the mourners were seated, then entered the church through a side door. He sat alone in the choir loft, telling one of his brothers he would not sit in a church filled with homosexuals. He left before the service ended, refusing to greet mourners or to join the modest luncheon afterwards in the church basement.

John Hanson quietly sat in the front of the church with his two grown daughters. But his wife, Kathy, and their teenage sons did not attend. Kathy Hanson has said she wanted nothing to do with Dick Hanson, and the boys—who have been teased at school—have been advised to deny they were related to him.

Grant Hanson's wife, Joyce, stayed home with her five young children. She called Henningson with condolences before the service but said she couldn't overcome her fear of AIDS.

"I really cared for Dickie," she said. "Maybe I should have gone. Maybe it would be different if it was just me, but I have to think about the kids."

In contrast, Henningson was surrounded by family members. His parents drove over from Ortonville, in neighboring Big Stone County. A few of his uncles were there, and his two brothers and their families. His sister called from Portland, Ore., to say she would be praying for him during the service.

"This is not a family that will abandon him," Ailys Henningson said of her son.

Behind the two families, the pews of the simple church were packed with about 150 mourners—public officials, anti-establishment radicals, farmers and homosexuals sitting shoulder-to-shoulder in their Sunday best.

"There's one thing we all have in common," said the Rev. Earl Hauge, a farmer and former state legislator, who presided over the service in the absence of Barsness Pastor Carl Listug, who was on vacation. "We have all been irritated by Dick at one time or another.

"There are times when we wanted to be left alone and left in peace, but he was always pushing us to carry on the cause. And he was an irritant to himself. If you had trouble accepting him, remember it took almost 10 years for him to accept himself that he was different, perhaps gay."

State Rep. Glen Anderson, DFL-Bellingham, and state Sen. Gary DeCramer, DFL-Ghent, were there. Gov. Rudy Perpich and his wife, Lola, sent a lush bouquet of pink and white roses for the altar. Other DFL leaders sent condolences from the party's central committee meeting in Grand Rapids. There were representatives from the Minnesota AIDS Project and the Minnesota Health Department.

But the majority of mourners were women, many of them well into the second half of their lives, the same women whom Hanson had found most responsive to his political radicalism and most accepting of his personal lifestyle.

Ten were selected by Hanson before his death to serve as honorary pallbearers. They were his political proteges: Alice Tripp, a sturdy second mother who stood with him to block construction of the United Power Association high-voltage transmission line; elegant Mary Stackpool of Glenwood, who made a bid for the state Senate last year under Hanson's tutelage; Lou Anne Kling, a former DFL county chairwoman from southwestern Minnesota who was involved in the Groundswell farm movement; and lively Nancy Barsness, who, with Hanson's backing, returned to college after her children were grown, graduating with straight As.

"Dick was well aware of the negative social pressures that discouraged women from seeking active public roles," Henningson said in a formal thank-you speech to the congregation. "He helped escort them along the way before he died, and he asked that these women be his escorts now as he begins his journey to a long and boundless life."

The other women were even older and less well known, but no less precious to Hanson. They were members of the Martha Circle of the Barsness Ladies Aid, a group Hanson's mother belonged to, and a group that, to him, represented respectability and acceptance.

While some paid their respects at the service, others worked downstairs in the church kitchen, preparing a meal of sandwiches and cakes. The get-well card Hanson received from the Martha Circle when he first was diagnosed with AIDS had remained one of his most cherished possessions.

"That card was the first indication that people here would not abandon him, but would show him true Christian love," Henningson said in his speech. "Dick was a strong and courageous man, willing to challenge authority and fight for justice. But he also was a sensitive soul who did not want to lose his friends here. I believe the welcome you extended gave him a great deal of his strength and peace in his fight with AIDS."

The ugly gossip found its way back to Henningson. A fisherman had been overheard at a local coffee shop, complaining that Lake Minnewaska would be contaminated with AIDS if Hanson's ashes were placed there.

For Henningson, it was just the piece of dark news he needed to trigger his anger and pull him out of a growing despondency. He had spent the previous week fighting for his right, as Hanson's partner and legal executor, to handle Hanson's death. Officials questioned his authority to make decisions about treatment, cremation and the disposal of the ashes, insisting on corroboration from a blood relative.

"There seemed to be great poles emerging at the time of his death, denying our relationship together and trying to shove Dick back in the closet again," Henningson said.

The two men met at a political convention in 1982. Hanson probably already was infected with the AIDS virus, although there was no way to know for sure—a test for the virus had not been developed.

Hanson had spent the previous three years exploring his homosexuality, "coming out and crashing out," as he called it, making up for 15 years of self-denial. He worked alone on the farm for weeks at a time, then traveled to Minneapolis or San Francisco or New York on political and sexual junkets.

"I can point to an awful lot of anonymous, unsafe sex," Hanson said a few months before his death. "The likelihood is I got AIDS because of being much more sexually active. But I don't know that it gains anything to know.

"I have given it a lot of thought. You try to go back and remember why you did something or not. There were social factors. It was just easier to have sex when I went to the Cities for the weekend. Being on the farm was not good for developing long-term relationships. And what would my family think if I brought home someone important to me? So I put a big blame, if there is any, on society's pressure that we had to be anonymous and closeted.

"There were a lot of people from Wisconsin, Iowa, the Dakotas doing the same thing. They were farmers, businessmen, teachers, priests. We just had an awful lot in common, living in an environment that wasn't acceptable to us being ourselves. So there was a lot more going on besides sex. Each time I went in it'd be like a therapy session. I saw each individual as someone who was special and I wanted to get to know a little bit. And there were a pretty good number of people I just visited with and got to know and never had sex with.

"I think of all those people. They had all those same emotions, the same need for some warm, loving embracing and healthy contact. It was good for me to discover that I could give something I didn't think was possible, that I wasn't just some freak not attracted by the opposite sex."

Henningson's sexual history was different. His marriage to a childhood friend had failed, and he had come to terms with his homosexuality through the Program in Human Sexuality at the University of Minnesota.

But gay liaisons had seldom worked for him. He had no tolerance for the fast-lane scene in the bars and bathhouses. After three unsuccessful involvements, he retreated into school, work and political activism—a route that led him to Hanson, whom he read about in a biography of power line protesters.

The men shared an uncannily similar background. Both were farm boys who never quite felt they belonged, who knew they were different before they even had a word for their homosexuality. Both became politically involved with the radical National Farmers Organization while still in grade school. Both were Vietnam War protesters, liberal Democrats and farm activists. Both felt rooted to life on the farm.

But they were temperamental opposites. Henningson's biting wit and quick temper was a balance to Hanson's sugary sincerity. Hanson's yen for the public limelight allowed Henningson to work in the background, where he was most comfortable. When Hanson was overcome with insecurity and self-doubt, he looked to Henningson for a gentle nudge of confidence. Hanson was the talker, Henningson the reader and writer.

Henningson was attracted to Hanson's vulnerability, a personal passivity with family and friends that contradicted his public image as a rabble-rouser.

Throughout his life, Henningson had been a caretaker—lending his car to friends against his father's advice, opening a counseling service for Vietnam veterans, working as an orderly in a Twin Cities nursing home.

Later, when Hanson became ill, it was natural for Henningson to assume the role of provider—earning the money that bought the groceries, laundering the soiled clothes and bedsheets, keeping a matter-of-fact attitude in the face of certain death, refusing to let Hanson wallow in depression or self-pity.

He was the one who said no when Hanson wouldn't, who reminded Hanson when to take a nap or wear a jacket. Once, when Hanson was patiently explaining his AIDS crusade to an abusive caller, Henningson simply unplugged the phone.

"I've always thought our relationship was preordained," Henningson said. "Dick probably got the virus in 1980, before we met. If he had to go through this AIDS bout the last year alone, he wouldn't have made it. So I think it was preordained. I would meet him and be there to take care of him.

"But I would lose my life, too, in the process. ... Giving up one's own life to allow another to die with dignity ... that's the purpose for my life."

Henningson said it's "likely" he caught the AIDS virus from Hanson. Though the two exchanged private vows of commitment five years ago, they agreed they could have outside affairs, a not-uncommon arrangement among gay couples.

"If it felt right, we have had light safe sex with others," Hanson said. "I encouraged that as part of a trusting relationship. I feel even post-AIDS there are people who need to not be rejected sexually."

Henningson agreed, knowing they had "reserved a part of our lives that wasn't going to be shared by others." He and Hanson discussed the risk of AIDS when they met, but decided their relationship was worth it.

"I'm half-Danish and, like the Scandinavians, there's a fatalism there," Henningson said. "If life dishes you out a lot of bad things, you roll with it because that's the way life is and there's not much you can do about it. Life's too short to lay guilt and all the rest of that. Nobody goes out and asks for AIDS. Nobody would want something like this. It's just something that happens and you have to deal with it."

The diarrhea struck Henningson in early spring. He paid it little mind at first, thinking he had caught a flu bug from Hanson's young niece. He had tested positive for the AIDS virus a year earlier, just after Hanson first fell ill. But with his background of limited sexual encounters, Henningson felt he was at minimal risk.

"My medical history didn't fit the profile and there was no reason to believe I'd go on to develop symptoms," he said. "So emotionally I was buffered."

But as the year wore on, and the strain of caring for Hanson became greater, Henningson couldn't shake the sickness. He had all the telltale signs: diarrhea, night sweats, alternating chills and fever. His weight began a steady drop, just as Hanson's had a year earlier.

Henningson is a small man who consciously kept his weight just below 130 pounds, fearing middle-age spread. By late spring, he was down to 120 and was sewing tucks in the waistlines of his pants. By early summer, he had lost 5 more pounds and was buying pants in smaller sizes. By midsummer, he weighed less than 110 and was wearing suspenders.

He was diagnosed as having ARC—AIDS-related complex—several months ago, but initially declined to discuss his condition publicly. At the time, he was applying for various loans to try to save the farm from foreclosure and, as he said, "They won't lend money to a dying man."

The farmhouse and surrounding 40-acre wetlands belong to Henningson now, signed over to him by Hanson a year ago and purchased for $8,000 under an agreement with the Federal Land Bank. With Hanson's impending death and his own deteriorating health, he realized it was futile to try to keep the cropland.

Instead, he decided to devote his dwindling energy to caring for Hanson, and to joining Hanson's crusade to educate others about AIDS.

"I realized how important it was in the face of this epidemic to get more public understanding about what has to be done," Henningson said. "Maybe not for me, but for the next generation of AIDS patients who will be getting sick in a year or so. It's a social obligation to them."

Henningson's regrets are few. He had no lofty career ambitions, content instead to study history and to write philosophy on his home computer. He never questioned his commitment to Hanson, despite its price. From the day they met, Henningson knew he wanted to spend the rest of his life with Hanson.

Now he wants to spend what is left reflecting on what their time together meant.

"It was like growing old together," he said. "The whole process was just speeded up for us. A couple usually has a lifetime to grow old together. We didn't have that time. We had to compensate for things we couldn't do anymore.

"There was no sex the last month. But that's like growing old, too. My parents have a plaque in their kitchen: "'Lovin' don't last, but good cookin' do.' Relationships change. You move past the passion of the first year and mellow out. You have to or you'll burn yourself out.

"We had stopped kissing on the lips. I didn't want to pass anything on to him. But that Tuesday in the hospital, when it looked like it would be terminal and it would go real fast, we just reached for each other. So then every time I'd be gone and come back into the room, I would kiss him.

"I realized what I missed was that close physical sharing we had. I guess I became more of a mother-comforter. I was so busy. I hadn't realized I missed it. So if there's any mourning I do—although I feel his spirit with me—it's a deferred realization of what we had been missing the last few months. As much as the homophobes try, they can't deny what we have is also a physical relationship."

Henningson has been left pale and tired by the last year. A disturbing rash marred his cheek—acne from the stress or, possibly, something more ominous, herpes or Kaposi's sarcoma, a cancer that attacks 40 percent of AIDS patients.

Yet a heaviness has lifted, leaving him with a sense of relief.

"I've seen spouses after a death, and they have a serenity about them," he said. "It's like they've accepted the death and still feel close to the spouse. They feel no compulsion to find anyone else. They still have a complete life in terms of feeling comforted by the closeness of the spirit.

"I've been a hermit all my life. Even as a child I was reclusive. The calling I had to live with Dick has been good. But if I now go back to being alone, it's not foreign to me. I spent most of my life that way."

He has pulled out his favorite books—acid essays by H.L. Mencken and "Mountain Dialogues" by Frank Waters—and has lined up agriculture research projects that will allow him to work at home. He was accepted into an experimental AZT project at the University of Minnesota Hospital and Clinic and will continue to seek treatment in Minneapolis, where an acquaintance is letting him live rent-free.

He will spend as much time as possible at the farm. Hanson's friends have become his, and can be counted on for companionship. Hanson's brother-in-law, Doug Jenniges, has offered to do the heavy labor, mowing the lawn through fall and plowing the driveway if Henningson tries to keep the farmhouse open through the winter.

Thoughts of his own illness, of Hanson's history repeating itself through him, don't greatly trouble him now. He might have a few years, he said. Or he might have a few months.

"I cry almost every day for might-have-beens," he said. "But it's just a momentary passing tear at something that's especially poignant. It's just a passing emotion, but it becomes part of your psyche in preparing for the future, and then it's not as terrifying.

"Oh, it'd be nice to think about living a lot longer and having all the time. But there's an attraction to going, too. We hear things about what's waiting for us and we have notions about it, and I'm curious to find out what it is. And if that happens sooner rather than later, that's fine.

"Meanwhile, Dick is there for me, not just on the other side, but here, now. That's something I find very comforting. And I know if I end up feeling more and more ill, there'll be someone out there waiting with an outstretched hand. And I have a very good idea who that'll be. So I won't be alone."

Henningson felt oddly light-hearted as he scattered Hanson's ashes into the stony creek. His bleached blue jeans were held up by suspenders, and a straw Panama hat kept the sun out of his eyes as he walked out to the creek where Hanson had played as a child. The waters there tumble rapidly during spring runoff, eventually spilling into the Minnesota River and along to the Mississippi.

"Dick got a lot of fish out of there and ate them, so throwing his ashes back there as fish food is just returning the favor," he said. "It's part of the natural cycle of the earth, ashes to ashes.

"That may sound a bit too flip, but that's how I felt."

That afternoon, he and Mary Hanson-Jenniges planted a memorial petunia next to the geraniums on Hanson's mother's grave. A few days later, a church member was mowing the cemetery lawn and cut too close around the tombstone. The petunia was mowed down.

Henningson was unperturbed. "The roots are strong. It'll grow back."

ANALYSIS

ONE CHALLENGE for the *Pioneer Press* was how to run such a long, three-part series over seven weeks. The decision was made to run the story over three separate Sundays in the paper's

"Focus" section, removing everything from the section but the editorial pages.

The series could have been even longer. After Hanson's death, Banaszynski wrote the fourth piece, dealing with Henningson, whose story she felt was left somewhat unanswered. His story, also ending in death is, if possible, even more heart-wrenching and sad than the three chapters that won the Pulitzer.

Although the paper received some initial opposition to the AIDS subject matter, the balanced and objective way it was written seemed to turn the tide. By the third part, readers were writing letters of praise over the series.

As Managing Editor Mark Nadler wrote at the time, "[Hanson] is the great tragedy of our times, and his is a story worth telling."

Or, perhaps, what Bert Henningson said later when Banaszynski called to tell him of her Pulitzer Prize: "Now the story will have legs. Now even more people will read it and know."

One of the first things to notice about this powerful three-part series is how each piece begins with an italic lead-in discussing where the story has been—and is heading.

The three parts form a well-thought-out beginning, middle and end—character introduction and development, followed by conflict and eventual resolution—the short story format prized by Jon Franklin, for example.

In the opening part, Banaszynski presents a solid summary lead on Hanson's deteriorating condition. Although not overtly foreshadowing the end, it allows readers to surmise—especially important as the second installment won't be published for another three weeks. This part is also used to introduce the two main characters, summarize their condition and "humanize" the AIDS epidemic.

The second installment brings the family and neighbors into the mix and shows how society does—and does not—deal with AIDS.

The third chapter takes an interesting turn, as Hanson's death is related in the italic lead, and becomes the main thrust of the final segment. Although his sudden death at that point caught Banaszynski by surprise, she reported his last hours and the memorial service extensively.

She also used the last chapter to summarize much of Hanson's life and how he met Henningson, concluding chillingly with how Henningson is beginning to deal with the ravages of his own AIDS condition.

Banaszynski moves her story along in a loose chronology but leaves plenty of room for transitions that develop the entire frightening picture of AIDS. Never losing sight of the goal, she quite properly forsakes lyrical language for a grim, unvarnished prose:

> He ... frequently lay huddled under heavy blankets as icy rivulets of sweat soaked through to the mattress. Sometimes he had diarrhea, while other times he would go two or three weeks between bowel movements. His weight plummeted from 160 to 112.
>
> He had grown suddenly old. He trembled with the sheer effort of sitting up and with a constant chill that was impervious to the muggy summer heat. His face at times looked ancient, the forehead protruding atop the fleshless skull, the eyes bulging over pronounced cheekbones.

Some of Banaszynski's observations really hit home hard:

> It was part of the hospital ritual—a shower and shampoo every other day if Hanson was up to it, a bed bath if he was not. It was the only physical intimacy the two men had left.

Banaszynski has noted one of her greatest challenges, recognizing she was becoming emotionally involved in the story, was to use that emotion "to breathe passion into my writing," yet remain detached enough to remain objective. (It might be instructive to recall how John Camp handled a similar situation in his 1986 series.)

For a paper of this size to have had both Camp and Banaszynski's feature writing abilities in the newsroom at the same time is impressive. Both also seem to have been very aware of the other and fed off the friendly rivalry. Banaszynski recalls Howell pointing out Camp as a "great profiler of place ... and he does killer action."

She also recalls Howell telling her she has the same ability in describing and profiling people and if the two skills could be merged, "it would be a thing of beauty."

Banaszynski also faced other significant hurdles in writing "AIDS in the Heartland," such as having to deal with a strongly divided family that didn't relish publicity. Some of the family were actively hostile to the press for publishing their family secret and many were turned off by the whole issue of homosexuality.

It reflects well on Banaszynski's dedication that, through honesty and patience, she eventually was able to interview each family member. Yet, after the first piece was published, she says it was still hard to persuade many family members to talk. "I promised each one of them that I would let them know, before publication, how they would fit into the story, how I was going to characterize them and quote them, and what others said about them. I did not let anyone see unpublished copy, or change it. But there were no surprises."

Banaszynski says the second part, published three weeks later, ran without knowledge of Hanson's worsening condition. "I still wanted a chance to write a third chapter ... what I thought of as the gay love story ... before we were pressed to deal with Dick's death," she relates. "But Dick, and death, weren't to have it that way."

With Hanson's death, the chances to write the love story vanished and Banaszynski decided to make Henningson the final "hinge" of the last piece:

"As much as that final chapter was about Dick dying, it was about those he left behind to live without him. And, primarily, it was about him and Bert, which became the door I needed to enter a room about their love story."

Rushing to write the final 165-inch story in three to four days, Banaszynski finally began to deal with the issue of the men's sexual practices, which led to a lot of newsroom negotiation. "Jean had a lovely and powerful photo of Dick and Bert kissing—a chaste, spousal kiss—the day before Dick fell into a coma," she says. "She argued passionately that it belonged in the package, was honest to the story and the men. I agreed with her wholeheartedly. Deborah Howell overruled us, arguing that we had asked the readers' patience and tolerance in going this far with us on an untasteful and controversial topic."

Banaszynski says she instead asked for more freedom to write "directly and unflinchingly about their sex lives," a request that was granted. Only Hanson's estimate of his hundreds of anonymous sex partners in gay bathhouses was edited out, again under the rationale of undermining the credibility of the story, she explains.

Although the decision was made to be judicious and tasteful

about Hanson's sexual history, Banaszynski didn't sugarcoat it, either, especially when he sounded a little too self-serving:

"If it felt right, we have had light sex with others," Hanson said. "I encouraged that as part of a trusting relationship. I feel even post-AIDS there are people who need to not be rejected sexually."

Many of the paper's readers initially complained the series glorified homosexuality and exploited a family's private pain. But in truth, the paper seemed to take care in presenting a powerhouse series with taste and concern for both the family and reader sensibilities, as the decision not to show the men kissing makes clear.

The series' powerful conclusion of Henningson spreading Hanson's ashes into the creek, then visiting his mother's grave is a poignant and resonant ending to the series, as is the final ironic quote that seems to offer future hope:

"The roots are strong. It'll grow back."

According to Banaszynski, that final scene "was an odd, serendipitous moment ... sort of a tie-together and a tribute to everything that had gone before—to Bert's quirky humor, to the family dynamics, and even to Dick's earlier insistence that this be a story not about death, but about life ... a day after Bert and Dick's sister, Mary, planted the petunia on his mother's grave, the groundskeeper came by on a riding lawn mower and inadvertently cut too close to the gravestone, lopping off the flowers. Bert told me the story, laughing his droll and ironic laugh at my expression of sympathy. He simply shrugged and smiled.

Banaszynski obviously immersed herself in the reporting and writing of this story, yet was able to meet her goal and "breathe passion" into her writing while keeping an objective eye on the truth. Her series is a stunning example of how such passion (and compassion), in the hands of a truly gifted reporter, can be harnessed to produce a masterful final product.

JACQUI BANASZYNSKI is currently a senior editor/enterprise for *The Oregonian.* She is a graduate of Marquette University in Milwaukee.

1989

DAVID ZUCCHINO

YOU CAN'T SAY David Zucchino exactly shies away from important stories. *The Philadelphia Inquirer* reporter has been a Pulitzer Prize finalist in many categories over the years: for reporting on the origin of violence in America (1995), covering war-torn Beirut (1983), and for his nine-part series, "Being Black in South Africa" (1989), the one that finally brought home the Pulitzer.

In 1988, the *Inquirer* decided to take a hard look at what was happening in the South African townships. Concern had been mounting over reports of detentions, disappearances and capricious security sweeps, all against the law to report under stringent new security rules. Having covered wars in both Beirut and Namibia, Zucchino was well equipped to write a series about what emergency rule in South Africa was doing to the black townships.

The *Inquirer* and Zucchino decided to violate the stifling government rules that prevented most coverage of 75 percent of South African citizens. "We decided to lift the veil," Zucchino recalled at the time.

"Under emergency rule it was difficult to get into the townships," Zucchino points out today. "There were so many aspects of importance to South Africans that technically you couldn't write about—such as security force actions, which just about covered the gamut. The security forces ran the townships, basically, and had a lid on them."

Zucchino says they decided to "burrow down and get in touch with ordinary South Africans," by visiting the townships and reporting on exactly what was going on—not what the government wanted printed.

To many reporters, that might sound like a writer just doing his job, but during 1988 in South Africa, "the government kept a short leash on your work permit so you had to go constantly to the Ministry of Information and Ministry of Foreign Affairs to have your work permit renewed," Zucchino explains.

The government would then "critique" the reporter's recent coverage, he says. "They were basically letting you know they were paying attention ... opening the mail, tapping the phones and ... following reporters around."

In this intimidating environment, Zucchino had to worry not only about having his credentials revoked and being asked to leave the country, but those who talked to him could be risking their lives.

Zucchino knew that wasn't an idle threat. Black activist Sol Tsotetsi was arrested as the reporter prepared a profile on him for this series, although Zucchino is certain the activist had previously been targeted for arrest. "I'm sure we were followed and watched and security people were aware I was reporting on him," Zucchino says.

"We got harassed quite a bit, particularly at the funeral [in the first profile], trying to get past the police and into the township. We were videotaped the whole time."

Despite this all-too-real danger, Zucchino found citizens willing to talk. He feels they trusted him because he was an American and a journalist. "Every time I went to the townships, people were excited to see an American reporter and were eager to talk."

Zucchino had made many white and black contacts during the two years he had reported on the anti-apartheid movement in South Africa. Many of these contacts now put him in touch with blacks willing to share their experiences with a white American journalist.

Being summoned by the government to "discuss" unpopular stories was nothing new to Zucchino, but this amazing series didn't even result in an official response from the South African government. "It certainly wasn't in their interest to publicize the stories any more," Zucchino feels. "They just kept their mouth shut."

How Zucchino was informed of his Pulitzer is a story in itself. "I was in a hotel covering the war in Namibia, in a place called Swakopmund," he laughs. "I got a midnight phone call from my editor telling me I had won. I didn't believe him [at first] because I didn't even know I was a finalist. I had been a finalist once before and hadn't won, so they didn't tell me anything [in advance] this time.

"So I immediately went down to the bar to celebrate and there was nobody there but me and the bartender. I was yelling and laughing and a guy said, 'what's going on?' I said I just won the Pulitzer Prize and he says, 'what the hell is the Pulitzer Prize?' I convinced him it was really important so he bought me a beer anyway!"

An empty bar in a far-off war zone actually seems like the *perfect* place for David Zucchino to celebrate journalism's highest honor.

Being Black in South Africa

The Philadelphia Inquirer

Sunday, December 11, 1988

OUT OF CHALLENGE CAME DEATH

TUMANHOLE, South Africa—It was not done the proper way, the old man said. The burial of his son had been spoiled, and it pained him that his final memory of the young man was so stained by discontent.

The damp dirt of his son's grave stuck to the shoes of Joseph Nakedi. His clothes smelled of tear gas. His wife was weeping. He could hear the rumble of police armored vehicles along the dirt path outside his shack.

Johannes Lefu Nakedi had just been buried on Oct. 10 in the windswept veld of the Orange Free State, his funeral watched from a safe distance by a crush of security police with shotguns and bullet-proof vests. The mourners had been tear-gassed. The priests had been bundled into a riot vehicle. "Hippos"—troop carriers—roared up and down the roads, scattering and panicking the black children of Tumahole township.

The confrontation seemed to define the short life of Lefu Nakedi, an activist who had challenged the system and was ultimately killed by it. He was just 23, fresh from another stretch of detention, when he was shot dead by the Green Beans—killed one midnight by the black township police in their distinctive green uniforms.

To the South African police, Nakedi was a terrorist. They said he had attacked a Green Bean with a knife and was shot dead to prevent the officer's murder. They said, too, that the young blacks of the Tumahole Youth Congress, which Nakedi had led, had supplied fellow blacks with hand grenades for use against the authorities.

But Joseph Nakedi believes his son was murdered. The police could not break or silence him even after 15 months in detention, the old man thought, so they lured him into a trap and killed him.

Now Nakedi, a common laborer, totaled up the many ways that "the system"—as blacks call white rule—had encroached on his life. Long before Lefu was killed, there were regular visits by the security police in the dead of night. His shack was watched, photos were taken. Lefu was detained for 13 months, then for two months. Another son, Benedict, was detained for 13 months. It seemed to Joseph Nakedi that the police lived at his place.

And the infringements did not end even with the claiming of his son's life by the system. It claimed his funeral, too.

Since June 1986, South Africa's black townships have been smothered by a state of emergency that now intrudes on the most prosaic aspects of daily life. The emergency dictates whether a book may be read, a pamphlet distributed, a meeting held, a speech delivered, a detainee visited, a funeral held. People may be detained without charge or trial or access to a lawyer. Police need no warrant to break in and search a home. Sometimes an activist is taken away and simply disappears.

Tens of thousands of black families in South Africa have suffered somehow because of emergency rule. About 32,000 people have been detained, and civil rights groups say at least 1,200 of them are still in custody. Countless others live in fear that they or someone they know will be detained, questioned, restricted, banned, informed upon, wounded or killed.

'Total Onslaught'

The government says emergency rule is necessary to protect the majority of the country's 26 million blacks from intimidation and death at the hands of black revolutionaries bent on a "total onslaught" against law and order. No government, it says, would fail to take the same action against terrorists who openly seek to overthrow the state. Ordinary laws are not sufficient to deal with these radicals, Pretoria says, but law-abiding blacks need not fear detention or harassment.

Joseph Nakedi has broken no laws. Nor had his son, he insists, but what happened to them happens often to black activists who challenge the state.

Lefu worked at an advice office run by the Tumahole Civic Association, an affiliate of the restricted United Democratic Front. The office supplies legal advice and small sums of money for families of detainees and others affected by apartheid laws or emergency rule. The government portrays such offices as instigators of unrest.

Suspicious

The authorities are particularly suspicious of Tumahole. In 1984, the township, about 75 miles south of Johannesburg, was the first in South Africa to resist rent increases, thus helping to trigger the great township revolt of 1984 to 1986. It is still known as a "hot" township. At least 60 local activists have been detained, and 10 more have been shot dead by the police in the last four years.

Four weeks after Nakedi was killed, another Tumahole Youth Congress leader was shot dead by the Green Beans. The Civic Association released a statement the next day: "We perceive a concerted effort by agents of the system to break the resistance of the people by systematically eliminating activists."

A police spokesman in Pretoria declined to discuss the specifics of either killing beyond brief police statements already released. He said anyone who felt abused by the police could file a formal complaint.

Through the Civic Association, Joseph Nakedi has been provided a Johannesburg lawyer who intends to challenge the police in court. Nakedi said Lefu had been harassed by the Green Beans, who would stop him on the street, search him and threaten to kill him. He said that the night Lefu was killed, he was asked by a young woman to accompany him to a *shebeen*—a nightclub. The woman, Nakedi alleged, is a police informer.

At the shebeen, Lefu was shot in the eye, the back and the right arm. He died instantly.

"From that day on, the police have interfered in every single thing we have done," Nakedi said, speaking in the southern Sotho dialect of the area. "We did not have the right to bury our son in our own private way. We were not allowed even to mourn him in the proper way."

Night Vigil

The family tried to have a night vigil—the all-night venting of grief at the home of the deceased. The police imposed a time limit and restricted the number of mourners to 80. The Johannesburg lawyer, Priscilla Jana, managed to have the restrictions eased.

The funeral itself was even more heavily restricted. Because of bloody confrontations between mourners and police at highly politicized funerals during the 1984-1986 uprisings, the authorities severely restrict burials. In Nakedi's case, they even restricted access to the corpse at the funeral home. The family was permitted to see Lefu's body only after the lawyer intervened.

The police sent Nakedi a series of letters that quoted at length from the complex emergency laws. There were to be no more than 300 mourners. The memorial and burial could last no more than three hours, from 10 a.m. to 1 p.m. Only an ordained minister could speak. And "no ceremonial gathering, insofar as it takes the form of a memorial service for Johannes Lefu Nakedi ... shall be held out of doors."

Nakedi was issued 300 slips of white paper. Each contained a number from 1 to 300—one "ticket" for each guest—and the words *Funeral* and *The late Lefu NAKEDI*. They were stamped with something that offended Nakedi: the official blue stamp of the Suid-Afrikaanse Polisie, the police. Nakedi could not insult his friends and family with these things. He refused to hand them out.

On the day of the funeral, the police surrounded Nakedi's corrugated metal shack and ordered the mourners to disperse. Some of the *amaqabane*—the young men who call themselves "comrades"— began the *toyi-toyi*, the rhythmic chanting and dancing that so antagonizes the police. Tear gas was fired, and three young men were arrested.

The two priests were dragged into a riot vehicle and taken to St. John the Baptist Catholic Church at the edge of the township. There, a rushed memorial service began.

A white Dominican priest, the Rev. Jan Jansen, compared Lefu's work to the work of Jesus. "He sought the liberation of his own oppressed people," he said of Lefu, speaking in Southern Sotho. Though it was illegal, a few comrades stood up and said the revolution would continue in Lefu's name, that the "racist regime" would be toppled.

Across the street outside, police commanders stood in a drizzle, bored, and swung imaginary cricket bats at imaginary balls. An officer with a gun on his hip filmed the service with a video camera so that informers could later identify people in the crowd.

When the mourners emerged from the church, an officer told

Father Jansen that no one would be allowed to walk to the gravesite. They would have to take vehicles. But no one had a car; it was a small township.

A nun tugged at Father Jansen's arm. "Can't you talk to them?" she said of the police.

"No, I have tried," the priest said. "It's like Germany before the war. Orders are orders."

Soon some taxis were arranged and everyone piled in, some mourners standing on the bumpers. A few fell off and had to roll quickly out of the street to avoid the huge wheels of the armored vehicles that followed the procession. One Hippo had the words *Kiss Me* painted on the front.

The burial was a brief and chaotic affair held in an open field next to other graves in a pasture where cows grazed in the chilly spring air. The police watched through binoculars from atop their Hippos as Father Jansen said a few words and Lefu's damp-eyed mother, Lydia, wrapped in a wool blanket and supported by two women, tossed a handful of dirt on her son's coffin.

Sharp whistles and shouting broke out, like a sudden stiff wind. There were screams of *"Amandla!"* "power!"—and *"Voetsek!"*—an expression used to shoo away a dog. It was directed at the police, who stiffened at the sound but kept their distance.

Then it was over, and the taxis and the Hippos roared back to Nakedi's little shack. A funeral tent had been attached to the shack. Inside, guests ate a mourning meal of pap and mince—corn meal and ground meat—and tried to talk over the roar of the Hippos on the pathway outside.

In a burlap bag inside the shack were kept the dead man's clothes. Someone pulled them out. There was a scarlet shirt with a gunshot hole in the arm and a nylon ski jacket stained brown with dried blood.

Joseph Nakedi sat down in a heap. He was worn out. Everything had gone wrong. This was a miserable way to say goodbye to his son.

He knew this was not the end of it. Just two nights earlier, he said, the Green Beans had roused him from his sleep and told him they would rip down his shack if he caused any trouble. He did not consider himself a man easily cowed—a sign in his yard said "Beware of the owner—never mind the dog"—but he feared for himself and his family.

There was a living activist son to worry about: Benedict, just 18, but already familiar with a detention cell. The old man mentioned

something the Green Beans had done the other night. They had pointed to Benedict and said: "Careful—maybe he's next."

Monday, December 12, 1988

A BOND OF NECESSITY FOR BLACK AND WHITE

JOHANNESBURG—The madam insisted that Mary stay up with the
baby that night. Mary was weary. She wanted a break between housekeeping and babysitting.

By the next morning, Mary Thrusi had been fired. After 13 years
of working as a maid and a baby sitter for the madam, she was back
on the street. She had until the weekend to clear out her meager possessions from the servants' quarters in the garden behind the madam's
well-tended home.

Well, that's it, Mary thought: 60 years old, black, uneducated and
no more job.

It was just another working day in the South African suburbs.
With four million blacks working in white homes as domestics and
gardeners— "house girls" and "garden boys" as they are called by
the madam and the *baas*—somebody gets fired somewhere every day
of the week, Sundays and holidays included.

Behind the security walls of almost every middle-class white home,
there are silent black figures toiling at menial tasks for token pay.
They care little about unrest and riots and black revolution, for that
is the stuff of the townships, not the serene white suburbs. Mostly,
they care about finding a job and keeping it, about not offending the
madam, about receiving the pay envelope at the end of the month.

Some have dared to organize themselves, despite resistance by a
suspicious white government. The South African Domestic Workers'
Union had been organized for just over a year when a bomb blew up
its office in May 1987. Its current office is raided regularly by the
security police, who have detained several organizers without charge.
The police say the union people are encouraging unrest among naive
black folks, spreading propaganda, undermining the security of the
republic.

The week after she was fired, Mary Thrusi took a bus down to the
dim and shabby union offices. She told her story to Roseline Naapo,
a big, robust union organizer who did something that surprised
Mary: She picked up the phone and called the madam.

Lisa Thompson, a 34-year-old white employee of the state-run television network, listened politely as Naapo said she wanted to hear her side of the story. Thompson even agreed to Naapo's suggestion that she speak with Mary right then.

Mary knitted nervously at a scarf in her lap as Naapo handed her the receiver. She shook her head furiously.

"No!" she shouted, loud enough for her madam to hear over the phone. "Did you ever hear of a prisoner going back to jail to see the warden?"

Naapo shrugged. She handles 60 of these cases a month. She got back on the phone and persuaded Thompson to let her and Mary discuss the problem at Thompson's home the following week.

The meeting would reveal a delicate and paternalistic relationship between white boss and black servant. Mary would call her madam "my little girl," for she had been with Thompson since the white woman was 21 and just out of school. Thompson would call Mary "a member of my family." The two women would say they loved each other, though in a contrived and distant way.

There is a symbiotic cord that binds black domestics to white suburbanites in South Africa. After three centuries of dominance, many middle-class whites have become dependent on household help. Millions of unskilled, poorly educated blacks have come to depend on domestic work as their only reliable and enduring means of support—as well as a bed in the safe white suburbs, away from the turmoil of the townships.

The domestics union accepts the relationship and even many of its most condescending and demeaning traits. What it demands is not an overthrow of the entrenched domestic system, but better pay, security and working conditions.

The domestics union was founded in early 1986. Its founders knew all too well the fears and insecurities of both master and servant. The blacks are victimized, exploited, degraded, beaten. They can be fired for no reason other than madam is having a bad day.

The whites point to shoddy work, drunkenness, petty theft and murders by fired gardeners or the boyfriends of fired maids, which occur with a regularity that terrorizes the white suburbs. It is rarely a political thing, just a grudge gone violent. (Some black revolutionaries, however, have suggested that every maid in town poison the baas' tea.)

The typical domestic worker in South Africa is paid 150 rand ($63) a month. In Johannesburg, the average pay for a domestic is higher, about 200 rand ($81) a month. The union is seeking a national guaranteed minimum of 200 rand a month, with hopes of eventually raising the minimum to 300 rand.

The union also hopes to guarantee a 5 1/2-day workweek, three meals a day, maternity leave, pension plans and a three-day weekend off each month. Many employers already provide those benefits, but not uniformly. And thousands of servants get benefits for a while, then find they are suddenly withdrawn without explanation.

Even these meager conditions are better than virtually anywhere else in Africa. Servants in Kenya, Zambia and Zimbabawe—who work for expatriates as well as Africans and Asians—earn roughly half as much as those in South Africa, with fewer benefits. Unions—except those controlled by the state—are anathema to black-ruled governments, too.

It has been difficult to persuade South African servants to join the union, union officials said. Some fear they will be fired. Others are suspicious of anything that smells of politics.

The union has 66,000 members. The union believes there are four million domestic workers in the country—or 31 percent of the 13 million blacks who live in "white" South Africa rather than the all-black "homelands." That is nearly one servant for every one of South Africa's whites, plus a relative handful of well-to-do black employers.

Early one morning, Mary and Naapo drove to see Thompson. On the way, Naapo took the old woman's case history:

Began scrubbing floors for a white woman at age 13. Family "chucked out"—forcibly removed—from its home by the white authorities in the 1950s. A long series of madams: Mrs. Bryant, Mrs. Cadman, Mrs. Stephens, Mrs. Mitchell ... Earned 200 rand a month from Mrs. Thompson, plus food, lodging, TV set, pension plan.

For Naapo, it was a familiar story. She had been a domestic herself for 17 years, on and off. Now she had transformed herself into the sort of figure the authorities regarded with suspicion—a formerly docile worker turned political activist.

Naapo, had once been a policewoman. She resigned the day the bloody riots broke out in Soweto on June 16, 1976, in which security forces killed 176 blacks. She remembered seeing a white policeman in her armored vehicle shoot at a young girl. She said the officer told her: "A snake is a snake, young or old."

"That meant I was a snake too because I was the only black in the vehicle," Naapo, recalled.

Now she was going into the heart of Johannesburg's white suburbs, where virtually the only blacks are maids, gardeners and delivery men. Though she had visited white homes many times to negotiate servant disputes, she felt out of place, as if she were wearing the wrong clothes at a formal party.

Thompson was cool but polite. She was wary of Naapo, who had her own doubts about how willing this madam was to take Mary back.

Naapo suggested that the problem was a mere miscommunication.

"You're right," Thompson said. "Mary was *not* dismissed."

According to Thompson, Mary had walked out in a huff the day after the babysitting incident. But Mary had been given the entire afternoon off the previous day, Thompson said, and had been given adequate advance notice of the babysitting duties for the couple's 15-month-old son.

"She left me literally overnight—just disappeared. She said she never wanted to see this place again," Thompson said. Her fair face was reddening.

Mary shook her head. She said she had gone to visit a friend in the hospital that afternoon. She did not consider that time off—and then she was told to baby-sit until 10 p.m. without a break.

Mary conceded that when "the master"—Richard Thompson—phoned to say he would be getting home later than 10, she told him she was going to lock the baby in the house and go outside to her quarters to sleep. But of course she stayed with the child, she said.

"I was just tired and cross," she said.

Naapo cut in to ask both women how their relationship had been over 13 years.

"Very good," Thompson said.

"Very nice, OK," Mary said.

Thompson smiled. "She's been like a mother to me. I call her my black mother. She's the grandmother to my child."

Mary cut in and said: "Yes, you are like my own child." But then she turned to Naapo and said coldly: "But they gave me a good reminder that I'm black and I don't belong here."

"Did they say so verbally?" Naapo asked.

"No, it's just the way they acted. Madam wants me to die here and go out in a coffin. ... I'm old and stupid, that's what they think. Old things get thrown away."

Thompson rolled her eyes. "Now, really Mary, you're insulting me. Please don't," she said.

Suddenly the young boy, Jonathan, appeared in the living room and rushed toward Mary. The old woman gave out a cry and swept the boy in her arms and kissed him. "Oh, I've missed you, my baby!" she said.

Thompson's face softened. Mary looked over and begged her to let her visit the boy regularly, no matter what happened between the two of them.

"Oh, Mary, of course you can. You know you're always welcome here," Thompson said.

Everyone fell silent. Finally, Naapo spoke: "There is a lot of love in this house. Can't we consider the future and forget these little troubles?"

Mary and her madam looked at each other. The boy gurgled in Mary's lap. Both women nodded.

It was agreed that Mary would get a full month's pay for the partial month worked, her pension, plus 400 rand for a sewing machine attachment Thompson had promised her. She had earlier given Mary a sewing machine, along with the TV set.

Thompson handed two checks to Mary, who said, "Oh, thank you, thank you, Madam."

Naapo asked Thompson if she would rehire Mary right away. Thompson said she would have to talk to her husband and give an answer the following week. She was already interviewing new maids.

Mary kissed Jonathan goodbye. Everyone shook hands, relieved to be done with the whole awkward thing.

Mary was not optimistic about a definitive answer from Thompson. "That child is so disorganized, she'll never make up her mind."

She asked Naapo to take her to the sewing-machine outlet right away. She was eager to get the new attachment. The two women got in the car and drove quickly from the white suburb.

Tuesday, December 13, 1988

A COUNTRY FORSAKES A WAR VETERAN

MADIBOGO, South Africa—John Choeu was a young man when he fought in the great war for a country called South Africa. Now he is an old man who lives, not by choice, in a country called Bophuthatswana.

For four years, Choeu served in South Africa's Native Military Corps, fighting Rommel in North Africa. When he was discharged in

1946, he was paid a grand total of six British pounds. He says he was promised that the bulk of his 20-cents-a-day salary would come years later in the form of a pension.

Now South Africa is refusing to pay that pension for the simple reason that Choeu is no longer a citizen of South Africa—by South Africa's choice. When the white-ruled nation created Bophuthatswana as a black "homeland" in 1977, it stripped Choeu and 1.4 million other Tswana-speaking South African blacks of their citizenship.

Choeu refused his new homeland citizenship and, along with the rest of the world, does not recognize the Bophuthatswana government. But his adobe shack rests on Bophuthatswana soil, which was South African soil when Choeu was forcibly removed by the white authorities in 1959 from his shanty in a white town 30 miles south.

Madibogo, in South Africa's eastern Cape near the Botswana border, has the look of a place from a previous century. The homes are slapdash dwellings made of clay, zinc, clapboard or corrugated metal. There is no electricity, plumbing or telephones. There are few cars; the main forms of transportation are donkey cart and bicycle. In fact, some black veterans received bicycles in lieu of pay after World War II.

"I didn't choose Bophuthatswana," Choeu, a trim and nearly toothless little man of 70, said recently as a spring wind blew the dirt from the bald veld of Bophuthatswana against the worn walls of his home. "Bophuthatswana came and dropped on my head."

And that is the problem—for Choeu, and for six million other South African blacks assigned by tribe to one of four "independent" homelands scattered like seeds in remote wastelands across the South African landscape. Some have never been to their assigned homelands, but all are trapped in countless ways by complex apartheid laws.

Those laws control where they may live and work, how they are schooled, where they get medical treatment and public services, and who governs them. In Choeu's case, life has been reduced to all of that—plus, he has been denied the reward for risking his life for what he thought was his country.

"We all thought we were saving the world," Choeu said in lightly accented English.

Choeu has not taken the same journey through apartheid reform as blacks who live in South Africa outside the homelands. Those blacks, numbering about 13 million, have benefited in limited ways since 1982 under changes instituted by President Pieter W. Botha's government.

Many forms of petty apartheid governing public facilities have fallen, along with the hated "pass laws," which prohibited blacks from white areas without a passbook. Some blacks may now vote for the segregated local councils so despised by black activists.

The government calls its process apartheid reform. Critics, both black and white, say apartheid is merely being softened and refined, not dismantled. Racism with a smile, they call it.

In the homelands, blacks run their own affairs. But the governments are bogged down by corruption and inefficiency. They are heavily subsidized by South Africa because the homelands are set in rural areas of crushing poverty with no industrial base. And black tribal authorities have learned from South Africa how to deal with troublesome blacks like Choeu. Like South Africa, they invoke martial law, detain without warrant or trial, ban, restrict and censor.

When Choeu and fellow veterans raised money for a fund for widows and orphans of veterans in 1981, Choeu said the Bophuthatswana authorities confiscated the money and his personal records. Later, he said, they shot down the veterans' joint bank account in the "capital" of Mmabatho and kept the money. He has a file of official letters referring to the confiscations.

In October, Choeu gathered several fellow Native Corps veterans at his shack to discuss ways to continue pressing for their pensions. The meeting was broken up by homeland police and soldiers. Choeu was detained for the day and questioned about holding an "illegal gathering." He was warned to stop holding meetings, and then released.

Choeu went back home and continued writing letters to South Africa. A creased manila envelope holds a sheaf of letters and documents dating back to 1982, all of them from various government departments refusing him a pension for various reasons. In essence, South African law forbids the paying of a war pension to a foreigner. It says Choeu should apply to Bophuthatswana.

Choeu refuses. "I didn't serve Bophuthatswana. I don't know what Bophuthatswana is. I served South Africa," he said.

In his shack, Choeu's voice grew loud as he spoke. Three fellow veterans and two veterans' widows listened to him in the dim light of the shack, urging him on with murmurs of "Yes!" and "Right!" From the tiny kitchen, the soft voice of Choeu's wife, Jane, corrected him on the dates and places in his war stories.

Choeu spoke of white officers who gave speeches every day to black soldiers in the Libyan desert during the North Africa campaign. He said they offered promises straight from South Africa's prime minister, the white war hero Gen. Jan Smuts.

"General Smuts said there was a new South Africa waiting for us when we got back," Choeu said. "He said it would be free from east to west, north to south. But we are still slaves, whether it's in South Africa or this thing they call Bophuthatswana."

Choeu figures his nine children and 10 grandchildren are worse off than he ever was. He was educated. They are not—because, he says, the homeland schools are too expensive. None of his offspring has been able to find a job in the homeland. Choeu has supported himself over the years by making bricks and repairing machinery.

Bophuthatswana consists of seven landlocked enclaves, each cut off from the other by hundreds of square miles of South African territory. Only 6.6 of the homeland's 17,000 square miles are arable. Unemployment and poverty are so rampant that 65 percent of the labor force works inside South Africa.

Yet few people move from Bophuthatswana, for they are not officially welcome any place else. "We are all prisoners of this place," Choeu said.

South Africa has recently made it possible for some homeland citizens to restore their South African citizenship. One requirement is to move to South Africa. Choeu would gladly leave Bophuthatswana, but in order to live legally in South Africa he would need both a home and a job. Both are in critically short supply in black areas.

Choeu's complex troubles have attracted the attention of the Campus Law Clinic at the University of the Witwatersrand in Johannesburg. It has arranged for Choeu and 34 fellow veterans around Madibogo to get 40 rand ($16) a month for the next six months from the National War Fund, a private white veterans' group in South Africa.

According to Zilla Graff, the supervisor of the clinic, South Africa's Ministry of Foreign Affairs has said it would consider introducing legislation next year to amend the nation's war pension laws to allow payment for "foreigners" in the homelands. She puts the number of black veterans at 400 in Bophuthatswana alone.

"I think they feel it's a bit of a blot on their record," Graff said of the South Africans. "And of course it is. It's reprehensible the way these servicemen have been treated by their own government."

In Madibogo, ex-Private John Choeu, army serial No. 12273, is still writing letters and still getting nowhere. He still clings to his service medals, as if losing them would mean losing his soldier's identity. They are nearly as unblemished as the day he got them: the Africa Service Medal, the Africa Star, the George VI medal.

The pieces of metal represent a country that has rejected the old man, but the soldier in him treasures them.

"I'm proud of them," Choeu said, wiping the dust of Bophuthatswana from the objects. "They prove I served my country."

Wednesday, December 14, 1988

ON RACIAL TIGHTROPE, A POLITICIAN PROSPERS

DAVEYTON, South Africa—Tom Boya remembers getting a letter one day. He opened it and read: "This letter will explode in your face!"

He threw the letter on the floor and ducked under his desk. Nothing happened. He got up and laughed at himself. It was just another empty threat.

Threats and intimidation have defined the life of Silumko Tom Boya for the last nine years, ever since he was elected councilman and mayor of this black township 21 miles east of Johannesburg. As South Africa's most prominent black councilman, Boya represents all that radical blacks despise about fellow blacks—scorned as "collaborators" and "Uncle Toms"—who serve within apartheid structures.

Twice in 1985, Boya's home was surrounded and attacked by black mobs seeking to overthrow the black council and revolutionize Daveyton. Only the quick arrival of police saved Boya's house from being torched and saved the mayor from "necklacing," the public execution by a gasoline-soaked tire hung around the neck and set alight.

Dozens of black councilmen and police were murdered by mobs from 1984 to 1986, when South Africa's black townships erupted in rage. Black radicals attempted to render the country ungovernable. Unable to reach white targets, they turned their fury on blacks who they believed perpetuated apartheid by running segregated local affairs under the umbrella of white rule.

Today, men like Tom Boya are prospering. Although the Daveyton town hall is still guarded by police and concertina wire, Boya says he has dropped the 24-hour police detail that once shadowed him and guarded his home. Daveyton, he says, has been "pacified."

Boya has moved into a sprawling new brick home in Daveyton with a pool and sauna. He has a black maid, a color TV, and well-stocked bar, a new 190E Mercedes with leather seats and mobile telephone, and a profitable gas station business.

Yet Boya is no richer than any other black in political or social rights. He may not vote for national leaders, run for Parliament, live in a white neighborhood or send his children to white schools. In many towns, he may still not use a white restroom or eat in a white restaurant. And even his local political power is superseded by white authorities.

Boya says he is striving for the day when blacks will have true equality in South Africa. He preaches accommodation, not confrontation. Black self-rule on the local level, he says, is a necessary first step by blacks toward dismantling apartheid.

South Africa's white rulers believe that there are millions of conservative blacks like Boya willing to accept gradual apartheid reform by working within existing, segregated structures. Foreign Minister Roelof F. "Pik" Botha speaks often of a "great, silent black majority." Those are the kind of blacks—respectful of authority, black or white—who recently turned out to cheer President Pieter W. Botha on a visit to the shantytown of Crossroads.

South African society is polarized not only along black and white lines, but also within the nation's majority black population. There are 10 major black ethnic groups, with competing political factions within and between them. The most explosive issue dividing blacks is whether to topple white rule or reach an accommodation with it.

"These radicals who call me a lackey, they want change right now, today!" Boya said, touring Daveyton in his Mercedes, carrying on a hectic conversation interrupted by the ringing of the car phone. "I say build progress in slow steps, from within. Our goals are the same—a nonracial democracy. But we are miles apart in our tactics."

Boya is a freewheeling capitalist. He portrays himself as a self-made man who pulled himself up from poverty. He believes that blacks cannot seize political power until they have economic power.

He is vehemently opposed to economic sanctions against South Africa, saying they hurt blacks more than whites. He has made six visits to the United States to lobby against sanctions in speeches to business people and members of Congress. The trips were financed by United Municipalities of South Africa, a group of conservative blacks founded and headed by Boya.

The government has tried to lure Boya into joining the National Council, a proposed group of blacks that would negotiate a new constitution to include broader black participation. He has so far refused, saying that the government must first release all political prisoners and repeal major apartheid laws.

Boya, 38, first joined the Daveyton council as a young radical bent on destroying it. Over the years he has come to cooperate closely with white authorities, who have provided huge sums of money to upgrade the township. The 9-by-6-mile township has a swimming pool and a nine-hole golf course, a well-stocked public library and a small, all-black college. The roads are paved and the garbage is collected. With virtually every home wired with electricity, Daveyton is unique among South African townships.

In his chauffeur-driven Mercedes, Boya rode past Daveyton's new section of spacious brick homes and well-tended gardens. Black gardeners mowed yards and black nannies in kerchiefs played with children. A van from a swimming pool service made its daily rounds.

"Now these are our really wealthy chaps—our doctors and teachers and executives," Boya said. "These people have done it on their own. They've shown that blacks can make it in South Africa."

Many, like Boya, came from families who had their homes bulldozed and were forcibly removed from a "black location" called Etwatwa in 1955. They were evicted to permit the expansion of the nearby white town of Benoni. More than 23,000 blacks were dumped on the empty site that grew into Daveyton, home now to about 150,000 blacks.

On the edge of Daveyton, a jumble of shanties and lean-tos is spread across the dusty veld. Here, black squatters have been allowed to put up their shacks on land donated by the white authorities. While squatters across South Africa are being evicted and arrested, the squatters of Daveyton are legal residents.

Boya has set up a program that allows the squatters to make small monthly payments for their sites, which have plumbing, and for the loan of construction materials. The intent is for them to gradually replace their shacks with solid houses. Already, half-completed houses are rising next to the shanties of many squatters.

Boya, looking out of place in a tailored suit and shiny shoes, stepped from the Mercedes to show the squatter sites to a visitor. A crowd of curious children gathered, and Boya reached into his pockets and tossed pieces of candy to them.

"You think a squatter *wants* to live in a shack?" he asked. "Of course not! But you don't threaten them. You don't tear down their shacks. You give them time. You give them a way to build a proper house."

Boya walked over to shake hands with Rebecca Kgomo, who had emerged from the darkness of shack number 472. She said she had lived in the shack for four years since being evicted from white farmland. From her 349 rand ($145) a month maid's salary, she said, she hoped to save enough to one day build a house. For now, she lived in a wood-and-adobe shack whose corrugated iron roof was weighted down by scrap doors.

"You see? You see?" Boya said. "She's going to make it. It just takes time."

Boya hopped back into the car. He is an effervescent man, a born politician. He is not shy. His office is decorated with an oil portrait of himself, along with dozens of newspapers photos of himself giving speeches or meeting with politicians. The office also contains a photo of President Botha.

That night, Boya would deliver a speech to the German Chamber of Commerce. He would speak out against sanctions, while also encouraging the government to move "at a faster pace to accommodate blacks in the running of the affairs of our beloved country." The government-run television network planned to cover it.

On the car phone, Boya was discussing the speech with a friend. "Now be sure to catch me on TV, hey?" he said, and hung up.

The Mercedes swung past Daveyton's small town center. On the sidewalks, hawkers sold fruits and vegetables, chickens and used clothes. To encourage small-time capitalism, Boya has withdrawn the township's old hawker licensing system. Anyone is free to sell virtually anything.

As a boy, Boya said, he was harassed by the township authorities for selling apples on the street without a hawker's license.

"I was an enterprising young man," he said. "I was an early believer in the free market system."

Daveyton seems a place where blacks want nothing more than to get along, to make a decent living and hope things get better. The township's radicals have been jailed or gone into hiding. Other townships may have school boycotts and rent strikes, but Daveyton is serene.

"Why are we different?" Boya said, though the question had not been raised. "We give the people what they want. They don't want violence and revolution. They want security and good jobs and decent homes."

A report by the South Africa Institute of Race Relations recently said of Boya: "Although Mr. Boya's critics condemn his stance on national political issues as mere public posturing, he appears to be winning support in Daveyton."

In the Oct. 26 segregated elections, Boya was re-elected unopposed to his 10th term as a councilman. But last month, his rivals on the council engineered an upset by electing their candidate as mayor and unseating Boya, who had been South Africa's longest serving black mayor.

Even so, Boya remains a prominent black figure. He has been active in the town council and continues to give speeches. He still lobbies hard against sanctions, though he is careful, as always, to maintain his anti-apartheid credentials.

Earlier this month, the new white supremacist council in nearby "white" Boksburg voted to put back up "whites-only" signs on businesses, restrooms and parks. Boya, racing to eclipse more radical blacks, quickly helped organize a black boycott of white businesses in Boksburg.

The press was called in to witness a proposed sit-in by blacks at the town's white-only lake. The press showed up, but no blacks did. The sit-in fizzled.

Boya, not one to waste a good photo opportunity, suddenly decided to use a whites-only toilet. As camera crews waited outside, Boya ducked in and emerged a few minutes later with an announcement. "I drank the water," he said triumphantly, "and I washed my hands!"

Thursday, December 15, 1988

A MOTHER MUST LIVE FOR HER SONS

SOWETO—Twice, three times, Cecilia Ngcobo tried to wake herself. Each time she fell back into a slumber. She had come home from the night shift at dawn. Now it was 11 a. m. Time to get up.

"Wake up, Mama Cecilia," said her granddaughter. The girl fetched some hot tea. Now the old woman was awake. It was already hot. There was so much to do, so many troubles descending like summer smog on her and her sons.

She had to go visit Chris in prison. The twins, Gerry and Bheki, were slipping in and out of the gray matchbox house, always wary of the security police. Her youngest son, Moses, 13, had been grabbed on the arm by a policeman the week before, and his mother had to yank him back into the house.

The security police want the sons of Cecilia Ngcobo. The midnight visit and ransacked house are etched into the routine of her daily life.

She knows well the way to prison, just as she knows the many ways of maneuvering to keep her sons safe and alive after years of detentions.

By night, Ngcobo mops floors and cleans toilets inside a skyscraper in downtown Johannesburg. By day, she makes the rounds that every detainee mother must make—back and forth to prison, to the lawyers, to the police, and then back home to hold the house together as the police paw through the bedrooms and haul away books and papers.

It is a regimen that permits only snatches of sleep. "There is no sleeping time in Soweto," Ngcobo repeats often.

No one in "The Struggle"—the anti-apartheid movement—sleeps well these days. Since June 1986, at least 32,000 activists have been detained without charge or trial, according to human rights groups. An estimated 1,000 of them are still in detention. Among them is Chris Ngcobo, who turned 26 in prison. More detainees are rounded up every day.

Ngcobo, a stout woman of 53, has lost track of the number of times the police have visited her four-room house. Throughout South Africa's black townships, police raids are so common that people remark casually to their friends, "The System visited the house last night," as if to say, "The postman passed just now."

The System has visited Ngcobo many times, and much has been lost. In December 1984, her eldest son, Jabulani, was killed by the South African army in neighboring Swaziland, where the young man had fled to join the outlawed African National Congress. Cecilia Ngcobo found out about it when she saw his photo in the newspaper; he was identified by the authorities as a "terrorist" who had engaged in unspecified "terrorist activities."

She spent three months' wages to travel to Swaziland and spent two days persuading the authorities to let her see the body. Her son's body had more than one hundred bullet wounds, she says. She wondered why a man had to be shot so many times. "He even had bullet wounds in his hands," she recalls now.

Jabulani had made the entire family a target. Early on the morning of June 12, 1986, the first day of the ongoing state of emergency, security police dragged Bheki, now 28, from his bed at 4 a.m. while his mother was at work. He did not emerge from detention for 13 months. After searching for Chris the next three days, the police found him sleeping in a dormitory bed and hauled him away. He is still in Soweto's Diepkloof Prison.

Exactly one year after Bheki's detention, on the day in June 1987 when the emergency was renewed for another year, Bheki's twin, Gerry, was found hiding in a safe house in Soweto after an informer turned him in. He was detained for three months.

The family was not notified of the detentions. Like thousands of other detainee parents, Cecilia Ngcobo spent several days inquiring at local police stations before stumbling across official records of her sons' detentions.

The police did not need warrants to take the Ngcobo men away. Nor did they charge them with crimes. (After his release, Gerry was charged with possessing banned literature, but was acquitted in February.) Detainees have no right to see lawyers or family members, though many—including the Ngcobos—are ultimately granted such privileges.

Cecilia Ngcobo often wonders why, if her sons are considered dangerous enough to lock up for months and years, they are not charged with crimes and taken to court. Liberal white politicians have asked the same kind of questions in Parliament. The authorities have replied that the judicial system is not equipped to deal quickly with "suspected revolutionaries" who must be taken off the streets at once.

"The ordinary laws of the land ... are inadequate to enable the government to ensure the security of the public," President Pieter W. Botha told Parliament in ordering the state of emergency.

A government booklet that attempts to justify detentions says: "When national interests are of greater importance than individual interests, some rights of the individual must be curtailed."

Law and Order Minister Adriaan Vlok has told Parliament that police must be able to detain people without legal encumbrances when "it is absolutely necessary for the maintenance of public order [and] the safety of the public."

In a comment that has astounded detainee mothers like Ngcobo, Vlok also said that activists are detained for their own safety and to end the state of emergency.

Cecilia Ngcobo, laughing despite her troubles, wondered how tossing her sons in jail for no stated reason would protect them—and from what?

And how, she asked, does their detention end the emergency rule that allows them to be jailed in the first place?

Her sons are not criminals, she said. Gerry is an organizer for the legal black transport workers' union. Bheki is unemployed and looking for work. The police have repeatedly searched the house for banned ANC literature and automatic rifles, Ngcobo said, but they have found nothing.

South Africa's Human Rights Commission has said the real purpose of emergency rule is to intimidate blacks and to crush peaceful
dissent by artificially declaring black political opposition a crime.
(The government does not detain right-wing whites who openly
oppose its policies.) Court hearings and civil rights are inconvenient
and time-consuming, the commission has said, and so they are swept
aside.

"We are all subject to the whims of soldiers and policemen," the
Detainees Parents Support Committee said last year. The government
no longer has to listen to DPSC criticism; it effectively banned the
group's anti-apartheid activities in February.

The detainees' group was once able to assist Ngcobo. Now she is
on her own. She would like to quit her job to devote more time to her
sons, but she supports 20 family members who sleep on her floors
every night—three sons, six daughters and all of her grandchildren.

And still the police come. Earlier this year, they kicked down the
door and took away her books, including her Bible. More recently,
she said, they demanded that she tell them where to find Bheki and
Gerry. She refused. They asked for her sons' passports. She refused
that demand, too.

Even Moses, just 13, is afraid to stay in the house some nights. He
was dragged from bed recently, his mother said. A security officer
shouted at him: "Careful, boy, you're growing up to join the ANC.
We are watching you."

"Even when Moses is away [hiding], I'm so afraid for him I can't
sleep," Ngcobo said, squeezing the boy's hand. "He's so tall, he looks
older."

She says she screams at the police, orders them out of her house.
They do not frighten her, she said. Nor does she fear the punishment
dealt out to others who have spoken out against detentions—a black
youth murdered in Johannesburg and a black woman shot in the eye
in the Cape, both by mysterious gunmen never caught by the police.

"For my husband, for myself, I am not afraid. They only want my
sons," Ngcobo said. "Before, I was always afraid, always worrying.
But since they killed my first son, I know the world is evil. I accept
it."

She accepts, too, the narrowing of her personal life. Friends no
longer visit, for they fear the security police will detain them. Her
husband, Maxwell, a trucker, avoids political matters and thus shuns
the driving force in the lives of his wife and children.

"My husband wants nothing to do with these troubles—we need
his salary," Ngcobo said. "But my sons are committed to the strug-

gle. I am proud of them. They have suffered so much, now I want to suffer for all of them."

She hugged Moses and went on: "My sons are making a difference, working for something good. One day change will come and everything will be all right. I will live to see that day. My sons are bringing that day closer to me."

It was almost noon now. Ngcobo's eyes were red from lack of sleep. Her ankles were swollen. After 20 years as a cleaning woman, she has high blood pressure and arthritis.

She gulped her tea, trying to make her body come alive. She had to go see Chris in prison that afternoon and then be at work downtown by 6 p.m. There would be no time to sleep.

It hurt her to see Chris in prison and not be able to touch him because of the Plexiglass barrier in the visitors' room. But she took heart at the way he ignored the orders of the prison guards, as if they were invisible and only he and his mother were in the room.

"Chris is cheeky, like me," she said.

Ngcobo sighed and remembered what Chris had told her during their last visit: "Don't worry about me. Watch out for yourself, Mama, you look tired."

She had to admit it: She was exhausted. But the police had come just the week before, looking for Gerry. And Moses was certain to be snatched if she did not get him out of Soweto. She could not let the System wear her down now.

Tonight, perhaps, if the buses were running on time, she would be home from work by 5 a.m. If all was quiet, she would steal some sleep before the next knock of the police at the door.

Friday, December 16, 1988

A BAR OWNER QUIETLY PROSPERS WITHIN THE SYSTEM

SOWETO—Peggy "Bel-Air" Senne was born in a shebeen. He figures he'll die in one, too.

In South Africa's black townships, a shebeen is a place of booze— a bar, a tavern, a nightclub or a hole in the wall that serves drinks. In Soweto, the nation's largest township, the king of the shebeens is Peggy Senne, a bow-legged little man with a gravelly voice and bloodshot eyes from too many cigarettes and too many late nights out.

Booze is Senne's life, and he is proud of it. He calls himself a bootlegger, and the backyard shebeen called Peggy's Place has made him richer than most white men.

"I was born in a shebeen," he says, sucking on a cigarette in the cool of his living room, where the clinking of glasses and the hum of conversation filter in from Peggy's Place out back. "I went to school on shebeen money, got married on shebeen money, bought my first Bel-Air automobile on shebeen money. My kids went to college on shebeen money."

If there is a success story in Soweto, it might as well be Peggy Senne. He has thrived within apartheid's boundaries, a black man grown great in a one-color world. Born into segregation, he has chosen to flourish within it, not fight to escape it.

There are many blacks like Peggy Senne in South Africa. They accept their lot, and profit nonetheless. They build their lives quietly, within bounds, leaving to others the terrifying struggles of liberation and revolution.

Senne is wealthy enough that he could afford a big apartment in the so-called gray areas of downtown Johannesburg, where people of color have breached apartheid's walls. He could even afford to pay a white man to buy him a house in the exclusive white suburbs, where a few well-to-do blacks have infiltrated.

He stays instead in Soweto, for it took him a long time to arrive. His family was evicted in the 1950s from a place called Sophiatown, then evicted again in the early 1960s from an eyesore known as the Western Native Township. In 1962, he found himself dumped into a four-room matchbox house in Soweto.

So naturally he opened a shebeen. It began in his dining room with a few crates of beer. Now he sells 8,000 cases of beer a week, plus huge quantities of liquor and wine. The little house has since grown up around the shebeen. Senne now owns one of the biggest homes in Soweto, with a separate two-story living wing and a big garage.

The white authorities cracked down on his new shebeen, of course, but not in the bloody racial clashes that have ruptured South African society for so long. They would simply confiscate his cars or his beer in return for allowing him to remain open.

Challenging the System

In his own cautious way, Senne fought back. In 1979, he formed the Soweto Tavern Association to represent the shebeeners against the authorities. By 1984, he had persuaded the white government to legalize shebeens and charge them licensing fees and taxes. He had challenged the system, quietly but persistently, and finally it gave in.

"We all struggle in our own way," he says.

Senne has since stayed out of politics. He doesn't want any trou-

ble. He just wants to sell his booze and see his customers have a good
time.

"Look, I'm a shebeener, not a politician," he says. "Don't ask me
political questions. I just take what comes. You've got to survive,
man."

Even so, racial politics engulf Soweto. Senne does what he must
do. When the young radicals who call themselves "comrades" order
him to shut down in support of a boycott or a strike, he obeys. He
does not reopen until they tell him to. He does not, however, encourage young people to drink at Peggy's Place. He prefers mature customers, who don't talk politics.

He often wonders why the comrades are so bitter and so willing to
suffer for their cause. He believes that a black man is far better off in
South Africa now than when he was their age.

'Sky's the Limit'

"Our new generation sees no improvement," he says. "But if you ask
me, things are much better—and they'll continue to get better. Before,
you couldn't even buy the car you wanted. You couldn't form a company or apply for a loan. Now, the sky's the limit. I can go down to
the white bank and take out a loan. They don't care what color I am,
long as my credit's good."

Senne offers himself up as proof that a black man can prosper
despite apartheid. As a boy, he worked in his parents' shebeen. His
mother was a maid. His father couldn't buy a car.

"My father rode a bicycle. I have seven cars," he says. He claims
to be the first black man in South Africa to drive an American car—
a Chevy Bel-Air in the 1950s. Now his main car is a silver 1988
Mercedes-Benz.

Senne wears his success. On this particular evening he wears a yellow cardigan over a golf shirt, mustard slacks, tassled loafers, tinted
shades and gold—gold necklaces, gold bracelets, gold rings and a
gold wristwatch.

There are three main avenues to wealth in the townships. One is
elected office in the township council, where graft and bribes enrich
a black man willing to serve within apartheid's edifice. Another is
construction—for the thousands of blacks who can afford expensive
additions to their little township homes.

A third avenue is booze, either a liquor store or a shebeen. A township is a place of joy and despair, and thus liquor is always required.
Senne prides himself on his ability to recognize the distinctive drinking habits of blacks and to profit from them.

"A black doesn't drink like a white man," he says. "A white man can drink at home. A black man, he has to drink in a place where there's people and talking and noise. And a black man wants to be able to drink early in the day if he wants to, and all night if he wants to do that."

For those reasons, Peggy's Place opens early and closes late. "We're like a police station—we never close," he says. He and his wife take separate vacations so that Peggy's Place can always be open.

Resting on a sofa, Senne smokes his cigarette and totals up his blessings. He has a loving wife, Dorothy, better known as Cookie. He has four children—one a lawyer, he says proudly—and seven grandchildren. When he dies, he says, he will die a satisfied and comfortable man.

In the kitchen, Cookie is preparing dinner, humming softly. Inside Peggy's Place, some customers have already ordered drinks. The sound of their laughter is soothing.

Life is sweet, says Peggy Senne, looking out his living-room window at men unloading cases of beer from a truck guarded by a man with a shotgun. The beer bottles reach the floor of his garage with a satisfying clink, like the sound of money in the bank.

Saturday, December 17, 1988

A TENTATIVE STEP TOWARD FREEDOM

SPRUITVIEW—David Mkhabela has taken his leave of Soweto. After years of fear and intimidation, of corruption and filth, he has made his escape from that sad black reservoir.

Home now is a fine, modern brick house he has built in a place called Spruitview, known to all as a "model township" for South Africa's black elite.

Here, in a stretch of expensive homes rising from the grass veld 19 miles south of Johannesburg, live the first blacks officially allowed out of the cramped townships—freed from the areas created decades ago as black labor reserves.

So David Mkhabela, his supervisor's salary invested in a new home and a new life, finds now that he has escaped only Soweto, not South Africa. He is the first urban black South African in 75 years to actually own the ground beneath his home, but he has taken only one tentative step on the long and uncharted journey to true liberation.

And in doing so, he has broken with the great black masses and also with his two brothers, both revolutionaries who have suffered greatly at the hands of the white security police.

Mkhabela has invested in apartheid reform, but without illusions.

Like other successful blacks, he has cautiously accepted a less oner-
ous form of racial segregation. The white authorities have endorsed
Spruitview as the first of several clean, efficient "upmarket"—and
still segregated—black living areas. Blacks who can afford it are moving in.

Some blacks believe that those in Spruitview have somehow abandoned the township resistance movement, but for many the alternatives had become unbearable.

"I had to get out of Soweto. I could no longer survive there,"
Mkhabela was saying in the cool living room of his new home, 27
miles and a political chasm away from his tiny matchbox house in
Soweto outside Johannesburg. He spoke like a man released from
prison, but on parole.

As a black man who works as a supervisor for white-owned Anglo
American Corp.—the mining and industrial colossus viewed by some
blacks as an exploiter of black labor—Mkhabela had become a target. The young township revolutionaries who call themselves "comrades" had threatened him and his family. They demanded that everyone in Soweto honor the many "stayaways"—work boycotts—they
call to protest apartheid.

But Mkhabela, who is 40, had an important position and a family
to support. He had worked too hard for too long to lose his job over
a political protest.

"Those youngsters were quite angry, quite threatening,"
Mkhabela, said. He mentioned their "people's courts," kangaroo
courts where township justice is meted out with floggings and sometimes with executions. "They would introduce a new law and you
would be guilty of violating it."

He refused to sacrifice his job. But moving to another cramped,
volatile township near Johannesburg was out of the question. Each
one, like Soweto, has a housing shortage so acute that the waiting list
for homes runs into the thousands.

In late 1986, South Africa offered another of its slowly evolving
apartheid reforms. Blacks were given "freehold rights" to own residential land in urban South Africa for the first time since 1913.

Except for the handful of blacks who fell through bureaucratic
cracks in rural areas, blacks were not allowed to own property in
South Africa under the Natives Land Act of 1913 for fear that property rights would lead to political rights. A black could own a home
in a black area, but the land it rested on had to be rented from the
government—a policy some blacks called "the bricks but not the
dirt."

With freehold rights now available, a handful of blacks with money have begun to flee the townships for clean, spacious Spruitview. Mkhabela, was the first, moving into his 76,000 rand ($36,000) home in January. Of the 100 families who have followed, at least 90 have come from Soweto in search of safety and peace.

The new cars driven by Mkhabela and his neighbors carry a bumper sticker: "SPRUITVIEW—The New Garden Suburb for Peace and Security."

Although Spruitview is South Africa's only completed "model township," others are planned. Since Mkhabela, got his title in January, more than 400 other blacks have acquired titles to their homes in existing townships, according to Alec Weiss, a government housing official in Pretoria.

Spruitview is a centerpiece of the government's "hearts and minds" strategy designed to improve black living conditions while maintaining strict racial segregation. The strategy is coupled with an iron fist policy of smashing both violent and peaceful dissent through the government's looming security apparatus and emergency rule.

The government's deputy minister of economic affairs, T.G. Alant, said recently that freehold rights and other reforms were creating "an affluent black middle class, which serves as an inspiration to other blacks of what can be achieved."

Those blacks, he said, are a hedge against "the [black] anarchists [who] are bound to totally destroy the existing structures and then capitalize on the chaos."

In Spruitview, men such as Mkhabela resent being portrayed as government supporters. They regard Spruitview as only one step toward dismantling—rather than modifying—apartheid. They say they differ from the revolutionaries only in tactics and timetables, not in goals. They believe that they will achieve full political rights in their lifetimes.

"Something must replace this system because there is no hope for black people under the present state of affairs," Mkhabela said. "For the government, reform means trying to buy time. For me, it means moving ahead to a better life. We are showing that a black man can do better. He doesn't have to live in a matchbox house."

Mkhabela has chosen a life far different from that of his defiant brothers. Their divergent paths are one small measure of the divisions within a vast black nation of 26 million.

One brother, Ismail, is an activist in the Azanian People's Organization, the black consciousness movement founded by the black martyr Steve Biko. Ismail has been detained many times; his wife gave birth to their child while she was in detention. He once told his brother that he did not intend to die of natural causes but as a soldier fighting for black revolution.

Mkhabela's other brother fled Soweto after the 1976 student riots and joined other exiles fighting South Africa from neighboring Botswana.

"My brothers belong to the movement," Mkhabela said. "I highly appreciate their actions. Without their struggle, things would seem normal. And of course nothing is normal for black people in South Africa."

Mkhabela has struggled in his own way. Twelve years ago, he decided he wanted to work at either Anglo American or IBM after working a series of menial jobs. So day after day, he pestered the two companies. Finally, Anglo offered him a job reserved by custom for blacks: security guard.

He took it. Soon he was demanding to be moved up to something more challenging. "I confronted them by asking if my color was a stumbling block," he said.

Anglo eventually moved him to an entry-level position in the transport department. After seven years with the company, he was promoted to supervisor in charge of licensing company vehicles. He now directs a staff of 19, five of them whites.

"On paper, I am above the whites," Mkhabela said. "But in reality, they don't report to me but to other whites. If you are a black, they move you away from direct supervision of whites. They have to nurse their feelings."

He now fears that he has reached his ceiling at the company, despite its declared policy of promoting blacks to traditionally white jobs. "It's frustrating to know you can do your boss' job, but to get constantly shoved sideways while the whites move up. So I make a lot of noise," he said.

In Spruitview, at least, Mkhabela believes that he has taken charge of his own life. His new home and lot are more than double the size of his Soweto matchbox, which cost 1,300 rand ($620). The water, electricity and telephone services are reliable. The roads are paved. The garbage is collected regularly. He no longer worries about crime and political strife.

In his living room, Mkhabela sat on a new sofa next to walls painted a light salmon. The house smelled of new paint and carpets. A color TV and a stereo system had been set up. In the kitchen, a black housekeeper fussed over Mkhabela's 3-year-old daughter, Joan. Out back, black construction workers bought sodas from a small snack shop he runs from his garage.

In Soweto, he said, he could not have run such a shop without paying enormous bribes to black councilmen who dole out franchise rights. In Spruitview, he paid a nominal sum for a trader's license.

But in other ways, not much has changed. His five children still go to poorly run "Bantu" schools reserved for blacks. There are white schools close by, but the Mkhabela children must attend school in cramped Katlehong township down the road. There are mixed-race private schools available, but they are in Johannesburg, too far away.

Mkhabela wants to start a private school in Spruitview, but he has encountered government resistance. The message is clear: Black children should go to black schools. He senses apartheid's walls closing in again.

"If this is a so-called elite area, why shouldn't we have elite schools?" he asked, though he knew the answer.

He sighed and rested his head against the back of the sofa. It was the end of another long day—the hour's drive to work and back, the struggle to complete a new house, the bills to pay. He had too many battles: to raise himself up, to fight the system in his own quiet way.

Anyway, he said softly, it was better than Soweto. He smiled and raised Joan to his lap. He had chosen the right path—he was certain of that. He was certain of something else, too. When his girl was grown, no one would tell her where to live.

Sunday, December 18, 1988

FOR MANY, STRUGGLE IS FOR WORK

UITENHAGE—Every morning for nine months, Patrick Stalli was there at the gate. He would walk the four miles from home in the dark and join the thousands of other jobless black men pressing against the fortified gates of the towering Volkswagen plant.

Every day for nine months, he walked back home without a job. One morning, the white foreman said he needed 20 men. Thousands surged for the gate. Stalli pushed and clawed. Somehow his body popped through the tiny opening. He had a job.

"I was so desperate. I would do anything for a job. A little fighting and pushing was nothing to me," Stalli said recently, riding a bus at dawn to his 4.98-rand-an-hour ($2.08) job as a press operator who cuts out upholstery for car seats.

For millions of black South Africans, the concerns that eat away at
their daily lives have little to do with the struggle for political rights
or the faltering, bloody war of black revolution. Protest and confrontation are remote concepts. Life boils down to the basics—a
decent house and a job, any job.

Officially, the unemployment rate for registered black workers is
14.7 percent. But private research groups put the actual unemployment rate at up to 30 percent of adults among South Africa's 26 million blacks, or nearly five times the white rate. In the hardscrabble
eastern Cape, where Uitenhage forms a dingy island of auto plants
and tire factories, black union leaders say the unemployment rate is
nearly 50 percent.

Earlier this year, a research firm asked blacks in nearby Natal
province to list their most pressing fears. Ninety-four percent of those
polled led with the fear of losing their jobs. Only 49 percent said they
worried about living under white rule. Just 8 percent said they had a
"great desire" for more political rights.

Patrick Stalli, 28 and the possessor of an eighth-grade Bantu education—prescribed to blacks by whites—does not dream the dreams
of black freedom and black rule. He wants to make enough money to
repair his dilapidated car, to afford a bottle of beer when he gets off
work. He wishes his matchbox township house were nicer or at least
bigger. He longs for the six friends and relatives camping out in his
spare bedroom to find their own place to live.

Most of all, Patrick Stalli hopes he can hold on to his job. He has
been laid off twice because of a soft car market, and each time he felt
the sting of hunger and despair. He is back full time now, but only
until the next union strike or the next retrenchment.

"I am most fortunate to have a job," he said, dropping heavily
onto an old sofa at home, exhausted after another 9-hour shift. "All
of my friends, they are begging me to find them work at the plant. But
even this job is not enough. I need overtime just to have enough food
to eat."

Like most blacks, Stalli supports an extended family of 20 or more
people. An enduring African tradition requires those with jobs to support those without. Stalli sends money to his parents and siblings and
the parents and siblings of his wife. The relatives and friends staying
with him eat away at his meager food supplies.

A longing for something better gnaws at him. He is driven by
ambition—but for himself and his family, not for the millions of dis-
possessed blacks across the land. He cannot carry their burdens. He
has no time or energy for protests and boycotts and political meet-

ings. It is enough to worry about his own affairs.

"This job doesn't support me in the way I want to live," he said. "It just keeps me alive to come to work the next day."

It was payday, and Stalli opened his envelope inside his darkened home after work one evening. He could not understand where all his money went. With overtime, he had grossed 501 rand over two weeks. But deducted from his paycheck were income taxes, medical insurance, pension payments, union dues and unemployment insurance—plus deductions to the township for his rent and utilities. That left 296 rand to see him through the next two weeks.

In the house, a visiting union shop steward named Mlami Magioimesi tried to console Stalli. He mentioned that things had been much worse before the black union—the National Union of Metalworkers of South Africa—was formed in 1986. Until 1979, black unions were not permitted in South Africa.

"Power—political power, economic power—comes from the union," Magioimesi said. "The government knows that. It knows we have the power now to affect the national economy."

White corporations pushed the government to allow black unions in order to address their workers as a coherent body, to avoid wild-cat strikes and uncontrolled strife. But now the government, stung by the unions' militancy and their ability to halt production, is trying to crush them. It has restricted Cosatu, the Congress of South African Trade Unions, from political activity. It detains union leaders without charge for months at a time. It is trying to ram through legislation restricting the right of unions to strike. And it uses the police to break up job actions.

Even Volkswagen, a progressive employer by South African standards, has not moved fast enough for the union men like Magioimesi. Of the plant's 7,600 employees, 5,600 are low-paid, hourly workers. All of them are black. The remaining 2,000 are higher-paid, salaried employees. With a small but growing number of exceptions, they are white.

"Job reservation may be scrapped," Magioimesi said, referring to the recently rescinded law that prohibited blacks from holding skilled jobs reserved for whites. "But it's still there, only in a more subtle form. If you're black, it's still very difficult to move up."

Even so, many South African academics predict that black revolution will one day come not from the barrel of a gun, but on the factory floor. The South African Institute of Race Relations speaks of a "silent revolution" triggered by black unions and the black workforce. Blacks drive the economy with their labor. As consumers, they determine white marketing strategies by the beer they drink, the clothes they buy, the types of food they eat."

"The worker's life and the political life are one and the same. Through unity comes liberation," another black shop steward, William Smith, told Stalli at the plant the next day.

Stalli nodded, but he did not care much for political theory. He supported the union. Without it, he knew, he could be fired for no reason. When the union told him to strike, as it did only last June, he obeyed. But really, he confided, he didn't think strikes accomplished much. He would rather be working.

Kwanobuhle township woke up. Dogs barked. Donkeys brayed. It was 4:30 a.m.—time for Patrick Stalli to go to work.

Stalli stepped over the sleeping forms of his friends and relatives. He washed his face and brushed his teeth from a pail of cold water filled from a tap outside. His pregnant wife, Valencia, cooked breakfast on a paraffin stove. Stalli listened to the morning news on a radio powered by a car battery. The house has no electricity or plumbing.

Pulling on his blue Volkswagen overalls, Stalli took a few bites of corn porridge and gulped down a cup of instant coffee. His wife handed him his lunch packed into a plastic grocery bag, and Stalli walked down a dirt road to the bus stop.

It was now 5:30 a.m. The bus was late. A long queue had formed—auto workers with their grocery bags of food, domestics with their faces streaked a ghastly gray from skin lightener creams. Already, unemployed men were lounging on Kwanobohle's street corners. At last the bus arrived.

It was an important day. After work, Stalli would take his driver's test. If he passed, he would be able to apply for a higher-paying job as a forklift driver. The job was so important to Stalli that he had taken lessons from driving school on his own. He still owed the One Way Driving School 100 rand for four lessons.

On the assembly line inside, Stalli went through the monotonous motions of laying the mold, stretching the fabric, cutting the fabric. His movements were crisp and economical. He prides himself on not losing his concentration.

His white supervisor, Jeff Humphries, watched him. He said Stalli seemed ready for a promotion to the bonding machine that adheres the upholstery to car seats. That assembly line job pays the same as a forklift driver's.

"He's a good, dependable worker," Humphries, said. "He knows what he wants. He wants to move up."

Humphries mentioned that he would recommend moving Stalli up the line to the bonding machine the next month. But he said nothing to Stalli.

After the shift, Stalli went out and passed his driving test. He needed only the driving school certificate to apply for the forklift job, but he couldn't get it until he paid for the lessons.

On the way out of the plant, Stalli seemed distracted. He did not suspect that he might soon be promoted up the line. Anyway, he was determined to get off the line and move up to the reasonably stimulating job of driving a forklift.

Outside the plant, some of the men from the union were talking politics. Stalli ignored them and walked on to the bus stop, his head bent in thought. He was wondering how a man working the line was going to save up 100 rand.

Monday, December 19, 1988

TOEING A FINE LINE TO HOLD TOGETHER COMMUNITIES RENT BY APARTHEID

JOHANNESBURG—The Bible—where was the Bible? Sol Tsotetsi rummaged through a stack of papers and found the Book. He never left the office without his Bible.

As a fieldworker for the South African Council of Churches, Tsotetsi cherished the Bible as a sort of talisman. When he was stopped by police at a roadblock, he raised the Book in their faces. Inexplicably, the police would let him pass.

The security police, the notorious Special Branch, were another matter. They knew Sol Tsotetsi. They knew he was no minister. To them he was a communist, a troublemaker, a rabble-rouser, a terrorist. They were always on the lookout for him.

Tsotetsi was a man on the run, operating on the fringes of South Africa's state of emergency. Like about two dozen other church fieldworkers, he attempted to hold together South Africa's shattered black communities while avoiding the police and a detention cell.

The fieldworkers are among the last functioning foot soldiers in the war against apartheid. Thousands of other black activists have been silenced through detentions and bannings. Eighteen major anti-apartheid organizations have been virtually banned. Only the Council of Churches, a vehement opponent of white rule, still practices what passes for "legal" resistance in South Africa.

From early October through early November the life of Sol

Tsotetsi was a frantic journey through the shadows of black resistance and white might. Hounded by the Special Branch, he slept in a different house each night. He rarely dared to go home, or visit his 3-year-old son, or steal a few moments with his wife, herself an activist who knows the inside of a detention cell.

The days and nights of Sol Tsotetsi strip back the facade of normalcy in black South Africa. All the pain and sorrow of this racially divided land is exposed. Institutionalized racism still shreds black lives. Blacks still seethe with resentment and hate. The townships still smolder, but only men such as Tsotetsi still burrow deeply enough to notice.

The people visited by fieldworkers are detained without warrant, charge or trial. Their homes are invaded by the police in the dead of night. Their families are left without breadwinners. They are often hungry and homeless. Some are forcibly removed, their shacks torn down. Others are beaten and threatened by the police or vigilantes. All of them have had their limited civil rights stripped away by emergency decree.

Tsotetsi said fieldworkers provide "lipstick services." They can offer only cosmetic help—providing money for detainee families, shelter for the homeless, food for the hungry, legal assistance for victims of apartheid's burdensome laws. His enduring value, he said, is his ability to organize black communities as the authorities try to divide them.

"It used to be that when the system flexed its muscles, the people cringed," he said earlier this fall, sitting in the seat of a car that bounded over the dirt roads of a township. "The system was able to pick them off, one by one. But over the years we have been able to organize the people. Now when the system strikes, the people can absorb the blows."

The fieldworkers form the link between anti-apartheid groups and the ordinary blacks of the townships. The security police seek to break that link. They operate under the cloak of the emergency, which allows them to detain anyone at whim. Social work is permitted. Political activism is not.

If I help the homeless find a house, I am helping my fellow man," Tsotetsi said. "If I organize the people to fight for their homes, I am a terrorist."

On this particular day, Tsotetsi was traveling to Sebokeng, one of seven townships in the industrialized ghetto south of Johannesburg known as the Vaal Triangle. It was here, in the fall of 1984, that organized opposition to rent increases erupted into a nationwide revolt that was not put down until late 1986, after approximately 2,500 blacks had died.

The Vaal was still a volatile place. The night before, police had swept through Sebokeng. Several young men had been taken away to detention. Tsotetsi's own home is in Sebokeng, but he had escaped the police by spending the night with friends in Soweto, outside Johannesburg.

Now, Tsotetsi stopped at several houses, hoping to find "comrades," as young revolutionaries call themselves. These teenagers and young men are his grass-roots sources. From various comrades, he got the names and addresses of people detained the night before.

At each house, he was at first rebuffed. Black faces refused to open doors. Tsotetsi was accompanied by a white man, a reporter. Surely these men were police. Why else would a black man and a white man ride together in a car?

Tsotetsi spoke calmly. He joked with the people at the notion that he was a policeman. A tall, lean man of 34, he smiles easily. He has a round, gentle face and dresses in baggy slacks and a sport shirt. He looks like anything but a cop.

Soon the people in the houses were smiling back at him. Tsotetsi went inside each house and was served tea. He took notes on the detentions. At the end of each day he files a report for the Council of Churches. The reports are kept in a secret place, ready to be destroyed like a bookie's betting sheet, in the event of a police raid.

Tsotetsi left each family the name of a Johannesburg lawyer who would pursue the detentions with the police. He would take the detainees' names to the lawyers. In a few weeks, he would begin delivering small amounts of money to help the families weather the loss of breadwinners.

He arranged transportation for each family to Johannesburg to see its lawyer. "It is very important," he told one family. "Please, please, you must keep the pressure on."

Two days later, Tsotetsi was back in Sebokeng to see a local grocer whose son had been missing since he was detained in October 1986. The police had raided the grocer's house the night before. They had dragged him and his wife out of bed and forced him to lie face down in the yard while they ransacked the house. Then, they had left without a word.

The grocer agreed to speak to a reporter if his name were not published. He said the police had warned him to keep his mouth shut.

The man's son, who would be 23 if he were still alive, was an activist. A few days after he was dragged from home in 1986, the police told the grocer his son had escaped from prison.

He did not believe it. He knew from newspaper reports that other detainees had also "escaped," only to turn up dead much later. The reports regularly quoted allegations by human rights lawyers that missing detainees had died from police torture.

"I suspect my son is dead," the grocer told Tsotetsi. "Or else he has been seriously injured by them and they are afraid I will sue."

Tsotetsi assured the man that the Council of Churches lawyers were demanding an explanation from the police.

"Tell me," the man asked, "is there any other country in the world where a man prays his son is being held by the police?"

A few days later a funeral was scheduled, but Tsotetsi was afraid to go. A fellow activist had been shot dead by black police in the township of Tumahole, 50 miles south of Johannesburg. Tsotetsi wanted to pay his respects, but he knew the Special Branch would be at the funeral, arresting activists who showed up, videotaping the whole affair.

He stayed away. "I'm no good to the movement if I'm in prison," he said.

Instead, he visited the dead activist's parents and delivered a message from lawyers investigating the killing. He was often a conduit for information; the police tap the phones of most anti-apartheid lawyers and groups.

On his way back to Johannesburg, he stopped to visit families of detainees in the small township of Bophelong. The place holds frightening memories. In 1986, police opened fire on a meeting of activists there. Tsotetsi remembers feeling the shock waves of bullets whistling past his face and neck. To this day, he is amazed that he was not killed.

Driving away after his late October visit, he spotted a yellow police van heading his way. He backed up his car and drove quickly in the opposite direction. The detour added a half hour to his drive back to Johannesburg, but he was taking no chances. Just that morning, the comrades in Sebokeng had sent him a message: The system had visited his house.

Two days later, Tsotetsi was riding in a car through a township when he heard on the radio that the police had raided the Council of Churches offices in Johannesburg. He stayed away for several days.

When he finally slipped in early one morning, he noticed that the council had put up heavy burglar bars to block the entrance to its offices. "Well, now," he said dryly. "That ought to slow them down for at least a few seconds."

The life of Sol Tsotetsi is a road map of South Africa's recent, tur-
bulent history. He was born in Sharpeville, south of Johannesburg,
the son of a factory laborer. His earliest memories are of the
Sharpeville Massacre, the March day in 1960 when police opened fire
on a crowd of unarmed blacks at a police station not far from the
Tsotetsi house, killing 67 of them. Some were his neighbors.

He remembers being drawn to the black struggle by listening to
clandestine radio broadcasts from the outlawed African National
Congress in Zambia. As a teenager, he had a clenched black fist tat-
tooed on his left forearm. By 1976, he was involved in the student
protests against the teaching of Afrikaans in black schools.

That same year, he was charged with helping to burn down the
Sebokeng Council Hall and with recruiting for the banned ANC.
During his lengthy trial, his father died. His request to attend the
funeral was denied.

Tsotetsi was convicted and sentenced to seven years on Robben
Island, the maximum-security prison outside Cape Town. There, he
met the jailed ANC leader Nelson Mandela. Tsotetsi's commitment to
the struggle intensified; he knew he would resume organizing black
resistance the day he got out.

Soon after his release in 1984, Tsotetsi went to the Council of
Churches. He had been told that they assisted freed detainees. When
he offered a detailed political analysis of events in the Vaal for the
council, laced with sociological terms he had learned from a prison
correspondence course, he was offered a fieldworker's position at 700
rand ($320) a month.

He does not regret taking the job, though his activism has effectively cost him his son. He rarely visits the boy because the police
watch his mother's house, where his son lives.

"When I see him on one of these quick visits, he cries when I have
to leave," Tsotetsi said. "He doesn't understand why his daddy is
afraid to come home."

Between 1984 and 1986 Tsotetsi was detained several times.
Earlier this year, his house in Sebokeng was searched by the security
police. He had made the mistake of leaving his briefcase at home. "It
seems my briefcase has been detained," he said.

He accepts the costs of his activism. "What the police don't realize
is, all their harassment and assaults don't deter the people," he said.
"It only unites the resistance against the system. It makes us
stronger."

Tsotetsi enjoys challenging the police. During the height of the
1984-86 revolt, he said, he would slip into the sealed-off townships
by posing as a laborer. He would shuffle and address the police as

baas, thanking them profusely in Afrikaans for letting him pass. Later, he would laugh about it with his comrades.

He is more amused than incensed by petty apartheid. When he was asked by a white sandwich-shop owner in one of the Boer towns around the Vaal to eat his lunch outside, he thanked the man for reminding him that he doesn't like to eat with bigots.

Tsotetsi did not show up for an appointment at the Council of Churches offices one day last month. No one had seen him, or his Bible.

The next day, Nov. 8, one of the comrades from Sebokeng dropped by to say there had been a police sweeping the night before. Tsotetsi had been spending the night at a friend's house. The police broke in through the darkness. The system had caught up with Sol Tsotetsi again.

A few days later, a Johannesburg lawyer named Amichand Soman discovered that Tsotetsi was being held in the Protea police station in Soweto. He is a Section 29 detainee, Soman said. That means he is being held for interrogation. He has no right to see a lawyer. He could be held indefinitely.

The lawyer is worried. "It is something quite serious, this interrogation," he said. There is much to be learned from a man like Sol Tsotetsi.

ANALYSIS

ONE OF THE MOST IMPRESSIVE things about David Zucchino's story is that it was ever written at all. Knowingly violating government rules in an environment rampant with weapons and violence isn't for everyone.

He estimates the series took three months of reporting and 3-4 weeks to write. Zucchino says he tried to write the individual profiles as breaking news. "I think it helps sharpen and focus your work when you're under the gun. Plus, going out every day [into the townships] was the way I ran into these people and managed to gain their confidence."

Zucchino chose not to tape most of his interviews, pointing out that only one of his subjects had ever been interviewed before. "I really thought pulling out a tape recorder would totally intimidate them and cause them to freeze up," he says.

Zucchino says the decision to write "Being Black In South Africa" as individual profiles, rather than one long story, was made early on. "The idea was to keep the story focused on people and how events affected their lives. The problem with a series, [especially] if it's a complicated subject, is you've got to have several paragraphs boiling down the essence of the series in every story."

(Zucchino's right. The decision on how to run a long and powerful series—running one long story vs. several parts; using a pull out section vs. a broadsheet; italic/boldface precedes or not—can play a major role in the story's ultimate impact.)

Zucchino, like Isabel Wilkerson, wasn't looking to win many literary style contests with his writing. "It was pretty much, report the story and write it.

"The biggest problem was access, just getting to these people. ... In the cases where they did have phones, you didn't want to be talking on it because my phone was tapped."

Zucchino writes terrific descriptive leads, often more "newsy" than "feature." His profiles in this series are chock-full of detail. The sentences are simple, the wording economical. The first few sentences of the first profile follow a specific Zucchino model for this series: present the key character(s), preferably in a scene that sets the stage for the rest of the piece, add an explanatory "nut" graf early in the piece and weave the overall topic in and out of the narrative.

His lead in the series' first profile is typical of his no-nonsense style—descriptive, compelling, instructional:

It was not done the proper way, the old man said. The burial of his son had been spoiled, and it pained him that his final memory of the young man was so stained by discontent.

Most importantly, the opening paragraph makes the reader want to read the next one:

The damp dirt of his son's grave stuck to the shoes of Joseph Nakedi. His clothes smelled of tear gas. His wife was weeping. He could hear the rumble of police armored vehicles along the dirt path outside his shack.

Finally, Zucchino adds the delayed summary lead that ties it all together:

*Johannes Lefu Nakedi had just been buried on Oct. 10 in the
windswept veld of the Orange Free State, his funeral watched
from a safe distance by a crush of security police with shotguns
and bullet-proof vests. The mourners had been tear-gassed. The
priests had been bundled into a riot vehicle. ...*

Zucchino's nine-part series is an amazing journalistic effort,
all the more so when one considers the state of South Africa in
1988, the dangers he faced traveling throughout the country,
and the courage of the individual citizens who talked with
him—often at great personal risk.

Zucchino is funny, warm and easy to talk to. But you don't
walk into dangerous situations three different times and walk
out a Pulitzer Prize finalist each time without a lot of heart and
courage.

DAVID ZUCCHINO is currently foreign editor of *The
Philadelphia Inquirer.* He holds a bachelor's degree in journalism from the University of North Carolina and is the author of
Myth of the Welfare Queen, a book about the lives of welfare
mothers in Philadelphia.

1990

DAVE CURTIN

WHEN A SAVAGE PROPANE EXPLOSION ripped through Bill and Cindy Walter's family home on June 21, 1988, leaving Bill and his two children with horrifying burns, the *Colorado Springs Gazette Telegraph* asked reporter Dave Curtin to shadow the family for several months—focusing primarily on the children.

Having only been with the paper for six months, Curtin jumped when the assistant city editor gave him the chance to write such an intense story. He recalled the children's aunt being quoted after the fire: "If they survive, their burns are going to be so disfiguring that they're going to feel like these little monsters."

Curtin says that comment gave his story a peg and set the wheels in motion for a five-month story that followed the children everywhere, monitoring their progress—both physical and emotional. The end result, "Adam & Megan," is a marvelous piece of journalism that could have easily won a Pulitzer in the service, features or explanatory categories.

Although the paper had planned to educate the community on the children's plight, hoping to prevent them from being treated as "monsters," Curtin concedes he also had ethical concerns over the story. "I was with this family at the worst possible time of their lives and was worried ... about their being exposed to 100,000 readers."

Curtin credits his editor for coming up with the answer to his quandary: "To show what they overcame, you have to show what they went through," the editor told Curtin.

The day the Pulitzers were announced, Curtin didn't even know he was a finalist, much less a winner. "I was eating lunch across the street and one of the reporters came over to get me." Believing he was being summoned to cover a big story, Curtin hurried back, only to find himself locked out. "I had forgotten my ID badge and someone had to come down and get me."

367

Curtin immediately noticed someone had pulled the AP bulletin announcing the Pulitzers up on a terminal, with his name prominently displayed. He still thought it was a typical newsroom joke until he suddenly realized that 100 people had squeezed into the newsroom and were giving him a standing ovation.

Curtin has one more ironic memory about his Pulitzer Prize-winning story: It finished *third* in a Colorado state writing contest the same year.

Adam & Megan

Colorado Springs Gazette Telegraph

January 8, 1989

SIX-YEAR-OLD Adam Walter and his 4-year-old sister, Megan, were burned severely along with their father on June 21 when a propane-gas explosion ripped through their Ellicott home east of Colorado Springs. Their lives were drastically changed.

Now, the Bill and Cindy Walter family is looking to the new year with great hopes and optimism. This is the story of their courageous triumph over disfiguring burns, and of the strength they have received from the warm responses of friends and strangers.

Megan Walter carefully arranges brightly colored ornaments three and four deep on the Christmas tree branches within her reach. Consequently, all the branches at the 3-foot height bend toward the floor from the weight.

"Megan, we need to spread out the ornaments a little more," her mother, Cindy, says gently, rearranging the bulbs.

Members of the Walter family had hoped to be back in their ranch home for Christmas, but construction is not completed. They are trimming their tree in an Ellicott rental home on a crisp, clear night, as they listen to a church-service program over the radio.

In the room illuminated only by the blinking of the multicolored lights on the tree, Cindy turns on a cassette tape. It is one the children had made to their father, Bill, five months earlier when they were in hospitals 1,100 miles apart.

In the background on the tape is the humming and beeping of hospital monitors. The children's voices quiver, their breathing is labored. Their words are more like gasps.

In the explosion, all suffered third-degree burns: Megan over 75 percent of her body, Adam over 58 percent and Bill over 38 percent of his body.

Third-degree burns—the most severe—destroy all skin layers. Bill, Adam and Megan were in critical condition for several weeks.

The blast killed the family's black Labrador retriever, Max.

"Dad, I think you're the specialest dad in the world," Adam begins on the tape. "And you're the only one I have. I'm glad we're still one family. I'm glad I don't have a stepdad or a stepmom. I'm so glad you guys don't fight and that we can be together. And that we can see each other, and that we can pray for each other, and that we can try to get better."

Then Megan's voice comes onto the tape. She is whispering, "Mom, can Dad talk back to me?"

"No," Cindy is heard to explain in the background. "Dad will have to talk back to you later on another tape."

Then, Megan begins: "Dad, you know what? Max is dead, Dad. And do you know why he's dead? Because he was standing right behind Adam and the wind blew him. The wind blew him so hard that it blew him right out the door and he broke his back. And now he's dead, Daddy. I'm really sad about that. I bet Adam's sad, too. When Mom talked about it to me, I got really scared. I thought Max got his fur burned. Mom told me his fur didn't get burned, he just got killed. Don't be sad, Dad, because when we get home, we're gonna get another puppy. Do you know what Dad? When you come see me, I'm going to start walking and you're going to see me walk."

Bill, sitting by the twinkling Christmas tree, quietly weeps as he listens to the tapes.

"What's wrong with Dad?" Adam asks.

"This tape is very special to Dad," Cindy says. "He has special feelings when he listens to it."

June

It is another summer evening on the plains 16 miles east of Colorado Springs. Ominous, black clouds roll in as a weary Bill Walter comes in from the fields of the 1,120 acre ranch he manages. Bill, 36, the son of an Illinois dairy farmer, is a big man with a hearty laugh.

His 34-year-old wife, Cindy, arrives home with groceries in one arm and 7-week-old Abby in the other. Adam, 6, and Megan, 4, scramble into the house ahead of her. Cindy and the children have been in Colorado Springs shopping and getting Megan a new hairdo.

Cindy and Bill, married for 14 years, met at Grand Rapids (Mich.) School of Bible and Music. They sing in their church choir, and she is a director of the youth ministry.

The family likes living on the Ellicott ranch, their home of three years since moving from Savanna, Ill. In the mornings, sunlight decorates the sprawling fields. In the evenings, thunderclouds rattle the windows like a temperamental neighbor.

But most importantly, the children are happy here. Adam loves horses, riding his bicycle and helping his dad feed the cattle. When he grows up, he wants to be a policeman, "so I can go fast and not get a ticket."

Megan can't wait for Abby—"my baby"—to grow up so she'll have a girl to play with. Megan loves to play hide-and-seek and, like her mother, she is meticulous. She follows her mother around the grocery store straightening the cans on the shelves. And Megan loves to hug, especially Abby and the family dog, Max.

Now, Adam and Megan are sitting on the floor of the mud room at the top of the basement stairs to change their shoes before going out to play. Max is wagging his tail, waiting for them. Adam is hoping his mother will make his favorite dinner, macaroni and cheese. Megan wonders what will be for dessert. Even after breakfast, she had asked, "What's for dessert?"

Cindy removes Abby from the blanketed infant seat in front of the kitchen window and places her in her crib in the children's bedroom. As Cindy prepares dinner at 5 p.m., she realizes there is no hot water. Bill, still wiping the sweat from his sundrenched brow, heads down to the basement to light the pilot light on the hotwater heater. He doesn't know that propane has leaked into the basement. He lights a match.

Suddenly a fiery explosion rocks the house.

"There was a boom and I saw a fireball," Cindy says later. "I didn't know what happened. I thought the house was hit by lightning."

"Call the hospital!" Bill shouts breathlessly. Trying to run, he staggers up the basement stairs. Only the collar of his shirt is left dangling from his neck.

The children are swept up in the sudden tunnel of fire. Most of their clothes are plastered to the walls of the mud room. The rest are melted onto their bloody bodies.

Six windows and a door are blown out into the yard. The blanket that had covered Abby moments earlier shoots through a shattered window and lands about 100 feet from the house.

Megan, her eyes stinging, wonders why Mommy is talking on the phone *now*. She thinks her mother is calling a friend.

The children and their father blindly stumble to the shower. They stand under a stream of cold well water to douse their burns.

"Daddy, my knees are weak. I'm falling," Megan cries.

"Hold on to me, Meggy," Bill says. "Hold on to me for support."

"I'm cold!" cries Adam. He has little skin to keep him warm.

Paramedics wrap the screaming children in wet sheets and carry them to the ambulance. Megan is crying out that her eyes hurt. Her corneas are burned and doctors at first fear she will be blind. But that fear will disappear after further examination.

In the ambulance, paramedics work desperately to keep the three conscious.

When Cindy sees her children at the Penrose Hospital emergency room in Colorado Springs, they are burned beyond recognition. She can't tell Adam from Megan.

"They didn't look anything like them," Cindy later recalls. "But their eyes, their eyes were the same and I knew it was Adam and Megan inside."

Megan is calm. "Look, Mommy, my foot's burned," she says, not knowing that her entire body is burned.

Adam is calm until he sees how badly burned Megan is. Then he becomes hysterical. He is struggling against the doctors, battling the oxygen, fighting the intravenous tubes. "His eyes, they were crazy," Cindy remembers.

"Adam, it's Mommy," Cindy calls to her son. But she can't make contact with him.

Not far from his children, Bill is hallucinating from the morphine anesthetic and shivering so violently that he is bouncing on the gurney.

Cindy walks alongside Megan into the operating room. Just one tuft of hair is left from the girl's new hairdo. When Cindy tenderly strokes it, it falls out.

"They're very critical," Dr. John Marta, an anesthesiologist, tells Cindy. "They might not make it. They're your kids out here. But they're mine in there," Marta says, pointing to the operating room. "I'll do everything I can. But I can't make any guarantees."

Cindy to this point has had unfaltering strength in living out this horror story. But now, she feels her strength pouring out as if through a sieve.

She buries her head in her hands.

"I prayed," she says later. "I prayed that my children would die.

"I didn't want them to have to go through it. I knew they had accepted the Lord as their savior. I knew they were going to heaven, that they would be with him. I didn't want them to go through all the pain and disfigurement. I didn't pray for Bill to die. He wasn't going to leave me all alone."

"I have to change my thinking," Cindy thinks the next morning when her children are still alive. "The Lord has not taken them to be with him. We can work through this."

Later, Bill is put in a wheelchair and pushed in to see his children. Megan doesn't recognize her father.

"Megan, it's Daddy," Cindy says.

The girl seems unconvinced. Then Bill speaks.

"Megan, honey, I love you," Bill says.

Megan's eyes keep circling her father's face, trying to piece it back together as she remembered it. Finally, she speaks.

"Daddy, you stepped on me!" she moans, remembering the frantic moments on the basement stairs after the explosion.

Since Megan did not immediately recognize her father, Cindy decides to prepare Adam for Bill's visit.

"Adam, your Daddy's coming to see you," she tells him. "He'll look different. Just look at his eyes."

Six days after the explosion, Megan and Adam are transferred to the Shriners Burn Institute in Galveston, Texas, which is 1,100 miles away. But doctors warn they may not survive the flight.

Bill sees his children moments before they are boarded onto the specially equipped medical jet. "I knew it might be the last time," he says.

"Am I going to die?" Adam asks daily from his Galveston hospital bed. "I'm not going to see Dad again, am I? Either I'm going to die or Dad is."

Nanny—the children's grandmother, Audra Shoemaker—and Cindy cannot truthfully tell Adam that he is not going to die. Instead, they work to calm his fear by changing the subject—"The Lone Ranger" is on television. This seems to brighten the boy.

"How come he's called the *Lone* Ranger when he always has a friend with him?" Adam wants to know.

Adam and Megan will spend seven weeks in the burn institute. Both are suffering from pulmonary edema, an excessive buildup of fluid in the lungs. Megan has a partially collapsed lung, and Adam had a cardiac arrest earlier.

Doctors work around the clock to prevent a collapse of circulation, a shutdown of the stomach and bowel system, upper lung and wound infections, kidney failure, pneumonia and prolonged shock.

The children are covered with cadaver skin as a temporary covering, and they undergo several blood transfusions and skin-graft operations. Back in Colorado Springs on one July day, 104 people from the Walter family's church, Mesa Hills Bible Church, respond to a call for blood.

The children are suffering from relentless nausea, burning fever and excessive chills. An automatic cooling blanket and fans control Megan's 104-degree fever.

The children relive the explosion in nightmares that might recur for months or even years.

Adam says the hospital isn't the solution—it's the problem. "Get me out of this hospital," he demands of Nanny.

During the final weeks of their first stay at the Galveston hospital, Adam and Megan are taught to sit up, to feed themselves and eventually to walk.

One day, Megan sees her reflection for the first time in a bedside cart and exclaims, "I think my hair's growing faster than Adam's."

On a bright day, Megan announces her wedding plans. She will marry "Dr. Bill"—surgeon Bill Baumgartl. Cindy and Nanny tell her she can't marry Dr. Bill, but she can have him for a boyfriend for now. Megan considers this for a moment and then declares, "I'll be a kid nurse!" Surely, that would be next best to marrying Dr. Bill.

Each child is given 3,200 calories of milk a day as part of a special diet rich in calcium, protein and potassium. Megan and Adam are fed a pint of milk an hour, 24 hours a day, for six weeks through a gastric-nasal tube.

Burn victims use calories at two times the normal metabolic rate. Not only is their rate of protein breakdown increased, but they lose protein through their wounds, says Shriners dietitian Megan Duke.

Doctors have learned how to replenish the tremendous amount of fluids lost through burn wounds. Before that, some severely burned people starved to death because they couldn't be fed fast enough, Duke says.

Adam is horrified when he sees the silicone-rubber face mask he and his sister will wear. "Take it away," he demands. "It scares me."

The masks, made from plaster molds of the children's faces, put pressure on the skin to control scarring.

The children will wear the $800 masks 23 hours a day for 1½ to three years, until the scars are mature and can no longer be changed.

"It's hot, it's itchy, it burns, it makes people afraid. There's a lot of reasons not to wear it," says Roland Morales, the medical sculptor who made the masks.

"It comes down to the parents. Kids start telling their parents, 'I hate you,' and the parents let it go and say, 'A plastic surgeon will correct it later.' A lot of people think a plastic surgeon can correct anything. That's not true."

The children also will wear pressure garments called Jobskins. Invented 20 years ago by an engineer, Conrad Jobst, the $1,000 elastic suits are custom-made to tightly fit their bodies like second skins to control scarring.

When skin is severely burned down to the third underlayer, it loses the benefit of the tight skin pressure that once was on top. The underlayer literally grows wild as it heals and forms a scar. If no pressure is applied when a scar is forming, skin will grow into irregular knots and swirls.

Without the mask and Jobskins, ugly, disfiguring and constrictive scars will develop.

The Jobskin must be worn for 12 to 18 months. Before pressure garments were used, burn victims were forever unable to function and grotesquely scarred.

Megan and Adam will wear a mouth spreader, a taut rubber-band contraption that keeps the mouth opening from growing shut. "You won't be able to eat a Big Mac unless you wear it," Morales tells the children.

They also will wear pads underneath their arms to prevent their armpits from growing shut.

Meanwhile in Colorado Springs, Bill is able to feed himself applesauce for the first time since the explosion five weeks ago. He now can shake hands, brush his teeth and blow his nose.

On Aug. 11, Adam, Megan, Cindy and Nanny return from Galveston.

But before they had left the burn institute, Cindy and Nanny were reminded that the children are returning to a world that may not be ready for them—a world that values physical beauty. They were told that severely burned children are stared at and often avoided. Other children may ask them why they look like a Martian, or a mummy or a monster.

Cindy and Nanny learned that some children live through their burns only to die a slow, social death.

"Do you know how they're going to feel when they get home?" asks the children's aunt, Candy Entingh. "Like misfits. They're going to feel ugly, different, like they don't fit in. We want people to see them and say, 'Hi Adam! Hi Megan!'"

August

"Hey!" Danny Spanagel shouts to Adam. "You lost two teeth, too!"

They are at children's church at Mesa Hills Bible Church on West Uintah Street. Adam and Megan are being reunited with their friends for the first time since the explosion, eight weeks earlier.

Danny doesn't seem to notice Adam's face, blotched red with open wounds. Or his shaved head. Or his awkward two-legged hop forced by constrictive scarring of the joints.

Danny sees only that Adam has lost his two front teeth.

Adam smiles and pats his best friend on the shoulder as only 6-year-old pals can do.

There are three dozen children ages 4 to 8 sitting in tiny chairs in the crowded room.

When Megan walks in, she sees little girls with long, flowing hair. Their skins are silky, their complexions radiant. They are in their Sunday dresses.

Megan's head is shaved. Her scalp has been used for donor skin for most of her five skin grafts. Her hands are gnarled and knobby, her fingers webbed together. Her face is scarred. Her body is bandaged from neck to toe.

The children stare. A tear rides unevenly down Megan's pock-marked cheek.

"Hi Megan," comes the squeaky call of a young, hesitant voice from across the room. This starts a flurry of greetings, and Megan quietly acknowledges them.

On the bulletin board is a poster of the Walter family with the words, "Can You Help?" In the portrait, the family is smiling, unburned, unscarred.

The children in the class look at the poster, then at Adam and Megan.

"Kids are curious by nature," teacher Sybil Butler says after class. "They've heard Adam and Megan have been burned. Now here they are in front of them and they're trying to figure it out. I told them that Adam and Megan will look different. But they're still Adam and Megan."

After church, family members go to their temporary home—the house of "Auntie" Candy and Uncle David Entingh.

There, Adam and Megan are shuffling around in rigid, robotlike motions with their cousins. Adam can't push his Hot Wheels cars along the floor as he used to. So he cradles them in his bent arms, drops them on the floor and pushes them with his feet.

"Eight weeks ago, we didn't know if they were going to live," Bill says. "Now they're running around. It's a miracle."

Then Bill turns solemn. "You don't wake up everyday and say I might die today. People are too preoccupied with what they're doing—where they're going—to think like that. What happened to us took 30 seconds and changed our lives forever. Things will never be the same for us," he says.

"We don't want to just be alive," Cindy says. "We want to be normal."

September

"How come your face is the same?" Adam asks his father during a two-hour therapy session at Penrose Hospital. "How come you don't have to wear the Jobst thing?"

"Because I'm not burned as bad as you are," Bill tells him.

Later, as Bill waits for his therapists, he tries to explain Adam's questions.

"What he's getting at," says Bill, "is 'How come you weren't burned as bad? Weren't you in the same explosion? You lit the match.'"

Adam denies he is burned, his father explains, and becomes angry when he is reminded. Sometimes Adam goes into uncharacteristic rages when he is forced to wear the mask or when he must go through another painful daily bath, Bill says.

"Sometimes ... he'll yell and scream. I'll pick him up and Adam won't be inside."

One day, when Bill paddles him, Adam screams, "I hate being burned!"

"Then this look comes over his face like 'Oh-oh, I admitted it,'" Bill says.

Another day, Bill asks his son, "How come you never say 'Thank you' anymore?"

"Why should I say 'thank you' for something I don't want?" Adam fires back.

"It's like he's saying, 'I didn't ask for this,'" Bill says. "He doesn't want this anymore. He just wants to be a kid."

While Adam is at times overcome with denial and anger, Megan struggles with feelings of shame, Bill and Cindy say.

Earlier in the week, when the children were going to a monthly checkup in Galveston, Megan was following her Auntie Candy through the Colorado Springs airport. But Auntie wasn't aware that Megan, in her mechanical straight-legged gallop, was trying desperately to keep up with her. Finally, Megan stumbled, falling breathlessly to the cold tile floor. She was unable to pick herself up.

On the plane, a disheartened Megan muttered for an hour, "I want to be burned. I'm glad I was burned. Take my ears off."

In an effort to relieve such feelings, the family is seeing a psychologist. "The kids have feelings that they don't know why they have," Bill says. "Sometimes I think if the Lord took them, they wouldn't have to go through this. They're tired. Tired of the pain."

"They don't know this is going to last a long time," Cindy says. "They think it's just for now."

Across the Penrose Hospital therapy gym, therapist Cathy McDermott asks Megan to make a fist. The girl strains with all the fury a 4-year-old can muster and succeeds in cupping her hand. "That's very good!" Cathy says.

Recognizing her own progress, Megan wiggles the knuckles on her right hand as if to wave and exclaims, "Look!"

The children's burns cause severe pain when they try to move their arms, legs and fingers. Thick scarring of the joints keeps them from moving normally. Therapists will work to mold the scar tissue while it is still active. When the scars mature, they will turn white and cannot be changed.

Cathy asks Megan what she is going to do on her birthday. Megan shrugs and says, "I'll eat cake."

Megan also hopes she will get earrings for her birthday. "Before I was burned, I used to have lipstick," she says in her best ladylike manner.

Later, another therapist, Janese London, places Megan on a large mat and removes her bandages. She encourages Megan to lie on the mat and point her toes "like a ballerina."

"I don't want to be a ballerina," Megan says.

"Why?" Janese asks.

"Because," Megan giggles, "they wear purple shoes and a pink dress!"

Megan tells Janese that she bathed herself today. "But I couldn't put the shampoo on," she laments. Which reminds her, "I have more hair than my baby does," she says of her sister Abby. "I'm gonna have long hair. Before I was burned, I had it all the way past my back."

As the therapy session comes to an end, Adam and Megan eagerly ask if they get to dance. Their father asks also, because he knows how much dancing means to them: During these minutes, Adam and Megan can forget they are scarred and burned. They can forget the painful struggles of eating, brushing their teeth, bathing. They can escape.

Adam and Megan put on oversized sunglasses that dwarf their shaved heads, and therapist Patti Stafford leads them in energetic, gyrating moves to the thumping sound of "Walk Like an Egyptian."

The children's excited laughs fill the gym. Without realizing it, their sudden exuberance equates to therapeutic exercises that it is hoped will one day allow them to do the things others take for granted—walking normally, dressing without pain, grasping a fork and a spoon.

As the session ends, Patti waves goodbye and the music fades.

Adam and Megan silently continue their high-stepping, arm-flinging liveliness. Into the elevator, they're still dancing. Down three floors, they're still shaking their heads rhythmically to the imagined beat. Then they bop out of the elevator and into the parking lot of the hospital—the same hospital where 10 weeks ago, 80 friends had gathered to hold hands and pray for the two critically burned children. Praying that Adam and Megan would again smile and laugh. And dance.

Adam arrives at his seventh birthday party wearing the hated mask. Ten other first-graders are with him at The Boardwalk, an amusement center. Adam at first had demanded, "No girls." But his mother had explained that girls *will* be there and that he *will* be nice to them.

The party is the first time he has seen all but one of his school friends since the explosion.

Sharing the party is Adam's friend Roy Webb, also turning 7. Cindy didn't want Adam to think he was being showered with gifts because he had been burned. The joint party should help dispel such a notion.

"I don't want him to be ugly and I don't want him to be spoiled. I just want him to be normal," Cindy says.

"Mom, take my mask off so I can go play," Adam says. His mother relents. After all, it is his birthday.

"Adam wants to get this over with by forgetting about the mask," Bill says. "With Adam, it's 'bring on the scars. I'm going to play. This isn't going to last.'

"The first impression you get of someone is by the expression on their face," Bill says. "But if you can't see the face, Adam thinks the mask scares people."

The maskless Adam has made his way to a bumper car. His gloved hands clutch the levers. At first, the other children are afraid to bump into his car, afraid that perhaps his frail body will break. But Adam quickly sets them straight. He bumps their cars with reckless abandon and sports a large smile that everyone can see.

In contrast to her brother, "Megan wants to get it over with by wearing her mask," Bill says. "She is very conscious of being pretty. She wants everyone to know that she's a girl. She saw what the Jobst gloves did for my hands."

"Megan has been hiding behind her mask," Bill says. The masks must be removed to eat, and when it's time for meals, she says she's not hungry.

Megan arrives at the party fashionably late, with her mask on. She's wearing a party dress over her Jobskin and a ribbon—not in her hair, but atop her Jobst hood. Her fingernails are painted red, and her earrings sparkle.

Auntie had fashioned the ribbon, following an incident two nights earlier. A pizza delivery man, upon leaving the Entingh home, waved goodbye to Megan and said, "See ya later, fella!"

"I hate it when someone calls me fella," Megan says, rolling her eyes.

Her eyes tell it all. You can tell whether she is smiling or frowning underneath her mask by the glint or sorrow in those sky-blue eyes. At the moment, she is frowning.

Some of the children at the party shy away from the masked girl. But not Justin Herl, one of Adam's classmates. Without a word, Justin grabs Megan's gloved hand and, gently but deliberately, marches her to a video game. He has become her protector.

"Kids are so compassionate," says Jan Henderson, Adam's kindergarten teacher who is at the party. "How come we can't carry that compassion with us all our lives?"

In Galveston the night before she and Adam go through their monthly clinic at the Shriners Burn Institute, Megan stares at her dinner. She quietly describes the other children she has seen at the institute.

"I see little children with no feet and no hands." She pauses. "Children with their ears and noses burned off."

The family is eating at Western Sizzlin'. Megan sticks a piece of steak with her fork and struggles to lift it to her mouth. Others in the restaurant watch curiously. Although it is a battle for Megan to feed herself, Bill and Cindy believe their children must learn to do everyday tasks for themselves.

During dessert, a chocolate chip takes a long plunge from atop Megan's sundae to the table. It takes her 30 seconds to pick it up in gloved fingers and hoist it to her mouth. "I got it!" she boasts.

At the daylong clinic, Megan and Adam go through a painful, comprehensive examination. They will undergo the checkups indefinitely. The Shriners will pay for their care at the burn institute until they are 18 years old.

The possibility for reconstructive surgery won't be known for at least two years, when the scars mature, says Dr. Bill Baumgartl. But the surgeons are optimistic.

"They were burned very severely, and they were here initially for only two months," Baumgartl says. "People with half the burns have stayed six months. Their progress has been remarkable."

Therapist Stephanie Bakker, who three months ago had taught the children to walk again, today will lead them in exercises to increase their range of motion, strength and endurance.

"The family as a unit must be very involved with the burned victims," Stephanie says. "Cindy was a rock through the whole thing. She's a great source of strength. She was determined they were going to make it. ... She's been a real inspiration for the other parents, and she's been admired by all the staff. Because we're so impressed with Cindy and Bill, that tells you about the rareness of their strength," Stephanie says.

"These kids are really a pleasure to work with—their smile, their big hug. That's the reward for working here—seeing them go from critically ill to being independent children again."

When the children go to therapy, they think it's a place to play. But therapists with psychology backgrounds are trained to learn what the kids are thinking by how they play. "If a 4-year-old is playing with dolls, and the doll who's supposed to be mommy is nagging the doll representing the child saying, 'That's what happens when you don't mind Mommy,' we know that's something we have to work on," says Sara Bolieu, a hospital spokeswoman.

"Children think that everything bad that happens to them is a punishment," says Andrea Royka, head of the child-life development department. "We had one boy who dressed up for Halloween as Freddy Krueger, the burned character in 'Nightmare on Elm Street.' Then he was burned two months later. He thought God was punishing him for dressing up as Freddy Krueger.

"The kids will ask, 'When I'm 21, will my scars go away?' Then it's time for reality therapy."

Across the room, music therapist Rocio Vega hands Adam bongo drums and instructs, "Beat it like you're really mad."

The exercise serves as a release for anger and tension, she explains.

"Music therapy is actually psychology," she says. "The kids will handle stress through music, and often are encouraged to write their own songs. Maybe they're real angry and have no other way to express it. It's OK to be mad or sad, and Adam and Megan know that."

Therapists have made a "re-entry" video that will reintroduce Adam and Megan to their classmates at home.

"You can prepare a child only so much for going back to school," Andrea says. "But when you don't prepare everyone else ... everything we've done with Adam and Megan is shot. It's scary to the other children because their friends look different."

In Adam's re-entry video, the therapist tells Adam's firstgrade classmates that he is "scared about going back to school. He wants people to know he is the same inside although he looks different on the outside. Adam is still the same Adam, and Megan is still the same Megan."

At the end of the film, Adam, dressed in hospital pajamas, tells his classmates, "I hope I can see you soon. Maybe the first day, I won't come."

Adam and Megan usually do not display an abundance of affection for each other. But on this day, after having gone through so much together, they are being separated for the first time. Adam is going home. Megan is staying in Galveston 10 more days. She will have skin grafts tomorrow on her chest, elbows, knee and thigh. She is devastated by the unexpected turn of events and she is crying uncontrollably. Adam is trying not to cry.

Adam limps toward the van parked near the hospital entrance. Megan waddles after him the best she can. Because of contractures in the elbow joints, she can't straighten her arms and he can't bend his.

Megan stops at the curb. Adam, bawling, turns to his sister. As he works desperately to curl his frail arms around her, Megan tries just as hard to unfold her bent arms to receive him. Finally, they hug.

As the van rolls away, Adam tells his father through gasping sobs, "I didn't think it would be so hard."

October

Five days before Halloween, the family goes to see "Bambi" at the Super Saver Eight theater at Citadel Crossing.

The cashier looks down at the two masked children. "Oh, great masks," he says. "I've never seen one of those before. Those are funny. Hey, those are great."

As the family walks in, Cindy corrects him. "Those aren't Halloween masks. My children have been burned."

A pallor stretches across the cashier's face, and he is speechless. After the movie, he approaches Bill. "I'm sorry. I didn't know. I really didn't know."

After the movie, the family goes shopping for tricycles. Therapists at Penrose Hospital have recommended the tricycles for the children to exercise their knee joints and improve their ability to grip by grasping the handlebars.

For Adam, the decision to accept a tricycle is tough. He was adept at riding his bicycle "very fast." He already had picked out a new bicycle for Christmas. It was the bike of his dreams.

"It's *very* fast," he had said. "And it has *very* good brakes. ... It's an adult bike."

Bill explains to Adam that he's not yet strong enough to balance a bicycle and that he wouldn't be able to grip the handlebars.

After much consternation, Adam decides he'll accept a trike. But not until Bill tells him he can pick out any horn he wants.

While they are shopping, a small boy spots the children. "Look Mom, they're wearing masks," he says.

"They have to wear the masks," his mother explains, "because they have 'owies.'" The boy appears to accept the explanation.

Moments later, a little girl sees Megan and says, "Look Mommy, she has a pig nose."

Megan's feelings are hurt, and she runs to Cindy. "Mommy, I don't have a pig nose."

"No," Cindy assures. "You don't have a pig nose. She just doesn't know about your mask."

On a moonless night, the family returns to the Ellicott ranch for the first time since the explosion four months earlier. Megan naps during the 16-mile ride. When she awakens, she's home at last.

But she's troubled because it doesn't look like home.

The mud room—at the top of the stairs where Megan and Adam were nearly killed by the fireball—is dark, vacant and hollow. It echoes. The doors and windows, blown out by the blast, are boarded.

The washer, dryer and freezer have been moved into the kitchen.

Megan walks into the kitchen. Cindy opens a cupboard, and scorched, wilted rose petals come fluttering out. She had kept a basket of the petals on top of the refrigerator. "What a mess!" Megan says. She limps quickly across the kitchen and into the children's old bedroom. She is comforted when she sees her bedroom is undisturbed.

Adam, meanwhile, has romped straight to the big wooden toy box made by his father and is digging feverishly for his cars and trucks. Megan soon arrives at her toy box. Side by side, they are absorbed in their long-lost toys.

This is Bill's second visit to the house. He had been here a couple of weeks ago. He had spotted melted pieces of clothing and skin, plastered to walls from the force of the explosion, and removed what he could.

Now he hesitates before going into the basement. "How will this make me feel?" he asks himself. "Can I handle this?" But he continues down, each of the 11 steps taking him closer to the source of the tragedy that so drastically had changed their lives. A cardboard box next to where Adam had been seated on the stairs is unscathed. The blast also hadn't disturbed a plastic bag, tennis rackets and baseball mitts in the basement.

"Sometimes I think the kids would have been better off if they were standing right behind me," Bill says. "But I can't change it."

For Cindy, this is the fourth trip to the home since the explosion. She had gone to the house the day after to get some clothes, and at other times to clean up the rooms. "It doesn't bother me anymore," she says. "I didn't like to go at first because of the smell. It was the smell of burned flesh. It was a people smell. It was the same smell as in the burn unit."

The family walks out the door of the mud room and stands at the evergreen bush where Max had gone to seek his final refuge. Max, with broken back and scorched lungs, had crawled under the evergreen to die.

November

Adam and Megan are wearing new winter coats and mittens on a cold, windy day in Elliott. Their old coats were destroyed in the explosion. They each carry a sack lunch, and Adam carries a book bag for both on his back. Today is their first day of school.

Cindy and Bill escort them to their classrooms at Elliott Elementary School.

Adam and Megan are not wearing their masks so their new classmates can see that they have features and hair.

Without hesitation, Cindy introduces Megan to the hushed kindergarten class. Then she holds up Megan's mask and carefully explains that her daughter must wear it. "If she doesn't, the bumps on her face will get real big and ugly," Cindy says.

The 20 kids watch Cindy put the mask on Megan. "Megan knows that when she wears her mask, you can't see her smile," Cindy says. "If you don't know how she's feeling, ask her. Ask her if she's feeling sad or happy."

Teacher Jan Henderson asks the boys and girls whether they are glad to see Megan. They respond with a resounding "yes!"

"Megan, are you happy to be here?" Mrs. Henderson asks. Megan nods, but unconvincingly.

The teacher tries again. "Megan, are you happy or sad?"

"Happy," Megan says, softly.

Her classmates, still silent, continue to look at the masked girl for several minutes.

Down the hall, Cindy repeats the introduction in Adam's class, where he is a celebrity, at least for today, among the 18 first-graders who are competing for his attention.

"Adam's face is red because his blood is working hard to heal it," Cindy tells them. "Underneath his suit, his skin is OK. It's just real red. After a year, Adam can take the suit off. You can touch Adam's skin if you want. Adam will let you.

"If he needs help, he will ask, 'Will you please help me?' but don't rush up to do things for him because we make him do a lot of things for himself," Cindy says.

After Cindy and Bill leave, the first-graders are asked by teacher Lynda Grove what they learned.

"He can do most things we can do," says one student.

"You can touch his skin and it won't hurt," another says.

"He can do things by himself," another says.

When first-grade teacher Jolynn Olden brings her students into the room to meet Adam, she asks the children if they have questions for him.

"Can you go across the monkey bars?" asks one.

"Not yet," Adam replies.

"Can you go down the slide?" asks another.

Adam nods.

"Can you run?" another wants to know.

"Yes," Adam says.

Now the true measure of worth for a first-grader becomes evident. "Fast" to a 7-year-old is everything important.

"Can you run as fast as in kindergarten?" a youngster carefully queries. "Faster," Adam says unflinchingly.

"Can you ride a bike?"

"No," Adam answers reluctantly. "We're still working on balance."

Miss Olden turns Adam's answer into a lesson. "Class, what's balance?" she asks. The answer is universal. "It's staying up on two wheels," the pupils chime.

"Were you scared to come to school today?" a classmate asks.

"A little at first," Adams says. "But I got over it."

The questions continue to pour in. "Do you have fingernails? (Yes). What do you do at home? (Homework). Does your neck get tired of holding your mask up? (No)."

"Can we touch you?" one boy asks. Adam nods.

The children scramble to their feet and rush to circle Adam. All at once, they begin touching him. They are convinced that he's just like them.

A cutback in their daily therapy allows the children to attend school three days a week. Cindy and Bill want to get their children back into the mainstream as quickly as possible.

Though Adam and Megan are starting school 2½ months late, they have been working math problems and reading books at home in rare moments when not consumed by therapy and treatment.

Adam needs no practice at art. In art class today, the students are drawing what they will eat for Thanksgiving. Adam uses crayons to draw a dinosaur and what he describes as "worm pie."

Meanwhile, Megan is learning to write V's in her class. But gripping the pencil hurts her right hand. "Megan will learn by watching," says Luann Dobler, a student teacher.

In the cafeteria at lunch time, all the kids are eager to sit next to Adam. Roy Webb and Jason Harding are the winners. They and Adam recall the old days. "Do you remember when the girls attacked?" Adam asks. The two nod furtively and smile. Undoubtedly, it was a memorable event.

Two tables away, Megan wrestles with her sandwich Baggie over possession of a peanut butter and jelly sandwich. A third-grade boy who enters the lunchroom fails to notice Megan's effort to look pretty; she's wearing her ribbons, earrings and her best dress. Having not heard Cindy's earlier lesson, he asks no one in particular, "What's wrong with Megan? She doesn't look too good. Her face is all red."

The harsh words fail to distract the little girl. Minutes later in math class, Megan is called to the blackboard to draw two of anything. On this blustery, gray day of this devastating year, Megan shuffles up to the board and draws two smiling suns.

Epilogue
"You always hear the cliché, 'life isn't fair,'" says Bill Walter. "I guess I've learned that. Even though it isn't fair, it doesn't mean your world has to go to pieces. This has helped me gain a better appreciation of life, what's serious and what's not.

"For my children, for myself, for my family, it doesn't seem fair. But being a Christian, I feel there's a reason for things to happen. The lives you touch and those that touch you—I wonder what the purpose is behind it all?

"More than anything, it was such a shock to me. I never really felt it was my fault. Just a freak accident. When you read of people who are hurt or see it on TV, you feel bad about it, but only for a little while. Then you go on. You never think of something like this happening to you.

"I was the one who lit the match. It seemed so unfair to the children. I've woken up many times at night with a real great sorrow. If I could, I'd like to back up to June 21 and go on from there. But in reality, you can't change that. The Lord has given us the strength to pick up the pieces and go on. Bitterness isn't going to help anyone—my being bitter or Cindy and I being bitter toward each other. Why destroy the kids with bitterness?

"It's good to be alive. More and more, the kids see that. They realize life will come back to a point of being normal. At first, they doubted if anything was ever going to be good again. Now they see that it will be.

"One thing that's really neat is to know that our community—El Paso County, Colorado Springs, Calhan, Ellicott—was pulling for us. That's hard to express. I thank everyone so much. 'Thank you' seems awful small for what we feel at a time like this."

ANALYSIS

ONE OF DAVE CURTIN'S major accomplishments in writing
"Adam & Megan" was his capacity to spend extensive time
with the family over several months—eating, shopping, traveling with them—yet still maintain a professional distance so he
could write objectively. "I felt I could get as close to the family
as I needed and not hold any emotions back," he explains.
"Sometimes, I would come home at night and just cry at some
of what I had heard. When it came time to write, I made a conscious effort to distance myself a little bit and try not to make it
a tear-jerker."

Winning Adam and Megan's trust was crucial to the success
of the story. Curtin and photographer Tom Kimmell went to
great efforts to bond with the family. He says they were quickly accepted after they learned to play hide-and-seek with the
children and "slurp chocolate pudding with them." Curtin says
letting the children play with the cameras helped. "It became
kind of a game: We take a picture of the kids and they would
take one of us."

Still, Curtin says reporting the story required solid interviewing skills, plus sensitivity to the family. "There were some real
emotional moments, and some heart-felt things were said. I did-
n't want to barge in the house and whip out my notebook. I
started off with small talk, very conversational. When we started getting into heavy stuff, I would ask if they minded if I took
a few notes. Before long, they didn't even recognize the notebook was there."

Conversely, Curtin says he decided not to use a tape recorder
because he felt the family wasn't very media-savvy and taping
could prove to be counter-productive.

Curtin estimates he spent some five months on "Adam &
Megan": four months reporting (while working on other stories) and two weeks exclusively writing the story. A final two
weeks were devoted to final editing and fine tuning.

Curtin remembers some discussion over how to play the
story. "We didn't know if we wanted to present it in a special
pull-out form in the Sunday paper, which we ultimately did, or
in the regular broadsheet of the Sunday paper, or in a series
form."

The decision to write the story in a chronology was the obvious choice. "I essentially had an electronic diary in chronological form," Curtin says. "I just took my diary, polished up a few things and had my rough draft."

The chronology was only broken once, and it turned out to be a momentous decision. "My editor, Carl Skiff, took the end of my story and put it at the beginning." Not that Curtin jumped at the idea immediately. "When he first made the suggestion, I thought, 'what are you talking about?' He said, 'just try it. For one thing, it's seasonal ... and it tells the reader that this isn't going to be the grim story that it appears.'"

Curtin says he used two literary tactics often seen in fiction—characterization and conflict. "The characters emerged very quickly," he feels. "Adam would fly into these uncontrollable rages. ... Bill felt this tremendous guilt. ... Cindy has to be this rock-solid superwoman. ... Megan was worried that she didn't look like a little girl anymore." The pain within each of the main characters gives the story its sense of conflict.

Curtin begins the story with a larger-type, boldface summary lead over the story, ending with a positive note about how the family optimistically views the new year. "That was to set up the story right away, present the facts quickly to the reader," he explains.

Compare this decision with how two other stories in this anthology handled a potentially harrowing outcome. In "Mrs. Kelly's Monster" (1979), Jon Franklin says he intentionally wrote an italic precede badly, so the readers wouldn't know for sure what was coming next. Yet, the readers were told that Mrs. Kelly would die.

In "AIDS in the Heartland" (1988), Jacqui Banaszynski, also wrote an italic lead-in, but the readers were never told for sure the outcome—although it may have been obvious to many.

Adam & Megan begins with the Christmas tree scene, recaps the explosion and ends with the emotional tape Adam made for his dad after the explosion. A gripping photo of the children in their masks takes up two of the page's three columns, resulting in an unforgettable start.

After this powerful opening, notice how Curtin retreats to June, the month the explosion happened, setting the stage by telling a little about each family member and the house.

Curtin says he reconstructed some of the blast details by talking to the rescuers and others who were on the scene. Some of the details are compelling:

Only the collar of [Bill's] shirt is left dangling from his neck.

The rest [of the children's clothes] are melted onto their bloody bodies.

Just one tuft of [Megan's] hair is left from the girl's new hair-do. When Cindy tenderly strokes it, it falls out.

Curtin points out the reconstruction was helped because the family "trusted us with tape recordings and diaries." The father and two children were in different burn centers, 1,100 miles apart, their burns severe enough to prevent writing. They communicated by tape recordings through the mail. Curtin feels they often felt these recordings might contain their last words together.

Curtin's reporting and observational skills continually shine through in this story. Notice this detail from the Shriners Burn Institute in Galveston, Texas.

The children are covered in cadaver skin as a temporary covering. ...

And, finally:

During dessert, a chocolate chip takes a long plunge from atop Megan's sundae to the table. It takes her 30 seconds to pick it up in gloved fingers and hoist it to her mouth. "I got it!" she boasts.

Curtin says he often finds it hard to live up to "Adam & Megan," wondering if such a memorable story will ever come his way again. For the rest of us, one like this is more than enough for a lifetime.

DAVE CURTIN has been a police, general assignment and features reporter for the *Colorado Springs Gazette Telegraph*. He has a bachelor's degree in journalism from the University of Colorado at Boulder.

1991

SHERYL JAMES

SHERYL JAMES NOT ONLY won a Pulitzer in 1991 for "A Gift Abandoned," but followed that up the next year by being nominated again—for a story about the effort to use the organs of a dead boy to save other lives.

James had a specific reason for writing "A Gift Abandoned," noting that South Florida seemed to have an epidemic of abandoned babies turning up everywhere in the mid-1980s. "It seemed natural to try to profile one of these cases," James recalls. "And I was given that assignment."

The story took about eight months to produce and was originally scheduled to run as a Sunday front, but it kept growing. "As I kept reporting, I knew I had something more," she says. "I was automatically given the time and encouragement to develop this material to its potential."

James feels her editor, Sandra Thompson, was exceptionally supportive and played a vital role in the final editing of the 400 plus inches of copy. "She helped improve the copy without ever rewriting anything herself—something feature writers hate."

In James' case, winning the Pulitzer had a major effect on her life and career: "I was working on a story at my desk when the wire services starting reporting the Pulitzer winners. I didn't know I was even a finalist. ... One of my colleagues stood up, threw out her arms and shouted, 'Sheryl, you won!' I was shocked senseless and elated beyond words. It was like being Miss America."

Unlike Miss America, however, James was rewarded for a lifetime. "I immediately got a $10,000 raise. ... More importantly, though, I was able to get back home to my native Michigan in real style. Because of the Pulitzer, I was able to negotiate a deal with *The Detroit Free Press* where I could work out of my home four days a week. With two small children, I secured a wonderful lifestyle I wouldn't trade for anything."

A Gift Abandoned

The St. Petersburg Times

April 18–21, 1990

DAY ONE: JACK-IN-THE-BOX

THAT DAY, Ryan Nawrocki was just an ordinary sixth-grader living an ordinary life. He was 11 years old, with blond hair that hung straight and heavy over his forehead. He was a stocky kid, and it was easy to imagine him carrying a baseball mitt or playing video games after dinner. That day, Thursday, April 27, Ryan strode across the street from his house in Wildwood Acres, a complex of shoe-box-shaped duplexes on streets that curl into other streets lined with more shoe boxes. He headed toward a small courtyard where his 16-year-old sister, Melissa, was doing laundry in a small community building. Walking along a worn foot path, he passed the dumpster and a large oak tree.

He heard something. A kitten?

His eyes followed the sound to a videocassette recorder box lying on the ground beneath the oak tree about 10 feet from the dumpster. The flaps of the box were closed but unsecured. Ryan walked over to the box. He opened the flaps.

It was a painful, jolting sight: a newborn baby marked with dried blood and a cheesy substance, lying on a bloody towel. The baby gnawed on its fist and cried again.

Ryan tore over to the laundry room.

"There's a baby in a box over there!" he told his sister.

"You're lyin'," she replied.

"No, I'm not!"

His sister peered at Ryan, unsure. Then she stopped stuffing clothes into the washer. "If you're lyin', I'm gonna kill you," she announced, walking out the door.

Moments later, she reached the box. *"Oh, my God."*

Melissa rushed across the street to her apartment. Inside, her mother, Lisa Nawrocki, was watching *Night Court* on television. She looked up as her daughter ran in. The girl was almost hysterical. Melissa told her mother what they had found.

Call 911, Lisa Nawrocki, said. She told Ryan to bring the box over, but Ryan said, "I can't look at it! I can't look at it!"

His mother walked across the street, brought the box back and laid it on her living room floor. A licensed practical nurse, she checked the baby's vital signs. Melissa was too upset to speak plainly on the phone. Her mother took the receiver.

The baby was a boy, she told the 911 operator. His color was good, and he didn't seem to have any respiratory problems. His mother, whoever she was, must have cut his umbilical cord and tied the end off with blue thread or fishing line.

An ambulance was on the way, and Melissa ran next door to borrow a diaper from their neighbor, who had 1-year-old twins. Lisa carefully wrapped the child in it; the diaper nearly swallowed him, reaching from his kneecaps to his chest. It made him look even more pitiful, Lisa thought, as she picked him up and wrapped him in a plaid blanket.

She rocked and talked softly to the baby. The ambulance arrived within minutes—too soon for Lisa. She felt as if she could have held the baby forever.

The emergency services technicians, a man and a woman, came in. They checked the baby and fired off questions: Who delivered the baby? Did you name him? They seemed a little cold, Lisa thought. She placed the baby on the stretcher. He was sucking his thumb. The technicians put the stretcher into the ambulance and then drove off to Tampa General Hospital.

By then, things were hectic. Police lights flashed outside. Officers came in to interview the Nawrockis. Reporters and television cameras swarmed around with lights, microphones and notebooks. Neighbors streamed in. Everybody was asking questions. The same questions:

Who was the mother? The University of South Florida was nearby; was she a student, afraid to tell her parents, deserted by her boyfriend? How could any mother do such a thing? She oughta be strung up, someone said.

God only knows what was going on in her mind, Lisa Nawrocki, thought. *I hope she gets help because she needs it. I'm going to wonder about this baby for the rest of my life. I hope whoever adopts him never tells him he was found by a dumpster. That's a heck of a way to start life: Your mother threw you away.*

Detective Dennis Hallberg of the Hillsborough County Sheriff's Office got to the scene soon after the baby was found. After talking to the Nawrockis, he and other deputies swung into action. Speed was important. A woman had just given birth. She was most vulnerable, most likely to be found, right now.

Hillsborough County Health Department clinics were asked to look out for any white, female walk-ins. Meanwhile, officers knocked on neighborhood doors. Have you seen any pregnant women recently? they asked. Do you know any women who are expecting?

One person said there was a pregnant woman who lived over on Marta Drive. The officers found her; she was still pregnant. Someone else saw a young woman holding a baby on the corner earlier in the day. The deputies found her—and her baby.

Detective Hallberg studied the scene, trying to reconstruct what may have happened: A white woman had a baby. She cut and tied its umbilical cord, preventing the baby from bleeding to death. She placed the baby in a box. In broad daylight, she put the box under a tree, alongside a path that people used to go to the laundry room, about 50 yards away in a courtyard.

Did she walk here? Drive? Was she alone? Was she a scared, young kid? A cold, selfish woman? Was she locked in a terrible relationship with the father? Did she plan all this? Did she panic? Was she somewhere watching right at this moment?

At Tampa General Hospital, they called him Jack-in-the-box. They put him under a warmer to stabilize him, fed him and gave him routine injections. They dressed him up. The nurses fell in love with him, all 7 pounds, 7 ounces of him, especially Tina Davis. She helped care for him that night and the next day. She had worked with infants there for three years, but she felt different about this one.

He was such a *gift!* She just couldn't believe it. She and her husband had been trying to conceive a child for a long time. And here, she thought, some woman had this baby and just walked away.

Later that Thursday night, around the corner from where the baby was found, at 5812 Mar-Jo Drive, Judy Pemberton, 42, quietly watched television. Cats and kittens played here and there in the two-bedroom duplex apartment.

At 10:30 p.m., Judy's live-in boyfriend, Russell Hayes, 28, came home from his job at a nearby restaurant. He was a big, red-headed fellow with a ruddy, boyish face and small, serious eyes. He asked Judy how she was feeling. She looked better than she had that morning. Her blond, shoulder-length hair was softly curled, and she wore her normal, loose-fitting clothes. But there were circles under her deep-set, blue eyes.

Judy said she was feeling much better. "I finally started my period," she said. The cramps were gone. She got up to fix Russell dinner.

Russell was relieved. For the past 24 hours or so, Judy had been suffering terrible cramps. She even called in sick to work, the first time she had done that in nearly a year. She told Russell she was going through menopause. She hadn't had a period in 11 months. This was all part of it. You missed periods, then you had one, then you missed more. Don't worry.

People had been worried about Judy, though. Russell knew that. A few people had even wondered if Judy were pregnant. One of Russell's outspoken aunts had asked Judy outright. Judy said no. About three weeks earlier, Russell's other aunt, Mary Duncan, who had raised Russell from the time he was 5, talked to Russell about Judy's condition.

"Russell, something is wrong with Judy. Is she pregnant?" Mrs. Duncan said.

"No, not that I know of," Russell said.

"Well there's somethin' wrong with her. She needs to go to the doctor. Would you please talk to her?"

When Russell talked to Judy, she said, "No, I'm gettin' tired of people askin' me that, no I'm not pregnant."

Then, last night, Judy was in terrible pain at the bowling alley. Her friends were worried about her because she could hardly bowl. One woman found Judy in the bathroom doubled over in pain. Judy was worried, too, and asked her sister-in-law, Marcie Gilbert, who was also the bowling alley manager, to take her to the hospital if she got worse.

"I'm cramping so bad I can't hardly stand it," Judy told her. "I feel like I want to start (my period), but I can't."

"Judy, *quit bowling,*" Marcie said. "If you're trying to start and having major problems, don't bowl." Marcie knew Judy had not had a period in months. She had asked Marcie often about menopause.

"Maybe it's a cyst," Marcie said. "Judy, let's go to the doctor tomorrow."

"I can't afford it," Judy said. "I can't afford to skip work."

"You can't afford to be dead, either. If you've got something going on inside your body, nobody can see it but a doctor."

When Russell picked up Judy that night, Marcie made him promise to take Judy to the hospital if she didn't feel better.

But Judy said she was all right. And now, as she fixed dinner, she seemed fine. The couple ate and then fell into bed by 11:30 p.m. Both of them were dog tired.

Friday morning, Judy went to work. For the past year, she had been a general receptionist at Hallmark Packaging Corp., on nearby 39th Avenue N. She wore one of the same outfits she had worn often in the past year—striped blouse worn out over a pair of slacks. When she got to the office, everyone was talking about the baby that was found by a dumpster in Wildwood Acres. They were outraged. Personnel manager Kim Clark and Hallmark president Vincent Tifer stood by Judy's desk, and they all discussed it.

"They should hang the woman by the damn neck," Tifer said.

"How could any mother do this?" said Kim Clark, personnel director.

Judy loved children. She had recently brought to work the cute clothes she bought for her little granddaughter. Judy agreed with Clark and Tifer. How could any mother do this?

The news about this baby was distressing not just because it was a disturbing crime, but also because it was getting to be such a common one. In the previous two years, news stories about babies left in boxes, garbage cans, trash bins, cars and baskets have popped up with numbing frequency. In the 10 months since this baby was found, five others have been abandoned in the Tampa Bay area, including a baby dubbed "Seminole Sam" who was left on the doorstep of a Seminole Catholic Church last week. Each case is tragically unique, and yet part of a phenomenon, ugly and terrifying, that people simply do not understand.

Last March, a baby was found dead next to a Tampa trash bin. The previous fall, a baby was left outside an apartment complex; he survived. Before that, another dead infant was found near a dumpster. The year before, a baby was found dead in a motel trash can. Across the state, near Fort Lauderdale, a police officer saved a baby thrown in a dumpster by sucking mucus out of its mouth; the same man had saved another baby a year before.

Some mothers have seemed more caring, leaving their babies in places where they would be found. One baby boy was left, wrapped in a quilt, in a Sarasota hospital parking garage. Another was left in a north Naples sheriff's department substation. One boy was left in an unlocked car in Fort Pierce. He was wrapped in a sweatshirt sleeve and blanket, and his mother left a note: "My husband is on drugs and because of it I became on drugs, too. I don't want to give my baby away, but he won't be brought up right. I cleaned him up. May God forgive me."

Across the country, it's the same thing. Mothers leaving babies in odd places, or just tossing them away. How many? No one knows. No one keeps count. No federal or state agencies keep track of how many babies are abandoned. Such cases are usually included in child abuse and neglect figures.

Only one organization—the Denver-based American Humane Association—has studied child abandonment to any degree.

The Association estimates that abandoned children make up about 1 percent of all child abuse and neglect cases. Using that measure and survey results from 20 states, the Association estimates that 17,185 children were reported abandoned in 1986. That figure includes all children up to age 18 abandoned by their parents in one way or another. In Florida, 2,226 children through age 17 were abandoned from June 1988 to July 1989.

Since reports of child abuse and neglect have risen 225 percent since 1976, the Association assumes that child abandonment parallels that increase. How many of these are newborn infants? That is impossible to guess. In a March 1987 article on baby abandonment, writer Jo Coudert found 600 newspaper accounts of babies who were thrown into dumpsters, toilets and other such places in 1986.

This was just a "pieced together" survey by one writer. How many other abandoned babies are not reported or written about? How many are never found at all and end up ignominiously in the nation's landfills?

At 10 a.m. Friday, April 28, the day after the baby was found, detectives Larry Lingo, Albert Frost and Michael Marino decided to search the dumpster. The garbage pickup was late that day. The dumpster had not been taped off as part of a crime scene. It had yet to occur to the detectives there was a connection between the baby, placed 6 to 10 feet from the dumpster under the tree, and the dumpster. If garbage trucks had come at their customary time, the dumpster would have been empty.

Instead, it was half full. Detective Marino, dressed in a suit, put on rubber yellow gloves and climbed in. He handed items of trash to the other detectives, who laid them carefully on the ground. For half an hour, they found nothing unusual. Then Marino found a box. It contained a clear plastic garbage bag. Inside the bag were two bloody towels, bloody tissue paper, bloody sanitary napkins, cat food cans, and empty Banquet Salisbury Steak TV dinner box, and directions for blond hair dye.

The box was a xerographic paper box with a half-square cut out on one side. On another side was an address label.

The address was Hallmark Packaging, 1212 39th Ave. N, Tampa.

The box provided one more piece, and many more questions, to the puzzle: The mother brought two boxes to the dumpster. She put one in the dumpster and the other on the ground. Did that mean she randomly left the box with the baby on the ground as part of the trash? Or did she make a conscious decision to distance the baby from the dumpster? After all, isn't it likely trash pickup workers would have grabbed the box on the ground? Or would they have *looked inside first,* to make sure someone wasn't throwing away a perfectly good videocassette recorder?

Why did she throw away the possibly incriminating box of trash? Didn't she realize someone might find it?

Detective Frost followed the first solid lead: Hallmark Packaging.

Hallmark Packaging is in a small, narrow office in a row of matching offices. It manufactures trash can liners and grocery sacks. Detective Frost arrived about 10:45 a.m. He walked into the small reception office and approached the window that separated the reception room from the rest of the company. Sitting at a desk behind the window was a blond woman with deep-set blue eyes. She looked to be in her 40s. Frost introduced himself and told the woman he was investigating the baby that was abandoned the day before at Wildwood Acres Apartments. He asked her what her name was.

Judy Pemberton, she replied.

Frost asked where the company put their empty boxes.

"I don't know," Ms. Pemberton said. "You'll have to ask the guys in the back, but most of us throw them out front, in the dumpster."

"Do you know if there are any pregnant women at the company?"

"None that I know of," she said. "There was one woman in the back who was expecting, but she already had her baby."

"*You're* not pregnant, are you?" Frost joked.

Ms. Pemberton laughed. "No."

They talked about 15 minutes. Halfway through the interview, Frost started to wonder about this woman and noted in his report she should be interviewed again. Something wasn't right. It was the way she was answering his questions. Too fast, for one thing, or with another question. She avoided eye contact. She looked off across the warehouse or at her desk, especially when he mentioned the baby.

Plus, she didn't react the way most people might when a cop comes out of nowhere to ask about a baby abandoned so nearby. She didn't seem surprised, or particularly interested, or kind of excited the way people who aren't involved are. She didn't ask gossipy questions, like,

Gee, what did it look like? Was it really in the trash? Any idea who the mother is?

She asked only one question, as Frost left his card, and turned to leave.

"How's the baby?"

In the corner office, Vincent Tifer, president of Hallmark, agonized over what he had to do that afternoon: fire Judy Pemberton. The company was automating, putting in computers, and Judy just didn't take to them. It was a shame. Tifer hated to let her go. She had been a reliable, punctual, hard-working employee, always willing if she didn't do something right to do it again. She was well-liked around the office. Tifer was so relieved the day before, Thursday, when she called in sick, which she had never done before. He was interviewing several candidates to replace her, and it would have been awkward with her sitting there. She had no idea that she was going to lose her job.

Tifer knew this would be hard on Judy. She had had some tough times. Two years before, she had left her husband of 21 years and her home in Colorado. She came with her 20-year-old daughter to Tampa, where she was born and raised. She soon learned her daughter was pregnant. Judy supported the family, and for a time, the father of the baby, on low wages she made working for a temporary office services company. Since her office skills were limited, Hallmark did not pay much either: about $5 an hour.

Later, Judy's daughter broke up with her boyfriend and then moved with her baby back to Colorado. They left behind a lot of unpaid bills.

At the same time, Tifer knew Judy was having health problems. She discussed it with the women there. She had missed a lot of periods and said she was going through menopause.

Not that Judy was one of these chronic complainers. She really kept to herself until she got to know you. Then, she opened up and talked about her life—especially about Russell.

Russell! When it came to Russell Hayes, Judy was a love-struck teenager. They had been dating about a year, living together since January. An 8-by-10 picture of him in his National Guard uniform dominated one corner of her desk. Sometimes, Tifer saw her staring at it, all lovey-eyed, as he described it. When she and Russell went to a carnival or fair, she would bring in a stuffed animal he won for her. At night, she would put all her stuffed animals near the picture and say good night to them.

It was obvious to everyone at Hallmark that Russell was good for

Judy. They had fun. They bowled. They went out to eat often, which, she said, was why they both were gaining weight. Tifer got the impression it was the first time Judy had felt relatively carefree in a long while.

The last thing she needed, Tifer thought, as the work day drew to a close, was to lose her job. But he had no choice. After paychecks were passed out, Tifer asked Judy to come into his office. As gently as he could, he told her they had to let her go. He explained why.

Judy listened quietly. Tears trickled down her face. But, so like Judy, she didn't get emotional. She said she understood, and that it had been a pleasure working for him and the company. Then she left.

Tifer felt rotten.

In those first crucial days after the baby was found, progress on the police investigation was sluggish. The VCR box had an old serial number, so it would take time to trace where it was purchased. A couple of people called saying they had seen pregnant women near Wildwood Acres, one near a traffic accident, to no avail.

Human hair had been found, and there were fingerprints on the items found in the dumpster. DNA testing and other lab tests on these items would also take time. The baby had been featured on television and in newspapers in an attempt to solicit public involvement. The detectives knew that's what usually cracked these cases. Someone who knows the mother finally makes an anonymous call. Someone with a conscience. Someone who despite other loyalties cannot ignore that baby.

Hallberg, Lingo and the other detectives working the case waited for that call. The more time that passed, the less likely it would come.

Friday night, Judy Pemberton and Russell Hayes visited Raymond and Mary Duncan. The couple are Russell's aunt and uncle, but Russell thought of them as Mom and Dad. They had raised him since he was a little boy. He was very close to them. Judy had grown close to them, too. They were an affectionate family, and she seemed to soak in that affection, as if she had never known it before. The four spent a lot of time together at the Duncans' cozy, two-bedroom Tampa apartment.

In the year or so Russell and Judy had been dating, Mrs. Duncan had grown fond of Judy. At first, the 15-year age difference between Russell and Judy seemed more important, but the two seemed so well-suited. Russell enjoyed Judy's tomboyishness, her sarcastic wit, her interest in sports. Judy seemed both mother and girlfriend to Russell, dependent on him at times, lending her own shoulder at others. Russell seemed to understand her and accept her as she was. She had quite a temper sometimes. When she lashed out, cursing and saying things she didn't mean, Russell just let it bounce off.

This night, Mrs. Duncan was quieter than usual as Judy, Russell and one of Russell's aunts watched the 11 o'clock news. Mrs. Duncan put up a good front, but something was bothering her, deep. When the report about the baby was shown, Mrs. Duncan's eyes shifted from the TV to Judy. Judy was undeniably thinner than she was 24 hours before, Mrs. Duncan thought.

It's like she had a pin stuck in her. Her feet isn't swollen. Her hands isn't swollen. I'm a listener and a looker. And I can guess things. I just know.

What am I gonna do? I read every little thing about the baby, what they found. I never have seen anything that could connect me with it. All I can go by is a picture of the baby on television, and the circumstances what happened, and the weight loss. You don't lose that much weight overnight, see. I can tell.

Maybe I should go to her, but how would I do this? What if I'm wrong? I know in my heart I'm not wrong. I really in my heart know that's my grandbaby.

The baby looked rosy and chubby on television. The reporter was describing where and how the baby was found.

"I don't see how a mother could do that," Russell's other aunt said. "They oughta take and shoot that person."

Mary watched Judy. Judy was looking away from the television, and she was humming very softly.

DAY TWO: 'LOVE ME, DON'T LEAVE ME'

Detectives Dennis Hallberg and Larry Lingo were frustrated. Ten days after a newborn baby boy was abandoned at a Temple Terrace apartment complex, they had few clues about the mother. A box of evidence, found in a dumpster near where the baby was abandoned, was addressed to Hallmark Packaging Inc. in Tampa. A detective who interviewed Hallmark's receptionist noted in his report that she acted strange and should be interviewed again.

It was Tuesday, May 2, five days after the baby was found in Wildwood Acres Apartments. Mary Duncan and Judy Pemberton went for a walk in Lettuce Lake Park, near Wildwood Acres, where Judy lived with her boyfriend, Russell Hayes.

Russell had left Saturday to go to Starke for his two-week National Guard training. Mrs. Duncan, Russell's aunt, was growing more and more anxious. She couldn't understand why Judy was acting so normal, as if nothing had happened. Could Mrs. Duncan be mistaken? It was all so confusing. But she couldn't ignore what she knew in her heart: Judy had had a baby, and something, somehow, made her not want to see it or know it.

Mrs. Duncan felt torn in half.

Nobody knows the torture I'm going through. She's been over here so much before and after. I can't sleep at night. Raymond says, 'Somethin' wrong with you? What is it?' 'I'm all right, I'll be fine.'

If only I could see the baby's toes. All my family got that baby toe that turns inward like that. That's the first thing I want to see is those toes. But ...

And my boy's gone at the National Guard right now. If I could just talk to him. Maybe me and him could do something. But he's got another week to go.

Monday, May 8. Detectives Dennis Hallberg and Larry Lingo were discouraged. They had followed leads, dug through garbage and knocked on countless doors looking for the mother of the abandoned baby. They had come up with no more evidence than some cat food cans, some TV dinner packaging and directions for blond hair dye. And they were running out of time. It had been 10 days since the baby boy was found in the videocassette recorder box. The infant was in the custody of the Florida Department of Rehabilitative Services, living in a shelter home and completely shielded from publicity.

Chances of finding the mother seemed more remote as each day passed.

But then, at 3 p.m., the Hillsborough County Sheriff's Office received an anonymous call. It was perhaps only the third anonymous call they had received on this case—far fewer than they expected. The caller had information about the abandoned baby. There was a woman who recently had lost a lot of weight. She lived in the same complex where the baby was found, on Mar-Jo Drive. 5812.

Lingo followed up the lead. He had no reason to think this lead would prove any more fertile than the others. He pulled his car along the curb in front of the duplex, a brick rectangular building with a door on either end. The duplex on the left was 5810; the one on the right was 5812. There was a nice little garden with freshly planted flowers out front.

Lingo knocked on the door. No one answered. He knocked again. Nothing. He drove up the block to the apartment complex office and talked to the manager. He identified himself and asked to see the lease agreement of the tenants at 5812 Mar-Jo.

He checked the tenant's name: Judy Pemberton. He checked how long she had been living there: since June. He checked her employer.

Hallmark Packaging.

He thanked the manager, left, and drove slowly back to the duplex.

Hallmark Packaging. The same company that was on the label of the box found in the dumpster. Lingo knew the connection could not be coincidental, that he had, in all likelihood, found the mother. He went up to the duplex door again and knocked. This time, the door swung open.

Judy Pemberton? Lingo asked. Yes, the woman said.

Lingo was a little taken aback by the woman's apparent age. After years as a detective, little surprised him. But this woman was clearly older than the mid-20s to mid-30s the detectives had estimated the mother to be.

Lingo introduced himself and told her he was investigating the baby that was abandoned down the street April 27. Can I talk to you? he asked.

She agreed and stepped aside. Lingo stepped into the small living room. He immediately saw some clues. A videocassette recorder. Three cats and four kittens playing about everywhere. Judy Pemberton was short, a little plump around the middle. She wore a striped jump suit. And she had blond hair.

She politely answered Lingo's questions. No, she said, she did not live here alone, she lived with her boyfriend, Russell Hayes, who was at National Guard camp right now. Yes, she had been alone here since he left a week ago Saturday.

Her eyes avoided Lingo's. Yes, she had heard about the baby being abandoned, but she knew nothing more about it.

Her weight shifted from one foot to the other. She hesitated before answering the questions. Lingo gingerly moved into more personal territory. How was her health? Had she been sick recently or experienced any weight loss?

Yes, she said, she had lost about 10 pounds due to a diet and the start of her monthly period.

That was strange, Lingo thought. Bringing up something as personal as her monthly period.

Was there any unusual bleeding from this cycle?

No, she answered in a small, flat voice. Nothing unusual. Her period had ended three weeks ago.

Lingo couldn't quite read this woman. She was quiet—given the situation, this was no surprise. But she also seemed strangely compliant, as if she did not suspect why he was here. She did not seem to mind his questions. She answered them in a voice that did not project or rise and fall the way most people's speech does. She might have been answering a survey about laundry detergent.

Lingo asked about her job. Yes, she had worked for Hallmark Packaging until the previous Friday, when she was let go because they needed someone who could operate computers.

A kitten jumped up on the kitchen table. Judy retrieved it and put it back on the ground. Did Judy remember a detective coming to Hallmark the day after the baby was born, asking about a box that had been found? Yes, she remembered. Yes, she did bring a box home from work for her kittens, but she had placed it in the dumpster on her street, not the one three blocks away on Kitten Drive.

It was 4:10 p.m. Lingo asked her if he could search her apartment.

Well, go ahead, she said. Again, passivity, as if she were half sleep-walking. She signed a consent form. Lingo headed toward the bedrooms. She did not follow him. She did not talk. She did not sit down.

Lingo started with the master bedroom. The waterbed was unmade. Lingo saw a few blood stains. Either she hadn't changed her sheets in three weeks, or she was lying about when she had her period. Lingo searched the spare bedroom. He saw a box cut out on one side like the one they had found in the dumpster. It was filled with cat litter. In the bathroom, he found blue and white towels, matching those found in the dumpster. He also saw an open box of sanitary napkins.

He went to the refrigerator. He opened the freezer. Banquet TV dinners. Salisbury Steak.

It was all right there. Paint by numbers. Lingo excused himself and went to his car. He radioed Hallberg. Hallberg, out at MacDill Air Force Base, made it over to Mar-Jo Drive in about 10 minutes. Lingo and Judy stood in stone silence waiting for him.

When Hallberg arrived, Lingo showed him what he had found. They checked the VCR make and serial number: RCA, number 504620465.

A match.

All this time, Judy remained standing. She didn't act upset, angry or fearful. A little nervous one moment, almost nonchalant another. Lingo didn't tell her what he had found in the apartment. She didn't ask.

Lingo retraced his steps around the house with Hallberg: They looked at the sheets, the box, the towels, the frozen dinners. Judy walked with the detectives. They finished in the bedroom. All three faced one another, standing in an awkward triangle: the two taller men, Lingo with silver hair, Hallberg: a sandy blond, both wearing suits; and Judy, much shorter, her eyes cast anywhere but at the detectives' faces.

Kittens tumbled everywhere. Hallberg explained to Judy what they had found in the dumpster. He said that the towels matched the towels in her house. The box they had found was like the one in her house.

A kitten darted into the room. Judy stood with her arms at her sides. A few minutes later another kitten dashed by. Hallberg kept talking. Judy kept watching the kittens or looking away.

Hallberg finished.

The silence between them grew heavier with each moment. Finally, Judy raised her eyes. She looked at Hallberg, then at Lingo, back to Hallberg, back to Lingo. Then she seemed to sigh, almost visibly, Lingo thought.

One hand twisting in the other, she said, "Well, I might as well tell you, the baby is mine."

It was now 4:50 p.m. Judy quietly led the small procession back into the kitchen. She offered the detectives something to drink. They declined. They made small talk. A kitten scaled Hallberg's leg. Hallberg gently, rather stiffly, detached it. A moment later, a kitten jumped up on the counter. Judy gently rescued it.

Hallberg advised her of her constitutional rights and asked her to sign an interview consent form. She signed. Then she just started talking, in the same flat voice. Lingo relayed her story in his written report:

"Pemberton advised Detective Lingo on the 27th of April she woke up with pains and thought it was her normal menstrual cycle starting. She stated she had not had a regular period for a while and felt she was going through the change of life. She said she stayed home and did not go to work on the 27th. She stated at approximately 5 p.m., she had a sharp pain, went into the bathroom and the baby "just popped out." She said she attempted to clean him up, and her, and tied the umbilical cord with blue sewing thread. She then cut the cord with a pair of scissors and put the afterbirth into the toilet. She said she then attempted to stop her bleeding. She then put the baby in a box and the other towels and used pads in plastic garbage bags and put them in the box marked Hallmark Packaging. She then took both boxes to the dumpster. She put the box with the evidence in the dumpster and placed the baby on the ground outside of the dumpster. She then returned home and later went back to the dumpster to make sure someone had found the baby. She said she saw the police there and left. She didn't tell Russell about it that night, and he did not know that she was pregnant. The following morning, she did go to work and remembered the detective coming by asking about the box with Hallmark Packaging on it. She said she did not remember if she told him at that time that she lived in Wildwood Acres or if she told him she had any knowledge of a box.

"She advised she did not even realize she was pregnant herself until she had the baby. She said she was glad we came to her house because she was wanting to tell someone about it, and had someone not arrived at her house, she would have gone and told someone within the next couple of days. She said she worked for an OB-GYN (obstetric and gynecological) clinic in the past as a medical assistant and had been familiar in assisting in a birth. She apparently just acted out of experience when she tied the baby's cord and cleaned him up. Then she said she would like to have the baby back, and guessed she just panicked when she had the baby, and didn't realize what she was doing."

Judy was arrested. The detectives started packing up the VCR, the towels, the box. A crime lab technician came to collect the evidence. Hallberg then led Judy to his car. They drove to the Hillsborough County Sheriff Office's Criminal Investigations Bureau, off I-4 and Buffalo Ave.

On the way over, Judy kept any emotions she may have had beneath the surface. She asked Hallberg what would happen to her. Hallberg said she would be taken to the county jail and probably charged with child abandonment. Beyond that, he was not sure.

She said nothing else. They reached the sheriff's office. Judy told Hallberg she did not want to make any more statements before talking to an attorney. She asked to use the phone. She said she wanted to call her boyfriend's aunt and uncle. Hallberg led her over to a desk. He dialed the number for her.

She was silent for a moment. Then Hallberg heard Judy say in plaintive tones, "You know that baby that was found? He was mine." Silence, then "I don't know, I just panicked."

Judy's contradictory behavior mystified Hallberg: First she says she wants an attorney, then, with Hallberg right next to her, she admits to the crime all over again.

He heard her voice—shaky now, pleading. "Love me, don't leave me," she said.

She hung up the phone.

And then she began to cry.

It was midnight, May 8. George Cochran, 32, could not sleep. It was all catching up to him. Everything had happened so fast, only now was he able to catalog it, and he was having a hard time.

One: The baby found by his best friends, the Nawrockis, was abandoned by his next-door neighbor, Judy Pemberton.

Two: Judy, a woman who had seemed as innocuous as her kittens, as ordinary as anybody in the mall on a Saturday afternoon, had had a baby next door—maybe even while he was home—and put it in a box and left it by a dumpster. This was a woman who was pregnant nearly the entire time he had known her.

Cochran had been interviewed by newspaper and television reporters all evening. He and his wife, Megan, saw the TV report of Judy being escorted to jail. Megan choked up a little.

Late that night they had met a couple who said they were Russell's mom and dad. The woman spoke with a Southern twang. She asked about the cats and the plants. She was so nice. Upset. She chattered. She worried that she hadn't said the right things earlier to the reporters. "I hope they don't twist our words," she told the Cochrans. "We love Judy. Judy said she flipped out, she just lost it. We need to support her."

They talked out front for 30 minutes. The Cochrans said they would keep an eye on Judy's place.

Now, it was all settling in on Cochran. Megan was asleep. His sons, 6 and 4, mercifully had slept through everything that evening. Cochran, sat down, and began to sort his feelings out in writing.

It's May 8, 1989, 12:00 midnight. I can't sleep tonight because I try to figure the whole thing out. I lived beside a woman for about a year and didn't even know she had been pregnant. It makes me wonder how observant I really am or how naive and stupid I can be.

But then I start to wonder what kind of person has lived beside me for so long. I wonder how a woman who generally seemed to like children could just abandon a newborn like that. I speculate how a woman who just witnessed new life in a litter of kittens could just throw away a life. How can a woman who cared for animals like she did totally disregard a human life?

Why didn't she look pregnant? Why didn't she say she was pregnant? Was this a calculated move? If she just "flipped out," could she have at any time? How could she have wrapped a baby, tied the umbilical cord and taken it to the dumpster, only hours after having it? Did she have help? And what about the flower bed?

I recall the flower bed being put in around the same time the baby was found. I didn't think anything about it at the time. But now, I wonder if she expected the baby to die and the flower bed is a memorial. The baby wasn't actually put in the dumpster, but beside it. Did she intend that someone should find the baby? After all, she did take enough care to clean the baby and tie off the umbilical cord. Therefore, the flower bed could be a remembrance.

Tuesday, May 9, 6 a.m., Florida National Guard's Camp Blanding in Starke. Russell Hayes was training out in the field. They had just finished maneuvers when his first sergeant came up to him. Their conversation was short and explosive: "Do you know anything about your girlfriend having a baby?" "No," Russell said. "Call home," he said.

Russell dialed the Duncans' number. "What's the matter?" Russell asked. He knew, but he had to hear it from his aunt. "Did Judy have a baby?"

"Yes, son, she did," Mrs. Duncan said gravely. She told him everything. "Judy's in jail."

Russell started to cry. He didn't know anything about this, he said. He was hurt, he was shocked, he was mad, he was hurt.

"So am I," Mrs. Duncan said. "Try to calm down. I've talked to Judy. She said she didn't know what she was doing, she didn't know why she did it. Just get home, and we'll work this thing out."

Russell's first sergeant drove him back to Tampa. It was a quiet ride. They arrived at the Duncans' by 1 p.m. Russell was still in his uniform, dirty from his field exercises. Only Mrs. Duncan was home. They embraced. Why did she do it? Russell asked over and over. He hadn't even known she was pregnant.

"Did you see any blood afterward?" his aunt asked.

"No, I didn't," Russell said. "I wasn't home when she had it."

He didn't know what to do.

Mrs. Duncan told him to take some Tylenol and a warm bath. She fixed him a sandwich. But neither Mrs. Duncan nor Russell Hayes could ignore the irony of the situation.

One day in 1966 in Lakeland, when Russell was 5 years old, his mother left him with a babysitter. She was going to visit someone, she said.

She didn't come back. Not that day. Not the next day. Or the next day.

Russell's mother had abandoned him.

The babysitter called the police. Eventually Mrs. Duncan's brother—Russell's father, who was separated from his wife—picked up the boy and brought him to the Duncans'. He said he couldn't care for the boy himself. Would the Duncans take him?

Raymond Duncan agreed, but on one condition: If we're going to raise him, we're going to raise him as our own son. Russell's father agreed. And so, in a more benevolent way, Russell's father left him, too.

But Russell's father could not have chosen better parents. Raymond Duncan is a down-to-earth man, kind, calm and logical, not the kind to hold a grudge. He was a groundskeeper for the city of Tampa, until he retired a few years ago. Now, he is a groundskeeper for Myrtle Hill Garden of Memories Cemetery.

Mary, oval-faced and talkative, is the self-ordained nursemaid of her family. Through the years, she has taken care of many family members.

Russell was a blessing for the Duncans. They had wanted children very much. Mrs. Duncan became pregnant once, but she miscarried after four months.

But little Russell had serious problems at first. He hovered in corners and trembled. He didn't eat well. The Duncans fed him with love. They took him to amusement parks and fairs, and picnics. But he remained withdrawn. Mrs. Duncan worried and waited.

The Duncans bought Russell a swing and hung it on the pecan tree out in the yard. One day, Russell fell off the swing and hit his head. Mrs. Duncan rushed out to him. He cried and cried. She cleaned up the gash on his head, soothed him and held him close.

That was the turning point. Russell clung to her that day; he wouldn't let go. He's been like a son ever since.

The Duncans, neither of whom graduated from high school, were proud of Russell. He graduated in 1980 from Tampa Bay Technical Vocational School; he spent four years in the U.S. Army, and then joined the National Guard. He was a hard worker, always holding down a job. Right now, he made pasta and did other jobs at an Italian restaurant in Tampa.

Though Russell had had other girlfriends, he and Judy seemed made for one another. In December 1988, six months after they met, Russell asked Judy to marry him. They were on a cruise to Mexico. He gave her a diamond ring. The couple started living together in Judy's apartment in January 1989 and planned to marry a year later. Because Judy was 42, they did not plan to have children. Neither thought birth control was necessary.

Now, everything seemed out of control. Russell talked to Judy briefly on the phone. But the detectives told him to stay home until they could interview him. He wasn't allowed to see the baby, who was in HRS custody. Meanwhile reporters showed up, asking searching questions. Russell had never been interviewed by the media before. He answered the questions, all of them, in honest, short sentences. He was hurt, shocked and angry.

Reporters showed him a videotape of the baby—his son. "He's great," Russell told reporters. "I saw him, and I knew he was mine. I'm so happy he's healthy."

But Russell did not feel like a father. How could he? He had known about the baby for only a few hours. He didn't know what to feel. He didn't know what to do.

"Are you going to leave her?" a reporter asked about Judy.

After being raised with the Duncans' unconditional love and optimism, he had learned to support first and ask questions later. This is our problem, he thought, and we'll work it out somehow.

He answered the question without hesitation. "No."

Tuesday night, Marci Gilbert, Judy's sister-in-law, talked by phone to Judy, who had spent the night in jail.

"Get me out of here," Judy said.

Marci told Judy she was doing everything she could, but so far, Judy couldn't get out. Judy, charged with child abandonment, a felony, and child abuse, a misdemeanor, had been denied bail in a hearing on Monday, the night she was arrested. Marci told Judy she had contacted the public defender's office, and two lawyers there were taking her case.

"Right now," Marci said to Judy, "I need to know some details: Did you do it?"

"I guess I did. They're telling me I did."

"Did you do it deliberately?"

"I don't remember anything about what I did."

"You don't remember anything about birthing that baby?"

"I don't want to talk about any of it," Judy said. "I just want out of here."

Wednesday morning, May 10, Mary Duncan, Russell Hayes and Marci Gilbert met at the Hillsborough County Courthouse Annex in Tampa for Judy's bail hearing. They walked into courtroom No. 8— the courtroom of Hillsborough Circuit Judge Harry Lee Coe III. They waited while Coe heard several other cases. Finally, Judy's case was called.

Judy came through the back door. She wore blue prison clothes;

her and Russell's eyes met and held. It was the first time they had seen each other since all this had happened. A few moments later, Russell, Mrs. Duncan and Marci advanced up to Coe's bench. Russell embraced Judy, and the two stood, arm in arm. They said nothing.

Coe set bail at $6,000. Marci got the bond, using her home as collateral. About 8 that evening, she and Russell went back to the jail. After spending two days and two nights in jail, Judy—who had never seen a courtroom before, much less the inside of a jail—was released.

Marci could see that Judy was tired, anxious and irritable. Marci and Russell were drained and exhausted. Marci suggested they get something to eat. Judy resisted. She was afraid people might recognize her and taunt her. Marci assured her that wouldn't happen.

They went to the Frisch's on 56th Street and sat unnoticed at a back table. Judy barely touched her food. Marci took charge, but she went easy. She asked Judy whether she wanted to hire a private lawyer. Judy told her she didn't have the money to do that. Marci also suggested Judy get some counseling. Judy said she would.

Marci surveyed her sister-in-law and tried to make sense of all this. She had first heard about it on the 11 o'clock news the night Judy was arrested. The news floored her. But when Marci looked back, she realized there had been clues.

A few months before, Marci teased Judy about gaining weight, joking, "Are you pregnant?" And Judy nearly screamed, "No! I'm tired of people asking me that!"

Then there was that Wednesday night at the bowling alley, when Judy was in such pain, as if she wanted to start her period but couldn't, she said. Of course she couldn't—she was in labor!

Judy had called Marci Friday, the day after she had the baby.

"Well, I started," Judy said.

"You did? Is everything normal?"

"Well, it's a little heavy, but not bad."

Judy stopped in the bowling alley later that Friday and then on Sunday, when she bowled as usual. *How in the world could she have seemed so normal?*

There was little public sympathy for Judy Pemberton. Hallmark Packaging received nasty, anonymous calls just because Judy had worked there. People drove by Judy's duplex, honked and pointed. The Cochrans were asked what it was like to live next to a baby killer.

The emotional reaction to what had happened was strong enough to split families. Marci Gilbert was the only member of Judy's family—five siblings and their families—who remained loyal to her, but it was at some expense to her marriage. Marci's husband, Alan, had no sympathy for his sister. As a result, he and Marci lived with a tense truce.

Mary Duncan faced great hostility from the Duncan family. She spent hours on the phone trying to explain and defend Judy's actions and her loyalty to Judy, largely to no avail.

Women at the bowling alley where Russell and Judy bowled every week were drawn into the fire, too. A couple of them had wondered whether Judy was pregnant and even laughed when, after the baby was found, Judy came in the bowling alley looking unchanged. "Well it's not Judy's!" they joked. But the women had to admit they never really thought Judy was pregnant. Bonnie Tschuddy agreed to testify to this in court. She argued with her son, himself the father of two children, who could not accept his mother would defend Judy. Irene Staving also said she never guessed Judy was pregnant. When she was 42—Judy's age—and the mother of five children, she went to the doctor complaining of a chest cold.

The doctor told her she was four to six months pregnant.

On May 18, Judy and Mary Duncan and her husband, Raymond, drove to the W.T. Edwards District Administration Office for HRS, an imposing, five-story white building on Dr. Martin Luther King Jr. Blvd.

They pulled up to the curb. They got out of the car and approached the doors. Judy was quiet and tense. Mrs. Duncan was excited. She was also disappointed Russell wasn't here for such an important meeting. He said he couldn't get off work. Mrs. Duncan wondered if he was afraid. Or maybe he just wasn't ready.

The small group stepped inside the building. They took the elevator up to the third floor. They turned right, toward a big waiting room. They sat down. They waited for 20 minutes. They didn't talk much.

Finally, they were called into a small room with baby toys and chairs. Another woman and child were there. Judy slowed down, then stopped at the doorway.

"I don't know if I can do this or not," she said.

"Well, you do what you think you can do," Mrs. Duncan said.

A man came into the room, smiled, and handed to Mrs. Duncan a 3-week-old baby wearing a blue suit.

Mrs. Duncan beamed. "He looks just like Russell did when he was a baby!" she said. Then, unable to wait any longer, she checked his foot.

"Look at that toe!" she said. "See? Just like I said."

Judy inched into the room. She watched as Raymond Duncan took the baby. The baby began to cry. He instinctively handed the baby to a woman: Judy.

Judy took him in her arms.

She smiled.

"He's a cute little angel."

For an hour, they played with the baby. Mrs. Duncan watched Judy closely. She could see the hurt in her face. But she held up, Mrs. Duncan thought. *Judy's just not well right now. She knows she don't need the baby right now. She's admittin' to all of that. She's not doin' like some people—I'm all right. She knows she's not. And when you can admit somethin's wrong with you, you're already on the road to recovery. That's what I've always heard.*

"What are you going to name him?" a social worker asked.

Mrs. Duncan thought that was a good sign. "Either Russell Raymond or Raymond Russell, we aren't sure which," she said.

Later that day, Judy told a *St. Petersburg Times* reporter that they loved the baby, that he cried when Raymond Duncan held him, "but as soon as Mary or I took him back, he just hushed right up.

"He trusts us, I guess."

DAY THREE: TAKING THE STAND

The baby was abandoned in a box near a dumpster on April 27, 1989. On May 8, an anonymous call led detectives to Judy Pemberton, 42, who was arrested and charged with child abuse and abandonment. She went to jail and was released on bail. She returned home to Russell Hayes, the baby's father. Meanwhile, the baby stayed in state custody.

It was a strange, tense time for George and Megan Cochran. Their neighbor, Judy Pemberton, had been arrested, accused of abandoning her baby in a box next to a dumpster. She went to jail, was charged with a felony and released on bail awaiting trial. Now, she was back home again. Life was supposed to return to normal. But for the Cochrans, normal was not recognizable anymore. What should they think of Judy? What should they say to her?

George Cochran couldn't stop thinking about what his neighbor had done. He poured out his confusion in a diary, asking questions everyone else was asking, too:

May 11. I don't know why this whole thing bothers me, but I've

*become obsessed with it. I tape everything that goes with it. My God,
I even write down all this stuff. Why can't I let it go ? Do I really have
to know why she did it? Do I have to voice my approval or disapproval ? Why must I understand it all?*

There are no neat answers to those questions. Mothers who have
abandoned their babies offer insufficient, often unconvincing explanations. Some say they don't remember the act or don't understand
it, says Dr. Robert Sadoff, a forensic psychiatrist at the University of
Pennsylvania School of Medicine. Sadoff has treated 25 women who
have abandoned their babies. Most were young white women who
were poor and had little education. All of the babies died.

The women often deny they are pregnant, even to themselves,
Sadoff says. Then they may experience a traumatic, unattended birth,
which can trigger certain conditions—a post-partum psychosis or a
dissociative reaction—that result in an irrational act, such as abandoning the baby. Later, the mothers may say the babies, like their
pregnancies, were not real to them. They deny what they have done
until they are pushed to accept responsibility, Sadoff says.

"If you ask them, 'Do you realize you are killing a human being?'
they say, 'No, I'm just getting rid of something.' But if you push them,
'Do you realize you flushed your baby down the toilet?' they realize
it."

Judy's friends and family searched for answers.

Russell Hayes was mystified. He lived with Judy and never
dreamed she was pregnant. He wondered whether he was partly to
blame for the abandonment because he was not at home when Judy
gave birth. He couldn't get Judy to talk about what she had done. She
said she panicked, she didn't know why she had done it—that was all.
Perhaps knowing how the subject upset her, Russell dropped it.

Mary Duncan, Russell's aunt, thought Judy might have been afraid
she and her husband, Raymond, and Russell would disapprove of her
if they knew she was pregnant. Maybe she thought she would lose her
new-found family.

Marci Gilbert, Judy's sister-in-law, had known Judy for 16 years.
Judy had a bad temper and a sharp tongue at times. She could be self-
centered and immature; she acted more like 22 than 42, especially
with Russell. But Judy was not a baby killer.

Tampa psychiatrist Michael Maher looked for answers, too.

On July 20, Judy met the fourth and final time with Maher. Judy's
lawyers had asked Maher to evaluate her and to testify later in court
if necessary. Maher had counseled three other women who had abandoned babies and testified in two trials.

Maher surveyed the blond, quiet woman sitting in his office. The summer obviously had taken its toll on Judy. She wasn't getting any sleep. She looked exhausted. Her looming trial and sentencing haunted her. She swayed from being sweet and loving to blowing up at the slightest provocation, usually when the baby or her case was mentioned. At the same time, Judy and Russell had serious financial problems. Judy was in no condition to work. One of their cars was repossessed. Bills piled up. They had no medical insurance. Judy had not seen a doctor since the birth.

Maher had made some observations about Judy. Sitting in his office, she looked calm. But beneath that thin layer of calm, she was, Maher believed, immobilized. She could not think for herself. She was deceptively passive, answering Maher's questions fully but asking none of her own. She was neither hysterical nor distraught; she didn't cry or beg for help. She didn't seem remorseful.

But Maher thought she was very sorry and angry at herself for what she had done. She was terrified, and her only defense was her hostility.

Maher thought that Judy had experienced an unacknowledged pregnancy, literally a lack of conscious awareness that she was pregnant. Most women begin their pregnancies with conflicting emotions but soon resolve them. But a few women—teenagers especially—deny their pregnancies until the day they give birth. If a woman is alone when she gives birth to a baby she doesn't consciously expect, she may react by distancing herself from the baby—and by abandoning it. That's what Judy did, Maher thought.

Judy also mentioned to Maher that about 11 months before the baby was born, she had missed two menstrual periods. She took an over-the-counter pregnancy test; the results were negative. This likely reinforced her conclusion that she was in menopause, not pregnant.

But the real mystery, Maher thought, was why Judy denied the pregnancy for so long.

He looked at Judy's past: The end of a 21-year marriage. Her move from Colorado to Tampa. The financial struggle to support herself, her 20-year-old daughter and newborn grandchild. Then meeting and falling in love with Russell Hayes and beginning to enjoy life for the first time in years. Within a few months, the unplanned pregnancy. The pregnancy itself dramatically different from her first pregnancy 20 years before—no morning sickness or notable weight gain.

Maher hypothesized that Judy pushed the unthinkable out of her conscious mind. This set up the unexpected birth.

He also noted that it was after her daughter was born that Judy's husband apparently started leaving her alone often. Had Judy subconsciously felt abandoned because she had a baby?

Still, Maher knew there had to be deeper reasons for the denial, reasons that only long-term therapy could uncover. But he wondered: Judy was the youngest of six children. Her mother was 37 when Judy was born.

Describing this, Judy casually told Maher, "I was a late-in-life baby. My mother thought she was all done having children. Then I came along."

During the summer of anticipation and preparation for the trial, Russell and Judy anchored each week around their hour visit with the baby at the W.T. Edwards District Administration Office in Tampa, operated by HRS. They called him Rusty now, short for Russell.

Judy cradled Rusty, she cooed, she bought him clothes and talked about Cub Scouts and Little League baseball. She was ready to mother him, she insisted. She could handle it. But she was moody and volatile. She would get mad if she had to wait for the baby or if she wasn't the first to hold him. Once, she stomped out of the building.

She also had seen a counselor, as Maher had suggested. But she thought the counselor insinuated she was lying, and she stomped out of his office, too.

Clearly, thought Marci Gilbert, Mrs. Duncan and HRS workers, Judy would be unable initially to care for her child, no matter what happened in court. HRS was strongly considering giving temporary custody of Rusty to the Duncans. When Russell and Judy were ready, perhaps they could gain permanent custody of their son.

Mrs. Duncan was delighted. She had spent her life taking care of other people. Now, just as her house seemed empty, she was going to have another baby. *I guess the Lord says, "You still gotta take care of somebody,"* she thought. *"The Lord knew why I never had no kids; he was gonna send me all I can handle."*

Aug. 14, Hillsborough County Courthouse Annex, Tampa. Judy stood outside Courtroom 8 with Russell, Mrs. Duncan and Marci Gilbert. She hovered in a small alcove behind a bench. Her arms were folded, her face was a tense mask. The others surrounded and talked to her in low, gentle tones.

She was here for a pretrial conference. Judy was charged with child desertion, a third-degree felony—a serious charge, but the lowest of the six felony grades. Luckily, her baby had survived. If he had died, Judy could have been facing a murder charge.

Judy's lawyers were assistant public defender Brian Donerly, a veteran who usually handles high-profile murder cases. He had assisted in two other baby abandonment trials. He knew that such cases elicited strong emotion, making it hard to get a fair trial.

Andrea Wilson had six years' experience in the public defender's office. She handled most of the interviews with Judy. Wilson was skeptical of Judy's story at first, but grew to respect and believe her. Judy was straightforward, cooperative, occasionally wry and sarcastic and seemed to hide nothing. But each time they met between June and August, Judy was more agitated, exhausted and terrified. To calm Judy, Wilson often switched to safe topics: How's Russell? How's the baby?

Today Donerly and Wilson had to decide how to plead Judy's case. The best scenario: Judy would plead guilty. Psychiatrist Maher would testify. The judge would sentence Judy to probation and counseling.

But before they chose this route, Donerly and Wilson wanted some assurance from Hillsborough Circuit Judge Harry Lee Coe III that he would be lenient. Sentencing guidelines indicated Judy should be sentenced to probation, one year in jail or a combination of jail and probation. But Coe could give her the maximum sentence, five years in prison. And he had a reputation for giving harsh sentences.

Around the courthouse, Coe is known as "Hangin' Harry." The Florida Supreme Court recently has overruled three of Coe's sentences imposing death sentences against juries' recommendations.

Coe is tall, wiry, with wavy dark hair, sharp features and a blunt courtroom manner. Once a pitcher for the Tampa Tarpons minor league baseball team, he still aims straight and hard, right down the middle. Intolerant of theatrics, long-winded explanations and soft sentences, he is known as a bottom-line kind of judge. If you commit a crime, you deserve to go to jail.

Bottom line, even Judy admitted she had abandoned her baby.

At 9:30 a m., Wilson and Donerly stood with Judy in front of Coe. Wilson began talking about unacknowledged pregnancy. She described a recent news story about a woman who was with her husband at Walt Disney World, complained of back pains, went to a clinic and gave birth to a 6-pound baby.

"Dr. Maher obviously can tell you more about the way this happens than I can," Wilson said.

"Is she pleading guilty or not guilty?" Coe asked bluntly.

"Well, Judge, we wanted to see if we could get some indication of—"

"No. I'm not going to plea negotiate the case."

Silence. Wilson seemed a bit taken aback. She tried again. "Is there anything else that you would like to know about the circumstances and—"

"Well, I would want to hear from anybody that wants to be heard. But I'm not going to plea negotiate it. She's either guilty or not guilty, and I'll do what I think is appropriate after I hear from everybody."

"Your honor, we felt that it would be better for everyone involved if we could try to work the case out, we hope—"

"I'm not going to plea negotiate it."

Trial was set for Aug. 21.

AUG. 21. Judy sat with Donerly and Wilson at the defense table in court. She wore a black and white polka-dot skirt and blouse, nylons and black flat shoes. Her hair was pulled away from her face, which gave her an unexpectedly girlish look.

This was the first day of her trial. Everything was going dismally for the defense.

Donerly and Wilson had thought they had only one plea option: Not guilty by reason of insanity. They had filed the necessary motions, with Maher's diagnosis: Judy Pemberton suffered from post-traumatic stress syndrome, resulting from the traumatic, unattended birth. The syndrome is characterized by mood swings, memory loss, confusion, depression, lack of sleep—all symptoms Judy had exhibited.

Judy's legal defense was built around Maher's theory and the testimony of Judy's bowling partners, who said Judy had not looked or acted pregnant.

For 20 minutes, Donerly and Wilson argued with Coe about the insanity defense. Judy sat staring at the floor. At one point, she began shaking so violently the bailiff had to bring her a chair. Finally, Coe ruled out the insanity defense, saying Donerly and Wilson filed their motions too late. Donerly thought Coe was just using a technicality; lawyers using the insanity defense rarely meet filing deadlines, and judges rarely disallow the defense on that basis.

Coe also ruled that whether Judy knew she was pregnant was irrelevant. And he limited the kinds of questions the defense could ask potential jury members. For instance, Wilson was unable to ask whether jurors understood menopause.

The rulings smashed Judy's defense. Maher was out. The bowling partners were out. Extended discussion of menopause was out.

The prosecution had 11 witnesses testifying. Donerly and Wilson were left with only one.

Judy.

AUG. 22. Judy hunched over the defense table, her head in her arms or slightly raised, a pile of crumpled tissues in front of her. Wearing a blue print Western style dress, white stockings and white boots, she was soon to testify, all alone, in her own behalf. She did not look equal to the task.

Sometimes she looked like an old woman. Other times, she looked like a little girl. Maher had earlier prescribed 10 mild tranquilizers to help Judy sleep. She had decided to take some to get her through her testimony, and the drugs' effects were obvious. Judy's eyelids drooped, her body sagged, and she seemed remote—not quite connected to everything that was happening.

Donerly and Wilson did not know Judy would take the tranquilizers, but they figured it was better for her to be tranquilized than hysterical on the stand. Her erratic behavior during the past several weeks worried her lawyers. Earlier in the hallway, Judy leaned against Russell, muttering, "I'm going to prison," or asking Wilson, "Am I going to prison today?" Then, without warning, she called Coe "a bastard." Her lawyers knew these outbursts could dash any hope for sympathy. Who, they wondered, would testify: the friendly Judy or the hostile one?

Assistant State Attorney Rolando Guerra called one witness after another: detectives Dennis Hallberg, Larry Lingo, Albert Frost and others from the sheriff's office. The Nawrockis also testified, one at a time: 11-year-old Ryan, who found the baby, Ryan's sister, Melissa, and his mother, Lisa. All testimony was brief and straightforward, explaining how the baby was found in a videocassette recorder box under a tree near a dumpster; how another box containing bloody towels and other evidence was later found in the dumpster, Judy's arrest and confession, how nurses called the baby "Jack-in-the-box." The defense did not cross-examine most witnesses.

Guerra referred often to the table full of evidence: the VCR box Judy had placed her baby in, the box that contained the towels, photos, maps and other exhibits, all drawing a clear picture of events.

Judy quietly cried or stared off into space. She stuck her tongue out at a photographer. At one point she took her engagement ring off, gave it to the bailiff, whispering something. The bailiff found Russell, seated toward the back of the courtroom, and gave him the ring. Russell tried to catch Judy's eye, but she did not look at him.

Throughout everything, Russell, Mrs. Duncan and Marci Gilbert sat together toward the back of the courtroom, looking as if they were at a funeral.

Vincent Tifer, Judy's former boss at Hallmark Packaging Inc. in Tampa, was subpoenaed by the prosecution to testify against Judy. He had wanted to do the opposite. Tifer testified that Judy went to work the day after she had a baby and seemed normal—by implication, cold and remorseless.

Wilson cross-examined, asking one question. Did Judy look pregnant the day before she had the baby? No, Tifer said.

As Tifer stepped down, he said in a loud voice, hoping the jury would hear, "Good luck, Judy!"

Within two hours, the prosecution rested its case. Coe called a brief recess. Judy, Mrs. Duncan, Marc Gilbert, Michael Maher, Donerly and Wilson retreated to the public defender's office upstairs. This is where they went during breaks—away from the noisy crowd, and, especially, the media.

During the breaks in her three-day trial, Judy usually just lay down on a couch. One time, when the couch was being used, she curled up on the floor in Wilson's office with her head behind a filing cabinet. She cried, or asked, "Why are they treating me like I'm a monster?"

Another time, as Judy sat with Marc, Russell and Mrs. Duncan, she cried and said, "I don't know how any of you can love me after what I did."

That, Marci knew, was Judy's way of saying, "I'm sorry."

Russell was strong for Judy. When she was upset, he took her by her shoulders and said, "Judy, it's going to be okay." But he was scared, too. Shortly before Judy testified, Russell sat alone in the near-empty courtroom, before the trial resumed. He rubbed his face with his hand and shook his head. His face reddened.

"I just don't know what I'm going to do," he said.

"The first witness we intend to call," said Donerly, as the trial resumed, "is the defendant, Judith Pemberton."

The bailiff took Judy's arm. Judy shuffled to the stand. She took the oath in a barely audible voice. She sat down.

Andrea Wilson asked gently, "Judy, would you tell us your name, please?"

Judy started to cry. "Judith Pemberton."

"You need to speak up so we can hear you, Judy."

Judy sobbed. "I can't. I can't."

"Try again," Wilson said. "Tell us your name?"

Wilson was relieved. Judy finally gathered herself and answered basic questions. Her address, age, whether she had children.

Wilson asked Judy to describe her pregnancy with her daughter 20 years ago. Judy said she had all the signs. "The classic morning sickness, swelling feet. They got very large and very large stomach, very large breasts. In fact, I was quite sick during the whole pregnancy. I gained water to the extent that I had to take cholesterol and water pills to get rid of it."

"How long were you in labor?"

"Oh, about 24 hours."

"Did you know right away when you went into labor?"

"Oh, yes."

Wilson talked about May 13, 1988, when Judy met Russell Hayes.

"I remember exactly," Judy said. "It was at the bowling alley, and he was wearing black slacks and a black sweater, and I adored him at first sight. I knew he was right."

Wilson tried to establish that Judy and Russell had a stable, loving relationship, and that Judy thought she was in menopause. She also established that Judy had taken an over-the-counter pregnancy test.

"Of course," Wilson said, "we all know now that you (later became) pregnant. Did you ever feel that you were pregnant?"

"No, I didn't get big enough."

"Did you gain weight?"

"Some, yes, but I was also eating an awful lot because the man I was married to before was very much against gaining weight. He was a physical fitness—I hate to use the word 'nut,'—but he was very fanatical about physical fitness and any weight gain was a no-no."

"Was your relationship with Russell a little different?"

"Yes. He doesn't care. I mean, you know, he isn't exactly skinny himself, but he doesn't care."

Everyone in the courtroom laughed. Russell turned scarlet and lowered his head and he and Mrs. Duncan laughed. It was the only jovial moment in the trial.

Wilson compared the difference in symptoms. During Judy's first pregnancy, "Did you feel her move inside you?"

"Oh, yeah, you could see my stomach was undulating. She was just turning."

"Kicking?"

"Oh, yes, especially in my right ribs. She made them very sore."

"Did you feel any movement the second time?"

"With Rusty? No."

Judy clutched a tissue in her hand and occasionally raised it to her nose.

"Do you remember having the baby?" Wilson asked.

"I remember some—some pains, but when he came out, there he was. I don't remember having him but all of a sudden there he was."

"What did you think?"

"I didn't know where he came from."

"Did you know that it was your baby?"

"He must have been. He was attached to me. I don't remember, you know. I don't know. He was there."

"What did you do?"

"I cleaned him up as much as I could and tied the umbilical cord and wrapped him up."

"What were you thinking while you were doing those things?"

"I don't know. I don't think I was thinking. I was acting almost on instinct, I think."

"After you cleaned him and wrapped him, what did you do?" Wilson asked.

"From that point, I don't know. It's very unclear."

"Judy, how is it possible that you were pregnant and didn't know it?"

"I don't know. I have no idea."

"When you look back on what happened to you, do you see it clearly?"

"No. It's a dreamlike state."

"What do you mean?"

"It doesn't seem real."

"Do you see yourself in these dreams?"

"I see somebody in that dream, but I don't know if it's me."

Assistant State Attorney Rolando Guerra is a solid, stocky man with dark, perfectly trimmed hair and a confident, square-shouldered walk. Before he began cross-examining Judy Pemberton, he put the VCR box next to her on the stand, so close that the box crowded her.

This was the worst part of everything for Russell. He was so afraid for Judy up there. She hadn't been pushed very hard yet. Russell knew that was about to change.

Guerra grilled her on details of the birth, questioning her previous testimony that she didn't remember most of what happened that day.

You deliver the baby, tie the umbilical cord, clean the baby up, clean yourself up, Guerra began. "What did you do with the baby?"

"I put him on our bed."

"And you found the box. You open it up and you put the baby in the box?"

Judy nodded.

"Correct? You took—"

"So they say," Judy said.

Guerra showed her the towel. This is the one she wrapped the baby in, correct?

"I can't recall. I don't know. I suppose it is."

Judy said she didn't remember any of her actions, putting the baby in one box, the other items in the other box. Guerra kept trying.

"After you put the baby in the box, and you got that box of garbage, you went looking for the keys to your car, right?"

"I don't know."

"You don't recall that?"

Judy shook her head. "I don't recall a lot of that time."

When Detective Frost interviewed her at Hallmark Packaging the next day, Guerra asked a few minutes later, "You knew by that time you had had the baby?"

"I wasn't sure," Judy said.

"You weren't sure at that point?"

"No."

"Well, of course, you didn't have it any more, right?"

"I didn't think I had it in the first place, not knowing I was pregnant."

The day she was arrested, Guerra said, Judy denied knowing about the baby, but "when they told you all the evidence that they had against you, you finally told him, 'It's my baby,' didn't you?"

"I guess they shocked it out of me. I don't know. I was—"

"They shocked it out of you?"

A few minutes later, Guerra picked up a photograph. "This is your kitchen?"

"Yeah, it looks like it."

"When those kittens were born in that kitchen you didn't put them in a box and throw them in a dumpster, did you?"

"Objection, your honor!" Wilson said. "He is goading the witness, and it's totally irrelevant."

Coe overruled the objection.

"You didn't get rid of those little kittens when they were born, did you?" Guerra repeated.

"Oh, no, sir."

Guerra asked why Judy didn't call anyone. She didn't know.

"That baby wanted you, didn't it?" Guerra demanded. "You held it?"

"Only enough to clean it up."

"And then you just got rid of it and threw it like trash by the dumpster, right?"

"No, sir. I laid it on the bed to make sure it was taken care of."

"Just long enough to go get your kittens food, right?"

"Pardon?" The sarcasm was wasted on Judy.

"I have no further questions."

Judy's ordeal on the stand was over. For a moment, she sat there.

Then, unnoticed by nearly everyone, including the jury, she slowly stretched out her fingers and caressed the VCR box.

Judy's testimony covered familiar ground. But one item never came up: The dumpster was a central image in this case. Guerra worked on that, implying that putting a baby near a dumpster was the same as putting it in the dumpster. The defense had even filed a motion to prevent him from saying that the baby was placed in the dumpster.

But both sides missed the fact that the dumpster had not been taped off as part of the crime scene, that detectives did not at first connect the baby and the dumpster.

As the media waited in the hallways, Judy ranted in an adjacent room. She hated Guerra. She hated Coe. "Why won't they let me say what I want?" she shouted. "I'll go talk to those reporters! I'll tell them a few things!"

Judy giving television interviews in this condition was a worst-case scenario for Donerly and Wilson. They finally calmed her down and she went home. But she still fumed. In all the news stories and that day in court, everyone kept calling the baby "Jack-in-the-box," the name given to him by the hospital nurses.

That evening, Judy called the television stations. "Quit calling my baby Jack-in-the-box," she said. "That's not his name."

"His name is Rusty."

DAY FOUR: JUDGMENT DAY

Judy Pemberton abandoned her baby in a box April 27, 1989, at her apartment complex. She said neither she nor the baby's father, Russell Hayes, knew she was pregnant. Judy's lawyers had hoped to use an insanity defense at her trial. But on Aug. 21, Hillsborough Circuit Judge Harry Lee Coe III ruled out that option. On Aug. 22, Judy appeared as the only witness in her defense.

AUG. 23. TRIAL DAY NO. 3. Assistant State Attorney Rolando Guerra tossed the videocassette recorder box on the floor in front of the jury. Thud.

"We know that on April 27, Judith Pemberton deserted her child," he began in his closing arguments. "The only person you didn't hear from was that baby in that box ... dumped off with the night's trash. You didn't hear the anger, fear, the terror he felt when his own flesh and blood threw him away."

Defense attorneys Brian Donerly and Andrea Wilson appealed to

the jury's sense of compassion. "The point of this case," Donerly
began, "is not that she did so, but why she did so."

About 11:30 a.m., the six-member jury, four women and two men,
filed out of the courtroom to decide whether Judy was guilty of willfully and intentionally deserting her child.

Donerly and Wilson considered one hour the cutoff point. If the
jury was out that long or longer, the defense had a chance for acquit-
tal, however faint. But if the jury came back in 15 minutes ...

Donerly was much more optimistic about an appeal than he was
about the verdict. Judge Harry Lee Coe III had stripped Judy of her
insanity defense and her witnesses. She was left to testify alone. These
and other factors made for a strong appeal case, Donerly thought.

Judy simply assumed she was going out the back door. To prison.
Her supporters had stopped telling her everything would be okay.
The group waited in the hallway, making small talk as the jury delib-
erated.

Fifteen minutes.

Thirty minutes.

Forty-five.

At one hour, Donerly came by. The jury still out after an hour was
a good sign, he said. No one smiled.

As she waited with Judy, Marci Gilbert, Judy's sister-in-law, realized any doubts she had about Judy's story about the birth were gone.
Marci had taken the same kind of tranquilizers Judy took the day she
testified. She knew: You can't lie under those. Your mind don't work.
She couldn't have been lying. She was so doped, and her answers were
there, over and over. Guerra would rephrase the question and her
answers were always there. I wish Coe would have let me talk. I
would have asked him, "Your honor, how can anybody lie drugged
up?"

Marci still did not know why Judy abandoned her baby. But she
considered Judy's background. Marci had cared for Judy's mother for
10 years before she died. The woman once told Marci how difficult
it was having a sixth child at 37. As a child, Judy did things for attention. She held her breath until she passed out. Once, she cut up a bed
sheet. Judy was 20 years younger than her oldest sister. Judy competed—unsuccessfully, Marci thought—with her sister's children for her
mother's attention.

Marci's observations seemed to give weight to psychiatrist Michael
Maher's speculation: Judy's mother never really formed an emotional
attachment to her last child. Maybe she went through the motions,
but she was detached.

The way Judy seemed now.

One hour, 20 minutes. The bailiff motioned. Everyone filed back into the courtroom. The jury came in, and the verdict was read aloud: Judith Pemberton was guilty as charged.

There was little reaction in the quiet courtroom. Judy seemed only half-aware of the verdict. Sentencing was set for Sept. 22.

Coe allowed Judy to stay out of jail. She went home, facing another 30 days of uncertainty: Her fate was now in Judge Coe's hands.

SEPT. 22, 8:30 A.M. JUDGMENT DAY. Judy meandered near Coe's courtroom, waiting. Wearing red pants and a red and white striped blouse, she seemed resigned, almost cheerful, talking calmly to her friends.

She joked that her breakfast that day might have been her last good meal. "Have you ever seen that crap they serve in jail?" she asked one of her friends. When a television cameraman showed up, she said, "Great. Here comes my public." When Guerra walked by, she said, "He deserves an Academy Award for his performance."

Russell Hayes was not doing as well. He sat on a bench down the hallway, his head in his hands. Judy went to him. He leaned against her, and she gently rubbed his back.

"He's falling apart," she said to Mary Duncan, Russell's aunt, a few moments later. As Mrs. Duncan started toward him, Judy stopped her. "He wants to be alone, he really does. He's been so strong for so long. I said, 'Well, fall apart.' I've done enough falling apart. It's his turn."

Judy knew a pre-sentencing investigation recommended 18 months in prison. There was little hope that Coe would impose a lighter sentence. She did not want to go to prison, she said. She wanted to be with Rusty, now 5 months old. "The baby needs his mother. And I need him."

By now, Mary and Raymond Duncan were so sure they would get temporary custody of Rusty, Mrs. Duncan had furnished the second bedroom in their Tampa apartment with a baby bed, clothes and toys. Judy and Russell bought things for the baby, too. Russell showed off pictures of his son. One showed Rusty asleep on Judy's shoulder.

It was time, Mrs. Duncan thought, for him to come home.

Moments before Judy's case was called, she and Russell stood together in the middle of the busy hallway. They embraced and spoke in low tones to one another.

The bailiff gestured. Judy stiffened. Crowd around me, she told her friends, leaning forward slightly. They circled around her and moved into the courtroom. She hated those television cameras.

Judy had one last, faint hope for leniency. Witnesses not allowed to testify at trials often are allowed to testify at sentencing hearings. Tampa psychiatrist Michael Maher, who had evaluated Judy and other women who had abandoned their babies, was permitted to present to Coe his theories about unacknowledged pregnancy and about Judy. The first day of the trial, Coe had disallowed an insanity defense built on Maher's testimony.

As Maher spoke in clear, declarative tones, occasionally gesturing neatly with his hands, the courtroom grew exceptionally quiet.

Maher explained how some women, under very special and unusual circumstances, could continue through their pregnancies without a "conscious awareness of her pregnancy."

Coe was skeptical but intrigued.

A partial account of the exchange between the psychiatrist and the judge revealed two opposing views of the crime:

"Do you think that is a reasonable possibility in a 7-pound, 7-ounce child, with a thin defendant?" Coe asked. "She would not know that she was pregnant?"

"Yes, I do," Maher said. "It's my opinion that she had no awareness until after the actual delivery." Other women who experienced unacknowledged pregnancies often had at least some vaginal bleeding, some semblance of menstrual periods, during their pregnancies. Judy Pemberton did not—but, at 42, she thought she was in menopause.

Judy's lack of awareness of her pregnancy, Maher continued, "sets the stage for a traumatic delivery. ... She identified her menstrual cramping and thought, 'Well, maybe I am going to have my period again.' She gave me no indication whatsoever that it even occurred to her that she might be going into labor at that point.

"At approximately 4 o'clock in the afternoon, I would estimate, she went into the end stages of labor and delivered this infant after going to the bathroom, expecting to relieve herself.

"Given that she had no conscious awareness of this pregnancy until that time, that put her in a state of psychic shock that I would characterize technically as a severe dissociative reaction—somewhat similar to psychosis but not exactly the same, the sort of reaction people describe in a near-death situation, where they feel they are out of their body looking at what is happening as an observer."

"What do you call this lack of memory?" Coe asked.

"Dissociative reaction."

"When she says she doesn't remember, is that the dissociative reaction?"

"Yes, basically."

"Can a dissociative reaction be selective? Can you remember one thing and not remember another?"

"Yes. A dissociative reaction includes an element of amnesia ... but even more prominent, a confusion about the events."

"Well, I'm trying to understand," Coe said patiently. "She cannot remember having a child and not remember leaving it at the dumpster, but yet remember going to the store ... and a week later does remember the child. Does that all make sense to you?"

"Yes, and I think I can explain in the context of circumstances that were forcing her to accept that this was not a dream, this was reality, and that her internal awareness was developing. ... As that process continued, she was developing an acceptance of the infant."

Coe frowned. "When did this happen? When?"

"Probably a couple of days prior to when she was arrested, but really when she was arrested, when the police came to her home (and) confronted her with the evidence."

"How can you then explain this?" Coe asked. "It looks selective to me. There is no consistency there. ... She does something that is very logical but then something that is very unlogical. ... She ties off the cord but yet dumps the baby. She dumps the baby but yet goes back to check. You know ... her reactions seem to say she can have it both ways."

"It fits the pattern of these situations," Maher said. "The person suffering will often wander around the area, will return to the area out of some feeling that that is necessary."

"But still did nothing to correct the situation?"

"Yes."

Maher explained that Judy was suffering from post-traumatic stress disorder, the result of an "out of the ordinary experience, not simply losing a job or something like that. It's also associated with thoughts and memories and confusion and anxiety about the traumatic event, disturbing dreams about it, that sort of thing.

"She has a mild form of this disorder, and she is recovering from it quite well. ... She has to accept the ultimate responsibility for this. In my opinion she is doing that."

"Well," Coe said, raising his arms, "given all that you say is true, why wouldn't she come in here and say, 'I did it and I am sorry?' Why is she trying to alibi out of it? Why wouldn't she say, 'There is no excuse for it and I am sorry,' if that is the truth?"

"Because—" Maher began.

"Why didn't she take the stand and say, 'This happened and I am sorry that it happened and it's terrible and I will suffer the consequences?' Why wouldn't she do that if she is such a fine person?"

"I don't know, but I can tell you a very important part of that, which is—"

"—'Let me tell you why I did it,'" Coe interrupted. "'I did it because of the disassociative reaction, I was not in my right mind, I shouldn't have done it that way. I am sorry I did it that way, and I am ready to suffer the consequences?'"

"Because she doesn't know it and understand it that clearly yet. ... When I have talked to her about this in my office, she blames herself and feels guilty and denigrates herself because of this. It's clear to me she feels responsible ... but because of her confused memory, lack of awareness, because of her lack of conscience—"

"Well, I am not quite sure. Here we are having it both ways. Does she remember this or not today?"

"Not in the way you and I would remember an event in our past. She remembers it still with this veil of dreamlike confusion. ... "

"How can she then say to the police, first, 'I know nothing about it, it wasn't my child,' and then, 'Yes it's my child?'"

"Because her memory of it changed during that period of time."

"It seems to change for the best."

Donerly saw that Coe seemed to be losing patience. Donerly interjected, "Judy, in terms of showing regret, I think she has."

"When? When? When?" Coe asked, leaning forward. "Point it out to me."

"In my office, crying, collapsed on a couch. ... In her sessions with Dr. Maher and in multiple conversations with me and Mrs. Wilson over the last months," Donerly said.

Judy stood, leaning weakly against Russell or Marci. "I'm going to faint," she whispered to Marci. "I'm going to prison."

Later, Wilson, attempting to show the extent of Maher's belief in Judy, asked Maher whether he would recommend that Judy have her child "now, sometime or never."

"Sometime," Maher responded, "probably after appropriate evaluation."

"How can you say that?" Coe shouted, leaning forward again. "How in the world? That escapes me. Somebody can do something like that, even assuming there is a justification for it, and you can say, 'Let them have another shot at it?'"

The courtroom rang with laughter.

"Yes." Maher held his ground.

"Is there any possible way to say she wants that child? ... Why doesn't she react by loving the child?"

"She had very, very strong, opposite feelings."

"Why? Why? Why? It's very simple. She didn't want the child because it was very disruptive of her life. She had enough reason to reason that out."

"Well," Maher said, "I would say that she had an irrational fear that the child would mean that she would be abandoned."

Could Maher predict, yes or no, whether the baby was emotionally harmed by having spent the first hour or two of his life by a dumpster, abandoned by his mother?

No, Maher replied, he could not predict.

"So," Coe said, "it wouldn't bother you if we took every child out of Tampa General Hospital and put them by the dumpster for two hours. You don't think they would be harmed at all?"

"Sir, I would certainly not agree with that."

"Of course not."

Maher testified for about 20 minutes. Then everyone else was heard. Guerra argued for Coe to exceed the recommended sentence based on the vulnerability of the victim—a newborn infant left "with no food, to the elements, animals ..."

The defense and the baby's court-appointed guardian pleaded for a more workable situation. Judy would be devastated by prison; it would serve no purpose to put her behind bars. Or if she did go to prison, she probably would not serve more than a year. Then she would probably reunite with Russell. Russell could gain custody of his child right now. So Judy, in effect, would have her child with no controls, no guidance from HRS, no court-ordered counseling.

After everyone had made their recommendations, there was a moment of silence. Judy stared at the ground. Coe began to speak.

Maher's presentation was excellent, he said. But "I don't believe for a minute that she (didn't know she was) pregnant, and I do not believe for a minute that she did not know what she was doing."

Russell bowed his head and leaned forward on one arm.

"She most certainly knew what she was doing. It was a cold, calculated act," Coe continued. "Only when confronted with overwhelming evidence did she admit the child was hers. There are circumstances and factors that justify me going outside the guidelines— the nature of the crime, the emotional trauma at a young age, the breach of trust. ... All of this dictates that she receives the maximum possible sentence. I find myself hard pressed to find any compassion for somebody that thinks more of their cat than they do of their own child.

"I sentence her to five years in the Florida State Prison."

Russell turned and ran out of the courtroom.

Donerly and Wilson quickly asked that Judy be allowed to report to jail the next Tuesday, so that she could attend Rusty's custody hearing on Monday. Coe asked for Russell. Russell composed himself and came back into the courtroom. Coe established that Russell was a Tampa native and resident and would help assure Judy would not leave town.

"Well, I certainly commend you, sir," Coe said. "You have stuck by her and your child, and I commend you. Nothing that has been said or done here reflects on you."

Coe agreed to let Judy stay out of jail.

Court was dismissed.

People flooded the courtroom. Russell fell into the arms of a friend, sobbing. Judy collapsed on a bench, buried her head in her arms and said, "I'm not gonna go to any prison, because I'll be dead by this weekend, you can guarantee it."

There was no trace of the calm, rational Judy of an hour before. She didn't listen to anyone who tried to comfort her. She refused to get up for 10 minutes. Then Russell guided her out of the courtroom. When she got into the hallway, she stopped dead in her tracks. Russell tried to coax her forward. She yelled at him. She pulled away from him, he pulled her back. She wouldn't move her feet, so they slid along the floor, her body slanted away from Russell. A television cameraman filmed it all.

Other cameras waited outside. Judy wouldn't leave the building. She threatened to kill herself. She shouted at Russell, who finally surrounded her against a wall between his arms.

"You're acting like a child!" he yelled. "I've been here all along, haven't I? And I'm gonna be here for you!"

Judy escaped and ducked into the elevator. She retreated to Wilson's fifth-floor office, then returned several minutes later. She finally walked toward the door. In her little-girl voice, she stared ahead, and said, "Judge Coe said I knew what I was doing, but I didn't."

Nov. 9, 1989, 5 p.m. Three small bowls lie scattered on the concrete floor outside her apartment door. They are for her cats and any other cats that come by, for she cannot turn away a stray animal. On that, even her critics agree. Right now, the bowls are empty. There are no cats in sight.

Judy Pemberton answers the door, wearing an oversized orange

Florida Gators sweat shirt and royal blue sweat pants. Russell sits cross-legged on the living room floor, absorbed in a Nintendo game that Judy gave him for Christmas 1988. He looks up, smiles, says hi, and goes back to the game.

"He's addicted," Judy says, grinning at him.

She shows off their new home, a two-bedroom, third-floor apartment they moved to last summer. It is clean, orderly and modestly furnished, except for some antiques handed down from Judy's family: an imposing four-poster bed and vanity that swallow the small spare bedroom, a 1920s-era couch with velvet upholstery and curved, wooden legs; a 1922 Singer sewing machine.

In the kitchen, scores of decorative magnets pepper the freezer section of the refrigerator. In the living room is Russell's collection of sports mugs, neatly lined on shelves. Small, framed photographs of family members fill a small table nearby.

One photo shows Judy and Russell next to a sign reading "Bermuda Star Line, Vera Cruz." It was taken as they left on a Mexico cruise at Christmas, 1988—when, she says, she was five months pregnant and did not know it. Judy is wearing the same striped jump suit she wore the day she was arrested.

"I threw it out," she says. "I would have burned it, but I didn't have any gasoline."

The remark is evidence of the stress of the past six months. Judy still faces five years in prison, but Coe released her on her own recognizance while her case is appealed, which could take up to two years.

On Sept. 23, Hillsborough Juvenile Judge Vincent Giglio granted temporary custody of the baby, Russell Raymond Hayes, to Mary and Raymond Duncan. The court allowed Judy and Russell unlimited, supervised visits with the baby. Giglio also ordered them to take parenting classes, which they attend weekly. He did not address whether Judy and Russell can get custody; HRS says it is possible one day. After the hearing, Russell beamed. Judy jumped up and down. "I get to see my baby every day!" she said.

All of that is now six weeks past. Judy and Russell are trying to get on with their lives. Russell still works at the restaurant making pasta and doing other jobs. Judy has a part-time minimum wage job. The couple never had a great deal of money. But the long legal ordeal and Judy's inability to work for several months have depleted their finances.

Judy and Russell share a 1987 Chevy Sprint with a broken back window covered with plastic. Bill collectors call. They have no medical insurance, Judy has yet to see a medical doctor or psychiatrist. She says she can't afford it.

Judy's family, except for her sister-in-law Marci Gilbert, still shun her. "They don't understand why I did such a thing. I don't, either," she says. "My family, this is the way they are: They have to make up their own mind at their own pace. I've just learned to stay away from them."

She introduces one of her cats, Morris, an orange tabby, cradling him in her arms for a moment. She looks around for Baby, and finds him in the bathroom cupboard. "There you are!" she says, gently picking up the black cat. "This is his favorite hiding spot."

Judy sinks into an easy chair and tucks her bare feet beneath her. Lamp light falls kindly on her face. She wears little makeup. Her eyes are deep set and close together, the rims a bit red. Freckles that refuse to fade with age cover her face. She is plump, as she was during her pregnancy.

Russell gets up. "Why don't you stay?" she asks. It is more like a polite plea. Russell says "No," softly, then goes into the bedroom. A 5 o'clock news program blares on the television. Judy gets up, clicks off the TV, then returns to her chair.

She is suddenly nervous, knowing the conversation will veer from antiques, cats and bowling to the abandonment. She says she is afraid talking will hurt her case, her chances of getting custody of Rusty. She also is shell-shocked by the media attention she has received.

But beyond that, there appears to be in her a mountain of resistance about the abandonment, a sense that despite all that has happened, she has yet to emotionally confront and resolve what she did. She admits to the crime, she expresses remorse, but as she sits talking, her words seem weightless. She seems robotic. Her occasional hostile remarks when anyone mentions the baby suggest she still denies, hoping that if she denies long enough, all of this will go away, and life can be as it was before this thing happened to her.

She answers questions with full eye contact, but her answers seem flat, lacking emotion. Her voice is girlish, a voice you can imagine talking to stuffed animals.

She grew up in Temple Terrace, less than two miles away. She was a tomboy, always closer to her father and three brothers, who spoiled her, than her mother and two sisters. In high school, she was the kind of student you can't quite remember years later. "I went to school and went home," she says. "I kept to myself." Her father died 16 years ago; her mother died a few months before Rusty was born.

Judy graduated from King High School in 1964. She joined the Navy in 1965. She did well; she was a hospital corpsman (a medic) and reached the rank of E-5 (E-8 is the highest enlisted rank). While in basic training at Parris Island, S.C., she met Russell Pemberton, a Marine. They married in 1966.

Pemberton was "good lookin', very good lookin', Judy says. "He was one of the beautiful people." But the marriage was unhappy, almost from the beginning. "Families, birthdays and Christmas, they mean a lot to me," she says. But not to Pemberton. "His opinion of birthdays is it's no big deal being born. Christmas is no big deal because it's Christ's birthday, not yours. I rarely got a present from him. With Mother's Day, he'd say, 'You're not my mother.' Things like that, that's really, you know, gee whiz."

Their daughter was born in 1969. Three years later, the family moved to Europe for seven years. Pemberton, a career Marine by then, left the family frequently on military trips, sometimes for long periods of time. Their relationship was unhealthy for Judy, but for years, she denied it.

The marriage ended one night in September 1987 in a scene Judy barely describes. She only says that when her husband packed up to leave for his girlfriend's for the night, "I said, 'This is ridiculous, I'm outta here.'"

"I couldn't understand why I stayed in that relationship so long. Then it dawned on me," she says, her voice childlike and trusting. "Well, obviously, I had to wait for Russell to grow up. I didn't know that, but they say God has a plan for us. That was mine. That's the only thing I can figure."

Sitting there, her hands resting in her lap, Judy seems every bit her 43 years. She is mature, rational, ordinary. Yet six months before, she left her baby in a box by a dumpster. She looks mystified by this. She frowns slightly, as if trying to discern why someone else she doesn't know did that. She still says she remembers only bits and pieces about the day the baby was born. She slowly shakes her head when asked why she cleaned up the baby, tied the umbilical cord—and then left him, possibly, to die.

Did she mean for him to be found?

She just doesn't know.

"There must have been some part of me that wanted not to (throw the baby in the dumpster)," she said. "I feel at that point in time there were probably two Judys that existed, like you see in cartoons, the angel on one shoulder and the devil on the other. Maybe that's part of it. I'm sure there is a bad part in me somewhere."

Psychiatrist Michael Maher, who evaluated Judy after the abandonment, pointed out to Judy that she risked her own health. The day after she gave birth she went to work, and four days later she bowled with a 15-pound bowling ball. "I coulda died," she said. "I mean, that's scary."

Her two nights in the jail were just as scary, she says. "People coming and going, loud noises. Other people sat across the jail, they would look at me, and talk to each other and point. I just stayed to myself, I thought, 'They make one move toward me, I'm gonna go up to the guard.' They would bring newspaper articles up to me, but I wouldn't look at them, 'cause I just wanted nothing to do with them."

She doesn't remember much about testifying. She doesn't remember caressing the VCR box that was placed next to her on the stand. She listens to her statement to the police the day she was arrested read aloud. Nooo, she shakes her head again, at the part saying she checked later on the baby. "I'm pretty sure I didn't say that. I was just going to do laundry."

But when shown the police report, she responds "Yeah, I suppose it's possible. ..."

She does remember sticking out her tongue at a photographer. "That, believe it or not, is the extent of my bad nature—sticking my tongue out as I walk away from a fight."

What makes the least sense is that she abandoned the child of the nicest man she had ever known, a man she lived with and would soon marry. Why? She shakes her head, again. "It was an awful thing to do, an awful thing to do to Russell, you know. As crazy as I am about him, why wouldn't I be crazy about his child?

"I've often thought—well, you've seen that rocking chair," she gestures toward the spare bedroom, "I've thought, if I could have just had any sort of sense about me, any awareness, knowledge of what was going on, and be sitting there in the rocking chair when Russell came home—what a sight that would have been. He probably would have passed out, I'm sure. That would have been terrific, if it just would have happened that way. Or if someone had been around. But you know, I was there all by myself.

"How could something like this happen to a person? Not know you're pregnant? Some people say, 'Well, at your age, you weren't married, you wouldn't have Russell's child.' That's absolutely ridiculous, the way I feel about him? I wouldn't have cared diddly squat what anybody else thought about it."

Since Judy abandoned her baby, five other women have abandoned their babies in the Tampa Bay area. Two babies were found alive in dumpsters by passersby. Another was left, wrapped carefully in aprons, outside a New Port Richey nursing home.

On Oct. 23, Claire Moritt, an 18-year-old freshman at Hillsborough Community College, locked herself in the dormitory bathroom and gave birth to a full-term baby boy. The baby was later found dead in the toilet. Her friends in the dorm did not know what had happened until it was too late.

Judy followed news accounts about Moritt, who is charged with first-degree murder. Her trial is scheduled to begin in March in Tampa.

A year ago, Judy would have condemned Moritt, just as Judy has been condemned. Not now.

"I thought, 'I hope they're not too tough on her.' Since I've been all through this, I've learned that when something like this happens, don't judge them. There can be a lot of circumstances that can lead up to it. Anymore, I don't judge. I'm more tolerant of a lot of things. And people."

Is she a criminal? "Obviously, I must be. I did the act. But I'm not a bad person. I'm not the monster that most of the media made me out to be. There's a lot more to me than the things you saw on TV."

Moritt's baby died. "Mine lived. He could've died, yeah. I see him every day, the thought of that happening is just ..." She pauses. "It's just not acceptable at all."

It is nearly 7 p.m. Judy and Russell are going to the Duncans' nearby to see Rusty, as they do most every night. Judy, instantly at ease with safer subjects, shows a flowery greeting card, handling it as if it were a treasure. Inside, Russell's small handwriting asks, "Will you be my wife?"

Judy then flips through a pile of photos. She stops at one.

"This is my favorite," she says.

Rusty is lying on the couch, Russell is leaning over his son. They are laughing, looking into one another's eyes.

"We're pretty sure he's gonna grow up to be a terror," Judy says. "Russell says he's gonna grow up to be mean and ornery. I said, 'I hope so.' I just like ornery children, it shows a lot of spirit.

"I call him Sugar Bear. He's my Sugar Bear. I'll walk in and say, 'Hi Sugar Bear,' and he's all smiles. He reached for me one time a couple weeks ago. Oh God. It was wonderful."

Judy says she hopes Rusty never has to know about the day he was born. She hopes that by then, no one will remember it. But when she and the Duncans' took the baby to the bowling alley, someone called Channel 10. The TV station contacted HRS, which determined there were no violations.

Yes, it's possible someone will say something. Or Rusty will ask questions.

"I'd just tell him there was a big mistake made," Judy says. "You know. Something happened."

On Jan. 6, 1990 Judy Pemberton and Russell Hayes were married in a small, civil ceremony. The guests were a friend of Russell's, Raymond and Mary Duncan and Russell Raymond Hayes.

ANALYSIS

JAMES WAS an experienced feature writer when she started "A Gift Abandoned." "I like to show how ordinary people react under extraordinary conditions," she offers. "In the case of Judy Pemberton, we wanted to find out how a woman can do something as apparently monstrous as abandoning her baby."

James says she went into the story with no preconceived ideas about right vs. wrong. "I did in fact [come to] understand to a great degree how and why this happened. Judy had many things in common with other women who have abandoned babies."

Some of James' literary techniques are obvious, such as her chronological narrative approach, which she prefers to "the conventional quote-and-tell, present tense approach, which I find sterile and predictable."

James believes a chronology can read like a story, as long as extensive recreation can be used. "I used dialogue whenever possible, plenty of visual detail and I tried to take advantage of episodic structure, building up to the climax of Judy's sentencing," she explains. (The only break from the chronology is approximately half way through the Day One section, where James gives some statistics and information about the local and national scope of the problem. As the section was early in the series, she was able to skillfully work it in without jeopardizing the narrative.)

To make the series work, James adopted various other fiction techniques, such as character development and using others' thoughts about what was going on. Although using such recollections can often be a risky proposition, James felt there was no other effective way to achieve the narrative flow. Plus, the tactic has long been used in fiction. And without it, the story wouldn't have been nearly as strong. She also used extensive interviews, police reports, court files and transcripts.

James had to spend months trying to win the trust of Judy Pemberton. However, James points out that key family members did talk to her and were the major reason she was able to write most of the narrative without Judy. When she finally sat down to write the story, Sheryl James knew the story cold.

One of the major strengths of the series is the quality of the leads James produced each day. Each is descriptive and tells a small tale.

Her **Day One** lead, recounting how Ryan Nawrocki found the baby, is extremely descriptive, yet foreshadows how she plans on using character development and staging through the story.

The **Day Two** lead, under a recap, allows the reader to watch the mother-in-law's suspicions grow through an effective use of italic quotes.

On **Day Three**, James leads with the diary of neighbor George Cochran. Again, the suspicions of neighbors, in their own words and thoughts, grabs instant reader interest.

Day Four picks up the story in mid-trial. Each of the daily leads moved the story forward and allowed the reader to catch up without an elaborate explanation. The recaps were also important in keeping the reader committed to the story.

Not that it was all cut-and-dried. James admits having problems with how to handle the aunt's thoughts: "Her voice was so strong, her quotes so good, that I wanted to use them verbatim." To do that would have forced James to jump to the present long before she wanted to. The answer? "I went with italics. Those sections are literally unedited portions of my interview with her."

In a similar vein, James felt the judge questioning the psychiatrist was one of the most dramatic portions of the story. "Trying to 'report' on that would have been flat compared with letting it unroll as part of the film," she says.

SHERYL JAMES is currently a staff writer for *The Detroit Free Press*. She has a bachelor's degree in English from Eastern Michigan University and has published two short stories.

1992

HOWELL RAINES

FAR MORE THAN a profile, Howell Raines' highly-literate story spotlights the bonding between an affluent white Southern family and a struggling black maid who is desperately trying to improve her lot in life.

Raines had long realized that Gradystein Williams Hutchinson had helped form his views on segregation. He always wanted to locate her again "just for personal as opposed to journalistic reasons," he says.

When Raines' sister acquired "Grady's" phone number through a chance encounter with one of her relatives, he wasted little time calling her. "The telephone conversation, and the visit, particularly, was like picking up a conversation that had been interrupted five minutes ago," Raines recalls.

After the visit, Raines says he decided to write "Grady's Gift" as a "closing of the circle" of all the work he'd done on civil rights. "As I'd gotten older, I'd come to realize that my early relationship with Grady has prepared me for the civil rights story and made me receptive to it perhaps in a way many white Southerners might not have been. So it was a thank-you, in a sense, to both Grady and my parents."

He suggested the idea to the *Times Magazine* and they responded enthusiastically. In his soft-spoken, distinctive Alabama drawl, Raines chuckles for a second. "I've got to say, when you're a senior editor of the *Times,* as I was then, your ideas do get presented with enthusiasm."

Raines was told of his Pulitzer by Max Frankel, then the executive editor, of the *Times.* "In the old days people used to gather around the ... clacking Teletypes, and you'd see it in print," Raines explains. "I always had this fantasy that if I ever won one that was how I would find out."

The Pulitzer was also appreciated because Raines felt the time was gone for the foremost journalistic honor. "I had really passed the stage of my career when I thought I was likely to win a Pulitzer," he says candidly.

"Back when I was doing a lot of investigative and political reporting, I thought I had a pretty good likelihood because I was nominated once by the *Times* for an investigative piece I did on the Birmingham church bombings in 1963 and once by *The St. Petersburg Times* for political reporting."

Raines says he really understood the enormity of his win after serving as a Pulitzer juror and reading the entries. "You realize how much wonderful work there is and how few pieces are able to be recognized."

He feels inexperienced writers need to realize how much work is required to reach the stage of the masterful writers whose work appears in this volume. "I always tell young people to remember you've got a lot of bad writing to get out of your system and there is no way around it. You're seeing people [in this anthology] who are writing at a level that did not come to them as undergraduates. The only way to write well is to write a lot."

Admitting that the Pulitzer is a career affirmation that has served to "relax" him, Raines is pleased how much joy the award has brought Grady. "I brought her to New York for the Pulitzer Prize awards," he explains. "Now Grady ... always refers to it as 'when we won the Pulitzer Prize.'"

Has the Pulitzer changed anything else?

"As Russell Baker says, 'You always know what the first line of your obit will be,'" Raines jokes.

Grady's Gift

The New York Times Magazine

December 1, 1991

GRADY SHOWED UP ONE DAY at our house at 1409 Fifth Avenue West in Birmingham, and by and by she changed the way I saw the world. I was 7 when she came to iron and clean and cook for $18 a week, and she stayed for seven years. During that time everyone in our family came to accept what my father called "those great long talks" that occupied Grady and me through many a sleepy Alabama afternoon. What happened between us can be expressed in many ways, but its essence was captured by Graham Greene when he wrote that in every childhood there is a moment when a door opens and lets the future in. So this is a story about one person who opened a door and another who walked through it.

It is difficult to describe—or even to keep alive in our memories—worlds that cease to exist. Usually we think of vanished worlds as having to do with far-off places or with ways of life, like that of the Western frontier, that are remote from us in time. But I grew up in a place that disappeared, and it was here in this country and not so long ago. I speak of Birmingham, where once there flourished the most complete form of racial segregation to exist on the American continent in this century.

Gradystein Williams Hutchinson (or Grady, as she was called in my family and hers) and I are two people who grew up in the 50's in that vanished world, two people who lived mundane, inconsequential lives while Martin Luther King Jr. and Police Commissioner T. Eugene (Bull) Connor prepared for their epic struggle. For years, Grady and I lived in my memory as child and adult. But now I realize that we were both children—one white and very young, one black and adolescent; one privileged, one poor. The connection between these two children and their city was this: Grady saw to it that although I was to live in Birmingham for the first 28 years of my life, Birmingham would not live in me.

Only by keeping in mind the place that Birmingham was can you understand the life we had, the people we became and the reunion that occurred one day not too long ago at my sister's big house in the verdant Birmingham suburb of Mountain Brook. Grady, now a 57-year-old hospital cook in Atlanta, had driven out with me in the car I had rented. As we pulled up, my parents, a retired couple living in Florida, arrived in their gray Cadillac. My father, a large, vigorous man of 84, parked his car and, without a word, walked straight to Grady and took her in his arms.

"I never thought I'd ever see y'all again," Grady said a little while later. "I just think this is the true will of God. It's His divine wish that we saw each other."

This was the first time in 34 years that we had all been together. As the years slipped by, it had become more and more important to me to find Grady, because I am a strong believer in thanking our teachers and mentors while they are still alive to hear our thanks. She had been "our maid," but she taught me the most valuable lesson a writer can learn, which is to try to see—honestly and down to its very center—the world in which we live. Grady was long gone before I realized what a brave and generous person she was, or how much I owed her.

Then last spring, my sister ran into a relative of Grady's and got her telephone number. I went to see Grady in Atlanta, and several months later we gathered in Birmingham to remember our shared past and to learn anew how love abides and how it can bloom not only in the fertile places, but in the stony ones as well.

I KNOW THAT OUTSIDERS TEND to think segregation existed in a uniform way throughout the Solid South. But it didn't. Segregation was rigid in some places, relaxed in others; leavened with humanity in some places, enforced with unremitting brutality in others. And segregation found its most violent and regimented expression in Birmingham—segregation maintained through the nighttime maraudings of white thugs, segregation sanctioned by absentee landlords from the United States Steel Corporation, segregation enforced by a pervasively corrupt police department.

Martin Luther King once said Birmingham was to the rest of the South what Johannesburg was to the rest of Africa. He believed that if segregation could be broken there, in a city that harbored an American version of apartheid, it could be broken everywhere. That is why the great civil rights demonstrations of 1963 took place in Birmingham. And that is why, just as King envisioned, once its jugular was cut in Kelly Ingram Park in Birmingham in 1963, the dragon of legalized segregation collapsed and died everywhere—died, it seems in retrospect, almost on the instant. It was the end of "Bad Birmingham," where the indigenous racism of rural Alabama had taken a new and more virulent form when transplanted into a raw industrial setting.

In the heyday of Birmingham, one vast belt of steel mills stretched for 10 miles, from the satellite town of Bessemer to the coal-mining suburb of Pratt City. Black and white men—men like Grady's father and mine—came from all over the South to do the work of these mills or to dig the coal and iron ore to feed them. By the time Grady Williams was born in 1933, the huge light of their labor washed the evening sky with an undying red glow. The division of tasks within these plants ran along simple lines: white men made the steel; black men washed the coal.

Henry Williams was a tiny man from Oklahoma—part African, part Cherokee, only 5 feet 3 inches, but handsome. He worked at the No. 2 Coal Washer at Pratt Mines, and he understood his world imperfectly. When the white foreman died, Henry thought he would move up. But the dead man's nephew was brought in, and in the natural order of things, Henry was required to teach his new boss all there was to know about washing coal.

"Oh, come on, Henry," his wife, Elizabeth, said when he complained about being passed over for a novice. But he would not be consoled.

One Saturday, Henry Williams sent Grady on an errand. "Go up the hill," he said, "and tell Mr. Humphrey Davis I said send me three bullets for my .38 pistol because I got to kill a dog."

In his bedroom later that same afternoon, he shot himself. Grady found the body. She was 7 years old.

Over the years, Elizabeth Williams held the family together. She worked as a practical nurse and would have become a registered nurse except for the fact that by the early 40's, the hospitals in Birmingham, which had run segregated nursing programs, closed those for blacks.

Grady attended Parker High, an all-black school where the children of teachers and postal workers made fun of girls like Grady, who at 14 was already working part-time in white homes. One day a boy started ragging Grady for being an "Aunt Jemima." One of the poorer boys approached him after class and said: "Hey, everybody's not lucky enough to have a father working. If I ever hear you say that again to her, I'm going to break your neck."

Grady finished high school in early 1950, four weeks after her 16th birthday. Her grades were high, even though she had held back on some tests in an effort to blend in with her older classmates. She planned to go to the nursing school at Dillard University, a black institution in New Orleans, but first she needed a full-time job to earn money for tuition. That was when my mother hired her. There was a state-financed nursing school in Birmingham, about 10 miles from her house, but it was the wrong one.

BETWEEN THE DEPRESSION and World War II, my father and two of his brothers came into Birmingham from the Alabama hills. They were strong, sober country boys who knew how to swing a hammer. By the time Truman was elected in 1948, they had got a little bit rich selling lumber and building shelves for the A.&P.

They drove Packards and Oldsmobiles. They bought cottages at the beach and hired housemaids for their wives and resolved that their children would go to college. Among them, they had eight children, and I was the last to be born, and my world was sunny.

Indeed, it seemed to be a matter of family pride that this tribe of hard-handed hill people had become prosperous enough to spoil its babies. I was doted upon, particularly, it occurs to me now, by women: my mother; my sister, Mary Jo, who was 12 years older and carried me around like a mascot; my leathery old grandmother, a widow who didn't like many people but liked me because I was named for her husband.

There was also my Aunt Ada, a red-haired spinster who made me rice pudding and hand-whipped biscuits and milkshakes with cracked ice, and when my parents were out of town, I slept on a pallet in her room.

Then there were the black women, first Daisy, then Ella. And finally Grady.

I wish you could have seen her in 1950. Most of the women in my family ran from slender to bony. Grady was buxom. She wore a blue uniform and walked around our house on stout brown calves. Her skin was smooth. She had a gap between her front teeth, and so did I. One of the first things I remember Grady telling me was that as soon as she had enough money she was going to get a diamond set in her gap and it would drive the men wild.

There is no trickier subject for a writer from the South than that of affection between a black person and a white one in the unequal world of segregation. For the dishonesty upon which such a society is founded makes every emotion suspect, makes it impossible to know whether what flowed between two people was honest feeling or pity or pragmatism. Indeed, for the black person, the feigning of an expected emotion could be the very coinage of survival.

So I can only tell you how it seemed to me at the time. I was 7 and Grady was 16 and I adored her and I believed she was crazy about me. She became the weather in which my childhood was lived.

I was 14 when she went away. It would be many years before I realized that somehow, whether by accident or by plan, in a way so subtle, so gentle, so loving that it was like the budding and falling of the leaves on the pecan trees in the yard of that happy house in that cruel city in that violent time, Grady had given me the most precious gift that could be received by a pampered white boy growing up in that time and place. It was the gift of a free and unhateful heart.

GRADY, IT SOON BECAME CLEAR, was a talker, and I was already known in my family as an incessant asker of questions. My brother, Jerry, who is 10 years older than I, says one of his clearest memories is of my following Grady around the house, pursuing her with a constant buzz of chatter.

That is funny, because what I remember is Grady talking and me listening—Grady talking as she did her chores, marking me with her vision of the way things were. All of my life, I have carried this mental image of the two of us:

I am 9 or 10 by this time. We are in the room where Grady did her ironing. Strong light is streaming through the window. High summer lies heavily across all of Birmingham like a blanket. We are alone, Grady and I, in the midst of what the Alabama novelist Babs Deal called "the acres of afternoon," those legendary hours of buzzing heat and torpidity that either bind you to the South or make you crazy to leave it.

I am slouched on a chair, with nothing left to do now that baseball practice is over. Grady is moving a huge dreadnought of an iron, a G.E. with stainless steel base and fat black handle, back and forth across my father's white shirts. From time to time, she shakes water on the fabric from a bottle with a sprinkler cap.

Then she speaks of a hidden world about which no one has ever told me, a world as dangerous and foreign, to a white child in a segregated society, as Africa itself—the world of "nigger town." "You don't know what it's like to be poor and black," Grady says.

She speaks of the curbside justice administered with rubber hoses by Bull Connor's policemen, of the deputy sheriff famous in the black community for shooting a floor sweeper who had moved too slowly, of "Dog Day," the one time a year when blacks are allowed to attend the state fair. She speaks offhandedly of the N.A.A.C.P.

"Are you a member?" I ask.

"At my school," she says, "we take our dimes and nickels and join the N.A.A.C.P. every year just like you join the Red Cross in your school."

It seems silly now to describe the impact of this revelation, but that is because I cannot fully re-create the intellectual isolation of those days in Alabama. Remember that this was a time when television news, with its searing pictures of racial conflict, was not yet a force in our society. The editorial pages of the Birmingham papers were dominated by the goofy massive-resistance cant of columnists like James J. Kilpatrick. Local politicians liked to describe the N.A.A.C.P.

as an organization of satanic purpose and potency that had been rejected by "our colored people," and would shortly be outlawed in Alabama as an agency of Communism.

But Grady said black students were joining in droves, people my age and hers. It was one of the most powerfully subversive pieces of information I had ever encountered, leaving me with an unwavering conviction about Bull Connor, George Wallace and the other segregationist blowhards who would dominate the politics of my home state for a generation.

From that day, I knew they were wrong when they said that "our Negroes" were happy with their lot and had no desire to change "our Southern way of life." And when a local minister named Fred L. Shuttlesworth joined with Dr. King in 1957 to start the civil rights movement in Birmingham, I knew in some deeply intuitive way that they would succeed, because I believed that the rage that was in Grady was a living reality in the entire black community, and I knew that this rage was so powerful that it would have its way.

I learned, too, from watching Grady fail at something that meant a great deal to her. In January 1951, with the savings from her work in our home, she enrolled at Dillard. She made good grades. She loved the school and the city of New Orleans. But the money lasted only one semester, and when summer rolled around Grady was cleaning our house again.

That would be the last of her dream of becoming a registered nurse. A few years later, Grady married Marvin Hutchinson, a dashing fellow, more worldly than she, who took her to all-black night clubs to hear singers like Bobby (Blue) Bland. In 1957, she moved to New York City to work as a maid and passed from my life. But I never forgot how she had yearned for education.

Did this mean that between the ages of 7 and 14, I acquired a sophisticated understanding of the insanity of a system of government that sent this impoverished girl to Louisiana rather than letting her attend the tax-supported nursing school that was a 15-cent bus ride from her home?

I can't say that I did. But I do know that in 1963, I recognized instantly that George Wallace was lying when he said that his Stand in the School House Door at the University of Alabama was intended to preserve the Constitutional Principle of states' rights. What he really wanted to preserve was the right of the state of Alabama to promiscuously damage lives like Grady's.

IT IS APRIL 23, 1991. I approach the locked security gate of a rough-looking apartment courtyard in Atlanta. There behind it, waiting in the shadows, is a tiny woman with a halo of gray hair and that destructive gap in the front teeth. Still no diamond. Grady opens the gate and says, "I've got to hug you."

Grady's apartment is modest. The most striking feature is the stacks of books on each side of her easy chair. The conversation that was interrupted so long ago is resumed without a beat.

Within minutes we are both laughing wildly over an incident we remembered in exactly the same way. Grady had known that I was insecure about my appearance as I approached adolescence, and she always looked for chances to reassure me, preferably in the most exuberant way possible. One day when I appeared in a starched shirt and with my hair slicked back for a birthday party, Grady shouted, "You look positively raping."

"Grady," my mother called from the next room, "do you know what you're saying?"

"I told her yeah. I was trying to say 'ravishing.' I used to read all those *True Confession* magazines."

Reading, it turned out, had become a passion of Grady's life, even though she never got any more formal education. For the first time in years, I recall that it was Grady who introduced me to Ernest Hemingway. In the fall of 1952, when I had the mumps and "The Old Man and the Sea" was being published in *Life*, Grady sat by my bed and read me the entire book. We both giggled over the sentence: "Once he stood up and urinated over the side of the skiff. ... "

Partly for money and partly to escape a troubled marriage, Grady explains, she had left Birmingham to work in New York as a maid for $125 a month. Her husband had followed.

"So we got an apartment, and the man I worked for got him a job," Grady recalls. "And we got together and we stayed for 31 years, which is too long to stay dead."

Dead, I asked? What did that mean?

For Grady it meant a loveless marriage and a series of grinding jobs as a maid or cook. And yet she relished the life of New York, developing a reputation in her neighborhood as an ace gambler and numbers player. Through an employer who worked in show business, she also became a regular and knowledgeable attender of Broadway theater.

There were three children: Eric Lance, 37, works for the New York subway system; Marva, 33, is a graduate of Wilberforce University and works in the finance department at Coler Memorial Hospital in New York; Reed, 29, works for a bank in Atlanta, where Grady is a dietetic cook at Shepherd Spinal Center. It has not been a bad life and is certainly richer in experiences and perhaps in opportunities for her children than Grady would have had in Birmingham.

At one point Grady speaks of being chided by one of her New York-raised sons for "taking it" back in the old days in Birmingham.

"He said, 'I just can't believe y'all let that go on,'" she says. "I said: 'What do you mean y'all? What could you have done about it?' What were you going to do? If you stuck out, you got in trouble. I always got in trouble. I was headstrong. I couldn't stand the conditions and I hated it. I wanted more than I could have.

"I always wanted to be more than I was," she adds. "I thought if I was given the chance I could be more than I was ever allowed to be."

I felt a pang of sympathy for Grady that she should be accused of tolerating what she had opposed with every fiber of her being. But how can a young man who grew up in New York know that the benign city he saw on visits to his grandmother each summer was not the Birmingham that had shaped his mother's life?

Among black people in the South, Grady is part of a generation who saw their best chances burned away by the last fiery breaths of segregation. It is difficult for young people of either race today to understand the openness and simplicity of the injustice that was done to this dwindling generation. When you stripped away the Constitutional falderal from Wallace's message, it was this: He was telling Grady's mother, a working parent who paid property, sales and income taxes in Alabama for more than 40 years, that her child could not attend the institutions supported by those taxes.

Even to those of us who lived there, it seems surreal that such a systematic denial of opportunity could have existed for so long. I have encountered the same disbelief in the grown-up children of white sharecroppers when they looked at pictures of the plantations on which they and their families had lived in economic bondage.

For people with such experiences, some things are beyond explanation or jest, something I learn when I jokingly ask Grady if she'd like her ashes brought back to Pratt City when she dies.

"No," she answers quite firmly, "I'd like them thrown in the East River in New York. I never liked Alabama. Isn't that terrible for you to say that? You know how I hate it."

WORD THAT I HAD FOUND Grady shot through my family.
When the reunion luncheon was planned for my sister's house, my
first impulse was to stage-manage the event. I had learned in conversations with Grady that she remembered my mother as someone who
had nagged her about the housework. None of the rest of us recol-
lected theirs as a tense relationship, but then again, none of us had
been in Grady's shoes. In the end I decided to let it flow, and as it
turned out, no one enjoyed the reunion more than Grady and my
mother.

"You're so tiny," Grady exclaimed at one point. "I thought you
were a great big woman. How'd you make so much noise?"

My mother was disarmed. In the midst of a round of stories about
the bold things Grady had said and done, I heard her turn to a visitor and explain quietly, in an admiring voice, "You see, now, that
Grady is a strong person."

Grady is also a very funny person, a born raconteur with a reputation in her own family for being outrageous. It is possible, therefore, to make her sound like some 50's version of Whoopi Goldberg
and her life with my family like a sitcom spiced with her "sassy"
asides about race and sex. But what I sensed at our gathering, among
my brother, sister and parents, was something much deeper than
fondness or nostalgia. It was a shared pride that in the Birmingham
of the 50's this astonishing person had inhabited our home and had
been allowed to be fully herself.

"She spoke out more than any person I knew of, no matter what
their age," my sister observed. "She was the first person I'd ever
heard do that, you see, and here I was 18 years old, and you were just
a little fellow. This was the first person I'd ever heard say, 'Boy, it's
terrible being black in Birmingham.'"

As Grady and my family got reacquainted, it became clear that my
memory of her as "mine" was the narrow and selfish memory of a
child. I had been blind to the bonds Grady also had with my brother
and sister. Grady remembered my brother, in particular, as her confidant and protector. And although they never spoke of it at the time,
she looked to him as her guardian against the neighborhood work-
men of both races who were always eager to offer young black girls
"a ride home from work."

"Even if Jerry was going in the opposite direction," Grady
recalled, "he would always say: 'I'm going that way. I'll drop Grady
off.'"

In my brother's view, Grady's outspokenness, whether about her
chores or the shortcomings of Birmingham, was made possible

through a kind of adolescent cabal. "The reason it worked was Grady was just another teen-ager in the house." he said. "There were already two teen-agers in the house, and she was just a teen-ager, too."

But it is also hard to imagine Grady falling into another family led by parents like mine. They were both from the Alabama hills, descended from Lincoln Republicans who did not buy into the Confederate mythology. There were no plantation paintings or portraits of Robert E. Lee on our walls. The mentality of the hill country is that of the underdog.

They were instinctive humanitarians. As Grady tells it, my father was well known among her relatives as "an open man" when it came to the treatment of his employees. I once saw him take the side of a black employee who had fought back against the bullying of a white worker on a loading dock—not a common occurrence in Birmingham in the 50's.

The most powerful rule of etiquette in my parents' home, I realize now, was that the word "nigger" was not to be used. There was no grand explanation attached to this, as I recall. We were simply people who did not say "nigger."

The prohibition of this one word may seem a small point, but I think it had a large meaning. Hill people by nature, are talkers, and some, like my father, are great storytellers. They themselves have often been called hillbillies, which is to say that they understand the power of language and that the power to name is the power to maim.

Everyone in my family seems to have known that my great long afternoon talks with Grady were about race. Their only concern was not whether I should be hearing such talk, but whether I was old enough for the brutality of the facts.

"I would tell Howell about all the things that happened in the black neighborhoods, what police did to black people," Grady recalled to us. "I would come and tell him, and he would cry, and Mrs. Raines would say: 'Don't tell him that anymore. Don't tell him that. He's too young. Don't make him sad.' He would get sad about it." Grady told me in private that she recalled something else about those afternoons, something precise and specific. I had wept, she said, on learning about the murder of Emmett Till, a young black boy lynched in Mississippi in 1955.

To me, this was the heart of the onion. For while some of the benefits of psychotherapy may be dubious, it does give us one shining truth. We are shaped by those moments when the sadness of life first wounds us. Yet often we are too young to remember that wounding experience, that decisive point after which all is changed for better or worse.

Every white Southerner must choose between two psychic roads—the road of racism or the road of brotherhood. Friends, families, even lovers have parted at that forking, sometimes forever, for it presents a choice that is clouded by confused emotions, inner conflicts and powerful social forces.

It is no simple matter to know all the factors that shape this individual decision. As a college student in Alabama, I shared the choking shame that many young people there felt about Wallace's antics and about the deaths of the four black children in the bombing of the Sixteenth Street Baptist Church in September 1963. A year later, as a cub reporter, I listened to the sermons and soaring hymns of the voting rights crusade. All this had its effect.

But the fact is that by the time the civil rights revolution rolled across the South, my heart had already chosen its road. I have always known that my talks with Grady helped me make that decision in an intellectual sense. But I had long felt there must have been some deeper force at work, some emotional nexus linked for me, it seemed now on hearing Grady's words, to the conjuring power of one name—Emmett Till—and to disconnected images that had lingered for decades in the eye of my memory.

Now I can almost recall the moment or imagine I can: Grady and I together, in the ironing room. We are islanded again, the two of us, in the acres of afternoon. We are looking at *Life* magazine or *Look*, at pictures of a boy barely older than myself, the remote and homely site of his death, several white men in a courtroom, the immemorial Mississippi scenes.

Thus did Grady, who had already given me so much, come back into my life with one last gift. She brought me a lost reel from the movie of my childhood, and on its dusty frames, I saw something few people are lucky enough to witness. It was a glimpse of the revelatory experience described by Graham Greene, the soul-shaking time after which all that is confusing detail falls away and all that is thematic shines forth with burning clarity.

Our reunion turned out to be a day of discovery, rich emotion and great humor. Near the end of a long lunch, my sister and my brother's wife began pouring coffee. In classic Southern overkill, there were multiple desserts. Grady spoke fondly of my late Aunt Ada's artistry with coconut cakes. Then she spoke of leaving Birmingham with "my dreams of chasing the rainbow."

"I used to say when I was young, 'One day I'm going to have a big house, and I'm going to have the white people bring me my coffee,'" Grady said, leaning back in her chair. "I ain't got the big house yet, but I got the coffee. I chased the rainbow and I caught it."

OF COURSE, GRADY DID NOT catch the rainbow, and she never will. Among the victims of segregation, Grady was like a soldier shot on the last day of the war. Only a few years after she relinquished her dream of education, local colleges were opened to blacks, and educators from around the country came to Birmingham looking for the sort of poor black student who could race through high school two years ahead of schedule.

Grady's baby sister, Liz Spraggins, was spotted in a Pratt City high-school choir in 1964 and offered a music scholarship that started her on a successful career in Atlanta as a gospel and jazz singer. Grady's cousin Earl Hilliard, who is 10 years younger than she, wound up at Howard University Law School. Today he is a member of the Alabama Legislature. When Grady and I had lunch with the Hilliards, the family was debating whether Earl Jr. should join his sister, Lisa, at Emory or choose law-school acceptances at Stanford, Texas or Alabama.

If Grady had been a few years younger, she would have gone down the road taken by her sister and cousin. If she had been white, the public-education system of Alabama would have bailed her out despite her poverty. Even in 1950, fatherless white kids who zipped through high school were not allowed to fall through the cracks in Alabama. But Grady had bad timing and black skin, a deadly combination.

At some point during our reunion lunch, it occurred to everyone in the room that with all the people who knew Grady Williams as a girl, there was one group that could have sent her to college. That was my family. The next morning my sister told me of a regretful conversation that took place later that same day.

"Mother said at dinner last night, 'if we had just known, if we had just known, we could have done something,'" Mary Jo said. "Well, how could we not have not known?"

Yes, precisely, how could we not leave known—and how can we not know of the carnage of lives and minds and souls that is going on among young black people in this country today?

In Washington, where I live, there is a facile answer to such questions. Fashionable philosophers in the think tanks that influence this Administration's policies will tell you that guilt, historical fairness and compassion are outdated concepts, that if the playing field is level today, we are free to forget that it was tilted for generations. Some of these philosophers will even tell you that Grady could have made it if she had really wanted to.

But I know where Grady came from and I know the deck was stacked against her and I know who stacked it. George Wallace is old, sick and pitiful now, and he'd like to be forgiven for what he, Bull Connor and the other segs did back then, and perhaps he should be. Those who know him say that above all else he regrets using the racial issue for political gain.

I often think of Governor Wallace when I hear about the dangers of "reverse discrimination" and "racial quotas" from President Bush or his counsel, C. Boyden Gray, the chief architect of the Administration's civil rights policies. Unlike some of the old Southern demagogues, these are not ignorant men. Indeed, they are the polite, well-educated sons of privilege. But when they argue that this country needs no remedies for past injustices, I believe I hear the grown-up voices of pampered white boys who never saw a wound.

And I think of Grady and the unrepayable gift she gave with such wit, such generosity, to such a boy, so many years ago.

Grady told me that she was moved when she went to a library and saw my book, an oral history of the civil rights movement entitled *My Soul Is Rested*. It is widely used on college campuses as basic reading about the South, and of everything I have done in journalism, I am proudest of that book.

I was surprised that Grady had not instantly understood when the book came out in 1977 that she was its inspiration. That is my fault. I waited much too long to find her and tell her. It is her book really. She wrote it on my heart in the acres of afternoon.

ANALYSIS

RAINES SAYS he used an interesting strategy in writing "Grady's Gift," producing a relaxed 500 words each morning over a two-week period. "I had written a previous story in the late '80s, in which I went back and traced the families who were photographed by Walker Evans," he says. "And that material was so powerfully emotional to me that I got writer's block for the only time in my career."

He eventually returned to the story a year later, writing simple sentences, only attempting to produce a page or so daily.

Raines hastens to add his direction wasn't new. "Hemingway had this theory that you should quit writing while you're still going good because that created momentum for the next day."

The result for Raines, however, was "Grady's Gift," a stunning, emotional work, punctuated with spare, concise prose. Raines feels emotion is a powerful tool—when handled properly. "Some of this was so moving I would actually tear up at the typewriter. That's a personal response [but] you can't just gush; you've got to manage that emotion.

"The more powerful the emotion you're dealing with, the simpler the style can be."

Although it has an essay feel to it, focuses on an earlier time and is written in the first person, "Grady's Gift" is a memorable profile. Notice how it compares and contrasts to two other Pulitzer Prize-winning profiles in this anthology: Alice Steinbach's "A Boy of Unusual Vision" (1985), and George Lardner's highly-personal account of the brutal murder of his daughter, "The Stalking of Kristin" (1993). It combines some of the personal emotional elements of Kristin and much of the literary qualities of "Unusual Vision."

Raines manages to deal with black/white relationships in one of the South's most segregated cities and admits how his family's seeming generosity inadvertently might have prevented Grady from reaching her goal of a college education.

As Raines writes in the first person, and the story is as much about him as Grady, he is exceedingly careful not to overwhelm the flow of the narrative. His simple, brisk prose helps "Grady's Gift" read like a secret diary found squirreled away in a hidden drawer.

One only need look at Raines' lead to see all the ground he plans to cover. The reader is informed how Grady arrived at the Raines household and would change Howell's life, what Birmingham was like in the 1950s, and the big "reunion" after 34 years. Raines also lets us know how all this affected him—then and now.

Raines begins with a classic summary lead, but like much of his story, it's rich in texture and description. The first direct quote in the story (from Grady) appears halfway through the lead and brings the narrative back to the present:

"I never thought I'd ever see y'all again ... "

Immediately after the lead, Raines sets the stage for the reader, explaining the environment of segregated Birmingham and the dynamics of Grady's family. He quickly takes Grady from age 7 to 16, when she first came to work at the Raines house. The author then finishes setting the stage by describing his family heritage in the same precise, accelerated fashion.

In giving the reader a guided tour of living in Birmingham—both for whites and blacks—Raines also opens a window into his own Grady-inspired education of right vs. wrong:

In 1963, I recognized instantly that George Wallace was lying when he said that his Stand in the School House Door ... was to protect the Constitutional Principle of states' rights.

And Raines' reporting, writing and sense of detail is equally sharp:

There was also my Aunt Ada, a red-haired spinster who made me rice pudding and hand-whipped biscuits and milk-shakes with cracked ice, and when my parents were out of town, I slept on a pallet in her room.

Of course, Grady did not catch the rainbow, and she never will. Among the victims of segregation, Grady was like a soldier shot on the last day of the war.

Raines also uses introspection well in this story, informing the reader what it was like to be white and Southern, forced to make uncomfortable decisions:

Every white Southerner must choose between these two psychic roads—the road of racism or the road of brotherhood. Friends, families, even lovers have parted at that forking, sometimes forever.

Raines likes to repeat previous phrases and scenarios. For example, when he describes Grady early in the story, Raines writes:

She had a gap between her front teeth, and so did I. One of the first things I remember Grady telling me was that as soon as she had enough money she was going to get a diamond set in her gap and it would drive the men wild.

When Raines finally meets Grady again, he notices the gap in her teeth and repeats the observation in a spare economical phrase:

Still no diamond.

And on three different occasions in the story, including the last sentence of the narrative, Raines mentions the long, hot "acres of afternoon" he spent learning from Grady.

It's interesting to note that Raines effectively balances current and old quotes. It would have been easy for this story to become overly maudlin with a less firm hand on the rudder, but Raines carefully prevents that from happening.

Raines may have written a moving tribute to Gradystein Williams Hutchinson, the woman who taught him so much, but in doing so, he put his heart and soul in the story, turning a profile into a treasure.

HOWELL RAINES is currently editorial page editor of the *The New York Times*. He holds a bachelor's degree in English from Birmingham-Southern College and a master's degree in English from the University of Alabama in Tuscaloosa. Raines has written three books, including *Fly Fishing Through the Mid-Life Crisis,* "which so far as I can determine is the only book with fly fishing in the title that's ever been on *The New York Times* best-seller list," he muses.

1993

GEORGE LARDNER JR.

FOR MOST OF the journalists in this anthology, winning the Pulitzer Prize was a dream come true—a brief moment of triumph when time stood still. But for George Lardner Jr., whose winning story documented the senseless murder of his youngest daughter, the moment was tinged with sadness.

Even *writing* the story was agonizing. Lardner says, "I had to put it aside again and again. There were a lot of tears on the keyboard."

Lardner first decided to write the complete story when he traveled to Boston after Kristin's funeral. "I told my editors I wanted to look around and investigate the matter and see if I could write something—but I didn't know if I could do it." (The intense personal nature of the story resulted in its being run in the *Post*'s Outlook section, an area usually reserved for opinion and commentary.)

Talking to Brookline Police Lt. George Finnegan outside the courthouse seems to have made a strong impression on Lardner—and his duty. "He suggested I try to find out where Cartier got the gun," Lardner says. "He said, 'You're a reporter aren't you?' I was shamefaced. Here I was, a big-deal reporter for *The Washington Post* and I didn't even know what had been happening to my own daughter. I think it was then that I decided to stick with it."

Deciding to write it was one thing. Lardner soon learned that being *able* to write it was another: "I found it slow-going emotionally. ... One of the hardest things I had to do was to transcribe a tape our malfunctioning answering machine had made when Kristin called home in tears one day and my wife Rosemary asked her about Cartier. Rosemary put in a new tape and set aside the old one. We remembered it after the funeral. I stared at it for weeks before I could bring myself to listen to it."

Lardner had a specific goal in putting pen to paper. "I wanted to bring public attention to the shortcomings of the justice system, especially in dealing with violence against women," he says.

The result is a classic example of how a skillful writer can turn closely-felt passion or rage into an objective work that changes society. "The Stalking of Kristin" resulted in some significant changes in national stalking and domestic violence laws, and influenced the 1994 Crime Bill. "In floor statements, (Rep. Joe) Kennedy gave credit to what happened to Kristin and to the story," he explains.

Lardner hesitates, then laughs when asked if he knew early that "Kristin" had won the Pulitzer. "I don't think I'm supposed to say this ... (but) I got a call from Don Graham on my voice mail, saying, 'Come upstairs, I'd like to see you.' I went upstairs and he and Kay Graham were waiting for me. We won three Pulitzers that year so it was a really big day for the *Post*.

"I was stunned, elated and sad all at once," he recalls. "Winning a Pulitzer is every journalist's dream but I never knew that dreams could hurt so much. When I heard about it, I knew that I could tell Rosemary only by apologizing. And by saying that I thought Kristin would have been pleased. Rosemary cried anyway."

The Stalking of Kristin

The Washington Post

November 22, 1992

THE PHONE was ringing insistently, hurrying me back to my desk. My daughter Helen was on the line, sobbing so hard she could barely catch her breath.

"Dad," she shouted. "Come home! Right away!"

I was stunned. I had never heard her like this before. "What's wrong?" I asked. "What happened?"

"It's—it's Kristin. She's been shot ... and killed."

Kristin? My Kristin? Our Kristin? I'd talked to her the afternoon before. Her last words to me were, "I love you Dad." Suddenly I had trouble breathing myself.

It was 7:30 p.m. on Saturday, May 30. In Boston, where Kristin Lardner was an art student, police were cordoning off an apartment building a couple of blocks from the busy, sunlit sidewalk where she'd been killed 90 minutes earlier. She had been shot in the head and face by an ex-boyfriend who was under court order to stay away from her. When police burst into his apartment, they found him sprawled on his bed, dead from a final act of self-pity.

This was a crime that could and should have been prevented. I write about it as a sort of cautionary tale, in anger at a system of justice that failed to protect my daughter, a system that is addicted to looking the other way, especially at the evil done to women.

But first let me tell you about my daughter.

She was, at 21, the youngest of our five children, born in D.C. and educated in the city's public schools, where not much harm befell her unless you count her taste for rock music, lots of jewelry, and funky clothes from Value Village. She loved books, went trick-or-treating dressed as Greta Garbo, played one of the witches in "Macbeth" and had a grand time in tap-dancing class even in her sneakers. She made life sparkle.

When she was small, she always got up in time for Saturday morning cartoons at the Chevy Chase library, and she took cheerful care of a succession of cats, mice, gerbils, hamsters and guinea pigs. Her biggest fault may have been that she took too long in the shower— and you never knew what color her hair was going to be when she emerged. She was compassionate, and strong-minded too; when a boy from high school dropped his pants in front of her, Kristin knocked out one of his front teeth.

"She didn't back down from anything," said Amber Lynch, a close friend from Boston University. "You could tell that basically from her art, the way she dressed, the opinions she had. If you said something stupid, she'd tell you."

Midway through high school, Kristin began thinking of becoming an artist. She'd been taking art and photography classes each summer at the Corcoran and was encouraged when an art teacher at Wilson High decided two of her paintings were good enough to go on display at a little gallery there. She began studies at Boston University's art school and transferred after two years to a fine arts program run jointly by the School of the Museum of Fine Arts and Tufts University. She particularly liked to sculpt and make jewelry and, in the words of one faculty member, "showed great promise and was extremely talented."

In her apartment were scattered signs of that talent. Three wide-banded silver and brass rings, one filigreed with what looked like barbed wire. Some striking sculptures of bound figures. A Madonna, painstakingly gilded. A nude self-portrait in angry reds, oranges and yellows, showing a large leg bruise her ex-boyfriend had given her on their last date in April.

"It felt as though she was telling all her secrets to the world," she wrote of her art in an essay she left behind. "Why would anyone want to know them anyway? But making things was all she wanted to do. ... She always had questions, but never any answers, just frustration and confusion, and a need to get out whatever lay inside of her, hoping to be meaningful."

'I Told Her That He Could Kill Her'

Kristin wrote that essay last November for a course at Tufts taught by Ross Ellenhorn, who also happens to be a counselor at Emerge, an educational program for abusive men. He had once mentioned this to his students. He would hear from my daughter in April, after she met Michael Cartier.

By then, Kristin had been dating Cartier, a 22-year-old bouncer, for about 2½ months. She broke off with him in the early morning of April 16. On that night, a few blocks from her apartment, he beat her up.

They "became involved in an argument and he knocked her to the ground and started kicking her over and over," reads a Brookline police report. "She remembers him saying, 'Get up or I'll kill you.' She staggered to her feet, a car stopped and two men assisted her home.

"Since that night," the report continues, "she has refused to see him, but he repeatedly calls her, sometimes 10 or 11 times a day. He has told her that if she reports him to the police, he might have to do six months in jail, but she better not be around when he gets out.

"She also stated the injuries she suffered were hematomas to her legs and recurring headaches from the kicks."

Kristin didn't call the police right away. But she did call Ellenhorn in hopes of getting Cartier into Emerge. "I made clear to her that Emerge isn't a panacea, that there was still a chance of him abusing her," Ellenhorn says. "I told her that he could kill her ... because she was leaving him and that's when things get dangerous."

Cartier showed up at Emerge's offices in Cambridge, around April 28 by Ellenhorn's calculations. Ellenhorn, on duty that night, realized who Cartier was when he wrote down Kristin's name under victim on the intake form.

"I said, 'Are you on probation?'" Ellenhorn remembers. "He said yes. I said, 'I'm going to need the name of the probation officer.' He said, '[Expletive] this. No way.'" With that, Cartier ripped up the contract he was required to sign, ripped up the intake form, put the tattered papers in his pocket and walked out. "He knew," Ellenhorn says.

"He knew what kind of connection would be made." Michael Cartier was, of course, on probation for attacking another woman.

Cartier preyed on women. Clearly disturbed, he once talked of killing his mother. When he was 5 or 6, he dismembered a pet rabbit. When he was 21, he tortured and killed a kitten. In a bizarre 1989 incident at an Andover restaurant, he injected a syringe of blood into a ketchup bottle. To his girlfriends, he could be appallingly brutal.

Rose Ryan could tell you that. When Kristin's murder was reported on TV—the newscaster described the killing as "another case of domestic violence"—she said to a friend, "That sounds like Mike." It was. Hearing the newscaster say his name, she recalls, "I almost dropped."

When Ryan met Cartier at a party in Boston in the late summer of 1990, she was an honors graduate of Lynn East High School, preparing to attend Suffolk University. She was 17, a lovely, courageous girl with brown hair and brown eyes like Kristin's.

"He was really my first boyfriend," she told me. "I was supposed to work that summer and save my money, but I got caught up with the scene in Boston and hanging out with all the kids. ... At first, everything was fine."

Cartier was a familiar face on the Boston Common, thanks to his career as a freelance nightclub bouncer. He had scraped up enough money to share a Commonwealth Avenue apartment with a Museum School student named Kara Boettger. They dated a few times, then settled down into a sort of strained coexistence.

"He didn't like me very much," Boettger said. "He liked music loud. I'd tell him to turn it down."

Rose Ryan liked him better. She thought he was handsome—blue eyes, black hair, a tall and muscular frame—with a vulnerability that belied his strength. To make him happy, she quit work and postponed the college education it was going to pay for. "He had me thinking that he'd had a bad deal his whole life," she said, "that nobody loved him and I was the only one who could help him."

Cartier also knew how to behave when he was supposed to. Ryan said he made a good first impression on her parents. As with Kristin, it took just about two months before Cartier beat Ryan up. She got angry with him for "kidding around" and dumping her into a barrel on the Common. When she walked away, he punched her in the head; when she kept going, he punched her again.

"I'd never been hit by any man before and I was just shocked," she said. But what aggravated her the most, and still does, is that "every time something happened, it was in public, and nobody stopped to help."

Cartier ended the scene with "his usual thing," breaking into tears and telling her, "Oh, why do I always hurt the people I love? What can I do? My mother didn't love me. I need your help."

Shortly after they started dating, Ryan spent a few days at the Cartier-Boettger apartment. He presented her with a gray kitten, then left it alone all day without a litter box. The kitten did what it needed to do on Cartier's jacket.

"He threw the kitten in the shower and turned the hot water on and kept it there under the hot water," Ryan remembers in a dull monotone. "And he shaved all its hair off with a man's shaving razor."

The kitten spent most of its wretched life hiding under a bed. On the night of Oct. 4, 1990, Cartier began drinking with two friends and went on a rampage. He took a sledgehammer and smashed through his bedroom wall into a neighbor's apartment. And he killed the kitten, hurling it out a fourth-floor window.

"I'd left the apartment without telling them," Ryan said. "When I came back, the police were in the hallway. ... They said, 'Get out. This guy's crazy.' They were taking him out in handcuffs."

Three months later, Cartier, already on probation, plea-bargained his way to probation again—pleading guilty to malicious destruction. Charges of burglary and cruelty to animals were dismissed; the court saw nothing wrong with putting him back on the street.

"I thought he was going to jail because he violated probation," Kara Boettger said. So did Cartier. "[But after the January hearing] he told me ... 'Oh yeah, nothing happened. They slapped my wrist.'"

'He Was Born That Way'

When Michael Cartier was born in Newburyport, Mass., his mother was 17. Her husband, then 19, left them six months later; Gene Cartier has since remarried twice. Her son, Penny Cartier says, was a problem from the first.

"He'd take a bottle away from his [step]sister. He'd light matches behind a gas stove. He was born that way," Penny Cartier asserted. "When he was five or six, he had a rabbit. He ripped its legs out of its sockets."

"None of this," she added in loud tones, "had anything to do with what he did to Kristin. ... Michael's childhood had nothing to do with anything."

Life with mother, in any case, ended at age 7, when she sent him to the New England Home for Little Wanderers, a state-supported residential treatment center for troubled children. Staff there remember him—although Penny Cartier denies this—as a child abused at an early age. "That's the worst childhood I've ever seen," agrees Rich DeAngelis, one of Cartier's probation officers. "This didn't just happen in the last couple of years."

Cartier stayed at the New England Home until he was 12. In October 1982, he was put in the Harbor School in Amesbury, a treatment center for disturbed teenagers. He stayed there for almost four years and was turned over to his father, a facilities maintenance mechanic in Lawrence.

Michael Cartier was bitter about his mother. "I just know he hated her," Kara Boettger said. "He said he wanted to get a tattoo, I think maybe on his arm, of her hanging from a tree with animals ripping at her body."

Penny Cartier didn't seem surprised when I told her this. In fact, she added, after he turned 18, "he asked my daughter if she wanted him to kill me."

Cartier entered Lawrence High School but dropped out after a couple of years. "He was just getting frustrated. He couldn't keep up," said his father. By his second semester, he was facing the first of nearly 20 criminal charges that he piled up in courthouses from Lawrence to Brighton over a four-year period.

Along the way, he enjoyed brief notoriety as a self-avowed skinhead, sauntering into the newsroom of the *Lawrence Eagle-Tribune* with his bald friends in June 1989 to complain of the bad press and "neo-Nazi" labels skinheads usually got. "The state supported me all my life, with free doctors and dentists and everything," Cartier told columnist Kathie Neff. "My parents never had anything to do with that because they got rid of me. This is like my way of saying thanks [to them]."

Neff said Cartier cut an especially striking figure, walking on crutches and wearing a patch on one eye. He had just survived a serious car accident that produced what seems to have been a magic purse for him. He told friends he had a big insurance settlement coming and would get periodic advances on it from his lawyer. Gene Cartier said his son got a final payment late last year of $17,000 and "went through $14,000" of it before he murdered Kristin.

'No Acute Mental Disorder'

The high-ceilinged main courtroom in Brighton has a huge, wide-barred cell built into a wall. On busy days, it is a page from Dickens, crowded with yelling, cursing prisoners waiting for their cases to be called.

Cartier turned up in the cage April 29, 1991, finally arrested for violating probation. Ten days earlier, when Rose Ryan was coming home from a friend's house on the "T," Boston's trolley train and subway system, Cartier followed her—and accosted her at the Government Center station with a pair of scissors. She ducked the scissors and Cartier punched her in the mouth.

Even before that, Ryan and her older sister Tina had become alarmed. After a party in December, Cartier got annoyed with Rose for not wanting to eat pizza he'd just bought. She began walking back to the party when he backhanded her in the face so hard she fell down. "And I'm lying on the ground, screaming, and then he finally stopped kicking me after I don't know how long, and then he said, 'You better get up or I'll kill you.'"

The same words he would use with Kristin. And how many other young women?

Rose Ryan said Cartier threatened to kill her several times after they broke up in December, and in a chance encounter in March, told her he had a gun. The Ryan sisters called his probation officer in Brighton, Tom Casey. He told Rose to get a restraining order and on March 28, he obtained a warrant for Cartier's arrest. It took a month for police to pick him up even though Cartier had, in between, attacked Rose in the subway and been arraigned on charges for that assault in Boston Municipal Court.

"Probation warrants have to be served by the police, who don't take them seriously enough," said another probation officer. "Probationers know ... they can skip court appearances with impunity."

When Cartier turned up in Brighton, "he was very quiet. Sullen and withdrawn," Casey said. "It was obvious he had problems, deeper than I could ever get to." Yet a court psychiatrist, Dr. Mike Annunziata, filed a report stating that Cartier had "no acute mental disorder, no suicidal or homicidal ideas, plans or intents." The April 29, 1991, report noted that Cartier was being treated by the Tri-City Mental Health and Retardation Center in Malden and was taking 300 milligrams of lithium a day to control depression.

Cartier, the report said, had also spent four days in January 1991 at the Massachusetts Mental Health Center in Boston. He was brought there on a "Section 12," a law providing for emergency restraint of dangerous persons, because of "suicidal ideation" and an overdose of some sort. On April 2, 1991, he was admitted to the Center on another "Section 12," this time for talking about killing Rose Ryan with a gun "within two weeks." He denied making the threats and was released the next day.

Tom Casey wanted to get him off the streets this time, and a like-minded visiting magistrate ordered Cartier held on bail for a full hearing in Brighton later in the week. When the Ryan sisters arrived in court, they found themselves five feet away from Cartier in the cell. "Soon as he saw me," Tina Ryan said, "he said, 'I know who you are, I'm going to kill you, too,' all these filthy words, calling me every-thing he could ... ."

After listening to what the Ryans had to say, the judge sent Cartier to jail on Deer Island for three months for violating probation. The next month, he was given a year for the subway attack, but was com-mitted for only six months.

That didn't stop the harassment. Cartier began making collect calls to Ryan from prison and he enlisted other inmates to write obscene letters. The district attorney's office advised the Ryans to keep a record of the calls so they could be used against Cartier later.

Despite all that, Cartier was released early, on Nov. 5, 1991. "'He's been a very good prisoner and we're overcrowded,'" the Ryans say they were told.

Authorities in Essex County didn't want to see him out on the streets even if officials in Boston didn't care. As soon as he was released from Deer Island, Cartier was picked up for violating his probation on the ketchup-bottle incident and sentenced to 59 days in the Essex County jail. But a six-month suspended sentence that was hanging over him for a 1988 burglary—which would have meant at least three months in jail—was wiped off the books.

"That's amazing," said another probation officer who looked at the record. "They dropped the more serious charges."

Cartier was released after serving 49 of the 59 days.

Ryan had already been taking precautions. She carried mace in her pocketbook, put a baseball bat in her car and laid out a bunch of knives next to her bed each night before going to sleep. "I always thought that he would come back and try to get me," she said.

Portrait of My Daughter

Kristin loved to go out with friends until all hours of the morning, but she didn't have many steady boyfriends. Most men, she said more than once, "are dogs" because of the way they treated girls she knew.

She was always ready for adventure, hopping on the back of brother Charles's motorcycle for rides; curling up with Circe, a pet ball-python she kept in her room; and flying down for a few weeks almost every August to Jekyll Island, Ga., to be with her family, a tradition started when she was less than a week old. Last year she caught a small shark from the drawbridge over the Jekyll River.

"I think she'd give anything a go," said Jason Corkin, the young man she dated the longest, before he returned last year to his native New Zealand. "When she set her mind to something, she wouldn't give it up for anything."

She could also become easily depressed, especially about what she was going to do after graduation next year. As she once wrote. her favorite pastime was "morbid self-reflection." Despite that, laughter came easily and she was always ready for a conversation about art, religion, philosophy, music. "I don't really remember any time we were together that we didn't have a good time," said Bekky Elstad, a close friend from Boston University.

Left in her bedroom at her death was a turntable with Stravinsky's *Rite of Spring* on it and a tape player with a punk tune by Suicidal Tendencies. Her books, paperbacks mostly, included Alice Walker's *The Color Purple* and Margaret Atwood's *The Handmaid's Tale,* along with favorites by Sinclair Lewis, Dickens and E.B. White and a book about upper- and middle-caste women in Hindu families in Calcutta.

Her essays for school, lucid and well-written, showed a great deal of thought about art, religion and the relationship between men and women. She saw her art as an expression of parts of her hidden deep inside, waiting to be pulled out, but still to be guarded closely: "Art could be such a selfish thing. Everything she made, she made for herself and not one bit of it could she bear to be parted with. Whether she loved it, despised it or was painfully ashamed of it ... she couldn't stand the thought of these little parts of her being taken away and put into someone else's possession."

Buddhism appealed to her, and once she wrote this: "Pain only comes when you try to hang on to what is impermanent. So all life need not be suffering. You can enjoy life if you do not expect anything from it."

She met Cartier last Jan. 30 at a Boston nightclub called Axis, having gone there with Lauren Mace, Kristin's roommate and best friend, and Lauren's boyfriend. At Axis, Kristin recognized Cartier as someone she'd seen at Bunratty's, a hard-rock club where Cartier had been a bouncer. Cartier was easily recognizable; he had a large tattoo of a castle on his neck.

What did she see in him? It's a question her parents keep asking themselves. But some things are fairly obvious. He reminded her of Jason, her friend from New Zealand. He could be charming. "People felt a great deal of empathy for him," said Octavia Ossola, director of the child care center at the home where Cartier grew up, "because it was reasonably easy to want things to be better for him." At the Harbor School, said executive director Art DiMauro, "he was quite endearing. The staff felt warmly about Michael."

So, at first, did Kristin. "She called me up, really excited and happy," said Christian Dupre, a friend since childhood. "She said 'I met this good guy, he's really nice.'"

Kristin told her oldest sister, Helen, and her youngest brother, Charlie, too. But Helen paused when Kristin told her that Cartier was a bouncer at Bunratty's and had a tattoo.

"Well, ah, is he nice?" Helen asked.

"Well, he's nice to me," Kristin said.

Charlie, who had just entered college after a few years of blue-collar jobs, was not impressed. "Get rid of him," he advised his sister. "He's a zero."

Her friends say they got along well at first. He told Kristin he'd been in jail for hitting a girlfriend, but called it a bum rap. She did not know he'd attacked Rose Ryan with a scissors, that he had a rap sheet three pages long.

Kristin, friends say, often made excuses for his behavior. But they soon started to argue. Cartier was irrationally jealous, accusing her of going out with men who stopped by just to talk. During one argument, apparently over her art, Cartier hit her, then did his "usual thing" and started crying.

Cartier, meanwhile, was still bothering Ryan. A warrant for violating probation had been issued out of Boston Municipal Court on Dec. 19, in part for trying to contact her by mail while he was in jail. But when he finally turned up in court, a few days before he met Kristin, he got kid-glove treatment. Rather than being sentenced to complete the one-year term he'd gotten for the scissors attack, he was ordered instead to attend a once-a-week class at the courthouse for six weeks called "Alternatives to Violence."

"It's not a therapy program, it's more educational," said John Tobin, chief probation officer at Boston Municipal Court. "It's for people who react to stress in violent ways, not just for batterers. Cartier ... showed up each time. You don't send probationers away when they do what they're supposed to do."

What Tobin didn't mention was that Cartier had actually dropped out of his Alternatives to Violence course—and, incredibly, was allowed to sign up for it again. According to a chronology I obtained elsewhere, Cartier attended the first meeting of the group on Feb. 5 and skipped the class Feb. 12. His probation was revoked two days later. But instead of sending him back to jail, the court allowed him to start the course over, beginning April 1.

Cartier's probation officer, Diane Barrett Moeller, a "certified batterer specialist" who helps run the program, declined to talk to me, citing "legal limitations" that she did not spell out. Her boss, Tobin, said she was "a ferocious probation officer."

"We tend to be a punitive department," Tobin asserted. "We are not a bunch of social rehabilitators."

However that may be, it is a department that seems to operate in a vacuum. Cartier's record of psychiatric problems, his admissions to the Boston mental health center in January and April 1991 and his reliance on a drug to control manic-depression should have disqualified him from the court-run violence program.

"If we had information that he had a prior history of mental illness, or that he was treated in a clinic or that he had been hospitalized, then what we probably would have done is recommend that a full-scale psychological evaluation be done for him," Tobin told the *Boston Herald* last June following Kristin's murder. "We didn't know about it."

Probation officer Tom Casey in Brighton knew. All Tobin's office had to do was pick up the phone to find out what a menace Cartier was. Meanwhile, in Salem, where she had moved to work with her sister at a family-run business, Rose Ryan remained fearful. But she had a new boyfriend, Sean Casey, 23, and, as Rose puts it, "I think he intimidated Mike because he had more tattoos. Mike knew Sean from before."

Around March 1, Sean went to Boston to tell Cartier to leave Rose alone. As they were talking, Kristin walked by. Sean didn't know who she was, but recognized her later, from newspaper photos.

Cartier nodded at Kristin as she passed. "He said, 'I don't need Rose any more,'" Casey recalled. "'I have my own girlfriend.'"

'Call Your Daughter'

Cartier was a frequent visitor at the six-room flat Kristin shared with Lauren Mace and another BU student, Matt Newton, but he didn't have much to say to them or the other students who were always stopping by. He told Kristin they "intimidated" him because they were college-educated.

As the weeks wore on, they started to argue. When he hit her the first time, probably in early March, Kristin told friends about it, but not Lauren. She was probably too embarrassed. She had always been outspoken in her disdain for men who hit women.

"He hit her once. She freaked out on that ..." Bekky Elstad said. "She wanted him to get counseling. ... He told her he was sorry. He was all broken up. She wanted to believe him."

Kristin came home to Washington in mid-March, outwardly bright and cheerful. She was more enthusiastic than ever about her art. She was "really getting it together," she said. She had yet to tell her parents that she had a boyfriend, much less a boyfriend who hit her.

When she got back to Boston, Cartier tried to make up with her. He gave her a kitten. "It was really cute—black with a little white triangle on its nose," Amber Lynch said. "It was teeny. It just wobbled around."

It didn't last long. Over Kristin's protests, Cartier put the kitten on top of a door jamb. It fell off, landing on its head. She had to have it destroyed.

Devastated, Kristin called home in tears and told her parents, for the first time, about her new boyfriend. Part of her conversation with her mother was picked up by a malfunctioning answering machine.

Rosemary: What does Mike do?

Kristin: Well, he does the same thing Jason did actually. He works at Bunratty's.

Rosemary: He does what?

Kristin: He works at Bunratty's.

Rosemary: Oh. Is he an artist also?

Kristin: No.

Rosemary: Well, that's what I was asking. What does he—? Is he a student?

Kristin: No. He just—he works. He's a bouncer.

"Oh," Rosemary said, asking after a long pause why she was going out with a boy with no education. Kristin told her that she wanted to have a boyfriend "just like everyone else does."

When I came home, Rosemary said, "Call your daughter." When I did, Kristin began crying again as she told me about the kitten. She was also upset because she had given Cartier a piece of jewelry she wanted to use for her annual evaluation at the Museum School. He told her he'd lost it.

Gently, perhaps too gently, I said I didn't think she should be wasting her time going out with a boy who did such stupid things. We talked about school and classes for a few minutes more and said goodnight.

She went out with him for the last time on April 16, the day after one of his Alternatives to Violence classes. He pushed her down onto the sidewalk in front of a fast-food place, cutting her hand. She told him several times to "go home and leave me alone," but he kept following her to a side street in Allston.

"Kristin said something like, 'Get away from me, I never want to see you again,'" Bekky Elstad remembers. But when Kristin tried to run, he caught up with her, threw her down and kicked her repeatedly in the head and legs. She was crying hysterically when she got home with the help of a passing motorist. She refused to see him again.

But Cartier kept trying to get her on the phone. He warned her not to go to the police and for a while, she didn't. She felt sorry for him. She even agreed to take a once-a-week phone call from him the day he went to his Alternatives to Violence class.

He was rated somewhat passive at the meetings, but he got through the course on May 6 without more truancy. The next day, he walked into Gay's Flowers and Gifts on Commonwealth Avenue and bought a dozen red roses for Kristin. He brought in a card to be delivered with them.

Leslie North, a dark-haired, puffy-faced woman who had known Cartier for years, had helped him fill it out in advance. "He always called me when he had a fight with his girlfriends," she said. "He said that he was trying to change, that he needed help, that he wanted to be a better person. He said, 'I'm trying to get back with her.'"

Flower shop proprietor Alan Najarian made the delivery to Kristin's flat. "One of her roommates took them," Najarian remembers. "He was kind of reluctant. ... I think he must have known who they were from."

Police think Cartier may have gotten his gun the day of the murder, but Leslie North remembers his showing it to her "shortly after he and Kristin broke up," probably in early May.

Why did he get the gun? "He said, 'Ah, just to have one,'" North says. "I asked him, 'What do you need a gun for?' He said, 'You never know.' I didn't realize you're not supposed to get a gun if you've been in jail. I didn't tell anyone he had it."

"He told me he paid $750 for it," she continues. "I showed him just a little bit of safety ... how to hold it when you shoot. ... It looked kind of old to me."

The gun found in Cartier's apartment after he killed Kristin and himself was 61 years old, a Colt .38 Super, serial number 13645, one of about a 100 million handguns loose in the United States. It was shipped brand new on Jan. 12, 1932 to a hardware store in Knoxville, Tenn., where all traces of it disappeared.

North remembered something else she says Cartier told her after he got the gun. "He goes, 'If I kill Kristin, are you going to tell anyone?'"

"I said, 'Of course, I'm going to tell.' I didn't take him seriously. ... He said that once or twice to me."

A Call for Help

On May 7, the same day Cartier sent flowers to Kristin, he told her that he was going to cheat her out of the $1,000 Nordic Flex machine she'd let him charge to her Discover card. When she told him over the phone that she expected him to return the device, he laughed and said, "I guess you're out the $1,000."

Kristin was furious. She promptly called Cartier's probation officer, Diane Barrett Moeller, and gave her an earful: the exercise machine, the beating.

Kristin's call for help was another of the probation office's secrets. Tobin said nothing about it to the Boston press in the days after Kristin's murder, when it grew clear that there was something desperately wrong with the criminal justice system. Tobin told me only after I found out about it from Kristin's friends.

"Your daughter was concerned," Tobin said. "She put a lot of emphasis on the weight machine. Mrs. Moeller said, 'Get your priorities straight. You should not be worrying about the weight machine. You should be worrying about your safety. ... Get to Brookline court, seek an assault complaint, a larceny complaint, whatever it takes ... and get a restraining order.'"

According to Tobin, Kristin wouldn't give her name even though Moeller asked for it twice. "We can't revoke someone's probation on an anonymous phone call," he said. Kristin, he added, "did say she didn't want this man arrested and put behind bars."

Tobin also claimed that his office could have taken no action because Kristin was "not the woman in the case we were supervising," which is like saying that probationers in Boston Municipal Court should only take care not to rob the same bank twice.

The next day, Friday, May 8, instead of moving to revoke Cartier's probation, Moeller called Cartier and, in effect, told him what was up. Tobin recalled the conversation. "She told him to get the exercise machine back to her. She told him she didn't want to hear about it any more. And she ordered a full-scale psychiatric evaluation of him. She also ordered him to report to her every week until the evaluation is completed."

Cartier did all that while planning Kristin's murder.

When Cartier called Kristin again, she told him that if he didn't return the exercise machine, she was going to take court action. "He called back 10 minutes later from a pay phone," remembers Brian Fazekas, Lauren's boyfriend. "He said, 'Okay, okay, I'll return the stupid machine.'"

Kristin was skeptical about that. And she was worried about more violence. The warnings of her friends, her brother Charlie, her teacher Ross Ellenhorn and now Cartier's probation officer rang in her ears. Her art reflected her anguish. She had painted her own self-portrait, showing some of the ugly bruises Cartier had left. Hanging sculptures showed a male, arms flexed and fists clenched. The female hung defensively, arms protecting her head.

By Monday, May 11, she had made up her mind. She was going to rely on the system. She decided to ask the courts for help. She talked about it afterwards with her big sister, Helen, a lawyer and her life-long best friend. Kristin told her, sparingly, about the beating and, angrily, about the exercise machine. Helen kept the news to herself, as Kristin requested.

"She said she found out what a loser he was. She said, 'He's even been taking drugs behind my back,'" Helen recalls. He was snorting heroin, confirms Leslie North—it helped him stay calm, she remembers him saying.

Late in the day, Kristin went to the Brookline police station, Lauren Mace and Brian Fazekas beside her.

"The courts were closed by the time we got there. We waited outside," Lauren said. "An officer showed her [Cartier's] arrest record. When she came out, she said, 'You won't believe the size of this guy's police record. He's killed cats. He's beat up ex-girlfriends. Breaking and enterings.' The officer just sort of flashed the length of it at her and said, 'Look at what you're dealing with.'"

Brookline police sergeant Robert G. Simmons found Kristin "very intelligent, very articulate"—and scared. Simmons asked if she wanted to press charges, and she replied that she wanted to think about that. Simmons, afraid she might not come back, made out an "application for complaint" himself and got a judge on night duty to approve issuance of a one-day emergency restraining order over the phone. The next day, Kristin had to appear before Brookline District Judge Lawrence Shubow to ask for a temporary order—one that would last a week.

Other paperwork that Simmons sent over to the courthouse, right next door to the police station, called for a complaint charging Cartier with assault and battery, larceny, intimidation of a witness and violation of the domestic abuse law. It was signed by Lt. George Finnegan, the police liaison officer on duty at the courthouse that day, and turned over to clerk-magistrate John Connors for issuance of a summons.

The summons was never issued. Inexcusably, the application for it was still sitting on a desk in the clerk's office the day Kristin was killed, almost three weeks later.

Other officials I spoke with were amazed by the lapse. Connors shrugged it off. "We don't have the help," he said. "It was waiting to be typed."

Shubow was unaware of the criminal charges hanging over Cartier's head at the May 12 hearing. And Shubow didn't bother to ask about his criminal record.

Restraining orders in Massachusetts, as in other states, have been treated for years by most judges as distasteful "civil matters." Until Kristin was killed, any thug in the Commonwealth accused under the domestic abuse law of beating up his wife or girlfriend or ex-wife or ex-girlfriend could walk into court without much fear that his criminal record would catch up with him. Shubow later told the *Boston Globe*, "If there is one lesson I learned from this case, it was to ask myself whether this is a case where I should review his record. In a case that has an immediate level of danger, I could press for a warrant and immediate arrest."

Instead, Shubow treated Docket No. 92-RO-060 as a routine matter. He issued a temporary restraining order telling Cartier to stay away from Kristin's school, her apartment and her place of work for a week, until another hearing could be held by another judge on a permanent order, good for a year.

"The system failed her completely," Shubow told me after Kristin's death. "There is no such thing as a routine case. I don't live that, but I believe that. All bureaucrats should be reminded of that."

'I Had This Gut Feeling'

Downtown, in Boston Municipal Court, chief probation officer Tobin said that "if we had found out about the restraining order, we would have moved immediately." But Tobin's office made no effort to find out. Cartier's probation officer knew that the anonymous female caller lived in Brookline; a call to officials there would have made clear that Cartier had once again violated probation by beating up an ex-girlfriend. No such call was made.

Apparently, the probation officer didn't ask Cartier for the details either. According to a state official who asked not to be identified, Diane Moeller met with Cartier on May 14, just eight days after he completed her Alternatives to Violence course and three days after Kristin obtained her first restraining order. Moeller did nothing to get him off the streets.

"She was concerned about getting additional assistance for this guy," the state official said of the May 14 meeting. "No charges were filed."

In Brookline, Lt. Finnegan said he sensed something was wrong. He walked up to Kristin outside the courthouse on May 12. "I had this gut feeling," he said. "I asked her, 'Are you really afraid of him?' She said, 'Yeah.' I asked her if he had a gun. She said, 'He may.'"

Finnegan told her to call the police if she saw Cartier hanging around.

The phone rang at the Brookline police station shortly after midnight on May 19; Kristin's request for a permanent restraining order was coming up for a hearing that morning. Now, in plain violation of the May 12 order, Cartier had called around midnight, got Kristin on the line and asked her not to go back to court. She called the cops.

Sgt. Simmons, on duty that night as shift commander, advised Kristin to file a complaint and sent officer Kevin Mealy to talk to her; Mealy arrived at her apartment at 1:10 a.m. "Ms. Lardner said that Mr. Cartier attempted to persuade her not to file for an extension of the order," Mealy wrote in his report, which he filed as soon as he got back to the station house. "A criminal complaint application has been made out against Mr. Cartier for violating the existing restraining order."

Sgt. Simmons says, "I told Kevin, 'They've got a hearing in the morning.' The documents went over there. But who reads them?"

Kristin arrived at the courthouse around 11:30 a.m. May 19, accompanied by Lauren Mace and Amber Lynch.

"He [Cartier] was out in front of the courthouse when we got there," Lynch said. "We all just walked in quickly. We waited a long time. He kept walking in and out of the courtroom. I think he was staring at her."

There was no one in the courtroom from the Norfolk County D.A.'s office to advise Kristin. Brookline probation officials didn't talk to her either. They had no idea Cartier was on probation for beating up another woman.

Neither did District Judge Paul McGill, a visiting magistrate from Roxbury. Like Shubow, he didn't check Cartier's criminal record. Unlike Shubow, it didn't trouble him. To him, it was a routine hearing. Kristin was looking for protection. She was processed like a slice of cheese.

"She thought he was going to be arrested," Lauren said. Brian Fazekas said, "It was her understanding that as soon as he got the permanent restraining order, he was going to be surrendered" for violating probation.

"What he [Cartier] did on the 19th was a crime," David Lowy, legal adviser to Gov. William Weld and a former prosecutor, said of the midnight call. "He should have been placed under arrest right then and there."

The hearing lasted five minutes. It would have been shorter except for a typical bit of arrogance from Cartier, trying to stay in control in the face of his third restraining order in 18 months. He agreed not to contact Kristin for a year and to stay away from her apartment and school. But he said he had a problem staying away from Marty's Liquors, where Kristin had just started working as a cashier. "I happen to live right around the corner from there," Cartier complained, according to a tape of the hearing.

The judge told him to patronize some other liquor store, but not before more argument from Cartier about how he would have to "walk further down the street" and about how close it was to Bunratty's, only half a block away.

McGill ended the hearing by ordering Cartier to avoid any contact with Kristin, to stay at least 200 yards away from her and not to talk to her if he had to come closer when entering his home or the nightclub. And with that, Cartier walked out scot-free. Yet, Massachusetts law, enacted in 1990, provides for mandatory arrest of anyone a law enforcement officer has probable cause to believe violated a temporary or permanent restraining order. In addition, a state law making "stalking" a crime, especially in violation of a restraining order, had been signed by Gov. Weld just the day before, May 18, effective immediately.

McGill later said that if he'd known Cartier had violated his restraining order by calling Kristin that morning, he would have turned the hearing into a criminal session.

The application for a complaint charging Cartier with violating the order was moldering in clerk John Connors's offices. Like the earlier complaint accusing him of assault and battery, it was still there the day Kristin was killed.

Kristin "could have said something [in court], I suppose," Lauren said. "But she just figured that after that, he would be out of her life. She said, 'Let's go home.' She felt very relieved that she had this restraining order."

'What a Weirdo'

Kristin, who now had 11 days to live, talked enthusiastically about going to Europe after graduation, only a year away. After that she was hoping to go to graduate school. She had lost interest in boys, wanting to concentrate on her art.

"I spoke to her the night before [she was killed]," Chris Dupre said. "She was like the most optimistic and happiest she'd been in months. She knew what she wanted to do with herself, with her art."

She even had a new kitten, named Stubby because its tail was broken in two places. She was working part-time in the liquor store and hoping for more hours as summer approached. But she liked to stay home and paint or just hang out with friends now that classes were over.

Cartier was still skulking about, even after issuance of the permanent restraining order. One afternoon, Kristin stepped out of the liquor store to take a break. She saw Cartier staring at her from the doorway of Bunratty's.

On the afternoon of May 28, she and Robert Hyde, a friend who had just graduated from BU, decided to get something to eat after playing Scrabble (Kristin won) and chess (Robert won) at Kristin's flat. The two hopped on the back of his Yamaha and were off. First stop was the Bay Bank branch on Commonwealth Avenue, two doors from Marty's Liquors. As they turned a corner, Kristin saw Cartier looking in Marty's window. "Did you see that?" she asked Hyde moments later as they got off the bike. "Mike was peeking in the window. What a weirdo!"

Hyde didn't think that Cartier saw them, but later that night, after taking Kristin home, he went over to Bunratty's to play pinball. Cartier was there, and he began an awkward conversation to find out where Hyde lived.

"I thought it was kind of weird, but I didn't think too much of it," Hyde said. He shuddered about it after the shooting.

Cartier had always been disturbingly jealous—and unpredictable. "He'd get under pressure, he'd start breathing heavy and start talking all wild," a longtime friend, Timothy McKernan, told the *Lawrence Eagle-Tribune.*

He couldn't handle rejection either. Cartier "told his friends that she broke up with him because she wanted to see other people," Bekky Elstad said. "That's not true. But that's why he killed her, I think. If he couldn't have her, no one else was going to."

If Kristin was bothered by the stalking incident that Thursday, she seemed to put it out of her mind. The usual stream of friends moved through the flat all day. She called me that afternoon in an upbeat mood. We talked about summer school, her Museum School evaluation and a half dozen other things, including the next month's check from home. I assured her it was in the mail. She had a big smile in her voice. All I knew about Cartier was that she had gotten rid of the creep. When I made some grumpy reference to boyfriends in general, she laughed and said, "That's because you're my dad."

Cartier called his father that day, too.

Gene Cartier knew about Kristin and about the restraining order. "I asked him what happened," the older Cartier said. "He said, 'Well, me and my girlfriend had a fight.' I figured they argued. ... He loved animals, he loved children. He wouldn't hurt a fly."

A man with a persistent drinking problem, Gene Cartier at times seemed to confuse Kristin with other girlfriends his son had, but his son's last call about her stuck firmly in his mind. "He said, 'She's busting my balls again,'" Cartier recalled. "I think she was seeing another guy—in front of Michael—to get him jealous. ... He was obsessed with her."

Kristin went to bed that night with a smile. It had been Lauren's last day at Marty's and some of the students who worked there stopped by the flat. "We were having a really, really good time," Lauren Mace said. "I remember, I said, 'Good night, Kristin.' I gave her a hug. The next morning, I saw her taking her bike down the street, on the way to work. I did not see her again."

My Daughter's Death

Saturday, May 30, was a beautiful spring day in Boston, a light breeze rustling the trees on Winchester Street below the flat. Kristin was looking forward to a full day's work; Lauren was supposed to meet her at 6, when she was done at Marty's. Lauren had just graduated from BU; they were going to buy a keg for a big going-away party at the flat on Sunday.

One of the managers at the liquor store, David Bergman, was having lunch across the street at the Inbound Pizza when Kristin walked in. He waved her over to his table. She had a slice of Sicilian pizza and then, as he remembers, two more. "We talked for half an hour," Bergman said. "She was going to travel to Europe with her friend, Lauren. She had all these plans laid on."

After lunch, the day turned sour. Leslie North walked into Marty's with another girl. So, clerks say, did a man in his thirties with rotting teeth and thinning hair—North's boyfriend. He got in Kristin's checkout line and started cursing at her.

Not long after North and her friend left Marty's, J.D. Crump, the manager at Bunratty's, walked in for a sandwich from the deli counter. He'd known Kristin since she had dated Jason. "She said she was having a tough day," he told the *Globe*. "The customers were being mean. I told her it would get better."

When Crump spoke with Kristin on May 30, it was about 4:30. Cartier, meanwhile, was at a noisy show at the Rathskellar on Kenmore Square. Friends told the *Lawrence Eagle-Tribune* that he was acting strangely, greeting people with long hugs instead of the usual punch on the arm or a handshake.

"He wasn't the hugging type," Timothy McKeman told the *Eagle-Tribune*. "I think he knew what he was going to do." Cartier left suddenly, running out the door.

Kristin was scheduled to work until 6, but at 5 p.m., she was told, to her chagrin, to leave early, losing an hour's pay. "We had other cashiers coming in," the manager explained. Instead of hanging around to wait for Lauren, Kristin decided to go to Bekky Elstad's apartment and return at 6. It was a decision that seems to have cost her her life.

Lauren had come by around 5:40 p.m., and left when told Kristin had already gone. Kristin was still at Bekky's, keeping her eye on the clock and by now recounting how this "disgusting ... slimy person" had been cursing at her at the cash register.

"She was laughing about how gross he was and then his being with these two girls—friends of Michael's—who were so gross," Bekky Elstad said. "She seemed pretty much in a good mood."

It was getting close to 6. By now, Cartier was back in the neighborhood, looking for a crowbar. He first asked for one at the Reading Room, a smoke shop about a block away, "maybe 20 minutes before it happened," said the proprietor. "I asked him why he wanted a crowbar. He said he had to go hurt somebody." Then he went over to Bunratty's, in a fruitless search for the same thing.

At one minute to 6, Kristin was heading down Commonwealth Avenue toward Marty's. Cartier, approaching from the other direction, stopped at a Store 24 convenience shop on the other side of Harvard Avenue. J.D. Crump was in there, buying a pack of cigarettes. According to the police report: "Crump stated that while in Store 24 ... he saw Mike and asked him [whether] he was going to work that night. Mike said that he was but had [to] shoot someone first. Crump stated that he did not take him seriously and walked away from him."

The shots rang out seconds later. Mike Dillon, a clerk at Marty's who clocked out at 6, had just stepped onto the sidewalk when he heard the first shattering noise.

"It was very loud," he said. "I looked up immediately. I saw Kristin fall."

Dressed all in black, she dropped instantly to the pavement outside the Soap-A-Rama, a combination laundromat, tanning salon and video rental store four doors from Marty's.

"She was lying on her right side, curled up in kind of a fetal position," Mike Dillon said. "I kind of froze dead in my tracks."

Cartier must have seen her and hid in a doorway or alley until she passed by him. Witnesses said he came at her from behind and shot into the rear of her head from a distance of 15 or 20 feet. Then he ran into a nearby alley.

Al Silva, a restaurant worker, started to walk towards Kristin to see if he could help when Cartier darted back out of the alley, rushed past Silva, and leaned down over her.

"He shot her twice more in the left side of the head," Mike Dillon said. "Then I saw him run down the alley again. ... I was still in shock. I didn't know what to do. I took one of her hands for a second or so, I don't know why. Then I ran back to call the police, but I saw a woman in the flower shop. She was already on the phone."

Chris Toher, the proprietor at Soap-A-Rama, heard the first shot from the back of his store and hurried up to the doorway. "I saw him fire the final shots," Toher said. "It happened so fast she never had a chance. She was completely unconscious at the point he ran up to her. Her eyes were shut."

A brave young woman was dead.

A Killer's Farewell

The killer fled down the alley, which took him to Glenville Avenue where he lived in a red brick apartment building. Back on Commonwealth Avenue, police and an ambulance arrived within minutes. But the ambulance was no longer necessary.

Police questioned Crump at the Soap-A-Rama and learned where Cartier lived. Brooke Mezo, a clerk from Marty's who witnessed the interrogation, heard Crump say "that Michael had spoken to him in the past couple of weeks and said he couldn't live without her, that he was going to kill her. And he talked about where to get a gun."

That made at least two people who knew Cartier had or wanted a gun and was talking about killing Kristin. How many others should have known she was in grave danger?

Police quickly sealed off the area around Cartier's apartment. "He had apparently made statements to several people that he hated policemen and had no reservations about shooting a cop," homicide detective Billy Dwyer said in his report. "He stated that he would never go to prison again."

A police operations team entered Cartier's apartment at 8:30 p.m. He was dead, lying on his bed with the gun he used to kill Kristin in his right hand. He had put it to his head and fired once. Police recovered the spent shell from the bedroom wall. They found three other shell casings in the area where he murdered Kristin.

Later that night, Leslie North walked into Bunratty's, looking for Cartier. "I said, 'He shot Kristin,'" said J.D. Crump. "She didn't look surprised. I said, 'Then he went and shot himself.' At that point, she lost it. She started screaming, 'What a waste! What a waste! He's dead!'"

Crump later said, "I've had to live the past couple of weeks feeling I could have stopped him. I should have called his probation officer."

It's doubtful that would have done any good. The system is so mindless that when the dead Cartier failed to show up in Boston Municipal Court as scheduled on June 19, a warrant was issued for his arrest. It is still outstanding.

ANALYSIS

THE SINGLE MOST impressive element of George Lardner's story about the murder of his daughter is probably his ability to keep obvious strong emotions under tight control, creating a mesmerizing feature story that slowly weaves the reader into the mind of the killer (and the victim) through the shocking failures of the justice system.

The best feature stories often result from emotions such as outrage, fury and passion brought into a story, yet kept at arm's length by a skillful writer such as Lardner, who excels at letting the story tell itself.

Compare this story to "Death of a Playmate," Teresa Carpenter's 1981 Pulitzer winner about the brutal death of Playmate Dorothy Stratten. Both Carpenter and Lardner had to recreate the circumstances leading up to especially vicious killings without being able to talk to those most involved in what happened. Lardner and Carpenter approach their work in vastly different ways—but in the end they both paint a painful, but accurate, portrait of two brutal crimes.

Lardner's first-person descriptive lead captures his daughter's phone call with frightful accuracy. The use of first-person is very effective here, as it is in the handful of other spots where he had no choice but to insert himself into the text.

It's easy to speculate if the story would have been more effective if he had used first person throughout. Most likely, it would have been more emotional and poignant—but probably less objective.

Lardner follows his compelling lead with a matter-of-fact delayed summary of the actual killing, using painful details to bring the crime scene to life:

> ... police were cordoning off an apartment building a couple of blocks from the busy, sunlit sidewalk where she had been ... shot in the head and face.

Although mostly written as a chronology, "Kristin" doesn't begin that way. After the lead, Lardner offers an unusual and important sentence:

> But first let me tell you about my daughter.

Lardner's reporting is peerless throughout the article. He rarely errs from sober objectivity, using strong anecdotes and facts in his narrative to humanize both main characters—showing Kristin as feisty and spunky; Cartier as sadistic:

> She was compassionate, and strong-minded too; when a boy from high school dropped his pants in front of her, Kristin knocked out one of his front teeth.

> "He threw the kitten in the shower and turned the hot water on and kept it there under the hot water."

> Left in her bedroom at her death was a turntable with Stravinsky's "Rites of Spring" on it and a tape player with a punk tune by Suicidal Tendencies.

Lardner structured this story around five major transitions, weaving the piece away from a straight narrative flow, helping the reader fully understand all the key figures and plot turns.

For example, right after the first few graphs of the lead, Lardner gives the reader a summary of the life of Kristin, filled with poignant anecdotes and meaningful quotes. Next, he does the same thing for the killer, adding details about how he dismembered a pet rabbit, tortured and killed a kitten and emptied a syringe full of blood into a restaurant's ketchup bottle.

Good vs. bad. Light vs. dark. Gripping and unsettling, yet vital to the story.

Lardner presents additional chilling facts into the killer's psyche, but as a dispassionate reporter, not a grieving father. Powerful quotes from others help move the story forward.

His use of transitions also gives the reader some emotional relief from the accelerating pace of the story and adds depth to the narrative, coloring in otherwise gray areas with vivid details. These transitional areas, called "chapters" by Steve Twomey, can be effective in a story of this type.

Notice how Kristin only plays a minor role in the narrative now, replaced by detailed explanations about Cartier's deranged psyche, his rough childhood and courtroom history. Lardner is taking care of reporting nuts and bolts, streamlining the story for its swift rush to the end. And when Kristin returns to the narrative in a major way, the reader is fully aware of the danger she faces and the story reverts to a straight chronology.

Many of Lardner's quotes are thought-provoking and show fine reporting antennae. For example, he didn't have to add the final quote from Leslie North, lamenting Cartier's suicide:

"What a waste! What a waste! He's dead!"

But Lardner felt the quote stood in sharp contrast to North's lack of concern over Kristin's death.

Lardner's understated conclusion is a remarkable final reminder of the ineptness of a justice system that lead to Kristin's tragic death:

The system is so mindless that when the dead Cartier failed to show up in Boston Municipal Court as scheduled on June 19, a warrant was issued for his arrest. It is still outstanding.

GEORGE LARDNER is currently a reporter on the national news staff of *The Washington Post*. He holds both a bachelor's and master's degree in journalism from Marquette University and has turned "The Stalking of Kristin" into a book.

1994

ISABEL WILKERSON

BEING A 1994 PULITZER finalist in both the feature writing and national reporting categories, having already won the George S. Polk Award for regional reporting, and named Journalist of the Year by the National Association of Black Journalists, Isabel Wilkerson had to feel reasonably confident about her chances to snare a Pulitzer that year.

But watching the news of her Pulitzer win appear on the wire in New York, she had a strange reaction. "[The feeling] is very hard to describe," she says. "It's something every journalist is aware of and dreams of. And when it happens, you're really just numb—kind of an out-of-body experience."

"Ten [of my] stories were submitted in national and three for feature writing," Wilkerson explains, pointing out she considers herself more of a national reporter than a feature writer. Of the three stories in Wilkerson's Pulitzer Prize-winning package, the earliest one, her magnificent profile of 10-year-old Nicholas Whitiker, received the most publicity and attention. Wilkerson's profile was the first of the *Times'* series of 10 stories written by 10 different reporters in the paper's "Children of the Shadows" series.

The reporters were granted a lot of freedom, Wilkerson explains. "It was very broad. We were given themes that were assigned and the children or the subject had to reflect that theme. My theme was family—which was very broad, very amorphous."

Realizing it would be hard to keep her objectivity on such a heart-rending story, Wilkerson had to focus on writing the story, rather than trying to help the family herself. This most basic journalistic lesson paid off. "The Chicago bureau [Wilkerson was then bureau chief] became sort of a depot [for Nicholas]," she says. Readers started dropping off clothes, shoes, toys and a television for the family. Wilkerson laughs at

:he memory of a reader who flew in from New York to buy the children a bunk bed to sleep on.

Although she is proud of the Nicholas story, Wilkerson says she's even happier over her river stories, written on deadline under hectic conditions. While she had three months to prepare and write "Nicholas," Wilkerson only had 3-4 hours to write her "Cruel Flood" story about the Missouri River.

Her three stories offer a unique view of how everyday people deal with extraordinary circumstances. They're well-reported and wonderfully written—yet full of hope.

First Born, Fast Grown:
The Manful Life of Nicholas, 10

The New York Times

April 3, 1993

CHICAGO—A fourth-grade classroom on a forbidding stretch of the South Side was in the middle of multiplication tables when a voice over the intercom ordered Nicholas Whitiker to the principal's office. Cory and Darnesha and Roy and Delron and the rest of the class fell silent and stared at Nicholas, sitting sober-faced in the back.

"What did I do?" Nicholas thought as he gathered himself to leave.

He raced up the hall and down the steps to find his little sister, Ishtar, stranded in the office, nearly swallowed by her purple coat and hat, and principal's aides wanting to know why no one had picked her up from kindergarten.

'I DON'T KNOW.' It was yet another time that the adult world called on Nicholas, a gentle, brooding 10-year-old, to be a man, to answer for the complicated universe he calls family.

How could he begin to explain his reality—that his mother, a welfare recipient rearing five young children, was in college trying to become a nurse and so was not home during the day, that Ishtar's father was separated from his mother and in a drug-and-alcohol haze most of the time, that the grandmother he used to live with was at work, and that, besides, he could not possibly account for the man who was supposed to take his sister home—his mother's companion, the father of her youngest child?

"My stepfather was supposed to pick her up," he said for simplicity's sake. "I don't know why he's not here."

Nicholas gave the school administrators the name and telephone numbers of his grandmother and an aunt, looked back at Ishtar with a big brother's reassuring half-smile and rushed back to class still worried about whether his sister would make it home OK.

Of all the men in his family's life, Nicholas is perhaps the most dutiful. When the television picture goes out again, when the 3-year-old scratches the 4-year-old, when their mother, Angela, needs ground beef from the store or the bathroom cleaned or can't find her switch to whip him or the other children, it is Nicholas's name that rings out to fix whatever is wrong.

He is nanny, referee, housekeeper, handyman. Some nights he is up past midnight, mopping the floors, putting the children to bed and washing their school clothes in the bathtub. It is a nightly chore: the children have few clothes and wear the same thing every day.

CURBSIDE SERVICE. He pays a price. He stays up late and goes to school tired. He brings home mostly mediocre grades. But if the report card is bad, he gets a beating. He is all boy—squirming in line, sliding down banisters, shirt-tail out, shoes untied, dreaming of becoming a fireman so he can save people—but his walk is the stiff slog of a worried father behind on the rent.

He lives with his four younger half-siblings, his mother and her companion, John Mason, on the second floor of a weathered three-family walk-up in the perilous and virtually all black Englewood section of Chicago.

It is a foreign landscape of burned-out tenements and long-shuttered storefronts where drunk men hang out on the corner, where gang members command more respect than police officers and where every child can tell you where the crack houses are.

The neighborhood is a thriving drug mart. Dealers provide curbside service and residents figure that any white visitor must be a patron or a distributor. Gunshots are as common as rainfall. Eighty people were murdered in the neighborhood last year, more than in Omaha and Pittsburgh combined.

Living with fear is second nature in the children. Asked why he liked McDonald's, Nicholas's brother Willie described the restaurant playground with violence as his yardstick. "There's a giant hamburger, and you can go inside of it," Willie said. "And it's made out of steel, so no bullets can't get through."

The Family

MANY EYES, MANY HANDS. It is in the middle of all this that Angela Whitiker is rearing her children and knitting together a new life from a world of fast men and cruel drugs. She is a strong-willed, 26-year-old onetime waitress who has seen more than most 70-year-olds ever will. A 10th grade dropout, she was pregnant at 15, bore Nicholas at 16, had her second son at 17, was married at 20, separated at 21 and was on crack at 22.

In the depths of her addiction, she was a regular at nearby crack houses, doing drugs with gang members, businessmen and, she said, police detectives, sleeping on the floors some nights. In a case of mistaken identity, she once had a gun put to her head. Now she feels she was spared for a reason.

She has worked most of her life, picking okra and butterbeans and cleaning white people's houses as a teen-ager in Louisiana, bringing home big tips from businessmen when she waited tables at a restaurant in downtown Chicago, selling Polish sausages from a food truck by the Dan Ryan Expressway and snow cones at street fairs.

She is a survivor who has gone from desperation to redemption, from absent mother to nurturing one, and who now sees economic salvation in nursing. Nicholas sees brand-name gym shoes and maybe toys and a second pair of school pants once she gets a job.

STUDYING FOR MIDTERMS. She went through treatment and has stayed away from drugs for two years. Paperback manuals from Alcoholics and Narcotics Anonymous sit without apology on the family bookshelf. A black velvet headdress from church is on the windowsill and the Bible is turned to Nehemiah—emblems of her new life as a regular at Faith Temple, a Coptic Christian church on a corner nearby.

For the last year, she has been studying a lot, talking about novels and polynomials and shutting herself in her cramped bedroom to study for something called midterms.

That often makes Nicholas the de facto parent for the rest of the children. There is Willie, the 8-year-old with the full-moon face and wide grin who likes it when adults mistake him for Nicholas. There is Ishtar, the dainty 5-year-old. There is Emmanuel, 4, who worships

Nicholas and runs crying to him whenever he gets hurt. And there is Johnathan, 3, who is as bad as he is cute and whom everyone calls John-John.

That is just the beginning of the family. There are four fathers in all: Nicholas's father, a disabled laborer who comes around at his own rhythm to check on Nicholas, give him clothes and whip him when he gets bad grades. There is Willie's father, a construction worker whom the children like because he lets them ride in his truck.

There is the man their mother married and left, a waiter at a soul food place. He is the father of Ishtar and Emmanuel and is remembered mostly for his beatings and drug abuse.

The man they live with now is Mr. Mason, a truck driver on the night shift, who met their mother at a crack house and bears on his neck the thick scars of a stabbing, a reminder of his former life on the streets. He gets Nicholas up at 3 A.M. to sweep the floor or take out the garbage and makes him hold on to a bench to be whipped when he disobeys.

Unemployment and drugs and violence mean that men may come and go, their mother tells them. "You have a father, true enough, but nothing is guaranteed," she says. "I tell them no man is promised to be in our life forever."

There is an extended family of aunts, an uncle, cousins and their maternal grandmother, Deloris Whitiker, the family lifeboat, whom the children moved in with when drugs took their mother away.

To the children, life is not the neat, suburban script of sitcom mythology with father, mother, two kids and golden retriever. But somehow what has to get done gets done.

When Nicholas brings home poor grades, sometimes three people will show up to talk to the teacher—his mother, his father and his mother's companion. When Nicholas practices his times tables, it might be his mother, his grandmother or Mr. Mason asking him what 9 times 8 is.

But there is a downside. The family does not believe in sparing the rod and when Nicholas disobeys, half a dozen people figure they are within their rights to whip or chastise him, and do. But he tries to focus on the positive. "It's a good family," he says. "They care for you. If my mama needs a ride to church, they pick her up. If she needs them to baby-sit, they baby-sit."

The Rules
READY TO RUN, QUICK TO PRAY. It is a gray winter's morning, zero degrees outside, and school starts for everybody in less than half

an hour. The children line up, all scarves and coats and legs. The boys bow their heads so their mother, late for class herself, can brush their hair one last time. There is a mad scramble for a lost mitten.

Then she sprays them. She shakes an aerosol can and sprays their coats, their heads, their tiny outstretched hands. She sprays them back and front to protect them as they go off to school, facing bullets and gang recruiters and a crazy, dangerous world. It is a special religious oil that smells like drugstore perfume, and the children shut their eyes tight as she sprays them long and furious so they will come back to her, alive and safe, at day's end.

These are the rules for Angela Whitiker's children, recounted at the Formica-top dining-room table:

"Don't stop off playing," Willie said.

"When you hear shooting, don't stand around—run," Nicholas said.

"Why do I say run?" their mother asked.

"Because a bullet don't have no eyes," the two boys shouted.

"She pray for us every day," Willie said.

THE WALK TO SCHOOL. Each morning Nicholas and his mother go in separate directions. His mother takes the two little ones to day care on the bus and then heads to class at Kennedy-King College nearby, while Nicholas takes Willie and Ishtar to Banneker Elementary School.

The children pass worn apartment buildings and denuded lots with junked cars to get to Banneker. Near an alley, unemployed men warm themselves by a trash-barrel fire under a plastic tent. There is a crack house across the street from school.

To Nicholas it is not enough to get Ishtar and Willie to school. He feels he must make sure they're in their seats. "Willie's teacher tell me, 'You don't have to come by here,'" Nicholas said. "I say, 'I'm just checking.'"

Mornings are so hectic that the children sometimes go to school hungry or arrive too late for the free school breakfast that Nicholas says isn't worth rushing for anyway.

One bitter cold morning when they made it to breakfast, Nicholas played the daddy as usual, opening a milk carton for Ishtar, pouring it over her cereal, handing her the spoon and saying sternly, "Now eat your breakfast."

He began picking over his own cardboard bowl of Corn Pops sitting in vaguely sour milk and remembered the time Willie found a cockroach in his cereal. It's been kind of hard to eat the school breakfast ever since.

The Children

WHEN BROTHERS ARE FRIENDS. Nicholas and Willie on brotherhood:

"He act like he stuck to me," Nicholas said of Willie. "Every time I move somewhere, he want to go. I can't even breathe."

"Well, what are brothers for?" Willie asked.

"To let them breathe and live a long life," Nicholas said. "Everytime I get something, they want it. I give them what they want after they give me a sad face."

"He saves me all the time," Willie said. "When I'm getting a whooping, he says he did it."

"Then I get in trouble," Nicholas said.

"Then I say I did it, too, and we both get a whooping," Willie said. "I save you, too, don't I, Nicholas?"

"Willie's my friend," Nicholas said.

"I'm more than your friend," Willie shot back, a little hurt.

Once Willie almost got shot on the way home from school. He was trailing Nicholas as he usually does when some sixth-grade boys pulled out a gun and started shooting.

"They were right behind Willie," Nicholas said. "I kept calling him to get across the street. Then he heard the shots and ran."

Nicholas shook his head. "I be pulling on his hood but he go so slow," he said.

"Old slowpoke," Ishtar said, chiming in.

NO FRIENDS, ONE TOY. In this neighborhood, few parents let their children outside to play or visit a friend's house. It is too dangerous. "You don't have any friends," Nicholas's mother tells him. "You don't have no homey. I'm your homey."

So Nicholas and his siblings usually head straight home. They live in a large, barren apartment with chipped tile floors and hand-me-down furniture, a space their mother tries to spruce up with her children's artwork.

The children spend their free time with the only toy they have—a Nintendo game that their mother saved up for and got them for Christmas. The television isn't working right, though, leaving a picture so dark the children have to turn out all the lights and sit inches from the set to see the cartoon Nintendo figure flicker over walls to save the princess.

Dinner is what their mother has time to make between algebra and Faith Temple. Late for church one night, she pounded on the stove to make the burners fire up, set out five plastic blue plates and apportioned the canned spaghetti and pan-fried bologna.

"Come and get your dinner before the roaches beat you to it!" she yelled with her own urban gallows humor.

RHINESTONES IN CHURCH. Faith Temple is a tiny storefront church in what used to be a laundry. It is made up mostly of two or three clans, including Nicholas's, and practices a homegrown version of Ethiopian-derived Christianity.

At the front of the spartan room with white walls and metal folding chairs, sits a phalanx of regal black-robed women with foot-high rhinestone-studded headdresses. They are called empresses, supreme empresses and imperial empresses. They include Nicholas's mother, aunt and grandmother, and they sing and testify and help calm flushed parishioners, who sometimes stomp and wail with the holy spirit.

The pastor is Prophet Titus. During the week he is Albert Lee, a Chicago bus driver, but on Sundays he dispenses stern advice and $35 blessings to his congregation of mostly single mothers and their children. "Just bringing children to the face of the earth is not enough," Prophet Titus intones. "You owe them more."

Nicholas's job during church is to keep the younger children quiet, sometimes with a brother asleep on the one thigh and a cousin on the other. Their mother keeps watch from her perch up front where she sings. When the little ones get too loud, their mother shoots them a threatening look from behind the microphone that says, "You know better."

GRANDMOTHER, EMPRESS. On this weeknight, Nicholas and Willie are with cousins and other children listening to their grandmother's Bible lesson.

She is a proud woman who worked for 22 years as a meat wrapper at a supermarket, reared five children of her own, has stepped in to help raise some of her grandchildren and packs a .38 in her purse in case some stranger tries to rob her again. On Sundays and during Bible class, she is not merely Nicholas's grandmother but Imperial Empress Magdala in her velvet-collared cape.

The children recite Bible verses ("I am black but beautiful," from Solomon or "My skins is black," from Job), and then Mrs. Whitiker breaks into a free-form lecture that seems a mix of black pride and Dianetics.

"Be dignified," she told the children. "Walk like a prince or princess. We're about obeying our parents and staying away from people who don't mean us any good."

The boys got home late that night, but their day was not done. "Your clothes are in the tub," their mother said, pointing to the bathroom, "and the kitchen awaits you."

"I know my baby's running out of hands," she said under her breath.

This is not the life Nicholas envisions for himself when he grows up. He had thought about this, and says he doesn't want any kids. Well, maybe a boy, one boy he can play ball with and show how to be a man. Definitely not a girl. "I don't want no girl who'll have four or five babies," he said. "I don't want no big family with 14, 20 people, all these people to take care of. When you broke they still ask you for money, and you have to say, 'I'm broke. I don't have no money.'"

A SISTER SAFE. Ishtar made it home safely the afternoon Nicholas was called to the principal's office. Mr. Mason was a couple of hours late picking her up, but he came through in the end.

Nicholas worries anyway, the way big brothers do. He worried the morning his mother had an early test and he had to take the little ones to day care before going to school himself.

John-John began to cry as Nicholas walked away. Nicholas bent down and hugged him and kissed him. Everything, Nicholas assured him, was going to be O.K.

The Mississippi Reclaims Its True Domain

July 18, 1993

CHICAGO—No one alive has seen the Father of Rivers yawn this high or this wide. No one imagined the Mississippi or its relatives would take such liberties, consuming so many hamlets whole, or that, if they did, technology would be nearly helpless to stop them.

There have been floods before. People in Hannibal, Mo., or Keokuk, Iowa, or Quincy, Ill., can tell you about watching their fathers and uncles pack sandbags to protect the year's corn crop or the feed store. For generations, some farmers figured floods and droughts into the cost of doing business. But then the country's big plumbing system of levees and dams, made better after each flood, was supposed to keep the rivers in their place and maintain the comfortable paradox of living on a floodplain.

Now the unimaginable has happened. Across the Midwestern cornbelt it has rained in biblical proportions—49 straight days, often in torrents. The rivers, driven past their banks, have taken back land that long ago was theirs, invading 15 million acres of farmland in eight states, forcing 36,000 people from their homes, halting river traffic for 600 miles and causing billions of dollars in damage.

From the air, from Minnesota to Missouri, from Kansas to Illinois, it looks like someone has spilled gallons and gallons of coffee on the green patchwork quilt that happens to be farms and towns. In silt rivers now wide as lakes, treetops look like bushes in a swimming pool, bridges and highways and other brave monuments to engineering are reduced to thin, threatened slivers, and even their builders know the water could take them, too, if it wanted. The floods have made the broad, S-curved Mississippi and its otherwise perfectly ordered valley look more like the Florida Keys.

Unlike earthquakes and hurricanes, floods defy the human urge to quantify. There is no single measure—no Richter scale, or mile-per-hour wind as in the eye of a hurricane—to gauge a flood. There are only the hundreds of crests and toppled levees on the rivers and their swollen creeks, and the thousand heartbreaks of lost soybean fields and moated Main Streets.

If the floods of 1993 have reminded people of anything, it is that the Mississippi River was never the docile pensioner some had come to think it was. It is not, after all, the Swanee. The Mississippi is America's watery aorta, draining or potentially flooding rivers in 31 states from the Appalachians to the Rocky Mountains.

"It's like talking about God Almighty himself," said Shelby Foote, the Memphis writer, who has lived his whole life on the river.

The river, ecologists and farmers say, was never supposed to follow the tight course humans have expected it to, indeed ordered it to, with their walls of dirt and concrete levees. Of course, that has not stopped people from building homes and farms and cities along the river. The Mississippi Valley's thick black soil is considered the richest on earth, impossible for farmers to resist.

But to claim the land meant making a bargain with the river, confining it to an artificially narrow path so that farms could reach as far as the shore and places like New Orleans and St. Louis could live undisturbed while their goods were carried safely from port to port. The price that river people pay is sudden and catastrophic flooding when excess rainwater, forced into a narrow channel by the levees, runs out of places to go and cannot drain naturally into the soil.

Then the river goes faster and faster, and it goes where it wishes, as it did during the flooding of the lower Mississippi in 1927, where, as William Faulkner wrote, the river "was now doing what it liked to do, had waited patiently the 10 years in order to do, as a mule will work for you 10 years for the privilege of kicking you once."

Mr. Foote was a boy during that flood. He remembers when word came that the levee had broken at Mounds Landing in Scott, Miss., north of Greenville. "It was a slow creeping rise," he said. "You can't even see it rise but if you turn away and then you look back, you see it is a little higher. Everything in its path is submerged or invaded. It presses against every crack and crevice. It's like solid wind when it comes."

Because of its might and willfulness, some ecologists argue that the very way people define a river is not particularly useful. They say that the river is not just whatever water you see in the channel, but the banks, the floodplain, in fact, the valley itself, from bluff to bluff. It is anywhere the water has been and could potentially go—a river, Mark Twain said, "whose alluvial banks cave and change constantly, whose snags are always hunting up new quarters, whose sand bars are never at rest."

In earlier centuries, when towns in the bottomlands were invaded by river water, townspeople packed up and moved to higher ground—as Franklin, Mo., for example, on the Missouri River, did in 1826. (Even that move could not save Franklin this time, however; the town is under water again.) Now, more than 7 million people live directly along the Mississippi, including more than 2 million around its confluence with the Missouri in St. Louis, where the two rivers are now cresting and levees straining and crumbling.

"No one is going to move St. Louis just because it happens to be on the river," said David Johnson, an aquatic ecologist who is assistant director of the School of Natural Resources at Ohio State University. "It's a question of working with the river or fighting the river. Fighting the river is almost always going to be a losing battle."

He argues for restoring the kind of wide open spaces that the river once had before Europeans and the great cities came, wetlands where the water could collect in times of severe rains. The Army Corps of Engineers built reservoirs to catch the run-off, although the current flooding suggests they may not be enough. In defense of the complex and normally efficient flood control system, hydraulic engineers say that without the man-made reservoirs, the bloated river would now stretch from bluff to bluff, five miles across in spots, covering what we now know as Dubuque, Iowa, or St. Louis.

Return of the Marshes

"People think of the river as their enemy," said David Lanegran, a professor of geography and urban studies at Macalester College in St. Paul, Minn. "They fight the river, dike the river, pollute the river, ignore the river. Now the river is taking back its old places. You can see the old marshes coming back in the farmers' fields, all the places where the duck ponds used to be. It's almost like a ghost. The water is saying, 'This is where I used to be. This used to be my place.'"

That may be cold comfort to people whose homes and businesses are under water. But there are some important differences between this disaster and others.

Things have changed since the days of Mark Twain, when armed guards patrolled levees to insure no one tampered with them or when, according to his stories, just about the only time a crowd would gather on the river was for a dogfight or a lynching. The flood has been remarkable for the show of volunteerism and general goodwill; there have been few reports of looting, and many of people driving for miles to work through the night sandbagging someone else's levee. It is a contrast to the country's biggest disaster of last year, Hurricane Andrew, which brought looters, and merchants jacking up the price of generators and people posing as carpenters and bilking roofless homeowners.

In Des Moines, where flooding of the Raccoon River knocked out the fresh water supply of 250,000 people, leaving residents without water to drink or take showers or fight fires or flush toilets with, people have shared well water, grocery stores have discounted bottled water and every other morning three senior citizens drive to a nursing home for the handicapped, where they deliver fresh water and personally flush all 126 toilets.

Midwesterners do these kinds of things, people here say, because even most city people originally came from small, rural towns where everybody knows everybody and it is an insult to take advantage. "These are standard, practical and utilitarian Midwestern values," said Douglas Hurt, director of the graduate program in agricultural and rural studies at the Iowa State University. "If your neighbor needs help, regardless of the spats you've had, you help him."

If there is an economic beneficiary of this flood, it is the farm states of the eastern Midwest—Michigan, Ohio and Indiana, where farmers will get to take advantage of the run-up in crop prices due to low supply.

"That will make the flood even more painful for farmers in the floodplains," said William Heffernan, a professor and chairman of rural sociology at the University of Missouri in Columbia. "They will be watching the highest prices in years and they don't have anything to sell."

Lifting and Cleansing

As disastrous as a flood is to those in its path, it is nonetheless part of a natural cycle of renewal just as forest fires are. The river channels grow so wide and the currents so strong they lift topsoil, carry nutrients downstream and deposit them in new soil. Iowa's loss may be Missouri's gain, but then Iowa may get its own refill from Minnesota. The heavy rains that precede the flooding can also cleanse the river waters and make a better pool for fish to spawn.

The current crisis will undoubtedly set off wide debate over ways to improve the system with an eye not to just one city or river but to the 250 or so creeks and rivers that feed into the Mississippi.

Only fairly recently in the river's history, when Congress authorized a Federal levee project after the 1927 flood, has there been any system-wide approach to flood control. But that was based in part on bringing up to code the haphazard levees of assorted farm towns who in times of desperation built wherever they felt like it. New and better levees have gone up, but they, too, can fail.

"People expect more out of what was there than was ever intended," said Harry Kitch, chief of the central planning management branch of the Army Corps of Engineers. "Any one of our structures can be overtopped if you have a big enough flood. We do a great deal of sophisticated work in rebuilding them, but there can always be a bigger flood."

The great lesson of the floods may be that humans will have to do a lot more if they are to outwit nature, if that is even possible.

"I think we as moderns tend to think that geological and meterological changes have stopped," said Bruce Michaelson, a professor of English at the University of Illinois at Urbana, who is writing a book about Mark Twain, "that volcanoes will no longer erupt, that hurricanes will no longer come off the coasts and the great rivers of the world are going to stay quietly in their banks so we can cruise them in our boats and barges."

But just as the river that Mark Twain romanced and revered carried the pieces of wrecked houses and trees from floods upstream, so it does a century later—"the debris," Professor Michaelson said, "of battlefields between water and man."

Cruel Flood:
It Tore at Graves, and at Hearts

August 25, 1993

HARDIN, MO.—When the Missouri River barreled through town like white-water rapids this summer, and grain bins and City Hall and the Assembly of God church and houses and barns gave way and there were no telephones or electricity or running water, people in this tiny farm town thought they knew all about the power of nature.

Then the unthinkable happened. The river washed away about two-thirds of the graves at the cemetery where just about anybody who ever lived and died here was buried. The river carved out a crater 50 feet deep where the cemetery used to be. It took cottonwood trees and the brick entryway and carried close to 900 caskets and burial vaults downstream toward St. Louis and the Mississippi.

The remains of whole families floated away, their two-ton burial vaults coming to rest in tree limbs, on highways, along railroad tracks and in beanfields two and three towns away.

"You cannot accept the magnitude of it until you're standing in it," said Dean Snow, the Ray County coroner. He said it might take years to find all the remains.

REMINDERS OF LOSSES. Now people who lost everything else to the flood are left to weep for the parents they mourned decades ago, the stillborn children they never saw grow up, the husbands taken from them in farm accidents, the mothers who died in childbirth. It is as if the people have died all over again and the survivors must grieve anew.

Every day they show up at the county fairgrounds to get word of their lost loved ones, gathering at a bulletin board where the names of the dead who have been recovered and identified are posted. People have driven from Kansas City and St. Louis to check on half-brothers or second husbands. A man called from Sacramento, Calif., trying to find his parents. Another flew in from New Mexico to find his mother. She was missing too.

"People are just heartsick," said Ed Wolfe, who had five generations of relatives in the cemetery. "It's a trying, a testing time to have to go through this all over again."

About 1,500 people were buried at the Hardin Cemetery, once a pristine landscape nine acres across and now a muddy lake where minnows and snapping turtles live alongside broken headstones and toppled graves. The disaster was all the more astonishing because Hardin is not even a river town. It is some five miles north of the Missouri.

Since it was founded in 1810, the cemetery had survived tornadoes, floods and the Civil War. No other cemetery in the country has been uprooted like this, officials of the American Cemetery Association say. Local people see the occurrence as near-biblical.

"It makes you think, 'What is God saying to us?'" said Bess Meador, a retired nurse with two husbands in the cemetery. "What is it we're doing that we shouldn't be doing? You look at that cemetery and you feel so helpless."

Whether a resident lost a direct relative or not, everybody lost someone. Just about everybody in the cemetery was kin.

So far, the remains of about 200 people have been found, stored in open barns and refrigerated trucks at the county fairgrounds and at a nearby farm. About 90 have been identified.

PAINFUL MEMORIES. It is a slow, painful task, more common to a plane crash than to a flood, that has required survivors to come in and give disaster volunteers any identifying information they can remember about their relatives.

Two boxes of tissues sit on the counseling desk for the shower of tears as people dig deep for old memories. Mr. Wolfe had to call up painful details about his only son, Christopher, a stillborn, who would have been 18 years old this year and whose remains are among the missing.

"They wanted to know what kind of casket, what color casket," Mr. Wolfe said. "What color his eyes were, what color his hair was, what he was wearing, if he had a little pillow in his casket."

Some people were able to give only the barest description. Some could only remember that a relative had a gold tooth or a hip replacement. Others remembered everything. One man's survivors remembered that he was buried in his Kansas State shorts, with a Timex watch and had a slide rule in his shirt pocket. The relatives of another man said he had a tattoo on his right arm that said "Irene."

The ordeal has forced Carrie Lee Young, 81, to relive the day she learned that her husband, Roy, had died when a tractor-mower fell on him five years ago. "He was out mowing by the road," she said, her eyes welling with tears. "And he didn't come in for supper. I couldn't go out looking for him. He had the car. People went out looking for him. They found him late that night. We were getting ready for our

55th wedding anniversary. It would be our 60th this year."

Every Memorial Day, she would carry peonies from her garden to place on the grave he had picked out for himself. Now she fears he is floating somewhere in the Missouri. "I don't know where my husband is," Mrs. Young said. "It is just pitiful."

BAD NEWS FOR WIDOW. She searched in vain for his name on the list and asked a volunteer, Greg Carmichael, if he knew where her husband was. He checked the plot number and the map. "He's pretty well gone," Mr. Carmichael said.

"That's what I was afraid of," Mrs. Young said, looking away.

To this town of 598 people, the cemetery was more than a place to bury people. It was an archives, a genealogical museum, a family album without pictures. People could trace their family trees by just walking among the tombstones.

The other day, Mr. Wolfe stood on the jagged 10-foot cliff at the corner of the cemetery that the river had left alone. Vaults and caskets—most lacking any identification marks—jutted from the cliffside, rusting in the sand steppes sculptured by the river. There were pink silk carnations on the remaining graves and broken obelisks and tombstones on their backs in the ravine below as gray-brown water lapped against the shores.

Mr. Wolfe soberly toured the cemetery, introducing people he knew as if he were at a reunion. "That's grandma and grandpa Bandy," he said of one set of tombstones.

MEMORIES OF FATAL ACCIDENT. "Those were neighbors of ours," he said, pointing to the headstones of a mother, father and daughter.

Joined by Mr. Snow, he came upon the grave of a World War II veteran, "That's Della's husband," he said.

"Yeah, Bob's dad," Mr. Snow said. "He was working on his car and it fell on him."

This is the kind of town where husbands and wives buy burial plots together and engrave their names on tombstones long before they die.

"You see, that's why grandmother wants a positive identification of grandfather," Mr. Chamberlain, a funeral director volunteering here, said. "Because she wants to be placed next to him, not next to somebody else."

As people here await word on the recovery effort, some are trying to figure out what to do with the cemetery. Some want to extend it into the adjacent cornfields and maybe put water lilies in the lake the river made as a memorial to those lost to the floods. Others want to move the entire cemetery, including the intact graves, to higher ground. Some want to have a new mass funeral service after more bodies are found.

Some people said they could not even think about that. "I can't go through that again," said Ethel Kincaid, whose parents' remains are still missing. "I went through it once. It's just too painful."

County officials have been hauling in about eight caskets a day as farmers and other residents report sightings. Clara Heil, a farmer eight miles east of Hardin, awoke one morning to find 10 vaults in her yard.

The cemetery itself has attracted tourists from Illinois and Kansas and as far away as Vermont, who drive past police barricades and ignore the "keep out" signs to take pictures. "Is this where the caskets popped out?" a gawker from Vermont asked Mr. Snow, camera in hand.

BABY AND DAD GONE. But these are hallowed grounds to people like Mr. Wolfe. When Mr. Snow waved him onto the site, he anxiously paced the cemetery in search of his father and stillborn son. He got to the edge of the cliff and saw the earth carved out in the spot where they had been.

"My baby and my dad are gone," Mr. Wolfe said, his eyes red and watery. "We've been hoping for five weeks they were safe. The way things are broken up down there, I don't know if they'll ever be recovered."

He wiped his eyes and headed back to the road, walking over dead corn shucks and wheat stubble, to break the news to his wife.

ANALYSIS

THE THREE STORIES in Isabel Wilkerson's Pulitzer package are powerful examples of the value of both reporting and writing. Perhaps surprising to some, Wilkerson's favorite of the three isn't the highly-honored "Nicholas" story, but the "Mississippi Reclaims Its True Domain" article, primarily because of the impossible physical and deadline conditions it was written under. After several weeks of writing daily flood stories for the paper, she was asked on a Wednesday to prepare the lead story for the Sunday Weekend Review section—meaning she had less than 48 hours to report and write the story.

Today she can chuckle about the enormity of the task. "I had to come up with new people to interview ... so I found rural sociologists and geographers, who never get talked to."

Although deadline pressure was smothering, and new reporting had to be done, Wilkerson found the Weekend Review piece strangely easy to write. "It was a magical experience," she says. "I connected with all the people I interviewed. They had also been watching [what the river was doing] with pain and horror and awe."

Sharp-eyed readers will note Wilkerson didn't quote the very people you might expect—flood victims. The reason is simple: She had already been interviewing them for weeks and the *Times* wanted fresh voices. Also, for the Weekend Review perspective, experts were able to give a more tempered view of the floods.

Wilkerson also called on distinguished historian Shelby Foote, searching for a new angle. "You're not necessarily looking for information," she explains. "You're looking for a perspective and a wisdom that can lead you to what you think the story is."

Wilkerson had decided to use personification in the story, picturing the Mississippi as much more than just a river. Foote gave her a valuable quote in support of that theme:

It's like talking about God Almighty himself.

In both of her river stories, plus "Nicholas," Wilkerson seems to like showing how ordinary people bear up, and even persevere, under extraordinary hardship. "I [do] write a lot of stories that bring out the empathy in people," she admits.

But caring and compassion aren't always enough, Wilkerson says. "The reporting is the basis. If you don't have the details and the color and the impression and the eye, [all the effort won't] lead to this great story you're striving for."

Wilkerson's observational and reporting skills were never more evident than when she was returning to Chicago from Iowa to write her wrap-up story. Looking down on the river, she noticed the Mississippi's flooding resembled a huge coffee stain. Grabbing a pen and the back of her airline ticket, Wilkerson wrote:

From the air ... it looks like someone has spilled gallons and gallons of coffee on the green patchwork quilt that happens to be farms and towns.

In another case, Wilkerson's reporting acumen resulted in a simple fact powerfully driving home a message of people helping each other:

... every other morning three senior citizens drive to a nursing home for the handicapped, where they deliver fresh water and personally flush all 126 toilets.

In the "Nicholas" profile, Wilkerson notes that the small boy serves as family "nanny, referee, housekeeper, handyman." Her description of his walk is both riveting and chilling:

.. his walk is the stiff slog of a worried father behind on the rent.

In her river stories, Wilkerson frequently felt the need to add details and a historical perspective to the tragedy:

It has rained in biblical proportions—49 straight days, often in torrents. The rivers, driven past their banks, have taken back land that long ago was theirs, invading 15 million acres of farmland in eight states, forcing 36,000 people from their homes, halting river traffic for 600 miles and causing billions of dollars in damage.

The New York Times' Chicago bureau chief took a different direction in writing about Nicholas, deliberately not seeking much distance from the boy. "He and the family were the experts. What makes that story different for me is that I spent as much time looking for him—looking for a good subject as I did the actual reporting." "The best approach to a story like this," she counsels, "is to let the story tell itself."

Wilkerson estimates her three-month project broke down like this: six weeks trying to find the perfect subject; four weeks with the family and the last two weeks trying to write the story and "wean myself away" from the family.

Finally, notice the quality of Wilkerson's leads and endings in her three stories. Her feature leads are those of an experienced national reporter—long, detailed and descriptive, followed quickly by a delayed summary lead. But her endings show the soul of a feature writer—dramatic and touching.

And the text of her stories is the work of a Pulitzer Prize winner.

ISABEL WILKERSON is currently on leave from her position as senior writer for *The New York Times'* Chicago bureau to write a book about the migration of African Americans from the south to the north. She holds a bachelor's degree in journalism from Howard University.

1995

RON SUSKIND

SIMILAR IN SOME WAYS to Isabel Wilkerson's profile of 10-year-old Nicholas Whitiker last year, Ron Suskind introduces his readers to Cedric Jennings, a smart kid trying to survive in a tough inner-city high school where brains and persistence aren't always appreciated by other students.

Suskind says he originally set out to find kids who wanted to learn—even in the worst urban schools. In this quest, he follows Jennings through rugged Ballou High School in Washington, D.C., and to a summer program for disadvantaged children at prestigious M.I.T. University.

In the first story, "Against All Odds," Suskind paints a heroic picture of Jennings, showing how he overcame a dysfunctional family, squalid conditions and a second-rate education to stand on the verge of entering M.I.T. "My life is about to begin," he exults.

In his second piece, "Class Struggle," published four months after Jennings left for M.I.T., Suskind charts his sad return to Washington, D.C., uncertain of his next move, and if his life is beginning or ending.

Suskind's stories deeply touched the readers, a fact *Wall Street Journal* managing editor Paul Steiger stressed in his nominating letter to the Pulitzer committee. He pointed out Suskind's two-part story resulted in "hundreds of letters and scores of checks" flooding in to the *Journal,* including a bond trader sending one student $10,000. Eventually, trust funds were set up for several of the students. Later, as Jennings' situation became known nationally, the president of M.I.T. even visited the high school to meet with students and urge them to apply to M.I.T.

Both Steiger and Suskind were especially moved by a tearful phone call from one business executive who had read the story. "If one of these kids sat next to me on the subway, I'd move to another car," he admitted. "Now, I realize that in that terrible environment, I'd be just like them, certainly hopeless. And the ones who somehow achieve through it all, well, they're simply better than me."

After the national furor and publicity from his stories, not to mention the money and letters pouring in, Suskind was gratified to learn he was a strong contender for a Pulitzer—in both the feature and explanatory categories.

His former college roommate (and current *Journal* reporter), Tony Horwitz, was also a Pulitzer finalist, in national reporting, the same year. This made for some friendly taunting in the newsroom, Suskind admits. But when the big day came, Suskind only wanted to suffer in private. "The next thing I know," he laments, "I'm in the *Journal*'s ninth floor with a hundred people watching the ticker, which is the last thing you want to do."

Suskind says he received his first hint when Joseph Kahn called from *The Boston Globe* seeking a comment at 2 p.m., an hour before the official announcement. Suskind asked him what he wanted a comment for. At that point, Kahn rapidly terminated the phone call, only fueling Suskind's suspicions. (The *Globe* had also won a Pulitzer that year, after a long drought, and they seemed to be jumping the gun on the 3 p.m. news embargo.)

Suskind already had some Boston history, having become something of a *cause celebre* in Boston that year after writing a controversial story about the death of Boston Celtic's star Reggie Lewis. The Celtics threatened to sue, but never did.

Finally, at 3 p.m., Suskind reluctantly trudged to the newsroom. "It was like a mob scene," he recalled. "There I am sitting at the machine. At first, public service comes up. Then Horwitz wins, and a cheer goes up."

To make the agony even worse, Suskind now thinks he's in the explanatory category, and sees that category's winner zip by. From somewhere behind him, he hears a stage whisper: "Block the windows. We don't want him to jump."

Finally, after Suskind swears he saw, "next week's weather and the Mets' opening day roster go by," the name of the Pulitzer Prize winner for features crawls across the screen: Ron Suskind.

Against All Odds

The Wall Street Journal

May 26, 1994

WASHINGTON—Recently, a student was shot dead by a classmate during lunch period outside Frank W. Ballou Senior High. It didn't come as much of a surprise to anyone at the school, in this city's most crime-infested ward. Just during the current school year, one boy was hacked by a student with an ax, a girl was badly wounded in a knife fight with another female student, five fires were set by arsonists, and an unidentified body was dumped next to the parking lot.

But all is quiet in the echoing hallways at 7:15 a.m., long before classes start on a spring morning. The only sound comes from the computer lab, where 16-year-old Cedric Jennings is already at work on an extra-credit project, a program to bill patients at a hospital. Later, he will work on his science-fair project, a chemical analysis of acid rain.

He arrives every day this early and often doesn't leave until dark. The high-school junior with the perfect grades has big dreams: He wants to go to Massachusetts Institute of Technology.

Cedric is one of a handful of honor students at Ballou, where the dropout rate is well into double digits and just 80 students out of more than 1,350 currently boast an average of B or better. They are a lonely lot. Cedric has almost no friends. Tall, gangly and unabashedly ambitious, he is a frequent target in a place where bullies belong to gangs and use guns; his life has been threatened more than once. He eats lunch in a classroom many days, plowing through extra work that he has asked for. "It's the only way I'll be able to compete with kids from other, harder schools," he says.

The arduous odyssey of Cedric and other top students shows how the street culture that dominates Ballou drags down anyone who seeks to do well. Just to get an ordinary education—the kind most teens take for granted—these students must take extraordinary measures. Much of their academic education must come outside of regular classes altogether: Little gets accomplished during the day in a place where attendance is sporadic, some fellow students read at only a fifth-grade level, and some stay in lower grades for years, feeling hardened, 18-year-old sophomores mixing with new arrivals.

'Crowd Control'

"So much of what goes on here is crowd control," says Mahmood Dorosti, a math teacher. The few top students "have to put themselves on something like an independent-study course to really learn—which is an awful lot to ask of a teenager."

It has been this way as long as Cedric can remember. When he was a toddler, his mother, Barbara Jennings, reluctantly quit her clerical job and went on welfare for a few years so she could start her boy on a straight and narrow path. She took him to museums, read him books, took him on nature walks. She brought him to church four times each week, and warned him about the drug dealers on the corner. Cedric learned to loathe those dealers—especially the one who was his father.

Barbara Jennings, now 47, already had two daughters, her first born while she was in high school. Cedric, she vowed, would lead a different life. "You're a special boy," she would tell her son. "You have to see things far from here, far from this place. And someday, you'll get the kind of respect that a real man earns."

Cedric became a latch-key child at the age of five, when his mother went back to work. She filled her boy's head with visions of the Ivy League, bringing him home a Harvard sweat shirt while he was in junior high. Every day after school, after double-locking the door behind him, he would study, dream of becoming an engineer living in a big house—and gaze at the dealers just outside his window stashing their cocaine in the alley.

Seduced by Failure

Ballou High, a tired sprawl of '60s-era brick and steel, rises up from a blighted landscape of housing projects and run-down stores. Failure is pervasive here, even seductive. Some 836 sophomores enrolled last September—and 172 were gone by Thanksgiving. The junior class numbers only 399. The senior class, a paltry 240. "We don't know much about where the dropouts go," says Reginald Ballard, the assistant principal. "Use your imagination. Dead. Jail. Drugs."

On a recent afternoon, a raucous crowd of students fills the gymnasium for an assembly. Administrators here are often forced into bizarre games of cat and mouse with their students, and today is no exception: To lure everyone here, the school has brought in former Washington Mayor Marion Barry, several disk jockeys from a black radio station and a rhythm-and-blues singer.

A major reason for the assembly, though, has been kept a secret: To hand out academic awards to top students. Few of the winners would show up voluntarily to endure the sneers of classmates. When one hapless teen's name is called, a teacher must run to the bleachers and order him down as some in the crowd jeer "Nerd!"

The announcer moves on to the next honoree: "Cedric Jennings! Cedric Jennings!" Heads turn expectantly, but Cedric is nowhere to be seen. Someone must have tipped him off, worries Mr. Ballard. "It sends a terrible message," he says, "that doing well here means you better not show your face."

Cedric, at the moment, is holed up in a chemistry classroom. He often retreats here. It is his private sanctuary, the one place at Ballou where he feels completely safe, and where he spends hours talking with his mentor, chemistry teacher Clarence Taylor. Cedric later will insist he simply didn't know about the assembly—but he readily admits he hid out during a similar assembly last year even though he was supposed to get a $100 prize: "I just couldn't take it, the abuse."

Mr. Taylor, the teacher, has made Cedric's education something of a personal mission. He gives Cedric extra-credit assignments, like working on a sophisticated computer program that taps into weather satellites. He arranges trips, like a visit with scientists at the National Aeronautics and Space Administration. He challenges him with impromptu drills; Cedric can reel off all 109 elements of the periodic table by memory in three minutes, 39 seconds.

Most importantly, earlier this year, after Cedric's mother heard about an M.I.T. summer scholarship program for minority high schoolers, Mr. Taylor helped him apply.

Now, Cedric is pinning all of his hopes on getting into the program. Last year, it bootstrapped most of its participants into the M.I.T. freshman class, where the majority performed extremely well. It is Cedric's ticket out of this place, the culmination of everything that he has worked for his whole life.

"You can tell the difference between the ones who have hope and those who don't," says Mr. Taylor. "Cedric has it—the capacity to hope."

That capacity is fast being drummed out of some others in the dwindling circle of honor students at Ballou. Teachers have a name for what goes on here. The "crab bucket syndrome," they call it: When one crab tries to climb from a bucket, the others pull it back down.

Just take a glance at Phillip Atkins, 17, who was a top student in junior high, but who has let his grades slide into the C range. These days he goes by the nickname "Blunt," street talk for a thick marijuana cigarette, a "personal favorite" he says he enjoys with a "40-ounce" of beer. He has perfected a dead-eyed stare, a trademark of the gang leaders he admires.

Phillip, now a junior, used to be something of a bookworm. At the housing project where he lives with both parents and his seven siblings, he read voraciously, especially about history. He still likes to read, though he would never tell that to the menacing crowd he hangs around with now.

Being openly smart, as Cedric is, "will make you a target, which is crazy at a place like Ballou," Phillip explains to his 15-year-old sister Alicia and her friend Octavia Hooks, both sophomore honor students, as they drive to apply for a summer-jobs program for disadvantaged youths. "The best way to avoid trouble," he says, "is to never get all the answers right on a test."

Alicia and Octavia nod along. "At least one wrong," Octavia says quietly, almost to herself.

CEDRIC TRIES NEVER to get any wrong. His average this year is better than perfect: 4.02, thanks to an A+ in English. He takes the most advanced courses he can, including physics and computer science. "If you're smart, show it," he says. "Don't hide."

At school, though, Cedric's blatant studiousness seems to attract nothing but abuse. When Cedric recently told a girl in his math class that he would tutor her as long as she stopped copying his answers, she responded with physical threats—possibly to be carried out by a boyfriend. Earlier, one of the school's tougher students stopped him in the hallway and threatened to shoot him.

The police who are permanently stationed at the school say Ballou's code of behavior is much like that of a prison: Someone like Cedric who is "disrespected" and doesn't retaliate is vulnerable.

Worse, Cedric is worried that he is putting himself through all this for nothing. Scores are in, and Cedric has gotten a startling low 750 out of a possible 1600 on his PSATs, the pretest before the Scholastic Aptitude Test that colleges require. He is sure his chances of getting into the M.I.T. program, where average scores are far higher, are scuttled.

He admits that he panicked during the test, racing ahead, often guessing, and finishing early. He vows to do better next time. "I'm going to do better on the real SATs, I've got to," he says, working in Mr. Taylor's room on a computer program that offers drills and practice tests. "I've got no choice."

At his daily SAT Preparation class—where Cedric is the only one of 17 students to have completed last night's homework—Cedric leads one group of students in a practice exercise; Phillip leads another. Cedric races through the questions recklessly, ignoring his groupmates, one of whom protests faintly, "He won't let us do any." Phillip and his group don't bother trying. They cheat, looking up answers in the back of the book.

Janet Johns-Gibson, the class teacher, announces that one Ballou student who took the SAT scored a 1050. An unspectacular result almost anyplace else, but here the class swoons in amazement. "Cedric will do better than that," sneers Phillip. "He's such a brain." Cedric winces.

IN TRUTH, CEDRIC MAY NOT BE the smartest student in his class. In a filthy boys room reeking of urine, Delante Coleman, a 17-year-old junior known as "Head," is describing life at the top. Head is the leader of Trenton Park Crew, a gang, and says he and "about 15 of my boys who back me up" enjoy "fine buggies," including a Lexus, and "money, which we get from wherever." There is a dark side, of course, like the murder last summer of the gang's previous leader, Head's best friend, by a rival thug from across town. The teen was found in his bed with a dozen bullet holes through his body.

But Head still feels invincible. "I'm not one, I'm many," says the 5-foot-3, 140-pound plug of a teenager. "Safety, in this neighborhood, is about being part of a group."

Head's grades are barely passing, in the D range. Yet Christopher Grimm, a physics teacher, knows a secret about Head: As a sophomore, he scored above 12th-grade-level nationally on the math section of a standardized basic-skills test. That's the same score Cedric got.

"How d'you find that out?" barks Head when confronted with this information. "Well, yeah, that's, umm, why I'm so good with money."

For sport, Head and his group like to toy with the "goodies," honor students like Cedric who carry books home and walk alone. "Everyone knows they're trying to be white, get ahead in the white man's world," he says, his voice turning bitter. "In a way, that's a little bit of disrespect to the rest of us."

Phillip tests even better than Head, his two F's in the latest quarter notwithstanding. On the basic-skills test, both he and Cedric hit a combined score—averaging English, math and other disciplines—of 12.9, putting both in the top 10 percent nationwide. But no one seems to pay attention to that, least of all Phillip's teachers, who mostly see him as a class clown. "Thought no one knew that," Phillip says, when a visitor mentions his scores.

Heading over to McDonald's after school, Phillip is joined by his sister Alicia and her friend Octavia, both top students a grade behind him. Over Big Macs and Cokes, the talk shifts to the future. "Well, I'm going to college," says Alicia coolly, staring down Phillip. "And then I'm going to be something like an executive secretary, running an office."

"Yeah, I'm going to college, too," says Phillip, looking away.

"Very funny, you going to college," snaps Alicia. "Get real."

"Well, I am."

"Get a life, Phillip, you got no chance."

"You've got nothing," he says, starting to yell. "Just your books. My life is after school."

"You got no life," she shouts back. "Nothing!"

The table falls silent, and everyone quietly finishes eating. But later, alone, Phillip admits that, no, there won't be any college. He has long since given up on the dreams he used to have when he and his father would spin a globe and talk about traveling the world. "I'm not really sure what happens from here," he says softly, sitting on the stone steps overlooking the track behind the school. "All I know is what I do now. I act stupid."

Phillip of late has become the cruelest of all of Cedric's tormentors. The two got into a scuffle recently—or at least Phillip decked Cedric, who didn't retaliate. A few days after the McDonald's blowup, Phillip and a friend bump into Cedric. "He thinks he's so smart," Phillip says. "You know, I'm as smart as he is." The friend laughs. He thinks it's a joke.

Cedric is on edge. He should be hearing from M.I.T. about the summer program any day now, and he isn't optimistic. In physics class, he gamely tries to concentrate on his daily worksheet. The worksheet is a core educational tool at Ballou: Attendance is too irregular, and books too scarce, to actually teach many lessons during class, some teachers say. Often, worksheets are just the previous day's homework, and Cedric finishes them quickly.

Today, though, he runs into trouble. Spotting a girl copying his work, he confronts her. The class erupts in catcalls, jeering at Cedric until the teacher removes him from the room. "I put in a lot of hours, a lot of time, to get everything just right," he says, from his exile in an adjoining lab area. "I shouldn't just give it away."

His mentor, Mr. Taylor, urges him to ignore the others. "I tell him he's in a long, harrowing race, a marathon, and he can't listen to what's being yelled at him from the sidelines," he says. "I tell him those people on the sideline are already out of the race."

But Cedric sometimes wishes he was more like those people. Recently, he asked his mother for a pair of extra-baggy, khaki-colored pants—a style made popular by Snoop Doggy Dogg, the rap star who was charged last year with murder. But "my mother said no way, that it symbolizes things, bad things, and bad people," he reports later, lingering in a stairwell. "I mean, I've gotta live."

Unable to shake his malaise, he wanders the halls after the school day ends, too distracted to concentrate on his usual extra-credit work. "Why am I doing this, working like a maniac?" he asks.

He stretches out his big hands, palms open. "Look at me. I'm not gonna make it. What's the point in even trying?"

Outside Phillip's house in the projects, his father, Israel Atkins, is holding forth on the problem of shooting too high. A lyrically articulate man who conducts prayer sessions at his home on weekends, he gives this advice to his eight children: Hoping for too much in this world can be dangerous.

"I see so many kids around here who are told they can be anything, who then run into almost inevitable disappointment, and all that hope turns into anger," he says one day, a few hours after finishing the night shift at his job cleaning rental cars. "Next thing, they're saying, 'See, I got it anyway—got it my way, by hustling—the fancy car, the cash.' And then they're lost."

"Set goals so they're attainable, so you can get some security, I tell my kids. Then keep focused on what success is all about: being close to God and appreciating life's simpler virtues."

Mr. Atkins is skeptical about a tentative—and maybe last—stab at achievement that Phillip is making: tap dancing. Phillip has taken a course offered at school, and is spending hours practicing for an upcoming show in a small theater at the city's John F. Kennedy Center for Performing Arts. His teacher, trying hard to encourage him, pronounces him "enormously gifted."

At Ballou, teachers desperate to find ways to motivate poor achievers often make such grand pronouncements. They will pick a characteristic and inflate it into a career path. So the hallways are filled with the next Carl Lewis, the next Bill Cosby, the next Michael Jackson.

But to Phillip's father, all this is nonsense. "Tap dancing will not get him a job," he says. It is all, he adds, part of the "problem of kids getting involved in these sorts of things, getting their heads full of all kinds of crazy notions."

As Cedric settles into his chair in history class, the teacher's discussion of the Great Depression echoes across 20 desks—only one other of which is filled.

But Cedric has other things on his mind. As soon as school is over, he seeks out his chemistry teacher Mr. Taylor. He isn't going to enter a citywide science fair with his acid-rain project after all, he says. What's more, he is withdrawing from a program in which he would link up with a mentor, such as an Environmental Protection Agency employee, to prepare a project on the environment. Last year, Cedric had won third prize with his project on asbestos hazards. Mr. Taylor is at a loss as his star student slips out the door.

"I'm tired, I'm going home," Cedric murmurs. He walks grimly past a stairwell covered with graffiti: "HEAD LIVES."

The path may not get any easier. Not long after Cedric leaves, Joanne Camero, last year's salutatorian, stops by Mr. Taylor's chemistry classroom, looking despondent. Now a freshman at George Washington University, she has realized, she admits, "that the road from here keeps getting steeper."

The skills it took to make it through Ballou—focusing on nothing but academics, having no social life, and working closely with a few teachers—left Joanne ill-prepared for college, she says. There, professors are distant figures, and students flit easily from academics to socializing, something she never learned to do.

"I'm already worn out," she says. Her grades are poor and she has few friends. Tentatively, she admits that she is thinking about dropping out and transferring to a less rigorous college.

As she talks about past triumphs in high school, it becomes clear that for many of Ballou's honor students, perfect grades are an attempt to redeem imperfect lives—lives torn by poverty, by violence, by broken families. In Cedric's case, Mr. Taylor says later, the pursuit of flawless grades is a way to try to force his father to respect him, even to apologize to him. "I tell him it can't be," Mr. Taylor says. "That he must forgive that man that he tries so hard to hate."

Behind a forest of razor wire at Virginia's Lorton Correctional Institution, Cedric Gilliam emerges into a visiting area. At 44 years old, he looks startlingly familiar, an older picture of his son. He has been in prison for nine years, serving a 12- to 36-year sentence for armed robbery.

When Cedric's mother became pregnant, "I told her ... if you have the baby, you won't be seeing me again," Mr. Gilliam recalls, his voice flat. "So she said she'd have an abortion. But I messed up by not going down to the clinic with her. That was my mistake, you see, and she couldn't go through with it."

For years, Mr. Gilliam refused to publicly acknowledge that Cedric was his son, until his progeny had grown into a boy bearing the same wide, easy grin as his dad. One day, they met at a relative's apartment, in an encounter young Cedric recalls vividly. "And I ran to him and hugged him and said 'Daddy.' I just remember that I was so happy."

Not long afterward, Mr. Gilliam went to jail. The two have had infrequent contact since then. But their relationship, always strained, reached a breaking point last year when a fight ended with Mr. Gilliam threatening his son, "I'll blow your brains out."

Now, in the spare prison visiting room, Mr. Gilliam says his son has been on his mind constantly since then. "I've dialed the number a hundred times, but I keep hanging up," he says. "I know Cedric doesn't get, you know, that kind of respect from the other guys, and that used to bother me. But now I see all he's accomplished, and I'm proud of him, and I love him. I just don't know how to say it."

His son is skeptical. "By the time he's ready to say he loves me and all, it will be too late," Cedric says later, angrily. "I'll be gone."

IT IS A SATURDAY AFTERNOON, and the Kennedy Center auditorium comes alive with a wailing jazz number as Phillip and four other dancers spin and tap their way flawlessly through a complicated routine. The audience—about 200 parents, brothers and sisters of the school-aged performers—applauds wildly.

After the show, he is practically airborne, laughing and strutting in his yellow "Ballou Soul Tappers" T-shirt, looking out at the milling crowd in the lobby.

"You seen my people?" he asks one of his fellow tappers.

"No, haven't," she says.

"Your people here?" he asks, tentatively.

"Sure, my mom's over there," she says, pointing, then turning back to Phillip.

His throat seems to catch, and he shakes his head. "Yeah," he says, "I'll find out where they are, why they couldn't come." He tries to force a smile, but manages only a grimace. "I'll find out later."

Scripture Cathedral, the center of Washington's thriving apostolic Pentecostal community, is a cavernous church, its altar dominated by a 40-foot-tall illuminated cross. Evening services are about to begin, and Cedric's mother searches nervously for her son, scanning the crowd of women in hats and men in bow ties. Finally, he slips into a rear pew, looking haggard.

From the pulpit, the preacher, C.L. Long, announces that tonight, he has a "heavy heart": He had to bury a slain 15-year-old boy just this afternoon. But then he launches into a rousing sermon, and as he speaks, his rolling cadences echo through the sanctuary, bringing the 400 parishioners to their feet.

"When you don't have a dime in your pocket, when you don't have food on your table, if you got troubles, you're in the right place tonight," he shouts, as people yell out hallelujahs, raise their arms high, run through the aisles. Cedric, preoccupied, sits passively. But slowly, he, too, is drawn in and begins clapping.

Then the preacher seems to speak right to him. "Terrible things are happening, you're low, you're tired, you're fighting, you're waiting for your vision to become reality—you feel you can't wait anymore," the preacher thunders. "Say I'll be fine tonight 'cause Jesus is with me.' Say it! Say it!"

By now, Cedric is on his feet, the spark back in his eyes. "Yes," he shouts. "Yes."

It is a long service, and by the time mother and son pass the drug dealers—still standing vigil—and walk up the crumbling stairs to their apartment, it is approaching midnight.

Ms. Jennings gets the mail. On top of the TV Guide is an orange envelope from the U.S. Treasury: a stub from her automatic savings-bond contribution—$85 a week, about one-third of her after-tax income—that she has been putting away for nine years to help pay for Cedric's college. "You don't see it, you don't miss it," she says.

Under the TV Guide is a white envelope.

Cedric grabs it. His hands begin to shake. "My heart is in my throat." It is from M.I.T.

Fumbling, he rips it open.

"Wait. Wait. 'We are pleased to inform you ...' Oh my God. Oh my God," he begins jumping around the tiny kitchen. Ms. Jennings reaches out to touch him, to share this moment with him—but he spins out of her reach.

"I can't believe it. I got in," he cries out, holding the letter against his chest, his eyes shut tight. "This is it. My life is about to begin."

Desperately Trying to Stay on Course

ALICIA ATKINS GRASPS the fake gold necklace at her throat as if it is a talisman, a charm that will ward off the evil spirits lurking all around. The necklace spells out "ERA," and Alicia gave one to each of her five closest girlfriends—honor students all—at the start of the school year.

She had gotten the trinkets from a woman at her church, who had picked up a handful at a women's rights rally. But Alicia decided the letters would stand for something other than Equal Rights Amendment: "That we would be a group of smart girls at Ballou, who'd be sticking together and do well in school, that we would bring about, like, a new era for black people."

Fifteen-year-old Alicia hopes desperately it will protect them. Short, chatty and all dimples behind her big glasses, she is the self-appointed mother figure for this group of sophomores.

Alicia is most protective of 15-year-old Octavia Hooks—and for good reason. Alicia's home life may be chaotic, with seven siblings including her brother Phillip. But her father has a steady job, her mother is always at home. She is guided by her father's advice to set "attainable" goals; she wants to be an executive secretary with "a house with three bedrooms, a little yard with a swing, where I can walk outside and not be afraid. And when I get it—and I will—I'll live there, all by myself."

Octavia's life has no such order. She has lived in two of the city's worst public housing projects in the past two years. She and her five siblings are from two different fathers - one a drug addict who was beaten to death, the other an occasional visitor.

In the past year, though, Octavia has emerged as a blazing student. When the other girls get "A's," Octavia brings home the lone "A+." She talks of being an obstetrician. But she is often tired and carries an edge of neediness.

Her physics teacher, Christopher Grimm, is concerned. Mr. Grimm was reluctant last September to accept Octavia into a class of almost all seniors, so he gave her a math-proficiency test, expecting her to fail; she scored 100 percent. Now he is challenging her at every opportunity, and says her science-fair project—which uses fireworks and sensors to measure rocket thrust—was "a cinch for first place." But Octavia didn't show up on the day she was due to fire the rockets, and the project won't be finished in time for the fair. She will only say she had "family business" that day.

"Occy's one of those welfare babies," says Alicia, trying to make it sound like banter. "What they call 'at risk.'" But she is worried: Octavia's "mind's been all over the place. ... Things are going on."

Over fried chicken during lunch period, the talk turns to a 21-year-old man Octavia has been seeing. Alicia has been on tenterhooks, afraid her friend might be pregnant, "and, that'll be it. Her life'll be over." One day she says that "Occy's in denial" and that "I'm going to be the godmother." Octavia angrily denies being pregnant, and later Alicia says she "was mistaken, it was all just a joke."

But in physics class, Octavia bears down on a copy of Parents magazine. She lingers over "10 Essentials for a Safe Nursery." "It must be really hard," she says, pensively, "to make a place absolutely safe for an infant—so nothing could happen to them."

A few weeks later, long after the science fair, Octavia sits in physics class with her head on the desk. Three feet away, on a table against the wall, dangle two starter fuses for a rocket launcher. Mr. Grimm is beside himself: If she doesn't complete her experiment in a few days, his star student will fail physics for the quarter.

"It's so frustrating," he says. "You see them drowning, and you reach out and say, 'Just take my hand.' But they won't. They think they're supposed to drown."

Later, Alicia mentions that she and Octavia, together, came up with the idea of a "new era that we would lead." The necklaces, they both felt, would be a shield to keep them safe. Now, Octavia is the only girl without one. Alicia says she took it back after discovering her friend tried to sell it for $5.

Half-a-mile away, at Octavia's row house, her 36-year-old mother, Michelle Rindgo, sits in her "TAKE ME HOME I'M DRUNK" T-shirt on the couch. Ms. Rindgo reels off mistakes she has made: her first baby at 14, her years on welfare, her attempts, often futile, to keep her children "away from all the other kids who live around here who are going nowhere."

Like many living rooms in the projects, hers is wall-papered with certificates that local schools pass out frantically, honoring small victories, like attendance or citizenship, to build self-esteem. But this shrine offers scant comfort as her daughter grows into womanhood. "She's at the age—she's a pretty girl—and I worry," Rindgo says.

Octavia comes home, and packs clothes for a weekend away. She will be staying at the apartment of her 21-year-old sister, who has three out-of-wedlock babies. As she slips out the door, Ms. Rindgo calls to her: "You still a virgin, baby?"

"Yes, Mama," her daughter calls back. Then she disappears across a landscape of bursting Dumpsters and junked cars.

Class Struggle

September 22, 1994

CAMBRIDGE, MASS.—In a dormitory lobby, under harsh fluorescent lights, there is a glimpse of the future: A throng of promising minority high schoolers, chatting and laughing, happy and confident.

It is a late June day, and the 51 teenagers have just converged here at Massachusetts Institute of Technology for its prestigious minority summer program—a program that bootstraps most of its participants into M.I.T.'s freshman class. Already, an easy familiarity prevails. A doctor's son from Puerto Rico invites a chemical engineer's son from south Texas to explore nearby Harvard Square. Over near the soda machines, the Hispanic son of two school teachers meets a black girl who has the same T-shirt, from an annual minority-leadership convention.

"This is great," he says. "Kind of like we're all on our way up, together."

Maybe. Off to one side, a gangly boy is singing a rap song, mostly to himself. His expression is one of pure joy. Cedric Jennings, the son of a drug dealer and the product of one of Washington's most treacherous neighborhoods, has worked toward this moment for his entire life.

Ticket out of Poverty

Cedric, whose struggle to excel was chronicled in a May 26 page one article in this newspaper, hails from a square mile of chaos. His apartment building is surrounded by crack dealers, and his high school, Frank W. Ballou Senior High, is at the heart of the highest-crime area in the city. Already this year, four teenagers from his district—teens who should have been his schoolmates—were charged in homicides. Another six are dead, murder victims themselves.

For Cedric, M.I.T. has taken on almost mythic proportions. It represents the culmination of everything he has worked for, his ticket to escape poverty. He has staked everything on getting accepted to college here, and at the summer program's end he will find out whether he stands a chance. He doesn't dare think about what will happen if the answer is no.

"This will be the first steps of my path out, out of here, to a whole other world," he had said not long before leaving Washington for the summer program. "I'll be going so far from here, there'll be no holding back."

As Cedric looks around the bustling dormitory lobby on that first day, he finally feels at home, like he belongs. "They arrive here and say, 'Wow, I didn't know there were so many like me,'" says William Ramsey, administrative director of M.I.T.'s program. "It gives them a sense ... that being a smart minority kid is the most normal thing to be."

Stranger in a Strange Land

But they aren't all alike, really, a lesson Cedric is learning all too fast. He is one of only a tiny handful of students from poor backgrounds; most of the rest range from lower-middle-class to affluent. As he settles into chemistry class on the first day, a row of girls, all savvy and composed, amuse themselves by poking fun at "my Washington street-slang," as Cedric tells it later. "You know, the way I talk, slur my words and whatever."

Cedric is often taunted at his nearly all-black high school for "talking white." But now, he is hearing the flawless diction of a different world, of black students from suburbs with neat lawns and high schools that send most graduates off to college.

Other differences soon set him apart. One afternoon, as students talk about missing their families, it becomes clear that almost everyone else has a father at home. Cedric's own father denied paternity for years and has been in jail for almost a decade. And while many of the students have been teased back home for being brainy, Cedric's studiousness has earned him threats from gang members with guns.

Most worrisome, though, is that despite years of asking for extra work after school—of creating his own independent-study course just to get the basic education that students elsewhere take for granted—he is woefully far behind. He is overwhelmed by the blistering workload: six hours each day of intensive classes, study sessions with tutors each night, endless hours more of homework.

Only in calculus, his favorite subject, does he feel sure of himself. He is slipping steadily behind in physics, chemistry, robotics and English.

In the second week of the program, Cedric asks one of the smartest students, who hails from a top-notch public school, for help on some homework. "He said it was 'beneath him,'" Cedric murmurs later, barely able to utter the words. "Like, he's so much better than me. Like I'm some kind of inferior human being."

A crowd of students jostles into a dormitory lounge a few evenings later for Chinese food, soda and a rare moment of release from studying. Cliques already have formed, there are whispers of romances, and lunch groups have crystallized, almost always along black or Hispanic lines. But as egg rolls disappear, divides are crossed.

A Hispanic teenager from a middle-class New Mexico neighborhood tries to teach the opening bars of Beethoven's "Moonlight Sonata" to a black youngster, a toll taker's son from Miami. An impeccably-clad black girl from an affluent neighborhood teaches some dance steps to a less privileged one.

Tutors, mostly minority undergraduates at M.I.T. who once went through this program, look on with tight smiles, always watchful. The academic pressure, they know, is rising fast. Midterm exams start this week—along with all-nighters and panic. Some students will grow depressed; others will get sick from exhaustion. The tutors count heads, to see if anyone looks glum, confused, or strays from the group.

"They're going through so much, that a day here is like a week, so we can't let them be down in the dumps for very long," says Valencia Thomas, a graduate of this program and now a 20-year-old sophomore at nearby Harvard University. "Their identities are being challenged, broken up and reformed. Being a minority and a high achiever means you have to carry extra baggage about who you are, and where you belong. That puts them at risk."

Tonight, all the students seem to be happy and accounted for. Almost.

Upstairs, Cedric is lying on his bed with the door closed and lights off, waiting for a miracle, that somehow, he will "be able to keep up with the others."

It is slow in coming.

"It's all about proving yourself, really," he says quietly, sitting up. "I'm trying, you know. It's all I can do is try. But where I start from is so far behind where some other kids are, I have to run twice the distance to catch up."

He is cutting back on calls to his mother, not wanting to tell her that things aren't going so well. Barbara Jennings had raised her boy to believe that he can succeed, that he must. When Cedric was a toddler, she quit her clerical job temporarily and went on welfare so that she could take him to museums, read him books, instill in him the importance of getting an education—and getting out.

"I know what she'll say: 'Don't get down, you can do anything you set your mind to,'" Cedric says. "I'm finding out it's not that simple."

Cedric isn't the only student who is falling behind. Moments later, Neda Ramirez's staccato voice echoes across the dormitory courtyard.

"I am so angry," says the Mexican-American teen, who goes to a rough, mostly Hispanic high school in the Texas border town of Edinburg. "I work so hard at my school—I have a 102.7 average—but I'm realizing the school is so awful it doesn't amount to anything. I don't belong here. My father says, 'Learn as much as you can at M.I.T., do your best and accept the consequences.' I said, 'Yeah, Dad, but I'm the one who has to deal with the failure.'"

By the middle of the third week, the detonations of self-doubt become audible. One morning in physics class, Cedric stands at his desk, walks out into the hallway, and screams.

The physics teacher, Thomas Washington, a black 24-year-old Ph.D. candidate at M.I.T., rushes after him. "I told him, 'Cedric, don't be so hard on yourself,'" Mr. Washington recounts later. "I told him that a lot of the material is new to lots of the kids—just keep at it."

But, days after the incident, Mr. Washington vents his frustration at how the deck is stacked against underprivileged students like Cedric and Neda.

"You have to understand that there's a controversy over who these types of programs should serve," he says, sitting in a sunny foyer one morning after class. "If you only took the kids who need this the most, the ones who somehow excel at terrible schools, who swim upstream but are still far behind academically, you wouldn't get enough eventually accepted to M.I.T. to justify the program."

And so the program ends up serving many students who really don't need it. Certainly, M.I.T.'s program—like others at many top colleges—looks very good. More than half its students eventually are offered admission to the freshman class. Those victors, however, are generally students from better schools in better neighborhoods, acknowledges Mr. Ramsey, a black M.I.T. graduate who is the program's administrative director. For some of them, this program is little more than resume-padding.

Mr. Ramsey, 68, had hoped it would be different. Seven years ago, when he took over the program, he had "grand plans, to find late bloomers, and deserving kids in tough spots. But it didn't take me three months to realize I'd be putting kids on a suicide dash."

A six-week program like M.I.T.'s which doesn't offer additional, continuing support, simply can't function if it is filled only with inner-city youths whose educations lag so far behind, he says: "They'd get washed out and everything they believe in would come crashing down on their heads. Listen, we know a lot about suicide rates up here. I'd be raising them."

Perhaps it isn't surprising, then, that while 47 percent of all black children live in poverty in America, only about a dozen students in this year's M.I.T. program would even be considered lower-middle class, according to Mr. Ramsey. Though one or two of the neediest students like Cedric find their way to the program each year, he adds, they tend to be long shots to make it to the next step, into M.I.T. for college. Those few, though, Mr. Ramsey says, are "cases where you could save lives."

Which is why Cedric, more than perhaps any other student in this year's program, hits a nerve.

"I want to take Cedric by the hand and lead him through the material," says physics instructor Mr. Washington, pensively. "But I resist. The real world's not like that. If he makes it to M.I.T., he won't have someone like me to help him."

"You know, part of it I suppose is our fault," he adds. "We haven't figured out a way to give credit for distance traveled."

So, within the program—like society beyond it—a class system is becoming obvious, even to the students. At the top are students like the beautifully dressed Jenica Dover, one of the girls who had found Cedric's diction so amusing. A confident black girl, she attends a mostly white high school in wealthy Newton, Mass. "Some of this stuff is review for me," she says one day, strolling from physics class, where she spent some of the hour giggling with deskmates. "I come from a very good school, and that makes all this pretty manageable."

Cedric, Neda and the few others from poor backgrounds, meanwhile, are left to rely on what has gotten them this far: adrenaline and faith.

On a particularly sour day in mid-July, Cedric's rising doubts seem to overwhelm him. He can't work any harder in calculus, his best subject, yet he still lags behind other students in the class. Physics is becoming a daily nightmare.

Tossing and turning that night, too troubled to sleep, he looks out at the lights of M.I.T., thinking about the sacrifices he has made—the hours of extra work that he begged for from his teachers, the years focusing so single-mindedly on school that he didn't even have friends. "I thought that night that it wasn't ever going to be enough. That I wouldn't make it to M.I.T.," he says later. "That, all this time, I was just fooling myself."

As the hours passed he fell in and out of sleep. Then he awoke with a jolt, suddenly thinking about Cornelia Cunningham, an elder at the Washington Pentecostal church he attends as often as four times a week with his mother. A surrogate grandmother who had challenged and prodded Cedric since he was a small boy, "Mother Cunningham," as he always called her, had died two weeks before he left for M.I.T.

"I was lying there, and her spirit seemed to come to me, I could hear her voice, right there in my room, saying—just like always—'Cedric, you haven't yet begun to fight,'" he recounts. "And the next morning, I woke up and dove into my calculus homework like never before."

The auditorium near M.I.T.'s majestic domed library rings with raucous cheering, as teams prepare their robots for battle. Technically, this is an exercise in ingenuity and teamwork: Each three-student team had been given a box of motors, levers and wheels to design a machine—mostly little cars with hooks on the front—to fight against another team's robot over a small soccer ball.

But something has gone awry. The trios, carefully chosen and mixed in past years by the instructors, were self-selected this year by the students. Clearly, the lines were drawn by race. As the elimination rounds begin, Hispanic teams battle against black teams. "PUERTO RICO, PUERTO RICO," comes the chant from the Hispanic side.

Black students whoop as Cedric's team fights into the quarterfinals, only to lose. He stumbles in mock anguish toward the black section, into the arms of several girls who have become his friends. The winner, oddly enough, is a team led by a Caucasian boy from Oklahoma who is here because he is 1/128 Potawatomi Indian. Both camps are muted.

In the final weeks, the explosive issues of race and class that have been simmering since the students arrive break out into the open. It isn't just black vs. Hispanic or poor vs. rich. It is minority vs. white.

At a lunch table, over cold cuts on whole wheat, talk turns to the ultimate insult: "wanting to be white." Jocelyn Truitt, a black girl from a good Maryland high school, says her mother, a college professor, "started early on telling me to ignore the whole 'white' thing ... I've got white friends. People say things, that I'm trading up, selling out, but I don't listen. Let them talk."

Leslie Chavez says she hears it, too, in her largely Hispanic school. " 'If you get good grades, you're 'white.' What, so you shouldn't do that? Thinking that way is a formula for failure."

In an English class discussion later on the same issue, some students say assimilation is the only answer. "The success of whites means they've mapped out the territory for success," says Alfred Fraijo, a cocky Hispanic from Los Angeles. "If you want to move up and fit in, it will have to be on those terms. There's nothing wrong with aspiring to that—it's worth the price of success."

Cedric listens carefully, but the arguments for assimilation are foreign to him. He knows few whites; in his world, whites have always been the unseen oppressors. "The charge of 'wanting to be white,' where I'm from," Cedric says, "is like treason."

A charge for which he is being called to task, and not just by tough kids in Ballou's hallways. He has had phone conversations over the past few weeks with an old friend from junior high, a boy his age named Torrance Parks, who is trying to convert Cedric to Islam.

"He just says I should stick with my own," says Cedric, "that I'm already betraying my people, leaving them all behind, by coming up to a big white University and all, that even if I'm successful, I'll never be accepted by whites."

Back in Washington, Cedric's mother, a data-input clerk at the Department of Agriculture, is worried. She hopes Cedric will now continue to push forward, to take advantage of scholarships to private prep schools, getting him out of Ballou High for his senior year, "keeping on his path out."

"He needs to get more of what he's getting at M.I.T., more challenging work with nice, hard-working kids—maybe even white kids," she says. The words of Islam, which she fears might lead toward more radical black separatism, would "mean a retreat from all that." She adds that she asks Torrance: "What can you offer my son other than hate?"

She is increasingly frustrated, yet unable to get her son to discuss the issue. When recruiters from Phillips Exeter Academy come to M.I.T. to talk to the students, Cedric snubs them. "They have to wear jacket and tie there; it's elitist," he says, "It's not for me."

Still, in the past few weeks, Cedric has been inching forward. Perseverance finally seems to be paying off. He has risen to near the top of the group in calculus. He is improving in chemistry, adequate in robotics, and showing some potential in English. Physics remains a sore spot.

He also has found his place here. The clutch of middle- and upper-middle-class black girls who once made fun of him has grown fond of him, fiercely protective of him. One Friday night, when Cedric demurs about joining a Saturday group trip to Cape Cod, the girls press him until he finally admits his reason: He doesn't have a bathing suit.

"So we took him to the mall to pick out some trunks," says Isa Williams, the daughter of two Atlanta college professors. "Because he doesn't have maybe as many friends at home, Cedric has a tendency of closing up when he gets sad, and not turning to other people," she adds. "We want him to know we're there for him."

The next day, on the bus, Cedric, at his buoyant best, leads the group in songs.

Though he doesn't want to say it—to jinx anything—by early in the fifth week Cedric is actually feeling a shard of hope. Blackboard scribbles are beginning to make sense, even on the day in late-July when he is thinking only about what will follow classes: a late afternoon meeting with Prof. Trilling, the academic director. This is the meeting Cedric has been waiting for since the moment he arrived, when the professor will assess his progress and—most important—his prospects for someday getting accepted into M.I.T.

Cedric, wound tight, gets lost on the way to Prof. Trilling's office, arriving a few minutes late. Professor Trilling, who is white, ushers the youngster into an office filled with certificates, wide windows, and a dark wood desk. Always conscious of clothes, Cedric tries to break the ice by complimenting Mr. Trilling on his shoes, but the professor doesn't respond, moving right to business.

After a moment, he asks Cedric if he is "thinking about applying and coming to M.I.T."

"Yeah," Cedric says. "I've been wanting to come for years."

"Well, I don't think you're M.I.T. material," the professor says flatly. "Your academic record isn't strong enough."

Cedric, whose average for his junior year was better than perfect, 4.19, thanks to several A+ grades, asks what he means.

The professor explains that Cedric's Scholastic Aptitude Test scores—he has scored only a 910 out of a possible 1600—are about 200 points below what they need to be.

Agitated, Cedric begins insisting that he is willing to work hard, "exceedingly hard," to make it at M.I.T. "He seemed to have this notion that if you work hard enough, you can achieve anything," Prof. Trilling recalls haltingly. "That is admirable, but it also can set up for disappointment. And, at the present time, I told him, that just doesn't seem to be enough."

Ending the meeting, the professor jots down names of professors at Howard University, a black college in Washington, and at the University of Maryland. He suggests that Cedric call them, that if Cedric does well at one of those colleges, he might someday be able to transfer to M.I.T.

Cedric's eyes are wide, his temples bulging, his teeth clenched. He doesn't hear Mr. Trilling's words of encouragement; he hears only M.I.T.'s rejection. He takes the piece of paper from the professor, leaves without a word, and walks across campus and to his dorm room. Crumpling up the note, he throws it in the garbage. He skips dinner that night, ignoring the knocks on his locked door from Isa, Jenica and other worried friends. "I thought about everything," he says, "about what a fool I've been."

The next morning, wandering out into the foyer as calculus class ends, he finally blows. "He made me feel so small, this big," he says, almost screaming, as he presses his fingers close. "'Not M.I.T. material' ... Who is he to tell me that? He doesn't know what I've been through. This is it, right, this is racism. A white guy telling me I can't do it."

Physics class is starting. Cedric slips in, moving, now almost by rote, to the front row—the place he sits in almost every class he has ever taken.

Isa passes him a note: What happened?

He writes a note back describing the meeting and saying he is thinking of leaving, of just going home. The return missive, now also signed by Jenica and a third friend, tells Cedric he has worked too hard to give up. "You can't just run away," the note says, as Isa recalls later. "You have to stay and prove to them you have what it takes. ... We all care about you and love you." Cedric folds the note gently and puts it in his pocket.

The hour ends, with a worksheet Cedric is supposed to hand in barely touched. Taking a thick pencil from his bookbag, he scrawls "I AM LOST" across the blank sheet, drops it on the teacher's desk, and disappears into the crowd.

Jenica runs to catch up with him, to commiserate. But it will be difficult for her to fully understand: In her meeting with Prof. Trilling the next day, he encourages her to enroll at M.I.T. She shrugs off the invitation. "Actually," she tells the professor, "I was planning to go to Stanford."

On a sweltering late-summer day, all three air conditioners are blasting in Cedric's cramped apartment in Washington. Cedric is sitting on his bed, piled high with clothes, one of his bags not yet unpacked even though he returned home from Cambridge several weeks ago.

The last days of the M.I.T. program were fitful. Cedric didn't go to the final banquet, where awards are presented, because he didn't want to see Prof. Trilling again. But he made friends in Cambridge, and on the last morning, as vans were loaded for trips to the airport, he hugged and cried like the rest of them.

"I don't think much about it now, about M.I.T.," he says, as a police car speeds by, its siren barely audible over the air conditioners' whir. "Other things are happening. I have plenty to do."

Not really. Most days since returning from New England, he has spent knocking around the tiny, spare apartment, or going to church, or plodding through applications for colleges and scholarships.

The calls from Torrance, who has been joined in his passion for Islam by Cedric's first cousin, have increased. Cedric says he "just listens," and that "it's hard to argue with" Torrance.

But inside the awkward youngster, a storm rages. Not at home on the hustling streets, and ostracized by high-school peers who see his ambition as a sign of "disrespect," Cedric has discovered that the future he so carefully charted may not welcome him either.

Certainly, he will apply to colleges. And his final evaluations from each M.I.T. class turned out better than he—and perhaps even Prof. Trilling—thought they would. He showed improvement right through the very last day.

But the experience in Cambridge left Cedric bewildered. Private-school scholarship offers, crucial to help underprivileged students make up for lost years before landing in the swift currents of college, have been passed by, despite his mother's urgings. Instead, Cedric Jennings has decided to return to Ballou High, the place from which he has spent the last three years trying to escape.

"I know this may sound crazy," he says, shaking his head. "But I guess I'm sort of comfortable there, at my school. Comfortable in this place that I hate."

ANALYSIS

WHEN RON SUSKIND began reporting "Against All Odds," he says he wanted to convey the war-zone-type similarities between Bosnia and U.S. inner cities. His hard-news lead was designed with that in mind:

Recently, a student was shot dead by a classmate during lunch period outside Frank W. Ballou Senior High. It didn't come as much of a surprise to anyone at the school, in this city's most crime-infested ward. Just during the current school year, one boy was hacked by a student with an axe, a girl was badly wounded in a knife fight with another female student, five fires were set by arsonists, and an unidentified body was dumped next to the parking lot.

After making his point effectively, notice how Suskind quickly starts the next paragraph in a traditional feature style, writing a sentence that could have easily been his lead, if he hadn't wanted the harder start:

But all is quiet in the echoing hallways at 7:15 a.m., long before classes start on a spring morning.

In the concluding part of his two-part series, Suskind chooses a complete feature lead, placing Jennings at the beginning of his M.I.T. experience. In both stories, Suskind uses a compelling ending. But in "Class Struggle," his "circle" close is both powerful and poignant, returning a confused and uncertain Jennings to the hopeless atmosphere of Ballou:

"I know this may sound crazy," he says, shaking his head. "But I guess I'm sort of comfortable there, at my school. Comfortable in this place that I hate."

Despite the demanding two months he spent at Ballou, Suskind eschewed a tape recorder in favor of his notebook. He feels many reporters (including himself) "use less quotes and more description" than they plan in a story. "On the other hand," he notes, "the thing I think most reporters tend not to do is ... write down the little details that evoke place and setting."

As an example of the small, but telling detail, Suskind points to the next-to-the last paragraph of the first story, where Cedric has learned of his acceptance to M.I.T. Suskind notes how Jennings pulls away from his mother's touch, perhaps already leaving her behind. He counsels using subtlety and "not being too overt" in writing such a sentence:

Ms. Jennings reaches out to touch him, to share this moment with him—but he spins out of her reach.

"I can't believe it. I got in," he cries out, holding the letter against his chest, his eyes shut tight. "This is it. My life is about to begin."

Also notice how Suskind etches other memorable details into his work—such as Cedric walking by a stairwell adorned with "HEAD LIVES" graffiti; the yellow "Ballou Soul Tappers" T-shirt Phillip wears with pride at the Kennedy Center and Octavia's mother wearing a "TAKE ME HOME I'M DRUNK" T-shirt.

Such details can "become defining and tell whole stories," Suskind explains. "(Such as) Octavia in class reading *10 Essentials for a Safe Nursery.*" Just saying she was reading *Parents* Magazine wouldn't have been nearly as powerful, he believes.

Although his two stories were written powerfully and authoritatively, seemingly putting Suskind in the middle of every home and situation, *The Wall Street Journal* reporter admits his vigil at the school started haltingly.

"I started to talk to kids and at the beginning it didn't go very well," he explains. He found himself interviewing children with high GPAs in the stilted atmosphere of school conference rooms. He concluded they were being less-than-candid in their answers.

"I realized I needed to just hang around and that's what I did," he says. "I went into the halls, into the classrooms, hung out in the cafeteria, and after a while they got used to me being there."

Finally, Suskind started to figure out the dynamics of the school, and it wasn't pleasant. "In this place, scholarship is considered something of a dishonor," he explains. "Wanting so badly to leave this place behind is considered disrespectful to the many people who will never leave."

Suskind also learned some other Ballou facts of life. For basic survival, top students such as Cedric Jennings have to blend in as well as possible—not carry school books around, raise their hands in class or boast about their grades.

And on the very day he stumbled across Jennings, Suskind also learned all the problems weren't in the classroom, as some of the administrators at Ballou seemed to have views somewhat similar to the young toughs in the hall.

Suskind heard a kid arguing vociferously with the assistant principal over an "A" grade he had received in a class, fighting for the "A+" he felt was deserved. When Suskind asked who the student was, he recalls the following remarkable answer from the assistant principal: "Oh, that's Cedric Jennings. Stay away from him. He's nothing but trouble ... he's an honor student and he's proud of it. He draws a lot of fire around here."

As a white reporter spending months in a tough urban neighborhood, Suskind rarely dodged situations that drew a lot of fire. "If you're a white guy walking the projects, you've got to keep your wits about you, although it's not as dangerous as people believe," he explains.

Suskind once even had a chance to actually test out his "keep your wits about you" theory. "At one point I was actually looking for the apartment where Phillip lived in a very bad project," he remembers. "[I was in my] reporter's trench coat and driving a bland American car, essentially a surrogate cop."

The reporter next violated several of his internal survival rules by wandering aimlessly and looking confused while flipping through his notebook. Immediately, he looked up into the faces of two project residents who were sizing him up. "One of them says, 'FBI or DEA? You choose,'" Suskind laughs. "I said, 'I'm actually with Bnai Brith women.' He cracked up. He thought it was funny as hell."

When Suskind wrote his first draft of "Against All Odds," it was constructed far differently than the final version. Cedric Jennings, for example, was just one of many characters. "We stuck with the original plan of writing about an ensemble of kids," he says. "Each were weighted about equally, including some sophomores who were just deciding which way to go. In fact, the two girls, Alicia and Octavia, were part of the group, along with Cedric and Phillip."

When he turned in that story, Suskind recalls the page one editor of the *Journal* being pleased. "He called me up and said, 'this is great. Just what we decided we wanted. But, you know, the voice of this Cedric kid is particularly resonant, wouldn't you agree?' "

Suskind was dismayed but had to reluctantly concur. "The thing that made the story even better was not compromising even a little bit," he recalls. "I went back and spent a few more weeks with Cedric and Phillip and made Cedric the centerpiece of the story, with Phillip a supporting character."

His willingness to listen, yet not compromise the quality of the work, led to a stunning two-part series that impressed everyone—including the Pulitzer judges.

RON SUSKIND is assigned to *The Wall Street Journal*'s Washington Bureau. He earned bachelor's degrees in both government and foreign affairs from the University of Virginia, followed by a master's degree from Columbia University's Graduate School of Journalism. Suskind is currently writing a book on these two stories.

1996

RICK BRAGG

RICK BRAGG AND HOWELL RAINES have a lot in common. Both work for *The New York Times*. Both are Southerners with a courtly manner. And both have a rare ability to write truly lyrical copy that won the Pulitzer Prize.

"Howell Raines is the legend," Bragg believes. "He's the newspaper writer we all want to emulate, someone we would like to be."

Bragg is too modest to state the obvious.

Alert readers will have noticed by now that many of the Pulitzer Prize-winning features in this anthology could have won awards in other categories. In fact, many entries were initially considered in categories such as national, service and explanatory journalism before being moved to features.

But not Rick Bragg's winning package, an innovative mix of features, profiles and news features. Although none are the long, passionate "rainmaker" variety found elsewhere in this book, Bragg's magnificent feature stories could easily be called story features. The Pulitzer board agreed, citing Bragg for "elegantly written stories about contemporary America."

Now based at the *Times'* Southern Bureau in Atlanta, Bragg also worked for the *Times* as a metro reporter. "Like a lot of country boys, I was shocked by Manhattan, the Bronx, Brooklyn and everything else. But I loved the stories."

Perhaps as a result of his hard-news experience, Bragg doesn't have any second thoughts about his decision. "I consider myself a feature writer," Bragg says in a soft Southern drawl. "A lot of people are afraid of that word. The fact is, I make my living in this business by taking the news and wrapping people into it. If that's a feature writer, than I guess that's what I am.

"Some of [my stories] like the Oklahoma City story, was really a feature, but it was a deadline story. ... The story on Howard Wells [The sheriff who took the confession from Susan

Smith] wasn't a tight deadline story but it still had to be done shortly after the verdict. "But the others didn't take more than a few days to do."

Like previous *Times* writers, Bragg was aware he had made the final cut for the Pulitzer. "I knew I was a finalist after the ASNE award came out [his second] and they called to congratulate me. Of course, no one is supposed to tell you [you're a Pulitzer finalist] and of course 5,000 people do, so you can agonize for a month and a half."

Bragg says he felt the award would go to Rick Meyer of the *Los Angeles Times Magazine,* for the profile of a woman's efforts to communicate after being left mute and paralyzed by a stroke. "It was just an awfully strong story," Bragg concedes. "[But] what I think I had going for me were [my pieces] were a variety of big national stories. I'm not going to pretend I didn't want to win this thing," he laughs. "I'm not that big a liar."

Bragg vividly remembers the day he discovered the prize was forthcoming. "The day they were announced, I had flown to Dulles Airport to interview the head of the NRA [and] had gotten there early and was taking a walk near a mall in Fairfax, Va." Bragg decided to call his New York office, only to learn that one of his editors, Joe Lelyveld, was urgently trying to reach him.

Bragg recalls thinking: "I've either been fired or I won the Pulitzer." He nervously continued to walk ("in my *New York Times*-issue blue suit and my *New York Times*-issue black brogan shoes"), stopping to call from every gas station he passed.

"Finally, I got him," Bragg says. "All he said was, 'where are you going to be tomorrow? ... Can you meet me for lunch in New York?' And then I knew, but he still wouldn't tell me. He said, 'I will have to demystify you tomorrow.'"

But one more problem soon developed, and "this is the honest-to-God truth," Bragg swears. "I had not planned on being gone overnight. I didn't take a toothbrush, not even a clean pair of underwear."

To get to New York, Bragg spent hours sitting in airports, afraid to pick up the phone and share his news until it was confirmed. He eventually arrived in New York too late to even buy underwear. "So on one of the greatest nights of my life, I hang my shirt over the air conditioner so the air will blow on it. I take off my underwear and wash it with some of that beautifully-perfumed Sheraton shampoo and wash my socks in the sink.

The only way to get my underwear to dry is over the lamp shade."

Bragg did finally make it to that lunch for his "demystification," but it's not nearly as humorous a story as the actual trip.

All She Has, $150,000, Is Going to a University

The New York Times

August 13, 1995

OSEOLA MCCARTY spent a lifetime making other people look nice. Day after day, for most of her 87 years, she took in bundles of dirty clothes and made them clean and neat for parties she never attended, weddings to which she was never invited, graduations she never saw.

She had quit school in the sixth grade to go to work, never married, never had children and never learned to drive because there was never any place in particular she wanted to go. All she ever had was the work, which she saw as a blessing. Too many other black people in rural Mississippi did not have even that.

She spent almost nothing, living in her old family home, cutting the toes out of shoes if they did not fit right and binding her ragged Bible with Scotch tape to keep Corinthians from falling out. Over the decades, her pay—mostly dollar bills and change—grew to more than $150,000.

"More than I could ever use," Miss McCarty said the other day without a trace of self-pity. So she is giving her money away, to finance scholarships for black students at the University of Southern Mississippi here in her hometown, where tuition is $2,400 a year.

"I wanted to share my wealth with the children," said Miss McCarty, whose only real regret is that she never went back to school. "I never minded work, but I was always so busy, busy. Maybe I can make it so the children don't have to work like I did."

People in Hattiesburg call her donation the Gift. She made it, in part, in anticipation of her death.

As she sat in her warm, dark living room, she talked of that death matter-of-factly, the same way she talked about the possibility of an afternoon thundershower. To her, the Gift was a preparation, like closing the bedroom windows to keep the rain from blowing in on the bedspread.

"I know it won't be too many years before I pass on," she said, "and I just figured the money would do them a lot more good than it would me."

Her donation has piqued interest around the nation. In a few short days, Oseola McCarty, the washerwoman, has risen from obscurity to a notice she does not understand. She sits in her little frame house, just blocks from the university, and patiently greets the reporters, business leaders and others who line up outside her door.

"I live where I want to live, and I live the way I want to live," she said. "I couldn't drive a car if I had one. I'm too old to go to college. So I planned to do this. I planned it myself."

It has been only three decades since the university integrated. "My race used to not get to go to that college," she said. "But now they can."

When asked why she had picked this university instead of a predominantly black institution, she said, "Because it's here; it's close."

While Miss McCarty does not want a building named for her or a statue in her honor, she would like one thing in return: to attend the graduation of a student who made it through college because of her gift. "I'd like to see it," she said.

Business leaders in Hattiesburg, 110 miles northeast of New Orleans, plan to match her $150,000, said Bill Pace, the executive director of the University of Southern Mississippi Foundation, which administers donations to the school.

"I've been in the business 24 years now, in private fund raising," Mr. Pace said. "And this is the first time I've experienced anything like this from an individual who simply was not affluent, did not have the resources and yet gave substantially. In fact, she gave almost everything she has.

"No one approached her from the university; she approached us. She's seen the poverty, the young people who have struggled, who need an education. She is the most unselfish individual I have ever met."

Although some details are still being worked out, the $300,000— Miss McCarty's money and the matching sum—will finance scholarships into the indefinite future. The only stipulation is that the beneficiaries be black and live in southern Mississippi.

The college has already awarded a $1,000 scholarship in Miss

McCarty's name to an 18-year-old honors student from Hattiesburg, Stephanie Bullock.

Miss Bullock's grandmother, Ledrester Hayes, sat in Miss McCarty's tiny living room the other day and thanked her. Later, when Miss McCarty left the room, Mrs. Hayes shook her head in wonder.

"I thought she would be some little old rich lady with a fine car and a fine house and clothes," she said. "I was a seamstress myself, worked two jobs. I know what it's like to work like she did, and she gave it away."

The Oseola McCarty Scholarship Fund bears the name of a woman who bought her first air-conditioner just three years ago and even now turns it on only when company comes. Miss McCarty also does not mind that her tiny black-and-white television set gets only one channel, because she never watches anyway. She complains that her electricity bill is too high and says she never subscribed to a newspaper because it cost too much.

The pace of Miss McCarty's walks about the neighborhood is slowed now, and she misses more Sundays than she would like at Friendship Baptist Church. Arthritis has left her hands stiff and numb. For the first time in almost 80 years, her independence is threatened.

"Since I was a child, I've been working, washing the clothes of doctors, lawyers, teachers, police officers," she said. "But I can't do it no more. I can't work like I used to."

She is 5 feet tall and would weigh 100 pounds with rocks in her pockets. Her voice is so soft that it disappears in the squeak of the screen door and the hum of the air-conditioner.

She comes from a wide place in the road called Shubuta, Miss., a farming town outside Meridian, not far from the Alabama line. She quit school, she said, when the grandmother who reared her became ill and needed care.

"I would have gone back," she said, "but the people in my class had done gone on, and I was too big. I wanted to be with my class."

So she worked, and almost every dollar went into the bank. In time, all her immediate family died. "And I didn't have nobody," she said. "But I stayed busy."

She took a short vacation once, as a young woman, to Niagara Falls. The roar of the water scared her. "Seemed like the world was coming to an end," she said.

She stayed home, mostly, after that. She has lived alone since 1967.

Earlier this year her banker asked what she wanted done with her money when she passed on. She told him that she wanted to give it to the university, now rather than later; she set aside just enough to live on.

She says she does not want to depend on anyone after all these years, but she may have little choice. She has been informally adopted by the first young person whose life was changed by her gift.

As a young woman, Stephanie Bullock's mother wanted to go to the University of Southern Mississippi. But that was during the height of the integration battles, and if she had tried her father might have lost his job with the city.

It looked as if Stephanie's own dream of going to the university would also be snuffed out, for lack of money. Although she was president of her senior class in high school and had grades that were among the best there, she fell just short of getting an academic scholarship. Miss Bullock said her family earned too much money to qualify for most Federal grants but not enough to send her to the university.

Then, last week, she learned that the university was giving her $1,000, in Miss McCarty's name. "It was a total miracle," she said, "and an honor."

She visited Miss McCarty to thank her personally and told her that she planned to "adopt" her. Now she visits regularly, offering to drive Miss McCarty around and filling a space in the tiny woman's home that has been empty for decades.

She feels a little pressure, she concedes, not to fail the woman who helped her. "I was thinking how amazing it was that she made all that money doing laundry," said Miss Bullock, who plans to major in business.

She counts on Miss McCarty's being there four years from now, when she graduates.

Terror in Oklahoma City at Ground Zero

April 20, 1995

BEFORE THE DUST and the rage had a chance to settle, a chilly rain started to fall on the blasted-out wreck of what had once been an office building, and on the shoulders of the small army of police, fire fighters and medical technicians that surrounded it.

They were not used to this, if anyone is. On any other day, they would have answered calls to kitchen fires, domestic disputes, or even a cat up a tree. Oklahoma City is still, in some ways, a small town, said the people who live here.

This morning, as the blast trembled the morning coffee in cups miles away, the outside world came crashing hard onto Oklahoma City.

"I just took part in a surgery where a little boy had part of his brain hanging out of his head," said Terry Jones, a medical technician, as he searched in his pocket for a cigarette. Behind him, fire fighters picked carefully through the skeleton of the building, still searching for the living and the dead.

"You tell me," he said, "how can anyone have so little respect for human life."

The shock of what the rescuers found in the rubble had long since worn off, replaced with a loathing for the people who had planted the bomb that killed their friends, neighbors and children.

One by one they said the same thing: this does not happen here. It happens in countries so far away, so different, they might as well be on the dark side of the moon. It happens in New York. It happens in Europe.

It does not happen in a place where, debarking at the airport, passengers see a woman holding a sign that welcomes them to the Lieutenant Governor's annual turkey shoot.

It does not happen in a city that has a sign just outside the city limits, "Oklahoma City, Home of Vince Gill," the country singer.

"We're just a little old cowtown," said Bill Finn, a grime-covered fire fighter who propped himself wearily up against a brick wall as the rain turned the dust to mud on his face. "You can't get no more Middle America than Oklahoma City. You don't have terrorism in Middle America."

But it did happen here, in such a loathsome way.

Whatever kind of bomb it was—a crater just outside the building suggests a car bomb—it was intended to murder on a grand scale: women, children, old people coming to complain about their Social Security checks.

The destruction was almost concave in nature, shattering the building from the center, almost front to back, the blast apparently weakening as it spread to both sides of the structure. Blood-stained glass littered the inside. So complete was the destruction that panels and signs from offices several stories up were shattered on the ground floor.

People could not stop looking at it, particularly the second floor, where a child care center had been.

"A whole floor," said Randy Woods, a fire fighter with Engine No. 7. "A whole floor of innocents. Grown-ups, you know, they deserve a lot of the stuff they get. But why the children? What did the children ever do to anybody?"

Everywhere observers looked, there were the discarded gloves, some blood-stained, of the medical workers.

There seemed to be very little whole inside the lower floors of the building, only pieces—pieces of desks, desktop computers and in one place what appeared to be the pieces of plastic toy animals, perhaps from the child care center, perhaps just some of those goofy little things grown-ups keep on their desks.

Much of it was covered in a fine powder, almost like ash, from the concrete that was not just broken, but blasted into dust. One fire fighter said he picked through the big and small pieces almost afraid to move them, afraid of what he would find underneath. Here and there, in a droplet or a smear, was blood.

One woman, one of many trapped by rubble, had to have her leg amputated before she could be freed. Earlier in the morning, fire fighters had heard voices drifting out from behind concrete and twisted metal, people they could hear but could not get to.

A few blocks away, Jason Likens, a medical technician, wondered aloud how anyone could have walked away unhurt. "I didn't expect to find anybody living," he said.

He was sickened by what he saw, but did not know who to hate.

"I would get mad, but I don't know who to get mad at," he said.

Next door, a group of grim-faced medical technicians, police and others gathered just outside the foyer of a church, not to pray, but to watch over the dead that had been temporarily laid inside in black body bags.

The stained-glass windows of the brick building had been partly blasted out, with a few scenes hanging in jagged pieces from the frames, but it was still the most peaceful place for blocks.

"I hope this opens people's eyes," Mr. Woods, the firefighter, said. What he meant was, it should show people everywhere that there really is no safe place, if a terrorist is fanatical enough.

Like others, he believes it was intended to send a message to the United States: not even your heartland is safe.

A few blocks away, two elderly women slowly made their way up the street, their faces and clothes bloody.

They are retirees, living in an apartment building next door to the office building that was the target of the explosion. Phyllis Graham and Allene Craig had felt safe there. But this morning, as the glass went flying through their home, life changed forever.

"It all just came apart," Ms. Craig said. It was not clear if she meant her building, or something else.

Where Alabama Inmates Fade into Old Age

November 1, 1995

GRANT COOPER knows he lives in prison, but there are days when he cannot remember why. His crimes flit in and out of his memory like flies through a hole in a screen door, so that sometimes his mind and conscience are blank and clean.

He used to be a drinker and a drifter who had no control over his rage. In 1978, in an argument with a man in a bread line at the Forgotten Man Ministry in Birmingham, Ala., his hand automatically slid into his pants pocket for a knife.

He cut the man so quick and deep that he died before his body slipped to the floor. Mr. Cooper had killed before, in 1936 and in 1954, so the judge gave him life. Back then, before he needed help to go to the bathroom, Mr. Cooper was a dangerous man.

Now he is 77, and since his stroke in 1993 he mostly just lies in his narrow bunk at the Hamilton Prison for the Aged and Infirm, a blue blanket hiding the tubes that run out of his bony body. Sometimes the other inmates put him in a wheelchair and park him in the sun.

"I'm lost," he mumbled. "I'm just lost."

He is a relic of his violent past, but Mr. Cooper, and the special prison that holds him, may represent the future of corrections in a time when judges and other politicians are offering longer, "true-time" sentences, like life without parole, as a way to protect the public from crime.

This small 200-bed prison in the pine-shrouded hills of northwestern Alabama near the Mississippi line is one of only a few in the nation specializing in aged and disabled inmates, but that is expected to change as prison populations turn gradually gray.

While the proportion of older prisoners has risen only slightly in recent years, their numbers have jumped substantially. In 1989, the nation's prisons held 30,500 inmates 50 or older; by 1993, that number had risen to almost 50,500, according to the American Civil Liberties Union's National Prison Project.

But experts say the major increases are still to come.

"Three-strikes" sentencing for habitual offenders and new laws that require inmates to serve all or most of their sentences, instead of just a fraction, will mean "an aging phenomenon" in American prisons, said James Austin, the executive vice president of the National Council on Crime and Delinquency in San Francisco.

"There are going to be huge geriatric wards," said Jenni Gainsborough, a lawyer with the National Prison Project.

The older inmates will fill beds needed for younger criminals who are more of a threat, said Burl Cain, warden at the Angola State Penitentiary in Louisiana, the nation's largest maximum-security prison. "We need our prison beds for the predators who are murdering people today," he said.

Locked away for good, inmates will need special medical care and will have to be housed inside separate cellblocks, or separate prisons like Hamilton, to protect them from younger, stronger predators, said W.C. Berry, the warden at Hamilton.

"What else can we do with them?" he said.

Once Dangerous Now Helpless

One Hamilton inmate, Thomas Gurley, has Huntington's disease. He sits in a chair all day and shakes and stares. He was a kidnapper, but now he has trouble holding a spoon.

It may seem cruel to lock a man away and watch him slowly die, Mr. Berry said, but most of the men in his care could not survive in the general population. Some are missing legs, some have misplaced their minds, some are just too old. They have heart, kidney or liver failure and need machines to keep them alive.

Some victims' rights groups see the slow death of these men as poetic justice and say they should take their chances in the general population, to see what it is like to live in fear.

But Mr. Berry, who built a reputation as a no-nonsense police detective before coming here, has seen what men do to each other in prison. Inmates who are getting old write him letters and beg to transfer to his prison, which has been in operation since Federal lawsuits in the 1970's obliged the state to separate its weaker inmates.

"They sort of look out for each other here," he said. The inmates who can work strip beds and help clean up after the old, most help-less ones. When Mr. Gurley slips from his chair to the floor, other inmates lift him back in.

There are prison breaks, but the escapees do not usually get far. Two inmates, one blind, one mostly blind and unable to breathe on his own, made it as far as the town hospital. It is across the street.

"We had another one get out, and we found him at the end of the runway of the local airport," Warden Berry said. "He couldn't breathe that well. I told him that if he hadn't had to stop every fourth landing light to take a breath, he might have made it."

Mr. Cooper travels only in his mind. "I don't know if they'll ever set me free," he said, looking up from his bed, a pair of black-framed glasses sitting crooked on his face. "I don't know. I don't reckon so."

Some days, if he forgets enough, he already is.

Life at the End of the Whisky River

All Jessie Hatcher's life, the devil in him would come swimming out every time a drink of whisky trickled in.

"It was 1979, down in Pike County," he said, looking down some dusty road in his memory for the life he took. "Me and this boy was drinking. He thought I had some money, but I didn't have none. We took to fighting, and I killed him. Quinn. His name was Quinn. Killed him with a .32. I was bad to drink back then. I never drunk another drop."

Like Grant Cooper, he has a life history of violence. He shot a woman several times with a .22 rifle in 1978, but she lived and he served less than a year. He was drunk then. The murder of the man in Pike County sent him away for life.

He is 76 now and limps on a cane because of a broken leg that never healed right. He works all day in the flower garden, where he has raked the dirt so smooth you can roll marbles on it.

"My favorites are the saucer sunflowers," he said, "because they're so beautiful."

The young man, the one whose life was washed away on a river of whisky, seems to have vanished inside this wizened little man on his knees in the mud, plucking weeds and humming spirituals.

"They could take the fences down and I wouldn't run," he said. "This is the right place for me."

"Lock me down in one of them other prisons, and I'd drop like a top," he said, referring to the practice in general prisons of locking aged or infirm inmates in cells to protect them.

How to Best Use Precious Cell Space

The State of Alabama, often criticized for taking prison reform in the wrong direction with its return to leg irons and breaking rocks, is part of a more progressive trend with Hamilton, said Ms. Gainsborough of the Civil Liberties Union.

But while the prison is hailed as a humane answer, the practice of keeping old inmates until death is wasting crucial space, said Mr. Cain, the Angola warden.

"There comes a time when a man goes through what we call criminal menopause and he is unable to do the crime that he is here for," Mr. Cain said. "My prison is becoming an old folks' home."

He sees nothing wrong with letting an old killer die free after prison has taken most of his life from him. As politicians shout for life sentences, he watches helplessly as Angola, with 3,000 inmates doing life, fills beyond capacity.

"When the criminal is not able to commit that crime again, it's time to put someone in there who is killing now," said Mr. Cain, who keeps older inmates in a special ward. "As Jesus Christ said, 'Let the dead bury the dead.' We don't have room."

For some inmates at Hamilton, keeping them locked away for life is the only alternative. Jason Riley, 41, has been partially blind since a car hit him when he was 3. He killed two women by stabbing and strangling them, then cut his own arms to watch himself bleed. He has said he would kill again.

"I'll probably die here," said Mr. Riley, who carries a magnifying glass in his pocket to see with. One of his gray eyes looms huge behind it as he gazes at you. "I accept that, accepted it several years ago. Life would be easier for some of the other inmates if they would accept it, too."

The Repercussions of a Political Trend

Sentences, especially life sentences, used to be like rubber bands. They stretched or snapped short depending on the inmate's record in prison, crowding and, sometimes, whether the inmate could convince the parole board that he had found the Lord. Inmates like the 76-year-old Mr. Hatcher could usually walk after 20 years, even with a murder conviction. But that was before it became so popular for politicians to run on pro-death-penalty, throw-away-the-key platforms.

"I'd like to be free," Mr. Hatcher said, "for a little while."

He has a feeling he will be, he said, and winks, as if some higher power has whispered in his ear that this will happen.

Warden Berry, standing beside him, looks away. It is common for a man doing life without parole to have that feeling, even though he knows chances are he will leave on a hospital gurney, or with a blanket over his head.

"They think, 'I just want a few years at the end of my life, free,'" he said. "You'll see them, men in their 70's, suddenly start walking around out in the prison yard, trying to take care of themselves, to save themselves for it.

"And some we have who wake up in the middle of the night in a cold sweat, because the thought of going out terrifies them."

They know that they have lived so long inside, everything they knew or loved outside will be gone, he said. So when they walk out the door, they will be completely alone.

The Birmingham jail was full of martyrs and heroes in the 1960's. The Rev. Dr. Martin Luther King Jr. made history locked behind its walls.

William (Tex) Johnson, who snatched $24 from a man's hand and got caught, was in fancy company. But as the civil rights heroes rejoined their struggle, a white judge gave him 50 years.

He escaped three times. "You can't give no 21-year-old boy 50 years; I had to run," he said. While he was out, he committed 38 more crimes. Now he is at Hamilton, finishing his sentence. He will be released in 1998, but two strokes have left him mostly dead on one side. "I believe I can make it," he said. "I believe I can."

There will be nothing on the outside for him. Warden Berry said that when an inmate reached a certain point, it might be more humane to keep him in prison. Wives die, children stop coming to see him.

"We bury most of them ourselves, on state land," he said. The undertaking and embalming class at nearby Jefferson State University prepares the bodies for burial for free, for the experience.

"They make 'em up real nice," the warden said.

A Killer's Only Confidant: The Man Who Caught Susan Smith

August 4, 1995

THE CASE OF A lifetime is closed for Howard Wells. The reporters and the well-wishers have begun to drift away, leaving the Union County sheriff at peace. He will try to do a little fishing when the police radio is quiet, or just sit with his wife, Wanda, and talk of anything but the murderer Susan Smith.

It bothers him a little that he told a lie to catch her, but he can live with the way it all turned out. Mrs. Smith has been sentenced to life in prison.

Still, now and then his mind drifts back to nine days last autumn, and he thinks how it might have gone if he had been clumsy, if he had mishandled it. It leaves him a little cold.

For those nine days—from Mrs. Smith's drowning of her two little boys on Oct. 25 until she finally confessed on Nov. 3—he handled her like a piece of glass, afraid her brittle psyche would shatter and leave him with the jagged edges of a case that might go unsolved for weeks, months or forever.

"Susan was all we had," Sheriff Wells said, sitting in his living room the other day with a sweating glass of ice tea in his hand. If he had lost her to suicide, or to madness, because he had pushed too hard, there would have been nowhere else to turn. There had been no accomplices, no confidants, no paper trails.

The manhunt for the fictitious young black man she had accused of taking her children in a carjacking would have continued. The bodies of the boys would have continued to rest at the bottom of nearby John D. Long Lake, under 18 feet of water. The people of the county would have been left to wonder, blame and hate, divided by race and opinion over what truly happened the night she gave her babies to the lake.

Even if the car had been found, it would have yielded no proof, no clues, that everything had not happened just as she said, Mr. Wells continued. He would have been left not only with the unsolved crime but also with the burden of having driven a distraught and—for all anyone would know—innocent woman to suicide at the age of 23.

Mr. Wells says he has no doubt that he and other investigators walked a tightrope with Mrs. Smith's mental state and that as the inquiry closed around her, she planned to kill herself. For nine days she lived in a hell of her own making, surrounded by weeping, doting relatives she had betrayed in the worst way. "She had no one to turn to," he said.

So although he was her hunter, he also became the person she could lean on, rely on, trust. But unlike Mrs. Smith, he had no way of knowing that the boys were already dead, had no way of knowing that they were not locked in a car or a closet, freezing, starving.

Someday the Smith case will be in law-enforcement textbooks. The Federal Bureau of Investigation has already asked Mr. Wells to put down in writing the procedures he used in the case, as well as any useful anecdotes from it.

But the story of how he, with the help of others, was able to bring the investigation to a close in little more than a week begins not with anything he did but with who he is.

Mr. Wells, 43, is the antithesis of the redneck Southern sheriff. He has deer heads mounted on his wall but finished at the top of his class in the F.B.I. Academy's training course. He collects guns but quotes Supreme Court decisions off the top of his head.

"I'm not a smart fellow," he said. But tell that to the people who work for him and around him, and they just roll their eyes. When the attention of the nation turned to Union County in those nine days last fall, and in much of the nine months since, "we were lucky he was here," said Hugh Munn, a spokesman for the State Department of Law Enforcement.

People in the county say they like him because he is one of them. He knows what it feels like to work eight hours a day in the nerve-straining clatter and roar of the textile mills that dominate Union's economy; after high school, he worked blue-collar jobs until he was hired by the town's police force at the age of 23.

He went on to be a deputy in the county Sheriff's Department. Then, for several years, he stalked poachers and drug peddlers as an agent with the State Wildlife and Marine Resources Division.

When his brother-in-law quit as sheriff in 1992, Mr. Wells himself ran, as a 10-to-1 underdog. He promised not to operate under a good ol' boy system of favors gained and owed, and white voters and black voters liked his plain-spokenness and the fact that he was neither backslapper nor backscratcher.

He won, by just 10 votes. His mother, Julia Mae, was then in the hospital dying of cancer. She had lain there unmoving for hours but opened her eyes when he walked in after the election.

"Who won?" she asked.

His father, John, has Lou Gehrig's disease, and every day Mr. Wells goes by to care for him. The sheriff went without sleep when the Susan Smith saga began on Oct. 25 but did not skip his visits to his father.

The Wellses have no children. Wanda suffered a miscarriage a few years ago, so they have become godparents to children of friends and neighbors. The Smith case pitted a man who wants children against a woman who threw hers away.

His investigation had to take two tracks. One, using hundreds of volunteers and a national crime computer web, operated on the theory that Mrs. Smith was telling the truth. The other, the one that would build a bond between a weeping mother and a doubting sheriff, focused on her.

Mr. Wells says Mrs. Smith never imagined, would never have believed, that the disappearance of her children would bring in the F.B.I., the state police, national news organizations. He thinks that when she concocted her story, she believed that the loss of the boys would pass like any other local crime.

Like other investigators, he was suspicious of her early on. As he talked to her only minutes after she had reported her children missing, he asked her whether the carjacker had done anything to her sexually. She smiled.

It would be months before the comprehensive history of her troubled life, of suicide attempts, sexual molestation, deep depression and affairs with married men, including her own stepfather, became known. But as bits and pieces of it fell from her lips during questioning, and as cracks appeared in her already unstable mental state, Mr. Wells began to realize that Mrs. Smith, and the case, could come apart in his hands.

He had to hold her together even as he and other investigators picked her story apart, had to coax and soothe and even pray beside her, until he sensed that the time was right to confront her and try to trick her into confessing.

And he had to shield her from others, who might push too hard. Once, on Oct. 27, a state agent accused her outright. She cursed loudly and stormed away.

After that, the people who had contact with her were limited. With the assistance of Pete Logan, a warm, grandfatherly former F.B.I. agent now with the state police, Mr. Wells asked for her help in finding the boys, but did not accuse her.

The whole time, her family, her hometown and much of America were following her story, sharing her agony.

"She couldn't turn to her family, she couldn't ask for an attorney," said Mr. Wells. "She painted herself into a corner where no one could help her."

On Nov. 3, he told her, gently, that he knew she was lying, that by coincidence his own deputies had been undercover on a narcotics case at the same crossroad where she said her babies had been stolen, and at the same time, and that the officers had seen nothing. Actually there had been no such stakeout.

He prayed with her again, holding her hands, and she confessed. "I had a problem telling the lie," he said as his story unfolded in his living room the other day. "But if that's what it takes, I'd do it again."

After the confession was signed, as she sat slumped over in her chair, there was still one thing he had to know.

"Susan," he asked, "how would all this have played out?"

"I was going to write you a letter," she said, "and kill myself."

He feels sorry for her, and is disgusted by the men who used her and in their own ways contributed to the tragedy. But he is not surprised that a 23-year-old mill secretary could fool the whole nation, at least for a little while.

"Susan Smith is smart in every area," he said, "except life."

Another Battle of New Orleans: Mardi Gras

February 19, 1995

THE LITTLE SHOTGUN house is peeling and the Oldsmobile in front is missing a rear bumper, but Larry Bannock can glimpse glory through the eye of his needle. For almost a year he has hunkered over his sewing table, joining beads, velvet, rhinestones, sequins, feathers and ostrich plumes into a Mardi Gras costume that is part African, part Native American.

"I'm pretty," said Mr. Bannock, who is 6 feet tall and weighs 300 pounds. "And baby, when I walk out that door there ain't nothing cheap on me."

Most days, this 46-year-old black man is a carpenter, welder and handyman, but on Mardi Gras morning he is a Big Chief, one of the celebrated—if incongruous—black Indians of Carnival. He is an important man.

Sometime around 11 A.M. on Feb. 28, Mr. Bannock, will step from his house in a resplendent, flamboyant turquoise costume complete with a towering headdress, and people in the largely black and poor 16th and 17th Wards, the area known as Gert Town, will shout, cheer and follow him through the streets, dancing, drumming and singing.

"That's my glory," he said. Like the other Big Chiefs, he calls it his "mornin' glory."

He is one of the standard-bearers of a uniquely New Orleans tradition. The Big Chiefs dance, sing and stage mock battles—wars of words and rhymes—to honor American Indians who once gave sanctuary to escaped slaves. It is an intense but elegant posturing, a street theater that some black men devote a lifetime to.

But this ceremony is also self-affirmation, the way poor blacks in New Orleans honor their own culture in a Carnival season that might otherwise pass them by, said the Big Chiefs who carry on the tradition, and the academics who study it.

These Indians march mostly in neighborhoods where the tourists do not go, ride on the hoods of dented Chevrolets instead of floats, and face off on street corners where poverty and violence grip the people most of the rest of the year. The escape is temporary, but it is escape.

"They say Rex is ruler," said Mr. Bannock, referring to the honorary title given to the king of Carnival, often a celebrity, who will glide through crowds of tourists and local revelers astride an elaborate float. "But not in the 17th Ward. 'Cause I'm the king here. This is our thing.

"The drums will be beating and everybody will be hollering and"—he paused to stab the needle through a mosaic of beads and canvas—"and it sounds like all my people's walking straight through hell."

A man does not need an Oldsmobile, with or without a bumper, if he can walk on air. Lifted there by the spirit of his neighborhood, it is his duty to face down the other Big Chiefs, to cut them down with words instead of bullets and straight razors, the way the Indians used to settle their disagreements in Mardi Gras in the early 1900s. Mr. Bannock, shot in the thigh by a jealous old chief in 1981, appears to be the last to have been wounded in battle.

"I forgave him," Mr. Bannock said.

The tribes have names like the Yellow Pocahontas, White Eagles, the Golden Star Hunters and the Wild Magnolias. The Big Chiefs are not born, but work their way up through the ranks. Only the best sewers and singers become Big Chiefs.

By tradition, the chiefs must sew their own costumes, and must do a new costume from scratch each year. Mr. Bannock's fingers are scarred from a lifetime of it. His right index finger is a mass of old punctures. Some men cripple themselves, through puncture wounds or repetitive motion, and have to retire. The costumes can cost $5,000 or more, a lot of cash in Gert Town.

The rhythms of their celebration, despite their feathered headdresses, seem more West African or Haitian than Indian, and the words are from the bad streets of the Deep South. Mr. Bannock said that no matter what the ceremony's origins, it belongs to New Orleans now. The battle chants have made their way into popular New Orleans music. The costumes hang in museums.

"Maybe it don't make no sense, and it ain't worth anything," said Mr. Bannock. But one day a year he leads his neighborhood on a hard, forced march to respect, doing battle at every turn with other chiefs who are out trying to do the same.

Jimmy Ricks is a 34-year-old concrete finisher most of the year, but on Mardi Gras morning he is a Spy Boy, the man who goes out ahead of the Big Chief searching for other chiefs. He is in love with the tradition, he said, because of what it means to people here.

"It still amazes me," he said, how on Mardi Gras mornings the people from the neighborhood drift over to Mr. Bannock's little house on Edinburgh Street and wait for a handyman to lead them.

"To understand it, you got to let your heart wander," said Mr. Bannock, who leads the Golden Star Hunters. "All I got to do is peek through my needle."

> *I'm 52 inches across my chest*
> *And I don't bow to nothin'*
> *'Cept God and death*
> —from a battle chant by Larry Bannock

The more exclusive party within the party—the grand balls and societies that underlie the reeling, alcohol-soaked celebration that is Carnival—have always been By Invitation Only.

The origins of Carnival, which climaxes with Mardi Gras, or Fat Tuesday, are found in the Christian season of celebration before Lent. In New Orleans the celebration reaches back more than 150 years, to loosely organized parades in the 1830s. One of the oldest Carnival organizations, the Mystick Krewe of Comus, staged the first organized parade. Today, Mardi Gras is not one parade but several, including that of the traditional Zulus, a black organization. But Comus, on Fat Tuesday, is still king.

The krewes were—some still are—secret societies. The wealthier whites and Creoles, many of whom are descendants of people of color who were free generations before the Civil War, had balls and parades, while poorer black men and women cooked the food and parked the cars.

Mardi Gras had no other place for them, said Dr. Frederick Stielow, director of Tulane University's Amistad Research Center, the largest minority archive in the nation. And many of these poorer blacks still are not part of the party, he said.

"These are people who were systematically denigrated," said Dr. Stielow, who has studied the Mardi Gras Indians for years. So they made their own party, "a separate reality," he said, to the hard work, racism and stark poverty.

It might have been a Buffalo Bill Wild West Show that gave them the idea to dress as Indians, Dr. Stielow said, but either way the first "Indian Tribes" appeared in the late 1800s. They said they wore feathers as a show of affinity from one oppressed group to another, and to thank the Louisiana Indians for sanctuary in the slave days.

By the Great Depression these tribes, or "gangs" as they are now called, used Mardi Gras as an excuse to seek revenge on enemies and fought bloody battles, said the man who might be the biggest chief of all, 72-year-old Tootie Montana. He has been one for 46 years.

Mr. Bannock said, "They used to have a saying, 'Kiss your wife, hug your momma, sharpen your knife, and load your pistol.'"

Even after the violence faded into posturing, the New Orleans Police Department continued to break up the Indian gatherings. Mr. Bannock said New Orleans formally recognized the Indians' right to a tiny piece of Mardi Gras just two years ago.

> *Shoo fly, don't bother me*
> *Shoo fly, don't bother me*
> *If it wasn't for the warden and them lowdown hounds*
> *I'd be in New Orleans 'fore the sun go down*
> —Big Chief's battle chant, written by a chief while in the
> state prison in Angola

They speak a language as mysterious as any white man's krewe.

In addition to Spy Boys, there are Flag Boys—the flag bearers—and Second Line, the people, sometimes numbering in the hundreds, who follow the chiefs from confrontation to confrontation.

They march—more of a dance, really—from Downtown, Uptown, even across the river in the poor black sections of Algiers until the Big Chiefs meet at the corner of Claiborne and Orleans Avenues and, inside a madhouse circle of onlooker, lash each other with words. Sometimes people almost faint from the strain.

But it is mainly with the costume itself that a man does battle, said Mr. Montana. The breastplates are covered with intricate pictures of Indian scenes, painstakingly beaded by hand. The feathers are brilliant yellows, blues, reds and greens.

The winner is often "the prettiest," Mr. Montana said, and that is usually him.

"I am the oldest, I am the best, and I am the prettiest," he said.

A few are well-off businessmen, at least one has served time in prison, but most are people who sweat for a living, like him.

Some chiefs do not make their own costumes, but pay to have them made—what Mr. Bannock calls "Drugstore Indians." Of the 20 or so people who call themselves Big Chiefs, only a few remain true to tradition.

Mr. Bannock sits and sweats in his house, working day and night with his needle. He has never had time for a family. He lives for Fat Tuesday.

"I need my mornin' glory," he said.

A few years ago he had a heart attack, but did not have time to die. He had 40 yards of velvet to cut and sew.

ANALYSIS

IT'S EASY TO READ these elegant stories from Rick Bragg and lose sight of what an outstanding reporter he really is—in a polite, respectful and careful Southern manner.

Scores of reporters were unable to land the big interview with Howard Wells, yet Bragg succeeded mostly by being himself, and knowing how to work that to his advantage:

"Wells was gracious to reporters, but he still had a job to do and was reluctant to talk a lot while the trial was going on," Bragg says. He carefully noted the sheriff sat alone, off to one side of the courtroom, watching some of the horseplay and joking among members of the press corps. "You know how national reporters are, especially when they come to a small town," Bragg says. "They act like they came in off another planet."

Bragg, who admits he "looks at a courtroom like church," was quieter and more reserved than his colleagues. It paid off when "Wells told me he wanted me to do the interview because he thought I showed a little more respect."

And once Bragg gets an interview, the actual Q&A is only the first step. "When I interview someone, very seldom do I close my notebook and walk away. I'll go back (or call) three or four times," Bragg says, "You get that real good quote the third or fourth time."

Patience and persistence are major tools in Rick Bragg's arsenal. "It's like rowing a canoe," he advises. "There's got to be constant, steady strokes of questions if you want to get anywhere. You don't push as much as you nudge. A lot of reporters don't get long, descriptive, narrative quotes because they're mining for something. I will ask the tough questions. We must. But I am also trying to put colors to someone's personality."

He uses Howard Wells again as an example:

"Here you've got a guy who used to work at a mill, who grew up very blue collar, very much like me, in the Deep South. He spent months and months being hammered by reporters [from all over the world]. He wanted to tell his story but he wanted to tell it sitting in his living room drinking some iced tea. So, for an hour, he and I talked about our mommas, and our daddies, and his gun collection.

"There was nothing phony about it. I was interested. But as he was showing me a Winchester, he was popping Supreme Court decisions off the top of his head. And without asking a single question, I'm thinking, I have a crucial part of my story here."

Bragg is a firm believer in the value of filling a notebook with details and flavor that will help later in the writing process. "I did a story on an autistic boy who survived four days in a swamp in the Florida panhandle, a swamp that had killed tough men."

Discovering the boy had once stared for hours at a knot in the drawstring of his bathing trunks, Bragg tied that anecdote into his story, showing how the boy survived by keeping his wits and staring at a star, totally tuning out the gators and water moccasins swimming by. "That little detail made the story make sense to people," Bragg says. "And that's what I try hard to do."

Another thing Bragg tries hard to do is get people thinking in a descriptive manner. "I'll even recount something from my own background and tell a little story," he explains. "If you can get them thinking in pictures, in images ... you've got it."

It's not surprising Bragg has an ability to create such imagery. "I grew up in a family of story tellers, in the oral tradition." he points out. "They told stories with color and detail and image. My father could rivet you with a story. That's how I learned; I didn't learn how to tell a story by reading. That helped me more than anything I've ever read."

Some of Bragg's most simple and elegant language can be found in his story about elderly Alabama inmates. Notice the devastating effectiveness of these sentences:

His crimes flit in and out of his memory like flies through a hole in a screen door ...

Back then, before he needed help to go to the bathroom, Mr. Cooper was a dangerous man.

He was a kidnapper, but now he has trouble holding a spoon.

And from the story about Oseola McCarty:

... binding her ragged bible with scotch tape to keep Corinthians from falling out.

And from the story about Howard Wells:

The Smith case pitted a man who wants children against a woman who threw hers away.

Bragg's keen powers of observation and relevant insights are also memorable in the following passage:

He works all day in the flower garden, where he has raked the dirt so smooth you can roll marbles on it.
"My favorites are the saucer sunflowers," he said, "because they're so beautiful."
The young man, the one whose life was washed away on a river of whiskey, seems to have vanished inside this wizened lit-

tle man on his knees in the mud, plucking weeds and humming spirituals.

And, finally, an ending that says reams about Bragg's ability to squeeze (and use) every memorable detail out of a story:

The undertaking and embalming class at nearby Jefferson State University prepares the bodies for burial free, for the experience.
"They make 'em up real nice," the warden said.

"When I heard that quote, I knew it had to be the end [of the story]," Bragg says.
It's a fitting end here, as well.

RICK BRAGG is currently assigned to the Atlanta Bureau of *The New York Times*. He has won many major journalism awards and a Neiman fellowship from Harvard. He is the author of *All Over But the Shoutin'*.

1997

LISA POLLAK

EDITOR & PUBLISHER hit it right on the head: Lisa Pollak knows how to increase her job security with a new employer. Just win a Pulitzer after only a few months on the job.

Like Peter Rinearson and Dave Curtin, Pollak has possibly written her masterwork early in her career. Yet, her winning entry shows the sensitivity and wisdom of a much more experienced writer.

Her effort also brought the *The Baltimore Sun* their third Pulitzer in features, more than any paper except *The New York Times* (which has won four).

Pollak says she isn't sure if the Pulitzer history has much to do with how the *Sun* approaches features but observes her editors didn't blink much, "even when I asked to fly back to Ohio to do a second interview with the family."

Interestingly, Pollak says she didn't "spend nearly enough" time talking about her effort with colleague Alice Steinbach, the 1985 winner for "A Boy of Unusual Vision." In hindsight, Pollak says she wishes she had drawn more on Steinbach's experience.

Pollak counts Steinbach, Madeleine Blais (1980 winner), Dave Curtin (1990 winner) and Rick Bragg (1996 winner) among the writers she admires.

Although Pollak seems fairly down-to-earth about winning a Pulitzer so early in her career, she admits to being uncomfortable at how other people now relate to her, both in and out of the newsroom.

The 5,000-word story took some 4½ weeks to report and write, Pollak estimates.

The Umpire's Sons

The Baltimore Sun

December 29, 1996

HOW DO YOU SURVIVE the death of a child? How do you go on know-ing another child shares the same genetic disease? When you've trav-eled umpire John Hirschbeck's journey, being spit upon is just a foot-note.

The boy loves games of chance. He loves slot machines and play-ing cards and instant-win lottery tickets. He learned at an early age to count coins, and to bet them. He learned in the hospital that money comes in get-well cards.

Michael Hirschbeck learned to play gin in the hospital, too. His father taught him, during the long weeks of waiting, between the chemotherapy and bone marrow transplant and seizures and pneu-monia and days when he was too sick to even eat a cup of ice chips. He never asked a lot of questions, even the day his parents told him he had the same disease as his older brother, who was already dying, and that it would take his baby sister's bone marrow to save his life. He was 5 years old.

"If you want to cry, it's OK," John and Denise Hirschbeck told Michael, and he did, and so did they.

They didn't tell him he was only the 18th child with this disease to have a bone marrow transplant; or that his baby sister was a carrier of the disease; or that the doctors had anguished over whether the sis-ter's tainted marrow would help him.

They didn't tell him it might be too late to save his brother.

That was 1992, the summer Michael learned to watch baseball on television like the grownups do, patiently and for hours, while recov-ering from the transplant. That was the fall he watched the World Series with his father, the American League umpire who stopped working when his sons got sick. People might think the worst thing that ever happened to John Hirschbeck was getting spit on by Orioles second baseman Roberto Alomar during a game last season. But it wasn't, not even close. When the worst thing happened to Hirschbeck, when his children were diagnosed with a deadly neuro-logical illness, he was thankful for baseball. Not just for the season off, or the fund-raiser where famous players sold shirts and signatures to help pay medical bills—but for that simplest of baseball pleasures: games to watch with his son.

In the hospital, the Hirschbecks also played a game called Trouble. In Trouble, you use a die to move colored pegs around a board; when your peg lands on the same space as someone else's, it's trouble.

The game was Michael's favorite.

The object was to get home safe.

Brothers

Everywhere the older brother went, the younger brother followed.

John Drew Hirschbeck was born in 1984, Michael two years later; they were October babies with birthdays two weeks apart. They played video games and basketball and ran in the woods and rode bikes together. "If John was at our door, Michael was right behind him," said Joanie Ramson, whose son, Johnny, was the older brother's best friend. "I can remember Michael coming down the street with one training wheel on his bike, trying to keep up with them."

The Hirschbeck boys shared. They shared the love of their mother and father and younger sisters. They shared a big bedroom in a warm, tidy house in Poland, Ohio. They shared a mutated gene, passed silently from grandmother to mother to children, silently because it didn't kill girls, silently because it is so rare few people have ever heard of it. So difficult to say that it goes by initials: ALD.

"Adrenoleukodystrophy?" a librarian once asked Denise Hirschbeck. "You don't want to know about it."

The Hirschbeck boys were close, close as brothers could be, and yet they were different. John's eyes were blue, Michael's brown. John batted lefthanded; Michael batted right. John was the first child, the one with his father's name, the one who sat on a bar stool, drinking milk while daddy drank beer.

Little John, they called him. Little John, who memorized country songs and banged up a storm with his miniature tools and laughed so hard he made you laugh, too. Who had a steam shovel on his birthday cake and was going to drive John Deere tractors when he grew up. His parents smiled. "Why don't you do real good at something else and I'll buy you one," said his father. Little John could do anything. He was smart and adventurous and happy and healthy.

And then, mysteriously, silently, he wasn't.

The trouble started at school. In first grade, John had problems paying attention. His writing looked shaky, and he'd lose his place in his work. The doctors prescribed medicine for attention deficit disorder, but nothing changed. Spring training came, March of 1992, and on the family trip to Florida little John seemed confused and frightened. Once he saw a dead bee and thought bees were coming to get him. A stranger asked his age, and he couldn't answer.

He was 7.

The next month, he had a brain scan. The day the results came back, Denise called the umpires' locker room in Seattle. It was April 7, 1992, the night of the American League season opener, Mariners vs. Rangers. John Hirschbeck was getting ready to walk out to the field; he was working third base that night.

There are spots in his brain, Denise told John. White spots, where there should be gray.

After the game, the umpire flew home. The next day, when his oldest son disappeared into an MRI cylinder, John held tight to the boy's foot. The diagnosis was ALD. A year to live. No cure.

But there had to be something. John and Denise flew to Baltimore to talk with Dr. Hugo Moser, a renowned ALD specialist. The white-haired doctor with the German accent told the Hirschbecks about experimental treatments, including a restricted diet and a special oil. Moser also said there was a doctor in Minneapolis who did bone marrow transplants. A transplant might give John's body the enzyme his faulty gene couldn't produce—the enzyme that would keep toxic fatty acids from damaging his brain.

John and Denise Hirschbeck sat side by side in Moser's office at the Kennedy Krieger Institute, where blood samples from their four children—two sons, two daughters—had already been shipped and scrutinized. It was early in the conversation, and Moser hadn't yet told the Hirschbecks the most terrible news. It wasn't just John. Their daughters, 3-year-old Erin and baby Megan, were ALD carriers. Even worse, Michael, their 5-year-old, had the same disease as his brother. But before Moser could broach the subject, John broke in.

What about the blood work?

Years later, Moser would still remember how the umpire cried. How he sobbed, inconsolable. How he held the doctor's hand and begged him to say it wasn't true, that he wasn't going to lose both sons, not John, not Michael, too.

Family Man

I'm the luckiest man in the world. Isn't that what John Hirschbeck had told his priest? Four healthy kids, beautiful home in a comfortable town, umpiring in the big leagues, a great marriage.

She's the easygoing one, they agree, and he has the temper, but in many ways John and Denise Hirschbeck are the same. They met on a beach in Puerto Rico—she was a flight attendant, he was working winter league baseball—and were married two years later. "The right hand and the left," a friend calls them. They are happier sitting by the fireplace or playing with their kids than going out at night. They treasure their privacy in Poland, the small Midwestern town where Denise grew up. The Hirschbecks are generous with their children, affectionate and protective. They often speak in unison, her sweet, crisp voice blending with his deep one.

The disease, the doctors told them, was tough on marriages. How could it not be? You wake up in the morning and what is there to be happy about?

John: "People would say, 'Well, you two need to go out to dinner.' But what are you going to talk about at dinner? 'How's Michael doing today?' *Well, his hair started to fall out from chemo, and he's on new medication.* 'What about John?' *I'm not sure if he's seeing the same or if he's having trouble swallowing now.* Did we get to the cemetery? Did we get the plots picked out? Nothing's happy. Nothing. You wake up every day, every single day, with that sick feeling just wrenching your stomach."

The man didn't just *love* his sons, understand. He admired them. The way little John enjoyed every minute of life, every tractor-riding, Pee-Wee baseball-playing second. The way Michael took things in stride that would tear apart most adults.

Sometimes the umpire was in awe of Michael's guts. Sometimes he wished he lived every day to the fullest as much as little John did.

Tests and More Tests

Everywhere the older brother went, the younger brother followed. In the spring of 1992 they went to a hospital at the University of Minnesota, home of a pioneering children's bone marrow transplant program.

Every other week the Hirschbecks would make the 800-mile trip to Minneapolis, first for John's tests, then Michael's, then John's again. Michael showed no symptoms, but John, already disoriented and confused, was getting worse quickly. His mom would ask him to go in the basement and get something; he'd forget where the basement was. "He'd have such a troubled look on his face," said Mary Ina Jones, his maternal grandmother. "He looked at you as if to say, 'Help me, I don't know what's going on.' And you just put your arms around him and said, 'You're going to be OK, God loves you, and we're taking care of you.'"

John and Denise wanted little John to have a bone marrow transplant. It wouldn't be a cure, the doctors warned—just a way, maybe, to keep the disease from progressing. But there was a complication.

Little John had too much pressure in his brain; plans for a transplant were put on hold while doctors prescribed drugs to reduce it. The umpire buried his head in his hands. "My son is going to die," he told a friend.

Denise, armed with medical books and donor registry statistics, kept after the doctors. *When can John have a transplant?* she begged them. *If not now, when?* John was the confident older brother, Michael the tag-a-long puppy, but all at once, in the summer of 1992, everything changed. It was Michael whose body was strong enough for a transplant, Michael whose sister Megan was a genetic match, Michael who slept while marrow dripped through a tube into his body. In the hospital, John visited his brother and hung back, transfixed by the sight of Michael's bald head and puffy face. "You're going to have a transplant too," Denise told John. Back in the hotel room, she assembled a makeshift kitchen to cook the lowfat foods recommended to fight John's disease. She plugged in an electric skillet to make chicken breaded with fat-free cornflakes. She scrubbed dishes in the bathroom sink. She lost 15 pounds, because how could she eat food that her son couldn't?

It was Michael who got the transplant, but even that was a risky bet. The doctors had faced a choice between two donors: Michael's sister, who was an ALD carrier, or a stranger, whose marrow was more likely to be rejected by Michael's body. The first choice might not stop the deadly disease; the second might kill him anyway.

That was the summer Michael learned to love games of chance, the summer of cards and chemo and IVs and Trouble. Even with his sister's marrow, the side effects of the transplant were brutal. Mark Hirschbeck, the uncle whose visits usually perked up Michael's spirits, could see the nervousness in his nephew's eyes. "He wouldn't let on to anybody," said Mark, who is also a major-league umpire. "But I knew it was bad when he said he was too tired to play with me." Sometimes the only thing Michael felt like doing was lying in bed and watching baseball. Not cartoons or movies; Michael preferred baseball.

He stayed in the hospital so long that by the time he got home, baseball season was over. His face was still swollen and his hair was still patchy, but it was little John whose eyes were vacant, who wore diapers and needed help walking. Michael didn't shy away from his brother. He sat by little John's side for hours, stroking his arm and holding his hand. *Like a nurse,* thought his father.

John and Denise never stopped trying to save little John. To respect his dignity, they kept him shielded from gawking well-wishers. But he never missed an appointment with his tutor, even when his father had to pick him up and carry him to her office. John had been working with Patti Preston since first grade; for months they'd sung his favorite songs and read stories and colored pictures. Preston never gave up on little John, either. But eventually he could no longer sing, and he could only make a few strokes with the crayon before dropping it. One day his father called Preston in tears; they weren't coming anymore.

"John was disappearing," said Preston. "It was like his whole person just disappeared. John would say to little John, 'I love you. Your daddy loves you.' I would say it, too. 'I love you, John.'" Sometimes, there was nothing else to say.

John Drew Hirschbeck died on March 7, 1993, 11 months after being diagnosed with ALD, a week after his parents took him to their Florida condo for the family's annual spring-training trip. His father had been scheduled to work a baseball game that day, but little John's fever spiked and his breath slowed and his parents could do nothing but cradle him in their arms until he was gone. He was 8 years old.

Back in Ohio a few days later, at the burial, Michael stood close to his Uncle Mark, John Hirschbeck's younger brother. Who better to comfort a little brother than another one?

In the chilly Poland cemetery, 6-year-old Michael spoke aloud to his big brother. "I'm gonna miss you, John," Michael said. When he turned to hug his uncle, Michael was crying.

"We won't have to miss him," said Uncle Mark. "He'll always be with us."

His parents had little John's picture etched on his gravestone—a picture taken in kindergarten, so his eyes would be bright—and next to his small stone, they placed a larger one, a stone with their names on it.

They didn't want to leave him there alone.

The Relief of Work

Try to work, people had told John Hirschbeck, in the idle weeks before Michael's transplant. But the umpire worried: How do you work knowing your sons have a fatal disease? What if he started to cry, walked off the field, couldn't take it? So he went to Richmond, Va., a minor league city, and worked three games to test himself. Then he spent three weeks back in the majors and discovered it felt right to be working again. Sometimes, it was even a relief, focusing on nothing but pitch after pitch after pitch. Keeping control, an umpire's job.

Except for those few weeks before Michael's long stay in the hospital, John Hirschbeck spent the better part of a year away from baseball. Now it was spring of 1993, a week after his son's funeral. It was time to go back.

"I never wanted people to look at me and feel sorry for me, or say that, 'He's not the same umpire he was because of what he's gone through,'" he would say later. "Everything in the world that I had was because of baseball. I felt I had built up this reputation—that the guy works hard, and he hustles, and he cares about what he does—and it meant a lot to me. I didn't want to lose that. On the field, nothing would get to me. That's the way I looked at it. I had 21 hours a day to think about John, and for the three hours that I worked, that was going to be baseball time. I'd worry about handling John's death the other 21 hours."

Those first three hours came during a spring training game—White Sox vs. Yankees—in Florida. Hirschbeck was supposed to work third base. But if he was going back to work, he was going all the way. He switched to home plate, the more visible and challenging position. Before the game, managers and players came up to the plate to welcome him back. There was Buck Showalter, Wade Boggs, Don Mattingly, and others, all shaking his hand and telling him they were sorry. The umpire had tears in his eyes. How could he not be thankful for baseball?

But the first year back was hard. There were long hours of down time, hours to think and hurt and remember. On the road, away from Denise and Michael and Erin and Megan, he learned which friends he could talk to during those 21 hours and which were tired of listening. He learned that unless you've buried your child, you can't know how it feels.

It was before a game in Baltimore the summer after John died when Hirschbeck sought out Tim Hulett, the Baltimore Orioles infielder whose 6-year-old son Sam had been hit by a car and killed the year before. "I just remember thinking I wanted to talk to him," Hirschbeck says.

Hulett, now the athletic director of a Christian high school in Springfield, Ill., remembers, too. He remembers listening to Hirschbeck's story in a private room in Camden Yards. He remembers thinking that as painful as losing Sam had been, the Hirschbecks' agony must be many times worse. It wasn't just that they'd watched little John disappear before their eyes. It was that Michael had ALD, too.

The bone marrow transplant could keep Michael's disease from progressing, but only time could tell how healthy he would be. The first year after the transplant, Michael was relatively well. Relatively: He was taking 30 pills a day, tired easily and developed shingles, a painful skin condition. But then, on a hot August day before first grade, Michael collapsed while playing at his grandmother's house. It was a brain seizure—the first of many to come, each another frightening symptom of the disease that killed Michael's brother. The seizures were powerful. Sometimes they put him in the hospital for days. Sometimes they blurred his vision and robbed his memory.

Was Michael going to be OK? That was the question the Hirschbecks lived with every day. They could fly to Minneapolis for checkups; they could read the case studies of ALD, boys who had thrived after transplants. They could listen to the confident voices of the doctors, saying the MRI images of Michael's brain were unchanged, that the boy was making slow but steady progress every year.

But they could also see Michael struggling to read. They could see the lapses in his short-term memory. They could see him missing so many days of school that he had to repeat first grade. They could see that his MRIs were no worse, but no better.

Was Michael going to be OK? For the Hirschbecks, the answer was always the same:

We don't know.

But the umpire promised himself: On the field, it wouldn't get to him. On the field, no one would know. The promise was tested during the 1995 World Series, Hirschbeck's first World Series in 13 years as a major league umpire.

Three years had passed since Michael's transplant. By October of 1995, Michael was taking high doses of powerful antiseizure medication—and now there were other problems. The boy who loved to eat was getting skinny and had no appetite. He was increasingly agitated, confused and disoriented. Normally polite, he stared blankly at family friends. The night his father worked the plate in the fourth game of the World Series—a series that pitted Cleveland, Michael's favorite team, against Atlanta—Michael didn't even seem to care. He stayed in the hotel in Cleveland with his grandmother while his mother went to the game. Michael, missing a baseball game, let alone a World Series game that his dad was working? Never in a million years. *It was like his whole person just disappeared.*

Denise didn't want John to be alarmed; these were the biggest games of his life, she knew. But, of course, he saw what was happening. "Let's just get through the Series," he told her. "Then we'll be home."

He concentrated. He focused. One pitch at a time, he got through it. Atlanta beat Cleveland in six games. And Michael's symptoms turned out to be a reaction to the powerful seizure drugs. The worries didn't end—but the crisis did.

This past baseball season was the umpire's fourth since little John died. Every day off, he went to the cemetery in Poland. Every game day, he carried a pager, in case Michael got sick. On special occasions, he took Michael to his games. "I'm going out on the road," Michael would tell Patti Preston, who'd been little John's tutor and was now his.

On the road, Michael came into his own. He was the brown-eyed charmer who beat the umpires at gin and helped them prepare the baseballs by rubbing them with mud before games. He shook hands with strangers and chatted with Kirby Puckett and politely told umpires "good game" after they worked. His father always got him seats behind the screen, where no foul ball could hurt him. Michael watched the games, but he also watched his father—the umpire with silver initials on the back of his navy hat. *JDH.*

John Drew Hirschbeck.

When Michael went on the road, his brother did, too.

Back in the Game

After the transplant, it was a while before Michael felt well enough to play with the kids again. When he did, the first person he thought of was his brother's best friend.

"Can I call Johnny?" he asked Denise.

Johnny Ramson knew Michael had the same disease that killed his brother. Johnny's mother had told him that a bone marrow transplant was going to save Michael's life. Even so, Johnny kept an eye out for Michael. Sometimes, while they were playing, he told Michael to slow down and take it easy.

Playing with Johnny helped Michael go on with life. Playing baseball did, too. The doctors warned that sports might be difficult for Michael—ALD had left him with blind spots in his vision, and he was prone to overheating and seizures. But how could Michael not play Pee-Wee baseball? He loved it so much that he'd joined his big brother's team a year early, at age 5.

After little John died, John Hirschbeck devised a plan to make sure

Michael—who'd already lost so much—wouldn't lose baseball. John would anonymously sponsor Michael's Pee-Wee team and pick his own coaches, dads who would understand Michael's weaknesses and encourage him.

Dads who would understand the double meaning of the team's name: John Deere.

Playing baseball, Michael was just like any other kid. He was a strong boy, a right-handed pull hitter, a team cheerleader who occasionally had to be told to stop singing "We will, we will, rock you" while his team was losing. Other boys got distracted during games—digging in the dirt or playing with a bug. But Michael's attention never strayed.

The effects of his disease meant that Michael sometimes misjudged balls in the field, and he couldn't always make contact at the plate. A few times, he had a seizure the night before a game. But the next day, he'd come downstairs with his uniform on, ready to play.

Denise: "I can picture him right now. He goes running up to the plate. He's got that little smile and he gets in his stance and he's so excited, beaming from ear to ear."

John: "If he strikes out, he just runs back and sits down. I see other kids cry and get upset. But he just sits and puts his helmet down. He would never think of slamming his helmet. He just sits there like a big-league ballplayer would."

Usually, big-league players wear the same numbers on their uniforms every season. But after John died, Michael wore different numbers every year. He liked to wear the age that John would be, if he were on the team.

Another Seizure

In September, Michael was in a Minneapolis hotel room, getting ready to go to a baseball game with his dad, when a seizure hit him. He felt the familiar dizziness before the left side of his body stiffened. His eyes went blank. The phone rang, but Michael, sprawled in a chair, didn't move.

"Michael, would you get the phone for Dad?" John Hirschbeck called from the bathroom.

But there was no answer.

The umpire ran to Michael's side, and in the dazed empty eyes he saw it again: The reason he carried a pager everywhere he went. The reason a phone ringing during the school day could make him jump. The reason a blank stare at the dinner table induced panic—even though the doctors said Michael had been steadily improving for several years. In Michael's eyes, John Hirschbeck saw the question, and he saw the answer:

We Don't Know

Hirschbeck tucked Michael in bed. The seizures usually passed quickly, but they left Michael shaky and exhausted. A mile away, at the Metrodome, workers were preparing the field. Seattle was playing Minnesota, a Sunday afternoon game, and Hirschbeck was scheduled to work the plate. He had promised himself: On the field, it wouldn't get to him.

For a while, Hirschbeck watched Michael sleep. Then, after an hour or so, he carried his son to the ballpark. Michael was still too tired from the seizure to watch the game, so a bed was fashioned from towels and blankets on the carpeted floor of the umpires' room. While his father worked, Michael slept. The clubhouse manager woke him up once for medication, but he drifted off again. Jamie Moyer, a Mariners pitcher who wasn't working that day, looked in on Michael four or five times and flashed Hirschbeck the thumbs-up sign from the dugout between innings.

At one point, Ken Griffey Jr. came up to bat for the Mariners. Before he stepped in the box, he spoke to the umpire.

I just saw Michael, and he's still sleeping, Griffey said. He's fine.

Thanks, said Hirschbeck, crouching down for the next pitch.

The Big Leagues

Everywhere the older brother went, the younger brother followed.

John and Mark Hirschbeck were the first brothers in history to umpire at the same time in the major leagues. John, the older brother, went to umpire school first; Mark, six years younger, chose the same career as his brother.

Today, John works in the American League; Mark works in the National League. Like most umpires, the Hirschbecks are seldom the focus of the game. And when they are, it's usually because people disagree with them.

On Sept. 27, in a dispute over a called third strike, John Hirschbeck ejected Roberto Alomar from a game against Toronto. During the argument that followed, Alomar spit in Hirschbeck's face. Afterward, the second baseman tried to explain what he'd done. "He had a problem with his family when his son died," Alomar told reporters. "I know that's something real tough in life, but after that he just changed, personality-wise. He just got real bitter." The next day, after hearing Alomar's words, Hirschbeck charged into the players' clubhouse, threatening to kill Alomar. He was restrained by another umpire and sat out that day's game.

In the weeks after the spitting incident, as the story continued to make headlines, Mark Hirschbeck worried about his brother. He called John three and four times a day, just to check on him. He stood up for John, telling a reporter that Alomar's five-game suspension was too lenient.

The suspension was set for spring and allowed Alomar to play in the postseason; the Orioles went on to face the Cleveland Indians in the division playoffs. The series featured a matchup of brothers: Roberto Alomar playing second base for the Orioles, his older brother Sandy Jr. catching for the Indians.

On Oct. 5, after being booed at each at-bat in Cleveland, Roberto Alomar hit the winning home run for the Orioles, sending Baltimore to the American League Championship Series. After the game, Sandy Alomar Jr. went into the visitors clubhouse to see his little brother. Sandy Jr. hugged Roberto and touched his face. The second baseman cried.

Seventy-five miles away, in Poland, Ohio, Michael Hirschbeck was absorbed in the playoffs, which he watched as much as he could on television. His mind didn't wander. His eyes stayed bright. During the day, he played cards and went to school with his sisters. At night, he slept in the bedroom he used to share with his brother.

Buying Time

Four and a half years after his transplant, Michael still loves games of chance. Last Christmas he got his own Las Vegas-style slot machine. If players bet with their own quarters, they can keep the winnings, but if they bet with Michael's quarters, the jackpot is all his.

On Oct. 23, in the middle of the World Series, Michael celebrated his 10th birthday. When his grandmother, Mary Ina, asked him what he wanted, he said: "You know, Grandma, I really have all the things I want." So she made him a money tree. It was a white branch dangling with rolls of quarters and silver dollars and instant-win lottery tickets. He loved it.

But he didn't scratch off the tickets right away, his grandmother noticed. He tucked them in his wallet, to save for later.

The bone marrow transplant bought Michael time—a lifetime, his parents pray. Every year Michael does better in school and has fewer seizures. Every year his parents get on their hands and knees and do more work at little John's gravesite. A few months ago, near the end of the baseball season, they planted a red maple and two weeping hemlocks.

"Everybody tells us that as time goes on, it gets easier," says Denise. "I don't find that it gets easier. Holidays are hard. Birthdays are hard." "Every day is hard," says John. "Every day."

Don't let a dead child be forgotten, says the newspaper column on the refrigerator in the Hirschbecks' sparkling kitchen. The kitchen is the center of life in their house, where breakfasts are gulped and spelling words are learned and medication is doled out along with the hugs. There are six seats at the table, and one of them will always be little John's. Maybe someday John and Denise will sit 8-year-old Erin and 5-year-old Megan down at that table and explain to them what it means to be ALD carriers—that ALD could affect their health when they are older, that they could pass the disease on to their own children.

But John and Denise aren't worrying about that yet. They have enough to think about.

Michael is in the third grade now. He takes eight pills a day; in school, he watches the clock and quietly excuses himself at medication time. Because of his vision, he gets his classwork enlarged, and every day he leaves the room to see a tutor. He recently came home ecstatic, with his first perfect report card.

In private, there are times when Michael cries. "I miss John," he tells his mother. But the odds are, if you ever get to meet him, Michael will shake your hand and beam. When you say goodbye, he'll hug you long and hard. When he laughs, he'll make you laugh, too.

And if you ask, he might even give you a tour of his bedroom.

This is some of John's stuff. Some of it is mine, but some of it is his. Here's my piggy bank, and it's all filled with quarters. Here are my baseball cards. I love to collect baseball cards. I love anything baseball. Lofton and Belle are like my top cards, and baseball's like my top thing. Someday when I'm older I can show my kids I have these cards to look at. Some are to look at, and some are to put away. I got all my cards sorted. If I want to know if I have a certain card, a Roberto Alomar card, let's say, then I can look under the Orioles and then I could find it. ... That bed should have been my brother's. ... I have the biggest room, because it should have been my brother's too, but he got sick and he died. ... Here's his picture. ... John's in our family but he's just not here. He's our angel.

ANALYSIS

Editor & Publisher called "The Umpire's Sons" a "compelling portrait of a baseball umpire who endured his son's death while knowing that another son suffered from the same deadly genetic disease."

Yet, at first glance a profile about how prominent baseball umpire John Hirschbeck is dealing with the family tragedy, the story ends up far more complex—involving the entire family dynamics.

Lisa Pollak's story also has some similarities to Alice Steinbach's "Boy of Unusual Vision." Both stories are comparatively short, use repetition, transition and punctuation well (specifically colons). Steinbach's story was ostensibly about ten-year-old Calvin Stanley, a boy who was blind from birth. Yet, as the story unfolded, the story seemed as much about his courageous mother. Pollak's story could have just as easily been called "The Umpire."

It's not surprising Pollak also admires the work of Dave Curtin—she brings many of the same skills to a tragic story Curtin brought to "Adam & Megan." Pollak's ability to write such a literate emotional story while keeping her own emotions in check is commendable, and why the story works so well.

Using a marvelous "games of chance" anecdotal lead, Pollak manages to explain the entire story and develop a solid summary lead into the all-important first few grafs.

Pollak's prose is enhanced through the use of proven literary techniques. The "games of chance" opening allowed her to describe how much of a gamble life still is for Michael Hirschbeck. Pollak also brings the thought back near the end of her story, in a final look at how iffy the situation remains:

It was a white branch dangling with rolls of quarters and silver dollars and instant-win lottery tickets. He loved it.

But he didn't scratch off all the tickets right away ... he tucked them in his wallet, to save for later.

Pollak's insertion of the game Trouble into the story, with its object to "get home safe" was also a nice stroke, one that foretold that Michael might still have a chance at life. (Such foretelling is important to keep nervous readers committed in stories such as this. Readers will recall that in "Adam & Megan," a special introduction and the family decorating the Christmas tree assured readers the children wouldn't die. Jon Franklin, on the other hand, prepared readers for the inevitable in "Mrs. Kelly's Monster," dropping several hints that Mrs. Kelly wouldn't survive the brain surgery.

Pollak also uses repetition effectively:

Everywhere the older brother went, the younger brother followed ...

Her phrase is intriguing, especially the way she uses it to focus on brothers, but not always the same pair. She offers it initially to talk about the umpire's two sons, John and Michael. The second time, it refers to how the umpire and his own brother relate to each other.

A second, more subtle form of repetition is the spoken and unspoken thoughts:

Was Michael going to be OK?

We don't know.

Again, it's more the skillful way Pollak uses repetition than the sheer number of mentions. A few strategically placed references work perfectly.

Another, more ominous and chilling example:

The Hirschbeck boys **shared.** *They* **shared** *the love of their mother and father and younger sisters. They* **shared** *a big bedroom in a warm, tidy house in Poland, Ohio. They* **shared** *a mutated gene ...*

Pollak's use of italic, both in the middle of quotes, thoughts and narrative creates a sense of dialogue even where there isn't any. It's an effective tactic in this story:

I'm the luckiest man in the world.

What about the blood work?

When can John have a transplant ... if not now, when?

It was like his whole person just disappeared.

Don't let a dead child be forgotten.

The use of italic reaches a logical conclusion with Pollak's powerful ending, an understood quote from young Michael Hirschbeck about his brother. Pollak's understated use of the mention of the Roberto Alomar baseball card is delicious irony, as the son seemingly is unaware that Alomar spat in his father's face. It's one of those anecdotes that only results from superior interviewing.

Pollak says she admires the way some writers use colons as a writing tool, specifically Madeleine Blais and Alice Steinbach. And in her Pulitzer effort, Pollak uses colons liberally as well. Young writers might pay attention how she simply puts a colon behind the names John: and Denise: and lets them talk at selected spots in the story. It's one more graceful way to handle attribution in such a powerful, quote-driven story.

Again similar to Steinbach's "Boy of Unusual Vision," Pollak breaks her story up into a half a dozen little interconnected vignettes that, rather than draining coherence from the story, somehow stitch it all together into a wonderful, touching, exhilarating literary ride, a fitting finish to a book containing the best newspaper feature stories of the past two decades.

LISA POLLAK has a master's degree in journalism from Northwestern University and has worked for the Raleigh *News & Observer* and *Charlotte Observer*. In 1995, she won the Ernie Pyle award for human interest writing.

ACKNOWLEDGMENTS

The editor and publisher thank the following newspapers for their help and courtesy in allowing the works in this anthology to be reprinted:

© 1978 *The Baltimore Sun* for "Mrs. Kelly's Monster" by Jon Franklin. Reprinted with permission from *The Baltimore Sun.*

© 1979 *The Miami Herald* for "Zepp's Last Stand" by Madeleine Blais. Reprinted with permission from *The Miami Herald.*

© 1980 Teresa Carpenter (special thanks to *The Village Voice*) for "Death of a Playmate." Reprinted with permission from Teresa Carpenter.

© 1981 The Associated Press for "The Federal Bureaucracy" by Saul Pett. Reprinted with permission from the Associated Press.

© 1982 *The New York Times* for "Toxic Shock" by Nan Robertson. Reprinted with permission from *The New York Times.*

© 1983 *The Seattle Times* for "Making It Fly" by Peter Mark Rinearson. Reprinted with permission from Seattle Times Company.

© 1984 *The Baltimore Sun* for "A Boy of Unusual Vision" by Alice Steinbach. Reprinted with permission from *The Baltimore Sun.*

© 1985 *The St. Paul Pioneer Press* for "Life on the Land: An American Farm Family" by John Camp. Reprinted with permission from the *St. Paul Pioneer Press.*

© 1986 *The Philadelphia Inquirer* for "How Super Are Our Supercarriers?" by Steve Twomey. Reprinted with permission from *The Philadelphia Inquirer.*

© 1987 *The St. Paul Pioneer Press* for "AIDS in the Heartland" by